BY SCHISM RENT ASUNDER

TOR BOOKS BY DAVID WEBER

Off Armageddon Reef
By Schism Rent Asunder

BY SCHISM
RENT
ASUNDER

DAVID
WEBER

TOR®

A TOM DOHERTY ASSOCIATES BOOK
NEW YORK

BY SCHISM RENT ASUNDER

Copyright © 2008 by David Weber

Edited by Patrick Nielsen Hayden
Maps by Ellisa Mitchell and Jennifer Hanover

A Tor Book
Published by Tom Doherty Associates, LLC
175 Fifth Avenue
New York, NY 10010

www.tor-forge.com

Tor® is a registered trademark of Tom Doherty Associates, LLC.

Library of Congress Cataloging-in-Publication Data

Weber, David, 1952–
    By schism rent asunder / David Weber.—1st ed.
        p.   cm.
    "A Tom Doherty Associates book."
    ISBN-13: 978-0-7653-1501-4
    ISBN-10: 0-7653-1501-7
    I. Title

PS3573.E217 B9 2008
813'.54—dc22

                                              2008016957

First Edition: July 2008

Printed in the United States of America

0   9   8   7   6   5   4   3   2   1

This one is for Sharon. Well, they all are, really, and I don't usually do public love letters, but this year is an exception. Thank you for marrying me all over again. I love you.

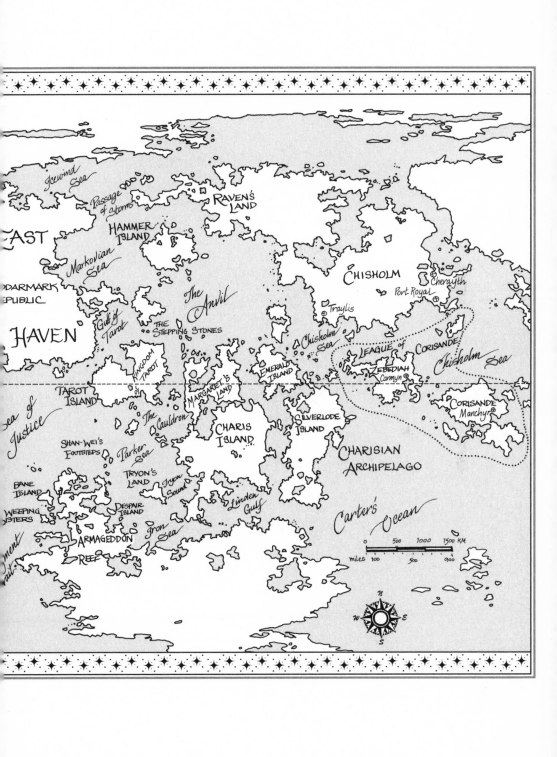

Icewind Sea

Passage of Storms

RAVEN'S LAND

HAMMER ISLAND

EAST

Markovian Sea

ODARMARK EPUBLIC

HAVEN

Gulf of Tarot

The Anvil

THE STEPPING STONES

CHISHOLM

Cheralyth

Port Royal

Traylis

Chisholm Sea

LEAGUE of

CORISANDE

Chisholm Sea

KINGDOM of TAROT

EMERALD ISLAND

ZEBEDIAH Carmyn

TAROT ISLAND

MARGARET'S LAND

Sea of Justice

The Cauldron

CHARIS ISLAND

SILVERLODE ISLAND

CORISANDE Manchyr

SHAN-WEI'S FOOTSTEPS

Parker Sea

CHARISIAN ARCHIPELAGO

BANE ISLAND

TRYON'S LAND

Tryon Sound

WEEPING OYSTERS

DESPAIR ISLAND

Linden Gulf

Carter's Ocean

ment rait

ARMAGEDDON REEF

Iron Sea

500   1000   1500 KM

miles 100   500   900

N
W   E
S

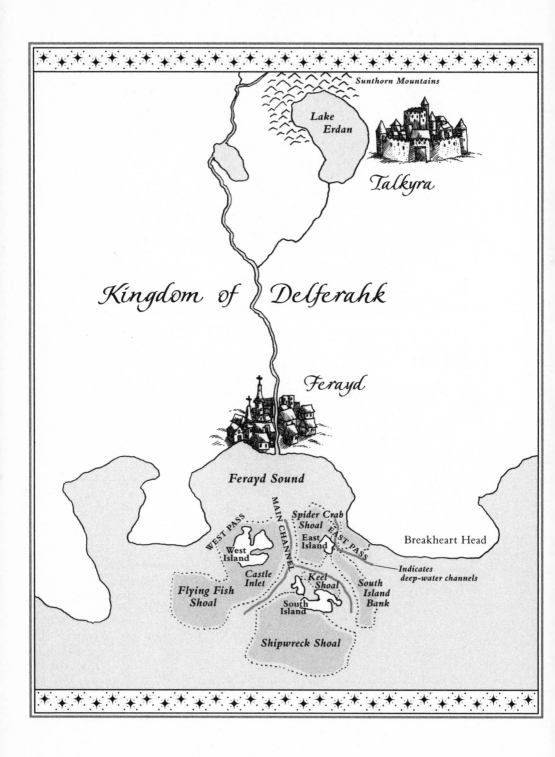

Sunthorn Mountains

Lake
Erdan

Talkyra

Kingdom of Delferahk

Ferayd

Ferayd Sound

WEST PASS

MAIN CHANNEL

Spider Crab
Shoal

East
Island

EAST PASS

Breakheart Head

West
Island

Castle
Inlet

Keel
Shoal

Indicates
deep-water channels

Flying Fish
Shoal

South
Island

South
Island
Bank

Shipwreck Shoal

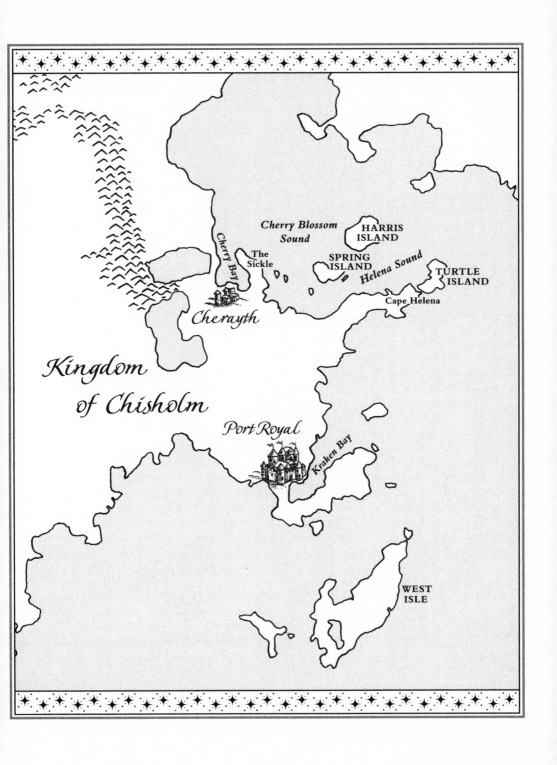

Cherry Blossom
Sound

HARRIS
ISLAND

SPRING
ISLAND

Helena Sound

TURTLE
ISLAND

The
Sickle

Cherry Bay

Cape Helena

Cherayth

Kingdom
of Chisholm

Port Royal

Kraken Bay

WEST
ISLE

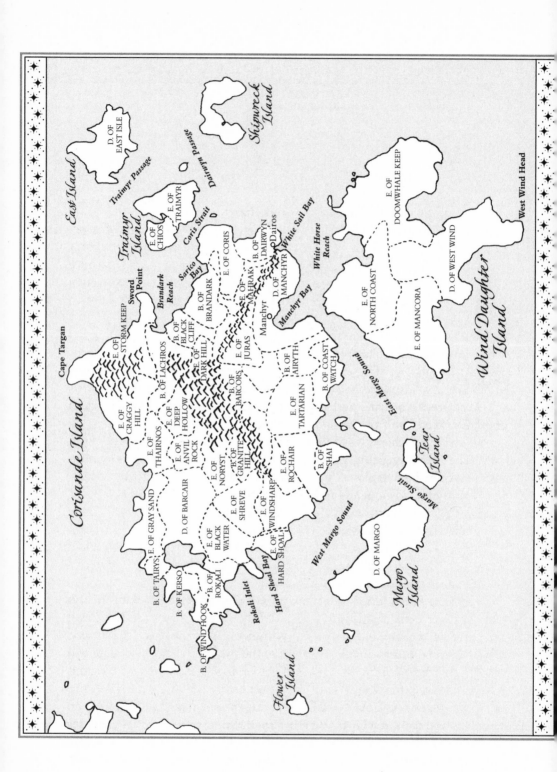

Corisande Island

East Island

D. OF
EAST ISLE

Shipwreck Island

Traimyr Passage

Traimyr Island

E. OF
TRAIMYR

E. OF
CHIOS

Coris Strait

Dairwyn Passage

Cape Targan

Sword Point

E. OF
STORM KEEP

Brandark Reach

Sarico Bay

E. OF CORIS

DAIRWYN

D. OF
MANCHYR

White Sail Bay

West Wind Head

D. OF
DOOMWHALE KEEP

E. OF
CRAGGY HILL

B. OF
LACHROS

B. OF
BLACK CLIFF

B. OF
BRANDARK

E. OF
DARK HILL

MAHRAK

B. OF
DAIRWYN

Dairos

Manchyr

White Horse Reach

E. OF
NORTH COAST

D. OF WEST WIND

E. OF
THAIRNOS

E. OF
DEEP HOLLOW

E. OF
ANVIL ROCK

B. OF
GRANITE HILL

E. OF
JURAS

B. OF
BARCORS

Manchyr Bay

E. OF MANCORA

E. OF GRAY SAND

D. OF BARCAIR

E. OF
NORYST

E. OF
SHREVE

E. OF
ROCHAIR

B. OF
AIRYTH

B. OF COAST WATCH

E. OF
TARTARIAN

East Margo Sound

Wind Daughter Island

B. OF TAIRYS

B. OF KERSO

B. OF
ROKALI

E. OF
BLACK WATER

E. OF
WINDSHARP

B. OF
SHAI

Tear Island

Rokali Inlet

Hard Shoal Bay

HARD SHOAL

West Margo Sound

Margo Strait

B. OF WINDHOOK

D. OF MARGO

Margo Island

Flower Island

I t was very quiet in the inverted recon skimmer.

It tended to be that way in orbit, aside from the quiet chirping of an occasional audio signal from the skimmer's flight computers, and those only seemed to perfect the silence, rather than interrupt it. The man who had once been Nimue Alban leaned back in the pilot's couch, looking down through the clear armorplast of his canopy at the planet beneath him, and treasured that quiet, serene calm.

I really shouldn't be here, he thought, watching the gorgeous blue-and-white-swirled marble of the planet called Safehold while his skimmer swept steadily towards the dark line of the terminator. *I've got way too many things to be doing back in Tellesberg. And I've got no business at all hanging around up here, stealth systems or no.*

All of that was true, and it didn't matter. Or, rather, it didn't matter enough to keep him from being here, anyway.

In one sense, there was absolutely no need for him to be up here physically. The Self-Navigating Autonomous Reconnaissance and Communication platforms he'd deployed were capable of transmitting exactly the same imagery to him, without any need for him to see it with his own eyes . . . if, indeed, that could be said to be what he was doing. And the SNARCs were far smaller, and even stealthier, than his recon skimmer. If the kinetic bombardment system that lunatic Langhorne had hung in orbit around Safehold really did have first-line passive sensors, it was far less likely to detect a SNARC than the skimmer, and he knew it.

Yet there were times when he needed this silent, still moment, this vacuum-clear eyrie from which he could look down upon the last planet mankind could claim. He needed the reminder of who—what—he truly was, and of what he must somehow restore to the human beings thronging that planet so far below him. And he needed to see its beauty, to . . . cleanse his thoughts, recoup his determination. He spent so much time poring over the take from his network of SNARCs, studying the spy reports, listening in on the plans and conspiracies of the enemies of the kingdom he had made his home that it sometimes seemed that that was all there was to the universe. That the sheer weight of opposition towering up all about him was too vast, too deep, for any single creature to oppose.

The people around him, the people he'd come to care for, were the true antidote to the despair which sometimes threatened him as he contemplated the enormous scope of the task to which he had been summoned. They were the ones who reminded him why humanity was *worth* fighting for, reminded him of the heights to which mankind could aspire, of the courage and the sacrifice—the trust—of which Homo sapiens was capable. Despite the way their history and their religion had been cynically manipulated, they were as strong and vital, as courageous, as any humans in the history of the race which had once been his own.

Yet, even so, there were times when that wasn't quite enough. When his awareness of the odds against their survival, his sense of desperate responsibility, and the sheer loneliness of living *among* them but never truly being one *of* them pressed down upon him. When the burden of his potential immortality against the ephemeral span of the lives to which they were condemned filled him with an aching grief for losses yet to come. When his responsibility for the wave of religious strife even now beginning to sweep around that blue and white sphere crushed down upon him. And when the question of who—and what—he truly was filled him with a loneliness that sucked at his soul like the vacuum outside his skimmer.

It was against those times that he needed this moment, gazing down upon the world which had become *his* charge, *his* responsibility. Needed to once more look upon the reality, the fledgling future, which made all the present's harsh demands worthwhile.

It really is a pretty world, he thought almost dreamily. *And looking at it from up here puts it all into perspective, doesn't it? Beautiful as it is, important as the human race may be to me, it's only one world among billions, only one species among hundreds of millions, at the least. If God can put that much effort into His universe, then I can damned well do whatever He demands of me, can't I? And*—his lips quirked in a wry smile—*at least I can be pretty sure He understands. If He can put all of this together, put me right smack in the middle of it, then I've just got to assume He knows what He's doing. Which means all I really have to do is figure out what* I'm *supposed to be doing.*

He snorted in amusement, the sound loud in the cockpit's silence, then shook himself and let the flight couch come upright once again.

Enough planet-gazing, Merlin, he told himself firmly. *It's going to be dawn in Tellesberg in three more hours, and Franz is going to be wondering where his relief is. Time to get your molycirc butt home, where it belongs.*

"Owl," he said aloud.

"Yes, Lieutenant Commander?" the distant AI in the cavern under Safehold's tallest mountain replied almost instantly over the secure communications link.

"I'm headed home. Run a hundred-klick sweep around the alpha base and make sure there's no one hanging around to notice the skimmer on its way to the garage. And take a look at my balcony, too. Make sure no one's in a position to see me when you drop me off."

"Yes, Lieutenant Commander," the AI acknowledged, and Merlin reached for the skimmer's controls.

YEAR OF GOD 892

Bright morning sunlight glittered on the crossed golden scepters of the green banner of the Church of God Awaiting. The twin-masted courier ship flying that wind-starched banner as she scudded along on the brisk breeze was little more than seventy feet long, built for speed rather than endurance . . . or even seakeeping and stability. Her crew of sixty was small for any galley, even one as diminutive as she was, but her slender, lightly constructed hull was well suited for rowing, and her lateen sails drove her in a rapid flurry of foam as she went slicing across the brilliant sun-splintered water and foaming white horses of the thirty-mile-wide passage between Callie's Island and the northeastern shore of Eraystor Bay.

Father Rahss Sawal, the small fleet vessel's commander, stood on his tiny quarterdeck, hands clasped behind him, and concentrated on looking confident while he gazed up at the seabirds and wyverns hovering against the painfully blue sky. It was harder than it ought to have been to maintain the outward assurance (it would never have done to call it *arrogance*) proper to the master of one of Mother Church's couriers, and Sawal didn't much care for the reason he found it so.

The Temple's messengers, whether landbound or afloat, enjoyed absolute priority and freedom of passage. They carried God's own messages and commands, with all the authority of the archangels themselves, and no mortal had the temerity to challenge their passage wherever God or His Church might send them. That had been true literally since the Creation, and no one had ever dared to dispute it. Unfortunately, Sawal was no longer certain the centuries-old inviolability of Mother Church's messengers continued to hold true.

The thought was . . . disturbing, in more ways than one. Most immediately, because of the potential consequences for his own current mission. In the long run, because the failure of that inviolability was unthinkable. Defiance of the authority of God's Church could have only one consequence for the souls of the defiers, and if their example led others into the same sin . . .

Sawal pushed that thought aside once more, telling himself—*insisting* to himself—that whatever madness had infected the Kingdom of Charis, God would never permit it to spread beyond Charis' borders. The universal authority of Mother Church was the linchpin not simply of the world in which he lived, but of God's very plan for Man's salvation. If that authority were challenged, if it failed, the consequences would be unthinkable. Shan-wei, lost and damned mother of evil, must be licking her fangs at the very possibility in the dark, dank corner of Hell to which the Archangel Langhorne had consigned her for her sins. Even now she must be testing the bars, trying the strength of her chains, as she tasted the overweening, sinful pride of those who sought to set their own fallible judgment in place of God's. Langhorne himself had locked that gate behind her, with all the authority of eternity, but Man had free will. Even now, he could turn the key in that lock if he so chose, and if he did . . .

Damn *those Charisians*, he thought grimly. *Don't they even realize what door they're opening? Don't they* care? *Don't*—

His jaw tightened and he forced himself to relax his shoulders and draw a deep, cleansing breath. It didn't help very much.

His instructions from Bishop Executor Thomys had been abundantly clear. Sawal was to deliver the bishop executor's dispatches to Bishop Executor Wyllys in Eraystor at all costs. That phrase—"at all costs"—had never before been part of Sawal's orders. There'd never been any need for it, but there was now, and—

"Deck there!" The shout came down from the crow's nest. "Deck there! Three sail on the port bow!"

▼   ▼   ▼

"Well, well," Commander Paitryk Hywyt, Royal Charisian Navy, murmured to himself as he peered through the spyglass. "*This* should be interesting."

He lowered the glass and frowned thoughtfully. His orders were perfectly clear on this point. They'd made him more than a little nervous when he first received them, but they were definitely clear, and now he discovered that he was actually looking forward to obeying them. Odd. He wouldn't have thought that was likely to happen.

"It's a Church courier, all right," he said a bit louder, and Zhak Urvyn, HMS *Wave's* first lieutenant, made a distinctly unhappy sound.

"Some of the men may not like it, Sir," Urvyn said softly. Hywyt glanced sideways at him, then shrugged.

"I've got a feeling the men's attitude may just surprise you a bit, Zhak," he said dryly. "They're still about as pissed off as I've ever seen them, and they know who that courier's really working for this morning."

Urvyn nodded, but he looked gloomier than ever, and Hywyt grimaced mentally. It wasn't the *men* Urvyn expected to be unhappy; it was Urvyn himself.

"Bring her three points to port, if you please, Lieutenant," Hywyt said, speaking rather more formally than was his wont. "Let's lay out a course to intercept her."

"Aye, aye, Sir." Urvyn's expression was worried, but he saluted and passed the order to the helmsman while other hands pattered across the wooden decks to tend sheets and braces.

Wave changed course, slicing across the water close-hauled on the port tack, and Hywyt felt a familiar surge of pleasure as his vessel responded. The sleek, flush-decked, twin-masted schooner was just over ninety-five feet long on the waterline, and mounted fourteen thirty-pounder carronades. Unlike some of her sisters, *Wave* had been designed and built from the keel up as a light cruiser for the Royal Charisian Navy. Her revolutionary sail plan made her faster and far more weatherly than any other ship Hywyt had ever encountered, far less commanded, and she'd already taken no less than seven prizes—almost half of those captured by the entire blockading squadron— here in Emeraldian waters since the Battle of Darcos Sound. That was what speed and handiness meant, and the comfortable sound prize money made falling into their purses had helped overcome any lingering qualms his crew might have cherished. They *were* Charisians, after all, he thought with a gleam of humor. Charis' numerous detractors were wont to refer to the Kingdom as a "kingdom of shopkeepers and moneylenders," and *not* in tones of approval. Hywyt had listened to their rancorous envy for years, and he had to admit there was at least a little truth to the stereotype of the Charisian constantly on the prowl for ways to make a quick mark.

Of course, we're also very good *at it, aren't we?* he reflected, and felt himself smiling as the courier boat with the dark green flag drew rapidly nearer.

He couldn't be positive the other ship had come from Corisande, but no other explanation seemed very likely. The dispatch boat had obviously approached through Dolphin Reach, which certainly meant it had also crossed the Sea of Zebediah. No courier from Haven or Howard would have been coming from that direction, and Hywyt rather doubted Sharleyan of Chisholm was particularly interested in corresponding with Nahrmahn of Emerald at the moment. And judging from the way the fellow had chosen the strait between Callie's Island and the Emeraldian coast, he definitely didn't want to attract the attention of the blockade squadron.

Unfortunately for him, he already had, and it was evident that his ship, for all its sleek design, was quite a bit slower than *Wave* under these conditions.

"Clear for action," he said, and watched the gap between the two ships narrow as the drum began to beat.

▼   ▼   ▼

Rahss Sawal tried very hard not to swear as the Charisian schooner swept to-wards him. Obviously, his information was even more out-of-date than he'd feared when Bishop Executor Thomys gave him his orders. He hadn't expected to see Charisian warships actually *inside* Eraystor Bay proper. Then again, he hadn't expected to see the gold kraken on black of the Charisian flag flying above what used to be the Emeraldian fortress on Callie's Island, either.

The dispersal of the Charisian warships was the clearest possible evidence of the totality of their victory at the Battle of Darcos Sound. The true extent of the allied fleet's defeat had still been unclear when Sawal left Manchyr. That it had been crushing was obvious, but everyone in Corisande had clung to the hope that the majority of the ships which had not returned had found refuge in Emerald, where they were even then helping Nahrmahn defend their anchorage.

Obviously not, Sawal thought sourly.

He could see exactly four ships now, counting the schooner charging down on his own command, and every one of them flew Charisian colors. They were spread out widely, as well, to cover as much of the bay as they could, and they wouldn't have been doing that if there'd been any possibility at all that someone might consider attacking them. That, coupled with the fact that all the island fortifications Sawal could see from his quarterdeck had clearly become *Charisian* bases, not Emeraldian ones, made it abundantly clear that there *was* no "allied fleet" any longer, much less one that was still defending its anchorage.

Sawal had never before encountered one of the Charisians' new schooners, and he was astonished at how close to the wind the thing could sail. And by the size and power of its sail plan. His ship had the same number of masts, but the Charisian had to have at least twice the sail area. It also had the stability and size to *carry* more sail, and it was driving far harder under these conditions than his own ship could manage.

The number of gun ports arranged along its side was at least equally impressive, and he felt his stomach muscles tighten as the stubby muzzles of cannon poked out of them.

"Father?"

He glanced at his own second-in-command. The one-word question made the other priest's tension abundantly clear, and Sawal couldn't blame him. Not that he had an answer for what he knew the man was actually asking.

"We'll have to see what we see, Brother Tymythy," he said instead. "Hold your course."

▼   ▼   ▼

"He's not changing course," Urvyn said.

As redundant statements of the obvious went, that one took some beating, Hywyt thought.

"No, he isn't," the commander agreed with massive restraint as the range fell steadily. It was down to less than three hundred yards and still dropping, and he wondered how far the other skipper was going to go in calling what he undoubtedly hoped was *Wave*'s bluff. "Pass the word to the Gunner to stand ready to fire a shot across his bow."

Urvyn hesitated. It was a tiny thing. Someone else might not have noticed it at all, but Urvyn had been Hywyt's first lieutenant for over six months. For a moment, Hywyt thought he would have to repeat the order, but then Urvyn turned heavily away and raised his leather speaking trumpet.

"Stand ready to fire across his bow, Master Charlz!" he shouted, and *Wave*'s gunner waved back in acknowledgment.

▼   ▼   ▼

"I think he's—"

Brother Tymythy never completed that particular observation. There was no need. The flat, concussive thud of a single gun punctuated it quite nicely, and Sawal watched the cannonball go slashing across the waves, cutting its line of white across their crests as cleanly as any kraken's dorsal fin.

"He's *fired* on us!" Tymythy said instead. His voice was shrill with outrage, and his eyes were wide, as if he was actually surprised that even *Charisians* should dare to offer such insult to Mother Church. And perhaps he was. Sawal, on the other hand, discovered that he truly wasn't.

"Yes, he has," the under-priest agreed far more calmly than he felt.

I didn't really believe they'd do it, he thought. *I'm sure I didn't. So why am I not surprised that they have? This is the beginning of the end of the world, for God's sake!*

He thought again about the dispatches he carried, who they were addressed to, and why. He thought about the whispered rumors, about exactly what Prince Hektor and his allies had hoped for . . . what rewards they'd been promised by the Church.

No, not by the Church, Sawal told himself. *By the Knights of the Temple Lands. There* is *a difference!*

Yet even as he insisted upon that to himself, he knew better. Whatever technical or legal distinctions might exist, he knew better. And that, he realized now, with something very like despair, was why he truly wasn't surprised.

Even now, he couldn't put it into words for himself, couldn't make himself face it that squarely, but he knew. Whatever might have been true before the massive onslaught Prince Hektor and his allies had launched upon the Kingdom of Charis, the Charisians knew as well as Sawal who had truly been behind it. They knew the reality of the cynical calculations, the casual readiness to destroy an entire realm in blood and fire, and the arrogance which had infused and inspired them. This time the "Group of Four" had come too far out of the shadows, and what they had envisioned as the simple little assassination of an inconvenient kingdom had turned into something very different.

Charis knew who its true enemy had been all along, and that explained exactly why that schooner was prepared to fire on the flag of God's own Church.

The schooner was closer now, leaning to the press of her towering spread of canvas, her bow garlanded with white water and flying spray that flashed like rainbow gems under the brilliant sun. He could make out individuals along her low bulwarks, pick out her uniformed captain standing aft, near the wheel, see the crew of the forward gun in her starboard broadside reloading their weapon. He looked up at his own sails, then at the schooner's kraken-like grace, and drew a deep breath.

"Strike our colors, Brother Tymythy," he said.

"Father?" Brother Tymythy stared at him, as if he couldn't believe his own ears.

"Strike our colors!" Sawal repeated more firmly.

"But, but the Bishop Executor—"

"Strike our colors!" Sawal snapped.

For a moment, he thought Tymythy might refuse. Tymythy knew their orders as well as Sawal did, after all. But it was far easier for a bishop to order an under-priest to maintain the authority of Mother Church "at any cost" than it was for Father Rahss Sawal to get the crew of his vessel killed as part of an exercise in futility.

If there were any hope of actually delivering our dispatches, I wouldn't strike, he told himself, and wondered whether or not it was the truth. *But it's obvious we can't keep away from them, and if those people over there are as prepared to fire into us as I think they are, they'll turn this entire vessel into toothpicks with a single broadside. Two, at the outside. There's no point in seeing my own people slaughtered for nothing, and we aren't even armed.*

The flag which had never before been dipped to any mortal power fluttered down from the courier boat's masthead. Sawal watched it come down, and an ice-cold wind blew through the marrow of his bones.

It was a small thing, in so many ways, that scrap of embroidered fabric. But that was how all true catastrophes began, wasn't it? With small things, like the first stones in an avalanche.

Maybe I should have made them fire into us. At least then there wouldn't have been any question, any ambiguity. And if Charis is prepared to defy Mother Church openly, perhaps a few dead crewmen would have made that point even more clearly.

Perhaps they would have, and perhaps he *should* have forced the Charisians to do it, but he was a priest, not a soldier, and he simply couldn't. And, he told himself, the mere fact that Charis had fired upon the flag of Holy Mother Church should be more than enough without his allowing his people to be killed, on top of it.

No doubt it would, and yet even as he told himself that, he knew.

The lives he might have saved this morning would be as meaningless as mustard seeds on a hurricane's breath beside the horrendous mountains of death looming just over the lip of tomorrow.

.II.
Royal Palace,
City of Manchyr,
Princedom of Corisande

Hektor Daykyn's toe caught on the splinter-fringed gouge a Charisian round shot had plowed across the deck of the galley *Lance*. It was one of many such gouges, and the Prince of Corisande reached out to run his hand across a shattered bulwark railing where the mast had come thundering down in splintered ruin.

"Captain Harys had his hands full bringing this one home, Your Highness," the man walking at his right shoulder said quietly.

"Yes. Yes, he did," Hektor agreed, but his voice was oddly distant, his eyes looking at something only he could see. The distant focus in those eyes worried Sir Taryl Lektor, the Earl of Tartarian, more than a little bit. With the Earl of Black Water's death in battle confirmed, Tartarian had become the senior ranking admiral of the Corisandian Navy—such as it was, and what remained of it—and he didn't much care for the way his prince seemed to occasionally . . . wander off into his own thoughts. It was too unlike Hektor's normal, decisive manner.

"Father, can we *go* now?"

Hektor's eyes blinked back into focus, and he turned to look at the boy beside him. The youngster had Hektor's dark eyes and jawline, but he had the copper-bright hair of his dead northern mother. He was probably going to favor his father in height, too, although it was a bit early to be sure about that. At fifteen, Crown Prince Hektor still had some growing to do.

In more ways than one, his father thought grimly.

"No, we can't," he said aloud. The crown prince frowned, and his shoulders hunched as he shoved his hands into his breeches' pockets. It wouldn't be quite fair to call his expression a pout, but Prince Hektor couldn't think of a word that came closer.

Irys, you're worth a dozen of him, the prince thought. *Why, oh why, couldn't you have been born a man?*

Unfortunately, Princess Irys hadn't been, which meant Hektor had to make do with his namesake.

"Pay attention," he said coldly now, giving the boy a moderately stern glare. "Men *died* to bring this ship home, Hektor. You might learn something from their example."

Hektor the younger flushed angrily at the public reprimand. His father observed his darkened color with a certain satisfaction, then reminded himself that publicly humiliating the child who would someday sit on his throne and rule his princedom was probably not a very good idea. Princes who remembered that sort of treatment tended to take it out on their own subjects, with predictable results.

Not that the odds of this particular crown prince having the opportunity to do anything of the sort were particularly good. Which had quite a lot to do with the damage to the battered galley on which Hektor stood.

He turned in place, looking up and down the full length of the ship. Tartarian was right, he reflected. Getting this ship home must have been a nightmare. Her pumps were still working even now, as she lay to her anchor. The long, crawling voyage home from Darcos Sound—almost seven thousand miles—in a ship which had been holed at least a dozen times below the waterline, and a third of whose crew had been slaughtered by the Charisian artillery, was the stuff of which legends were made. Hektor hadn't even tried to count the shot holes *above* the waterline, but he'd already made a mental note to have Captain Zhoel Harys promoted.

And at least I have plenty of vacancies to promote him into, *don't I?* Hektor thought, looking down at the dark discoloration where human blood had soaked deeply into *Lance*'s deck planking.

"All right, Hektor," he said. "We can go, I suppose. You're late for your fencing lesson, anyway."

▼   ▼   ▼

Some hours later, Hektor; Admiral Tartarian; Sir Lyndahr Raimynd, Hektor's treasurer; and the Earl of Coris, his spymaster, sat in a small council chamber whose window overlooked the naval anchorage.

"How many does that make, My Prince?" Earl Coris asked.

"Nine," Hektor said, rather more harshly than he'd intended to. "Nine," he repeated in a more moderate tone. "And I doubt we're going to see many more of them."

"And according to our latest messages from the Grand Duke, *none* of the

Zebediahan-manned galleys have made it home even now," Coris murmured.

"I'm well aware of that," Hektor said.

And I'm not very surprised, either, he thought. *There never were many of them, and despite anything Tohmys may have to say, I'll wager his precious captains surrendered just about as quickly as Sharleyan's Chisholmians.* He snorted mentally. *After all, they love me just about as much as Sharleyan does.*

Actually, that probably wasn't *quite* fair, he reflected. It had been over twenty years since he had defeated and deposed—and executed—the last Prince of Zebediah. Who hadn't been a particularly good prince before the conquest even when he'd had a head, as even the most rabid Zebediahan patriot was forced to admit. Hektor might have displayed a certain ruthlessness in rooting out potential resistance and making sure the entire previous dynasty was safely extinct, and he'd been forced to make examples of the occasional ambitious noble since then. But at least they'd gotten honest government since becoming Corisandian subjects, and their taxes weren't actually all that much higher than they had been. Of course, more of those taxes were spent in Corisande than in Zebediah, but if they insisted on losing wars, they couldn't have everything.

And whatever the common folk might think, Tohmys Symmyns, the Grand Duke of Zebediah, and his fellow surviving aristocrats knew which side of their bread the jam was on. Symmyns' father, for example, had been a mere baron before Hektor elevated him to the newly created title of grand duke, and the current grand duke would retain the title only as long as he retained Hektor's confidence. Still, there was no denying that his Zebediahan subjects were somewhat less enthusiastic than his native-born Corisandians about shedding their blood in the service of the House of Daykyn.

Something about how much of their blood had been shed *by* the House of Daykyn over the last few decades, probably.

"Frankly, Your Highness," Tartarian said, "I'll be astonished if we see any more of them, Corisandian-crewed *or* Zebediahan-crewed. *Lance* is the next best thing to a wreck. Given her damage and casualties, it's a miracle Harys got her home at all, and he didn't set any record passage doing it." The admiral shook his head, his expression grim. "If there were any of them with worse damage, they almost certainly went down before they could reach Corisande. Either that or they're beached on an island somewhere between here and Darcos Sound, at any rate."

"That's my opinion, as well," Hektor agreed, and inhaled deeply. "Which means that whenever Haarahld gets around to us, we're not going to have a navy to fend him off."

"If the reports are accurate, no conventional galley fleet would be able to stop him anyway, Your Highness," Tartarian said.

"Agreed. So we're just going to have to build ourselves a 'new model' galleon fleet of our own."

"How likely is Haarahld to give us the time to do something like that, My Prince?" Coris asked.

"Your guess is as good as mine, Phylyp. In fact"—Hektor's smile was alum-tart—"I rather hope your guess is *better* than mine."

Coris didn't quail, but his expression wasn't particularly happy, either. Phylyp Ahzgood, like his counterpart in Charis, had not been born to the nobility. He'd received his title (following the unfortunately deceased previous Earl of Coris' involvement in the last serious attempt to assassinate Hektor) in recognition of his work as Hektor's spymaster, and he was probably the closest thing Hektor had to a true first councilor. But he'd slipped considerably in the prince's favor as the devastating degree to which Haarahld of Charis' naval innovations had been underestimated began becoming painfully clear. It was entirely possible that his head was still keeping company with the rest of his body only because everyone else had been taken equally by surprise.

"Actually, I think we may have at least a little time in hand, Your Highness," Tartarian said. The admiral seemed blissfully unaware of the undercurrent between his prince and Coris, although Hektor rather doubted he truly was.

"As a matter of fact, I think I may agree with you, Admiral," the prince said. "I'm curious as to whether or not your reasoning matches mine, though."

"A lot depends on Haarahld's resources and how focused he can keep his strategy, Your Highness. Frankly, from the reports we've received so far, it doesn't sound as if he lost very many—if any—of those damned galleons. On the other hand, he didn't exactly have a huge number of them before the battle, either. Let's say he has thirty or forty. That's a very powerful fleet, especially with the new artillery. In fact, it could probably defeat any other fleet on the face of Safehold. But as soon as he starts splitting it up to cover multiple objectives, it gets far weaker. And despite what's just happened to all of our navies, he has to take at least some precautions to cover his home waters and protect his merchant shipping.

"As I see it, that means he *probably* only has the capability to launch one effective offensive at a time. I'd love for him to try to conduct multiple campaigns, but I don't think he's stupid enough to do that. And while we're thinking about the sorts of campaigns he can fight, let's not forget that he doesn't really have an army at all, and Corisande isn't exactly a small piece of dirt. It's over seventeen hundred miles from Wind Hook Head to Dairwyn, and more like two thousand from Cape Targan to West Wind Head. We may be a lot less densely populated than someplace like Harchong or Siddarmark, but that's still a lot of territory to cover. He can raise an army big enough to meet his needs against us and Emerald both, if he really tries, but that's going to take time and carry Shan-wei's own price tag. And it's going to cut into his ability to continue his *naval* buildup, as well.

"Even in a best-case situation—best case from his perspective, I mean—it will be five-days, or even months, before he's prepared to launch any serious overseas attacks. And even when he is, Emerald is much closer to him than we are. He's not going to want to leave Prince Nahrmahn unneutralized in his rear while he sends the majority of his fleet and every Marine he can scrape up to attack *us*. That probably means he'll deal with Emerald first, and while I don't think much of the Emeraldian Army, it does exist. If it decides to fight, it's going to take him at least another couple of months, minimum, to take just the major ports and cities. Subduing the entire island, assuming Nahrmahn's subjects decide to remain loyal to him, is going to take even longer.

"So, if he pursues a conventional strategy, I doubt very much that he's going to be able to get around to us at all this year."

"Cogently argued," Hektor said. "And, overall, I find myself in agreement with you. But don't forget that Haarahld of Charis has already demonstrated that he's perfectly prepared to pursue *un*conventional strategies, Admiral."

"Oh, I won't, I assure you, Your Highness. No one associated with the Navy is likely to forget that anytime soon."

"Good." Hektor smiled frostily, then waved one hand.

"For the moment, though, let's assume your analysis is reasonably accurate. Even if it's not, we undoubtedly have at least a month or two before Haarahld's going to be able to come calling. Oh, we may see some cruisers prowling around the coast, snapping up any merchant shipping foolish enough to cross their paths, but it's going to take him longer to put together a serious expedition. And if it takes him long enough, we may have a few nasty surprises of our own for him when he gets here."

"What sort of surprises, My Prince?" Coris asked.

"At least Black Water's dispatches with the sketches of the new Charisian guns got here safely," Hektor pointed out. "It's a pity the actual prize ships managed to end up in Eraystor for some mysterious reason, but thanks to his sketches and Captain Myrgyn's accompanying report, we know about the new gun mounts and carriages and the bagged powder charges. I'd love to know more about this new gunpowder of theirs, as well, but—"

Hektor grimaced amd shrugged slightly. That was the one part of Myrgyn's report which had been less than rigorously complete.

"I think we can still take advantage of what we do know about their artillery improvements even without that, though," he continued after a moment. "The question is how long we'll have to put them into effect."

"I've already discussed the new guns with the Master of Artillery, Your Highness," Tartarian said. "He's just as upset as I was that the same ideas never occurred to us. They're so damned *simple* that—"

The earl stopped himself and shook his head.

"Sorry, Your Highness." He cleared his throat. "The point I was going to make is that he's already making the molds for his first pour of new-style guns. Obviously, he's going to have to do some experimenting, and the new guns are going to have to be bored and mounted. All the same, he's estimating that he should be able to deliver the first of them within a month and a half or so. I told him"—Tartarian looked Hektor in the eye—"that I understood it was only an estimate and that there'd be no repercussions if it turned out that, despite his best efforts, his estimate was overly optimistic."

Hektor grimaced again, but he also nodded.

"While the Master of Artillery is working on that," Tartarian continued, "I've already started looking at ways to modify galleons to mount the new weapons. I don't think it's going to be as simple as just cutting ports in their sides, and I'm not prepared to even guess at this point how long it's going to take to actually refit a ship with them. We'll do the best we can, but we're not going to be able to build a fleet to meet Haarahld at sea in less than at least a year or two, Your Highness. I'm sorry, but that's just the way it is."

"Understood. I'm not any happier about the numbers than you are, Admiral, but we'll just have to do the best we can in the time we have. What I think that's going to mean, at least in the short term, is that as the new guns come from the foundry, they'll go first to our more critical shore batteries, and only then to new naval construction."

"If I may, Your Highness, I'd prefer to modify that slightly," Tartarian said. "I agree that the shore batteries have to have immediate priority, but every gun we can put afloat to support the batteries will be well worthwhile, as well. I'm of the opinion that we could probably build floating batteries—I'm talking about what would basically be nothing but big rafts, with bulwarks to protect their crews against small arms fire and light artillery—relatively quickly to help cover our critical harbors. And every galleon we can fit out with the new guns will be very valuable in terms of harbor defense."

"I see."

Hektor pursed his lips, considering the argument carefully, then shrugged.

"You may well be correct, Admiral. I rather suspect that the point is going to be moot, initially at least, though. Once you begin producing galleons to put the guns aboard, we'll have to reconsider our priorities, of course."

"Yes, Your Highness."

"Which brings us to you, Lyndahr," Hektor continued, turning to his treasurer. "I'm fully aware that we don't begin to have the money to pay for an entirely new navy. On the other hand, buying a new navy will probably be cheaper than buying a new princedom. So I need you to be creative."

"I understand, My Prince," Raimynd replied. "And I've been giving some thought to that very point. The problem is, there's simply not enough money in the treasury to begin to pay for an armaments program on this scale. Or perhaps I should say, there's simply not enough money in *our* treasury to pay for it."

"Ah?" Hektor cocked an eyebrow, and Raimynd shrugged.

"I believe, My Prince," he said in a rather delicate tone, "that the Knights of the Temple Lands aren't going to be . . . excessively pleased by the outcome of our recent campaign."

"That's putting it mildly, I'm sure," Hektor said dryly.

"I assumed that would be the case, My Prince. And it occurred to me that, under the circumstances, the Knights of the Temple Lands might recognize a certain commonality of interest with the Princedom, let us say. Indeed, I believe it would be quite reasonable for us to request them to help defray the costs we've incurred in our common endeavor."

Raimynd, Hektor reflected, should have been a diplomat rather than a coin-counter.

"I agree with you," he said aloud. "Unfortunately, the Knights of the Temple Lands are some distance away. Even with the assistance of the semaphore system and Church dispatch boats, it takes five-days to pass simple messages back and forth, much less gold or silver. And if Haarahld gets wind of actual shipments of bullion, I know *precisely* where his cruisers will be deployed."

"You're correct, My Prince. However, Bishop Executor Thomys is right here in Manchyr. I believe that if you were to approach him properly, explaining the exact nature of our need, you might be able to convince him to bolster our efforts."

"In exactly what fashion?" Hektor asked.

"I believe that if the Bishop Executor were willing, he could issue letters of credit against the Knights of the Temple Lands' treasury. We might have to discount their face value slightly, but it's more likely they'd circulate at full value, given the fact that everyone knows the Temple Lands' solvency is beyond question. We could then issue our own letters of credit, secured by the Bishop Executor's, to finance our necessary armaments program."

"And if the Bishop Executor is unwilling to commit the Knights of the Temple Lands?" Tartarian asked. Raimynd looked at him, and the admiral shrugged. "I agree with the logic of every single thing you've said, Sir Lyndahr. Unfortunately, the Bishop Executor may feel he lacks the authority to encumber the Knights of the Temple Lands' treasury. And, to be perfectly honest, if I were a foundry owner or a shipbuilder, I might find myself a little nervous about accepting a letter of credit on the Temple Lands which hadn't *already* been approved by the Knights of the Temple Lands themselves, if you take my meaning."

"An understandable point," Hektor said. "But not, I think, an insurmountable one. Lyndahr, I think this is a very good idea, one that needs to be pursued. And if Bishop Executor Thomys proves reluctant when we speak to him, I believe we should point out that while he can't legally commit the Knights of the Temple Lands, he *does* have the authority to commit the resources of the Archbishopric. He has the assets right here in Corisande to secure a large enough letter of credit to cover our first several months' expenses. By that time, we'll undoubtedly have heard back from the Knights of the Temple Lands themselves. I think they'll see the logic of your argument and approve the arrangement. If they don't, we'll simply have to come up with some alternative approach."

"Yes, Your Highness." Raimynd dipped his head in a sort of half bow.

"Very well," Hektor said, pushing back his chair, "I think that concludes everything we can profitably discuss this afternoon. I want reports—*regular* reports—on everything we've talked about. I realize our position is rather . . . unenviable, shall we say, at the moment." He showed his teeth in a tight grin. "However, if Haarahld will just take long enough munching up Emerald, I think we ought to be able to accomplish enough to at least give him a serious bellyache when he gets around to Corisande!"

.III.

Tellesberg Cathedral,
City of Tellesberg,
Kingdom of Charis

It was very quiet in Tellesberg Cathedral.

The enormous circular structure was packed, almost as crowded as it had been for King Haarahld's funeral mass, but the atmosphere was very different from the one which had prevailed on that occasion. There was the same undertone of anger, of outrage and determination, but there was something else, as well. Something which hovered like the sultry silence before a thunderstorm. A tension which had grown only more taut and sharper-clawed in the five-days since the old king's death.

Captain Merlin Athrawes of the Charisian Royal Guard understood that tension. As he stood at the entrance to the royal box, watching over King Cayleb and his younger brother and sister, he knew exactly what that vast, not-quite-silent crowd was thinking, worrying about. What he wasn't prepared to hazard a guess about was how it was going to react when the long-anticipated moment finally arrived.

Which, he thought dryly, *it's going to do in about twenty-five seconds.*

As if his thought had summoned the reality, the cathedral's doors opened. There was no music, no choir, on this occasion, and the metallic "clack!" of the latch seemed to echo and re-echo through the stillness like a musket shot. The doors swung silently, smoothly, wide on their well-oiled, meticulously maintained hinges, and a single scepter-bearer stepped through them. There was no thurifer; there were no candle-bearers. There was simply a procession—relatively small, for the main cathedral of an entire kingdom—of clergy in the full, glittering panoply of the vestments of the Church of God Awaiting.

They moved through the stained-glass sunlight pouring through the cathedral's windows, and the stillness and silence seemed to intensify, spreading out from them like ripples of water. The tension ratcheted higher, and Captain Athrawes had to forcibly remind his right hand to stay away from the hilt of his katana.

There were twenty clerics in that procession, led by a single man who wore the white, orange-trimmed cassock of an archbishop under a magnificently embroidered cope stiff with bullion thread and gems. The ruby-set golden crown which had replaced the simple bishop's coronet he had previously worn in this cathedral proclaimed the same priestly rank as his cassock, and the ruby ring of his office flashed on his hand.

The other nineteen men in the procession wore only marginally less majestic copes over white, untrimmed cassocks, but instead of crowns or cornets, they wore the simple white-cockaded priests' caps of bishops in another prelate's cathedral. Their faces were less serene than their leader's. In fact, some of them looked even more tense, more worried, than the laymen waiting for their arrival.

The procession moved steadily, smoothly, down the central aisle to the sanctuary, then unraveled into its component bishops. The man in the archbishop's cassock seated himself on the throne reserved for the Archangel Langhorne's steward in Charis, and voices murmured here and there throughout the cathedral as he sat. Captain Athrawes didn't know if the archbishop had heard them. If he had, he gave no sign of it as he waited while his bishops took their places in the ornate, and yet far humbler, chairs which had been arranged to flank his throne.

Then the last bishop was seated, and the silence was absolute once more, brittle under its own weight and internal tension, as Archbishop Maikel Staynair looked out over the congregation.

Archbishop Maikel was a tallish man, for a Safeholdian, with a magnificent beard, a strong nose, and large, powerful hands. He was also the single human soul in that entire cathedral who actually looked calm. Who almost certainly *was* calm, Captain Athrawes thought, wondering how the man managed it. Even faith had to have its limits. Especially when Staynair's right to the crown and cassock which he wore, the throne in which he sat, had not been confirmed by the Church's Council of Vicars. Nor was there even the most remote hope that the vicars ever *would* confirm him in his new office.

Which, of course, explained the tension which gripped the *rest* of the cathedral.

Then, finally, Staynair spoke.

"My children," his powerful, magnificently trained voice carried easily, helped by the cathedral's total, waiting silence, "we are well aware of how anxious, how worried and even frightened, many of you must be by the unprecedented wave of change which has swept through Charis in the last few months."

Something which not even Captain Athrawes' hearing could have quite called a sound swept through the listening parishioners as the archbishop's words recalled the invasion attempt which had cost them the life of a king. And as his use of the ecclesiastical "we" emphasized that he truly was speaking ex cathedra, formally proclaiming the official, legal, and *binding* doctrine and policy of his archbishopric.

"Change is something which must be approached cautiously," Staynair continued, "and change, solely for the sake of change, must be avoided. Yet even Mother Church's Office of Inquisition has recognized in the past that there are times when change *cannot* be avoided. Grand Vicar Tomhys' writ of instruction, *On Obedience and Faith*, established almost five centuries ago that there are times when attempts to deny, or evade, the consequences of necessary change become in themselves sin.

"This is such a time."

The stillness when he paused was absolute. What had been a state of tension had become a breathless, totally concentrated focus on Archbishop Maikel. One or two heads twitched, as if their owners were tempted to look up at the royal box, instead of at the archbishop, but no one did. Captain Athrawes suspected that it would have been physically impossible for anyone to actually look away from Staynair at this moment.

"My children," the archbishop shook his head gently, his smile sad, "we fully realize that many of you are concerned, possibly even angered, by the vestments we wear, the priestly office to which we have been summoned. We cannot find it in our hearts to blame any of you for that. Nonetheless, we believe what is transpiring in Charis today is the will of God. That God Himself has called us to this office. Not because of any special ability, eloquence, or grace which we might, as any mortal, possess, but because it is His will and

intent to put His house here on Safehold, and in the hearts of His children—
our hearts—into order.

"This is a day of great grief and sorrow for all of us, but it must also be a
day of renewal and rebirth. A day in which we—all of us, every man and
woman among us—reaffirm that which is true and just and good and reclaim
those things from those who would profane them. We must do that without
succumbing to the temptations of power, without listening to the voice of
self-interest, or tainting ourselves with hatred or a lust for revenge. We must
act calmly, deliberately, with due respect and reverence for the offices and institutions of Mother Church. But, above all, we must *act*."

Every member of his audience hung upon the archbishop's every word,
yet Captain Athrawes saw no lessening of their tension, no relief, despite
Staynair's calm, rational, almost soothing tones.

"My children, we have, with King Cayleb's permission, approval, and
support, brought before you today the text of our first official message to the
Grand Vicar and to the Council of Vicars. We would not have it appear that we
have hidden in the shadows, concealed from you any aspect of what we do
here, and why. You are God's children. You have the right to know what those
who have been entrusted with the responsibility of caring for your immortal
souls have been called to do by the demands of those pastoral responsibilities."

The archbishop held out his hand, and one of the other bishops rose. He
crossed to the archbishop's throne and laid an ornately sealed and signed document in that waiting hand. Ribbons, wax, and metallic seals dangled from it,
and the rustle of the thick, expensive parchment upon which it had been
penned was loud in the stillness.

Then he began to read.

"To His Grace, Grand Vicar Erek, of his name the seventeenth, of his Office the eighty-third, Steward and Servant of God and of the Archangel Langhorne, who is, was, and will be God's deputy here on Safehold, from
Archbishop Maikel Staynair, Shepherd of Charis, greetings in the name and
brotherhood of God."

The archbishop's reading voice was as powerful and well trained as his
normal speaking tones. It was the sort of voice which could have taken the
driest, least interesting of official documents and somehow made people realize those documents *mattered*.

Not that it took any special talent to make that clear to these people on
this day.

"It is with the most bitter and profound regret," Staynair continued reading, "that we must inform Your Grace that recent events here in Charis have
revealed to us a great evil which has infested God's Church."

The air in the cathedral stirred, as if every single one of his listeners had
inhaled abruptly and simultaneously.

"The Church and Council of Vicars ordained by the Archangel Langhorne in God's name have been corrupted," Staynair continued in that same calm, unflinching voice. "Offices, decisions, pardons, writs of approval and attestation, as well as writs of condemnation and anathematization, are sold and bartered for, and the very authority of God is twisted and abused for the ambition, arrogance, and cynicism of men who call themselves vicars of God.

"We send to you with this message evidence attesting to and confirming that which we now tell you in our own words."

He paused, very briefly, and then looked up, no longer reading, but reciting from memory as his eyes swept the strained, silent faces which filled that mighty cathedral.

"We indict Zahmsyn Trynair, called a Vicar of God and Chancellor of the Church of God, and with him Allayn Maigwair, Rhobair Duchairn, and Zhaspahr Clyntahn, who also call themselves Vicars of God, for crimes against this Kingdom, this Archbishopric, Holy Mother Church, and God Himself. We offer you proofs that they, acting in concert as the so-called 'Group of Four,' did, in fact, organize and direct the recent attack upon the people of Charis. That Zahmsyn Trynair, individually, and all of them, in concert, did, in fact, use their personas as 'Knights of the Temple Lands' to incite and command the Kings of Dohlar and Tarot, the Queen of Chisholm, and the Princes of Emerald and Corisande, to league together for the express purpose of utterly destroying this Kingdom with fire and the sword. That they misused, misdirected, and stole funds from Mother Church's own coffers to finance their plan to destroy Charis. That they, and others like them, have systematically and continuously abused their positions and their authority in the pursuit of personal power, wealth, prestige, and luxury.

"We can no longer turn an ear which does not hear, nor an eye which does not see, upon this ongoing pattern of vile corruption. The high offices of Mother Church are neither the negotiable virtue of some street-corner strumpet nor the plunder of footpads and thieves to be disposed of to receivers of stolen goods in dark rooms, hidden from all honest eyes. They are trusts from God, held in the service of God's children, yet in the hands of those vile men who have been permitted to poison God's own Church, they have become tools of oppression, abuse, and the casual ordering of mass murder.

"We, the Archbishop of Charis, speaking of, for, and with the consent of our dread sovereign, King Cayleb II, can and will abide no further degradation of Mother Church. The Mother of all men and all women has become the Harlot of Shan-wei herself, for she has permitted all of the evils enumerated in this message and its accompanying proofs not simply to exist, but to prosper. Accordingly, we can no longer hold ourselves, or our rulers, or the children of God in our care, slavishly obedient to the men who sell that harlot's favors to the highest bidder. We separate ourselves from them, and from you, and we cast you out, for you have permitted them to flourish like noxious weeds in the garden which God has entrusted to you.

"The Archbishopric of Charis, as the Kingdom of Charis, rejects the authority of murderers, rapists, arsonists, and thieves. If you cannot purge the Church of such cankers and poisons, then we will cleanse *ourselves* of them, and, God willing, in the fullness of time, we will purge Mother Church herself of those who profane the vestments and rings of their offices with every breath they breathe, every decision they make.

"We do not come lightly to this point, to this decision," Maikel Staynair told the far distant head of the Council of Vicars while his eyes bored into the faces, expressions, and souls of his flock. "We come to it with tears and sorrow. We come to it as children who may no longer serve a mother they have always loved because her only ambition has become the systematic enslavement and murder of her own children.

"Yet however it may grieve us, however deeply we may wish that it were not so, we *have* come to this point, to this decision. Here we will stand, for we can do no other, and we appeal to the ultimate judgment of the God who created us all to judge between us and the true fathers of corruption."

.IV.
Royal Palace,
City of Tellesberg,
Kingdom of Charis

Merlin Athrawes stood just inside the council chamber door, wearing the black and gold of the Charisian Royal Guard, and watched a young man gaze out a window across the Tellesberg waterfront at the latest in the line of rain squalls marching towards the city across Howell Bay. The youngster in question was dark-haired, dark-eyed, and on the tall side for an inhabitant of the planet of Safehold, and especially of the Kingdom of Charis. He was also barely twenty-three years old, which came to only twenty-one in the years of the planet on which (though he did not know it) his species had actually evolved. That made him very young indeed to wear the emerald-set golden chain whose glittering green fire was the emblem of a king.

Many people would no doubt have been struck by his youthfulness, the fact that, despite his already powerful physique, he clearly had filling out still to do. Others might have noted the restless energy which had driven him to the window after the better part of two hours of discussion and planning. They might have confused that restlessness with boredom or lack of interest . . . but only until they saw his eyes, Merlin thought. They were no longer as young as once they had been, those eyes, and the mouth below them was thinner, with the set of a man far older—wiser, tougher, and more ruthless—than his years. They were the eyes and mouth of Cayleb Zhan Haarahld Bryahn Ahrmahk, King Cayleb II, ruler of Charis, who had—in the space of barely three local months—won the three most crushing, one-sided naval victories in the entire history of Safehold, lost his father, inherited a crown, and thrown his defiance of the four most powerful men in the entire world into the teeth of God's own Church.

And they were also the eyes and mouth of a king whose kingdom still faced the short end of a battle of extinction unless he and his advisers could think of a way to avert that outcome.

Cayleb watched the distant rain for several more moments, then turned back to several of the advisers in question.

The group of men seated around the massive table weren't the entire Royal Council. In fact, they weren't even *most* of the Council . . . and they did include several people who weren't Council members at all. Cayleb was well aware that some of the Councilors who weren't present resented—or would resent—their exclusion when they discovered it. *If* they discovered it. But while his father's tutelage had seen to it that he was far from oblivious to the political imperatives of maintaining a broad base of support, especially in the present circumstances, he was also perfectly willing to live with that resentment for the moment.

"All right," he said, "I think that deals with all of the immediate domestic reports?"

He looked around the table, one eyebrow quirked, and the compact, distinguished-looking man sitting at its far end nodded. Rayjhis Yowance, the Earl of Gray Harbor, had served Cayleb's father as Charis' first councilor of Charis for the better part of fourteen years; now he served his new king in the same role.

"For the moment, at any rate, Your Majesty," he said. Despite the fact that he'd known Cayleb literally all his life—or possibly because of it—he had made it a point to address his youthful monarch with a greater degree of formality since Cayleb's ascension to the throne. "I believe Maikel here has at least one additional point he wishes to address, although I understand he's waiting for a few more reports before he does so." Gray Harbor's rising inflection turned the final part of the statement into a question, and he raised one eyebrow at the man sitting at the far end of the council table from the king in the white cassock of the episcopate.

"I do," Archbishop Maikel confirmed. "As you say, however, Rayjhis, I'm still waiting for two reports I've requested. With your permission, Your

Majesty, I'd like to reserve a few minutes of your time tomorrow or the next day to discuss this."

"Of course," Cayleb told the man who had been his father's confessor and who—despite certain . . . technical irregularities—had been elevated to Archbishop of all Charis.

"I also expect additional reports from Hanth in the next few days," Gray Harbor continued, and smiled thinly. "Current indications are that Mahntayl is considering a rather hasty relocation to Eraystor."

"Probably the smartest move the bastard's made in years," someone murmured so softly even Merlin's ears had trouble overhearing him. The voice, Merlin noted, sounded remarkably like that of the Earl of Lock Island.

If Cayleb had heard the comment, he gave no indication. Instead, he simply nodded.

"Well," he said, "in that case, I suppose it's about time we considered breaking up. It's coming up on lunch, and I don't know about the rest of you, but I'm hungry. Is there anything else we need to look at before we eat?"

"Zhefry reminded me of several items this morning, Your Majesty," Gray Harbor replied with a slight smile. Zhefry Ahbaht was the first councilor's personal secretary, and his ability to "manage" Gray Harbor's schedule was legendary.

"Despite his insistence, I think most of them can probably wait until after lunch," the earl continued. "He did, however, point out that the Group of Four ought to be getting their copies of the writs in the next five-day or so."

One or two faces tightened at the reminder. Cayleb's wasn't one of them.

"He's right," the king agreed. "And I wish I could be a fly on the wall when Clyntahn and Trynair open them." His smile was thinner—and much colder—than Gray Harbor's had been. "I don't imagine they'll be particularly pleased. Especially not with your personal log for the fire, Maikel."

Several of the other men sitting around the table smiled back at him. Some of their expressions were even more kraken-like than his own, Merlin noted.

"I don't imagine they've been 'particularly pleased' about anything that's happened in the past few months, Your Majesty," Gray Harbor agreed. "Frankly, I can't think of any message you could have sent them that could possibly have changed *that*."

"Oh, I don't know, Rayjhis." Admiral Bryahn Lock Island was the commander of the Royal Charisian Navy. He was also one of Cayleb's cousins. "I imagine that if we were to send them a mass suicide note, that would probably cheer them up immensely."

This time there were a few outright chuckles, and Cayleb shook his head admonishingly at Lock Island.

"You're a bluff, unimaginative sailor, Bryahn. Remarks like that demonstrate exactly why it's such a good idea for us to keep you as far away as possible from the diplomatic correspondence!"

"Amen to that!" Lock Island's pious tone was at least eight-tenths sincere, Merlin judged.

"Speaking of 'bluff, unimaginative sailors,'" Ahlvyno Pawalsyn said, "I have to say, although I'd really rather not bring this up, that your current plans for expanding the Navy worry me, Bryahn."

Lock Island looked at the other man and cocked his head. Ahlvyno Pawalsyn was also Baron Ironhill . . . and Keeper of the Purse. That made him effectively the treasurer of the Kingdom of Charis.

"I assume that what you mean is that figuring out how to *pay* for the expansion worries you," the admiral said after a moment. "On the other hand, what's likely to happen if we *don't* continue the expansion worries me a lot more."

"I'm not trying to suggest it isn't necessary, Bryahn," Ironhill replied mildly. "As the fellow who's supposed to come up with a way to finance it, however, it does leave me with some . . . interesting difficulties, shall we say?"

"Let Nahrmahn pay for it," Lock Island suggested. "That fat little bugger's still got plenty tucked away in his treasury, and he's got damn-all for a navy at the moment. We're already camped in his front yard, and he can't be any too happy about the way we've sewed Eraystor Bay shut like a sack. So why don't I just make his day complete by taking a couple of squadrons in close and sending a few Marines ashore to deliver a polite request from His Majesty here that he finance our modest efforts before we burn his entire miserable waterfront around his ears?"

"Tempting," Cayleb said. "Very tempting. I'm not sure it's a very practical solution, though."

"Why not?" Lock Island turned back to the king. "We won; he lost. Well, he *will* lose, whenever we finally get around to actually kicking his fat arse off his throne, and he knows it."

"No doubt," Cayleb agreed. "Assuming we add Emerald to the Kingdom, however, we're going to have to figure out how to pay for its administration. Looting its treasury doesn't strike me as a particularly good way to get started. Besides, it would be a onetime sort of thing, and just expanding the Navy isn't going to solve our problems, Bryahn. Somehow we've got to pay for *maintaining* it, too. With the Church openly against us, we don't dare lay up large numbers of ships. We'll need them in active commission, and that means we'll have a heavy, ongoing commitment on the Treasury. We couldn't rely on regular 'windfalls' the size of Nahrmahn's treasury even if we wanted to, so we're going to have to figure out a long-term way to pay for it out of our own ongoing revenue stream."

Lock Island's eyebrows rose as he gave his young monarch a look of respect. Ironhill, on the other hand, positively beamed, as did Gray Harbor, and Merlin nodded mentally in satisfaction, as well. All too many rulers twice Cayleb's age would have settled for whatever got them the ships they needed in the shortest possible time and let the future take care of itself.

"Actually, Your Majesty," another of the men seated at the table said, "I think paying for the Navy isn't going to be quite as difficult as it might first appear. Not, at least, as long as we're not trying to raise mainland-sized armies, at the same time."

All eyes turned to the speaker. Ehdwyrd Howsmyn was short, stout, and very well dressed. At forty-one years of age (thirty-seven and a half, standard, Merlin automatically translated mentally), he was the youngest man in the council chamber after Cayleb himself. He was also, almost certainly, the wealthiest. It was his foundries which had produced the artillery and the copper sheathing for the galleons Cayleb and his captains had used to smash the recent attack upon the kingdom. In fact, his shipyards had *built* half a dozen of those galleons, as well. Howsmyn was not officially a member of the Royal Council, or even of Parliament. Neither, for that matter, was Rhaiyan Mychail, the sharp-eyed (and almost equally wealthy) man sitting next to him. Mychail was at least twice Howsmyn's age, but the two of them were business partners of long-standing, and Mychail's textile manufactories and ropewalks had produced virtually all of the canvas for those same galleons' sails, not to mention most of the cordage for their standing and running rigging.

"Unless you and Master Mychail intend to build ships gratis, we're still going to have to figure out how to pay for them," Ironhill pointed out. "And without access to Desnair's gold mines, we can't just coin money whenever we need it."

"Oh, I'm well aware of that, Ahlvyno. And, no, I'm not planning on building them gratis. Sorry." Howsmyn grinned, and his eyes twinkled. "Neither Rhaiyan nor I have any intention of gouging the Treasury, of course. That'd be an outstandingly stupid thing for either of us to be doing at this particular moment. But we do have to manage to pay our own workers and our suppliers, you know. Not to mention showing at least a modest profit for ourselves and our partners and shareholders.

"What I was getting at, though, was that as long as the Navy can keep merchant shipping moving, the balance of trade is going to provide quite a healthy cash flow. And under the circumstances, I don't see me or any of my fellow shipowners complaining if the Crown decides to tack on a few extra duties and taxes on the Navy's behalf so that it *can* keep trade moving."

"I'm not as certain as you seem to be about that cash flow, Ehdwyrd." Ironhill's expression was far more somber than Howsmyn's. "If I were the Group of Four, the very first thing I'd do would be to demand that all of

Haven's and Howard's harbors be closed to our shipping immediately." He shrugged. "They have to be as aware as we are that the Kingdom's prosperity hinges entirely on our merchant marine. Surely they're going to do everything they can to cripple it."

Gray Harbor frowned, and some of the others went so far as to nod in sober agreement. Howard and Haven, the two main continents of Safehold, contained at least eighty percent of the planetary population. The kingdoms, principalities, and territories in which that population lived were the markets upon which Charis' merchant marine and manufactories had built the kingdom's wealth. If those markets were taken away, Charisian prosperity would be doomed, but Howsmyn only chuckled.

"The Group of Four can demand whatever they want, Ahlvyno. I doubt they're going to be stupid enough to issue that particular decree, but, then, they've already done some spectacularly stupid things, so it's always possible I'm wrong. In fact, I rather hope I am and that they *do* try it. Even if they do, though, it's not going to happen."

"No?" Ironhill sat back in his chair. "Why?"

"Why do I wish they would? Or why do I think it's not going to happen even if they do?"

"Both."

"I wish they would because giving orders you *know* won't be obeyed is one of the best ways I know to destroy your own authority. And the reason an order like that wouldn't be obeyed is that no one in Haven or Howard can possibly provide the goods those markets require. I don't mean just that they can't provide them as *cheaply* as we can, Ahlvyno, although that's certainly true, as well. What I mean is that they literally don't have the capacity to provide them *at all*. And that even if they had the capacity, or developed it as quickly as possible, they still wouldn't have the ability to transport those goods at anything like the economies of cost *we* can achieve." Howsmyn shook his head. "That's one of the minor details the Group of Four left out of their calculations, actually. I'm astonished Duchairn didn't warn the other three what would happen if they succeeded in what they had in mind."

"Would it really have been that bad for them, Ehdwyrd?" Gray Harbor asked, and Howsmyn shrugged.

"It would've been bad, Rayjhis. Maybe not as bad as *I* think it would have been, I suppose, if I'm going to be fair. After all, my perspective is bound to be shaped by my own business interests and experience. Still, I think most people—including a lot of people right here in the Kingdom—don't understand how thoroughly we've come to dominate the world's markets. There was a reason Trynair chose King Haarahld's supposed ambition to control the entire world's merchant traffic as his pretext for supporting Hektor and Nahrmahn against us. He knows there are plenty of people in

Dohlar, Desnair, Harchong—even the Republic—who deeply resent our domination of the carrying trade. And quite a few of them—the *smarter* ones, to be honest—resent their own growing dependency on our manufactories, as well.

"All of that's true, but their resentment can't change the reality, and the reality is that better than half—probably closer to two-thirds, actually—of the world's merchant galleons fly the Charisian flag. And another reality is that somewhere around two-thirds of the manufactured goods those galleons transport are made right here in Charis, as well. And a third reality is that it takes four times as long and costs five or six times as much to transport the same goods to their ultimate destinations overland as it does to ship them by sea. If, of course, it's even possible to ship them overland in the first place. It's just a bit difficult to get something from Siddarmark to Tarot by wagon, after all. There's this little thing called the Tarot Channel in the way."

One or two of the others looked dubious. Not at his analysis of the manufacture and transport of goods. That was something any Charisian understood on an almost instinctual level. Some of them clearly thought Howsmyn's assumptions were overly optimistic, however. Ironhill appeared to be one of them; Gray Harbor and Cayleb did not, and behind his own outwardly expressionless guardsman's face, Merlin frowned thoughtfully. He wasn't certain of Howsmyn's actual numbers. No one on Safehold kept that sort of statistic, so anything Howsmyn said could be no more than an informed estimate. On the other hand, he wouldn't be very surprised to discover that those estimates were, in fact, very close to accurate. No one got as wealthy as Ehdwyrd Howsmyn from international trade without a keen grasp of the realities of finance, shipping, and manufacturing.

And, Merlin reminded himself, *Charis was already well along the way towards a purely water-powered Industrial Revolution, despite the Church's proscriptions against advanced technology, even before I put in my own two cents' worth.*

"Over the past year and a half or so," Howsmyn continued, very carefully not looking in Merlin's direction, "our ability to produce goods, especially textiles, quickly and at even lower cost has increased dramatically. No one in Haven or Howard is going to be able to match our productivity for a long time to come, and that assumes that nothing happens"—he was even more careful not to glance at Merlin—"to further increase our manufactories' efficiency. And as I say, even if they could produce the goods we can produce, trying to transport them overland instead of shipping them by water would add enormously to their expenses. No." He shook his head. "If the Group of Four had succeeded in destroying Charis and our merchant marine, they would have created a huge problem for themselves. It truly would have been a case of killing the wyvern that fetched the golden rabbit."

"Even assuming all of that's true, that doesn't mean they won't try to do exactly what Ahlvyno's just suggested anyway," Gray Harbor pointed out, dutifully playing the role of Shan-wei's advocate. "They already tried to destroy us, after all, despite all of the dire consequences you're saying they would have faced as a result."

"I also admitted that they've already done some spectacularly stupid things," Howsmyn reminded the earl. "And they *may* try to close their ports to us, as well. But if they do, those ports are going to leak like sieves. There are going to be entirely too many people—including quite a few of the vicars' own bailiffs, for that matter—who want and need our goods for it to work. Not even the Church has ever really been able to control smuggling, you know, and trying to do something like that would be much, much harder than chasing a few independent smugglers."

"You probably have a point, Master Howsmyn," Archbishop Maikel said. "However, I suspect the Group of Four—and especially Grand Inquisitor Clyntahn—are, indeed, likely to make the attempt."

"I bow to your greater familiarity with the Council of Vicars' thinking, Your Eminence," Howsmyn said. "I stand by my analysis of what will happen if they do, however."

"Rahnyld of Dohlar's always wanted to increase his own merchant marine," Bynzhamyn Raice, Baron Wave Thunder, pointed out.

The bald, hook-nosed Wave Thunder had been King Haarahld VII's spymaster. He served Cayleb in the same role, and he seldom spoke up in meetings like this unless it had something to do with those duties. When he did open his mouth, though, he was almost always worth listening to, Merlin thought, and this time was no exception. The King of Dohlar was hemmed in on all sides by much more powerful neighbors like the Harchong Empire and Republic of Siddarmark. His chances of territorial expansion were effectively nil, which was why he'd attempted for years to emulate the maritime prosperity of Charis, instead.

"That was one of the pretensions which made Rahnyld such an enthusiastic supporter of the Group of Four's plans, after all," Wave Thunder continued. "Well, that and those loans of his from the Church. Under the circumstances, I'm sure the Church would be willing to forgive even more of his loans and actively subsidize his efforts to build up a merchant fleet big enough to cut into our own carrying trade, and the Church has a *lot* of money. If the Group of Four decides to make a major commitment to helping him, he could launch a lot of galleons."

"Unless my memory fails me, Bynzhamyn," Lock Island said, "we're still at war with Dohlar, and likely to remain so for quite some time. Something about our demand for Rahnyld's head, I believe."

Quite a few of the men around the table chuckled at that observation, Merlin noticed.

BY SCHISM RENT ASUNDER / 43

"Until and unless that state of war is terminated," the admiral continued, "any Dohlaran-flagged vessel is a legitimate prize of war. And even if, for some reason, peace should disastrously break out between us and Rahnyld, there've always been problems with piracy in the waters around Howard. I'd be astonished if some of those 'pirates' didn't somehow manage to come into possession of some nice little schooners, possibly even with some of the new guns on board."

The chuckles were louder this time.

"We're getting too far ahead of ourselves," Cayleb said. He looked at Howsmyn. "I'm inclined to think your analysis is basically sound, Ehdwyrd. That doesn't mean things won't change, and we've seen for ourselves over the last two years just how *quickly* they can change. Still, I think one of the other points you made is almost certainly valid. Navies are expensive, but as long as we have one and our enemies don't, we don't need a huge army to go with it, so at least we can avoid *that* expense. And under the circumstances, I think we can count on being able to finance the fleet somehow."

"For now, at least, we can, Your Majesty," Ironhill conceded. "The funds are there for the thirty additional ships Admiral Lock Island has under construction at the moment, at any rate. We can't lay down many more than that until we've launched the current vessels to clear the building ways, anyhow. But completing those ships is going to effectively finish the total elimination of the treasury surplus your father and grandfather had managed to build up before the current emergency."

"I understand." Cayleb nodded.

"Which, if Your Majesty will pardon me," Lock Island said with greater than usual formality, "brings us to the question of just what we do with the ships we already have while we wait for the new ones."

"You mean besides keeping a lid on other people's privateers and making certain the Church isn't able to land an overwhelming army to slaughter our people, burn our cities to the ground, and remove all of our heads?" Cayleb inquired mildly.

"Besides that, of course, Your Majesty."

"Bryahn, I'm perfectly well aware that you want to exterminate Prince Nahrmahn." There was a slight but unmistakable edge of patient exasperation in Cayleb's tone. "For that matter, I'd rather enjoy the process myself. But the truth is that our own navy consists of less than sixty obsolete galleys and only thirty-four galleons, at least until more of the new construction comes forward and we get the damaged ships back from the repair yards. That's going to leave us stretched dangerously thin if we go after Nahrmahn and Hektor simultaneously."

"Then let's go after them one at a time," Lock Island argued with respectful stubbornness. "And since Nahrmahn is the closer, and since we're already blockading Eraystor Bay, let's start with him."

"I think you're entirely right that we need to go after them one at a time," Cayleb replied. "Unfortunately, I also think Hektor is the more dangerous of the two. Unless I miss my guess"—it was his turn to avoid looking in Merlin's direction—"he's already laying down and converting as many galleons of his own as he can. And if Black Water's reports on our new artillery got home to him, he's going to know how to arm them effectively, as well. He'll have to start from scratch with the new guns, but I trust no one in this room is foolish enough to think Hektor is stupid or that his artisans and mechanics have been stricken with some sort of mysterious incompetence overnight. Nahrmahn doesn't begin to have Hektor's building capacity and foundries, so if we're going to go after one of them, we need to start with Corisande, not Emerald. And then there's that little matter of the army we don't have. Taking islands away from Nahrmahn and sealing off Eraystor is one thing; finding enough troops to put ashore to take the *rest* of his princedom away from him is going to be something else, I'm afraid."

Lock Island looked moderately rebellious, and he wasn't the only one who felt that way, Merlin decided.

"In Bryahn's support, Your Majesty," Wave Thunder said, "don't forget who it was that tried to have you assassinated." Cayleb looked at him, and the spymaster shrugged. "He tried it *before* you and your father completely destroyed his navy; now that he doesn't have one anymore, there has to be even more pressure to consider . . . unconventional measures. If we give him long enough, he's likely to try it again."

"Then it's just going to be up to you and the Guard"—this time Cayleb did glance at Merlin—"to see to it that he *fails* again, Bynzhamyn."

"That may not be quite as simple a matter as we'd all prefer, Your Majesty. In fact, that's part of what I want to discuss with you later," Archbishop Maikel said, and all eyes turned to him. "Before, Nahrmahn was forced to hire mercenaries, professional assassins, if he wanted you or your father dead," the archbishop continued. "Today, alas, there are far more potential assassins in Charis than ever before. Indeed, protecting you against *Nahrmahn's* efforts to murder you may be the least of the Guard's concerns."

And that, Merlin thought, *is probably an understatement. Unfortunately.*

The majority of Cayleb's subjects strongly supported their youthful king and his new archbishop in his confrontation with the Church of God Awaiting. They knew precisely what the Church—or, at least, the "Group of Four" which actually created and manipulated the Church's policies—had intended to happen to their kingdom and their families when they chose to break Charis' power once and for all by turning it into a wasteland of slaughtered people and burned towns. They supported the scathing indictment Maikel had sent to Grand Vicar Erek in their collective name, for they'd made a clear distinction between God Himself and the corrupt, venal men who controlled the Church.

But if the majority of Charisians felt that way, a significant minority did not, and almost a quarter of the kingdom's clergy were outraged and furious at Cayleb's "impious" challenge to the Church's "rightful, God-given authority." It would have been nice if Merlin had been able to convince himself that all of those people who disapproved were just as corrupt and calculating as the Group of Four themselves. Unfortunately, the overwhelming majority of them weren't. Their horror at the thought of schism within God's Church was completely genuine, and their outrage at the ruler who'd dared to raise his hand against God's will sprang from a deep-seated, totally honest faith in the teachings of the Church of God Awaiting. Many—*most*—of them saw it as their sacred duty to resist, by any means they could, the abominations King Cayleb and Archbishop Maikel sought to impose upon the kingdom.

For the first time in living memory, there was an actual, significant, *internal* threat to the life of a king of Charis, and Staynair's regretful expression showed that the archbishop understood exactly why.

"I know, Maikel," Cayleb said. "I know. But we can't undo what we've already done, and even if I thought it was what God wanted, we couldn't turn back from the journey we've begun. Which doesn't mean"—he looked back at Wave Thunder—"that I want any mass arrests. I've never been very fond of iron heels, and I can't convince people who hate and fear what they think I'm doing that they're wrong about my policies or the reasons for them if I start right out trying to crush every voice of disagreement."

"I've never suggested that we ought to, Your Highness. I only—"

"His Majesty is right, My Lord," Staynair said quietly, and Wave Thunder looked at him.

"It's the question of conscience, of the relationship between each individual human soul and God, which stands at the heart of the Group of Four's hostility towards us," the archbishop continued in that same firm, quiet voice. "Trynair and Clyntahn, each for reasons of his own, are determined to preserve Mother Church's total control over the thoughts, beliefs, and actions of all of God's children. They've seen fit to dress their ambition in the fine clothes of faith and concern for the salvation of souls, to pretend they're motivated only by priestly duty, and not the obscene wealth and decadent lives they live, when, in fact, their own arrogance and corruption have turned Mother Church herself into a tool of oppression and greed.

"We know that." He looked around the suddenly quiet council chamber. "We've seen it. And we believe we're called by God to oppose that oppression. To remind Mother Church that it's the *souls* of God's people which matter, and not the amount of gold in her coffers, or the personal power and wealth of her vicars and the luxury in which they live. But to do that successfully, we must remind all of Mother Church's children of those same things. We cannot do that by resorting to oppression ourselves."

"With all due respect, Your Eminence," Wave Thunder said into the stillness which seemed only deeper and quieter as thunder rumbled and rolled once more in the distance, "I don't disagree. But, by the same token, we can't protect the King if we're not willing to act strongly and publicly against those who would destroy him. And if we lose the King, we lose everything."

Cayleb stirred, but Wave Thunder faced him stubbornly.

"At this moment, Your Majesty, that's true, and you know it. We've already lost your father, and Zhan is still a child. If we lose you, who holds the Kingdom together? And if this Kingdom stumbles, who will be left to 're-mind' Mother Church of anything? Right now, on this day, any hope of human freedom dies with *you*, Your Majesty. For now, at least, that statement is the terrifying truth. And it's also the reason you *must* let us take the necessary precautions to keep you alive."

Cayleb looked around the table, and stark agreement with Wave Thunder looked back at him from every face. Even the archbishop nodded in grave acknowledgment of the baron's point.

"I will, Bynzhamyn," Cayleb replied, after a moment. He glanced at Merlin again, then back at Wave Thunder.

"I will," he repeated, "and anyone who actually lends himself to treason against the Crown, to violence against the Crown's ministers, or against any of the Kingdom's subjects, will be dealt with sternly, regardless of the reasons for his actions. But there will be no preemptive arrests because of what men *might* do, and no one will be punished unless their conspiracies or their crimes are first proven before the King's Bench in open court. No secret courts, no summary imprisonments or executions. I refuse to become another Clyntahn simply to protect myself against him."

Wave Thunder's expression was a long way from anything Merlin would have called satisfied, but at least the baron let the argument drop. For now, at any rate.

"All right," Cayleb said more briskly. "I still hear lunch calling, and it's getting louder, so let's go ahead and wrap this up. Ahlvyno, please give me a report by the end of this five-day on the exact state of the Treasury, allowing for the completion and manning of the galleons we currently have under construction. Take Ehdwyrd at his word and propose a reasonable schedule of new duties and taxes, as well, based on the assumption that our trade will at least hold level. Bryahn, I'd like you and Baron Seamount to give me your best estimates of what we're going to need Ahlvyno to somehow figure out how to pay for after we finish the present building program. You'd better get Sir Dustyn involved in that, as well. Ehdwyrd, I'd like you and Rhaiyan to give some additional thought to what you were saying earlier about the likely consequences of any effort by the Group of Four to close Haven and Howard to our trade. Assume they're actually going to do it, then come up with the most effective ways for us to undermine any embargo and make sure their efforts don't succeed. You might also consider how we could motivate our merchants and shipping houses to fund presentation galleons for the Navy, as well. As you say, our survival depends upon their prosperity, but their prosperity depends upon our survival. I think it's fair for them to contribute a little more to protecting their shipping than we might expect out of, say, a dragon-breeder from somewhere back in the hills. And, Rayjhis, I think you'd better check with Dr. Mahklyn. I'd like the College's input on some of our estimates on shipping, trade, and taxation, as well."

Heads nodded around the table, and Cayleb nodded back.

"In that case, I think we're mostly done here. Rayjhis, I'd like you and Archbishop Maikel to remain behind for a moment, if you would."

"Of course, Your Majesty," Gray Harbor murmured, and chairs moved back from the table as the others took their cue and rose.

▼   ▼   ▼

The council chamber door closed behind the others, and Cayleb looked at Merlin.

"Why don't you come over and join us, now that it's safe?" he asked with a smile, and Gray Harbor chuckled.

"As you command, Your Majesty," Merlin replied mildly, and crossed to settle himself into the chair Howsmyn had occupied a few minutes before.

Had anyone else been present, that hypothetical other observer probably would have been more than a bit surprised to see King Cayleb's bodyguard sitting at the council table along with the king's two most trusted official advisers as if he were their equal in the king's eyes. After all, it was clearly Captain Athrawes' responsibility to keep Cayleb alive, and *not*—despite his recent promotion, in keeping with his position as the king's personal armsman—to advise him on high matters of state.

Of course, that same hypothetical other observer would be operating on the mistaken assumption that Captain Merlin Athrawes of the Charisian Royal Guard was alive. Well, that he was a human being, at least. He might actually be *alive* after all; Merlin's internal jury was still out on that particular question.

Not even Gray Harbor and Staynair knew the complete truth about him. For that matter, Cayleb himself didn't know the *complete* truth. The king knew Merlin was considerably more than human, but not that he was in fact a PICA—a Personality Integrated Cybernetic Avatar—whose artificial body was home to the electronically recorded personality, memories, emotions, hopes, and fears of a young woman named Nimue Alban who had been dead for the last eight or nine centuries.

But what Gray Harbor and Staynair did know, and what they, along with Cayleb and the handful of others who shared the same knowledge, went to great lengths to keep anyone else from discovering was how central Captain Athrawes' "visions" and bits and pieces of esoteric knowledge had been to Charis' ability to survive the Group of Four's massive onslaught. Everyone in the kingdom knew Merlin was a *seijin*, of course—one of the deadly warrior-monk martial artists and sometime spiritual visionaries who came and went (usually apocryphally) through the pages of Safeholdian history. Merlin had chosen that particular persona carefully before he ever arrived in Charis, and his reputation as one of the deadliest warriors in the world (although, to be strictly accurate, he wasn't simply *one* of the deadliest warriors in the world, given his . . . abilities) made him the perfect choice for Cayleb's personal armsman. Which just happened to put him permanently at the king's elbow, deep at the heart of all of Cayleb's councils and plans, and yet simultaneously made him almost a piece of the furniture. Constantly available for advice or consultation, yet so invisible to outside eyes that no one ever wondered just what he was doing there.

Now Cayleb looked at him and arched an eyebrow.

"What did you think of Ehdwyrd's analysis?" he asked.

"I think I'm not equipped to argue with him in that particular area of expertise," Merlin replied. "I doubt anyone in the entire Kingdom is, at least until Mahklyn's passion for recording numbers gives us an objective base of statistics. I'd have to agree with him, though, that it would be extraordinarily difficult for the Group of Four to effectively close Howard and Haven to our merchants. How successful their efforts would be in the end if they decided to try anyway, and whether or not Baron Wave Thunder's concerns about subsidies to Rahnyld are realistic, is more than I'm prepared to say, however."

Napoleon tried it against England, with his "Continental System," Merlin reflected. *It didn't work out all that well for him, which is probably a good sign for Howsmyn's theories. Then again, there was a lot more to Earth at that point than just Europe. In this case, it would be as if Napoleon controlled all the major ports of North America, South America, and Asia, including Russia, China, and the Ottoman Empire, as well. And, for that matter, the Church's control goes a lot deeper than Napoleon's did. Which is only going to get worse as the religious aspect of this confrontation gets clearer and clearer to everyone involved.*

"I'm inclined to agree with Ehdwyrd," Gray Harbor offered. Cayleb and Staynair both looked at him, and the first councilor shrugged. "I don't doubt the consequences here in Charis would be . . . serious if the Group of Four could pull it off. In fact, they could well turn out to be catastrophic. But I'm inclined to think Ehdwyrd's arguments about the availability and cost of our goods would make things almost as bad for the mainland realms, as well. Almost certainly bad enough to lead to major covert resistance to any such decree, in fact. For that matter, it could well lead to *open* resistance in a lot of cases. Unless, of course, the Church goes ahead and declares Holy War. Under those circumstances, things could get a lot dicier."

"Maikel?" Cayleb turned to his archbishop, and there was rather more concern in the king's brown eyes than he would have let most people see.

"My opinion hasn't changed, Cayleb," Staynair said with a serenity Merlin envied, even as he wondered how justifiable it was. "Given the way the Group of Four approached this entire bungled affair, they're going to be feeling a lot of internal pressure. Remember, they've always had enemies of their own in the Council of Vicars. *They* haven't forgotten that, at any rate, and some of those enemies have significant power bases of their own. Our little note to the Grand Vicar is going to both weaken them and embolden their enemies, as well. Against that backdrop, they're going to have to move at least a bit cautiously, unless they choose to risk everything on some dramatic, do-or-die gesture of defiance. They've never done that in the past. Indeed, if they'd had the least notion their attack on the Kingdom could possibly turn into the diaster it has, they would never have undertaken it. Or, at least, never so offhandedly and casually. Having already fed one hand to the slash lizard, I believe they're unlikely to want to raise the stakes any higher than they absolutely must, for a time at least."

"I hope you're right about that," the king said. "I really do hope you're right about that."

So do I, Merlin thought dryly. *Which is why I hope you and Maikel were both right about setting forth your position vis-à-vis the Church quite so . . . forthrightly.*

"My hope is the same as yours, Your Majesty." The archbishop smiled slightly. "Time will tell, of course. And"—his smile broadened and his eyes twinkled—"I'm very well aware that the nature of my own concerns lends itself to operating on the basis of faith rather better than yours does."

"My own impression is that His Eminence is probably right about the Group of Four's disinclination to rush into some sort of white-hot religious confrontation, at least in the short term," Merlin said, and saw Cayleb's almost subliminal grimace. Merlin hadn't actually advised against Staynair's letter to the Grand Vicar, but he hadn't exactly been one of its stronger supporters, either.

"I think that's inevitably where we're headed, unfortunately," he continued now. "Completely ignoring our own correspondence with them, the mere fact that we're no longer obeying their orders would push them into that, and things are going to get extraordinarily ugly when it happens. For now, though, habit, if nothing else, is going to keep them trying to 'game the situation' the way they've always done it in the past. That's how they got themselves into this mess, of course, but I think it's going to take at least a few more months for it to penetrate just how completely the rules have changed. Which means we should have at least a little time to press our own preparations."

"Which brings me to the real reason I asked you and Rayjhis to stay behind, Maikel," Cayleb said.

He leaned back in his chair and ran the fingers of his left hand across the emerald sets of the chain he had inherited so recently from his father. He did that a lot, as if the chain were a sort of talisman, a comforting link between his father and himself. Merlin was confident that it was an unconscious mannerism on his part, but the *seijin* felt a familiar pang of personal grief as it reminded him of the old king's death.

"Bryahn is right about the necessity of dealing with Nahrmahn and Hektor," the new king continued. "There's always Gorjah, as well, but Tarot can wait. At least, though, we know where we are with Nahrmahn and Hektor. Our options there have the virtue of straightforwardness, you might say. But then there's Chisholm. Have the two of you given any more thought to my proposal?"

"As a general rule, Your Majesty," Gray Harbor said dryly, "when the King 'requests' that his First Councilor and his Archbishop 'give some thought' to one of his proposals, they do that."

"All right." Cayleb flashed a smile, although Merlin was well aware that in quite a few Safeholdian kingdoms, that degree of levity and informality from a first councilor might well have resulted in the summary replacement of said first councilor. "Since I'm the King, and since you've been thinking about it like dutiful servants, what conclusions have you reached?"

"Honestly?" Gray Harbor's amusement transmuted itself into sobriety, and he raised one hand and waggled it back and forth in a gesture of uncharacteristic uncertainty. "I don't know, Cayleb. In many ways it would be an ideal solution to at least one major chunk of our problems. It would probably reassure several people who are currently concerned about the succession, at any rate, and Bynzhamyn is right about just how frightening that entire question is right now. But it would also result in some significant upheavals, and there's always the question of whether or not Sharleyan would even consider it. She's going to be in enough trouble with the Group of Four when they find out about her navy's performance against us. And, of course," he showed his teeth in a thin smile of approval, "your decision to return her surrendered vessels with no strings attached is only going to increase the suspicions of someone like Clyntahn and Trynair."

"Trynair, at least, is likely to recognize exactly why you did it," Staynair put in. "Clyntahn, on the other hand, is more problematical. He's more than *smart* enough to understand. The question is whether or not his bigotry and prejudices will *let* him understand."

Staynair's certainly right about that, Merlin reflected. *It would be so much simpler if we knew which Clyntahn is going to turn up at any given moment. Is it likely to be the self-indulgent glutton? Or the undeniably brilliant thinker? Or the religious fanatic zealot Grand Inquisitor? Or the cynical schemer of the Group of Four?*

"And Sharleyan and Green Mountain are going to recognize exactly the same thing," Gray Harbor pointed out. "That's going to be a factor in how they may react to your . . . modest proposal. Turning up the pressure on them may not have put them in the most receptive possible state of mind."

"From what I've seen of Queen Sharleyan and Baron Green Mountain, I wouldn't think that would be too much of a problem," Merlin said. "Both of them understand the sorts of constraints we're facing. I won't say they're likely to be delighted by any effort on our part to manipulate them, but they're certainly going to realize there was nothing personal in it."

Both Gray Harbor and Staynair nodded in acceptance of his observation. They were well aware that Merlin's "visions" had allowed him to follow the inner workings and private discussions of Queen Sharleyan of Chisholm and her own most trusted advisers in a way no one else could have.

"Having said that," Merlin continued, "I don't have the least idea how she would react to what you have in mind. I don't think the possibility's even crossed her mind. Why should it have?"

"That's certainly a reasonable question," Gray Harbor said wryly. "On the other hand, there was the way she reacted to your father's proposal for a more formal alliance, Cayleb."

"The situation's changed just a bit since then," Cayleb replied. "And let's not forget who Father chose as his ambassador."

The youthful monarch's jaw tightened in briefly remembered pain. Kahlvyn Ahrmahk, the Duke of Tirian and his own cousin, had represented King Haarahld in his effort to secure a defensive alliance against Corisande with the Kingdom of Chisholm. Of course, when Haarahld selected Tirian, he hadn't realized that the cousin he loved like a brother was already plotting against him in cooperation with Prince Nahrmahn of Emerald. Nor had Haarahld even begun to suspect that Kahlvyn intended to assassinate both Haarahld and Cayleb.

"There is that," Gray Harbor acknowledged in a painfully neutral voice, and his own eyes were dark and shadowed. Kahlvyn Ahrmahk had been Cayleb's magnificent older cousin, far more of an uncle and almost a second father than a mere cousin, but he had been Rayjhis Yowance's son-in-law, the husband of Gray Harbor's daughter, and the father of his two grandsons.

And it had been Rayjhis Yowance's thrown dagger which had ended the Duke of Tirian's traitorous life.

"So, bearing that in mind, who would you choose for your ambassador this time?" Merlin deliberately made his own voice a bit brisker than usual. "I assume you've given some thought to that?"

"I have, indeed." Cayleb smiled. "Given the nature of the proposal—and, ungentlemanly though it may be, the desirability of maintaining enough pressure to . . . encourage Sharleyan and Green Mountain—I thought we might send them a truly senior representative. Someone like"—he turned his smile on Gray Harbor—"my esteemed First Councilor."

"Now, just a minute, Cayleb!" Gray Harbor twitched upright in his chair, shaking his head. "I see where you're headed, but I couldn't possibly justify being absent long enough for a mission like this! It's the next best thing to ten thousand sea miles from Tellesberg to Cherayth. That's better than a month and a half's voyage just one way!"

"I know." Cayleb's smile faded into an entirely serious expression. "Believe me, Rayjhis, I know, and I've thought long and hard about it. Unless I miss my guess, you'd be gone for at least three or four months, even assuming everything went perfectly. And you're right, the prospect of having you out of the Kingdom for that long isn't likely to help me sleep soundly. But *if* we could possibly make this work, it would go an enormous way towards determining whether or not we manage to survive, and you know it. God knows how much I'd miss you, but Maikel could substitute for you as First Councilor while you were gone. He knows everything you and I have discussed, and his position would put him above the normal political dogfights someone else might have to referee if they tried to temporarily take your place. In fact, he's the only other suitable candidate for ambassador I've been able to come up with, and to be totally honest, we can afford to have you out of the Kingdom at this particular moment far more than we can afford to have *him* out of the *Archbishopric*."

Gray Harbor had opened his mouth as if to argue, but he closed it again, his expression thoughtful, with Cayleb's last sentence. Then, despite manifest reservations, he nodded slowly.

"I see your reasoning," he acknowledged, "and you're right about Maikel covering for me. I don't think a single king or prince in the entire world has ever asked his archbishop to act as a mere first councilor, you understand, but I can see quite a few advantages to the arrangement—especially in our present circumstances. Having the Church and the Crown genuinely working in tandem certainly isn't going to *hurt* anything, at least! And he does know all of our plans, and Zhefry could handle all of the routine documents and procedures under his direction." The first councilor's lips twitched. "God knows, he's been doing that for *me* for years!"

"The key points are that we can manage without you if we have to," Cayleb said, "and that I can't think of anyone who'd have a better chance than you of convincing Sharleyan. And the more I've thought about it, the more I think convincing her is probably at least as important as making Hektor of Corisande a foot or two shorter."

"And the prospect of getting to help you make Hektor shorter would probably be one of the major attractions of the scheme, as far as she's concerned," Gray Harbor agreed.

"That thought had crossed my mind." Cayleb gazed at the first councilor for another second or two, then cocked his head. "So, are you ready to go play envoy?"

.V.
HMS *Destroyer,*
Eraystor Bay,
Princedom of Emerald

"Admiral Nylz is here, Sir. Captain Shain is with him."

Admiral Sir Domynyk Staynair, the newly created Baron of Rock Point, looked up from his examination of the double-barreled flintlock pistol as his flag lieutenant poked his head respectfully through the flag cabin door aboard HMS *Destroyer.*

"Thank you, Styvyn," he said. "Ask them to join me, please."

"Of course, Sir."

Lieutenant Styvyn Erayksyn bowed very slightly before he withdrew, and Admiral Rock Point smiled. Young Erayksyn was connected to at least two-thirds of the aristocrats of the Kingdom of Charis. Indeed, he was far better born than his admiral, despite the recent creation of Rock Point's own title, although that sort of thing was less uncommon in Charis than in most other Safeholdian kingdoms. And, Rock Point supposed, the fact that he himself was the younger brother of the Archbishop of Charis would normally have been more than enough to offset Erayksyn's bluer blood. Of course, in this case, given the . . . irregularities of Maikel's elevation to his archbishopric, that was a bit more problematical than usual.

If Erayksyn was remotely aware of the superiority of his birth he gave absolutely no sign of it. It did, however, grant the efficient, intelligent lieutenant a certain undeniable comfort level when it came to dealing with superior officers in general.

The admiral set the pistol aside rather regretfully, settling it back into its fitted velvet nest beside its mate in the hand-rubbed wooden case on his desk as the door closed behind the flag lieutenant. That brace of pistols was one of the latest brainstorms from Baron Seamount's fertile imagination, and Rock

Point had always appreciated the baron's ever-active approach to life and to his duties. It was an attitude which would have served him poorly in many navies, but not in the Royal Charisian Navy—or, at least, not in the *current* Royal Charisian Navy—and the new weapon was typical of Seamount's efforts.

Before the introduction of the flintlock, firearms like the pistol Rock Point had just been examining would have been impractical, at best. Now, they were completely practical . . . aside from the diversion of manufacturing capability they represented, at least. Rock Point suspected that it had been difficult for Seamount to sit on the artisan who'd built the matched set of pistols in their box on the desk. Traditionally, presentation weapons were seen as opportunities to show off the maker's artistic talents, as well as his practical ability. Under those rules, the pistols ought to have been finely engraved, and—undoubtedly—inlaid with gold and plaques of ivory. This time, the only decoration lay in the small golden medallions set into the pistols' butts, bearing the crossed cannons and kraken of the coat of arms his monarch had awarded to him with his title.

I guess Ahlfryd knows me better than most, Rock Point told himself with a fond smile. *He knows how little use I have for wasted finery.*

Even more than that, the admiral thought as he closed the box and latched it, Seamount knew how much he treasured functionality and practicality, and the sleek, beautifully blued pistols had both of those in abundance. They cocked with a glassy-smooth, satisfying "click," the triggers broke cleanly and crisply, and the rich scent of gun oil clung to the pistol case like subtle perfume. With rifled, side-by-side fifty-caliber barrels, an admiral who no longer possessed two working legs would still hold four men's lives in his hands, even if his footwork was no longer up to the highest standards of swordsmanship.

"Admiral Nylz and Captain Shain, Sir," Erayksyn murmured as the cabin door opened once more and he ushered the visitors into Rock Point's flag cabin.

"Thank you, Styvyn," Rock Point said, then smiled at his two subordinates as the flag lieutenant disappeared once more.

"Kohdy, Captain Shain," he said then. "Please, sit down." He waved one hand at the chairs waiting for them. "I'm sorry I wasn't on deck to greet you."

"No apologies are necessary, My Lord," Admiral Kohdy Nylz replied for both of them as they sat down, and Rock Point smiled again, this time a bit more crookedly, as he glanced down to where the calf of his right leg used to be.

"How *is* your leg, Sir?" Nylz asked, following the direction of his superior's eyes.

"Better." Rock Point looked back up with a small shrug. "They've fitted me with my peg, but they're still tinkering with it. Trying to get the angle right on the foot pad, more than anything else." He raised his truncated leg from the footstool on which it had rested and flexed the knee. "I'm lucky to still have the knee, of course, and the stump is healing well, but I'm getting a lot of irritation from the peg itself. I understand"—he shrugged again, this time ironically—"that Earl Mahndyr is having some of the same difficulties."

"So I've heard," Nylz acknowledged with a slight smile of his own. Rock Point's shattered lower leg had been amputated after the Battle of Darcos Sound, in which the fire of his flagship had already removed the *left* leg of Gharth Rahlstahn, the Earl of Mahndyr, who had commanded the Emeraldian Navy at the same battle. Rock Point's flagship in that battle, HMS *Gale*, had been damaged even more severely than her admiral, and would remain in dockyard hands undergoing repair for at least several more five-days yet.

"All things considered, I'm happier losing a leg than an arm," Rock Point said. "A sea officer doesn't spend a lot of time running foot races, anyway."

Nylz and Shain chuckled politely, and Rock Point snorted at their dutiful response to his minor jest. Then his expression sobered.

"So, what's this about young Hywyt?"

"I have his written report, Sir," Nylz said, opening the bulky dispatch case he'd brought with him and extracting a thin sheaf of paper. "It contains all the details, but the gist is simple enough. A Church dispatch boat tried to get past him to Eraystor. When it refused to halt, he fired a single shot across its bow, at which point its commander was wise enough to haul down his flag and surrender."

He makes it sound so simple, Rock Point thought. *And, really, I suppose it is. Of course, the* consequences *aren't going to be.*

"So there were no casualties?" he asked aloud.

"No, Sir," Nylz replied. "Not this time."

Rock Point grimaced at the qualifier, but he couldn't object to it. There *was* going to be a next time, after all, and eventually some stubborn, stiff-necked, intransigent Church courier was going to refuse to strike his flag and there were going to be quite a lot of casualties.

"Well," he observed, "it sounds like Hywyt did exactly what he was supposed to do. I'm assuming from what you've said, and the way you said it, that you agree with that conclusion?"

"Completely, Sir," Nylz said firmly.

"How did his people take it?"

"Well, overall, Sir." Nylz twitched his shoulders slightly. "Most of them appear to have taken it pretty much in stride. In fact, some of them seemed disappointed that they didn't get to fire into Father Rahss' ship after all. I got the impression when Hywyt delivered his personal report to me that at least one of his officers was . . . less excited, let's say, about the possibility, but if Hywyt had ordered them to fire, they would have."

"Good," Rock Point said, and wondered as he did whether or not he truly meant it.

He turned his chair slightly, listening to the creak of its swivel, so that he could gaze out the broad expanse of *Destroyer*'s stern windows at the panoramic, sun-dancing blue mirror of Eraystor Bay. From where he sat, he could see the northern end of the tadpole shape of Long Island, and the sheltered water between Long Island, Callie's Island, and South Island had been turned into a Charisian anchorage once the fortifications on those islands had surrendered to the Marines.

In some ways, Rock Point was still a bit bemused by how readily those batteries and fortresses had surrendered when summoned. Colonel Hauwyrd Jynkyn, Rock Point's senior Marine officer, had never been able to assemble more than two or three battalions' worth of Marines from the fleet's shipboard detachments. Rock Point had been able to reinforce them with drafts of seamen, of course, especially from the surviving galleys, with their manpower-intensive crews. Still, it had been a distinctly motley landing force, even backed up by the heavy artillery ferried ashore from the fleet's galleons.

It was tempting to feel a degree of contempt for the Emeraldian commanders who'd hauled down their flags when faced by Jynkyn's summons to surrender. On the other hand, most of the fortifications had been badly undermanned themselves, with enough gunners to man the artillery against a naval attack, but insufficient infantry to hold out against a serious assault from the landward side. And with the destruction of the Emeraldian Navy, there'd been no way to prevent Rock Point from finding places he could put his troops and artillery ashore without interference from the defenders.

Besides which the totality of Emerald's naval defeat had devastated the defenders' morale before the first landing party ever set foot on any of those islands.

But all of that had been no more than the preliminaries. Most of the Charisian Navy and Marines were undoubtedly focused on finishing off their adversaries in Emerald and the League of Corisande, but that was going to take at least a little while, since there was the minor problem of exactly what the kingdom was going to use for an army. Seizing island bases, sealing off major ports with blockading squadrons, and annihilating the merchant fleets of their enemies was one thing, and Rock Point had no doubt the Navy and Marines had the resources to manage those tasks. Actually invading someplace like Emerald—or, even worse, Corisande—was something else entirely.

And even if—when—we manage to deal with Nahrmahn and Hektor, it's still only the beginning, he thought grimly. *I wonder how many of our people really understand that? Right this minute, they're still so infuriated by what the Group of Four tried to do to us that I don't doubt Hywyt's men were ready to fire into that dispatch boat. But what happens later, when they realize—really realize, deep down inside—that our true enemy, our dangerous enemy, isn't Hektor or Nahrmahn. It's the Church herself.*

No admiral, no general—no *kingdom*—had ever before faced that reality. Charis did, and a part of Sir Domynyk Staynair felt an icy shiver of dread whenever he thought about the dark, trackless future into which he and his kingdom were voyaging.

"Did Hywyt happen to capture whatever dispatches they were carrying?" he asked, and his eyebrows rose as Nylz gave a harsh crack of laughter.

"I asked something amusing?" he inquired, and the other admiral shook his head.

"Not really, My Lord," he said, although he was still smiling. "It's just that the Church is going to have to rethink some of its standard procedures, I suspect. It seems Father Rahss didn't have a dispatch bag at all, much less a weighted one. All the documents he was charged to deliver were locked in a strongbox in his cabin. A strongbox which was bolted to the deck, as a matter of fact."

"*Bolted* to the deck?" Rock Point blinked, and Nylz nodded.

"Obviously, the Church hasn't given any thought to the possibility that any of *her* couriers might be intercepted. Their procedures for handling their dispatches have been more concerned with the documents' internal security during transit than they have with keeping them out of anyone else's unauthorized hands. So, instead of carrying them in a weighted bag, they lock them up in the captain's quarters. And"—he shook his head—"it takes two keys to unlock the box. The captain has one; the purser has the other."

Rock Point looked at him for a moment, then shook his own head, wondering how long it would take the Church's thinking to adjust to the new reality and change the way her dispatch boats handled her correspondence.

"I assume Commander Hywyt managed to secure both keys?" he said mildly.

"Actually, I believe he said something about prybars, Sir," Captain Shain said, speaking up for the first time and smiling wickedly. "From what he had to say to me while he was waiting to see Admiral Nylz, this Father Rahss at least managed to get his key thrown over the side before *Wave's* people went aboard. I don't know if he actually thought that was going to stop Hywyt, but apparently he just about died of apoplexy when Hywyt broke the strongbox open. I think he more than half expected lightning to strike Hywyt dead on the spot."

"Which, obviously, it didn't," Rock Point said dryly. He supposed he was pleased to see Shain's amusement at the thought, yet he couldn't help wondering if the rest of his officers and men would share the flag captain's reaction.

"I've brought the captured documents with me, My Lord," Nylz said, reaching down and patting his dispatch case. "I've also had duplicate copies made, just in case. Unfortunately, they appear to be in some sort of cipher."

"I suppose that's not too surprising," Rock Point said. "Irritating, but not surprising." He shrugged. "We'll just have to send them back to Tellesberg. Perhaps Baron Wave Thunder and his people will be able to decipher them."

And if they can't, I'm sure Seijin *Merlin can*, he reflected.

"Yes, My Lord."

"Please pass my compliments to Commander Hywyt for a job well done. He and his people seem to have developed a knack for being in the right place at the right time when there's prize money to be won, don't they?"

"So far, at least," Nylz agreed. "I am getting a few requests to let someone else have a crack at *Wave*'s station, though."

"It's not her station, Sir," Shain snorted. "It's her *speed*. Well, that and the fact that Hywyt really does have a knack for this sort of work."

"He'd better enjoy it while he can," Rock Point said. Nylz raised an eyebrow, and Rock Point smiled. "I just received dispatches of my own from Earl Lock Island. Among other things, he's asked me to nominate commanding officers for some of the new galleons, and it sounds to me as if young Hywyt might be the sort of captain we're looking for."

.VI.
Royal Palace,
City of Eraystor,
Princedom of Emerald

Prince Nahrmahn of Emerald was not a happy man.

There were many reasons for that, starting with what had happened to his navy, followed by the fact that he no longer had control even of Eraystor Bay, beyond the reach of the waterfront's defensive batteries. And by the fact that he could hardly expect King Cayleb to overlook his own attempted assassination or the part one Prince Nahrmahn had played in arranging it. Then there was the way in which he and his entire princedom had been forced to become the junior partners—almost the vassals—of Hektor of Corisande under the Group of Four's master plan for the destruction of Charis.

And, of course, there'd been this morning's delightful interview with Bishop Executor Wyllys.

He stood gazing out the palace window at the vast blue expanse of the bay. Emerald's merchant marine had never been very large, compared to that of Charis, or even Corisande, but these days the waterfront wharves were crowded with merchant ships which dared not put to sea, and more of them lay to anchors and buoys farther out. The naval yard's anchorages and slips, on the other hand, were virtually empty. Nine galleys—the total surviving strength of Nahrmahn's navy—huddled pathetically together, as if for some sort of mutual comfort.

There were two additional galleys anchored off to one side, and Nahrmahn glowered at the big, twin-masted ships. They were the only prizes the Duke of Black Water's fleet had managed to capture before Haarahld and Cayleb of Charis annihilated his own ships in return. They'd just happened to be here in Eraystor when the hammer came down on Black Water, although Nahrmahn didn't expect any of his erstwhile "allies" to believe in the coincidence which had "fortuitously" left him in possession.

Nahrmahn had gone down to examine the captured ships personally the day they'd arrived. He was no experienced naval officer himself, but even he'd been able to follow the explanations about the peculiar Charisian artillery mountings and the reasons for the new weapons' effectiveness. Not that understanding made him feel any better, especially when he reflected upon the fact that as the geographically closest member of the alliance against Charis, he was virtually certain to be the first recipient of King Cayleb's attention. As, indeed, the seizure of his capital city's outlying island defenses only emphasized.

He turned as the chamber door opened and Trahvys Ohlsyn, the Earl of Pine Hollow, and Commodore Hainz Zhaztro came through it.

Pine Hollow was Nahrmahn's cousin, as well as his first councilor, and one of the relatively few courtiers whose loyalty the prince truly trusted. Zhaztro, on the other hand, was the senior—in fact, the *only*—Emeraldian squadron commander to have returned from the Battle of Darcos Sound. There were those, Nahrmahn knew, who cherished suspicions about Zhaztro—about his courage, as well as his loyalty—simply because he *was* the most senior officer to come home again. Nahrmahn himself, somewhat to the surprise of many, did not. The fact that Zhaztro's flagship had suffered over thirty percent casualties and was so badly damaged that she'd gradually settled to the bottom after she'd managed to claw her way back to the naval yard was all the recommendation the commodore had needed as far as Nahrmahn was concerned.

"You wanted to see both of us, My Prince?" Pine Hollow said with a bow, and Nahrmahn nodded.

"Yes," he said with uncharacteristic shortness, and waved for the two of them to join him by the window.

Pine Hollow and Zhaztro obeyed the beckoned command, and the first councilor wondered if the naval officer realized how atypical Nahrmahn's attitude had been for the past several five-days. Unless Pine Hollow was mistaken, his short, round prince was actually losing weight. Some people probably wouldn't have been particularly surprised to find a prince in Nahrmahn's position doing that, but Pine Hollow had known his cousin from childhood, and he couldn't remember *anything* that had ever managed to put Nahrmahn off his feed. Nor did the prince fit the image of a depressed man sinking listlessly into despair. As a matter of fact, Nahrmahn actually seemed more focused, more energetic, than Pine Hollow had ever before seen him.

"I've just finished entertaining Bishop Executor Wyllys," the prince told his two subordinates as he looked back out the window. "He was here to express his . . . unhappiness over what happened to his dispatch boat yesterday."

Pine Hollow glanced at Zhaztro, but the commodore only gazed calmly and attentively at Nahrmahn. The naval officer's phlegmatic personality was part of what had commended him so strongly to Nahrmahn, the first councilor suspected.

"I explained to His Eminence," Nahrmahn continued, "that this sort of thing happens when someone else's navy is in control of one's home waters. He responded to that by telling me that it had never before happened to one of *Mother Church's* vessels, a fact of which"—he turned to smile thinly at the others—"it may astound you to learn, I was already aware."

Despite himself, Pine Hollow felt his eyes widen at Nahrmahn's desert-dry tone.

"The question I have for you, Commodore," the prince said, "is whether or not there's any way you can think of that we could somehow guarantee the security of future Church dispatch vessels arriving here at Eraystor?"

"Honestly? No, Your Highness," Zhaztro said without hesitation. "Up until yesterday, I would have said there was at least an even chance the Charisians would allow Church-flagged couriers to pass through the blockade unhindered. In fact, I would have said the chances were considerably better than even, frankly." He shrugged very slightly. "Apparently, I would have been wrong. And given their presence here in the bay, and their obvious willingness to risk the Church's anger, I don't see any way we can prevent them from doing exactly the same thing over again anytime they want to."

"I see." Nahrmahn's tone was calm, Pine Hollow noted, without even a hint of displeasure at Zhaztro's devastating frankness.

"If I might make a suggestion, Your Highness?" the commodore said after a moment, and Nahrmahn nodded for him to continue.

"Eraystor isn't the only port in Emerald," Zhaztro pointed out. "And Cayleb doesn't begin to have enough ships to shut down every fishing port along our coasts, as we're already demonstrating. There are several places where I feel confident couriers could make a safe landfall and send any dispatches overland to the capital."

"That's exactly what I was thinking myself," Nahrmahn agreed. "In fact, I've already made that suggestion to the Bishop Executor. He didn't seem overly pleased by the prospect." The prince's thin smile showed the tips of his teeth. "I think he feels it comports poorly with the Church's dignity to require her messengers to 'creep around in the shadows like poachers avoiding the bailiff,' as he put it."

Nahrmahn's voice was even drier than before, Pine Hollow noticed, and the first councilor felt a distinct flicker of uneasiness. Nahrmahn's position was grim enough without his openly antagonizing the Church's official representative in Emerald.

And, of course, the position of Emerald's first councilor depended almost entirely upon that of its prince.

"I'm sorry to hear His Eminence feels that way," Zhaztro said politely, and Nahrmahn actually chuckled.

"I'm sure you are, Commodore."

The prince shook his head, then shrugged.

"Well, Commodore, that was really the only question I had for you. I can't say your answer surprises me, but that's certainly not your fault. Would you be so good as to draw up a list of the best alternate landing sites for future Church messengers so that I could get it to the Bishop Executor by tomorrow morning?"

"Of course, Your Highness."

Zhaztro bowed, clearly recognizing his dismissal, and withdrew. Nahrmahn watched the door close behind him, then looked at his cousin.

"I can't say I'm delighted about the attached price tag, Trahvys," he observed almost whimsically, "but at least the reaming Haarahld and Cayleb gave us has brought one worthwhile officer to my attention."

Pine Hollow nodded. Zhaztro's apparent immunity to the gloom, doom, and despair which had sent most of the Emeraldian Navy's surviving senior officers' morale plunging was remarkable. The commodore had to be aware of the near hopelessness of Emerald's position, but instead of dwelling upon it, he was actively seeking ways to strike back at Charis. As he had just finished pointing out, the Royal Charisian Navy lacked sufficient ships to blockade every Emeraldian port, and Zhaztro was busy fitting out light, jury-rigged cruisers as commerce raiders in every harbor with a boatyard. Most of them would be little more than lightly armed, outsized rowing skiffs or hastily converted—and even more lightly armed—merchantmen. Neither type could hope to stand up to any sort of regular man-of-war, even one without the devilish new Charisian artillery, but they could capture and destroy lumbering, lightly armed—or completely *unarmed*—merchantmen, and commerce raiding was probably the one way in which Emerald could hope to actually hurt—or inconvenience, at least—Charis.

Not that it was going to do any good in the end, of course.

Nahrmahn continued to gaze out the window for two or three more minutes without speaking. Pine Hollow knew the prince's eyes were following the grayish-tan pyramids of the Charisian galleons' weathered sails as they glided slowly, slowly across Eraystor Bay.

"You know," Nahrmahn said finally, "the more I think about how we got into this mess, the more pissed off I get."

He turned away from the Charisian warships and looked his cousin in the eye.

"It was *stupid*," he said, and that, Pine Hollow knew, was the deepest, most damning condemnation in Nahrmahn's vocabulary. "Even if Haarahld hadn't been building all those damned galleons, with all those damned new guns of his, it would still have been stupid. It's obvious Trynair and Clyntahn never even tried to find out what was actually happening in Charis, because they didn't really care. They had their own agenda, and their own objectives, and so they simply said the hell with thinking things through and started moving their chess pieces around like blind, fumbling idiots. Even if things had worked out the way they'd expected, it would have been using a sledgehammer to crack an egg. And the way it *did* work out, they only pushed Haarahld into smashing *everyone* who could have hurt him! Oh," he made an impatient gesture, "we didn't know what he was up to, either, before he handed us all our heads. I'll admit that. But we at least knew he was up to *something*, which was more than that idiot Hektor seemed aware of! And who did Trynair and Clyntahn decide to back? Hektor, that's who!"

Pine Hollow nodded, and Nahrmahn's lips worked as if he wanted to spit on the floor. Then the prince drew a deep breath.

"But there's another reason it was stupid, too, Trahvys," he said in a much softer voice, as if he were afraid someone else might hear him. "It was stupid because it shows all the world exactly what the 'Group of Four's' precious members really think."

His eyes had gone very still, dark and cold, and Pine Hollow's stomach muscles tightened.

"What they think, My Prince?" he asked very carefully.

"They think they can destroy anyone they want to," Nahrmahn told him. "They whistled up—what was it Earl Thirsk said Cayleb called us? Ah, yes. They whistled up a pack of 'hired stranglers, murderers, and rapists' and ordered us to cut Charis' throat. They couldn't have cared less what that meant—for us, as well as for Charis. They decided to burn an entire kingdom to the ground and kill thousands of people—and to use *me* to do it, Shan-wei take their souls!—as if the decision were no more important than choosing what bottle of wine to order with supper, or whether to have the fish or the fowl for the main course. *That's* how important the decision was for them."

He'd been wrong, Pine Hollow thought. Nahrmahn's eyes weren't cold. It was simply that the lava in them burned so deep, so hot, that it was almost—*almost*—invisible.

"Nahrmahn," the earl said, "they're the Church. The vicarate. They can do whatever—"

"*Can* they?" Nahrmahn interrupted him. The pudgy Prince of Emerald raised his right hand, jabbing his index finger at the window. "Can they?" he repeated, pointing at the Charisian galleons' sails. "I don't know about you, Trahvys, but *I'd* have to say their plans didn't work out exactly the way they'd intended, did they?"

"No, but—"

"It's not going to end here, you know." Nahrmahn's voice was calm again, and he seated himself on the padded window seat with his back to the wall, gazing up at his taller cousin. "Given even the Church's purely secular power, the odds against Charis' survival are high, of course. But Cayleb's already proven Charis isn't going down easily. I would rather have preferred being here myself to see how it all works out, of course. But even though I won't be, I can tell you this much already. It's going to take *years* for anyone to overcome the defensive advantages Charis already enjoys, and it's going to take a lot more ships, and a lot more men, and a lot more gold than the Group of Four ever imagined in their worst nightmares. Cities are going to be burned, Trahvys. There are going to be murders, atrocities, massacres, and reprisals . . . I can't even begin to imagine everything that's going to happen, and at least I'm *trying* to, unlike the 'Group of Four.' And when it's all over, there won't be a single prince or king in all of Safehold who doesn't know his crown depends not on the approval of God, or even the acceptance of the Church, but on the whim of petty, corrupt, greedy, *stupid* men who think they're the Archangels themselves come back to Safehold in glory."

Trahvys Ohlsyn had never before heard anything like that out of his prince, and hearing it now frightened him. Not just because of its implications for his own power and survival, either. He'd always known, despite the way his rotund little ruler's allies and opponents alike persistently tended to underestimate him, that Nahrmahn of Emerald was a dangerously, dangerously intelligent man. Now it was as if his own impending defeat and probable demise had cracked some inner barrier, loosed some deep, hidden spring of prophecy, as well.

"Nahrmahn, think about what you're saying, please," the earl said quietly. "You're my Prince, and I'll follow wherever you may take Emerald. But remember that, whatever else they may be, they speak with Mother Church's voice, and they control all the rest of the entire *world*. In the end, Charis can't—"

"Charis doesn't *have* to," Nahrmahn interrupted again. "That's the very point I'm making! Whatever happens to Charis, whatever the Group of Four may think, this is only beginning. Even if they manage to completely crush Charis, it's *still* only beginning. This isn't God's will, it's *theirs*, and that's going to be obvious to everyone, not just to someone like me, or like Greyghor Stohnar in Siddarmark. And when it becomes obvious, do you really think the other princes and kings are simply going to go back to sleep, as if this never happened? As if Trynair and Clyntahn hadn't *proved* no crown is secure, no city is safe, if it's foolish enough to rouse the ire of the Group of Four or whoever replaces them on the Council of Vicars?"

He shook his head slowly, his expession grim.

"The one thing in the entire world the Church simply can't afford to lose is its moral authority as God's voice, His steward among His people, Trahvys." His voice was very, very soft. "That's been the true basis for the world's unity—and the Church's power—since the Day of Creation itself. But now the Group of Four has just thrown that away, as if it were so unimportant, so *trivial*, that it wasn't worth so much as a second thought. Only they were wrong. It wasn't unimportant; it was the only thing that could have saved them. Now it's gone, and that, Trahvys—*that*—is something they will never, ever be able to get back again."

.VII.
Breygart House,
Hanth Town,
Earldom of Hanth

M ove, damn you! I want this street *cleared!*"
        Colonel Sir Wahlys Zhorj reined his horse around so angrily that the animal sunfished under him. He reacted—predictably, in Captain Zhaksyn Maiyr's opinion—by pulling the reins even shorter and leaning forward to slap the back of the horse's head.

Sir Wahlys (only Maiyr wasn't supposed to know that the "Sir" was self-bestowed) snarled and jabbed his index finger in the general direction of the waterfront.

"I don't give a *damn* how you do it, Captain, but you get this street cleared all the way to the wharves, and you do it *now!*"

"Yes, Sir," Maiyr replied in a stony voice. Zhorj gave him one more fulminating glance, then jerked his head at his small party of aides and went cantering back towards the center of town, leaving Maiyr to his own devices. Which, in a lot of ways, suited Maiyr just fine.

Of course, in other ways, nothing about this entire bitched-up situation suited Zhaksyn Maiyr at all.

He turned a glare of his own towards the shouting, smoke, and general hullabaloo of the street Zhorj had ordered him to clear. It was going to be an unmitigated pain in the arse however he went about it, he reflected. And whatever "Sir" Wahlys might think, it wasn't going to make the situation any better.

He isn't really idiotic enough to think it'll do any good, Maiyr thought angrily. *He just doesn't have any better ideas. Which isn't all that surprising, either, I suppose.*

The truth was that Colonel Zhorj was a reasonably competent field commander, with a genuine talent for managing the logistics of a mercenary cavalry company, which happened to include Maiyr's mounted arbalesteers. No one knew exactly where he'd come from originally, but his reputation as someone prepared to ask very few questions of his employer had preceded him. And for the last couple of years, he'd been Tahdayo Mahntayl's senior troop commander here in the Earldom of Hanth.

And mightily unpopular he's made himself . . . and all the rest of us, Maiyr thought bitterly.

"All right," he told his troop sergeant, "you heard the Colonel. If you have any bright ideas, this is the time to trot them out."

"Yes, Sir," the gray-haired sergeant said sourly. He was a highly experienced man, and his expression was even sourer than his tone as he looked past Maiyr at the defiant riot and shook his head. "As soon as one occurs to me, you'll be the first person I tell."

"Well, *that's* remarkably helpful," Maiyr observed dryly.

"I'm sorry, Sir." The sergeant's voice was a bit chastened, and he shook his head again, in quite a different manner. "I just don't see any way to do it without leaving blood in the street, and I thought we were supposed to be avoiding that."

"Apparently, the Colonel has just changed our orders in that regard." Maiyr and the noncom exchanged speaking glances, and then the captain shrugged.

"Well, whether it's a good idea or not, we've got our orders. On the other hand, I'd just as soon not kill anyone if we can help it."

"Yes, Sir." The sergeant's agreement was obvious, although Maiyr doubted he felt that way for the same reason the captain did. The sergeant simply understood that bloodshed begat bloodshed, and that there was no nastier kind of fight than one against a true general insurrection. Maiyr, on the other hand, was familiar with the House of Ahrmahk's reputation, and he thought giving King Cayleb any more reason to come personally looking for one Zhaksyn Maiyr was an enormously bad idea.

Besides, it went against the grain to kill people with as many legitimate reasons for hating their local earl as these people had.

"Most of them aren't that well armed," he thought aloud for the sergeant's benefit. *After all*, he added to himself, *we've spent the last two years confiscating every weapon we could get our hands on.* "They're also on foot. So we'll try a show of force, first. I want half of our troopers mounted. They'll take the center of the street and try to push the rabble in front of them. I don't want any casualties we can avoid, so tell them that they're to fire over the rioters' heads unless we're actually taking fire from them. Make *sure* that's understood."

"Yes, Sir."

"I want the other half of our men *dis*mounted. I know they'll bitch about walking to work, but if these people scatter into the alleys and warehouses, we need someone who can follow them—at least long enough to make sure they keep running. Tell them to take their staffs with them. I don't want edged weapons used except in direct self-defense."

"Yes, Sir."

The "staffs" in question were heavy, three-and-a-half-foot-long lengths of seasoned ironwood. They might not be edged, but they were easily capable of breaking bones or crushing skulls. Still, he hoped the rioters would recognize that he and his men were doing their best to avoid general bloodshed.

Not that there was really much likelihood of that.

"We'll push straight down the street towards the harbor," he continued. "I want the squad leaders to make sure the buildings on either side of the street are really *cleared*. I don't expect them to stay that way for long once we've moved on, but let's at least give it our best shot, Sergeant."

"Yes, Sir. Whatever you say." The sergeant was obviously content to leave the responsibility up to Maiyr. As far as he was concerned, orders didn't have to make sense, as long as there was at least a reasonable chance of carrying out the ones he'd been given.

"All right, Sergeant," Maiyr sighed. "Let's get them saddled up."

▼　▼　▼

Tahdayo Mahntayl, who would have been the Earl of Hanth for two years in exactly one more month, stood with Sir Styv Walkyr on one of Breygart House's balconies glaring west towards the smoke and tumult rising between them and the Hanth Town waterfront. The broad waters of Margaret Bay stretched as far as the eye could see beyond the wharves and warehouses. The bay could be as stormy a body of water as anyone was likely to find, Walkyr thought, but today, it was far calmer than Hanth Town.

"God*damn* them!" Mahntayl snarled. "I'll teach them better this time!"

Walkyr bit his tongue rather firmly. The "earl" obviously hadn't managed to school his unruly subjects in the last two years. Exactly what made him think he was going to manage it in the next two *days* escaped Walkyr.

"Who the hell do they think they *are*?" Mahntayl went on. "This is all that bastard Cayleb's fault!"

"Well," Walkyr said as reasonably as he could, "it's hardly a surprise, is it? I mean, you know how it must have stuck in his and his father's craws when the Church rammed the decision in your favor down their throats."

"What d'you mean, 'the decision in my favor'?" Mahntayl snarled. "I had the better claim!"

It was even harder for Walkyr to hold his tongue this time around. The truth, as Mahntayl surely knew inside, was that his claim had been as completely and totally specious as Sir Hauwerd Breygart and his supporters had insisted all long. Walkyr had no idea where Mahntayl had gotten hold of the forged correspondence which purported to establish his claim to the earldom, but that it *was* a forgery was beyond question, whatever the Church had decided after receiving sufficient inducement from Nahrmahn of Emerald and Hektor of Corisande.

Apparently, Mahntayl had begun to entertain a few delusions upon that head, however. For years, as Walkyr knew perfectly well, all the so-called "Earl of Hanth" had really hoped for was that he'd be a big enough nuisance that Breygart—or possibly Haarahld of Charis—would decide to buy him off just to make him go away. But then, contrary to all expectations, the Church had abruptly and unexpectedly decided in favor of his obviously fraudulent claim, and his horizons had suddenly expanded. Now that he'd had two years in Hanth, he wasn't prepared to give up his purloined title. In fact, he was no longer prepared even to admit that it had been fraudulently obtained in the first place.

Unfortunately, Walkyr thought dryly, *his loving subjects—and Cayleb Ahrmahk—aren't in agreement with him on that minor point. And if Tahdayo still had the sense God gave a slash lizard, he'd already have taken Cayleb's offer and found a fast ship to somewhere else.*

Which is exactly what I ought to be doing, whatever he finally chooses.

"I only meant to say," he said now, mildly, wondering what cross-grained, quixotic instinct kept him here in Hanth still trying to save Mahntayl's hide, "that Haarahld and Cayleb took the decision against Breygart personally. We both knew that at the time, Tahdayo." He shrugged. "Obviously, now that he's come to the point of open conflict with the Church, he doesn't see any reason to pussyfoot around where a situation in his own backyard is concerned. And with Emerald's and Corisande's navies mostly either at the bottom of the sea or anchored off Tellesberg as prizes, there's no one who's going to be able to stop him."

"So, after coming this far, I should just cut and run with my tail between my legs?" Mahntayl demanded harshly.

"I prefer to think of it as salvaging what you can now that the luck's turned against you. If there's any way you could stand off Cayleb's entire navy—and his Marines—*I* don't know what it is."

"Bishop Mylz swears the Church will protect us."

From his expression, even Mahntayl must have recognized how lame his own tone sounded, Walkyr thought. Bishop Mylz Halcom was one of only four of the Archbishopric of Charis' bishops who had refused the summons to Tellesberg to endorse Maikel Staynair's elevation. His diocese included Hanth and most of the other earldoms and baronies along the eastern shore of Margaret Bay. Clearly, he had hopes of establishing some sort of citadel for what he insisted on referring to as the "true Church" here in Margaret's Land until the Council of Vicars could somehow come to his aid.

Which only means he's as delusional as Tahdayo. Maybe even more so.

"I'm sure Bishop Mylz means what he says," he said aloud. After all, one couldn't exactly call a bishop of Mother Church a frigging lunatic even if— or perhaps *especially* if—he was one. "But whatever his intentions and hopes may be, I'm not sure he fully understands the gravity of the situation, Tahdayo."

"So you think Cayleb can successfully defy even God Himself, do you?"

"I didn't say that," Walkyr replied patiently. "What I said was that the situation is grave, and it is. Does Bishop Mylz have an army tucked away somewhere? Does he have the troops and warships to support us against the Royal Charisian Navy and the entire Kingdom? Because, if he doesn't, then in the short term, yes—Cayleb *can* defy God's Church."

Which isn't quite the same thing as defying "God Himself," is it?

"I'm not going to run like a whipped cur! I'm the Earl of Hanth! If I have to, I can still *die* like an earl!" Mahntayl snarled, then turned and stormed off the balcony back into Breygart House.

Walkyr watched him go, then turned back to the smoke rising from the warehouse district. All reports indicated that Mahntayl's dwindling cadre of loyalists had already lost control of Mountain Keep and Kiarys, two of the three major towns outside the earldom's capital of Hanth Town, itself. And the reports from Zhorjtown suggested that the situation wasn't much better there. Worse, both Mountain Keep and Kiarys backed up against the Hanth Mountains, and Mountain Keep controlled the Hanth end of the one really practicable pass from the Earldom of Lochair, on Howell Bay. Which meant the best overland escape route had already been closed . . . not to mention the fact that it gave Cayleb control of yet another potential *invasion* route.

I don't care what Bishop Mylz and the other Temple Loyalists may think, Styv Walkyr thought grimly. *However things work out in the end, Cayleb's defiance of the Church is already an established fact here in Charis. And, frankly, the way Tahdayo's spent the last two years squeezing the people of "his" earldom, they'd be ready to sign on with Shan-wei herself if it meant getting his arse kicked out of Breygart House!*

Walkyr had no idea how the tempest sweeping across Safehold would finally end—or, for that matter, if it ever *would* end. But of one thing he was absolutely certain. Whatever finally happened, Tahdayo Mahntayl would *not* be the Earl of Hanth when it was over.

And Tahdayo knows that, somewhere inside, whether he's willing to admit it or not.

The smoke seemed to be thicker, he observed. And he heard more than a few gunshots. Obviously, Colonel Zhorj's troopers had missed at least a few matchlocks, which had apparently come out of hiding. It wouldn't be enough to take Hanth Town away from the present management—not today, at least. But the time limit Cayleb had given Mahntayl was running out fast. In fact, it had only two five-days to go.

Whether Tahdayo accepts it in the end or not, I'm not going to be here when his time runs out. Cayleb's obviously willing to let him run rather than risk higher casualties— especially civilian ones—here in Hanth if he decides to fight. But if Tahdayo doesn't accept the offer, Cayleb will come in here and kick *his arse out of Breygart House. And in the process, he'll undoubtedly make him a head shorter. Which is probably the same thing that will happen to* me, *if I hang around.*

He shook the head which was still (for the moment, at least) attached to his neck and wondered why in the world he was even hesitating. It wasn't as if he'd ever seen Tahdayo as anything more than a way to make a few marks, himself. Still, he'd been with Tahdayo for almost seven years now. Obviously, that meant more to him than he'd previously suspected.

Which is remarkably stupid of me.

Well, he still had at least one five-day in hand to work on restoring "the Earl of Hanth's" sanity. And he'd had the forethought to send quite a bit of his own share of the loot he and Mahntayl had squeezed out of Hanth to bankers in the Desnarian Empire. If he had to run without Mahntayl, he had a sufficient nest egg to keep him in comfort for the remainder of his life. Which would be a considerably *longer* life if he departed in time.

Maybe I can convince him the Church really will restore him—eventually—to "his" earldom. For that matter, Walkyr's eyes narrowed, *he probably really would be of considerable value to the Church as the pretender to—no, not the pretender to, the "legitimate Earl of"—Hanth. Especially if the reason he was driven out had nothing to do with the fact that his loving subjects hate his guts and had everything to do with his persecution for his steadfast loyalty to Mother Church.*

Walkyr's lips pursed thoughtfully. That really was an excellent notion, he thought. And the possibility of Mahntayl's still being recognized as the Earl of Hanth (by *someone*, at least) and probably being supported as befitted his title might well be enough to let Walkyr convince the man it was time to go.

And if the Church does decide to support his claim, I can probably make the Group of Four see that it would be worth their while to keep someone who can manage him riding herd on him. For a price, of course.

Walkyr's eyes brightened at the prospect, and he scratched his chin thoughtfully, still gazing at the smoke and listening to the gunshots, while he considered the best way to present his argument to the "earl."

JUNE, YEAR OF GOD 892

.I.

The Temple of God,
City of Zion,
The Temple Lands

The atmosphere in the conference chamber was less than collegial.

All four of the men sitting around the fabulously expensive table with its inlaid ivory, rock crystal, and gems wore the orange cassocks of vicars. The silken fabric was rich with embroidery, glinting with the understated elegance of tiny, faceted jewels, and the priest caps on the table before them gleamed with gold bullion and silver lace. Any one of them could have fed a family of ten for a year just from the value of the ruby ring of office he wore, and their faces normally showed the confidence and assurance one would have expected from the princes of God's Church. None of them was accustomed to failure . . . or to having his will thwarted.

And none of them had ever before imagined disaster on such a scale.

"Who the fuck do these bastards think they *are?*" Allayn Maigwair, Captain General of the Church of God Awaiting, grated. By rights, the thick, expensive sheets of parchment on the table before him should have burst into spontaneous flame under the heat of the glare he turned upon them.

"With all due respect, Allayn," Vicar Rhobair Duchairn said harshly, "they think they're the people who just destroyed effectively every other navy in the world. *And* the people who understand *exactly* who sent those navies to burn their entire kingdom to the ground."

Maigwair turned his glare on Duchairn, but the Church of God Awaiting's Treasurer General seemed remarkably unfazed by his obvious anger. There was even more than a hint of "I told you so" in Duchairn's expression. After all, he'd been the only member of the "Group of Four" who'd persistently advised against taking precipitous action against the Kingdom of Charis.

"They're fucking *heretics*, that's what they are, Rhobair," Zhaspahr Clyntahn half snapped in a dangerous voice. "Don't ever forget that! I promise you the *Inquisition* isn't going to! The Archangel Schueler tells us how to deal with Shan-wei's foul get!"

Duchairn's lips tightened angrily, but he didn't reply immediately. Clyntahn had been in an ugly mood for five-days, even before the messages from Charis arrived. Although he was famed for his bouts of temper and his ability to hold grudges forever, neither Duchairn nor anyone else had ever seen the

Grand Inquisitor as furious—or as *persistently* furious—as he'd been ever since the Church's semaphore system reported the disastrous consequences of the battles off Armageddon Reef and in Darcos Sound.

Of course we haven't, Duchairn thought disgustedly. *This entire disaster is the consequence of our letting Zhaspahr rush us into his damned "final solution of the Charisian problem!" And no wonder Maigwair's just as pissed off as Zhaspahr. After all, he* was *the one who made it all sound so simple, so foolproof, when he laid out his brilliant plan for the campaign.*

He started to say exactly that aloud, but he didn't. He didn't say it for several reasons. First, however little he wanted to admit it, because he was frightened of Clyntahn. The Grand Inquisitor was undoubtedly the most dangerous single enemy within the Church anyone could possibly make. Second, however much Duchairn might have argued initially against taking action against Charis, it hadn't been because he'd somehow magically recognized the military danger no one else had seen. He'd argued against it because, as the Church's chief accountant, he'd realized just how much of the Church's revenue stream Clyntahn proposed to destroy along with the Kingdom of Charis. And, third, because the disaster which had resulted was so complete, so overwhelming, that the Group of Four's hold upon the rest of the Council hung by a thread. If they showed a single sign of internal disunion, their enemies among the vicarate would turn upon them in a heartbeat . . . and the rest of the vicars were just as frightened as Duchairn himself. They were going to be looking for scapegoats, and the consequences for any scapegoats they fastened upon were going to be . . . ugly.

"They may very well be heretics, Zhaspahr," he said instead. "And no one disputes that matters of heresy come rightfully under the authority of your office. But that doesn't make anything I just said untrue, does it? Unless you happen to have another fleet tucked away somewhere that none of the rest of us know anything about."

From the dangerous shade of puce which suffused the Grand Inquisitor's heavy face, Duchairn thought for a moment that he'd gone too far, anyway. There had always been a dangerous attack dog (some had even very quietly used the term "mad dog") edge to Zhaspahr Clyntahn, and the man had demonstrated his utter ruthlessness often enough. It was entirely possible that he might decide his best tactic in this instance lay in using the power of his office to turn upon the other members of the Group of Four and transform them into his own scapegoats.

"No, Rhobair," a fourth voice said, preempting any response Clyntahn might have been about to make, "it doesn't make what you've just said untrue. But it *does* tend to put our problem rather into perspective, doesn't it?"

Zahmsyn Trynair had an angular face, a neatly trimmed beard, and deep, intelligent eyes. He was also the only other member of the Group of Four whose personal power base was probably as strong as Clyntahn's. As Chancellor of the Council of Vicars, it was Trynair who truly formulated the policies which he then slipped into the mouth of Grand Vicar Erek XVII. In theory, that actually made him more powerful than Clyntahn, but his power was primarily political. It was an often indirect sort of power, one which was most effective applied gradually, over the course of time, whereas Clyntahn commanded the loyalty of the Inquisition and the swords of the Order of Schueler.

Now, as Duchairn and Clyntahn both turned to look at him, Trynair shrugged.

"Zhaspahr, I agree with you that what we've seen in the past few five-days, and even more what's contained in these"—he reached out and tapped the parchment documents which had occasioned this particular meeting—"certainly constitute heresy. But Rhobair has a point. Heretics or not, they've destroyed—not defeated, Zhaspahr, *destroyed*—what was for all intents and purposes the combined strength of every other navy of Safehold. At this moment, there's nothing we can do to attack them directly."

Maigwair stirred angrily, straightening in his chair, but Trynair pinned him with a single cold stare.

"If you know of any existing naval force which could possibly face the Charisian Navy in battle, Allayn, I suggest you tell us about it now," he said in a chill, precise tone.

Maigwair flushed angrily, but he also looked away. He was well aware that his fellows regarded him with a certain contempt, even though they were normally careful about showing it. The truth was that it was his position as the commander of the Church's armed forces, and certainly not his inherent brilliance, which made him a member of the Group of Four. He'd enjoyed his chance to take center stage when it came to coordinating the attack on Charis precisely because it had finally allowed him to seize the limelight and assert his equality among them, but things hadn't worked out quite as well as he'd planned. Trynair watched him coolly for a handful of seconds, then returned his attention to Clyntahn.

"There are those on the Council, as I'm sure we're all well aware, who are going to seek any opportunity to break our control, and Staynair's 'open letter' to the Grand Vicar hasn't exactly done anything to *strengthen* our position, has it? Some of those enemies of ours are already whispering that the current . . . unfortunate situation is entirely the result of our own precipitous action."

"The Inquisition knows how to deal with anyone who seeks to undermine the authority and unity of the Council of Vicars in the face of such a monumental threat to the soul of every living child of God." Clyntahn's voice was colder than a Zion winter, and the zealotry which was so much a part of his complex, often self-contradictory personality glittered in his eyes.

"I don't doubt it," Trynair replied. "But if it comes to that, then we may well find ourselves replicating this . . . this *schism* within the Council itself. I submit to you that any such consequence would scarcely be in the best interests of the Church or of our ability to deal with the heresy in question."

Or of our own long-term survival, he very carefully did not add aloud, although all of his companions heard it anyway.

Clyntahn's puffy, heavy-jowled face was like a stone wall, but, after several tense seconds, he nodded minutely.

"Very well." Trynair managed to show no trace of the profound relief that grudging acquiescence engendered as he surveyed the other three faces around the table. "I think we have two separate but related problems. First, we must decide how Mother Church and the Council are going to deal with *these*." He tapped the parchment documents again. "And, second, we must decide what long-term course of action Mother Church and the Council can pursue in the face of our current military . . . embarrassment."

Duchairn wasn't quite certain how he refrained from snorting derisively. Trynair's "separate but related problems" just happened to constitute the greatest threat the Church of God Awaiting had faced in the near millennium since the Creation itself. Hearing the Chancellor talk about them as if they were no more than two more in the succession of minor administrative decisions the Group of Four had been required to make over the past decade or so was ludicrous.

Yet what Trynair had said was also true, and the Chancellor was probably the only one of them who could genuinely hope to manage Clyntahn.

The Treasurer General reached out and drew the nearest document closer. He had no need to consult its text, of course; that much was already branded indelibly into his memory, but he ran his fingertips across the seals affixed to it.

Under other circumstances, it would have been unexceptionable enough. The language was the same as that which had been used scores—thousands— of times before to announce the demise of one monarch, duke, or other feudal magnate and the assumption of his titles by his heir. Unfortunately, the circumstances were anything but normal in this instance, for the monarch in question, Haarahld VII of Charis, had not died in bed.

And there is that one minor *difference between this writ of succession and all the others,* Duchairn reminded himself, letting his fingers trace the largest and most ornate seal of all. By both law and ancient tradition, no succession was valid or final until it had been confirmed by Mother Church, which was supposed to mean by the Council of Vicars. But this writ of succession already bore Mother Church's seal, and Duchairn's eyes slipped to the second—and, in his opinion, more dangerous—succession writ.

Neither of them could have been more politely phrased. No one could point to a single overtly defiant statement. Yet the seal affixed to the first writ of succession belonged to the Archbishop of Charis, and in the eyes of Mother Church, there *was* no Archbishop of Charis. Erayk Dynnys, who had held that office, had been stripped of it and was currently awaiting execution for the crimes of treason, malfeasance, and the encouragement of heresy. The Council of Vicars had not yet even considered a replacement for him, but the Kingdom of Charis clearly had . . . as the second writ made abundantly clear.

It was, for all the blandness of its phrasing, a clear-cut declaration of war against the entire Church of God Awaiting, and just in case anyone had failed to notice, there was always the *third* document . . . the original copy of Staynair's letter to Grand Vicar Erek.

Duchairn was certain that the blandness of the two writs of succession, the contrast between their traditional phraseology and terminology and Staynair's fiery "letter," was intentional. Their very everyday normality not only underscored the deadly condemnation of Staynair's accusations, but also made it clear that Charis intended to continue about its own affairs, its own concerns, without one iota of deference to the desires or commands of the Church it had chosen to defy.

No, not simply *defy*. That was the reason the writs of succession had been written as they had, sent as they had. They were the proof that Charis was prepared to *ignore* Mother Church, and in many ways, that was even more deadly.

Never in all of Safehold's history had *any* secular monarch dared to name the man of his own choice as the chief prelate of his realm. *Never.* That was the Council of Vicars' official position, although Duchairn was well aware of the persistent, whispered rumors that Mother Church's traditions had not always supported that view of things.

But this was no hypothetical age which might have existed once, centuries ago. This was the *present*, and in the present, it was a patently illegal act. Yet the writ of appointment naming Maikel Staynair Archbishop of all Charis carried not simply Cayleb Ahrmahk's signature, but also the signatures and seals of every member of his Royal Council, the Speaker of the House of Commons . . . and of nineteen of the twenty-three other bishops of the Kingdom of Charis. The same signatures and seals had been affixed individually to Staynair's "letter," as well, which was even more frightening. This wasn't one man's, one king's, one usurping archbishop's, act of defiance; it was an entire *kingdom's*, and the consequences if it was allowed to stand were unthinkable.

But how do we keep *it from standing?* Duchairn asked himself almost despairingly. *They've defeated—as Zahmsyn says,* destroyed—*the navies of Corisande, Emerald, Chisholm, Tarot, and Dohlar. There's no one left, no one we can possibly send against them.*

"I think," Trynair continued into his colleagues' angry, frightened silence, "that we must begin by admitting the limitations we currently face. And, to be honest, we have no choice but to confront openly both the failure of our original policy and the difficulties we face in attempting to recover from that failure."

"How?" Maigwair demanded, obviously still smarting from Trynair's earlier remarks.

"The charge which is most likely to prove dangerous to Mother Church and the authority of the Council of Vicars," Trynair replied, "is that the attack directed against Charis has somehow pushed Cayleb and his adherents into this open defiance and heresy. That had we not acted against Haarahld's earlier policies as we did, Charis would not have been lost to us."

He looked around the table once more, and Duchairn nodded back shortly. Of course that was what their enemies were going to say. After all, it was true, wasn't it?

"I suggest to you," Trynair said, "that these documents are the clearest possible proof that there is no accuracy at all to such a charge."

Duchairn felt his eyebrows trying to arch in astonishment, but he somehow kept his jaw from dropping.

"It's obvious," the Chancellor continued, still sounding as if what he was saying actually had some nodding acquaintance with reality, "no matter whose name is signed to this so-called 'open letter,' that the hand truly behind it is Cayleb's. That Staynair is simply Cayleb's mouthpiece and puppet, the sacrilegious and blasphemous mask for Cayleb's determination to adhere to his father's aggressive and dangerous foreign policy. No doubt some people will see Cayleb's undeniable anger over his father's death and the attack which we supported as impelling him to take such defiant steps. However, as has been well established, it was not Mother Church or the Council of Vicars, but the Knights of the Temple Lands who supported the resort to arms against Haarahld's overweening ambition."

Clyntahn and Maigwair swallowed *that*, too, Duchairn noted, even though it just happened that the "secular" magnates of the Temple Lands also all happened to be members of the Council of Vicars, as well. It was true that the legal fiction that they were two separate entities had served the purposes of the vicarate often enough over the years. Yet the very frequency with which that particular ploy had been used meant everyone *recognized* it as a false distinction.

None of which seemed to faze Trynair, who simply went on speaking as if he were making some sort of genuine differentiation.

"Nowhere in any of the correspondence or diplomatic exchanges between the Knights of the Temple Lands and any of the secular rulers involved was there any discussion of Crusade or Holy War, which would surely have been the case had Mother Church moved against apostates and heretics. Clearly, Cayleb and his supporters are in possession of much of the correspondence between the Knights of the Temple Lands' secular allies and their naval commanders. As such, they must be aware of the fact that Mother Church was never involved at all and that, in fact, the entire war had its causes in purely secular motives and rivalries. Yet their immediate response has been to impiously and heretically name an apostate bishop to the primacy of the Archbishopric of Charis in defiance of the Council of Vicars as God's chosen and consecrated stewards and to flatly reject Mother Church's God-given authority over all of God's children."

He leaned back in his chair, his expression suitably grave, and Duchairn blinked. He'd never heard such a heap of unadulterated claptrap in his entire life. And yet . . .

"So what you're saying," he heard his own voice say, "is that the actions they've taken prove they were already lost to apostasy and heresy before anyone ever moved against them?"

"Precisely." Trynair waved one hand at the documents. "Look at the number of signatures, the number of seals, on these writs and Staynair's letter. How could anyone have possibly generated such a unified, prompt response to any perception of Mother Church's hostility? At least some of the nobles of Charis must be aware of the fact that the Council of Vicars and Grand Vicar Erek never authorized, far less demanded, any attack on their kingdom. And even if they weren't, Mother Church's own bishops *must* know the truth! Yet here they are, supporting Cayleb's illegal and impious actions. If, in fact, it were no more than a response to the attack of a purely secular alliance, Cayleb could never have secured the support of such an overwhelming majority in so short a time. The only possible explanation is that the entire kingdom has been falling steadily into the hands of the enemies of God and that those enemies have seized upon the current situation as a pretext for open defiance of the legitimate stewards of God and Langhorne here on Safehold."

Duchairn sat back in his own chair, his expression intent. It wasn't just claptrap—it was, in fact, outright dragon shit—but he saw where Trynair was headed.

And so, apparently, did Clyntahn.

"I see what you mean, Zahmsyn." There was an unpleasant glow in the Grand Inquisitor's eyes. "And you're right, of course. No doubt Cayleb and his lackeys were as surprised as anyone by the scale of their naval victories. Obviously the overconfidence and arrogance that's generated has led them to openly embrace the heretical attitudes and goals which they've been secretly nurturing for so long."

"Precisely," Trynair said again. "Indeed, I think it's highly likely—almost a certainty—that the Ahrmahk dynasty, and others who have fallen into the same sin, have been headed in this very direction ever since Haarahld insisted Archbishop Rojyr name Staynair Bishop of Tellesberg. Obviously that insistence was part of a long-standing plan to subvert Mother Church's loyalties in Charis . . . as the rest of the Council is well aware that Zhaspahr has warned everyone so many times might be the case."

Duchairn's eyes narrowed. He couldn't very well dispute Trynair's thesis, since Erayk Dynnys' failure to remove Staynair from his see and purge his archbishopric's ecclesiastic hierarchy of its Charisian elements had been one of the many crimes of which he had been convicted.

On the other hand, of the nineteen bishops who had concurred in Staynair's illegal elevation, only six were native-born Charisians, which left the question of how Haarahld, and now Cayleb, had influenced the others into supporting the Ahrmahks' criminal actions. That was a fact to which the Group of Four would undoubtedly be well advised to avoid drawing attention, he thought.

"Even so," he pointed out aloud, "that leaves us with the problem of how we respond. Whether they've been secretly planning this for years or not doesn't change the consequences we have to deal with."

"True." Trynair nodded. "However, despite the gravity of the situation, there's no need for panic or overly precipitous action. Although we may not currently possess the naval strength to act directly against Charis, Cayleb has no army. His fleet may suffice—for now—to keep the armies Mother Church may summon to her banner away from the shores of his kingdom, but he cannot threaten Mother Church's own security here in Haven or Howard. And let us not forget that Charis is a small kingdom, when all's said and done, while nine in ten of all the human souls of Safehold are found in the kingdoms and empires of Haven and Howard. Even if Cayleb controlled every ship on God's seas, he could never raise the troop strength to attack here. And so, ultimately, time must be on our side. We can always build new ships, in the fullness of time; he cannot somehow create the manpower required for him to raise whole armies, however much time he may have."

"Building fleets isn't something to be accomplished in a day, or even a five-day," Duchairn pointed out.

"Allayn?" Trynair looked at Maigwair. The Captain General straightened a bit in his chair, and his eyes lost some of their earlier sullenness. "Do we have the capacity to build a new navy?" the Chancellor continued. "And if we don't, how long will it take to create that capacity?"

"If you're asking whether or not Mother Church and the Temple Lands have the capacity to build a navy, the answer is no, not immediately," Maigwair admitted. "We could almost certainly build that capacity, but it would require us to import the carpenters, designers, and all the other skilled workers

shipyards require. Or enough of them to train our own workforce, at least."
He shrugged. "The Temple Lands have never been a naval power, for obvious
reasons. The only 'seacoast' we have is on Hsing-wu's Passage, and that's
frozen every winter."

Trynair nodded. So did Duchairn. Despite his personal opinion of Maigwair's intellect, the Church's Treasurer had to admit that when it came to *im-
plementing* tasks, the Captain General frequently showed the traces of genuine
ability which had gotten him elevated to the vicarate in the first place.

Of course, he thought sardonically, *the fact that Allayn's uncle was Grand Vicar
the year he was elevated to the orange also had just a little bit to do with it. And the problem's never been that Maigwair can't carry out instructions; it's that he's pitiful when it
comes to deciding which tasks ought to be undertaken to begin with.*

"I was afraid you were going to say that, Allayn," Trynair said. "I believe
it might well be worthwhile to begin building up that workforce as quickly as
possible, but I'd already assumed we'd be forced to look elsewhere in the
short term. So what are our prospects in that direction?"

"None of the mainland realms have the concentrated shipbuilding capacity Charis possesses," Maigwair replied. "Desnair certainly doesn't, and neither does Siddarmark."

"*Umpfh!*" The irate grunt came from Clyntahn, and everyone looked at
him. "There's no way *I* want to rely on Siddarmark for naval support, shipyards or no shipyards," the Grand Inquisitor said bluntly. "I don't trust
Stohnar as far as I can fart. He's likely to take our money, build the ships, and
then decide to throw in with Charis and use them against us!"

Duchairn frowned. The Siddarmark Republic and its growing power
and apparent territorial ambitions had concerned the Group of Four and its
predecessors for decades. Indeed, Siddarmark had been considered an actual,
immediate threat, potentially at least, while Charis had been regarded more
as a long-term cancer which must be excised *before* it became a threat. And
Lord Protector Greyghor Stohnar, the current ruler of Siddarmark, was a
dangerously capable man. Worse, he'd been *elected* to the protectorship. That
gave him a much broader base of support than would have been the case for
many an hereditary ruler who might have aroused the Church's ire. Against
that backdrop, it was scarcely surprising Clyntahn should react strongly
against the possibility of actually increasing Siddarmark's military potential.
Still . . .

"If we obviously exclude Siddarmark from any shipbuilding programs,"
he said in a painfully neutral tone, "Stohnar, for one, is unlikely to miscon-
strue our reasoning."

"Fuck Stohnar," Clyntahn said crudely, then grimaced. "Of course he's
unlikely to misunderstand," he said in somewhat more temperate tones. "On
the other hand, he already knows we don't trust him. God knows we've never

made any great secret of it among ourselves or in our correspondence with him. Since the enmity's already there, I'm in favor of depriving him of any additional weapons he might use against us rather than worrying about how the injury to his tender sensibilities might turn him against us."

"Zhaspahr has a point, I think," Trynair said. "And we can still . . . soften the blow, I suppose, by spreading some of the gold we're not using on ships in Siddarmark around to Siddarmark's wheat farmers. For that matter, they have plenty of excess pikemen we could hire when the time comes."

"All right, then," Maigwair said, "excluding Siddarmark, and leaving Desnair and Sodar aside because they have almost as little naval capacity as we do, that really leaves only Dohlar, the Empire, and Tarot. And, of course, Corisande and Chisholm."

The last sentence was a sour afterthought, and Duchairn snorted mentally. Corisande's shipbuilding capacity was going to become a moot point as soon as Cayleb and Charis got around to dealing with Hektor, which was probably true for Tarot, as well. And unless Duchairn much missed his guess, *Chisholm's* building capacity was more likely to be added to that of Charis than brought to the support of Mother Church.

Dohlar and the Empire of Harchong were very different matters, however. Dohlar, at the moment, no longer *had* a navy, courtesy of the Royal Charisian Navy, but King Rahnyld had been attempting to increase his shipbuilding capacity for many years. And Harchong—the largest and most populous of all Safehold's kingdoms and empires—had the biggest fleet of any of the mainland realms.

"Rahnyld is going to want revenge for what happened to him," Maigwair continued, putting Duchairn's thoughts into words. "If we agree to subsidize the rebuilding of his navy, I'm sure he'll jump at it. And he'd be even happier to build ships expressly for Mother Church's service, since Dohlar would get to pocket every mark of their price at no cost to his own treasury.

"As for Harchong, most of its navy is laid up. I have no idea how much of it may be serviceable and how much of it's hopelessly rotten by now. But the Empire at least has shipyards, which we don't. And I don't think any of us would have any qualms about the Emperor's reliability."

Which was certainly true, Duchairn reflected. Harchong was the oldest, wealthiest, largest, and most conservative realm in existence. It was also arrogant, disdainful of all outsiders, and run by an efficient but deeply corrupt bureaucracy. From the Group of Four's perspective, however, what mattered just now was that the Harchong aristocracy's allegiance to Mother Church was ironclad. That aristocracy could always be relied upon to come to Mother Church's defense in return for Mother Church's validation of its privileges and power over the hapless serfs who drudged away their lives on its huge, sprawling estates.

"I'll have to do some research before I could give you any hard and fast numbers," Maigwair said. "I believe that between Harchong and Dohlar, we could probably come close to matching Charis' present building capacity, though. Charis will probably do everything that it can to increase its capacity, of course, but it simply doesn't have the manpower—or the wealth—to match the extent to which we could expand Harchong's and Dohlar's ship-yards."

"What about Trellheim?" Clyntahn asked, and Maigwair's face tightened in scorn, or possibly disgust.

"None of those lordlings have more than a handful of galleys apiece," he said, "and the lot of them are nothing more than common pirates. If they had the ship strength to make their raids on Harchong's coastal shipping more than a nuisance, the Emperor would already have conquered them outright long ago."

Clyntahn grunted again, then nodded in agreement.

"So it would appear to me," Trynair said in his patented summarizing fashion, "that we're in agreement that one of our first steps must be to under-take a major naval expansion through Harchong and Dohlar. Until Allayn's had an opportunity to conduct his research, we don't know how long that's going to take. I'd be surprised, however, if it takes less than a year or two, at the very best. During that time, we will remain secure against attack here, but we'll be unable to take the offensive against Charis. So our immediate con-cern is how to address that period in which we can't effectively attack them—with fleets or armies, at least—and how to deal with our fellow vicars' reaction to these . . . tumultuous events."

"It's clearly our responsibility to prevent any weaker souls among the vic-arate from overreacting to the current provocation, despite the undoubted se-riousness of that provocation," Clyntahn said. "Charis has bidden defiance to the Church, to the Archangels, and to God Himself. I believe we must quench any sparks of panic among those weaker souls by making it clear to the entire vicarate that we have no intention of allowing that defiance to stand. And that we intend to deal . . . firmly with any additional outbreaks of defiance. That will be the Inquisition's task."

The Grand Inquisitor's face was hard and cold.

"At the same time, however, we must prepare the entire Council for the reality that it will take time for us to forge the new weapons we need for our inevitable counterstroke," he continued. "That may be difficult in the face of the deep concern many of our brothers in God will undoubtedly feel, and I believe your earlier point was well taken, Zahmsyn. We must make it clear to those . . . concerned souls that Charis' apparent strength, and Charis' initial victories, are not a threat to us, but rather a sign to Mother Church. A warn-ing we must all heed. Indeed, if one considers the situation with unclouded eyes, secure—as one ought to be—in one's faith, the hand of God Himself is abundantly clear. Only the achievement of such an apparently overwhelming triumph could have tempted the secret heretics of Charis into openly revealing themselves for what they are. By permitting them their transitory victory, God has stripped away their mask for all to see. And yet, as you say, Zahmsyn, He's done this in a way which still leaves them unable to truly threaten Mother Church or undermine her responsibility to guide and protect the souls of all His children."

Trynair nodded again, and an icy quiver ran through Duchairn's bones. The Chancellor, he felt certain, had evolved his explanation as if he were solving a chess problem, or perhaps any of the purely secular machinations and strategies his office was forced to confront daily. It was an intellectual ploy based on pragmatism and the naked realities of politics at the highest possible level. But the glitter it had lit in Clyntahn's eyes continued to glow. Whatever the Chancellor might think, and however capable of cynical calculation the Grand Inquisitor might be when it suited his purposes, the fervent conviction in Clyntahn's tone was most definitely not feigned. He had embraced Trynair's analysis not simply out of expediency, but because he *believed* it, as well.

And why does that frighten me so? I'm a Vicar of Mother Church, for God's sake! However we came to where we are, we know what God demands of us, just as we know that God is all-powerful, all-knowing. Why shouldn't *He have used our own actions to reveal the truth about Charis? Show us how deep the rot truly runs in Tellesberg?*

Something happened deep in Rhobair Duchairn's heart and soul, and another thought occurred to him.

I have to think about this, spend time in prayer and meditation, pondering the Writ *and* The Commentaries. *Perhaps people like the Wylsynns have been right all along. Perhaps we* have *grown too arrogant, too enamored of our power as secular princes. The Charisians may not be the only ones whose mask God has decided to strip away. Perhaps this entire debacle is God's mirror, held up to show us the potential consequences of our own sinful actions and overweening pride.*

It was not, he knew, a suggestion to be brought forth at this moment, in this place. It was one to be considered carefully, in the stillness and quiet of his own heart. And yet . . .

For the first time in far too many years, in the face of obviously unmitigated disaster, Vicar Rhobair Duchairn found himself once more contemplating the mysterious actions of God through the eyes of faith and not the careful calculation of advantage.

Queen Sharleyan's Palace,
City of Cherayth,
Kingdom of Chisholm

Trumpets sounded and the batteries protecting the Cherry Bay waterfront blossomed with smoke as they thudded their way through a sixteen-gun salute. Indignant seabirds and wyverns made their opinion of the goings-on abundantly clear as they wheeled, screeched, and scolded across a sky of springtime blue. The brisk wind out of the east lofted them easily as it blew across the sheltering peninsula known as The Sickle, which shielded Cherry Bay and the city of Cherayth from the often rough weather of the North Chisholm Sea, and the air was refreshingly cool.

Queen Sharleyan of Chisholm stood at a window high up in Lord Gerait's Tower on the seaward side of the palace which had been her family's home for two centuries, looking out over the orderly stone houses, streets, warehouses, and docks of her capital as she watched the four galleons sailing majestically into its harbor. The winged tenants of Cherry Bay might be filled with indignation at the disturbance of their normal routine, but they had no idea just how disturbing *she* found all this, she reflected.

Sharleyan was a slender, not quite petite young woman who'd just turned twenty-four. Despite the occasional fawning versification of particularly inept court poets, she wasn't a beautiful woman. Striking, yes, with a determined chin, and a nose which was just a bit too prominent (not to mention a bit too hooked). But her dark hair, so black it had blue highlights in direct sunlight and so long it fell almost to her waist when it was unbound, and her huge, sparkling brown eyes somehow deceived people into thinking she *was* beautiful. Today, Sairah Hahlmyn, her personal maid since she was nine, and Lady Mairah Lywkys, her senior lady-in-waiting, had dressed that hair in an elaborate coiffure, held in place by jeweled combs and the light golden circlet of a presence crown, and those lively eyes were dark and still and wary.

The man at her side, Mahrak Sahndyrs, Baron Green Mountain, was at least eight or nine inches taller than she was, with blunt, strong features and thinning silver hair. Sharleyan had been Queen of Chisholm for almost twelve years, despite her youth, and Green Mountain had been her first councilor all that time. They'd weathered many a political storm together, although neither of them had ever anticipated one like the hurricane which had swept across half of Safehold in the last six months.

"I can't quite believe we're doing this," she said, eyes on the lead galleon as it followed a flag-bedecked galley of the Royal Chisholmian Navy towards its assigned anchorage. "We have to be insane, you know that, don't you, Mahrak?"

"I believe that was the point I made to you when you decided we were going to do it anyway, Your Majesty," Green Mountain replied with a crooked smile.

"A *proper* first councilor would have already taken the blame for his monarch's temporary lapse into insanity onto his own shoulders," Sharleyan said severely.

"Oh, I assure you, I will in *public*, Your Majesty."

"But not privately, I see." Sharleyan smiled at him, but her expression couldn't hide her tension from someone who'd known her literally since she'd learned to walk.

"No, not privately," he agreed gently, and reached out to rest one hand lightly on her shoulder. That wasn't the sort of gesture he would have allowed himself in public, but in private there was no point pretending his youthful queen had not long ago become the daughter he'd never had.

"Have you had any further thoughts about what this is all about?" she asked after a moment.

"None we haven't already discussed to death," he told her, and she grimaced, never taking her eyes away from the arriving ships.

They had, indeed, "discussed it to death," she thought, and neither of them—nor any of the other councilors and advisers she truly trusted—had been able to come up with a satisfactory theory. Some of those advisers, the ones who had argued most strenuously in favor of refusing this meeting, were certain it was simply one more trap designed to drag (or push) Chisholm deeper into the Charisian quagmire. Sharleyan wasn't certain why she didn't agree with that interpretation herself. Certainly, it made sense. The "spontaneous" return of her surrendered warships must have already tainted Chisholm with suspicious distrust in the eyes of the Group of Four. The fact that she'd dared to receive Sir Samyl Tyrnyr as King Cayleb of Charis' ambassador, despite the minor fact that she was still technically at war with Cayleb's kingdom, could only have underscored that distrust. And now this.

Somehow, I doubt that rendering formal honors to Charisian warships here in my own capital's harbor while receiving the First Councilor of Charis as Cayleb's personal envoy is going to do a thing for me in that pig Clyntahn's eyes, she thought. *The doomsayers are right about that much, at least. On the other hand, how much worse can it get?*

It was a more than academic question, under the circumstances. She had no doubt at all that the Group of Four must have realized she and her admirals had dragged their heels in every possible way after receiving their orders to support Hektor of Corisande against Charis. Indeed, it would have been amazing if Sharleyan hadn't, given the fact that she was probably the only monarch Hektor hated more than he'd hated Haarahld VII, or the fact that she probably hated *him* even more than he hated *her*. Still, the fact that so many of her navy's warships had surrendered intact had probably been going a bit too far, even for someone as experienced in the cynical realities of politics as Chancellor Trynair. And Cayleb's "generosity" in returning those surrendered ships to her without even seeking reparations for her part in the attack which had killed his father, along with several thousand of his subjects, had been a shrewd move on his part.

She wanted to resent the way he'd deliberately maneuvered her into a position which could not but make the Group of Four furious with her. What had started as a simple move to conserve her own military power by "cooperating" with Hektor as grudgingly as possible started to look dangerously like active collusion with Charis in the wake of Cayleb's "spontaneous" gesture. No one in the Temple was likely to forgive that, which could all too easily have fatal consequences for her own kingdom in the fullness of time.

But she could scarcely complain over the fact that Cayleb had done precisely what she would have done, had their roles been reversed. Anything which might divert at least some of the Group of Four's attention and resources from Charis had to be worthwhile from Cayleb's perspective. And, again from his perspective, any lever he could use to . . . encourage Chisholm into some sort of active alliance *with* Charis, rather than against it, had to be tried. Indeed, what she felt far more strongly than any sort of resentment was an unbegrudged admiration for how well Cayleb clearly understood that.

And be honest, Sharleyan, she thought. *From the very beginning, you would have preferred aligning yourself with Charis to finding yourself "allied" with Hektor and Nahrmahn. If you'd thought Haarahld had a single chance of surviving, you would have proposed an alliance to him, and you know it. That's the real reason you accepted Cayleb's "gift" when he returned your galleys. And it's the real reason you let him send Tyrnyr to Cherayth, as well. There's a part of you that still prefers Charis to Hektor, isn't there? And it's just possible Cayleb does have a chance of surviving—maybe even winning—after all.*

She watched the galleons which represented that chance of victory moving sedately towards their anchorage, and wondered what the Earl of Gray Harbor had come all this way to say to her.

▼   ▼   ▼

This was Rayjhis Yowance's third visit to Cherayth, although both of his earlier trips had been made as an officer in the Royal Charisian Navy, not as the kingdom's first councilor. First councilors, after all, never left home. That was why kingdoms had little things called "ambassadors" to do the traveling instead, since first councilors were far too busy, and their duties were far too important, for them to go haring off on quixotic quests.

Of course they are! he snorted mentally. *Which is how* you *happen to be here, isn't it, Rayjhis?*

His lips twitched at the thought, but he suppressed the smile reflex sternly as he followed the chamberlain down the palace corridor. However accommodating Sharleyan had been, it would never do to suggest that he saw anything humorous in her agreeing to meet with him. Especially in her agreeing to meet with him privately, accompanied only by her own first councilor. And especially not when she'd had less than a five-day's notice he was coming, given how closely he'd followed on the original messenger's heels.

Cayleb's like his father in a lot of ways, but he has his own inimitable style . . . and far too much energy for an old man like me, Gray Harbor reflected. *I'm beginning to appreciate what Merlin and Domynyk had to say about trying to ride herd on him at sea. He's not really anywhere near as . . . impulsive as he sometimes seems, but Merlin's right. Given two possible approaches to any problem, he'll always opt for the more audacious one. And once he's made up his mind, he's not about to waste time, is he?*

There were worse traits a king could have, especially when he was engaged in a battle for survival. But it did make keeping up with him more than a little wearing.

The chamberlain slowed, looked over his shoulder at the Charisian with an expression which had been carefully trained to conceal any trace of what its owner might have thought about his monarch's decisions, and then turned a final bend and stopped.

There were two guardsmen, sergeants, in the silver and royal blue of Chisholm posted in front of the door, and their expressions weren't quite as neutral as the chamberlain's. They clearly nursed significant reservations about allowing the first councilor of the kingdom whose navy had just smashed a sizable portion of the Chisholmian fleet into firewood into their queen's presence. The fact that they'd been ordered to stay *outside* the small presence chamber didn't make them any happier, and the fact that they'd been expressly forbidden to search Gray Harbor or relieve him of any weapons made them unhappier still.

The earl was well aware of what they must be feeling. In fact, he sympathized deeply with it, and he made a quick decision.

"Just a moment, please," he said, stopping the chamberlain just before the man knocked on the polished door. The chamberlain looked surprised, and Gray Harbor smiled crookedly. Then he carefully lifted his dress sword's baldric over his head and passed the sheathed weapon to the nearer of the two guardsmen. The Chisholmian's eyes widened slightly as he accepted it, and then Gray Harbor unhooked his belt dagger and passed it across as well.

The guardsmen's expressions changed as he voluntarily surrendered the blades they'd been forbidden to take from him. They still didn't look especially cheerful about the entire notion of this meeting, but the senior of them bowed deeply to him, acknowledging his concession.

"Thank you, My Lord," he said, then straightened and personally knocked on the door.

"Earl Gray Harbor has arrived, Your Majesty," he announced.

"Then by all means, let him in, Edwyrd," a musical soprano replied, and the guardsman opened the door and stood aside.

Gray Harbor stepped past him with a murmured word of thanks and found himself in a paneled presence chamber. There were no windows, but it was brightly lit by hanging lamps, and a fire crackled quietly on a hearth. It wasn't a particularly large fire, especially for one burning in a hearth which could easily have accommodated most of a topsail yard, but its heat was surprisingly welcome. It was technically spring here in Chisholm, but Cherayth was over two thousand miles above the equator, and Gray Harbor's Charisian blood found it distinctly cool.

He made his way calmly down the runner of royal blue carpet, and his eyes were busy. Sharleyan's chair was just too simple to call a throne, but a small platform elevated it just enough to make it clear this was a crowned head of state, even if she had chosen to receive him rather informally. Baron Green Mountain stood beside her, watching alertly as Gray Harbor approached. Then Sharleyan frowned.

"My Lord," she said before he could speak, her voice less musical and considerably sharper than it had been, "I gave strict instructions that you were to be permitted your weapons for this meeting!"

"I realize that, Your Majesty." Gray Harbor stopped in front of her and bowed, then straightened. "I deeply appreciate your graciousness in that regard, too. However, when I arrived here, I could tell your guardsmen were uneasy. They couldn't possibly have been more courteous, and neither of them gave any sign, by word or deed, that they intended to disobey your instructions," he hastened to add, "but I felt it would have been churlish on my part to cause them distress. Their devotion to you was readily apparent—I've seen its like before—and I chose to offer them my weapons, even though they hadn't requested it."

"I see." Sharleyan sat back in her chair, gazing at him thoughtfully, then smiled slightly. "That was a gracious gesture on *your* part," she observed. "And if, in fact, no insult was offered to you, then on behalf of my guardsmen—who are, as you observed, devoted to me—I thank you."

Gray Harbor bowed again, and Sharleyan glanced at Green Mountain for a moment. Then she returned her attention to the Charisian.

"I trust you'll understand, My Lord, that Baron Green Mountain and I must view your presence here with mixed emotions. While I'm deeply grateful for the return of my ships and sailors, for the honorable treatment they were given as Charis' prisoners, and for your King's decision against seeking any sort of reparations, I'm also aware that all his decisions were made with a full awareness of their practical consequences. Particularly, shall we say, where the demands—and suspicions—of certain rather insistent 'Knights of the Temple Lands' are concerned."

She smiled tightly as she acknowledged openly for the first time that the Group of Four had compelled her to join Charis' enemies, and Gray Harbor smiled back.

"It pains me to say it, Your Majesty," he said, "but honesty compels me to admit that His Majesty thought about that rather carefully before he returned your vessels. Indeed, he was fully aware that it would have the consequences you've just mentioned. It may have been . . . ungallant of him to put you in that position, but it's also true that when he made the decision, you were part of an alliance which had attacked his Kingdom without warning or provocation and"—he looked her squarely in the eye, his smile fading—"killed his father."

Sharleyan's face tightened. Not with anger, although Gray Harbor saw anger in it, but in pain. The pain of memory at his oblique reminder of how her own father had died in battle against "pirates" subsidized by Hektor of Corisande when she was still a girl.

"Nonetheless," he continued, "it is, as I'm certain Sir Samyl has made clear, His Majesty's earnest desire to see Chisholm as a friend and an ally, rather than a foe. Your realm and his have much in common and little cause for enmity, beyond the machinations and demands of those who are the natural enemies of both. To speak frankly, both His Majesty and Your Majesty have ample reasons to hate Hektor of Corisande and to regard him as a mortal threat to your own security. And, to speak even more frankly"—he looked into her eyes once more—"Grand Inquisitor Clyntahn regards both Charis and Chisholm with deep suspicion and distrust. If Charis is destroyed for no better reason than the arrogance, bigotry, and blind intolerance of the so-called Group of Four, it can be only a matter of time before Chisholm follows."

Sharleyan's tight expression smoothed into total *non*-expression as Gray Harbor took her own open acknowledgment of how she had been compelled to join with Hektor to an entirely new level.

"My King has instructed me to be forthright in this matter, Your Majesty," he told her—quite unnecessarily, he was certain, after his last sentence. "For whatever reason, the Group of Four, on behalf of the Church, has decided Charis must be destroyed. We were not informed of any point of doctrine or practice in which we were deemed to be in error. We weren't summoned to explain any actions, weren't charged with any violation of Church law or of the Proscriptions. Nor were we offered any opportunity to defend ourselves before any tribunal or court. They simply decided to destroy us. To burn our cities. To rape and murder our people. And they compelled *you* to join with your own Kingdom's worst enemy and assist him in carrying out that onslaught.

"His Majesty understands why you felt you had no choice but to acquiesce in the demands levied upon you. He neither faults you for your decision, nor believes for a moment that you felt anything but regret and unhappiness at the idea of attacking his Kingdom.

"But His Majesty also knows that if the Group of Four can do what it's already done, then no kingdom, no realm, is safe. If corrupt and venal men can use the power of God's own Church, whatever legal technicalities they may use to mask the Church's participation in an act of murder and rapine, to destroy *one* blameless kingdom, then in the fullness of time they will, as inevitably as the sun rises in the east, use it to destroy other kingdoms. Including your own."

He paused, watching the queen and her first councilor. Chisholm was as distant from the Temple and the Temple Lands as Charis, and Sharleyan and Green Mountain both knew that Clyntahn's automatic suspicion of Chisholm ran almost as deep as his suspicion of Charis. That suspicion, after all, was precisely what Cayleb's return of her surrendered ships had been calculated to play upon, and neither the queen nor her first councilor could possibly be unaware of it.

"The truth is, Your Majesty," he said after a moment, "that once a kraken tastes blood, there's no stopping its attack. Once the Group of Four—once Vicar Zhaspahr—has broken one kingdom, he'll see no reason he shouldn't apply the same technique to every other realm he distrusts or fears. That's the road upon which the Group of Four has set out, and their final destination lies in the smoldering ruins of Charis and Chisholm . . . unless they can somehow be stopped."

"And you—your King—believe they *can* be stopped?" Green Mountain spoke for the first time, his eyes intent, and Gray Harbor nodded.

"He does, and so do I. We have this advantage, which Chisholm shares, in that no army can simply march across our frontiers. The Group of Four cannot attack either of us without a navy, and as you and your own 'allies' have recently discovered, the sheer distances involved favor the defense. You and your captains and admirals have seen what our new ships and artillery can accomplish, as well. My King believes that together, Charis and Chisholm can indeed defy the Group of Four."

"Let's be honest here, My Lord," Sharleyan said, leaning forward, her own eyes narrow. "Whatever Archbishop Maikel's letter to the Grand Vicar may have said, or how it may have said it, we're not speaking solely of the Group of Four. For reasons which undoubtedly seemed good to them, and with which, to be honest, I find myself sharing a certain agreement, your King and his Archbishop have effectively bidden defiance to the entire Church, to the Grand Vicar himself. If Chisholm joins with Charis in an alliance against Hektor—and the Group of Four—it will inevitably, in the fullness of time, become an alliance against Mother Church herself. Against the Council of Vicars and the Grand Vicar, Langhorne's anointed steward here on Safehold. Is your King prepared for *that*? Prepared to defy the entire Church, embrace an unhealable, *permanent* schism within the body of God's people?"

"Your Majesty," Gray Harbor said quietly, "Safehold has already selected its own archbishop. For the first time in over five hundred years, a kingdom of Safehold has practiced the ancient right of our forefathers and named an archbishop of its own choosing. If that constitutes schism, then so be it. We do not defy God, Your Majesty; we simply defy the corruption, the decadence, which has infested God's Church, and *that* we will fight to the death. Indeed, my King bade me say this to you about his decision and all which will inevitably flow from it: 'Here I stand. I can do no other.'"

Silence filled the presence chamber as Sharleyan and Green Mountain gazed at him. Then, finally, Green Mountain cleared his throat.

"What you say about our distance from the Temple, about our ability— joined together—to defend ourselves against attack, may be true. The Church's reaction to the defiance you propose to bid it will certainly put that truth to the test, however. And in the face of that storm, only the strongest tree could hope to survive. It's one thing to speak of alliances in the normal sense of the world, My Lord, for the truth is, as we all know, that in the normal sense of the world, there will always be a tomorrow. Interests change, objectives flow, this month's or this year's ally becomes next month's or next year's foe, and so the dance continues, with partners changing as the music changes.

"But what you propose, what your *King* proposes, can have only one tomorrow. The Group of Four, and the Church, will never forget or forgive someone who bids them defiance, and not simply because of the calculation of corrupt men. Since the Day of Creation, the Church has been the keeper of men's souls, the proclaimer of God's will, and there are men and women of good faith within the Church who will fight to the death to preserve her overlordship in God's name, not the name of corrupt ambition. The war you propose to fight will have to end not in treaties and negotiations between diplomats dancing the measures we all know, but in utter defeat or victory. There can be no lesser end for either side than that, for the Church will never yield, never accept any other victory than the restoration of her supremacy as God's bride, and she will be no normal alliance, with changing partners.

Which means that if Charis is to have any hope of final victory, *her* alliances must be equally firm, equally final."

"My Lord," Gray Harbor said, "this isn't a war we 'propose to fight.' It's a war which has already *begun*, whether we ever wanted to fight it, or not. But even though you're entirely correct about the stakes, about the way in which the Church will view its nature and the way in which she will fight it, we hope and believe that, in time, there can be an end. That it need not continue unabated until all of those on one side are dead or enslaved. What that end may be, or when it will come, is more than anyone in Charis would dare to predict, yet my King agrees that any alliances must be strong and permanent enough to endure that sort of bitter test. In fact, he believes that what is truly needed isn't an alliance at all."

"It isn't?" Despite her best effort, Sharleyan couldn't quite keep her surprise out of her tone, and Gray Harbor smiled.

"As Baron Green Mountain just said, Your Majesty, alliances come and go. Which is why I wasn't sent to you to propose an *alliance* at all. Instead, my King proposes a marriage."

Sharleyan jerked upright in her chair, her eyes wide, and Green Mountain inhaled sharply. The queen's surprise was obvious, but as Gray Harbor watched her first councilor, he found himself wondering if Green Mountain hadn't suspected where Cayleb was headed from the outset.

"I've brought with me King Cayleb's personal letters and documents setting forth his proposals, Your Majesty," the earl continued, still watching Green Mountain's expression. "Fundamentally, however, they're very simple. Stripped of all the high-flown legal language, what King Cayleb proposes is the unification of Charis and Chisholm through marriage. You would retain the crown of Chisholm for the remainder of your life; he would retain the crown of Charis for the remainder of his life. Should either of you predecease the other, the surviving spouse would hold both crowns for the remainder of his or her life, and upon his or her death, both crowns would pass as one to the heirs of your joint bodies. An imperial parliament, navy, and army would be created to govern and protect both kingdoms in concert during your lifetimes and afterwards. The peers of Charis and Chisholm would be seated in the House of Lords of that parliament, and both Charis and Chisholm would elect members to the House of Commons."

He paused, once more meeting Sharleyan's gaze levelly, then bowed.

"I fully realize, as does His Majesty, that no one in Chisholm has ever contemplated such a . . . sweeping change in the relationship between your Kingdom and Charis. Clearly, this isn't the sort of decision which can be made by a single person in a single day, even if that person be a king or a queen, and the nature of the threat your Kingdom would be embracing is not one to be lightly shouldered.

"But that threat already looms over both Chisholm and Charis. We can either confront it together, or separately. His Majesty believes our chance of survival and victory is far greater together, and this proposal is the strongest surety he can offer that if, indeed, we face this peril together, we will go *on* together to whatever victory or other end awaits us."

.III.

Ehdwyrd Howsmyn's Foundry,
Delthak,
Earldom of High Rock,
Kingdom of Charis

A nd how has your day been?" Rhaiyan Mychail asked genially as he stepped into Ehdwyrd Howsmyn's office.

"Hectic," Howsmyn said with a grin, standing to clasp forearms with his longtime business associate. "On the other hand, there could be a lot worse reasons for putting up with all of the headaches."

"True." Mychail returned Howsmyn's grin. "The sound of all those gold marks falling into my cash box at night is *such* a cheerful one!"

Both men laughed, and Howsmyn twitched his head at the office window. The two of them walked across to stand looking out it, and Mychail's expression sobered as he shook his head.

"It's hard to believe that all you had here two years ago was a single small furnace and a lot of empty dirt," he said.

"I feel the same way a lot of the time," Howsmyn acknowledged. "And, like you, I have no objection at all to how much richer this is making me. But at the same time. . . ."

He shook his head, and the gesture was far less cheerful than Mychail's had been.

His older friend didn't respond at once. Instead, he simply stood there, looking out over what was without doubt already one of the largest—if not *the* largest—foundries in the entire world.

Howsmyn's new and growing facility sat on the western shore of Ithmyn's Lake, the vast lake formed at the confluence of the Selmyn River and the West Delthak River in the Earldom of High Rock. The West Delthak was a brawling, powerful river flowing out of the South Hanth Mountains, but frequent shallows and cataracts made anything but small, local boat traffic impossible. The *lower* Delthak, however, was navigable, even for galleons, between Ithmyn's Lake and Larek, the small (but growing) port at the river's mouth, sixty-four miles to the south. That had been a major factor in Howsmyn's decision to buy the land from Earl High Rock, since it meant ships could sail all the way up the river to what was literally his front door. The extensive deposits of high-quality iron ore in the mountains to the west had been another factor, of course, although he hadn't actually done very much to develop the site until the sudden need for enormous quantities of artillery had burst upon the Kingdom of Charis.

Now engineers in Howsmyn's employ had already begun construction of a series of locks to improve navigation on the West Delthak and facilitate development of the mountains' iron deposits. Still more engineers had been busy farther down the river, and much of its water had been diverted through dams and channels by a swarming army of workmen to create an entire series of holding pools. Aqueducts from the highest pools and channels from the lower ones led to almost two-dozen overshot waterwheels, all of them churning steadily to power the equipment Howsmyn's mechanics had installed, and fresh mill races were under construction, as well. Smoke fumed from blast furnaces, more smoke rose from the foundries themselves, and as Mychail watched, a team of workers tapped the ore bath of a puddling furnace. The ferociously incandescent molten iron—wrought iron, now, softer and more malleable than cast iron—spilled through the tap into a collecting ladle for further processing.

Elsewhere, a much larger ladle of fiery, molten iron moved steadily towards the waiting molds. The ladle was suspended from an iron framework, which was in turn mounted on a heavy, multi-ton freight wagon. The wagon's wheels had flanged rims, instead of the smooth ones one might have expected, but that was to insure that they followed the iron rails linking the furnaces and the rest of the foundry's facilities. Draft dragons leaned into their collars, moving their burden with brisk efficiency, and Mychail inhaled deeply.

"Believe me, I understand," he said quietly. "When I look at this"—he jutted his chin at the swarming, incredibly noisy activity beyond Howsmyn's window—"I feel this enormous surge of optimism. Then I think about the fact that the Group of Four has the combined resources of every mainland realm to draw upon. That's a *lot* of foundries, Ehdwyrd, even if none of them can hold a candle to what you're doing here."

The truth was that all the techniques being employed out there had been known to ironmasters virtually since the Creation. But most of the iron which had ever before been required had been produced in much smaller operations, and without the consistent application of power from the perpetually rotating waterwheels Howsmyn and his mechanics had integrated into *this* foundry.

Well, Mychail corrected himself, *there are a few changes in "technique," if I'm going to be honest. So I suppose it's fortunate that none of them had to be tested under the Proscriptions.*

Howsmyn had gone further than anyone else in finding ways to use the power of his waterwheels. As one result, his furnaces burned hotter, and he'd been forced to find more refractory materials for the firebrick those furnaces required. Which, in turn, had inspired him to try to drive temperatures still higher. Mychail was one of the very few people who knew about Howsmyn's latest project—a further development of the puddling hearth but one which used hot furnace gases to preheat the ductwork by which the furnace was fired. Unless Mychail was sorely mistaken, production rates would be going up once more. And if Howsmyn's more optimistic predictions proved justified, he might actually find himself producing true steel, not simple wrought iron, in quantities such as no other ironmaster had ever even contemplated.

Fortunately, the Church had never set any sort of standard for the materials from which firebrick had to be made, or the temperatures to which furnaces might be heated, which meant Howsmyn's increased efficiency had slipped past almost unnoticed by Safehold at large . . . and by the Inquisition, in particular. The same broader and more innovative use of the power of his waterwheels had allowed him to achieve still other efficiencies as well, such as the grooved, geared rollers which let him produce iron bars far more quickly and economically than the traditional methods of hammering or of cutting strips from a rolled plate.

"I know your output is a lot higher on a manpower basis," Mychail continued. "But they don't have to match your output if they can bury you under sheer numbers of foundries."

"I know. Believe me, I know. On the other hand"—Howsmyn raised one hand and pointed out beyond the current outer ring of furnaces, to where still more walls and foundations marked additional expansion which was already well underway—"within four months, we're going to have increased our present capacity by another fifty percent. I'm expanding both my Tellesberg foundry and the one in Tirian, as well, too."

Mychail nodded, turning his head to watch yet another cargo vessel moving steadily up the Delthak from Larek. He wondered what this one carried as it steered towards the cluster of ships already moored at Howsmyn's lakeside docks. More coke for the furnaces? Copper and tin for Howsmyn's bronze works? Or more timbers, brick, and cement for the ongoing construction tasks?

Housing for Howsmyn's employees was also going up. Like Mychail himself, Howsmyn held strong opinions on the quality of housing his workers required. From a purely selfish viewpoint, the better the housing, the more strictly Pasquale's injunctions on sanitation were followed, the healthier the workforce he could expect, and the healthier his workforce, the more productive it would be. But there was more to it for Ehdwyrd Howsmyn, just as there was for Mychail, himself.

Rhaiyan Mychail was perfectly well aware that even here in Charis, altogether too many wealthy merchants and manufactory owners had absolutely no regard for their employees as fellow human beings. He and Howsmyn both detested that view. Indeed, Mychail had been an outspoken critic of that sort of thinking literally for decades, and he felt reasonably confident that that was one of the reasons King Haarahld had approached him and Howsmyn when he needed to create the manufacturing basis for his new navy.

And those idiots who try to screw every single hundredth-mark out of their workers deserve the loyalty they get in return, since it's absolutely nonexistent, he thought caustically. *Funny how starvation and loyalty don't seem to go hand in hand, isn't it? But see to it that they have affordable housing and healers, that there are schools available for their children, that they have the wages in their pockets to buy food and clothing, and that they all know you're constantly looking for foremen and supervisors from among anyone with the wit and ambition to better themselves in your employ, and it will repay you a hundred times over just from a purely selfish viewpoint.*

That was a lesson Ehdwyrd Howsmyn wasn't going to forget, even here, even in the face of the crisis the entire kingdom faced. It was, in fact, one he had learned from Mychail, and he'd taken it even further in at least one respect. Howsmyn had established an investment pool for his employees—one which actually allowed them to buy a share in the ownership of the foundries and manufactories in which they worked—and the employees at each of his enterprises were allowed to elect a single steward who represented their interests at the managerial level, as well. Any steward actually had the right to meet directly with Howsmyn, if the situation was serious enough for the workers who'd elected him to demand it.

That entire concept had been an unheard-of concession, even in Charis, until Howsmyn initiated it. Now it was actually spreading beyond his own enterprises, and the older man felt a glow of almost paternal pride as he gazed out at the growing sprawl of manufacturing capacity which was going to cement Ehdwyrd Howsmyn's claim to be the wealthiest man in Charis in the very near future.

"What's your cannon production up to now?" he asked after a moment.

"Not where we need it to be—yet," Howsmyn replied. "That is what you were asking, isn't it?"

"More or less," Mychail admitted.

"Actually, between the operation here and my other foundries, we're producing just over two hundred pieces a month," Howsmyn said. Mychail's eyebrows rose, and he pursed his lips in a silent whistle, but the younger man shook his head. "That's *all* of them, Mychail—long guns, carronades, field pieces, wolves, the lot. At the moment, we're better than half of the Kingdom's total production, too. And to be honest, we can't increase production of bronze guns much beyond where we are right now. There's simply not enough copper and tin available. Of course, the mines' production is going up rapidly now that the new gunpowder is available for blasting, as well as artillery, but we're still going to bottleneck on the lack of metal at any moment."

"What about the iron guns?" Mychail asked.

"That's a considerably brighter picture, actually." Howsmyn smiled. "Those iron deposits Earl High Rock wanted developed are starting to come in very handy, although I hadn't really anticipated operating them myself. I'd planned on leasing the rights, but it's turned out to be a lot simpler to just hire experienced mining operators and put them to work for me." He shook his head. "We won't really hit our stride with them until the canals are completed, of course, but when they're opened, production is really going to climb. Of course, I couldn't have done any of this without the new artillery contracts from the Crown."

"Of course," Mychail agreed. After all, he'd experienced exactly the same thing. His ropewalks had increased production by almost three hundred percent, and his textile manufactories were growing even more rapidly.

The new cotton gins made raw fiber available in enormous quantities, and the productivity of the powered looms and spinning machines Merlin Athrawes' "suggestions" had made possible was mind-boggling to someone who'd grown up with traditional methods. The new methods were also considerably more dangerous for workers, though. He was doing everything he could think of to limit those dangers, but the sheer number and extent of the drive shafts and belts required to transmit power from waterwheels to the new machinery had to be seen to be believed. Every foot of the power train was a broken or amputated limb just waiting to happen, and the powered looms themselves could inflict permanently crippling damage on someone who got careless even for a moment.

Well, Ehdwyrd and his people have been dealing with that for years now. The rest of us are just going to have to learn to cope, as well, he thought.

Even though he knew the argument was true, it didn't make him feel much better about the men and women who'd already been injured working with the new equipment. At least he and Howsmyn both had long-standing pension programs to support workers who were injured in their employ. And, unlike some of their fellows, they hadn't even considered using *children* in the new manufactories.

Which means we're not going to get hurt as badly as some of the others when the Crown's new laws against child labor go into effect next year, he thought, with a certain undeniable satisfaction. He and Howsmyn had fought hard to get them applied immediately, and he knew Cayleb had wanted to do just that, but his council had talked him into allowing for the adjustment period.

And whatever drawbacks the new technology might have, its advantages were almost unbelievable. Mychail was producing textiles at less than a quarter of his pre-Merlin costs, and even with all of his investment in new machinery, *that* was going to have a pronounced effect on his bottom line. In fact, he and his trading factors were already hearing screams of outraged fury from his mainland competitors as he and the rest of the Charisian textile industry began flooding "their" markets with quality goods whose prices they simply couldn't come close to matching, despite the Charisians' shipping costs.

Of course, we're not exporting very much canvas *just now, are we?* he reminded himself sardonically. The Royal Charisian Navy was buying every scrap of sailcloth he could produce, and as more and more of the powered looms came into operation, the superiority of the canvas he was able to offer became more and more pronounced. With its tighter weave, the new, machined canvas made for much more efficient and longer lasting sails. Coupled with the anti-fouling copper sheathing, most of which was still coming from Howsmyn, it made the Navy's ships' speed advantage even more pronounced.

The demand far outstripped his ability to supply it, even now. And the Navy had first call on the new canvas, which meant most of the kingdom's merchant shipping still had to "make do" with the older, looser weave. On the other hand, his capacity was increasing almost as rapidly as Howsmyn's, so it wouldn't be long before he was able to branch out into supplying the civilian market, as well. He looked forward to that.

"How are you coming with the production problems on the iron guns?" he asked Howsmyn.

"Actually, we haven't had anywhere near as many of those as I'd been afraid we might." Howsmyn shrugged. "Not on the cast-iron ones, that is. I'm not saying it's as easy with the iron as with the bronze, but our bell-founding techniques have converted remarkably well. I'm starting to experiment with wrought iron, too, but that's incredibly expensive at the moment. It uses an enormous amount more coke, and the furnace time for the repeated firings drives up the cost even more. And then we have to hammer the slag out of the blooms, and even with the new, heavier drop hammers, *that* takes an incredible amount of time, which drives costs up still higher. If I can find a way to do all *that* more efficiently . . ."

His voice broke off as he frowned thoughtfully into a vista only he could see. Then he shook himself.

"I think we may be able to bring the wrought iron costs down, eventually. At least to something not more than twice the cost of bronze, let's say, though that may be a *little* overly optimistic. In the meantime, though, the cast iron's going to be a lot *cheaper* than bronze, and I think we just about have the problems in producing guns out of it licked."

"I'll take your word for that," Mychail said. "Iron-making isn't my area, after all."

"I know." Howsmyn turned to look back out the window, frowning thoughtfully. "You know, one of the things Merlin's in the process of doing is changing the way all of us think about things like this," he said slowly.

"Meaning what?" Mychail's tone was one of agreement, but he still looked sideways at the younger man and arched an eyebrow.

"I was talking about it with Rahzhyr Mahklyn over at the Royal College," Howsmyn replied. "I've always been on the lookout for ways I could be a little more productive, a little more efficient. But it's all been . . . I don't know. Not even trial and error, but just a case of seeing obvious possibilities within the existing, allowed techniques, I suppose. Now I'm finding myself actively thinking about *why* one thing works better than another. What is it about a given technique that makes it superior to another? For example, I know that puddling cast iron produces wrought iron by gathering the impurities into the slag, but *why* does heating the iron in a hollow hearth while you stir it have that effect? And how do you take the next step into producing *steel* in larger, more useful ingots?"

"And do you have answers for your questions?" Mychail asked softly.

"Not yet—certainly not for *all* of them, at least! But sometimes I find the implications of just thinking such questions a little bit frightening. There's so much we do today just because it's permitted under the Proscriptions. Which is almost just another way of saying 'because that's the way we've always done it.' Like using bronze, instead of iron, for artillery. Sure, bronze has advantages of its own, but there's never been any reason we couldn't have used iron if we'd really wanted to. We just *didn't*."

"You said you've discussed this with Rahzhyr. Have you happened to mention your thoughts to someone else? Like Archbishop Maikel?"

"Not directly, no." Howsmyn turned back from the window to face his old friend and mentor. "I don't really think it's necessary, do you? The Archbishop is a very perceptive man, Rhaiyan."

"That's true." Mychail nodded. "On the other hand, the things you're talking about, the questions you're asking yourself. . . . You do realize how someone like Clyntahn would react to what you've just said?"

"Of course. And I'm not going to go around saying it to just anyone, either. There's a reason it's taken me this long to mention my thoughts even to *you*, you know! But despite everything the Archbishop's said, he's clearly aware that before it's over, this schism between us and the Temple is going to end up being about far more than simply the corruption of the Council of Vicars. You do realize that, don't you?"

"Ehdwyrd, *I* realized that the first day we sat down with *Seijin* Merlin and he started sharing his thoughts with us."

"And does it bother you?" Howsmyn asked softly.

"Sometimes," Mychail admitted. He glanced back out the window at the smoke, heat, and furious activity, then looked back at Howsmyn.

"Sometimes," he repeated. "I'm twice your age, after all. That means I'm a lot closer to giving account to God and the Archangels than you are. But God didn't give us minds just so we could refuse to use them. Mahklyn and the College are right about that, and Archbishop Maikel is right that we have to make choices. *We* have to recognize what it is God expects of us. That's the reason He gave us free will—the Inquisition itself says that. And if I've made the wrong choices, it's only been after trying as hard as I possibly could to make the *right* ones. I'm just going to have to hope God understands that."

"This whole war is going to go places Clyntahn and his cronies never even imagined," Howsmyn said. "In fact, it's going to go places *I* can't even imagine, and at least I'm trying to."

"Of course it is. In fact, I think there are probably only two people—possibly three—in the entire Kingdom who do truly understand where we're all bound," Mychail said.

"Oh?" Howsmyn smiled crookedly. "Let me guess—the Archbishop, the King, and the mysterious *Seijin* Merlin?"

"Of course." Mychail returned his smile.

"It *has* occurred to you, I suppose, that when the day finally comes that Clyntahn discovers everything Merlin's taught us, he's going to denounce the *seijin* as a demon?"

"Of course he is. On the other hand, I have a far livelier respect for the judgment—and, even more, for the integrity—of Archbishop Maikel, and he's actually *met* Merlin. For that matter, when was the last time you knew King Haarahld to be mistaken in his judgment of someone's character?" Mychail shook his head. "I'll trust the judgments of those two men—and of King Cayleb, for that matter—over the judgment of that pig in Zion, Ehdwyrd. If I'm wrong, at least I'll find myself in better company in Hell than I would in Heaven!"

Howsmyn's eyes widened ever so slightly at Mychail's blunt-toned forthrightness. Then he snorted.

"Do me a favor, Rhaiyan, and don't say anything like that to anyone else, all right?"

"I'm older than you are, Ehdwyrd; I'm not *senile* yet."

"What a relief!"

"I'm sure." Mychail chuckled dryly, then used his chin to point back out the window. "But to return to my earlier question, the iron guns are going to work out, you think?"

"Oh, I never really had any doubt about that. They're going to be heavier than bronze for a given weight of shot, of course, but they're also going to be a lot cheaper. Not to mention the fact that they're not going to be competing for the limited supply of copper."

"So things are going pretty well, overall?"

"Aside from the fact that we really need to be producing the guns at least twice as fast, you mean?" Howsmyn responded with a snort.

"Aside from that, of course," Mychail acknowledged, smiling crookedly.

"I wouldn't say they're going 'well,' " Howsmyn said more soberly. "Not given what we're up against. But I'd have to say they're going better than I ever anticipated they might. The biggest problem from the perspective of the new artillery, actually, is the competition for the rifles. Not only do they both use up enormous quantities of iron and steel, but they require a lot of the same skilled labor. We're training new people as quickly as we can, but it's still a problem."

"And so is keeping someone from hiring them away from you as soon as they're trained, right?"

"I see you've had some of the same sort of krakens circling around your operations." Howsmyn chuckled.

"Well, of course. After all, it's so much cheaper to let someone *else* train them, then hire them away!"

"I don't think that proposition's worked out quite as well as some of the competition hoped it might." There was an undeniable note of satisfaction, almost smugness, in Howsmyn's voice, and Mychail laughed out loud.

"It never ceases to amaze me just how stupid some of our oh-so-esteemed colleagues are," the textile magnate said. "Or, at least, how stupid they think *mechanics* are! Do they think someone capable of becoming a skilled artisan gets that way without having a *brain* that works? Our people know they're better off working for us than for almost anyone else. Not to mention the fact that every working man and woman in Charis knows we've *always* treated our people as well as we could. It's not exactly something we woke up yesterday and decided to try for a change . . . unlike certain other employers. That idiot Erayksyn actually tried to hire two of my foremen away from the Weaving Street manufactory last five-day."

Howsmyn snorted with harsh contempt. Wyllym Erayksyn might as well have been a Harchong nobleman, for all the concern he'd ever evinced for his labor force. In fact, Howsmyn was more than half prepared to bet most Harchongese worried more over their serfs than Erayksyn and his sort did about their theoretically free workers.

"I'll bet *that* was a resounding success," he observed.

"Not so that anyone would notice." Mychail smiled thinly. Then the smile turned into a slight frown. "I wish there weren't so many others who shared Erayksyn's attitude, though. Especially with the way all the new possibilities for making money are going to play into their basic greediness. Oh," he waved one hand when Howsmyn opened his mouth, "I know he's probably the worst of the lot. But you can't deny there are a lot of others who feel basically the same way. The people who work for them are just one more expense, not fellow humans, and they're going to do their damnedest to drive *that* cost down along with all the others."

"They may think that way now," Howsmyn replied, "but I don't think that attitude's going to get them what they expect it to. I may have trouble getting my hands on all the skilled workers I need—and so may you—but that's because there simply aren't enough of them. We've never had trouble convincing people to work for us, and Erayksyn isn't the only one who's found out that hiring them *away* from us is a lot harder than they expected it to be. Think about that sanctimonious bastard Kairee! And the handful they have managed to hire away weren't exactly our best people, either. Given the pressure all these new innovations are going to put on the supply of trained workers, the cost of labor's not going to do anything but climb, however much they may want to drive it back down again. Given the greater output per worker, the *relative* cost is going to decline, of course, but people like Erayksyn and Kairee are going to find that the labor force they've abused for so long is going to be going to be working for people like you and me, not them."

"I hope you're right, and not just because of our bottom lines," Mychail said.

"You're the one who taught me to take the long view—yes, and the one who taught me to never forget that just because a man may be poorer than I am, he's no less a man, with no less a right to his dignity." Howsmyn's expression was unusually sober as he met Mychail's eyes. "That's a lesson I hope I never forget, Mychail. Because if I do, I don't think I'll like the man I've turned into as well as I like the one I am right now."

Mychail started to speak, then gave his head a little shake and squeezed Howsmyn's shoulder, instead. The textile manufacturer had lost both of his sons almost twenty years before when the galleon upon which they had been embarked disappeared at sea with all hands. In many ways, Howsmyn had stepped into the aching void their deaths had left in Rhaiyan Mychail's life. He'd become virtually a surrogate father to Mychail's younger grandchildren, his wife had become an adoptive aunt, and three of those grandsons were currently Howsmyn employees, learning the ironmaster's trade. Right off the top of his head, Mychail couldn't think of a single person who would have been a better mentor for them.

"Well, this is all very edifying, of course," he said then, with a deliberate lightness. "But my official reason for coming to visit you is that we need to discuss exactly how we want to handle the management breakdown for that new shipyard in Tellesberg."

"You've already managed to put together the partnership?" Howsmyn's eyebrows rose in surprise, and Mychail nodded.

"Ironhill's announcement that the Crown would underwrite forty percent of the initial investment did the trick," he said.

"And in return for that forty percent, exactly what does Cayleb get?" Despite his own undoubted patriotism, Howsmyn sounded more than a bit skeptical.

"Obviously, the Navy gets first call on the building slips," Mychail replied calmly. "And I'm sure we'll find ourselves under pressure to give Ironhill 'family discount' prices. On the other hand, the agreement specifically calls for us to buy back the Crown's interest. So in three or four years—five, at the outside, I'd estimate—we'll have complete ownership, free and clear."

"Well, that's better than I'd been afraid of." Howsmyn rubbed his chin thoughtfully, then nodded. "It sounds fair enough to me. Mind you, I'll want to look at the proposed agreements in writing!"

"I expected no less." Mychail smiled. "Which is why I just happened to have brought a draft of the agreement with me."

" 'Just happened,' is it?"

"You know I've always been in favor of killing as many wyverns as possible with a single rock," Mychail replied. "And, speaking of single rocks, one of the *unofficial* reasons for my visit is to remind you that it's Styvyn's birthday next five-day and that Alyx and Myldryd expect you for dinner."

"What? *Next* five-day?" Howsmyn blinked. "Surely not! Didn't he just *have* a birthday?"

"The fact that you can ask that question is an indication you're no longer as young as you think you are," Mychail said. "Yes, next five-day. In fact, he'll be eleven."

"Well, why didn't you tell me that first? That's vastly more important than any picayune worries about manufacturing artillery! Just how many godsons do you think I have? And it's not exactly as if *you* have an unlimited supply of great-grandchildren, either, now is it?"

"No." Mychail shook his head with a small smile. "So, should I tell Myldryd you'll be there?"

.IV.
Galleon *Southwind*,
Margaret Bay;
Gray Ship Tavern,
Hanth Town, Earldom of Hanth

I still say we should make for Eraystor," Tahdayo Mahntayl grumbled as the galleon *Southwind* left Hanth Town's smoke-smutted skies astern.

It required a great deal of self-discipline for Sir Styv Walkyr to manage not to roll his eyes heavenward or utter any heartfelt prayers for strength. The fact that he'd at least gotten Mahntayl to finally agree it was time to go *some-where* rather than kicking his heels in Hanth Town while he waited for Cayleb to get around to removing his head helped.

Some, at least.

"First," he said patiently, "the Captain isn't too keen on trying to run the blockade into any of the Emeraldian ports. Second, it's not going to be so very much longer before Cayleb and Lock Island get around to invading *Emerald*, too. Do you really want to be there when he does that?"

"I'm not so sure his precious invasion of Emerald is going to go all that smoothly," Mahntayl replied almost petulantly. "Nahrmahn's army is a lot more loyal than those traitorous bastards *I* had."

"I don't really care how loyal his troops are, not in the long run," Walkyr told him. "He doesn't have enough of them, Cayleb's troops are even more loyal to him, and I strongly suspect that the Charisian Marines are going to have a few surprises of their own for Nahrmahn. Somehow it just strikes me as unlikely that Haarahld's navy got *all* the new toys."

Mahntayl snorted angrily, but at least he didn't disagree, and Walkyr shrugged.

"It's like I've been saying all along, Tahdayo. There are very few people whose heads Cayleb wants more than he wants yours. Wherever you go, it needs to be someplace he's not likely to come calling anytime soon. That doesn't exactly describe Emerald, and I don't think it's going to describe Corisande very much longer, either. So that only leaves someplace on the mainland. And if we have to go to the mainland anyway, Zion is the only logical destination."

"I know, I know! You've certainly explained your reasoning to me often enough."

Mahntayl's jaw clenched as he glanced back once again at the city he'd once thought would be his for the rest of his life. Which was the real root of the problem, Walkyr reflected. Not only was Mahntayl furious over having his prize snatched from his hands, but he'd been so confident of the future that he'd made no provision for what might happen if Charis actually won against the alliance the Group of Four had hammered together.

And I have no intention of telling him about the provision I most certainly did make, he told himself once more.

"Well, it's hard for me to think of anyone the Chancellor and the Grand Inquisitor are going to be happier to see than you," he said instead. "The proof that not all of Cayleb's nobles support his blasphemy is going to be welcome, and I'm sure they'll be willing to support your efforts to liberate Hanth as soon as possible."

Mahntayl snorted again, but his expression also lightened. Despite his truculent mood, he wasn't immune to the reflection that the Temple's purse was more than deep enough to support him in the style to which he had become accustomed. Assuming, of course, that he could become a sufficiently valuable figurehead for them.

"Well," he said at last, turning his back upon the shrinking vista of his onetime capital with a certain finality, "I certainly can't argue with any of that. And the truth is," he continued with the air of a man making a clean breast of it, "that I should have listened to you a lot sooner than I did."

You've got that much right, at least, Walkyr thought sourly.

"It's not easy to convince yourself to cut your losses," he said out loud. "I know that, and it's especially true when someone's worked as long and hard as you did for Hanth. But what you've got to focus on now is coming back again someday. And you might want to think about this, too. I'm certain you'll be the first Charisian noble to reach Zion, the first native son to put your sword at Mother Church's service. When the time finally comes to replace all those traitorous, heretical nobles who've chosen to cast their lots with Cayleb and Staynair, you may well find yourself the most senior of all the available candidates. If that's the case, Hanth isn't all you'll receive as compensation for your losses and a richly deserved reward for your loyalty."

Mahntayl nodded again, soberly, with an expression of truly noble determination.

"You're right, Styv. You're right." He reached out and clasped the other man's shoulder. He stood that way for several seconds, then exhaled a long breath.

"You're right," he repeated, "and I won't forget it, if the time ever does come that I'm in a position to reward you properly, I promise. But in the meantime, I think I'm going below. Somehow"—he smiled humorlessly—"I'm not enjoying the scenery very much at the moment."

▼   ▼   ▼

"God*damn* that gutless bastard!" Mylz Halcom snarled as he watched *Southwind*'s topsails shrinking out on the dark blue waters of the bay.

He stood at an upper window of The Gray Ship, a none too prosperous tavern on the outskirts of Hanth Town. Its location and general air of dilapidation didn't do much to attract trade, but at least it was out of the way of most of the shooting he could still hear as the last of Tahdayo Mahntayl's mercenaries tried to get out of town. That was about the best he could say for it . . . and he couldn't say a lot more for his own state at the moment, if he was going to be honest. Very few people would have recognized the powerful Bishop Mylz if they'd seen him. His luxuriant, carefully trimmed beard had disappeared, the dramatic silver at his temples had been darkened by dye, and his exquisitely tailored cassock had been exchanged for the far simpler clothing of an only moderately successful farmer, or perhaps a minor merchant.

"Surely we've known for five-days that this was coming, My Lord," the much younger man standing with him observed. Father Ahlvyn Shumay looked even less like the Bishop of Margaret Bay's personal aide than Halcom looked like the bishop in question. "It's been obvious from the beginning that Mahntayl's only true loyalty is to himself."

"And that's supposed to make me feel *better*?" Halcom growled. He swung away from the window, turning his back on the fleeing galleon, and faced Shumay squarely.

"Not 'better,' My Lord." Shumay actually managed a smile. "But the *Writ* does remind us that it's best to face the truth head-on rather than deluding ourselves with wishful thinking, even on God's behalf."

Halcom glared at him for a moment, but then the peppery little bishop's shoulders relaxed at least marginally, and he produced a grimace that held at least a hint of an answering smile.

"Yes, it does say that," he acknowledged. "And I suppose I need to keep reminding myself that stripping away delusion is one of your best functions, even if it does make you an intolerable young whippersnapper on occasion."

"I try, My Lord. To serve a useful function, that is—not to be intolerable."

"I know you do, Ahlvyn." Halcom patted him lightly on the shoulder, then inhaled deeply, with the air of a man deliberately turning his thoughts away from anger and into some more productive endeavor.

"At least the way Mahntayl's finally cut and run simplifies our own options just a bit," he said. "Note that I didn't say it *improves* them; only that it *simplifies* them."

"Forgive me, My Lord, but I'm afraid I don't see how anything is particularly 'simple' these days."

"Simpl*er* isn't the same thing as *simple*." Halcom showed his teeth in a brief flash of a grin. "On the other hand, there's not much question that if Mahntayl isn't going to stand and fight, we can't either. Not here, not now."

Shumay's eyes widened ever so slightly. Halcom's insistence that they could somehow build a fortress for the true Church here in his diocese had been as unyielding as stone. The fiery sermons he'd preached in Hanth Cathedral had focused on both their responsibility and their ability to do just that.

"Oh, don't look so surprised," Halcom half scolded. "There was never really much hope of holding off Cayleb and that damned traitor Staynair. If I'd ever once admitted that, though, Mahntayl would have disappeared even sooner. And if there wasn't much hope of it, there was still at least a *chance* . . . as long as Mahntayl didn't run. But as you yourself just pointed out, there's no point deluding ourselves when reality hits us across the face. None of the other nobles in the diocese have the backbone to stand up to Cayleb, either—assuming any of them even wanted to in the first place. And, to be honest,

most of them don't want to. For that matter, at least two-thirds of them probably *agree* with him, the traitorous bastards. At the very least, they're going to
take the easy way out and give him whatever he wants. Probably they figure
that if—when—Mother Church crushes him in the end, they'll be able to
claim they only gave in to force majeure, despite their deep and heartfelt opposition to his apostasy. Mahntayl was the only one of them who couldn't
reach an accommodation with Cayleb, even if he'd wanted to . . . assuming
someone could somehow give him a sufficient infusion of guts to get him to
stand and fight. That's the real reason you and I have been anchored here in
Hanth ever since Darcos Sound."

"I . . . see, My Lord," Shumay said slowly, as he found his brain reorder-
ing the events of the past few months, and what his bishop had had to say
about them at the time, in light of Halcom's admission.

"Don't misunderstand me, Ahlvyn." Halcom's face had hardened once
again, this time with harsh determination. "There's no question in my mind,
nor doubt in my heart, about what it is God, Langhorne, and Mother Church
expect of us. The only *questions* are how we go about accomplishing our tasks.
Obviously, Mahntayl's . . . departure strongly suggests that building any center of open resistance to this accursed 'Church of Charis' here around Margaret Bay isn't the way to do it. So the problem becomes what we do next."

"And may I assume you have an answer to that in mind, My Lord?"

"I had been thinking in terms of fleeing to Emerald," Halcom admitted.
"Bishop Executor Wyllys could probably be counted upon to give us sanctuary, and I'm sure we could make ourselves useful to him in Emerald. But in
the last few days, I've come to the conclusion that Emerald isn't our best destination, either."

"May I ask why, My Lord?"

"For two reasons, really. First, I'm none too certain the Bishop Executor
is going to be in a position to offer *anyone* sanctuary for much longer." Halcom grimaced. "That pusillanimous worm Walkyr's been right about at least
one thing all along, and that's the fact that Nahrmahn isn't going to be able to
hold Cayleb off for long. Worse, I'm very much afraid Nahrmahn's been
making plans of his own where Mother Church is concerned."

"Surely not, My Lord!"

"And why shouldn't he have been?" Halcom snorted. "Certainly not because you think he has some deep-seated moral fiber which is going to prevent
him from seeing the same opportunities Cayleb's obviously seen! I've always
suspected Nahrmahn was a lot brighter than he's chosen to encourage his enemies to believe he is. That isn't necessarily the same thing as principled, unfortunately, and a smart man without principles is dangerous. *Very* dangerous.

"If Nahrmahn hopes to reach any sort of accommodation with Cayleb,
however unlikely that might seem, he must realize Cayleb and Staynair are

going to require him to join their open defiance of Mother Church. And if he's aware of that much, then he has to have made plans to . . . neutralize anything Bishop Executor Wyllys might try to do to stop him. And, to be perfectly honest, the fact that the Bishop Executor's most recent letters to me have all insisted nothing of the sort is happening only makes me even more anxious. With all due respect to the Bishop Executor, all his confidence suggests to me is that Nahrmahn's succeeded in keeping his own preparations completely out of sight. Which means they're likely to succeed, at least in the short term."

Shumay regarded his superior with horror, and Halcom reached out and laid a comforting hand on his shoulder.

"Don't make the mistake of thinking Cayleb and Staynair are alone in their madness, Ahlvyn," he said gently. "Look at how quickly, and with how little resistance, the entire Kingdom's followed their blasphemous example. I'm not saying the rot's spread as widely and as deeply in Emerald as it obviously has here in Charis, but the Charis Sea and Emerald Reach aren't broad enough to prevent the poison from reaching Emerald at all. And Nahrmahn's an even greater slave to worldly ambition than Cayleb. He's not going to be blind to the opportunity to make himself master of the Church in Emerald, whatever else happens. When you add that to all of the pressure he's going to be under from Cayleb and Charis, how can you expect anything *but* for him to strike at the legitimate authority of Mother Church whenever the moment seems most propitious to him?"

"But if that's the case, My Lord," Shumay said, "then what hope do we have?"

"We have something much better than mere hope, Ahlvyn. We have God Himself on our side. Or, rather, we're on His side. Whatever may happen in the short term, the final victory will be His. Any other outcome is impossible, so long as there are men who recognize their responsibility to Him and to His Church."

Shumay looked at Halcom for several seconds. Then he nodded—slowly at first, and then harder, with more assurance.

"You're right, of course, My Lord. Which brings us back to the question of exactly what we *do* do, since a retreat to Emerald seems much less attractive than it did before your explanation. Should we follow Mahntayl to Zion?"

"No." Halcom shook his head. "I've given this a great deal of thought. In fact, that brings me to my second reason for deciding Emerald isn't our best destination. Where we need to be, Ahlvyn, is where God can make the best use of us, and that's right here in Charis. There are others who'll need us in the Kingdom, even—or perhaps especially—in Tellesberg itself. The ones Cayleb's and Staynair's creatures have labeled 'Temple Loyalists.' Those are the people we need to find. They're going to need all the encouragement they can get, and all the leadership they can find. More than that, they remain the true children of God in Charis, and as the good sheep they need—and deserve—shepherds worthy of their loyalty and faith."

Shumay was nodding again, and Halcom raised one hand in a gesture of warning.

"Make no mistake, Ahlvyn. This is another battle in the terrible war between Langhorne and Shan-wei. None of us truly expected it to erupt once again so openly, certainly not in our own lifetimes, but it would be a failure of our faith to refuse to recognize it now that it's come upon us. And just as there were martyrs, even among the Archangels themselves, in the first war with Shan-wei, there will be martyrs in this one. When we venture into Tellesberg instead of sailing to Zion, we'll be stepping into the very jaws of the dragon, and it's entirely possible those jaws will close upon us."

"I understand, My Lord." Shumay met the bishop's gaze levelly. "And I'm no more eager to die, even for God, than the next man. If that's what God's plan and Mother Church require of us, though, what better end could any man achieve?"

.V.
Madame Ahnzhelyk's,
City of Zion,
The Temple Lands

Subtle perfume drifted on the air circulating through the sumptuously decorated and appointed apartment. The overhead fan, powered by a servant in the basement who patiently and endlessly turned the crank at the far end of the pulleys and shafts, rotated almost soundlessly. The street outside was a broad avenue—well paved, spotlessly swept and washed each day, fronted by expensive homes, and scrupulously maintained. Birds and softly whistling wyverns perched in the ornamental pear trees in the wide islands of green marching down the center of that street, or fluttered around the feeders set out by the inhabitants of those expensive residences.

Most of those residences were the Zion townhouses of minor branches of the great Church dynasties. Although it was definitely one of the fashionable neighborhoods, it was far enough from the Temple to be a merely "respectable" address, and more than a few of the townhouses had passed into other hands, either because the original owners' fortunes had improved enough for them to move up to more stylish quarters elsewhere, or because their fortunes had declined enough to force them to sell.

Which was how this particular residence had passed many years ago into the possession of Madame Ahnzhelyk Phonda.

There were those sticklers in the neighborhood who found Madame Ahnzhelyk's presence objectionable, but they were few, and as a rule they kept their opinions to themselves, for Madame Ahnzhelyk had friends. *Powerful* friends, many of whom remained . . . clients, even today.

Still, she understood the virtue of discretion, as well, and her establishment offered that same discretion to her clientele, along with the services of her exquisitely beautiful and well-trained young ladies. Even those who deplored her presence among them understood that establishments like hers were a necessary and inevitable part of the city of Zion, and unlike certain shabbier establishments, at least Madame Ahnzhelyk allowed no gaming or drunken brawls. *Her* clientele, after all, came only from the upper echelons of the Church's hierarchy.

She was, almost certainly, one of the wealthiest women in the entire city. Indeed, she might be *the* wealthiest woman in terms of her own personal worth, rather than her position in one of the great Church families. There were persistent rumors that before she'd chosen her vocation and changed her name, she could have claimed membership in one of those families, although no one really believed it. Or was prepared to admit it, if they did.

At forty-five, her own working days were behind her, although she retained the slender figure and much of the ravishing beauty which had made her so successful before she moved up into the managerial ranks. On the other hand, her phenomenal success had not depended solely upon physical beauty or bedroom athleticism, although she'd possessed both of those qualities in abundance. More importantly, though, Ahnzhelyk Phonda also possessed a sharp, insightful intelligence married to a trenchant sense of humor, a keen sense of observation, a genuine sense of compassion, and the ability to hold her own in any discussion, no matter the subject, with wit and charm.

Many a lonely bishop, archbishop, or even vicar had availed himself of her exquisite companionship over the years. Had she been the sort of woman who was inclined to dabble in politics, the many and varied Church secrets which had been confided to her over those same years would have made devastating weapons. That, however, was a dangerous game, and one Madame Ahnzhelyk had been far too wise to play.

Besides, she thought broodingly, gazing out at the quiet neighborhood beyond her window, she'd had a better use for most of those secrets.

"You sent for me, Madame?"

She turned from the window in a graceful flutter of filmy skirts and whispering silk on satin skin. Despite her age, she continued to exude an aura of sensuality, a mature sense of her own passionate nature no youngster could have matched. She appeared incapable of moving gracelessly even if she'd wanted to, and a flicker of what might have been envy showed in the eyes of the plainly dressed servant woman in the doorway.

"Yes, Ailysa," Madame Ahnzhelyk said. "Please, come in."

Ahnzhelyk's courtesy, even with her servants, was natural and instinctive, but there was never any question who was the mistress and who the servant. Ailysa obeyed the polite command, carrying her sewing bag, and closed the door behind her.

"I have several minor repairs, I'm afraid," Ahnzhelyk said, raising her voice very slightly as the door closed.

"Of course, Madame."

The door latched, and Madame Ahnzhelyk's expression changed. The calm, elegant air of superiority vanished, and her expressive eyes seemed to deepen and darken as she held out her hands. Ailysa looked at her for a moment, and then her own mouth tightened.

"Yes," Ahnzhelyk said softly, taking the other woman's hands in her own and squeezing them tightly. "It's been confirmed. The day after tomorrow, one hour after dawn."

Ailysa inhaled deeply, and her hands squeezed Ahnzhelyk's in reply.

"We knew it had to come," she said quietly, and her voice had changed. The lower-class servant's accent had disappeared into the clear, almost liquid diction of one of the Temple Lands' most exclusive finishing schools, and some indefinable change in body posture mirrored the change.

"I still hoped," Ahnzhelyk replied, her eyes glistening. "Surely, *someone* could have sought clemency for him!"

"Who?" Ailysa's eyes were harder and drier than Ahnzhelyk's, but there was more anger in them, as well. "The Circle couldn't. Whatever I may have wanted, I always knew that, and why. And if *they* couldn't, then who else would have dared to? His own family—even his own brother!—either voted to confirm the sentence or abstained 'out of the lingering bonds of affection' between them." She looked as if she wanted to spit on the chamber's gleaming wooden floor. "Cowards. Cowards every one of them!"

Ahnzhelyk gripped her hands more tightly for a moment, then released them to put one arm around her.

"It was the Grand Inquisitor," she said. "None of them dared to defy him, especially after what the Charisians did to the invasion fleet . . . and after Cayleb named Staynair as his successor and Staynair sent that dreadful letter to the Grand Vicar. The entire Council is terrified, whether they want to admit it or not, and Clyntahn's determined to feed them the blood they want."

"Don't make excuses for them, Ahnzhelyk," Ailysa said softly. "Don't even make excuses for *him*."

"He was never a *bad* man," Ahnzhelyk said.

"No, not a bad man, only a corrupt one." Ailysa drew another deep breath, and her lower lip trembled for just a moment. Then she shook herself almost sternly. "They're *all* corrupt, and that's why not one of them would stand in his defense. The *Writ* says all men reap as they have sown, and he never sowed anything strong enough to stand in the face of this storm."

"No," Ahnzhelyk agreed sadly, then squared her shoulders and walked across to the window seat and stretched out along it, leaning back against the upholstered arm at one end where she could look out on the soothing tranquillity of the street once again.

Ailysa followed her, and smiled slightly as she saw the three gowns hung ready for mending. Unless she very much missed her guess, Ahnzhelyk had deliberately torn at least two of them, but that was typical of her. When she summoned a seamstress to repair damaged clothing, the clothing in question *was* damaged . . . however it had happened to get that way.

Ailysa opened her bag and started removing needles, thread, scissors, and thimbles . . . all of which, except the thread, she reflected wryly, had been made in Charis. One of the things which had inspired Ahnzhelyk to suggest her current role was the fact that she actually was an extraordinarily skilled seamstress. Of course, that was because it had been a wealthy woman's hobby, not because it had been a servant's livelihood.

Ailysa sat in a far humbler but still comfortable chair and began working on the first of the gowns while Ahnzhelyk continued gazing pensively out the window. Several minutes passed in silence before Ahnzhelyk stirred and turned her head, propping her chin on a raised palm as she regarded Ailysa.

"Are you going to tell the boys?" she asked quietly, and Ailysa's needle paused for just a moment. She looked down at it, biting her lip, then shook her head.

"No. No, not yet." Her nostrils flared, and she began once again setting neat, perfect stitches. "They'll have to know eventually, of course. And Tymythy already suspects what's happening, I think. But I won't risk telling them until I've got them someplace safe. Or at least"—she smiled with bitter, barren humor—"someplace *safer*."

"I could get you aboard ship tomorrow." Ahnzhelyk's statement sounded tentative, but Ailysa shook her head again.

"No." Her voice was harsher. "It wasn't much of a marriage in all too many ways, but he is my husband. And at the end of his life, I think perhaps he's finally found at least a trace of the man I always knew was hidden somewhere down inside him." She looked up at Ahnzhelyk, her eyes brimming with tears at last. "I won't abandon that man if he's finally found him."

"It's going to be horrible," Ahnzhelyk warned. "You know that."

"Yes, I do. And I want to *remember* it." Ailysa's face had hardened. "I want to be able to tell them how it was, what they did to him in 'God's name.' " The last two words dripped acid, and Ahnzhelyk nodded.

"If that's what you want," she said gently.

"I want to be able to tell them," Ailysa repeated.

Ahnzhelyk only gazed at her for several seconds, then smiled with an odd mixture of fondness, sorrow, and memory.

"It's such a pity he never knew," she said. Ailysa looked at her, as if perplexed by the apparent change of subject.

"Knew what?"

"Knew about us. Knew about how long we've known one another, what we kept hoping we'd see in him. It was so hard not to just take him by the front of his cassock and try to shake some sense into him!"

"We couldn't risk it. Well, *you* couldn't." Ailysa sighed. "Perhaps *I* could have. Perhaps I *should* have, but he was always too busy playing the game. He never heard me when I threw out a hint, never recognized a suggestion. They just went right past him, and I was afraid to be too explicit. And"—it was her turn to smile sadly—"I always thought there'd still be time. I never imagined he might come to *this*."

"Neither did I," Ahnzhelyk said, and leaned back in the window seat, folding her hands in her lap.

"I'll miss your letters," she said.

"Lyzbet will take my place," Ailysa said. "It will take her a few months to get all of the delivery arrangements settled fully into place, but she knows what to do."

"I wasn't talking about that." Ahnzhelyk smiled crookedly. "I was talking about *your* letters. Quite a few of the others really do hold my past against me, you know. Those who know of it at all. You never did."

"Of course I didn't." Ailysa laughed quietly, softly. "I've known you since you were less than a year old, 'Ahnzhelyk!' And your 'past' is what made you so effective."

"But it felt so strange, sometimes, discussing him with you," Ahnzhelyk said wistfully.

"Yes, it did. Sometimes." Ailysa bent back to her stitchery. "In many ways, you were more his wife than I ever was. You certainly saw more of him after the boys were born than I did."

"Did you resent that?" Ahnzhelyk's voice was quiet. "I never dared to actually ask you that, you know."

"I resented the fact that the power games he played here in Zion were more important to him than his family," Ailysa replied, never looking up from her work. "I resented the fact that he pursued his comfort in brothels. But that was his world, the one he was born to. It wasn't your fault or your doing, and I never resented *you*."

"I'm glad," Ahnzhelyk said softly. "I'm glad, Adorai."

Captain Sir Dunkyn Yairley stood on the quarterdeck of HMS *Destiny*, hands clasped behind him while he enjoyed Margaret Bay's brisk predawn air. The sky to the east, beyond the shadowy, still all but invisible bulk of Margaret's Land, was turning pale gold and salmon, and the thin banners of clouds were like high, blue smoke against the steadily paler heavens. The moon was still just visible, peeking over the edge of the western horizon, but the stars had all but vanished, and the breeze moved *Destiny* along at a steady five or six knots, with all sail set to the topgallants.

Yairley was proud of his command. The fifty-four-gun galleon was one of the most powerful warships in the world, and Yairley had been in command for less than five five-days. His previous command, the galley *Queen Zhessyka*, had distinguished herself at the Battle of Darcos Sound, and *Destiny* was his reward. He suspected that the ship would have gone to someone else, despite his performance in battle, if he hadn't also spent two and a half years in command of a merchant galleon. Regular navy officers with experience handling square-riggers, instead of galleys, weren't all that common, after all.

Serves Allayn right, he thought smugly. His older brother had thought that taking a three-year hiatus to accept a merchant berth would be the kiss of death for his naval career, but he'd been wrong. *I told him the merchant service experience would look good to the High Admiral, give me that "well-rounded" look he's always so happy to see. Of course, I have to admit that I didn't expect it to look good for the reasons it actually did. Who'd have thought that* galleons *would make* galleys *obsolete?*

His brother certainly hadn't expected it . . . which was why Allayn had gone back to school to learn to handle galleons while Dunkyn got *Destiny*. He tried not to gloat too hard whenever he ran into his beloved brother. Really he did!

Sir Dunkyn's lips twitched at the thought, and he sucked in an enormous lungful of air, marveling at how wonderful the world seemed this fine morning.

The ship's bell chimed, sounding the half hour, and Sir Dunkyn looked back up at the strengthening dawn. The land to port remained a blue mystery, bulking against the morning sky as the sun began to lift itself over the edge of the world, but it was beginning to become more visible. It wouldn't be long before Yairley could begin making out details, and he felt a twinge of something very like regret. Within the hour, his quiet quarterdeck would be invaded by others, and a few hours after that, *Destiny* would once again become captive to her anchor and the land.

And she'd stay that way for up to the next three five-days . . . or even longer, if it turned out Yairley's passenger required his ship's services or those of her Marines.

Don't be silly, he told himself sternly. *She isn't really* your *ship, you know. King Cayleb is kind enough to lend her to you, and even* pay *you to command her, but in return, he expects you to do the occasional odd job for him. Unreasonable of him, perhaps, but there it is.*

He smiled again, then turned to look at the midshipman of the watch, standing by the starboard ratlines to give his captain sole possession of the weather side of his quarterdeck.

"Master Aplyn-Ahrmahk!" he called.

"Yes, Sir?"

The midshipman came trotting across the deck planking, and Yairley suppressed an urge to shake his head in familiar bemusement. Young Hektor Aplyn was the youngest of *Destiny*'s midshipmen, yet all five of the others, including lads as much as six years his senior, deferred to him almost automatically. To his credit, he seemed totally unaware of their attitude. He wasn't, of course, which only made Yairley think better of him for acting as if he were. It couldn't be easy for a boy who had just turned twelve to resist the temptation to make seventeen- or eighteen-year-olds dance to his tune, yet that was precisely what Midshipman Aplyn had done.

Only, of course, it wasn't really "Midshipman Aplyn." These days, the youngster was properly styled "Master Midshipman His Grace the Duke of Darcos, Hektor Aplyn-*Ahrmahk*."

King Cayleb had exercised an ancient, purely Charisian tradition in Aplyn's case. So far as Yairley was aware, no other realm in all of Safehold followed the Charisian practice of adopting commoners into the royal house in recognition of outstanding service to the Crown and to the royal house. *Only* commoners could be so adopted (which was how the Earldom of Lock Island had been created generations ago, Yairley reflected), and they became members of the royal house in every sense. The sole restriction was that they and their children stood outside the succession. Aside from that, young Aplyn-Ahrmahk took precedence over every other Charisian noble except for the equally young Duke of Tirian, and any children he might someday produce would also be members of the royal house.

Personally, Yairley felt quite confident that the youngster was delighted to have been packed off to sea again as quickly as possible. In the Navy, the tradition was that a senior officer never used a junior officer's title if the junior officer in question was a peer of the realm whose title took precedence over that of the senior officer in question. Instead, his naval rank was used, and since young Aplyn-Ahrmahk's title took precedence over that of *every* senior officer in the King's Navy—including High Admiral Lock Island—he could slot quite handily back into the far more comfortable role of simple "Master Midshipman Aplyn-Ahrmahk," which had to be an enormous relief.

Of course, on purely social occasions, the rules were different. Which probably meant it was a good thing the crew of a King's ship didn't have a lot of opportunities to socialize ashore. And Yairley intended to see to it that the duke spent as many of those rare social occasions aboard ship as possible.

Let's spare the boy what we can, at least until he's, oh, fourteen, let's say. The least we can do is give him time to finish learning proper table manners before he has to sit down to dinner with other *dukes and princes!*

Which just happened to be one of the things in which Yairley was personally tutoring the youngster.

Aplyn-Ahrmahk finished crossing the deck and touched his left shoulder in formal salute. Yairley returned it gravely, then twitched his head at the steadily solidifying land to port.

"Go below, if you would, Master Aplyn-Ahrmahk. Present my compliments to the Earl and inform him that we will be entering harbor at Hanth Town as scheduled."

"Aye, aye, Sir!"

Aplyn-Ahrmahk saluted again and headed for the after hatch.

He didn't move like a twelve-year-old, Yairley reflected. Maybe that was part of the reason the older midshipmen found it so easy to accept him as their equal. Aplyn-Ahrmahk was a slightly built youngster, who was never going to be particularly tall or broad, but he seemed unaware of that. There was a confidence, a sense of knowing who he was, despite his quite evident ongoing discomfort with his exalted patent of nobility. Or perhaps it was simply that, unlike those other midshipmen, young Aplyn-Ahrmahk knew he would never again in his life have to face anything worse than what had already happened to him aboard HMS *Royal Charis*.

I suppose, Yairley thought more grimly, *that having your own king die in your arms tends to help you put the rest of the world into perspective.*

▼   ▼   ▼

The man who still thought of himself as Colonel Hauwerd Breygart, Royal Charisian Marines, not yet as the Earl of Hanth, stood at *Destiny*'s bulwark as Captain Yairley worked his vessel carefully through the crowded waters of the harbor. Normally, it wouldn't have been that much of a challenge, but so far as Breygart could tell, every square yard of the harbor's surface was covered by a sailing dinghy, launch, rowboat, skiff, or raft . . . and every one of those ramshackle vessels was packed with the cheering, shouting citizens of Hanth Town.

"They seem happy to see you, My Lord," Lieutenant Rhobair Mahkelyn, *Destiny*'s fourth lieutenant, remarked. As Yairley's most junior commissioned officer, Mahkelyn had been detailed as Breygart's aide aboard ship. He was a personable young man, in many ways, although Breygart couldn't quite rid himself of the suspicion that Mahkelyn was one of those people who kept track of the favors his superiors owed him.

"I'd like to believe it was a spontaneous demonstration of their deep-seated affection for me and my family," the newly recognized earl replied dryly, raising his voice to make it heard through the torrent of voices. "On the other hand, I've had enough reports of Mahntayl's tenure to know what it really is. And, frankly, I suspect they'd be cheering just as lustily for *anyone* who was going to replace that bastard's sorry arse here in Hanth Town."

"There's probably some truth to that, My Lord," Mahkelyn acknowledged after a moment.

"There's Shan-wei's own amount of truth to it," Breygart—who supposed he really ought to start thinking of himself as Earl Hanth—said bluntly. "And a few months down the road, when I haven't been able to magically fix everything Mahntayl's buggered up, I'm probably going to be a lot less popular with my beloved subjects."

This time, Mahkelyn obviously didn't know exactly what to say. He contented himself with a nod and a small semi-bow, then excused himself with some murmured remark about his duties. Breygart—*No, damn it,* Hanth, *you dummy!*—watched him go with a certain amusement.

Didn't want to risk putting your foot in it by agreeing with me, hey, Master Mahkelyn? he thought derisively. Then he turned his head as someone else stepped up to the bulwark beside him, gazing across at the humanity-littered harbor waters.

"Good morning, Your Grace," the earl said, and Hektor Aplyn-Ahrmahk grimaced.

"Good morning, My Lord," he replied, and Hanth chuckled at his tone of voice.

"Still an uncomfortable fit, is it, Your Grace?"

"My Lord?" Aplyn-Ahrmahk looked up at him, and Hanth chuckled again, louder.

"The title, lad," he said after a moment, his voice low enough to insure no one else overheard the informality. "It chafes, doesn't it? Feels like it should belong to someone else?"

The midshipman continued gazing up at him for several moments. Hauwerd Breygart was not exceptionally tall, but he was a hard-muscled, fit man who'd seen almost twenty years service as a Marine. Compared to the slightly built boy beside him, he was a solid, chunky presence, and he watched the emotions flickering across Aplyn-Ahrmahk's face. Then the midshipman nodded.

"It does, My Lord," he acknowledged. "Captain Yairley's working on me, but there's never been a single noble in my entire family. Not even a simple knight, as far as I know! What do *I* know about being a 'duke of the realm'?"

"Probably a bit less than I know about being an earl," Hanth said with a grin. "Which, to be blunt, means not one Shan-wei-damned thing!"

"Less than that," Aplyn-Ahrmahk told him with a crooked grin.

"Well, I guess we'll just both have to get used to it, Your Grace." Hanth looked back across the harbor at the somewhat battered Hanth Town waterfront. There'd been more than a little arson involved in the final fighting against Mahntayl's abandoned mercenaries, and the gutted walls of at least half a dozen warehouses stood gaunt and charred under the morning sun.

One more thing to rebuild, he thought.

"But at least you always knew you were in the succession, My Lord," Aplyn-Ahrmahk pointed out, and Hanth nodded.

"That I did. But, to be honest, I never expected for all five of the siblings and cousins between me and the title to up and die on me. Never wanted them to, for that matter." He shook his head, his expression glum. "I never could convince that idiot Mahntayl that I didn't *want* the damned earldom. I think that's why he tried so hard to have me assassinated even after the Church gave it to *him*, instead. He never understood that the only reason I contested his claim in the first place was that I just couldn't stand by and watch someone like him ruin it. Which is exactly what he's spent the last couple of years doing, when all's said."

Hektor Aplyn-Ahrmahk doubted that very many people would believe the earl's claim that he'd never really wanted the title. Aplyn-Ahrmahk, on the other hand, *did* believe him.

"I remember something the King—King Haarahld, I mean—said to me once, My Lord," he told the salt-and-pepper-bearded veteran standing beside him. "He said there were really only two sorts of officers—or noblemen. One felt that the rest of the world owed him something because of who he was; the other felt that *he* owed the rest of the world *everything* because of who he was. I know which sort His Majesty was. I think you're the same sort."

"That's a compliment I'll treasure, Your Grace," Hanth said, looking back down at the serious-faced youngster at his side. "And, if you'll forgive me for saying so, I think I know which sort you'll turn out to be, as well."

"I mean to try, at any rate," Aplyn-Ahrmahk replied. "And I had a good example. The *best* example."

"Yes. Yes you did," Hanth agreed, and for just a moment, he decided, all of the proper protocol he and young Aplyn-Ahrmahk were still learning could go to Hell. He reached out, wrapping one arm around those straight, slim shoulders, and the two of them stood there side by side, gazing out at the cheering, shouting faces of the nameless subjects to whom he owed so much.

.VII.
Royal Palace,
City of Tellesberg,
Kingdom of Charis

S o, Merlin, what interesting things have you been seeing lately?"

King Cayleb's smile was crooked as he and his personal bodyguard stood on the palace balcony while night settled in. Cayleb often dined in his chambers, and his valet, Gahlvyn Daikyn, had just finished supervising the removal of the supper table. He'd be back shortly to oversee Cayleb's preparations for bed. Neither Cayleb nor his father had ever seen any reason to maintain the army of personal servants some other rulers, especially on the mainland, required to wait upon their every need, but Daikyn had been with Cayleb since he was a boy. Breaking him of the habit of making certain "the young master" had brushed his teeth before turning in was a far more formidable challenge than the mere bagatelle of dealing with the Group of Four!

Now Cayleb shook his head in fond exasperation, then drew a deep, lung-swelling breath as he and Merlin gazed out over his capital city. Whatever might be happening in the Temple, and whatever might be happening in the halls of diplomacy throughout Safehold, the Tellesberg waterfront was a hive of activity. The destruction of their enemies' fleets had freed the merchant ships which had been huddled at wharf-side and lying to anchor off the idled port while they waited out the war. Now all of those ships' owners were frantic to get them back out to sea with the cargoes which had accumulated in Tellesberg's warehouses. And the possibility that the ports of Haven and Howard might be closed against them undoubtedly played a part in their thinking, Merlin thought. They wanted to get their cargoes landed, sold, and paid for before any embargo was proclaimed.

It's going to be interesting to see if Howsmyn's predictions about trade patterns hold up, he reflected.

"Actually, I've seen quite a few 'interesting things,'" he said aloud in a mild tone. "I'm planning on writing most of them up for Bynzhamyn. I assume you want the summary version?"

"You assume correctly."

Cayleb turned, leaning back against the balcony's waist-high balustrade and propping his elbows on it, to gaze at Merlin. He'd never heard of Self-Navigating Autonomous Reconnaissance and Communication platforms, nor had he ever heard of the almost microscopically small parasite sensors a SNARC could deploy. But, like his father before him, he'd come to rely on the accuracy of Merlin's "visions." And, unlike most of the other handful of people who knew about those visions, Cayleb had a very shrewd notion that there was nothing particularly "miraculous" about them, although there *was* the tiny problem that Merlin had explained they violated the Proscriptions of Jwo-jeng. Which, miraculous or no, would have made them—and Merlin—anathema in the eyes of the Inquisition.

Continuing to accept Merlin's aid after discovering that minor fact hadn't been the easiest thing Cayleb Ahrmahk had ever done in his life, but he was no more inclined than his father had ever been to look back and second-guess his decisions.

"Where would you like me to start?" Merlin asked politely.

"Well, you could begin with Queen Sharleyan, I suppose. If, of course, there's not something more interesting you want to tell me about."

Cayleb's expression was almost as pointed as his tone, and Merlin chuckled. Marriage of state or no, Cayleb was remarkably nervous about the Chisholmian queen's reaction to his proposal. The fact that he'd never even seen a portrait of her didn't appear to make his internal butterflies any smaller or better behaved, either.

He really is very *young for a reigning king, isn't he?* Merlin thought. Then his chuckle faded. *And he's awfully young to be making a cold-blooded political marriage. Of course, I think he's going to be pleasantly surprised when he finally gets a look at her.*

"Actually," he said, "I think she's considering the notion very carefully. And favorably, I suspect, although she's playing that very close to her tunic at the moment. She hasn't openly committed herself one way or the other, even with Green Mountain, and he's the closest thing to a father she has. But she's been spending quite a bit of time in her chamber reading over your letters. And"—Merlin's sapphire eyes gleamed—"she's been spending quite a bit of time looking at that painting of you we sent along, too."

"Oh, God!" Cayleb rolled his eyes. "I *knew* I should never have let you and Rayjhis talk me into sending her that thing! If she thinks that absolutely vacuous expression is an accurate reflection of my mental processes, she's going to run the other way as quickly as she can—probably screaming as she goes!"

"Nonsense!" Merlin said bracingly. "I think it's a very good likeness, myself. Of course, I'm not a young and beautiful princess."

Not anymore, at least, he added mentally. *But trust me, Cayleb. You're obviously not the best judge of how any female is going to react to* that *portrait. And it's not even particularly prettied-up.*

"Are you saying *she* is?" Despite Cayleb's light tone, Merlin knew the question was more serious than the youthful king wanted to admit, and he decided to take pity upon the young man.

"To be completely honest, I wouldn't say she's 'beautiful,' Cayleb. She's an extraordinarily handsome young woman, though, and I very much doubt any man could fault her figure, or the way she carries herself. And if she isn't beautiful, she has something far more important than that: character and intelligence. This is no pretty little doll you're talking about, believe me. I strongly suspect that most people forget she *isn't* beautiful when they spend much time in her company . . . and that's going to be as true when she's an old woman as it is right now."

"Really?" Something in Merlin's voice told Cayleb he was being completely candid, and the king let down his own guard, accordingly. "Is that really true, Merlin? You're not just trying to make me feel better about this?"

"It's true, Cayleb. In fact, from what I've seen of Sharleyan, she's almost certainly the best possible match you could make. Oh, I think Rayjhis is probably right when he says there's no *need* for you to marry her to pull Chisholm into alliance with Charis. The truth of the matter is that neither of you has anywhere else to go, and I'm sure the logic of that will be just as compelling to Sharleyan and her councilors as it is to you and Rayjhis.

"Where I think he's wrong is in his argument that you shouldn't hurry to commit yourself because your . . . marital availability, let's say, is such a valuable diplomatic card. That might be true in the normal course of politics, but in this case, and completely ignoring the fact that you need to produce an heir of your own as quickly as possible, who would you marry? Hektor's daughter Irys? She'd make a formidable Queen of Charis, and she's probably as smart as Sharleyan, but there's no way you'd be able to keep the poison out of your wine cup eventually. So, what about Nahrmahn's older daughter, Princess Mahrya? She's smart, too, although not as smart as Sharleyan or Irys, but she's also extremely attached to her father. If he winds up getting a head or so shorter, she's not going to forgive you for that. And, frankly, I don't think you're going to need a dynastic marriage to keep Emerald in line after the conquest."

" 'After the conquest,' " Cayleb repeated. "I like the sound of that, even if I do suspect that everyone's showing just a little too much blithe confidence in our ability to hammer Nahrmahn anytime we feel like it. But getting back to Sharleyan—?"

"I'm simply saying you need to realize that this young woman has an enormous amount to offer you if you're smart enough to make her your *partner*, not just your wife. From the handful of things your father ever said to me about your mother, I think they probably had the sort of marriage *you* need to forge if she does say yes. Don't ever make the mistake of thinking of this as a simple transaction to formalize an alliance, Cayleb. *Listen* to this woman. Despite her birth, no one handed her *her* throne, and from all I can see, no one expected her to keep it, either. But she's still here, and the men who thought they could control her or usurp her throne aren't. She's a formidable force in her own right, even if the Group of Four has made the mistake of taking her and her entire kingdom far too lightly, and I think your enemies will find the two of you together will be a far more dangerous combination than both of you would be separately."

"That's exactly what I'm hoping for," Cayleb said quietly.

"Well, I can't say for certain, obviously, but if I were an odds-maker, I'd say the odds are good that she's going to accept. It makes so much sense in so many ways, and it does, indeed, answer the question of whether or not Charis and Chisholm will both be seriously committed to the alliance between them."

"And to squashing the sand maggot that *lies* between us." Cayleb's voice was considerably harsher than it had been. "I want that, too, Merlin. I want it so badly I can *taste* it."

"More than you want Emerald?" Merlin challenged in a neutral tone, and Cayleb barked a laugh.

"I want Emerald, all right. For a lot of reasons. I haven't forgotten who helped Kahlvyn hire the assassins who tried to kill me. And, looking at it logically, Emerald is far more valuable to us . . . and a far more dangerous jumping-off point for future attacks *on* us. Not to mention the fact that Emerald, unlike Corisande, falls very naturally and neatly into our sphere of trade and development. But, from everything you've said, everything Bynzhamyn's spies have told us, Hektor's always been the moving force against us."

"I wouldn't go quite *that* far," Merlin said. "I'll admit he's a far more cold-blooded and ambitious sort than Nahrmahn is, though. He's an odd sort of fellow in a lot of ways, actually. At home, he's what you might think of as a benign tyrant; he won't suffer any challenge to his authority, and he's not at all averse to making that point . . . firmly, but he gives his people genuinely good government. Don't make the mistake of thinking that he's not truly popular with his own people, either, Cayleb. But when it comes to foreign policy, he's a totally different man, one who's driven by ambition and sees absolutely no reason to worry about little things like morality.

"To be honest, I think a lot of *Nahrmahn's* hostility towards Charis has always been due to the fact that he's a student of history. He knows Charis has been steadily expanding in his direction for centuries, and he doesn't want to be one more swallowed-up territory. But don't ever underestimate that man.

I don't think he's as naturally cold-blooded as Hektor, and his 'ambitions' have always been more modest and pragmatic—and, probably, more defensive, in a lot of ways—than Hektor's. But he's capable of being as ruthlessly cold-blooded as they come, whether it's natural for him or not, and he's also a much, much more intelligent man than most people—including your father, I think—have ever given him credit for. In fact, I think in many ways, he's been gaming and manipulating Hektor from the outset. I told you about that conversation he had with Pine Hollow about his post-war territorial ambitions. That was as clear—and accurate—an analysis of the Group of Four's actual objectives as I've ever heard. That man knew *exactly* what he was doing, and the fact that he didn't *want* to be doing it—or not, at least, with Hektor in charge—didn't keep him from playing every angle he could find."

"Oh, I'm not going to take Nahrmahn lightly, I assure you. I suspect he's used that 'fat, indolent hedonist' image to fool a lot of people. In fact, I think you're right; he did manage to fool even Father, at least to some extent. Which, trust me, was *not* an easy thing to do. But, as you just pointed out yourself, he's been reacting more defensively, at least as *he* sees it. And let's be fair here—he's right in our backyard. It's less than seven hundred and fifty miles, as the wyvern flies, from East Cape to Eraystor Bay, but it's over five *thousand* miles from East Cape to Manchyr, which means Nahrmahn has a legitimate interest—an *inevitable* legitimate interest—in the same area we're interested in. Hektor doesn't. Like you say, he's in this solely out of ambition and greed. He wants our carrying trade to increase his own military power, and what *he* has in mind is a Corisandian Empire stretching from Tarot to Chisholm."

"Well, we certainly can't have a *Corisandian* Empire 'stretching from Tarot to Chisholm,' can we?" Merlin murmured, and Cayleb laughed again, this time a bit less harshly.

"At least *my* ambitions stem from self-defense, Merlin! And if we're seriously contemplating holding off the Church—or the Group of Four, if there's any difference—we're going to need all the manpower and resources we can get our hands on. We certainly can't afford to leave the Church any powerful potential allies inside our defensive perimeter."

"No, you can't do that," Merlin agreed.

"Which brings us back to exactly what Hektor is up to. Have there been any significant changes?"

"No." Merlin shook his head. "The only real change is that Bishop Executor Thomys has gotten off the fence and agreed to underwrite the first wave of letters of credit out of his own resources. Well, out of Archbishop Borys' resources, I suppose, if we're going to be sticklers for accuracy. But Thomys is right. There's no way the Archbishop won't back him up on this one, and Raimynd is right about the Group of Four. The *Church* may not openly fund Hektor, although I'm beginning to think they're more likely to come into the open officially than we'd thought they might be. But, whatever the Church does, the 'Knights of the Temple Lands' are going to be perfectly ready to underwrite as many letters of credit as Hektor wants. Either Hektor wins, in which case every mark would be a mark well spent, from their perspective. Or else Hektor loses, in which case we conquer Corisande, and most of those letters of credit turn into waste paper and end up not costing them a hundredth-piece."

"That does sound like them," Cayleb said sourly, then turned back to the railing, leaning forward and propping his folded arms on it.

Night had finished falling while they were talking, and Tellesberg, like every other Safeholdian city, was miserably illuminated by the standards of Nimue Alban's birth world. The only sources of light were burning wood, wax, or oil, and most of the city was an indistinguishable dark mass. Only the waterfront area, where the longshoremen continued to labor frenetically by lantern light, was what might be called well lit.

"I don't like Hektor's resiliency," the king said after a moment. "He and Tartarian are right about how big a bite Corisande is going to be. If it turns into a conventional land war, we could be tied down there for years, despite all our advantages. And if that happens, someone like Hektor is going to figure out how to duplicate almost all of those advantages, which will only make it even bloodier in the end."

"You could always consider a diplomatic resolution," Merlin pointed out. "He's working hard to build a matching navy, and his foundries are going to be going into full production on modern artillery any day now. But the truth is that Charis has such a commanding head start that, even with the Church's backing, he's not going to be able to build into a realistic threat for a long time. Especially not if we keep a close eye on him and you're prepared to prune back his naval strength if it starts to look threatening."

"Forget it." Cayleb snorted. "My house has a long memory for injuries and enemies, Merlin. I suspect Hektor has an even longer one. Besides, even if I wanted to bury the hatchet with him, he'd never believe it. Just as I'd never believe it about him. And I'm not about to leave him at my back, especially not with any modern navy at all, while the Group of Four works at convincing every major realm in Haven and Howard to come at us from the front! I might settle for letting him abdicate and . . . relocate him and his entire family. I'd hate forgoing the sight of his head on a pike outside his own palace, you understand, but I don't want to get bogged down in a quagmire in Corisande any more than the next person does, so if there's another way to get him out of the kitchen, I'll probably settle for it. But that's as far as I'm prepared to stretch my forgiveness. If that means risking the complications of a long war, then so be it. I'll take the chance of giving the Group of Four time before I leave Hektor or any of his get sitting on a throne behind me."

The last sentence came out in the voice of a man swearing a solemn oath, and Merlin nodded. The truth was that he found himself strongly in agreement with Caleb where Hektor was concerned.

"If that's what you want to do, Caleb, then I think you're going to have to figure out how to move against him as quickly as you can," he said. "If Sharleyan is thinking the way I think she's thinking, and if she's as decisive about your proposals as she usually is about decisions, then you'll probably find Chisholm even more ready than you are to move against Corisande. But Tartarian's also right. Even with Chisholm, I don't see any way you can project more than one overseas offensive at a time. Not if the offensives in question both involve *armies*, at any rate."

"Which brings us back to Nahrmahn," Caleb agreed. He pursed his lips thoughtfully, then straightened.

"I know it would give Bynzhamyn apoplexy—*he* doesn't trust Nahrmahn as far as he can spit—but, to be honest, I'd far rather reach a diplomatic solution with *him* than with Hektor. If nothing else, he's close enough, and Emerald is small enough, we could almost certainly crush him if he decided to get adventuresome again."

"Indeed?" This was the first time Merlin had heard Caleb even mention the possibility of any sort of negotiated resolution where Emerald was concerned.

"Don't get me wrong," Caleb said more grimly. "I *do* plan to add Emerald to Charis. Nahrmahn may have been worried about that all along, but the truth is that from every perspective, especially the strategic one, we can't afford to leave Emerald independent. The only real question is how we go about changing that status. Given what Nahrmahn was just a party to, whether it was his idea or not, I'm perfectly willing to do it the hard way, if that's what it takes. On the other hand, I'm not *quite* as wedded to the notion of seeing his head on a pike as I am to seeing Hektor's head there."

"From what I've seen of Nahrmahn's recent coversations, I'm not too sure he's aware of that fine distinction," Merlin observed.

"Which doesn't bother me a bit at this point." Caleb smiled evilly. "The more concerned he is about his head now, the more likely he is to be . . . amenable to sweet reason when the time comes, shall we say? And I want him to clearly understand that all the winning military cards are in *my* hand, not his. If—and note that I say *if*, Merlin—I end up offering him any terms short of unconditional surrender and a scaffold with a view, it won't be a discussion between equals, and I intend for him to understand that. Clearly."

Merlin simply nodded. This was a game Caleb had learned at his father's shoulder, and Haarahld VII had been one of the most accomplished practitioners of . . . practical diplomacy Safehold had ever produced. Obviously, Caleb intended to continue the tradition. In fact, his version of diplomacy

appeared to be considerably brawnier and more bare-knuckled than his father's had been.

*But if Haarahld had found himself in the position Cayleb's in, I think he'd be
making a lot of the same decisions,* Merlin reflected.

"Be thinking about everything you've seen about what Nahrmahn and
what's-his-name, Zhaztro, are up to," Cayleb said. "Tomorrow morning, you
and I are going to sit down with Bryahn, and I'm going to tell him I've decided to let him go calling on Nahrmahn, after all. Between the three of us,
I'm sure we can come up with a suitable way to turn up the heat in
Nahrmahn's kitchen."

.VIII.
Erayk Dynnys' Cell and the Plaza of Martyrs,
The Temple of God,
City of Zion,
The Temple Lands

Erayk Dynnys used his silver-headed cane to lever himself to his feet as he
rose from the kneeler before the simple icon of Langhorne. The knee
which had been half-crippled since his fall a year and a half earlier had been
giving him even more trouble, of late. Not, he reflected, looking out his narrow window, that it was going to be a problem much longer.

His lips twitched in what might almost have been a smile as he stepped
back from the window and examined the small, spartan cell which had been
his home for the past three and a half months. Its bare, undressed stone walls,
narrow, barred windows, and thick, securely locked door were a far cry from
the luxurious apartment he had enjoyed as the Archbishop of Charis, before
his other, more serious fall. And yet . . .

He turned to the small desk under the single window and settled himself
into the chair behind it. Ever since his imprisonment, the only reading material he had been permitted was a copy of the *Holy Writ* and the twelve thick
volumes of *The Insights*.

He touched the golden scepter of Langhorne, embossed into the finely
tooled leather cover of the *Writ*. He had not, he conceded, spent very much
time reading that book over the last few decades. *Consulting* it when he required a specific passage for an episcopal decree, perhaps. Scanning for the
scriptural basis for a pastoral message, or one of his infrequent sermons.
But he hadn't truly *read* it since he'd gained the ruby ring of a bishop. It
hadn't been *irrelevant*, exactly, but he'd studied it exhaustively in seminary,
preached from it regularly as an under-priest. He'd already known what it

contained, hadn't he? Of course he had! And the duties and responsibilities of a bishop, and even more of an archbishop, demanded too much daily attention. There'd been no time to read, and his priorities had been those of his office.

It made a fine excuse, didn't it, Erayk? he asked himself as his fingertip stroked the scepter which was the emblem of the order to which he had belonged . . . until it cast him forth. *It's a pity you didn't spend more time with it. At least then you might have been a bit better prepared for this moment.*

And perhaps it wouldn't have made any difference after all, for the *Writ* and *The Insights* both assumed that those called to serve as shepherds in God's name would be worthy of their calling.

And Erayk Dynnys had not been.

I wonder what would happen if Clyntahn made all the Church's bishops and archbishops spend a few months alone with the Writ *on a diet of bread and water?* he thought whimsically. *Probably not anything he'd like! He has enough trouble on his hands just with the Wylsynns without adding an entire flock of bishops who actually read the* Writ.

Well, it wasn't going to matter very much longer to Erayk Dynnys either way. All too soon, he would know what God had truly expected of him in his life. It would not, he was grimly certain, be an accounting he would enjoy hearing, for whatever it was God had expected of him, he had failed. Failed as all men must who presumed to claim to speak for God when, in fact, they had forgotten Him.

Dynnys had done what he could to amend his failures, since his fall from power, yet it was pitifully little against what he ought to have been doing for years. He knew that now. And he knew that even though the charges brought against him by the Grand Inquisitor were false in every particular, what was about to happen to all of Safehold was truly as much his fault as that of any other living man.

Much to his surprise, the only archbishop who had dared to visit him since his arrest had been Zhasyn Cahnyr, the lean, almost stringy Archbishop of Glacierheart. They'd detested one another cordially for years, and yet Cahnyr had been the only one of his fellows who had called upon him, daring the wrath of Clyntahn and the Group of Four to pray with Dynnys for the redemption of his soul.

It was odd. Cahnyr had been permitted to see him only half a dozen times, and he had been allowed to remain no longer than an hour on any occasion. And yet, Dynnys had found himself drawing immense comfort from those visits. Perhaps it had been because the archbishop was the only human being he'd seen since his imprisonment who had not been interrogating, threatening, or haranguing him. He'd simply been there, the only member of the Church's entire hierarchy prepared to discharge his priestly office by ministering to the soul of one of the Inquisition's prisoners.

His example had shamed Dynnys, and all the more so because of the contempt Dynnys had once felt for the pastoral "simplemindedness" of Cahnyr's approach to his episcopal duties.

I could've learned something from him, if I'd only bothered to listen. Well, I've still learned something, and as the Writ *says, true knowledge and understanding never come too late for the profit of a man's soul.*

He opened the *Writ* to one of the marked passages, from the ninth verse of the fifteenth chapter of *The Book of Langhorne.*

"For how will a man profit if he gains all the world's power, yet loses his soul? And how much will he pay, how much gold will he bring, for his soul? Ponder that well, for whoever is ashamed of the teachings God has sent through my hand, that man also will I be ashamed of on the day he stands before the God who created him, and I will neither hold forth my hand as his shield nor speak for him in that dread judgment."

That, he thought, was a passage Zhaspahr Clyntahn might profitably spend a few hours contemplating.

He turned the book's pages, listening to the crisp flutter of the thin, expensive paper. There were so many things in that book, so much he would not have time enough to ponder as it deserved. And there were a few things *missing*, as well.

He reached the end of the *Book of Chihiro.* By ancient tradition, there was always a blank page between *Chihiro* and the beginning of *Hastings*, but there was no blank page in Dynnys' copy of the *Writ.* Not anymore, at any rate.

He ran an index finger down the gutter between printed pages, feeling the raggedness where a single *un*printed page had been removed, then drew a deep breath and closed the book once again.

He sat back, and wondered if Adorai had received any of his letters. He'd considered writing to others among his onetime friends, or to the other members of his family, but decided not to. None of them had dared to emulate Cahnyr, and none of them had so much as spoken in his defense. It had scarcely come as any surprise, given the charges against him and the identity of his accuser, yet that had made his sense of abandonment hurt no less. That wasn't the reason he hadn't written to them, however. Whether they'd abandoned him or not, they were still his family, and he'd known every word of every letter he might write would be scrutinized by the Inquisition. Given the near-panic which had gripped the entire Temple since word of Charis' smashing naval victories—and even more, Staynair's letter to the Grand Vicar—had reached Zion, Clyntahn would be looking for additional victims. Searching for additional blood with which to placate his fellow vicars. Dynnys had no intention of helping him to offer up the other members of his own family simply because of some incautious word, some phrase which could be taken out of context, in a letter from him.

But he did hope that at least one of his letters had reached Adorai. He doubted any of them had, whatever the Inquisitors might have promised him. After all, what promise was binding to an apostate heretic? To a man convicted—and Dynnys had been convicted long before any formal trial—of selling his protection to the very spawn of Shan-wei? Of deliberately lying to the Council of Vicars and to the Grand Inquisitor to conceal his own sins and the even greater sins being practiced by the heretics and blasphemers of his fallen archbishopric? Why should any of *his* letters be delivered to anyone?

They'd taken all of them, though, whether to deliver, to somehow use against him, or simply to dispose of unsent. And they'd denied him any paper, except to write those letters upon. But they hadn't realized he had another source of paper. Nor had they suspected that Zhasyn Cahnyr had been more than simply a visitor. That Glacierheart's primate had very quietly volunteered to take messages from him.

At first, Dynnys had suspected some sort of complex trap, organized by the Inquisition. That notion had lasted perhaps all of thirty seconds before he realized how patently absurd it was. At that point, he'd begun to worry about the deadly risk Cahnyr had offered to run for him, and he'd turned the archbishop down with a smile he hoped told the other man how unspeakably grateful he'd felt.

But then, as he'd studied the *Writ* with newly refreshed eyes, and especially as he'd perused the sections of *The Insights* written by Grand Vicar Evyrahard, he'd realized it wasn't that simple. Not just a question of Cahnyr's carrying letters which might somehow serve Dynnys' own needs or ends.

Evyrahard's had been a short grand vicarate, and as Dynnys pored over his brief contribution to *The Insights* from the perspective of his own current plight, he'd realized exactly why that had happened. Saint Evyrahard could not have been a welcome presence in the Temple's corridors of power. Clearly, he'd had no notion how "the game" was played, and, equally clearly, his efforts at reform had made him dangerous enemies in plenty. Indeed, Dynnys suspected that much of Clyntahn's hatred for the entire Wylsynn family was an almost institutional thing, going clear back to Evyrahard the Just's grand vicarate.

And as he'd read Saint Evyrahard's century-old words, and remembered the clear-eyed commitment and faith of that long-dead Grand Vicar's distant grandson, Paityr, he'd recognized something he himself had never truly had. Something he wished desperately *had* been his. And in that recognition, he'd realized there were, indeed, two letters he needed delivered. Two letters no Inquisitor could ever be permitted to see. And so, he'd found his notepaper in the *Writ* itself. He couldn't believe God or the Archangel Langhorne would begrudge him its use, not given the task for which he had needed it.

Cahnyr hadn't so much as flinched when Dynnys handed him the tightly folded piece of paper when they clasped hands in greeting at his next visit. Dynnys was certain he'd seen the other man's cheek muscles tighten, seen the sudden flicker of anxiety in Cahnyr's eyes, but all the archbishop had done was to slip the note unobtrusively into a cassock pocket.

Despite everything else that had happened, Dynnys had no fear Cahnyr might have delivered his note to the Inquisition's hand, or betrayed his confidence. No. Here at the very end of his life, Erayk Dynnys had finally met the duties of his office, and he had prayed nightly that Zherald Ahdymsyn and Paityr Wylsynn would heed the final directives he'd sent them.

It wasn't very much, not at the end of everything, after a life he'd wasted so profligately. It was simply the only thing he could have done.

He folded his hands before him, leaning his forehead against them in silent prayer. He didn't know how long he sat there, praying, before the sudden, loud "clack" of his cell door's lock yanked him up out of his state of meditation.

He straightened slowly, with as much dignity as he could muster, and turned to face the two upper-priests in the flame-and-sword-badged purple of the Order of Schueler. The Inquisitors wore the stark black stoles and gloves of the executioners they were, and their eyes were pitiless and cold. The half-dozen Temple Guardsmen behind them were expressionless, their faces masks for whatever they might have been feeling, but there was no doubting the satisfaction and icy hatred in the Inquisitors' stony gazes.

"It is time," the senior of them told him flatly, and he nodded.

"Yes, it is," he replied with a calmness which astounded him. He thought he might have seen surprise flicker in the backs of the Schuelerites' eyes, as well, and the possibility gave him a curious satisfaction.

One of the guardsmen stepped forward with a heavy set of manacles. His eyes were reluctant, almost apologetic, and Dynnys looked at the senior Inquisitor.

"Are those truly necessary?" he asked.

The Inquisitor returned his gaze for several long, taut moments. Then, slowly, he shook his head.

"Thank you," Dynnys said, and stepped forward, leaning on his cane as he took his place at the center of the hollow square of guardsmen. It wasn't exactly as if he might somehow have miraculously run away and escaped his fate simply because they hadn't chained his hands. Besides, there was the . . . agreement he'd struck with Clyntahn to be considered, wasn't there?

"Shall we go, Father?" he asked, looking back at the senior Inquisitor.

▼ ▼ ▼

It was a beautiful morning, the sewing woman called Ailysa thought. More than a bit cool, as May often was, here in the City of Zion, with a brisk breeze blowing in off Lake Pei, but filled with sunlight. The vast, beautiful Plaza of

Martyrs was drenched in that rich, golden radiance, and the sounds of the early-morning city were hushed, stilled. Even the birds and wyverns seemed subdued, muted, she thought.

But that was almost certainly just her imagination. God's winged creatures had no concept of what was about to happen here on this beautiful spring morning. If they had, they would have fled as quickly as they could fly.

Unlike them, Ailysa knew exactly what was going to happen, and her stomach muscles were tight with tension and incipient nausea. Ahnzhelyk had been right about how horrible this day was going to be, but Ailysa had meant what she'd said. She *had* to be here, however dreadful it might prove to be.

The crowd was vast, filling a good half of the enormous plaza before the Temple's soaring colonnade. She'd tried to decide what that crowd's mood was. She'd failed.

Some of them—many of them—were as silent as she herself was, standing there in their jackets or shawls, waiting. Others chattered to one another as if this were to be some sort of sporting event, yet the very brightness of their chatter, their smiles, said otherwise. And then there were the *others*, the ones who waited in a silent anticipation fueled by rage and fired by a savage demand for the Church's justice.

Justice, she thought. *This wouldn't be justice even if he'd actually done the things he was accused of!*

A sudden stir warned her, and she looked up, biting her lower lip, as the procession of guardsmen, Inquisitors, and, of course, the victim appeared on the Temple's steps and began the descent to the platform which had been erected so that the spectators could be sure they wouldn't miss a single grisly detail.

Voices began to cry out from the crowd, from the ones who'd waited in anticipation for so long. Jeers, catcalls, curses. All the pent-up hatred, all the bitter-tasting fear which Charis' rebellion against Mother Church had awakened, was in those half-inarticulate screams of fury.

The ex-archbishop appeared not to notice. He was too far away for Ailysa to see his face clearly, but his shoulders were square, his spine straight, as he limped along on his cane in the plain, scratchy burlap robe of a condemned heretic. He carried himself well, she thought, her heart swelling with a pride she was surprised to feel even now, and the bright sunlight wavered through the sudden welling of her tears.

He and his guards and executioners reached the platform where all of the hideous tools had been assembled to carry out the penalties assigned for heresy and blasphemy by the Archangel Schueler. His stride seemed to hesitate for just a moment as he stepped up onto it, and if it had, who should blame him? Even from here, Ailysa could see the heat-shimmer above the braziers whose glowing coals embraced the waiting irons and pincers, and those were but one of the horrors awaiting him.

If he did hesitate, it was only for a moment. Then he moved forward once again, taking his place before the waiting, shrieking multitude who had come to see him die.

Another figure appeared. As the executioners, he wore the dark purple of the Order of Schueler, but he also wore the orange priest's cap of a vicar, and Ailysa's mouth tightened as she recognized Vicar Zhaspahr Clyntahn.

Of course, she thought. *This is the first time in the entire history of Mother Church that one of her own archbishops has been put to death for heresy and blasphemy. How could the Grand Inquisitor not appear? And how could a man like Clyntahn possibly stay away from the judicial murder of the sacrifice for his own crimes?*

The Grand Inquisitor unrolled an archaic, formal scroll, and began to read from it. Ailysa tuned him out. She had no need to listen to a recitation of the alleged crimes for which Dynnys was to be executed. Not when she knew that the one crime of which he was truly guilty was being the Group of Four's perfect scapegoat.

It took quite a while for Clyntahn to finish the lengthy litany of condemnation, but he came to the end at last, and turned to Dynnys.

"You have heard the judgment and sentence of Holy Mother Church, Erayk Dynnys," the vicar intoned, his voice carrying well, despite the breeze. "Have you anything to say before that sentence is carried out?"

▼   ▼   ▼

Dynnys looked out across the vast plaza, and a corner of his mind wondered how many times he'd walked across those same stones, passed those same statues, those same magnificent sculptures and fountains? How many times had he passed under the Temple's colonnade, taking its majesty and beauty for granted because he had so many "more important" things to think about?

His thoughts had floated back through those other days, other visits to this place, as Clyntahn read off the list of offenses for which he was to die. Like Ailysa, if he'd only known, he had no need to actually listen to them. He knew what they were, and as the Inquisition had demanded, he had duly confessed to all of them. There'd been no point refusing to. Eventually, he knew, they would have brought him to confession. That was something at which the Inquisition was well skilled, and even if he'd somehow managed *not* to confess, it wouldn't have changed his fate.

Still, there could be one mercy yet. He remembered the upper-priest's cold promise, the message from Clyntahn himself which the Grand Inquisitor was unwilling to deliver in person. Confession, and the proper public admission of his guilt, would buy him a strangling garrote and a quick death before the full catalog of punishments the Archangel Schueler had decreed were visited upon his no longer living body.

Dynnys had understood Clyntahn's minion perfectly.

Public contrition, the admission of guilt and entreaty for forgiveness, were an important part of the Inquisition's punishment of sin. God's mercy was infinite. Even on the lip of Hell itself, a soul touched by true remorse, true contrition, might yet find forgiveness and sanctuary in Him. And so tradition decreed that anyone condemned before the Inquisition was entitled to make public repentance and to recant his sins before execution of his sentence.

It was a tradition which was sometimes ignored. Dynnys had always known that, even before his own fall from grace. To his shame, he'd never been so much as tempted to speak out against that practice. It hadn't been his business, and the Inquisition was jealous of its responsibilities and prerogatives. If it chose to silence some criminal lest he use his final moments to spew forth protests of innocence, accusations of torture, fresh declarations of heresy or fresh blasphemies, then surely that was the Inquisition's business.

But it was also a tradition the Inquisition had learned to use well for its own advantage. A prisoner who acknowledged his guilt, besought forgiveness, proclaimed his penitence, and thanked Mother Church—and the Order of Schueler—for saving his immortal soul, even if it had to come at the expense of his mortal body, *proved* the justice of the Inquisition. It was the demonstration that no one had acted in haste, that true justice and the holy purpose of God had been duly and properly served.

And so, Dynnys had given the Inquisitor his word. Had promised to say what was "proper."

To give Clyntahn what he'd known the Group of Four wanted from him, obedient to their final script.

▼　▼　▼

"Yes, Your Grace." Ailysa's stomach clinched more tightly still as Dynnys faced Clyntahn on the platform. "Of your kind permission and Mother Church's grace, I would take this final opportunity to express my contrition and acknowledge my guilt before God and man, seeking God's forgiveness."

"If that is your true desire, then speak, and may God hear your words and measure the truth in your heart," Clyntahn replied.

"Thank you, Your Grace."

Dynnys' voice wasn't as deep, or as powerful, as Clyntahn's, yet it carried well against the breeze. He moved closer to the lip of the platform, leaning on his cane, gazing out across the crowd which had stilled its own shouts into silence as it awaited his public admission of guilt. The grim implements of torture loomed behind him, pregnant with their promise of cleansing agony, but he seemed unaware of them now.

Ailysa looked up at him, wishing she dared to come closer, yet already half-sick with what she knew was about to happen.

And then, he began to speak.

▼　　▼　　▼

"Your Grace, you have asked if I have anything to say before I die for my crimes, and I do. I freely admit my most grievous failure in my duties as an archbishop of Mother Church. It was my solemn charge to be both shepherd and father to the flock Mother Church had entrusted to me in God's name. It was my responsibility, and my privilege, to safeguard their souls. To teach them aright, to keep them in the way of God and the teachings of Langhorne. To discipline, as a father must, when discipline is necessary, knowing that only in that way can those committed to his charge be brought to proper understanding in God's unending love in the fullness of time.

"Those were my responsibilities to Mother Church and to the souls of the Archbishopric of Charis, and I have most grievously failed to meet them."

Dynnys never looked away from the crowd in the plaza. Never so much as glanced at Clyntahn, lest it be obvious he was seeking the Grand Inquisitor's approval of all he said. Yet even without turning his head, he could see Clyntahn from the corner of his eye, and the satisfaction hiding behind the vicar's solemn expression was obvious. He knew what was coming next, for he had Dynnys' promise.

Too bad, Your Grace, the condemned ex-archbishop thought with a sort of grim, cold, terrified exaltation. *Some things are more important than what you want . . . and why should any condemned and apostate heretic keep a promise to a lying bastard like you?*

"A true shepherd dies for his flock. As the Archangel Langhorne himself said, 'There is no greater love in any man than his willingness to die for others,' and as Charis' archbishop, I ought to have been willing to listen to Langhorne's words. I was not. I feared the personal consequences of my failures as a child of God and an archbishop of Mother Church. And so, when Vicar Zahmsyn came to me, expressing the concerns, the suspicions and fears, which the reports of others had aroused in Charis' case, I did not tell him that each and every one of those reports was a lie."

▼　　▼　　▼

Ailysa's head jerked up in astonishment. Surely, she hadn't heard him correctly! He couldn't *possibly* have said—

Then her eyes darted to Clyntahn, saw the Grand Inquisitor's sudden dark-faced fury, and knew she hadn't misunderstood a thing.

▼   ▼   ▼

"Instead of telling him the allegations of heresy, apostasy, and violations of the Proscriptions of Jwo-jeng were lies, false reports spread by Charis' enemies and carried throughout the Temple by corrupt priests of Mother Church in return for gold from those same enemies, I promised to investigate. To make 'examples' of those falsely accused of sin. And I fully intended to keep those promises."

Dynnys forced himself to continue to speak calmly and distinctly. Sheer stunned disbelief seemed to have paralyzed Clyntahn and his Inquisitors, at least briefly, and Dynnys looked out into the equally stunned silence of the Plaza of Martyrs and made his voice ring out clearly.

"For myself, I amply deserve the penalty I am to suffer this day. Had I discharged my duties to my archbishopric, thousands might not have already died, and more thousands might not be about to die. But whatever *I* may deserve, Your Grace, whatever punishment *I* may merit, the souls you and the Council of Vicars entrusted to my care are, as you know full well, innocent of the crimes you have charged against them. Their only crime, their only sin, has been to defend themselves and the families they love against rape, murder, and destruction at the orders of the corrupt and greedy—"

One of the Inquisitors reacted at last, spinning around to Dynnys and driving a gloved fist into the ex-archbishop's face. The steel studs reinforcing the glove's fingers pulped Dynnys' lips, and the blow's savage force broke his jaw in at least three places. He went to his knees, more than half-stunned, and Clyntahn pointed down at him in a rigid gesture of anathema.

"*Blasphemer!* How *dare* you raise your voice against the will and plan of God Himself?! Servant of Shan-wei, you prove yourself, your guilt, and the damnation awaiting you with every word you speak! We cast you out, we commit you to the outer darkness, to the corner of Hell reserved for your dark mistress! We expunge your name from the children of God, and strike you forever from the company of redeemed souls!"

He stood back, and the upper-priests seized the semi-conscious, bleeding man who had once been the Archbishop of Charis and yanked him to his feet. They ripped the burlap robe from his body, stripping him naked before the stunned, mesmerized crowd, and then they dragged him towards the waiting instruments of torture.

▼   ▼   ▼

The sewing woman known as Ailysa pressed both hands to her trembling mouth as she watched the executioners chaining their victim's unresisting body to the rack. She was weeping so hard she could scarcely see, but the sobs were silent, too deep, too terrible, to be shared.

She heard the first deep, hoarse grunt of agony, knew it was only a matter of time before grunts became screams, and even now, she could scarcely believe what he'd done, what he'd said.

Despite all she'd said to Ahnzhelyk, she had never wanted anything more than she wanted to flee this place of gathering horror. Of horror made still worse by the final gesture of Erayk Dynnys' life.

But she couldn't. She *wouldn't*. She would stay to the very end, and, as she had told Ahnzhelyk, she would know what to tell her sons. *His* sons.

Sons, she thought, who need never feel shame for the name they bore. Not now—not ever. Never again after *this*.

For the first time in too many years, the sewing woman known as Ailysa felt a deep, fierce pride in the man she had married, and whose agonizing death she stood to witness for her sons and for history.

.IX.
Grand Council Chamber,
Queen Sharleyan's Palace,
City of Cherayth,
Kingdom of Chisholm

There was a certain undeniable tension as Queen Sharleyan and Baron Green Mountain walked into the council chamber.

There were several reasons for that. First, every member of the Queen's Council knew the First Councilor of Charis had been an honored guest in the palace for over two and a half five-days, despite the minor technicality of the state of war which still existed between the two kingdoms. Second, although all manner of rumors had been flying through Cherayth ever since Gray Harbor's arrival, their monarch had not seen fit to share with anyone— except, *possibly*, Green Mountain—precisely what she and the Charisian first councilor had been discussing. Third, Bishop Executor Wu-shai Tiang's imperious demand in the name of the Knights of the Temple Lands that Gray Harbor be taken into custody and handed over to him had been courteously but firmly rebuffed. And, fourth . . . fourth, their slender, dark-haired queen had chosen to wear not her simple presence coronet, but the Chisholmian Crown of State.

Sharleyan was fully aware of that tension. She'd anticipated it, and, in some ways, she'd deliberately provoked it. Politics, she'd discovered many years ago under Green Mountain's careful tutelage, was at least half a question of proper stage management. And the higher the stakes, the more critical that management became.

Especially with Uncle Byrtrym sitting out there, she thought unhappily as she crossed regally to the elaborately carved chair at the head of the huge, oval table. She let her eyes stray to Byrtrym Waistyn, the Duke of Halbrook Hollow, the commander of the Royal Army . . . and her mother's only brother.

She settled into her chair and turned her head to give the middle-aged man in the green cassock and brown cockaded priest's cap of an upper-priest a sharp glance.

Carlsyn Raiyz had been Sharleyan's confessor since only a very few months after she'd taken the throne. She hadn't exactly chosen him for herself, given her youthfulness, but he'd always met the responsibilities of his position admirably. And although he had to be aware of his youthful ruler's . . . misgivings about the Church's current leadership, he'd never made an issue of them. She hoped he wasn't going to now, but she wasn't as confident of that as she would have preferred to be. On the other hand, his expression was remarkably serene for a spiritual counselor whose charge hadn't even mentioned to him what brought the first councilor of a kingdom which had rebelled against that leadership to speak with her so earnestly. Or discussed her reasons for telling a bishop executor of holy Mother Church why he couldn't have that first councilor as a prisoner.

"Father?" she said quietly.

Raiyz gazed at her for perhaps two heartbeats, then smiled very slightly, rose, and looked around the table at the faces of Sharleyan's councilors.

"Let us pray," he said, and inclined his own head. "O God, Who sent Your Archangels to teach men the truth of Your will, we beseech You to lend Your grace to our beloved Queen, and to the men gathered in this place at this time to hear her will, to bear witness to it, and to advise her. In these troubled times, You and the Archangels remain the final refuge, the final help, of all men and women of goodwill, and no other help is required. Bless our Queen's deliberations, grant her wisdom to choose aright in the grievous decisions which lie before her, and give her the peace of knowing Your love and guidance. In Langhorne's name, amen."

Well, that was certainly hopeful, Sharleyan thought as she joined the members of her council in signing themselves with Langhorne's scepter. *On the other hand, he didn't exactly come out doing handsprings of delight, either, did he?*

She waited while Raiyz sat back down, then swept the faces of the men seated around the table with eyes which warned them she was in no mood to tolerate intransigence this day. She felt the tension click up another few degrees as that message went home. She was not only the youngest person in that council chamber, but also the only *female* person present, and she found herself suppressing a huntress' smile as she contemplated that fact and their reaction to her unyielding gaze. Some of her "advisers," she knew, had never really fully resigned themselves to having a queen, rather than a king.

Unfortunately, she thought at them with an undeniable edge of satisfaction, *Father and Mother had* me, *instead, didn't they? And between us, Mahrak and I—and Uncle Byrtrym—made it stand up. It's been a bumpy ride, hasn't it, My Lords? Of course, you're about to find out just how truly* "bumpy" *things can get.*

"My Lords," she said after a moment, into the taut silence, her voice clear and strong, "we have summoned you here today to inform you of certain matters which we have been contemplating for some days past now. As always, we will welcome your wisdom and your advice concerning the decision to which we have come."

If the chamber had been tense before she spoke, that was nothing compared to the jolt which ran through her listeners as she used the royal we. They heard that particular usage from her very rarely, at least when they sat in council with her. Coupled with her decision to wear the Crown of State, and the phrasing of her final sentence, it told every one of them that Sharleyan had, indeed, already come to her decision about whatever it was she intended to "discuss" with them.

It wouldn't be the first time it had happened. Sharleyan Tayt had all of her dead father's incisiveness and possibly even more strength of will. When she'd found herself on the back of the slash lizard following his death, she'd recognized that she simply could not afford to allow her councilors to regard her as a child, even though that had been precisely what she was when the crown landed on her head. There had been relatively few reigning queens in the history of Safehold. Indeed, Sharleyan was only the second in the entire history of Chisholm, and Queen Ysbell had been deposed after barely four years on the throne. That had not been an encouraging precedent after King Sailys' death, and more than one of his councilors had been prepared to "manage" his daughter for him. Some of them, Sharleyan knew, had cherished the hope she might follow in Ysbell's footsteps. Even of those who hadn't been willing to go quite that far, some had entertained notions of seeing her properly married off to someone—like themselves, perhaps, or one of their sons—who could provide the necessary masculine guidance she would undoubtedly need.

Well, My Lords, she thought with a certain grim amusement, watching them as they tried with varying degrees of success to hide their consternation at what she'd just said, *I had all the "masculine guidance" I needed from Mahrak, didn't I?*

It had been Green Mountain who'd warned the grieving child who'd just lost a father and inherited a crown that she must choose between merely *reigning* and *ruling.* Even then, and despite her own crushing sense of loss, she'd been old enough to understand what the first councilor was telling her, and she'd had absolutely no intention of permitting Chisholm's governance to fall into the hands of any of the various great lords already licking their chops as they prepared to grapple for control of the kingdom. And the only way to prevent that potentially disastrous factional strife had been to make it abundantly clear that there was already a "faction" firmly—even ruthlessly—in control.

Her.

Some of them had found that lesson harder to learn than others, and the most uneducable had been eased off the Queen's Council. One of them, the Duke of Three Hills, had proved sufficiently persistent in his refusal to accept that "a mere girl" had the ability to rule in her own right that she'd been forced to remove him from the Council with a minimum of gentleness and a maximum of firmness. When he'd attempted to reverse her decision by extra-legal methods, her army and navy had argued the point with him. In the end, his had been only the third death warrant Sharleyan had personally signed, and his power base had disintegrated with his death.

Signing that warrant had been the hardest thing she'd ever done—then—but she'd done it. And, in a perverse sort of way, she knew she would always be grateful to Three Hills. He'd shown the one person to whom it really mattered—Sharleyan herself—that she had the steel in her spine to do what needed to be done. And what had happened to him had been sufficient to inspire the remaining holdouts to . . . reevaluate their positions in the recognition that Queen Sharleyan was *not* Queen Ysbell.

Still, she wasn't surprised by the evident dismay she saw from some of them today. Obviously, the men behind those particular faces suspected that they weren't going to care for the decision she'd reached today.

And they're right, she thought. *In fact, they're far righter than they could even guess at this point.*

"As all of you are aware," she continued after several moments, "King Cayleb of Charis has sent us his own first councilor as his personal emissary. I am aware that some members of this Council felt it would be . . . imprudent, shall we say, to receive Earl Gray Harbor. Or, for that matter, any representative of Charis. I'm also aware of the reasons they had for feeling that way. But, My Lords, even the soundest of ships and even the most skilled of captains cannot survive a storm simply by ignoring it. I'm sure we would all prefer calm to storm, but we live in the times in which we live, and we can but pray for God's guidance to make the best choices we may in the face of the challenges the world sends us.

"At this time, again as all of you are aware, we remain technically at war with Charis. Unfortunately, that war has not prospered. And I suspect it will surprise none of you to discover that the decision to join that war in the first place was never truly our own."

Several councilors, including her uncle, stirred uneasily in their chairs, and two or three pairs of eyes swiveled sideways to Father Carlsyn. The priest, for his part, only sat with his hands folded on the table in front of him, head cocked slightly to one side, while he listened to the queen and watched her with bright, alert eyes.

"In fact, of course," she continued, "Chisholm 'agreed' to join the League of Corisande and the Princedom of Emerald only at the . . . strong urging of the Chancellor of the Knights of the Temple Lands. The Knights desired us to assist Prince Hektor against Haarahld of Charis for reasons which no doubt seemed good to them, but which—let us be honest here among ourselves, My Lords—were never truly critical, or even relevant, to Chisholm's own interests. We had no just cause for enmity with Charis on our own part, and we had many reasons for regarding our 'ally' Hektor with suspicion and caution.

"Nonetheless, we acceded to Chancellor Trynair's urging when Archbishop Zherohm delivered his message to us on behalf of the Knights of the Temple Lands." Her uncle, she observed, winced visibly at her repeated use of "Knights of the Temple Lands." She wished that could have come to her as a surprise. "There were several reasons for that, but—being honest, once again—the primary reason was fear. Fear of what the Knights might do to Chisholm if we declined to do as they 'requested' in this instance."

She paused, with a wintry smile which should have turned every square inch of exposed skin in that council chamber blue. Her uncle's face had tightened at the word "fear," and one or two other faces had turned into blank walls.

Well, that's scarcely a surprise, she told herself tartly.

She was aware of a bright, singing tension deep inside her. It was a sensation she'd felt before—the taut recognition that she danced upon the edge of a sword. Every monarch must know that feeling, sometimes, at least, she thought. There had been times—like the signing of Duke Three Hills' death warrant—when she'd faced it, rendered her decision, and then retired to her private chambers to throw up. Those times had been more common in the first year or two after she took the crown, however. Now, it was something to be embraced. The proof she was doing her job, meeting the challenges the world sent to her. And, she admitted to herself, there was something almost addictive to it and to the hard-won knowledge that she was *good* at the task to which birth had called her. To the awareness that the issues she grappled with, the decisions she made, were *important*. That she *had* to get them right if she was going to meet her father's spirit with the ability to look into his eyes without shame. It wasn't the power itself which gave her that sense of being alive, so much as it was the determination to do her very best, the satisfaction she took from knowing that she had. It had to be the same sort of emotion a star athlete felt when he pushed himself ruth-lessly in training to reach a higher plateau of performance. The satisfaction he felt within *himself*, not the one which came from the cheering adulation of his fans. Or perhaps, as she often thought, it must be akin to what a champion swordsman felt in that first, breathless moment when he stepped into the lists at a competition.

Or, she admitted to herself, *what a duelist feels like when his opponent draws his sword.*

"My Lords," she allowed her voice to turn chiding, "does anyone around this table pretend to truly believe that Haarahld of Charis intended to *invade* Corisande? That he had some sort of malign intent to seize control of all the world's commerce?"

"With your permission, Your Majesty," Duke Halbrook Hollow said, keeping his voice almost painfully neutral, "that seems to be exactly what's happening now."

"Yes, Your Grace," she acknowledged. "It does indeed seem to be what's happening now. But the critical word is 'now,' is it not? Charis has just beaten off the attack of no less than five navies, including our own, and King Cayleb is obviously aware of the pretext upon which the attack, and the re-sultant death of his father"—she let her eyes bore into her uncle's—"was or-chestrated by . . . the Knights of the Temple Lands. What Charis never sought to seize in time of peace may very well have become something she has no option but to seek in time of war if she hopes to survive the attack upon her."

Please, Uncle Byrtrym, she thought pleadingly behind the confident façade of her calm eyes and firm mouth. *I know what you're thinking. Please, support me in this.*

The duke opened his mouth, then closed it once more.

"The plain truth of the matter, My Lords," she continued as her uncle backed away from the challenge, for the moment at least, "is that I was con-strained against my will to attack a peaceful neighbor. And another plain truth is that the attack which was intended to overwhelm and destroy Charis failed miserably. Those truths, among others, are what King Cayleb sent Earl Gray Harbor to Chisholm to discuss."

The distant sound of a hunting wyvern's piercing whistle, coming through the council chamber's window, was plainly audible in the intense si-lence which hovered above the table. All eyes were riveted to Sharleyan, and one or two faces were undeniably pale.

"My Lords, the . . . Knights of the Temple Lands decreed Charis' de-struction. They failed. I believe they will continue to fail. And I believe that if they *don't* fail, if they can decree the destruction of one realm for arbitrary reasons of their own, they can—and will—decree the destruction of others. I used the example of a ship at sea, and I chose it deliberately, for many reasons. We've navigated through many a storm together, since that day I first came to the throne, but the hurricane which is about to sweep across the face of Safehold is unlike any other storm we have ever seen. There will be no safe harbor against it, My Lords. It must be met and survived at sea, in the very teeth of its thunder and lightning and wind. Never doubt that. Never forget it. And, My Lords"—her eyes were hard as polished brown agates—"never forget who set that storm in motion."

Duke Halbrook Hollow's shoulders tightened, and his jaw clenched. He'd been dismayed enough when she refused to hand Gray Harbor to Tiang, but he'd swallowed it. And so had Tiang, although the Harchong-born bishop executor's fury had been obvious. Unfortunately for him, he'd demanded she surrender Gray Harbor to him, as Mother Church's representative in Chisholm, without reflecting upon the fact that—as Sharleyan herself had just stressed—it was "the Knights of the Temple Lands," and not the Church of God Awaiting, which had declared war upon Charis. Without specific directions from Zion and the Temple, Tiang had been unwilling to abandon the legal fiction that there was a difference between them.

Which doesn't mean anyone in the entire world believes there is, she told herself grimly, watching her uncle's expression and body language.

"I'm quite certain all of you have guessed that King Cayleb sent Earl Gray Harbor to us with the proposal of an alliance," she continued, speaking clearly and unhurriedly. "He's already returned our warships—such of them as survived the battle to which we were *ordered* to commit them, at any rate— and he's pointed out, with reason, that Chisholm and Charis have far more in common, when it comes to threats and enemies, than could ever divide us."

"Your Majesty, I beg you to think most carefully about these matters," Halbrook Hollow said, meeting his niece's eyes. "You've been very careful to refer only to 'the Knights of the Temple Lands,' and no one in this chamber can doubt the reason you have. Yet it isn't the Knights to whom Charis has bidden defiance. It's Mother Church herself. Whatever his reasons, and however warranted he may believe himself to be, Cayleb hasn't restricted himself to denouncing the attack launched upon him. No, Your Majesty. He's seen fit to defy Mother Church's authority to name her own archbishops. He's accused Mother Church herself of corruption and tyranny, and of betraying the will of God. He's informed the Grand Vicar himself that Charis will never again submit to the authority of Mother Church. Whatever justification he may feel he has—whatever justification *we* may feel he has—he's surely gone too far when he threatens the sanctity and supremacy of God's own Church."

He started to say something more, then cut himself off with a hard, tight shake of his head. It was a sharp, abrupt gesture, and silence gripped the council chamber once again in its wake. But now that silence was brittle, broken into fragments and heaped in the corners of every councilor's mind.

"Your Grace—Uncle," Sharleyan said softly, "I know how you feel on this issue. Believe me, I *know*. And I would not, for all the gold and power in the world, cause you the pain I know this is causing. Yet I have no choice. Chancellor Trynair and Vicar Zhaspahr have left me none. Either I must assist in the murder of an innocent victim, knowing Charis will be but the first of many victims, or else I must defy . . . the Knights of the Temple Lands."

"You're talking about *God's* Church, Sharleyan," Halbrook Hollow half whispered. "You can call it the Knights of the Temple Lands, if you wish, but the truth won't change."

"And neither will the fact that *they* started this war, Uncle Byrtrym. Neither will the fact that they sent no warning, no demands, no tribunals to investigate. They never even bothered to truly examine the facts at all. They simply *ordered* five realms to destroy a sixth, as if it were of no greater concern than deciding which pair of shoes to wear. Because it wasn't even worth their time to make certain that all of the thousands upon thousands of God's children they proposed to kill really needed to die. Because it was *their* decision, not His. Never His. *That* is the truth, as well, and you know it as well as I do."

"But even if that's all true," he replied, "think about where this must end. If you ally with Charis and Charis loses, then Chisholm will be destroyed as well. Yet terrible as that is, if you ally with Charis and Charis *wins*, you—*you*, Sharleyan—will be as responsible before God as Cayleb himself for destroying the authority of the Church Langhorne himself commanded us to obey in God's name for the preservation of our very souls."

"Yes, Uncle, I will be," she acknowledged quietly. "But the Church Langhorne commanded us to obey lies in the grip of *men*, and those men have betrayed their own responsibilities to God. If I support them, I acquiesce—I become their *accomplice*—in the murder of innocents and the perversion of God's *will* in the name of God's *Church*. I can't do that. I won't. Before God Himself, I won't."

Halbrook Hollow's face was drawn and white, and Sharleyan shook her own head sadly, but firmly.

"I said King Cayleb has proposed an alliance between our kingdoms," she said then, looking around the council chamber once more. "That statement was true enough, but it falls short of the full truth. Because, My Lords, the *full* truth is that Cayleb has proposed not mere alliance, but marriage."

An invisible lightning bolt struck that council chamber. Men jerked back from the table, faces startled, shocked, even frightened. Other men sat suddenly straighter, eyes brighter. But whatever their response, it was obvious not one of them had suspected what she had just told them.

Duke Halbrook Hollow stared at his niece in horror. She looked back at him, seeing the beloved uncle who, with Green Mountain, had been her strong shield and buckler. Who had helped to raise her. Who had watched with obvious pride as the child-princess became a queen in truth.

"Understand me, My Lords"—her voice was tempered steel—"there is no burden I will not bear in the service of Chisholm and of the people God has entrusted to my care. There is no danger I will not face. There is no choice I will refuse to make. I have thought, I have pondered, I have prayed, and only one answer presents itself. There is only one decision I can make without betraying my duty to God, my duty to Chisholm, and my duty to myself, and I have made it."

Halbrook Hollow was shaking his head mutely, again and again, his eyes like holes burned into his face. Sharleyan made herself ignore that, and her voice continued, strong and unflinching.

"Cayleb of Charis has offered honorable marriage, complete equality between Chisholm and Charis, and I have decided to accept that offer. *I have decided.* I do not intend to debate that decision. I do not intend to discuss it. And I *will* not change it. As Cayleb has said, and as God Himself has witnessed, *here* I stand."

.X.
Tellesberg Palace,
City of Tellesberg,
Kingdom of Charis

It was very late—or possibly very early, depending upon one's perspective—and Merlin Athrawes sat at the desk in his modest, if comfortable, quarters in Tellesberg Palace while his long fingers skillfully reassembled the pistol on his desk. If anyone had happened to open the door at that particular moment, they might have been just a bit curious as to why Captain Athrawes had chosen to perform that intricate task in the dark. Of course, the room *wasn't* dark for someone with a PICA's built-in light-gathering optics, but that didn't really matter one way or the other. Despite the fact that Merlin's eyes were open and clearly gazing at the pistol upon which he was working, he was actually watching something else entirely.

The most recent imagery from the SNARCs he had deployed across the surface of Safehold played itself behind those open eyes while he worked. As the struggle against the Group of Four and its proxies broadened and the events he found himself trying to keep track of snowballed, there was more and more of that imagery. In fact, there was quite simply too much of it for him to properly review, even with Owl's assistance. And the fact that, as the commander of Cayleb's personal guard detachment, he had even less free time in which to do the reviewing didn't help.

The last of the current day's imagery from Emerald finished, and he grimaced.

"Write that up for Wave Thunder, Owl," he directed. "Standard format."

"Yes, Lieutenant Commander," the distant AI said obediently, and Merlin nodded in satisfaction. The computer would use the graphics interface in the cavern in the Styvyn Mountains which Merlin had converted into his forward base here in Charis to produce a complete summary of the day's events in Emerald, in Merlin's handwriting, on proper Safeholdian stationery, complete with the occasional, carefully inserted correction and blot. When it was done, Owl would use another of the stealthed SNARCs to deliver it (and the other summaries Merlin had asked for) through Merlin's open window via tractor beam. Owl's writing standards weren't quite up to Merlin's own, but it was one way to get the necessary information written down and delivered to Wave Thunder. By now, the baron had to be wondering just how *Seijin* Merlin found time to jot down so many notes, but if he was, he'd very carefully not asked.

Merlin smiled in amusement at the thought, then refocused his attention on the pistol as he completed its reassembly. There'd really been no point in taking it apart in the first place, but he'd enjoyed the minor task. He'd discovered that he liked the way fine machinery fitted together, the way smooth and reliable function emerged from the careful assembly of all of the puzzle's many pieces. Besides, he'd wanted to see how the inside of this one actually looked.

The pistol in his hand was a perfect duplicate of one of the pair of pistols Seamount had presented to Merlin at the same time he presented a rather more finely ornamented pair to Cayleb. Appearances, however, could be deceiving, and *these* pistols had been manufactured by Owl, using the same fabrication unit in Nimue's Cave which had produced Merlin's battle steel katana, wakazashi, and armor. Outwardly, they might be indistinguishable from the originals, but internally there was one significant difference.

Every member of Cayleb's personal detachment had been issued his own pair of pistols. The decision had been made not to divert any significant manufacturing capacity away from the desperately needed rifled muskets, but given the nature of the Royal Guard's duties, Lock Island, Seamount, and Howsmyn had pretty much insisted upon producing enough of them for the Guard. They were part of the Guard's uniform now, and Seamount had designed sturdy, practical leather holsters for them. Overall, Merlin heartily approved, but even though the rifled pistols were deadly accurate, they still possessed one significant drawback. For all of its greater efficiency and reliability as compared to a *match*lock, a flintlock remained vulnerable to misfires, which wasn't something Merlin was prepared to put up with when it came to protecting Cayleb Ahrmahk's life.

Which was why *his* pistols, unlike those of anyone else on the entire planet, had hidden power cells built into their butts. When Merlin squeezed the trigger, the flintlock hammer snapped down, just like it was supposed to. And, at the same instant, the electronic igniter installed at the base of the pistol barrel flashed white-hot. One way or the other, Merlin reflected, that pistol *would* fire when he needed it to.

He chuckled softly at the thought, then slid both pistols into their waiting holsters, got up and walked across to his chamber's window to gaze out across the darkness of Tellesberg, sleeping under the light of the large single moon the "Archangels" had named Langhorne. It was a peaceful scene, and for just a moment, he felt a familiar, soul-deep longing for the merely mortal body of flesh and blood which had been Nimue Alban's. He could do marvelous, miraculous things with his PICA's molecular circuitry, sensors, and synthetic muscles. He could go without sleep, he could—theoretically, at least—live literally forever . . . assuming that he was, indeed, alive in the first place. But he could never again know what it was to collapse into peaceful, genuine sleep knowing it would wash away the fatigue he no longer felt. That had been taken from him forever with the death of Nimue's body.

Oh, stop whining *about it!* he told himself sharply. *Any time now you're going to start waxing maudlin over the fact that you're not subject to* tooth decay, *either!*

The thought made him chuckle, and he squared his shoulders, turning resolutely away from the window as he prepared to dive back into the SNARCs' reports once more.

▼   ▼   ▼

Cayleb Ahrmahk's eyes opened. He peered up into the darkness, then sat up as the crisp knock sounded again on his bedchamber door.

"Enter!" he called before whoever it was could knock a third time.

No one was going to get past bodyguards under the command of Merlin Athrawes unless they had a most legitimate reason for being here, and Cayleb's dignity wasn't so fragile that he had to insist on mountains of formal protocol. He climbed quickly out of bed, reaching for the robe Gahlvyn Daikyn had left in case he needed it. He was only halfway into it when the door opened.

"Your Majesty."

Merlin stood on the threshold, bowing slightly, and Cayleb's eyes widened. Even now, he didn't know everything Merlin was up to, but the fact that Captain Athrawes needed quite a lot of time to do whatever it was had been made abundantly clear. And since it seemed so much more convenient for him to do whatever it was in the hours of darkness, the night duty outside Cayleb's bedchamber almost always went to Lieutenant Franz Ahstyn, Merlin's second-in-command in Cayleb's personal guard detail.

Which made Merlin's sudden appearance . . . interesting.

And I hope "interesting" is all *it's going to be*, Cayleb reflected, remembering other midnight messages Merlin had brought him.

"Come in, Merlin," he said out loud, for the benefit of the other guardsmen, as he finished donning the robe and tied its sash. "Close the door."

"Of course, Your Majesty," Merlin murmured, stepping inside and pulling the door closed behind him.

"And now," Cayleb said a bit tartly as the door closed, "suppose you tell me why you've gotten me up in the middle of the night *this* time?"

"Because, Your Majesty, it isn't 'the middle of the night.' In fact, it's only about an hour until dawn, and it happens that in Chisholm, they're five hours ahead of us."

Cayleb's spine snapped straight and his eyes widened.

"I debated not telling you about it until after you decided to get up," Merlin continued. "Then it occurred to me that however justified I might be in waiting, you, with the impetuosity of youth, would probably fail to see it that way. Indeed, the more I thought about it, the more it occurred to me that, with that undeniable degree of unreasonableness I've noted in you before, upon occasion, you might have felt I'd been remiss, somehow, not to awaken you immediately. Still, it did seem that *one hour*, either way, wouldn't have made that much difference. But, despite my own feelings on the matter, as a loyal servant of the Crown, it was clearly my duty to—"

"Unless you want to discover whether or not it's possible for a mere mortal to throttle a *seijin*, I'd recommend telling me what you came here to say! And *not* what you came here to say about whether or not you should have waked me up!"

"Well, if you're going to be *that* way," Merlin sniffed. Cayleb balled one hand into a remarkably sinewy fist, and Merlin smiled.

"All right, Cayleb," he said in a much gentler voice. "I'm sorry. I just couldn't help teasing you."

"You," Cayleb said through gritted teeth, "have a very peculiar sense of humor. Did you know that?"

"Yes, I do." Merlin reached out and laid one hand on the king's shoulder.

"She's decided to say yes," he said.

"Quietly, damn your eyes!" Sir Dunkyn Yairley hissed. "You're *seamen*, not drunk whores at a wedding!"

Someone laughed softly, secure from identification in the darkness. Yairley couldn't be certain, but he rather suspected the sound had come from Stywyrt Mahlyk, his personal coxswain. It had certainly come from aft, and Mahlyk had the tiller as the launch moved steadily and, for the most part—despite Yairley's injunction to its crew—quietly through the water.

The chuckle certainly hadn't come from the seaman whose incautiously moving foot had elicited Yairley's gentle remonstrance when it knocked over one of the cutlasses piled on the launch's floorboards with a loud clang. On the other hand, that worthy, having been methodically kicked by two of his crewmates for his clumsiness, was unlikely to be making any more noise anytime soon, and Yairley knew it. Besides, these were all handpicked men, chosen for their experience. They knew what they were about.

So did Yairley, although it felt . . . peculiar to be personally leading what amounted to a glorified cutting-out expedition. As the captain of one of the Royal Charisian Navy's more powerful galleons, he'd thought this sort of nonsense was behind him. Unfortunately, this particular "cutting-out expedition" consisted of well over three hundred Marines and the next best thing to four hundred seamen, and that was a captain's command, wherever the men in question had come from.

He peered astern from his place in the launch's bow, trying to see the other boats. The overcast night was darker than the inside of Shan-wei's boot, and he could barely make out the two closest ones. All the others were completely invisible, and he told himself that was a good thing. If *he* couldn't see them, it was extremely unlikely that the defenders of North Bay could see them, either. Which, after all, was the entire point of launching the raid after moonset. Not that knowing all of that made him feel any happier about his own blindness.

Stop fretting, Dunkyn! he scolded himself. *You've got more than enough men for this business. You just don't like being out here.*

Well, no, if he was going to be honest, he *didn't* like being out here. That wasn't something an officer in the Royal Charisian Navy was supposed to admit, even to himself, however. They were all supposed to be brave, daring, and perpetually eager to close with the foe. Sir Dunkyn Yairley understood his duty, and he was prepared to do it unflinchingly, yet deep inside, he'd always questioned his own courage. He didn't really know about anyone else, but he'd never seen the signs of his own sweaty palms and knotted stomach muscles in his fellow officers.

That's just because they're better at hiding it than you are, he told himself. Which was all very well, and probably even true, but didn't make him feel one bit better at the moment. Of course—

"There, Sir!"

The whispered half exclamation interrupted his thought, and he turned his head as the young midshipman crouched in the bow beside him tapped his shoulder and pointed. Yairley peered in the indicated direction, straining his older, less acute eyes, then nodded sharply.

"Good lad, Master Aplyn-Ahrmahk," he said quietly, then looked aft to where he couldn't quite see Mahlyk in the stern sheets. "Come two points to starboard," he said. "And show the others a light."

He thought about the youngster beside him while he listened to the whispered repetition running aft, relayed from one rower to another until it reached Mahlyk. Bringing a royal duke—however he'd gotten to be one—along on a mission like this might not be the best way for a man's career to prosper. The Charisian tradition had always been that members of the royal house served their time in the Navy and took their chances just like anyone else, yet Yairley couldn't quite rid himself of the suspicion that a man who got the member of the royal house in question killed on his watch might find himself under just a *little* bit of a cloud. Still, keeping the lad wrapped up in cotton-silk wouldn't be doing him—or anyone else—any favors, either. And the captain had gone far enough to assign young Aplyn-Ahrmahk as his personal aide, which should keep him out of at least some potential trouble. And—

His thoughts broke off as he saw the faintest of glows when the seaman beside Mahlyk opened the shutter of the closed lantern for the benefit of the boats following astern of them while using his own body to shield it from anyone ashore.

A moment later, the launch altered course, the men pulling more strongly as Mahlyk steered for the dim points of light the alert midshipman had pointed out to Yairley.

▼   ▼   ▼

Major Bahrkly Harmyn tipped back in his chair, stretched, and yawned mightily. It was almost Langhorne's Watch, that period between midnight and the first true hour of the day. In theory, Harmyn should be spending that time meditating on all of God's gifts and his duty to the Archangels and to God. In fact, he was spending it trying to stay awake.

He finished yawning and let the chair tip forward again. The oil lamps filled his sparsely furnished office with light, although it was scarcely what anyone would have called bright. Somewhere on the other side of the office door, there were two clerks and an orderly, who were undoubtedly also doing their best to stay awake. Of course, they might be finding it a little easier than Harmyn was. They probably hadn't spent most of the night before drinking in one of the waterfront taverns the way Harmyn had.

The way I wouldn't *have, if I'd had any idea* I *was going to get stuck with the duty tonight*, he thought sourly.

Unfortunately, his superiors hadn't asked him about that when his name came up as the replacement for Major Tyllytsyn. Tyllytsyn wasn't going to be holding down the night watch for a while. Still, he was more fortunate than his horse had been. The beast had put its foot into a lizard hole and, like its rider, broken a leg. But while Tyllytsyn's leg had been set and wrapped up in plaster, the horse had simply been put down. And one Major Harmyn had been informed that he was going to be holding down Tyllytsyn's night duties until the colonel told him differently.

At least it's not likely anything's going to happen, he thought.

▼   ▼   ▼

Captain Yairley watched and waited impatiently as HMS *Torrent*'s second cutter blended out of the night. He was glad to see it—Lieutenant Symyn, *Torrent*'s first lieutenant, was officially his second-in-command—but at least one launch and the thirty-five men in it had obviously gone astray.

Not surprisingly. Indeed, if no one had gone astray, *that* would have been grounds for outright astonishment, not simple surprise. Every officer in the Charisian Navy knew the first law of battle was that anything which could go wrong, would. Besides, actually keeping a couple of dozen launches, cutters, and gigs together while rowing for almost twelve miles through a pitch-black night would have qualified as a miracle in any sea officer's book.

The problem was that Yairley couldn't see a thing beyond his immediate position, except for occasional dim smears of light. He'd put together the simplest plan he could, then briefed all of the officers involved in tonight's festivities as carefully as possible before they ever embarked. Each of them had had his particular role explained to him at least twice, and each of them had also been given his contingency instructions in case someone else failed to reach his intended destination in time. That didn't necessarily mean the officers in question had actually understood their instructions, however. And even if they had, there was no way of predicting what sort of navigational errors the vagaries of wind and tide might have induced. It was even theoretically possible that *only* the five boats Yairley could actually see had managed to reach their assigned objective at all.

Stop that! He shook his head. *Of course they're out there . . . somewhere. And every one of them is waiting for your signal.*

Symyn's cutter came alongside Yairley's launch. Hands reached out, easing the two boats together, and Yairley leaned across towards the lieutenant.

"I think we're in position," he said quietly. "I'm not positive, though. This"—he waved one hand at the wharf in whose shadow the boats bobbed up and down on the swell—"should be the east pier if we *are* where we're supposed to be."

Symyn nodded as if he hadn't already known that perfectly well, and Yairley felt his mouth twitch in a tight grin.

"Whether it's the *east* pier or not, it's *a* pier, and it'll just have to do. You take your cutter and *Defender*'s launches and swing around to the far side. I'll take the other boats down this side."

"Aye, aye, Sir," Symyn acknowledged. Hissed orders were passed, and Symyn and the assigned boats moved steadily away.

Yairley gave them several minutes to get into position on the far side of the pier. Then his launch led the remaining boats down the nearer side towards shore, keeping to the densest, darkest shadows cast by the galleons moored to it on either side.

▼   ▼   ▼

The pair of sentries on the east pier stood gazing glumly out into the darkness. There were very few duties which could possibly match the boredom quotient of watching over the deserted waterfront of a thoroughly blockaded port. Normally, they could at least have looked forward to the possibility of being summoned by the local city watch to help deal with a drunken brawl somewhere. But the seamen whose ships had been caught inside the blockade had run out of money with which to carouse, and the local government had decreed a curfew, if only to get the pestiferous merchant crews off the streets at night. Which meant they had absolutely nothing to do except stand there, looking out to sea as if their single-handed devotion to watchfulness could somehow prevent a Charisian attack.

Besides, while they stood out here in the dark, they knew perfectly well that the company of army troops which was supposed to be waiting, poised in instant readiness to respond to any alarm they might raise, was undoubtedly shooting dice in the barracks. It wasn't so much that they begrudged fellow soldiers their entertainment as it was that they resented being excluded from it. Still—

One of them heard something over the sigh of wind and steady slopping of waves. He didn't know what it was, but he began turning in its direction just as a brawny arm went around his neck from behind. His astonished hands flew up instinctively, prying at that strangling bar of bone and muscle, but then a needle-pointed dirk drove up under his ribs to find his heart, and he abruptly lost all interest in whatever it was he might have heard.

His companion on the far side of the pier had even less warning than that, and Captain Yairley grunted in approval as he climbed up the ladder from his launch, Aplyn-Ahrmahk at his heels, and observed the two bodies.

"Good work," he told the much-tattooed senior seaman who had led the removal of the sentries. The grin he got in reply would have done credit to a kraken, and Yairley wondered once again exactly what the man had done before joining the Navy.

Probably better not to know, he told himself once more, and stood back as the rest of the launch's crew swarmed up onto the pier.

He counted noses as carefully as he could in the darkness while the seamen and Marines formed up into their prearranged groups. Cutlasses and bayonets glinted dully in the dim lights of the pier's lanterns, and he watched as the Marines carefully primed their muskets. The fact that the newfangled "flintlocks" didn't need a lit length of slow match was a blessing, since it meant they could be carried ready to fire without looking like a lost flock of blink lizards through the darkness. On the other hand, it also increased the possibility of accidental discharges because it deprived a musketeer of that visual cue that his weapon was ready to fire. Which was why Yairley had given specific, bloodthirsty orders about the dreadful fate awaiting anyone who had dared to prime his musket during the long boat trip in.

Besides, if I'd let them, the spray would damned well have soaked the priming.

"Ready, Sir," Lieutenant Symyn said quietly, and Yairley turned to find the younger officer at his elbow. Symyn, he observed sourly, was almost beaming in anticipation.

"Good," he said, instead of what he was actually thinking. "Remember, wait until you hear the grenades."

"Aye, aye, Sir," Symyn said, as if Yairley hadn't made exactly that same point in the pre-attack briefings at least three times.

▼   ▼   ▼

In point of fact, the sentries on the pier had been doing their fellows an injustice. There were no dice games tonight, because their previous evening's entertainment had been interrupted by an unanticipated visit from the company commander, who had been less than amused. After a few pithy observations on their state of discipline, their readiness, and probable ancestry, Major Tyllytsyn had informed them of the unpleasant fate in store for anyone else he found diverting himself during duty hours. Despite his subsequent broken leg (which one or two unworthy souls had suggested might represent divine retribution), they had no doubt he'd passed his observations on to Major Harmyn. Who, unfortunately, had a reputation for being even less understanding than Major Tyllytsyn. Under the circumstances, it had seemed wise to exercise a little discretion for the next five-day or so.

So, instead of clumping together in the middle of their barracks floors with their dice boxes and cards, they were engaged in dozens of homey little tasks—mending uniforms, polishing brightwork, cleaning gear, or honing the edges of cutlasses, dirks, and swords.

The sound of breaking glass intruded rudely. Heads turned towards the sound and eyebrows rose in surprise that turned abruptly into something else as the iron spheres with their sputtering fuses thumped down on the floor.

One trooper, faster than his companions, dove towards the nearest grenade. He snatched it up and whirled to throw it back out the window, but he didn't have quite enough time. He got the throw off, but the grenade had traveled less than four feet when it exploded, killing him almost instantly.

It wouldn't really have mattered if the fuse on that particular grenade had been a bit longer. It was only one of a dozen, and the barracks' peaceful order disintegrated into chaos, horror, and screams as all of them detonated almost simultaneously.

▼   ▼   ▼

"*Now!*" Lieutenant Hahl Symyn shouted as the grenade explosions echoed from behind him.

His waiting parties of seamen had already broken down into two-man teams. Now the member of each team with the slow match lit one of his fellow's prepared incendiaries, then stood back while doors were kicked in and windows were smashed. The blazing compounds of pitch, naphtha, and a sprinkling of gunpowder sailed through the sudden openings into the dockside warehouses, while other teams charged the galleons and harbor craft tied up alongside the pier.

Smoke billowed up and lurid flames began to leap, turning the pitch-black night into something very different. More flames erupted as other incendiaries ignited their targets, and scattered voices began to shout in alarm as the town of North Bay abruptly awakened. Muskets cracked as the Marines detailed to Symyn's support attacked the harbor batteries from behind. Only two guns in each battery were actually manned after nightfall, and the handful of sleepy gunners were no match for the Marines storming in among them out of the darkness. Still more fires ignited along the harbor front, and a sharp, thunderous explosion echoed as one of the incendiaries found an unexpected store of gunpowder in a harbor barge beside a galleon undergoing conversion into a commerce raider. The explosion set the ship heavily ablaze and hurled flaming fragments into three other vessels and onto at least a half-dozen warehouse and tavern roofs.

"Look, Sir!" one of Symyn's men shouted, and the lieutenant saw the bright, sudden sparkle of more musketry against the pitch-blackness to the west of the city.

"It's the Marines!" he shot back. "No telling how long Major Zheffyr will be able to slow the bastards up, so hop to it!"

"Aye, aye, Sir!"

▼   ▼   ▼

Major Harmyn lurched to his feet as the explosions and screams erupted. He grabbed up his sword belt and dashed for the office door, swinging the belt around him as he ran. His clerk and orderly were still coming out of their chairs as he erupted into the anteroom.

"Get your weapons, goddamn it!" Harmyn barked, and charged out the office block's front door onto the parade ground between the two long rectangles of the barracks.

Flames were already beginning to dance and glare through the barracks windows, and he heard a second wave of explosions as the Charisian seamen threw another dozen grenades into each building. Some of the wounded's shrieks ended abruptly, but other sounds of agony replaced them.

Harmyn's belly knotted as he realized the attackers had already completely eliminated his borrowed company as a cohesive fighting force. He didn't know how many of "his" men were actually dead or wounded, but even the ones who weren't would be too demoralized and terrified to offer any sort of effective resistance.

And even if Tyllytsyn might have been able to rally them, I *won't be,* he thought grimly. *They don't even* know *me, so why in Hell should they listen to me in a mess like this?*

The beginning sputter and crackle of musketry from the west told him no one was likely to arrive to reinforce him, so—

Major Bahrkly Harmyn hadn't thought about the way he'd just silhouetted himself against the lit window of the orderly room behind him. Nor did he ever . . . just as he never heard the sharp "crack" of the rifled musket which killed him.

▼   ▼   ▼

Sir Dunkyn Yairley allowed himself to feel a profound sense of relief as he observed the same musket fire Symyn had seen and Harmyn had heard. Obviously, the Marines *had* gotten into position to cover the road from the main fortress west of the town. According to their spies' reports, there were at least three thousand men in that fortress' garrison. It was unlikely Major Zheffyr's two hundred Marines could hold them off forever, but surprise and confusion ought to keep them tied up for at least a while. Besides, Zheffyr's rate of fire and ring-mounted bayonets ought to go a fair way towards equalizing the odds between them.

A cannon boomed from the fortress. Yairley had no idea what the gunners behind it thought they were firing at. God knew the fortress' garrison had to be hopelessly confused by the sudden eruption of explosions and flames from the quietly sleeping town below its lofty headland perch. For all Yairley knew, they actually thought they'd seen Charisian galleons standing in to the attack.

At least two dozen ships were thoroughly ablaze. More were smoldering, and the stiff breeze was blowing sparks, cinders, and flaming debris from one ship to another. The warehouses which served the harbor were taking fire nicely, as well. Yairley hoped the flames wouldn't spread to the city proper, but he wasn't going to lose any sleep over the possibility.

He looked out across the black mirror of the harbor, painted crimson with the rising torrents of flame, and saw more of his boats pulling strongly towards the merchant vessels anchored farther out. He also saw more than a few boats pulling *away* from those vessels, as their vastly outnumbered anchor watches of merchant seamen beat hasty retreats.

They're probably going to hear about things like "deserting their posts" later this morning, Yairley thought. *Not that they could have accomplished anything—except getting themselves killed—if they'd stayed.*

"All right, Master Aplyn-Ahrmahk," he said to the midshipman at his side. "Let's see to starting a few more fires of our own, and then I think it'll be time to go."

"Aye, aye, Sir!" Aplyn-Ahrmahk replied with a huge grin, and twitched his head at Stywyrt Mahlyk. "Come along, Cox'in!" he said, and went trotting along the waterfront, blowing on his slow match while Mahlyk hauled out the first incendiary and Yairley tagged along behind.

.XII.
Royal Palace,
City of Eraystor,
Princedom of Emerald

Prince Nahrmahn looked up from the latest dispatch and grimaced. "Well," he said mildly, "that's irritating."

The Earl of Pine Hollow couldn't quite hide his disbelief as he looked across the table at his cousin. Nahrmahn saw his expression and snorted in harsh amusement. Then he laid the dispatch on the tabletop beside his plate and reached for a fresh slice of melon.

"I take it you were expecting a somewhat . . . stronger reaction, Trahvys?"

"Well . . . yes," Pine Hollow admitted.

"Why?" Nahrmahn popped a bite of melon into his mouth and chewed. "Aside from the fact that Bishop Executor Wyllys' permission to use the church semaphore network means we got the news a little quicker than we might have, there's no real surprise here. Is there?"

"I suppose not," Pine Hollow said slowly, trying to analyze Nahrmahn's mood. There was something . . . peculiar about it.

"Militarily, burning North Bay to the ground—although, mind you, I expect we'll find the damage is less extensive than these first reports might indicate—doesn't make a lot of sense," Nahrmahn acknowledged. "*Politically*, though, it makes perfect sense."

"Meaning what, My Prince?"

Personally, Pine Hollow couldn't see any sense in the attack at all. Aside from two small war galleys which had been anchored there, and half a dozen of the merchantmen Commodore Zhaztro had been converting into light cruisers for commerce-raiding purposes, most of the damage which had been inflicted struck him as pure, wanton destruction. The merchant ships tied up at North Bay's wharves and the idle warehouses, filled with goods which were simply collecting dust in the face of the Charisian Navy's blockade, hadn't been what *he* would have considered militarily important targets, at any rate. Not only that, but North Bay was the next best thing to seven hundred miles from Eraystor, and not exactly the largest and most important town in the princedom, either.

"Meaning that Cayleb—or, more probably, Admiral Rock Point, acting within the general scope of Cayleb's instructions—is sending me a message."

Nahrmahn cut another piece of melon and regarded it critically for a moment before sending it after its predecessor. Then he looked back across at Pine Hollow.

"They're demonstrating that as long as they have control of the sea, they can do this to us whenever they want. You might think of it as a pointed reminder that despite everything Commodore Zhaztro can do, we can't really hurt *them*, but they can certainly hurt *us*. It's a point I was discussing with Bishop Executor Wyllys just yesterday, as a matter of fact."

"Really?" Pine Hollow's eyes had narrowed speculatively. He'd known about the meeting between Nahrmahn and Bishop Executor Wyllys Graisyn, the highest-ranking churchman in the princedom, given Archbishop Lyam Tyrn's abrupt decision to return to Zion to . . . confer with his colleagues as soon as word of Darcos Sound reached Eraystor. But his cousin hadn't told him what that meeting had been about. Until now, at least, he thought as Nahrmahn gave him a somewhat off-center smile.

"The good Bishop Executor is concerned about the degree of our commitment to the ongoing war against Charis."

"*Commitment?*" Pine Hollow blinked, then shook his head in disbelief. "He thinks that after Darcos Sound and Haarahld's death we think Cayleb is going to welcome us as *allies?*" he asked incredulously, and Nahrmahn chuckled mirthlessly.

"I think that letter from Archbishop Maikel—excuse me, from the apostate heretic and traitor, Maikel Staynair—to the Grand Vicar has Graisyn a bit . . . rattled, let's say. I don't think he put any more credence in the reports about Haarahld's violations of the Proscriptions than we ever did. Not, at least, as long as it was supposed to be a nice, simple matter of wrecking Charis from one end to the other according to Clyntahn's timetable. Now that the boot is on the other foot and those idiots in the Group of Four have managed to drive Cayleb into outright public defiance, he's feeling just a tad *exposed* here in our welcoming bosom."

"Nahrmahn," Pine Hollow's tone was as worried as his expression as his initial incredulity faded into something else, "it's not safe to be—"

"What?" The prince's eyes challenged him across the table. "Honest? Straightforward?"

"I'm only saying I'd be astonished if the Inquisition didn't have ears closer to you than you know," Pine Hollow said soberly.

"I know exactly who the Inquisition's chief agent here in the palace is, Trahvys. In fact, he's been reporting exactly what I wanted reported for about three years now."

"You *bribed* an agent of the *Inquisition?*"

"Oh, don't be so shocked!" Nahrmahn scolded. "Why *shouldn't* Clyntahn's spies be bribable? Only a drooling idiot who was also blind and deaf—which no agent of the Inquisition is likely to be, I think you'll agree—could be unaware of the graft and bribery that goes on every day in the Temple itself! When the entire Church hierarchy is as corrupt and venal as a batch of dockside pimps selling their own sisters, why shouldn't their agents be just as corruptible as their masters in Zion?"

"You're talking about God's Church," Pine Hollow pointed out stiffly.

"I'm not talking about God, and I'm not talking about His Church," Nahrmahn shot back. "I'm talking about the Church that's been taken over by people like Zhaspahr Clyntahn, Allayn Maigwair, and Zahmsyn Trynair. Do you really think for a moment that the Group of Four gives a good goddamn what *God* wants the Church to be doing? Or that anyone else on the Council of Vicars is going to risk his own sweet, rosy arse by standing *up* to Clyntahn and the others just because they happen to be lying, self-serving bastards?"

Pine Hollow was considerably more than simply shocked. Nahrmahn had grown steadily more open in his disgruntlement with the Temple since Darcos Sound, but he'd never before expressed himself that frankly about the

Church and the men who controlled its policies. Oh, he'd never made any secret of his opinion of Vicar Zhaspahr and his cronies, either, at least with his cousin, but he'd never openly extended his contempt for the Grand Inquisitor and the Group of Four to the entire Church hierarchy!

"What's the matter, Trahvys?" Nahrmahn asked more gently. "Are you shocked by my lack of piety?"

"No," Pine Hollow said slowly.

"Yes, you are," Nahrmahn corrected in that same gentle voice. "You think I don't believe in God, or that I've decided to reject His plan for Safehold. And you're afraid that if Graisyn or the Inquisition figure out the way I actually feel, they'll decide to make an example out of me . . . and maybe out of you, as well, since you're not only my first councilor but my cousin."

"Well, when you put it that way, you may have a point," Pine Hollow conceded even more slowly.

"Of course I do. And I'm not surprised that *you're* surprised to hear me say it, either. It's the first time I've ever expressed myself quite this frankly to anyone, except possibly Ohlyvya. But I think it's time I discussed the matter with someone besides my wife, under the circumstances. Well, someone besides my wife and Uncle Hanbyl, I suppose, if I'm going to be completely accurate."

"Under *which* circumstances?" Pine Hollow asked warily, and there was active alarm in his eyes now.

There was a reason his anxiety level had just soared to entirely new heights, because Hanbyl Baytz, the Duke of Solomon, was not simply his and Nahrmahn's uncle. Despite the fact that he was over seventy, Solomon remained vigorous and sharp as a razor. Physically, he was very nearly Nahrmahn's antithesis; in every other sense, he and the prince were very much alike, except for the fact that, unlike his nephew, Solomon abhorred politics. Little though he might like the "great game," though, there'd never been the least question about either his competence or his loyalty to the family interests, or to Nahrmahn himself. Which was why he was the commander of the Emeraldian Army. It was a post to which he was well suited, and one which allowed him to spend as little time as humanly possible in Eraystor, dealing with politics.

Which, Pine Hollow reflected now, *has served Nahrmahn well upon occasion. Uncle Hanbyl is the dagger in his sheath, but he's so much "out of sight, out of mind" that even clever people have a tendency to leave him out of their calculations.*

"There are two separate things to consider here, Trahvys," Nahrmahn said, in response to his question. "Well, three, actually."

He pushed his plate aside and leaned forward, his face and body language both unwontedly serious.

"First, from a political and military standpoint, Emerald is fucked," he said bluntly. "And, no, I didn't need Uncle Hanbyl to tell me that. Anytime Cayleb wants to put troops ashore, supported from the sea, he can do it. That's one of the things that little business in North Bay was supposed to bring to my attention, in case it had managed to escape me thus far. For the moment, he's probably still building up his troop strength; God knows the Charisian Marines are good, but he didn't have a lot of them when this whole business started. On the other hand, we have even less in the way of an army, don't we? Especially given how much of it was serving as Marines when our navy suffered its little mishap. It's not going to be all that much longer before he's ready to come calling here in Eraystor, probably with a siege train of artillery in tow to knock on any doors that get in his way, and I doubt very much that Uncle Hanbyl is going to be able to do much more than inconvenience him when he does.

"Second, from a diplomatic standpoint, our *good* friend Hektor isn't about to stick his neck out to help us in any way. And I'll be deeply surprised if Sharleyan doesn't decide she'd rather be allied to Charis than to us or to Hektor, under the circumstances. Which means we're . . . 'swinging in the wind,' is the term I want, I believe. We're the most exposed, we're the ones who tried to assassinate Cayleb, and we're the ones who don't have a single hope this side of Hell that anyone is going to come sailing to our rescue.

"And, third . . . *third*, Trahvys, every single word Staynair and Cayleb have said about the Group of Four, the Grand Vicar, and the Church herself is true. You think that just because I recognize the corruption of men like Clyntahn and Trynair and their sycophants on the Council of Vicars I don't believe in *God*?" The prince's laugh was a harsh bark. "Of course I believe in *Him*—I just don't believe in the bastards who've hijacked His Church! In point of fact, I think Staynair and Cayleb have the right idea . . . *if* they can make it stand up. And that's exactly why Graisyn is so concerned, the reason he keeps pushing us so hard to figure out some way to take the offensive, keeps probing to see how 'loyal' I am to Hektor."

"And how loyal *are* you, My Prince?" Pine Hollow asked softly.

"To Hektor?" Nahrmahn's lip curled. "About as loyal as *he* is to *us*—which is to say I'm just as loyal as it will take to get into reach of his throat with a nice sharp knife. Or do you mean to the Church?"

Pine Hollow said nothing. He didn't need to, for his expression said it all.

"My loyalty to the Church extends exactly as far as the reach of the Inquisition," Nahrmahn said flatly. "It's time we stop confusing the Church with God, Trahvys. Or do you think God would have permitted Charis to completely gut the combined fleets of an alliance that outnumbered it five-to-one if Haarahld had actually been defying His will?"

Pine Hollow swallowed hard, and the pit of his stomach was a hollow, singing void. Deep inside him somewhere a schoolboy was repeating the catechism in a desperate gabble of a voice while he hunched down and stuffed his fingers into his ears.

"Nahrmahn," he said very, very quietly, "you can't be thinking what I think you're thinking."

"No?" Nahrmahn tilted his head to one side. "Why not?"

"Because, in the end, Charis is *going* to lose. It can't be any other way. Not when the Church controls all of the great kingdoms completely. Not when its purse is so deep and so much of the world's total population lives on Haven and Howard."

"Don't be too certain of that." Nahrmahn leaned back, his eyes intent. "Oh, I know the 'Group of Four' sees it that way. Then again, we've just had a rather pointed lesson in the fallibility of their judgment, now haven't we? I suspect they're about to find out that the world is less monolithic than they'd been assuming, and that's going to come as an even more unpleasant shock to them. All Cayleb really needs to do is to survive long enough for his example to spread, Trahvys. *That's* what has Graisyn running so scared. I'm not the only ruler or noble who understands what's going on in the Council of Vicars right now. If Charis is able to defy the Church, others are going to be tempted to follow Cayleb's example. And if that happens, the Church is going to find herself much too busy putting out local forest fires to put together the kind of fleet it would take to break through the Royal Charisian Navy. And that assumes Charis is trying to stand off the Church all by itself."

"But—"

"Think about it, Trahvys," Nahrmahn commanded, overriding Pine Hollow's attempt to object. "It's not going to be long before Sharleyan becomes at least Charis' de facto ally. For all I know, she may choose to make it official and join him in openly defying Clyntahn and his cronies. When that happens, Hektor is going to find himself flanked by enemies, cut off from anything the Church could do to help him. And when Sharleyan and Cayleb split Corisande and Zebediah up between them, and when Cayleb adds *us* to Charis proper, he and Sharleyan between them will control over a third of the total surface of Safehold. Of course they won't have anywhere near as large a fraction of the world's *people*, but they *will* have most of the world's naval power, a lot of room to expand into, and all of the resources they'll need for their economies . . . or their military power. How easy do you think the Church is going to find it to squash him after that?"

Pine Hollow sat silent, his eyes worried, and Nahrmahn waited while his cousin worked his way through the same logic chain. The earl, Nahrmahn knew, was cautious by nature. More than that, Pine Hollow's younger brother was an upper-priest of the Order of Pasquale, serving in the Republic of Siddarmark and about due to be elevated to the episcopate. It was entirely possible that Nahrmahn's frankness was more than Pine Hollow was pre-pared to accept.

"No," the earl said finally. "No, the Church isn't going to find it easy. Not if it works out the way you're predicting."

"And *should* the Church find it easy?" Nahrmahn asked softly, deliber-ately pushing his cousin still further.

"No," Pine Hollow sighed, and his expression was no longer uncertain, although Nahrmahn doubted the profound sorrow it mirrored struck Pine Hollow as an improvement. "No. You're right about that, too, Nahrmahn. The Group of Four aren't the true problem, are they? They're the symp-tom."

"Exactly." Nahrmahn reached out and placed one plump hand on Pine Hollow's forearm. "I don't know whether or not it's possible for the Church to reform herself internally. I do know that before the Group of Four and the other vicars like them allow that to happen, there's going to be bloodshed and slaughter on a scale no one's ever seen since the overthrow of Shan-wei."

"What do you want to do about it?" Pine Hollow managed a wan smile. "It's not like you to drop something like this on me across the breakfast table unless you've already got a plan in mind, My Prince."

"No, I don't suppose it is." Nahrmahn sat back again and reached for his temporarily abandoned plate. His eyes fell to his hands as he meticulously sliced the remaining melon into bite-sized pieces.

"I need to send a message of my own to Cayleb," he said, never looking away from his knife and fork. "I need someone who can convince him I'm prepared to surrender to him. That he doesn't need to keep burning my cities and killing my subjects to make his point."

"He's made it pretty clear he wants your head, Nahrmahn. From the tone of his comments, I don't think he's going to be very happy about settling for anything short of that."

"I know." The prince's smile was more of a grimace than anything else, but there might have been a little actual humor in it. "I know, and I suppose that if he really *insists* upon it, he'll undoubtedly get it in the end, anyway. It's a pity Mahntayl decided to run off to the mainland rather than coming here. I might have been able to convince Cayleb of my sincerity by offering him the 'Earl of Hanth's' head as a substitute, as it were. Still, I may be able to demonstrate to him that a man of my talents and experience would be more valuable working for him than fertilizing a garden plot somewhere behind his palace."

"And if you can't?" Pine Hollow asked very quietly.

"If I can't, I can't." Nahrmahn shrugged far more philosophically than Pine Hollow felt sure he would have been able to manage under the same cir-cumstances. "I can always hope he'll settle for life imprisonment in some only moderately unpleasant dungeon somewhere. And even if he doesn't, at least Cayleb isn't the sort to carry out any sort of reprisals against Ohlyvya or the children. Which"—he looked up and met Pine Hollow's eyes squarely—"is about the best I could hope for anyway, if he has to land an invasion force. Except that, this way, we get to skip the bit where thousands of my subjects get killed first."

Pine Hollow sat looking into his cousin's eyes and realized that possibly for the first time since Nahrmahn had ascended to the throne of Emerald, his prince had abandoned all pretense. It came as something of a shock, after all these years, but Nahrmahn was serious.

"You can't just make peace with Cayleb, even surrender to him, without Graisyn and the rest of the clergy going up in flames behind you," the earl said. "You know that, don't you?"

"Graisyn, yes. And probably most of the bishops, at the very least," Nahrmahn conceded. "On the other hand, most of our upper-priests—even our itinerant bishops—are Emeraldians. We're almost as bad as Charis in that respect. Frankly, that's one of the things that has Graisyn running so scared, and I strongly suspect he has good reason for it. At any rate, I've . . . discussed this matter with Uncle Hanbyl at some length."

"I see." Pine Hollow leaned back, the fingers of his right hand drumming slowly, rhythmically, on the arm of his chair while he thought.

Nahrmahn's point about the composition of the Emeraldian clergy was well taken. Whether or not the division between the lower-ranking, native-born clergy and their foreign-born ecclesiastical superiors would even begin to translate into the sort of support for schism which Cayleb had discovered in Charis was another, more complicated calculation. And, the first councilor admitted to himself, it wasn't one to which he himself had given the careful consideration it no doubt merited.

Probably, he acknowledged to himself, *because I didn't want to think about this possibility at all until Nahrmahn rubbed my nose in it.*

But if Nahrmahn had discussed it with Duke Solomon, and if Solomon had said what Nahrmahn appeared to be suggesting he had, then Pine Hollow was prepared to assume that the prince's estimate of how the clergy would react—and whether or not Nahrmahn could survive their reaction—was probably accurate. And when it came right down to it, the Church's reaction was the only potential domestic opposition he truly had to fear. Like the Ahrmahks in Charis, although for rather different reasons and in rather a different fashion, the House of Baytz had centralized political power in its own grasp. Nahrmahn's father had deprived the feudal magnates of their personal standing armies (not without a certain degree of bloodshed, in some cases), and Nahrmahn had gone even farther in subordinating the aristocracy to the Crown. Not only that, but the Commons in the Emeraldian Parliament, such as it was and what there was of it, had strongly supported both Nahrmahn and his father in their efforts to restrict the power of their nobly born landlords. That tradition of support would *probably* carry over to Nahrmahn's response to the present crisis, as well.

And in this case, both the aristocracy and the commoners of Emerald would almost certainly find themselves in general agreement. If the religious elements were subtracted from consideration, both of them would undoubtedly support a settlement with Charis—probably even an outright surrender *to* Charis. Despite the traditional rivalry between Emerald and Charis, the Ahrmahks had a reputation as reasonable rulers. It would be difficult to convince anyone, on a purely secular level, that finding themselves under Cayleb of Charis' rule would be any sort of personal disaster. And completely rational self-interest and the desire to avoid the destruction and bloodshed of an outright Charisian invasion would make convincing them of that even more difficult.

That was obviously Nahrmahn's reading of the situation, at any rate, and the prince had an impressive track record when it came to assessing and accurately predicting the reactions of Emerald's usual power brokers.

On the other hand, he has *been wrong a time or two before,* Pine Hollow reminded himself. *Not often, though. And unlike some people, he doesn't have a tendency to convince himself that what he wants the truth to be automatically* is *the truth.*

Assuming he wasn't wrong, and assuming the preparations Pine Hollow had no doubt Solomon was even then very quietly making were effective, then Nahrmahn could almost certainly survive negotiating with Cayleb. Whether or not he could survive the *outcome* of those negotiations with his head still attached to the rest of his body was another question entirely, of course. And in all honesty, Pine Hollow wasn't prepared to offer any better than barely even odds in favor of the possibility that he could, which could have most unpleasant consequences for the first councilor, as well. Still . . .

"If you really mean all of that," the earl heard his own voice saying, "then I suppose you should probably send the most senior diplomat you can to open the negotiations. Someone highly enough placed in your confidence that Cayleb might actually believe anything he said for at least five seconds or so."

"Really?" There was a most atypical warmth in Nahrmahn's smile. "Did you have anyone in mind, Trahvys?" he asked.

.XIII.
Tellesberg Cathedral
and
Royal Palace,
City of Tellesberg,
Kingdom of Charis

The organ began its majestic prelude, and the hundreds of people crammed into Tellesberg Cathedral rose to stand in their pews. The glorious notes sped through the incense-scented air on golden wings of sound, and then the choir burst into song.

The cathedral's doors swung open, and the familiar Wednesday morning procession of scepter-bearers, candle-bearers, and thurifers moved forward into the welcoming splendor of that majestic hymn. Acolytes and under-priests followed the procession's advance guard, and Archbishop Maikel Staynair followed behind them, in turn.

Merlin Athrawes watched from his post in the royal box, twenty feet above the cathedral's floor, with familiar mixed feelings. The Church was so much a part of every Safeholdian's life that moments like this were inescapable, and sheer immersion seemed to be wearing away at least some of his original outrage.

But only some *of it,* he told himself. *Only some of it.*

The procession moved steadily, majestically forward, and the archbishop moved at its heart. But Maikel Staynair's idea of a proper procession wasn't quite like that of other archbishops, and Merlin smiled as Staynair paused to lay one hand on the curly-haired head of a little girl in blessing as her father held her up.

Other hands reached out to touch the archbishop as he passed, and other children's heads awaited his blessing. Those sophisticated other archbishops would undoubtedly have looked down upon Staynair's "simpleminded" pastoral abandonment of an archbishop's proper dignity. Then again, those sophisticated other archbishops would never have been the focus of the intensely personal love and trust Maikel Staynair evoked from the people of *his* archbishopric. Of course, there were—

Merlin Athrawes' thoughts broke off with guillotine suddenness as purposeful movement swirled abruptly in the cathedral's nave.

▼   ▼   ▼

Archbishop Maikel laid his hand on another youngster's head, murmuring a word of blessing. He knew his frequent stops provoked generally tolerant exasperation among his acolytes and assisting clergy. On the other hand, they knew better than to protest, of course, even if it did make the proper choreography of the Church's ironclad liturgy a bit more difficult. There were some responsibilities—and joys—of any priest's calling which Maikel Staynair refused to sacrifice to the "dignity" of his ecclesiastic office.

He turned back to the procession, bowing his head while one corner of his mind once more reviewed the day's sermon. It was time he began emphasizing that—

The sudden coalescence of movement took him as much by surprise as it did anyone else in the cathedral. His head snapped back up as someone's hands closed upon his arms. The two men who had abruptly forced their way into the procession jerked him around, turning him to one side, and he was far too astonished to offer any sort of resistance. No one *ever* laid hands upon the clergy of Mother Church. The action was so totally unheard of that every worshipper in the cathedral was just as astounded as Staynair. Only those closest to him could actually see what was happening, but the abrupt interruption of the procession turned heads, snapped eyes around.

The archbishop's mind worked more rapidly than most, yet he was only beginning to realize what was happening when he saw the dagger in the third man's hand. The dagger which, in defiance of every tradition of the Church of God Awaiting, had been brought into the cathedral concealed under an assassin's tunic.

"In the name of the *true* Church!" the assassin shouted, and the dagger started forward.

▼ ▼ ▼

Cayleb Ahrmahk's mind also worked more rapidly than most. The king came to his feet, one hand reaching out in futile protest as the dagger flashed.

"*Maikel!*" he cried, then flinched back as a cannon fired less than six inches from his ear.

That was what it felt like, at any rate. Cayleb lurched away from the concussive impact hammering at his eardrum, and it fired again.

▼ ▼ ▼

Maikel Staynair felt no fear as the dagger drove towards him. There wasn't really enough time for that, not enough time for his mind to realize what was happening and inform the rest of him that he was about to die. His stomach muscles had just begun to clench in a useless, fragile defensive reaction when, abruptly, the assassin's head disintegrated. The heavy bullet continued onward, thankfully missing anyone else as it splintered one of the pews, and a gory fan of blood, brain tissue, and splinters of bone sprayed across the pew's occupants.

The sound of the pistol shot interrupted the organ music and the choir as if it were the organist who'd been shot. The magnificent interplay of music and voices chopped off in a welter of beginning screams and shouts of confusion. Most of those in the cathedral still had no notion that anything was happening to the archbishop. Instead of looking in Staynair's direction, heads popped around as all eyes flew to the royal box and the tall, blue-eyed Royal Guardsman who'd vaulted onto the box's palm-wide, raised railing.

He balanced there, impossibly steady on his precarious perch, his right hand shrouded in a thick, choking cloud of powder smoke, and then the pistol's *second* barrel fired.

▼   ▼   ▼

Staynair's eyes closed in automatic reflex as his would-be killer's blood spattered across his face and white, magnificently embroidered vestments. His brain was finally beginning to realize what was happening, and his muscles tensed as he prepared to yank away from the hands which had seized him.

Before he could move, a second thunderclap exploded through the cathedral, and he heard a choked-off scream as the man holding his right arm released him abruptly.

▼   ▼   ▼

The heavy pistol in Merlin's right hand bucked with his second shot.

He'd had no option but to go for the head shot the first time he fired. He'd *had* to put the dagger wielder out of action permanently and instantly, despite the very real danger that the heavy bullet would continue onward to kill or wound some innocent bystander. Neither of Staynair's other assailants had so far produced a weapon, however, and he'd dropped the glowing dot of the aim point projected across his vision onto the second man's back. The bullet smashed into his target's spine and drove downward through his torso at the sharp angle imposed by Merlin's elevated firing position. The resistance of bone and human tissue slowed the big, mushrooming projectile, and his target released Staynair, staggered half a stride forward, and went down.

Merlin's left hand came up, holding the second pistol. The cloud of gun smoke spewed out by the two shots he'd already fired hung in front of him. It would have been all but totally blinding to a human being, but Merlin Athrawes wasn't a human being. *His* eyes saw through the smoke with perfect clarity as he balanced on the royal box's rail, and his left hand was as inhumanly rock-steady as his right.

His aim point tracked across onto the remaining attacker. *This* one, he wanted alive. A leg shot ought to do the job, he thought grimly, then swore mentally as the final assailant produced a dagger of his own. The other members of the procession had finally realized what was happening. Two of them turned to grapple with the third man, but they weren't going to have time.

The attacker's left hand was still clamped on to Staynair's left arm as the dagger rose, and no one could possibly reach him before that blade came down once more.

▼   ▼   ▼

Staynair felt the grip on his right arm disappear and shifted his weight, preparing to yank away from the grip on his *left* arm. But then there was a *third* explosion, and abruptly there were no more hands upon him.

▼   ▼   ▼

Merlin began to vault over the railing to the floor below, then paused.

Let's not do anything outright impossible in front of this many witnesses unless we really have to, he told himself.

The little voice in his brain seemed preposterously calm to him, but it made sense, and he slid the still-smoking pistol in his right hand into its holster. Then he crouched, gripping the box railing in his right hand, and lowered himself over the edge. He let his fingers slide down a smooth, waxed upright until his feet were only five or six feet above the cathedral's marble floor, then let himself drop with cat-like grace.

He landed on the seat of a pew which had magically cleared itself when its occupants saw him coming. They shrank back, staring at him, eyes huge, as he descended out of the hovering cloud of powder smoke, and he nodded courteously back to them.

"Excuse me," he said politely, and stepped out into the nave.

The cathedral was filled with shouts of confusion—confusion that was tinged with gathering anger as people began to realize what had happened—but Merlin ignored the background bedlam as he made his way up the nave.

His uniform would have been enough to clear a path for him under most circumstances. Under *these* circumstances, the pistol still in his left hand, one hammer still cocked while smoke still plumed from the fired barrel, was even more effective, and he reached Staynair's side quickly.

The archbishop was down on one knee, ignoring the under-priest trying to urge him back to his feet as he turned the second of his assailants up on his side. As Merlin watched, Staynair felt the side of the fallen man's throat, obviously searching for a pulse. He didn't find one, of course, and he shook his head slowly, heavily, and reached up to close the corpse's staring, surprised-looking eyes.

"Are you all right, Your Eminence?" Merlin demanded, and Staynair looked up at him with an expression of regret.

"Yes." His voice was a little shaky. Merlin had never heard that particular note in it before, but under the circumstances, he supposed it was reasonable that even Maikel Staynair's monumental calm should be just a bit frayed. The archbishop cleared his throat and nodded.

"Yes," he said more firmly. "I'm fine, Merlin. Thanks to you."

"Then unless you want a riot, I think you'd better stand back up and show yourself to the congregation before they decide *you're* dead, too," Merlin suggested as gently as he could through the steadily growing roar of angry, frightened, confused voices.

"What?" Staynair gazed at him for a moment, obviously still more than a bit confused himself. Then his eyes cleared with understanding, and he nodded again, more crisply.

"You're right," he said, and stood.

"We have to get you to someplace safe, Your Eminence!" one of the under-priests said urgently. Merlin found himself in strong agreement, but Staynair shook his head. The gesture was vigorous, purposeful.

"No," he said firmly.

"But, Your Eminence—!"

"No," he repeated, even more firmly. "I appreciate the thought, Father, but *this*—" one hand waved at the cathedral and the ripples of fury spreading steadily outward as those closest to the attempted assassination shouted explanations to those farther away "—is where I need to be."

"But—"

"No," Staynair said a third time, with a note of finality. Then he turned, pushed his way through the scepter-bearers and candle-bearers still standing in shocked immobility, and started back up the nave.

The other members of the procession stared at one another, still too badly shaken and confused to know exactly what to do, but Merlin straightened his shoulders and started after the archbishop. His own thoughts were still only beginning to catch up with Staynair's, but as they did, he realized the archbishop was right. This *was* where he needed to be . . . in more than one way.

Merlin carefully closed the priming pan and lowered the hammer on his remaining pistol's single unfired barrel. He holstered the weapon without breaking stride and continued down the nave behind Staynair, watching the worshippers to either side narrowly. The odds of there being a *second* assassination team were undoubtedly slim, yet Merlin intended to take nothing— *nothing* else, *at least*, he told himself grimly—for granted where Maikel Staynair's safety was concerned.

Those closest to the nave saw the archbishop walking past them, alone, followed only by the single grim-faced, blue-eyed guardsman, and waves of relief rippled outward from them, following on the heels of the shocked confusion and anger which had already swept the cathedral. Staynair's face was less grim than Merlin's, and he seemed to find it rather easier than Merlin would have to keep himself from flinching as more hands than ever reached out, touching him as their owners sought physical reassurance that he was unharmed.

Letting those people reach out to the archbishop, actually touch him, was one of the hardest things Merlin had ever done, yet he forced himself not to interfere. And not just because he knew Staynair would not have thanked him for the interference. Merlin would have found it remarkably easy to live with the archbishop's subsequent ire, if only he hadn't realized Staynair was right about that, too.

It's not even as if he'd reasoned it out, Merlin thought. *It's who he is—what he is. Pure instinct. Well, instinct and faith.*

Staynair reached the sanctuary rail, unclipped the gate in it—probably the first time in at least a decade that one of his acolytes hadn't performed that task for him—and stepped through it into the chancel itself. Merlin stopped at the rail, turning back to face the rest of the cathedral, but he also watched through the remotes his SNARCs had deployed throughout the enormous structure as Staynair genuflected to the enormous mosaics of Langhorne and Bédard, then stood to face the assembled congregation himself.

The bedlam faded slowly and unwillingly as the worshippers saw him standing there. The blood spray from his would-be killers showed dark across his vestments, and there was still blood on his face, as well, yet it was obvious that none of it was *his* blood, and several people cried out in relief as they realized that.

Relief, however, did nothing to cancel anger, and Merlin could feel the rage crouched in the hearts and minds of those hundreds of people as they realized how close to assassination their archbishop had truly come. There were more shouts, now—shouts of more clearly articulated, more sharply directed, anger.

"My children!" Staynair said, pitching his own powerful voice to break through the gathering storm swell of vengeful outrage. "My children!"

His words rang out, cutting through the background noises, and quiet descended upon the cathedral once more. It wasn't *silence*—there was still too much anger, too much shock, for that—but at least the noise level dropped, and Staynair raised his hands.

"My children," he said in a marginally quieter voice, "this is a house of God. In this place, in this time, surely vengeance must be His, not ours."

A fresh ripple went through the cathedral, as if the people listening to him couldn't quite believe what they'd just heard, and he shook his head sadly.

"Whatever others may believe, my children, God is a god of love," he told them. "If justice must be dealt, then let it be dealt, but don't poison yourselves with vengeance. Surely it's tragic enough that three of God's children should already have died here in His house without the rest of them staining themselves with hatred!"

"But they tried to kill you!" someone, lost in the vast depths of the cathedral, shouted back, and Staynair nodded.

"They did," he acknowledged, "and they have already paid the price for that." The regret, the sadness, in his voice was completely genuine, Merlin realized. "The men who made that attempt are already dead, my son. So who would you have us take vengeance upon for their crime?"

"The Temple Loyalists!" someone else replied hotly, but Staynair shook his head once more.

"No," he said firmly. "We know only that three men made this attempt. We know nothing as yet of who they were, *why* they attempted such a thing, or of whether or not they acted on their own. We know *nothing* about them, my children, not even—whatever some of you may think—that they had any connection whatsoever with the Temple Loyalists here in Tellesberg. In the absence of that knowledge, there can be no justification for striking out at anyone, and even if there could, vengeance is not the proper province of any child of God, under any circumstances. *Justice* may be, but justice is the province of the Crown. We will leave justice to our King, confident in his ability to know and to do that which is right. We will *not* seek vengeance. We will *not* turn ourselves into something we would never wish to be."

Voices murmured, some of them still with more than a hint of rebellion, yet no one dared to disagree with their archbishop.

"My children," Staynair said more softly, "I know you're angry. I understand why. But this is a time for sorrow, not anger. Whatever you may think of the men who made this attempt today, they were still your fellow children of God. I have no doubt that they did what they did because of their own faith in God. I don't say I believe it truly was what God desired of them, but it was what they have been *told* God wants. Shall we condemn them for acting as their faith demanded, when our own faith has demanded that we turn our faces away from the Council of Vicars and the Temple? We may find it necessary to oppose men who believe as they believed. In the war which the Group of Four has declared against us, it may even be necessary for us to slay men who believe as they believed. But despite that grim necessity, never let yourselves forget that they who oppose you are just as human, just as much God's children, as you yourselves. What they do may be evil in our eyes, and wrong in God's eyes, but if you let yourselves be filled with hate, if you turn them into something less than human in order to make it easier to kill them, then you open *yourself* to the very evil which you have condemned in them."

The murmuring voices had faded into stillness as he spoke, and he gazed out at them sadly.

"We live in a time when godly men and women must make *choices*, my children. I beg of you, as you love me—as you love yourselves, love your wives and husbands and children, as you love God Himself—make the *right* choices. Choose to do that which must be done, but do it without poisoning yourselves, your souls, or your ability to love one another."

The silence was almost absolute now, and Staynair looked to where the stalled procession still clustered about the bodies. A half dozen of Merlin's fellow guardsmen had joined the procession. Now, as they stooped to lift and remove the bodies, Staynair beckoned to the acolytes and under-priests.

"Come," he told them, standing before the congregation, splashed with the drying blood of the men who had attempted to kill him. "Come, we have a mass to celebrate, brethren."

▼   ▼   ▼

"Maikel," King Cayleb said very, very seriously, "you realize what they took advantage of when they planned this, don't you?"

"Of course I do, Your Majesty," the archbishop replied serenely. They sat on the balcony of Cayleb's personal suite in the palace, looking out over the city in the golden light of early evening, and Merlin stood behind the king's chair. "But, to anticipate your argument, I'm far too old and set in my ways to start trying to change them now."

"Maikel, they tried to *kill* you," Cayleb said, sounding like someone trying very hard *not* to sound exasperated . . . and failing.

"I know," Staynair said in that same, serene tone.

"Well, exactly what do you think is going to happen to the Church of Charis—and this Kingdom—if the *next* time they try, they succeed?" Cayleb demanded.

"If that happens, you'll just have to choose my successor, Your Majesty. You'll find a complete list of nominees in my desk. Father Bryahn knows where to find it."

"*Maikel!*"

"Calmly, Your Majesty," Staynair said with a small smile. "I truly realize what you're saying. And I'm not trying to minimize the impact my death would have on our efforts to defy the Grand Vicar and the Group of Four. Nor, for that matter, am I unaware of the way in which my death at the hands of real or supposed Temple Loyalists would inflame public opinion. Nonetheless, I'm a priest before I'm a politician. Even before I'm an archbishop. I serve God; I don't ask Him to serve *me*, and I refuse to live my life in fear of my enemies. Moreover, I refuse to allow my enemies—or my friends—to *believe* I live in fear of them. This is a time for boldness, Cayleb, not for timidity. You've grasped that well enough in your own case. Now you have to understand that it applies to *my* case, as well."

"That's all very well and good, Your Eminence," Merlin put in respectfully. "For that matter, I don't disagree with you. But there *is* one distinction between you and the King."

"And that 'distinction' is precisely what, *Seijin* Merlin?" Staynair asked.

"His Majesty is constantly and openly surrounded by bodyguards," Merlin replied. "It may be time for him to take risks, even bold ones, but reaching him with an assassination attempt would be extraordinarily difficult. I leave it to you to . . . evaluate just how difficult it would be to reach you. Again."

"As always, you make a valid point," Staynair conceded. "It doesn't change my own reasoning, however. And I might also point out that outside the cathedral during services, I'm constantly protected by the Archbishop's Guard, myself."

"Which doesn't address Merlin's point at all," Cayleb said sternly. He sat back in his chair, glowering at his archbishop. "I'm strongly inclined to *order* you to change your procedures."

"I earnestly hope you'll be able to resist that temptation, Your Majesty. It would grieve me deeply to disobey a royal command."

"And you would, too," Cayleb growled. "That's the only reason I'm still 'inclined' to give you the order instead of just going ahead and doing it!"

"It's not my intention to make problems for you, Your Majesty. It *is* my intention to discharge my pastoral duties in the fashion in which I believe God expects me to discharge them. I recognize the risks involved. I simply refuse to allow them to tempt me into being less of God's priest than He demands."

Cayleb's expression turned even more sour, and his nostrils flared. But then he shook his head.

"All right. *All right!*" He threw up his hands. "You know you're being an idiot. *I* know you're being an idiot. But if I can't stop you, I can't. The one thing I *am* going to do, however, is to take a few precautions of my own."

"Such as, Your Majesty?" Staynair asked a trifle warily.

"First, I'm placing a permanent guard around the cathedral," Cayleb said grimly. "I may not be able to stop people from smuggling daggers into mass with them, but I can damned well keep anyone from smuggling in a barrel or two of gunpowder when no one's looking!"

Staynair looked a bit unhappy, but he nodded in acquiescence.

"And, second, Maikel—and I warn you now, I'll entertain no arguments from you on this point—I'm placing a couple of General Chermyn's scout-snipers inside the cathedral itself."

The archbishop seemed to stiffen, but Cayleb stuck a finger under the older man's nose and shook it.

"I told you I'm not listening to any arguments," he said sternly, "and I'm not. I'll keep them as much out of sight as I can, probably in one of the upper balconies. But they're *going* to be there, Maikel. They won't be *seijins*, of course, so don't expect them to duplicate Merlin's little feat without managing to kill any innocent bystanders, but at least they'll be there just in case."

For a long, tense moment it looked as if Staynair were going to argue, anyway. Then his shoulders slumped slightly, and he sighed.

"Very well, Cayleb," he said. "If you truly insist."

"I do."

Cayleb's voice, like his expression, was unyielding, and Merlin agreed with him. Of course, it was unlikely, to say the least, that two or three marksmen—or even a dozen of them—could have prevented this morning's assassination attempt from succeeding. Only Merlin's enhanced reaction speed and the fact that he'd seeded the cathedral with remote sensors had let *him* realize what was happening in time to do anything about it. Marksmen limited to their natural senses and reflexes were unlikely, to say the least, to duplicate his accomplishment.

On the other hand, he told himself grimly, *there are a few additional precautions I can take. And His Eminence Archbishop Too-Stubborn-for-His-Own-Good isn't going to be able to do anything about them, either, because unlike Cayleb, I have absolutely no intention of discussing them with him in the first place!*

He allowed no sign of his thoughts to show in his own expression, despite a certain sense of satisfaction at having found a way around Staynair's stubbornness. Owl was already redeploying and beefing up the sensor net inside and around Tellesberg Cathedral. King Cayleb's guardsmen might not be able to tell which of the archbishop's parishioners had decided to attend mass tastefully accoutered with the latest thing in hidden daggers, but Owl's sensors certainly could. And one Merlin Athrawes would have absolutely no hesitation about confronting anyone who'd absentmindedly brought one along.

That was the easy part, but he had no intention of stopping there.

Owl was already busy duplicating Staynair's vestments on a stitch-by-stitch, gem-by-gem basis. When he was done, it would be literally impossible for even Staynair to tell the difference between the AI's handiwork and the originals. Even any tiny, darned spots would be exactly duplicated. But unlike the originals, the copies would be made of the latest in antiballistic fabrics, seeded with nanotech which would literally transform any portion of their surface into plate armor in the face of *any* impact. And once his vestments had been replaced, it would be time to start on his regular cassocks, as well. Owl ought to have the entire project finished by the end of the current five-day.

And then, Your Eminence, the next *son-of-a-bitch who tries to stick a knife into you is going to find himself confronted with a "miracle" Clyntahn and his friends will find difficult to explain away,* Merlin thought coldly.

Of course, I doubt that the son-of-a-bitch in question will live long enough to realize just how surprised he really is.

Which suited Merlin Athrawes just fine.

JULY, YEAR OF GOD 892

.I.
Royal College,
City of Tellesberg,
Kingdom of Charis

Rahzhyr Mahklyn squinted at the sheet of paper on his desktop. Despite the best lenses the opticians could grind, his nearsightedness was growing steadily worse, and the lighting didn't help. The oil lamps were filled with the finest first-grade kraken oil, and the reflectors behind them had been burnished to mirror brightness, but it was still a dim substitute for natural sunlight.

Of course, if I'd just go home at a reasonable hour, I could work on this during daylight and not have to worry about lamps, couldn't I?

His lips twitched at the thought, especially given the fact that he knew every one of his colleagues would have said exactly the same thing to him, although probably somewhat more acerbically than he just had. Still, the nascent smile faded, it wasn't as if there were anything waiting for him at home since his wife's death. Ysbet had been his constant companion, fellow scholar, collaborator, and best friend, as well as his wife, for over thirty years, and if he was going to be honest, her death was one of the main reasons he *didn't* go home when the rest of the Royal College of Charis shut down for the night.

He sighed and sat back, pushing his wire-frame glasses up onto his forehead and massaging the bridge of his nose wearily. The new system of "Arabic numerals" Merlin Athrawes had introduced to the kingdom had been an incredible boon to Charis' merchant houses and manufactories. In some ways, the "abacus" had been an even greater boon, yet Mahklyn was virtually certain no one outside the Royal College had yet begun to grasp all of the *other* things they made possible. There were even a handful of statements in the *Holy Writ* and *The Testimonies* which were beginning to make sense to him for the first time, with their hints of mathematical operations he'd never been able to make work using the old, cumbersome system of notations. The possibilities were literally dazzling, although he suspected that only a batch of old fogies like himself and his College colleagues could appreciate the vistas he saw opening before him.

Yet, at least. Unless he was very mistaken, that was about to change radically.

Just the ability to keep accurate records and actually understand what the numbers mean, how they change over time, is going to completely change the way kings and emperors think. In fact, I wonder if even Cayleb and Ironhill appreciate the advantage for his clerks and his quartermasters, far less the Treasury!

Well, if anyone would, it would be Cayleb. For all of his own lack of interest in pure scholarship, he was his father's son in so many ways it was almost frightening, and he'd already made his continued commitment to the Royal College abundantly clear. In fact, he'd offered to move the entire College out of its tall, narrow, shabby, teetering converted waterfront counting house and its attached warehouse and into luxurious new quarters in Tellesberg Palace.

To be honest, Mahklyn thought, puffing out his cheeks and then dropping his glasses back onto the bridge of his nose, the offer was tempting. If nothing else it would keep him from climbing all those stairs every morning! But the Royal College had been in the same buildings ever since Cayleb's grandfather first founded it. By now, Mahklyn and his fellows knew every cranny, exactly where every record was filed or tucked away. Besides, despite the Crown's patronage, and despite its very name, Haarahld VI had insisted when he first endowed it that it must be independent of the royal government. That it was not to become a mere adjunct or tool of the House of Ahrmahk, but rather serve the kingdom as a whole. Mahklyn wasn't afraid Cayleb wanted to change that, but he *was* afraid that such close proximity to the throne would inevitably lead to a greater degree of dependence upon it.

Still, does it really matter all that much? he asked himself. *There's so much happening now, so many things that have broken loose in the last couple of years. I doubt half a dozen people in the entire Kingdom, outside the College itself, even begin to suspect all that's about to break loose, either. Or, thank God, how much of that we owe to* Seijin *Merlin. If any of those "Temple Loyalist" idiots knew about* him, *there'd be hell to pay, and no mistake. But with so much happening, so much coming together, I doubt we'd have* time *to become "subservient" to the Crown!*

He chuckled dryly at the thought and bent over his desk once more, frowning as he contemplated the formula he'd been playing with for the last several hours. He tapped his teeth gently with the end of his pen holder, then dipped the nib and started writing slowly once again.

He never quite identified the sound which pulled him out of his reverie an hour or so later. It hadn't been very loud, whatever it was. Probably, he decided later, it had been the sound of breaking glass.

At the time, all he knew was that he'd heard *something* which wasn't part of the old building's normal nighttime creaks and groans. Space near the harbor was always at a premium in Tellesberg, which helped explain why the city had so many tall buildings. Some of them were even taller than the College, in fact, and many of them were even older structures. But some of the builders had been a little less than scrupulous in their building practices. Certainly the College was constantly showing new cracks in its walls and emitting nocturnal sounds which could be downright alarming. In this case, however, and even though it didn't sound especially threatening (whatever it was), it wasn't supposed to be there, and Rahzhyr Mahklyn was a naturally curious man.

He sat for several seconds, waiting for the sound to repeat itself, but it didn't. Finally, he shrugged and returned his attention to his work, but he wasn't able to slide back into it the way he usually could. The oddity of that unidentifiable sound continued to pick at one corner of his mind, continued to challenge him to figure out where it had come from.

Oh, all right, Rahzhyr! he told himself finally. *You know you're not going to get anything else done until you go and find out.*

He laid his pen down once again, stood, walked across his small fourth-floor office, and opened the door onto the building's central stairwell.

The blast of heated air roaring up the hollow core of that stairwell nearly knocked him off his feet.

Rahzhyr Mahklyn stared in disbelief at the dense torrents of smoke already funneling up like the fumes from one of Ehdwyrd Howsmyn's furnaces. The brick building was close to eighty years old. Its wooden framing timbers, walls, and floors were bone-dry and heavily painted, its hollow core was like one vast chimney, and the hungry, crackling roar of the voracious flames told Mahklyn the structure was already doomed.

And so, a small, still voice told him in the back of his mind as he slammed the door shut once again, was he. His office was on the College's top floor. That stairwell was the only way out, and if anything in this world was clear, it was that he couldn't possibly get down those stairs through that inferno.

I suppose I'm coming after all, Ysbet, he thought almost calmly as he backed up against the office's outer wall.

Smoke was beginning to curl under the office door, as if the fact that he'd opened it had shown the fiery monster the path in, and he thought he could feel the searing heat on the far side of that flimsy portal radiating against his face. Perhaps it was only his imagination. But if it was, it wouldn't be imaginary heat for long, and Mahklyn made up his mind.

It's better than burning to death, he thought grimly, and opened his office window wide. The cobblestone street below was already lit with the hellish red glare of the flames consuming the College's lower floors. The cobbles didn't look very inviting, to say the least, but at least it ought to be quicker and less painful than burning.

Yet he hesitated. Perhaps it didn't make any sense, but somehow these last few moments of life were unutterably precious. Or perhaps it was simply that his excellent imagination insisted on projecting what would happen when his frail, elderly body slammed into that stony street.

A contrarian to the end, aren't you, Rahzhyr? Still, when the flame actually eats through that door, I think you'll find it easier. And, of course, you can always plan on landing headfirst and—

"I beg your pardon, Dr. Mahklyn, but don't you think we should be going?"

Rahzhyr Mahklyn jumped at least a foot straight up as the deep, calm voice seemed to speak out of the thin air beyond his window. Then, as he stared in disbelief, Captain Merlin Athrawes of the Charisian Royal Guard swung easily down and through the open window from the edge of the building's roof. His boots thumped on the office floor, and Mahklyn gaped at him as the *seijin* stroked his waxed mustachio thoughtfully.

"Yes, *definitely* time we were going," the guardsman said, as if he were simply observing that it looked like they might have rain.

"How—? Where—?"

"I'm afraid we're a little short on time for detailed explanations, Doctor. In fact, we're a little short on time for anything except—"

Mahklyn squawked in astonishment as King Cayleb's personal bodyguard snatched him up in what another era on another planet would have called a "fireman's carry." Mahklyn was elderly, and he knew he was growing frail, but he also knew he weighed far more than Merlin seemed to realize. The shoulder under him could have been carved out of marble for all that it gave under his weight, and then Merlin was clambering back out through the window opening.

Well, you were going to jump anyway, weren't you? a lunatic voice gibbered in the back of his brain, and he screwed his eyes tightly shut as Merlin calmly turned sideways and reached for the side of the building.

Later, Mahklyn was unable to reconstruct exactly what happened next. Possibly that was because of the way his all-too-rational mind insisted on trying to make sense of something which was patently impossible. Or, possibly, it was because smoke inhalation had already begun to blur his perceptions, caused him to begin imagining things. Of the two, he considerably preferred the second explanation. Probably because he was confident it wasn't the right one.

At any rate, he found himself smoothly descending the outside of the Royal College's home over that impossibly strong shoulder. It was as if Captain Athrawes were actually driving his fingers and toes *through* the outer wall as easily as if it were made of paper or thatch instead of bricks and mortar. That was the only explanation for how he could possibly have found purchase points exactly where he needed them all the way down that sheer wall. Except, of course, that it *wasn't* possible . . . was it?

Possible or not, it obviously worked. Only minutes after Merlin had miraculously appeared in his office, Rahzhyr Mahklyn found himself standing in the street watching the building which contained the better part of his life's work go up in a roaring torrent of flame.

"My God, my God," he heard himself muttering over and over again. "What a disaster! My God, how did something like this *happen?* We never allow lit lamps or candles unless someone is actually using them! *Never!*"

"You didn't this time, either, Doctor," Captain Athrawes said grimly.

"What?" Mahklyn blinked at him. "What did you say?"

"I said you didn't leave any lit candles behind, Doctor." The *seijin* turned to look at him levelly. "And this was no accident, either. That fire was deliberately set."

"What?" Mahklyn shook his head violently. "No, that's not possible. It couldn't be!"

"Why not? This building, your College," Merlin waved one hand at the roaring, crackling inferno as the first of the city's fire pumps came thundering up behind a pair of foothill dragons, "has been denounced by the Temple Loyalists from the very beginning, Doctor. It's one of their pet horrors, the home of all that 'unclean knowledge' that 'led the Crown into apostasy,' isn't it? Why shouldn't one of their zealots decide to burn it to the ground?"

Mahklyn stared at him as the firemen began coupling hoses between the pump and the closest fire department cistern while others took their places at the pump handles. It was obvious they couldn't save the College, but they might save the buildings to either side if they could get enough water on them quickly enough.

"Surely it hasn't come to the point that people are willing to *murder* one another so casually!" the doctor exclaimed.

"You think not?" Merlin raised an eyebrow, and his eyes were hard. "You may, perhaps, remember the fact that less than three five-days ago they tried to murder Archbishop Maikel in the nave of his own cathedral?"

"Well, yes, of course it was, but he's the *Archbishop!* If anyone's going to be a logical target—assuming there could be any such thing for something like this—then obviously it would be him. But to murder someone like me? A no one? As if it were no more than swatting a fly? Surely not!"

"If it hasn't come to that yet, it soon will." Merlin's deep voice was harsh as crushed stone. "And you're scarcely 'a no one,' either, Doctor! I'll grant you, whoever set this particular fire probably didn't have murder on his mind, but not because they wouldn't think killing you was worthwhile. I simply doubt that they could have realized the opportunity even existed. How many people outside the College itself know the hours you keep?"

"Not very many," Mahklyn conceded, swinging away from the other man to stare at the flames once again.

"Then probably our friend with the tinderbox didn't know it, either. He probably thought the building would be empty at this time of night."

"I suppose that makes me feel a *little* better," Mahklyn said bleakly. "But if whoever it was wanted to destroy the College, he's succeeded. All our records, all our documents, all our *work* is inside that building, *Seijin* Merlin. *Everything,* you understand? Gone."

"The records and the documents, yes, Doctor." Mahklyn turned back to look at Merlin once more, startled by the gentleness which had suddenly in-fused the guardsman's voice. Merlin looked back steadily, and his shoulders twitched in an odd little shrug. "The records may be gone, but the minds which created them, or studied them, or worked with them, are still here."

"We can't possibly reconstitute all of that—"

"Probably not, but at least you can make a start on it. And, if you'll permit me to say so, what you really need is to find yourselves some youngsters with the same mindset. Get *them* involved. Give them some starting points and some guidance, then stand back and see where they take it. You might be sur-prised. And at least you know Cayleb is prepared to support and fund you openly. Let him, Doctor. You've got too much rebuilding to do to worry about the independence from the Crown that might have been so important forty years ago."

Mahklyn stared at him, listening to the mocking roar of the furnace con-suming his life's work. The insulating effect of shock and the first outriders of grief were already beginning to pass, and as he met Merlin's eyes in the lurid glare of the flames, he knew why that was. They were being displaced by an-other emotion—rage. Raw, bloody-fanged rage. Rage such as he had never before felt in his entire life.

"Yes, Doctor," Captain Athrawes said, nodding almost as if he could read Mahklyn's mind. "Whatever else happens, you can't let *these* people"—he ges-tured at the booming flames—"win, can you?"

▼   ▼   ▼

Bishop Mylz Halcom watched the additional fire engines charging through the city streets. Despite the lateness of the hour, the seething torrent of crimson flame and midnight-black smoke had summoned quite a crowd out into the streets, as well. Many of the spectators were hurrying forward to assist the fire-men in fighting the flames, although it must be obvious to all of them that the Royal College itself was already doomed. The majority were simply gawking in awe at the holocaust. It wouldn't be long until they figured out exactly how the fire had started, though, and Halcom nodded to himself in satisfaction.

All the loyal sons of Mother Church had needed was a little leadership, a little direction to point the way for their outraged faith to strike back at the abomination of the so-called "Church of Charis'" schismatic heresy.

And what could have been a more suitable target? he asked himself. *It's time Cayleb and his sycophants discover just how hot the true faithful's rage really burns. That accursed* seijin *may have managed to save that traitor Staynair's life, but they know now that one setback isn't going to cause us to just give up! Perhaps this little bon-fire will help them . . . reassess their decision to raise impious hands against God's true Church.*

And if it doesn't, I'm sure we'll be able to find one that will . . . eventually.

S o you're certain it was deliberately set?" King Cayleb asked grimly.
He and Merlin sat in comfortable chairs in the sitting room of the
king's personal suite in Tellesberg Palace, and Merlin's black and gold uniform smelled of smoke. No, actually it *reeked* of smoke, Cayleb corrected
himself, which wasn't all that surprising. Despite the firemen's best efforts,
the entire block around the Royal College had burned along with it, and after
he'd handed Mahklyn over to the half squad of the Guard which Cayleb had
sent in his wake by more . . . conventional methods, Merlin had been deeply
involved in trying to save what could be saved.

"Yes." Merlin sighed and rubbed his mustachios, which seemed a little
singed on one side. "I'm certain it was. The buildings were tinderboxes
stuffed full of kindling, but they wouldn't have gone up that quickly without
some help. I'd say the fire started in at least four or five places simultaneously.
Probably from burning lanterns thrown in through the ground-floor windows." He shook his head. "Those savants of your father's didn't even have
bars on the windows, for God's sake! Talk about babes in a boat. . . ."

"I know." Cayleb ran the fingers of both hands through his dark hair,
then shook his own head half helplessly. "I know! But Father was never able
to convince them that anybody could possibly hate *them* just because they insisted on asking questions."

"Well, I'd say they're convinced now," Merlin replied. "And I should've
seen this coming. I should've been keeping a closer eye on them, especially
after what almost happened to Maikel, because Mahklyn's right. We've just
finished losing an enormous stockpile of knowledge and information. I told
him it could be re-created, and probably it can—or a lot of it, at any rate. But
we've lost *years* of lead time, Cayleb. It would be hard for me to think of any
other target they could have attacked—aside from Maikel, of course—which
would have hurt us equally badly."

"I know," Cayleb repeated yet again. "But don't feel too badly about not
having seen it coming ahead of time. Not even *your* 'visions' "—he grinned
crookedly at Merlin—"can see everything. We're going to be surprised more
than once before this is over, so we might as well start getting used to it now.
And at least you were able to get there—and please note that I am *not* asking
how!—in time to save Dr. Mahklyn. That's a huge blessing right there."

Merlin nodded, although he still looked distinctly unhappy with himself, and then Cayleb's nostrils flared as he inhaled deeply.

"And while we're busy looking for silver linings, there's not going to be any more nonsense about where their precious College is going to be located from now on, either. I want them inside these walls, and I want bodyguards assigned to every member of the faculty, and to their families, whether they want them or not!"

"That's going to be a lot of bodyguards," Merlin observed mildly.

"Do you disagree?" Cayleb challenged.

"I didn't say that. I only said it was going to be a lot of bodyguards, and it is. As a matter of fact, I think it's probably a very good idea, at least for the faculty members and their immediate families. But you're going to have to draw a line somewhere, Cayleb. Right now, I suspect, these Temple Loyalists are still trying to make a point, to convince all of us that the schism was a terrible mistake we should undo as quickly as possible. But they're going to get even more violent as they begin to realize how irrelevant their 'message' is as far as most of your subjects are concerned. The more isolated they become, the more powerless they feel, the more likely they are to do things like tonight. And once it truly begins sinking in that they aren't going to change enough minds to matter, no matter what they do, they're going to go looking for ways to *punish* people, not for ways that might simply frighten them into heeding 'the true will of God.' Which means that, sooner or later, you're going to reach a point at which you simply *can't* provide bodyguards for all of their likely targets."

"Then what should I do instead?" Merlin felt certain Cayleb would not have let any of his other advisers hear that particular note of frustration and semi-despair. "Go ahead and take Bynzhamyn's advice and start arresting people on suspicion? Crack down on anyone who disagrees with me? *Prove* I'm some sort of tyrant, intent on usurping the Church's rightful authority for purely selfish reasons of my own?"

"I didn't say that, either," Merlin replied gently. "I only said there are limits, which is true. And the corollary of that, whether we like it or not, is that we simply can't protect everyone. You just said it yourself, Cayleb. There are going to be more incidents like tonight and, eventually, people *are* going to get killed when they happen. You're going to have to accept that. And you're going to have to decide whether or not trying to limit the damage justifies resorting to repression, after all."

"I don't want to. As God is my witness, I don't want to."

"Which probably says good things about you as a person. And, in my opinion, for what it's worth, it says good things about you as a king, as well. Justice isn't something to be lightly bartered away, Cayleb, and the faith your subjects have in your own and your family's sense of justice is one of the greatest legacies your father left you. I can't say you'll never reach a time when you have no option but to arrest first and figure out what to do second, but I will say that I think you have to avoid it for as long as you can without compromising your safety, or the safety of the Kingdom as a whole. And that's going to be a judgment call—one *you'll* have to make."

"Oh, thanks," Cayleb said with a sardonic smile.

"Well, you *are* the king. I'm only a lowly bodyguard."

"Of course you are, Master Traynyr."

Merlin chuckled just a bit sadly as he remembered the first time King Haarahld had used that title for him. And, in all fairness, there were times he *did* feel like a puppetmaster. The problem was that he could never forget his "puppets" were flesh and blood, or that they had minds, wills, and destinies of their own.

And that, in the end, they all have the right to make up their own minds, he reminded himself. *Don't you* ever *forget that, Merlin Athrawes, or Nimue Alban, or whoever you really are.*

"I did see to it that Dr. Mahklyn got bedded down here in the Palace tonight," he said aloud after a moment. "With your permission, I think it might not be a bad idea to offer quarters here to his daughter and his son-in-law, as well. At least until we're confident that the people who set the College on fire tonight really didn't know he was in his office."

"So you do think there's at least a possibility they were deliberately trying to kill him?"

"Of course there's a possibility of it, Cayleb. I just don't think the people behind this could have known he was sitting there like a wyvern on the pond, and if they didn't know he was there, they couldn't exactly have set out deliberately to kill him. I'm not saying they would have shed any tears if they'd managed to catch him in their little sausage roast, because I'm damned sure they *wouldn't* have. I'm only saying I don't think they set out to do that on purpose. This time."

"I hope you're right about that. And while we're on the little matter of things I hope, is Dr. Mahklyn likely to be doing any mental sums about your . . . opportune arrival and peculiar abilities, shall we say?"

"Oh, I think you can count on it, after he's had a chance to get his brain put back into order. That's a very, very bright man, Cayleb. I don't think his brain ever really shuts down, and sooner or later—probably sooner—he's going to want to know how I got there, how I got onto the roof, and how *we* got down the outside of the building."

"And is there any disconcerting evidence I need to worry about concealing? Any more krakens with harpoons driven completely through them, for instance?"

"I don't think you need to worry about that this time around," Merlin said reassuringly. "The walls were already coming down before I left, and the Fire Brigade's planning on demolishing the rest of them as soon as the embers cool enough. I'm fairly sure that any . . . peculiarities I might have left behind have been thoroughly consumed by the fire, and if they haven't, they'll be gone when the demolition's done."

"Well, that's a relief, at least. Now all we have to do is worry about how we fob off one of the smartest men in Charis, who also happens to be the head of the Royal College, whose full-blooded support, I remind you, we're going to need in the not so distant future. Any suggestions on how to go about doing *that*, Merlin?"

"Actually, I do have a suggestion."

"Spit it out, then!"

"I don't think you should try to fob him off at all," Merlin said seriously. "We're both in agreement that he's an extraordinarily smart fellow. Probably smarter than either of us, when you get right down to it. So, the odds are he's going to figure out a lot of it on his own over the next several five-days. I think we should just go ahead and tell him."

"Tell him what? How much? After all," Cayleb observed wryly, "it's not as if you've told *me* everything."

"I know." Merlin's expression was apologetic, and he shook his head. "And I promise, I really will tell you as much as I can as soon as I can. But as far as Dr. Mahklyn is concerned, I think we need to tell him at least as much as Rayjhis and Bynzhamyn know. Probably as much as Ahrnahld and the rest of your personal detail know. And, eventually, I'd like him to know as much as *you* know, if it turns out that he's . . . philosophically flexible enough to handle it."

" 'Philosophically flexible,' " Cayleb repeated with an almost dreamy expression. "Now there's a handy term for it. You have a way with words, I see, *Seijin* Merlin."

"One tries, Your Majesty. One tries."

.III.
Archbishop's Palace,
City of Tellesberg,
Kingdom of Charis

Archbishop Maikel Staynair listened to the soft hum of the cat-lizard in his lap as he stroked the short, silky white plush of its fur. The cat-lizard lay on his back with all six feet in the air, and his golden eyes were half-slitted in shameless bliss as the archbishop's long fingers caressed his belly fur.

"Like that, do you, Ahrdyn?" Staynair chuckled.

The cat-lizard didn't deign to acknowledge his remark. Cat-lizards, after all, as every cat-lizard obviously knew, were the true masters of creation. Human beings existed for the sole purposes of feeding them, opening doors for them, and—above all else—petting them. At this particular moment, the world was in its proper place, so far as Ahrdyn was concerned.

The archbishop smiled at the thought. He'd been Ahrdyn's pet (and there was no point thinking of the relationship in any other terms) for almost ten years now, since shortly after his wife's death. At the time he'd acquired Ahrdyn, he'd thought the cat-lizard was female. Even cat-lizards found it difficult to tell males from females until they were a couple of years old, and he'd named his new pet after his wife. By the time he'd realized his mistake, Ahrdyn had settled into his name and would undoubtedly have refused, with all the monumental stubbornness of his breed, to answer to anything else.

Fortunately, Ahrdyn Staynair had been a woman of rare humor, and Staynair had no doubt she was amused by the mix-up. Certainly her daughter, who now shared her name with the cat-lizard, was. The furry Ahrdyn had been her gift to her lonely father. She, too, had assumed he was female, and she knew enough of cat-lizards to refuse to waste time trying to change this one's mind. So did Staynair's son-in-law, Sir Lairync Kestair, although he *had* been heard to remark—mostly when his wife was absent—that Ahrdyn the cat-lizard was far less stubborn than his two-legged namesake. And that both of them were less stubborn than any one of Staynair's four grandchildren.

The archbishop's smile softened at the memory, but then it faded into a pensive frown as thoughts of his own grandchildren reminded him of the enormous threat looming over the entire Kingdom of Charis and *all* of its children. Those grandchildren were hostages to fortune, and whenever he thought about them, he understood exactly why some men dared not raise their hands against the Church's corruption.

But it's also the reason other men can't refuse to raise their hands, he thought. *And neither Ahrdyn nor Lairync has ever questioned my decision.*

Knuckles rapped discreetly on his door, and Staynair stirred in his chair. Ahrdyn's eyes opened fully as his mattress shifted under him, and the archbishop picked him up.

"Time for work, I'm afraid," he said. The cat-lizard yawned, showing off its pink, forked tongue, then gave his cheek a quick, affectionate lick.

"Bribery will get you nothing, you furry little fiend," Staynair told him, then lowered him to the floor. Ahrdyn flowed down and padded off towards the basket in one corner, and Staynair cleared his throat.

"Enter!" he called, and watched thoughtfully as the two unlikely visitors were escorted into his office in the Archbishop's Palace.

The two men were studies in physical contrast in many ways, and other differences went far deeper. Yet the two of them had requested a *joint* meeting with Staynair, which suggested several interesting possibilities.

None of which, he reminded himself, *is likely to be accurate, given how little information you have upon which to base any of them.*

Bishop Executor Zherald Ahdymsyn was well past middle age, and prior to the recent . . . unpleasantness, he'd had a solid, well-fed look. In fact, he'd always enjoyed the comforts of a good table, and he'd been carrying a bit more weight than the Order of Pasquale's healer-priests would have approved. He'd been very careful of his physical appearance, as well. He'd been aware that *looking* the part of a bishop executor was a significant advantage, and his grooming had always been impeccable. Now, although he was still attired in the white cassock of his episcopal rank, he was leaner, and there was an odd fragility to his movements. It wasn't precisely that he'd aged, but rather that he had been forced to cope with something totally unexpected and, in the process, had discovered that the world was not in fact the neat, well-organized, *controlled* place he'd thought it was.

The man with him, Father Paityr Wylsynn, was much younger, no more than a dozen years, at most, older than King Cayleb himself. Ahdymsyn's hair was dark, where the silver of age had not overtaken it, but Wylsynn's was a curly shade of red which was as rare as his gray, northern eyes here in Charis. Where Ahdymsyn was almost as tall as Staynair, Wylsynn was a head shorter than the archbishop, and where Ahdymsyn moved with that strangely fragile air, Wylsynn was as poised and energetic as he'd ever been.

They were accompanied by two armsmen in the orange and white of the Archbishop's Guard. The armsmen in question walked a respectful pace behind the visitors, yet their presence was not the simple ceremonial act of respect it might have been. Especially not now, after the assassination attempt had come so close to success. Staynair's armsmen and guardians were in no mood to take additional chances where his safety was concerned, and the archbishop felt confident both his visitors were aware of that.

Ahdymsyn and Wylsynn stopped in front of his desk, and he rose to greet them.

"Bishop Executor," he said, inclining his head very slightly to Ahdymsyn, and then looked at Wylsynn. "Father."

He did not offer his ring to be kissed.

"Archbishop," Ahdymsyn replied for both of them.

Staynair's eyebrows didn't arch, and he managed to keep any sign of surprise from touching his expression. It wasn't easy. Granting him that title, even in a private interview, would have serious consequences for Ahdymsyn if word of it ever reached the Temple.

"Please, be seated," Staynair invited, waving at the chairs in front of the desk behind which Ahdymsyn had once sat as Erayk Dynnys' deputy here in Charis.

Staynair had appeared before that desk more than once to be "counseled"—and reprimanded—by Ahdymsyn, and the bishop executor's awareness of the change in their respective fortunes showed in the other man's slight, ironic smile. Father Paityr, on the other hand, simply sat, with a composure and something very close to serenity which seemed almost unaware of the earthquake upheaval the Church of Charis had undergone since *his* last visit to this office.

Staynair gazed at them for a moment, then nodded to the armsmen. They hesitated a moment, eyes unhappy, and the archbishop raised both hands and made shooing motions at them until they finally gave up and withdrew from the office, closing the door silently behind them.

"I must confess," the archbishop continued, resuming his own seat as the door closed, "that I was somewhat surprised when the two of you requested this meeting. Your message made it clear you had some fundamental point which both of you wished to discuss with me, but it was curiously silent as to exactly what that point might be."

His tone made the last sentence a question, and he raised his eyebrows politely. Ahdymsyn glanced at Wylsynn, then drew a deep breath, reached into a cassock pocket, and extracted a folded piece of paper.

"I don't doubt you were surprised . . . Your Eminence," he said, and this time Staynair allowed his eyes to narrow at the bishop executor's chosen mode of address. Ahdymsyn obviously saw it, because he smiled slightly and shook his head.

"At first, as I sat in my comfortable, if involuntary, quarters in Tellesberg Palace, Your Eminence, I had no intention of granting even the least appearance of acquiescence to your patent usurpation of Archbishop Erayk's legitimate authority here in Charis. Of course, at the time I became King Cayleb's . . . guest, I had no more idea than anyone else in the Kingdom as to why and how such a massive attack had been launched against it. It's become rather clearer since then that the 'Knights of the Temple Lands' must have put their 'allies' into motion against Charis well before Archbishop Erayk could have reached Zion with any formal report of his last pastoral visit."

He paused, and Staynair cocked his head.

"Is there a reason the timing of their actions should affect your attitude towards—what was it you called it?—my 'patent usurpation of Archbishop Erayk's legitimate authority'?"

"In itself, no." Ahdymsyn's half smile guttered and went out. "It did play a part, however. Your Eminence, I won't pretend that many of my decisions when I sat in the chair in which you now sit weren't motivated by . . . pragmatic concerns, let us say, as much as, and even more than, by spiritual or doctrinal concerns. Despite that, however, I trust you'll believe me when I say I never for a moment considered any of the actions and innovations here in Charis, disturbing though some of them may have been, as rising to a level which would require or justify the apparent choice of solutions of the 'Knights of the Temple Lands."

"I do believe that," Staynair said quietly, and it was true. He'd never considered Ahdymsyn an *evil* man, although in some ways the very banality of his venal motivations had been almost worse.

"I'm sure you also realize," Ahdymsyn continued, "that Father Paityr's report to the Inquisition emphasized his own belief that none of the innovations upon which he'd been asked to rule constituted violations of the Proscriptions of Jwo-jeng. I believe he was even more shocked by the attack launched against Charis than I was."

Staynair glanced at Wylsynn, and the young upper-priest looked back levelly. No doubt Wylsynn had been more surprised than Ahdymsyn, Staynair thought. Unlike the bishop executor, there'd never been any question of the sincerity and depth of Paityr Wylsynn's personal faith. He had to be aware of the frequently sordid considerations which underlay the official pronouncements of the Council of Vicars and the policies of the Group of Four, but Staynair had no doubt at all that the young priest had been both shocked and horrified by the Group of Four's proposed solution to the "Charisian problem."

"Despite that," Ahdymsyn went on, "both of us found ourselves in rather uncomfortable positions. Mind you, Your Eminence, no one offered to abuse or mistreat us in any way. Indeed, I doubt two prisoners have ever been more comfortably housed in the history of Safehold, although one or two of the guardsmen were undeniably a bit . . . testy after those lunatics tried to murder you right here in the Cathedral." Ahdymsyn shook his head, as if he could not believe, even now, that someone had tried to assasinate an archbishop— *any* archbishop—in his own cathedral. "Still, there was no question in our minds that we were in fact prisoners, however courteous everyone was in pretending otherwise."

"I can well understand that," Staynair replied. "In fact, that's precisely what you have been, and for several reasons. First, because of your positions in the Church hierarchy here in Charis, of course. Secondly, because there would have been so many reasons—many of them quite valid, even in King Cayleb's eyes—for you to have actively opposed our actions here of late. That opposition would have been inevitable, and, quite candidly, both of you, for different reasons, perhaps, would have carried considerable weight with some of our local clergy. And, third, to be completely frank, and whether you find this easy to believe or not, it's constituted an attempt to protect you, as well. To make it clear even to the Group of Four that you had had no part in those same actions."

Despite his own open acknowledgment of what the Grand Inquisitor and his colleagues had intended for Charis, the skin around Ahdymsyn's eyes seemed to tighten briefly as Staynair used the term "Group of Four." He made no protest against the archbishop's choice of words, however.

"No one ever explained that particular aspect of it to us, Your Eminence. Nonetheless, I was aware of it. And to match frankness for frankness, I was none too confident it would do any good, in my own case, at least. It's the tradition in your own navy, I believe, that a captain is responsible for whatever happens aboard his ship. The Council of Vicars will—quite rightly, to be fair—hold me at least partly accountable for what's transpired here.

"Despite that, it was always my intention to disassociate myself from your Kingdom's defiance of Mother Church. I could scarcely hold your legitimate self-defense against unprovoked attack against you, but in rejecting the authority even of the Grand Vicar, I felt you'd gone too far. Not simply in doctrinal terms, but in terms of the inevitable consequences not simply for Charis, but for all of Safehold.

"And then, yesterday, I received this."

He held up the folded paper he'd taken from his pocket.

"And that is?" Staynair asked politely.

"A personal letter from Archbishop Erayk," Ahdymsyn said very quietly. "One addressed jointly to Father Paityr and myself."

"I see."

Staynair managed to keep his fresh surprise out of his voice or expression, although the possibility of a letter from Erayk Dynnys to Ahdymsyn and Wylsynn had never occurred to him. Nor had there been any reason for him to suspect one had arrived. At Staynair's own insistence, Cayleb had directed that his "guests' " incoming mail was not to be tampered with. The king had insisted that any *outgoing* correspondence must be carefully examined and subject to censorship, but no one had attempted to restrict messages *to* Ahdymsyn or Wylsynn.

"Since the letter appears to be what inspired you to ask for this interview, may I assume you intend to share its contents with me?"

"You may, Your Eminence." Ahdymsyn's voice was heavy, his mouth grim.

"Your Eminence," he said, "Archbishop Erayk is dead."

"I beg your pardon?" Staynair sat suddenly straighter behind his desk.

"I said Archbishop Erayk is dead," Ahdymsyn repeated. "The news hasn't reached us here in Charis yet. I realize that. However, Archbishop Erayk's letter leaves me in no doubt that he is, indeed, dead by now. Executed by the Inquisition for malfeasance, apostasy, heresy, and treason against God's Church and against God Himself."

Staynair's face tightened. He needed no one to tell him what penalties

The Book of Schueler laid down for *anyone* convicted of those offenses, far less one of Mother Church's own archbishops.

"The archbishop's letter isn't lengthy, Your Eminence," Ahdymsyn said. "He was denied access to paper and ink for the purposes of correspondence and had to improvise to obtain even this single sheet. I'm not certain how he managed to get this one note out, either, given his strict confinement by the Inquisition. I feel certain his silence on that point was intended to protect whoever he entrusted it to. But what it does say is very much to the point."

"And that point is?" Staynair asked quietly.

"He begins by informing Father Paityr and myself of the grounds for his arrest and the sentence passed upon him. He asks us to forgive him—and to pray for his soul—despite his many failures. He also specifically asked me to leave this letter with *you*, for you to make use of in whatever way seems best to you, and he apologizes for his failure to protect and nurture the souls of his archbishopric in the way God demands of His priests. And"—Ahdymsyn looked levelly into Staynair's eyes—"he makes bold to give us one last directive as our archbishop."

"And that directive is?"

"He does not order us, for he says he feels he no longer has that right, but he urgently entreats us to remain here in Charis. He says that he fears that, should we return to Zion or to the Temple Lands, we, too, would be forced to answer to the Inquisition. He accepts his own fate, but as our priestly superior, he enjoins us to preserve our lives against unjust punishment and judicial murder by remaining beyond the Inquisition's reach. And he begs us to do whatever we may to atone for his failure—and ours—as the spiritual shepherds of Charis."

Staynair sat back in his chair, his eyes thoughtful. He would never have anticipated such a letter from Erayk Dynnys. Yet he had no doubt it was genuine, and he wondered what sort of spiritual pilgrimage Dynnys had experienced in the hands of the Inquisition to produce it. There was good in any man. Staynair believed that as firmly as he believed the sun would rise in the morning. But that good was more deeply hidden, more deeply buried, in some than in others, and he had thought the good in Erayk Dynnys was irretrievably buried under a mountain of careless venality and a lifetime's participation in the Temple's internal corruption.

But I was wrong, he thought. *The finger of God can touch anyone, anywhere, through the most unlikely of avenues. I've always believed that, too. And here at the end of Erayk Dynnys' life, God has incontestably touched him.*

The archbishop closed his eyes while he said a brief, intense prayer of thanks that even at the very end, Dynnys had found his way to God, clear-eyed despite the corrupting lenses through which he had been taught to look for Him. Then Staynair straightened and looked across at his visitors.

He understood now the peculiar fragility he'd sensed in Ahdymsyn. Like Dynnys—and unlike Wylsynn—Ahdymsyn was a man whose faith had taken second place to his secular responsibilities . . . and opportunities. In Dynnys' fate and letter, he'd seen the mirror of himself, and it must have been a terrifying glimpse. Yet, unlike Dynnys, he had the opportunity to profit from the experience in this world, not simply in the next. He could choose what decisions he would make in the life that remained to him, and it was obvious to Staynair that he found that possibility as frightening as it was exhilarating, as much a matter for shame as for a chance to make some sort of amends.

For young Wylsynn, however, it must have been quite a different shock. Staynair knew better than most that Wylsynn had entertained few illusions about the way in which the Church's actions so often betrayed the spirit of its own *Holy Writ*. But the *scale* of the corruption, and the horrific lengths to which the Group of Four had been prepared to go, must have hit him like a sledgehammer. And unlike Dynnys and Ahdymsyn, Paityr Wylsynn had never forgotten he was God's priest, never allowed the corruption around him and behind him to distract him from his spiritual duties.

And now one of the most blameless servants of Mother Church Staynair had ever known found himself directed by a fallen archbishop whose corruption must have been evident to Wylsynn all along to turn his back upon Mother Church. To deny her authority, reject her demands. A priest of the Inquisition had been commanded to defy the Grand Inquisitor himself by one of the Inquisition's very victims.

"May God have mercy on His true servant Erayk," Staynair murmured, touching first his heart and then his lips.

"Amen," Ahdymsyn and Wylsynn echoed.

"I am shocked and dismayed by Archbishop Erayk's fate," Staynair said then. "And yet, at the end of his life, I believe he rose to a level and an awareness of God which all too few of us ever attain.

"Nonetheless, I must tell both of you that one point of doctrine upon which I, and the Church of Charis, strongly disagree with the doctrine of the Council of Vicars is on the right—and responsibility—of any child of God to judge for himself or herself where the right truly lies and what it demands of him or her. The role of the Church is not to dictate, but to teach—to explain, educate, and enjoin. The role of the individual is to exercise his or her freedom of will in loving God and doing that which is right because it *is* right, and not simply because he is given no other choice."

Wylsynn stirred slightly in his chair, and Staynair looked at him.

"I tell you this, Father Paityr, because I refuse to mislead you or any other man as to my own stance upon this point. No man or woman can truly choose to serve God unless they are equally free to *refuse* to serve Him, and God desires for His people to come to Him clear-eyed and joyously, not cringing in terror of the Inquisition and the damnation of Hell. I intend to make it clear to all that I refuse to abuse the power of this office to dictate to the consciences of priests or the laity. That way lies the very corruption and casual abuse of power 'in the name of God' which has led us to this current break with the Council of Vicars. When Mother Church decides she may *command* whatever she desires of her children, then the feet of her priesthood are set firmly on the path into darkness. As Archbishop, at the head of the Church's hierarchy here in Charis, I may order policy, make decisions, and instruct both the episcopate and the priesthood. And, should those instructions be violated or ignored, I have the right and responsibility to remove those who cannot in conscience obey me from whatever offices they may hold within that hierarchy. But a priest is a priest forever, Father. Unless he be found incontestably guilty of sin and the misuse of his office, no man may *take* that office from him or deny him his vocation. Nor do I—or any man— have the right to excommunicate, torture, or kill any man or woman who simply does not or cannot believe that which *I* believe."

Wylsynn said nothing for a moment, then he inhaled deeply.

"Your Eminence, I'm a servant of the Inquisition. I believe you must recognize that I've always attempted to exercise the powers of my office in a way which meets my pastoral responsibilities and tempers discipline with love and understanding. Yet I've dedicated my entire life, my faith in God, to Mother Church's responsibility to preserve God's children from corruption. Not simply to *'convince'* them of what their actions should be, but to protect them from the lures of Shan-wei by whatever means may be necessary."

"I realize that, Father. That's the very reason I've been so explicit in defining that doctrinal difference. I have great respect for your personal faith and for your character, both as a man and as a priest. Nothing would give me greater pleasure than to see you become a part of the process of reforming the Church's abuses—*all* of her abuses—here in Charis and elsewhere. I fully recognize what a tower of strength you could become in that daunting task. But this isn't a cause upon which any man, be he ever so much a priest, can embark unless he feels confident that it's *his* cause, and God's, as well as mine. Do you feel that confidence, Father?"

"I don't know," Wylsynn said simply, quietly, meeting Staynair's level gaze with eyes of clear gray honesty. "I know the abuses of which you speak, of which Archbishop Erayk wrote, are real. I know what the Grand Inquisitor and Chancellor intended to happen to Charis, and I know it was wrong. Worse than wrong, it was evil, a betrayal of everything Mother Church is supposed to stand for and defend. Whatever else it might have been, I know it *could* not have been the will of God. Yet there's a great difference between agreeing that what they've done is wrong and agreeing that what you've done is *right*."

"I appreciate your honesty, Father. And I trust the clarity of your spiritual vision. I won't try to convert you to my view today. Obviously, until your own faith and your own conscience convince you that what we're trying to accomplish here in Charis *is* right, no one could expect you to lend yourself to it. But I ask you to consider what you yourself have seen, what Archbishop Erayk has written to you, the words and deeds of the Church of Charis, and the touch of God upon your own heart. Approach it in prayer and sober meditation, Father, not in a white heat. If you find in time that God moves you to embrace our efforts, then we will welcome you as a brother and a fellow servant of God. And if God doesn't move you to join us, we will respect and accept that decision, as well."

"And in the meantime, Your Eminence?"

"And in the meantime, Father, I would be most grateful if you would continue to exercise the office of Intendant here in Charis. As you say, no one in this Kingdom has ever entertained the least doubt of your determination to apply the Proscriptions honestly and fairly. It would be immensely reassuring to all of our people to know you continue in that position in this time of turmoil and change."

"If I were to agree to any such thing, Your Eminence, then I would continue to exercise that office in the way *I* see fit."

"Which is no more and no less than I would wish of you, Father."

"Even if it brings us into conflict, Your Eminence?"

"Father," Staynair said with a gentle smile, "given the way you've met your responsibilities in the past, I see absolutely no reason to believe that you would find yourself in conflict with me over the matter of the Proscriptions. If we disagree, then, obviously, each of us will attempt to convince the other, but I've never seen you make a capricious decision, or, for that matter, one with which I disagreed. I see no reason to expect you to make any such decision now.

"It's true that we may have some differences of opinion upon the proper use of the coercive authority of your office. As you say, you believe that the Church's responsibility is to protect against corruption by 'whatever means are necessary,' whereas I believe her responsibility is to teach and convince. That external compulsion cannot generate the *internal* strength to resist darkness and evil when they come upon each and every one of us in our daily lives. I suspect you may now find yourself somewhat more leery of the term 'whatever means are necessary' than you were before the Group of Four's invasion attempt, but I have no doubt we may yet find ourselves on opposite sides over some issue of doctrinal enforcement. If that time comes, I'll certainly attempt to convince you to accept my view of the situation, but you will always have the right to resign your office—and to publicly state your reasons for doing so. And I will never attempt to compel you to accept or publicly endorse my position on any matter in which your conscience cannot agree with me."

"With your permission, Your Eminence, I will say neither yes nor no today," Wylsynn said after a long, thoughtful moment. "As you yourself have suggested, this isn't a decision, a choice, which should be rushed into. I would prefer to meditate and pray that God will show me my direction before I give you an answer."

"I can ask no more than that of any priest, Father." Staynair smiled at the young man, then looked back to Ahdymsyn. "Nor can I ask more than that of any bishop executor," he said with another smile. "Obviously, I would welcome both of you for political reasons, as well as spiritual ones, but neither I nor King Cayleb will attempt to dictate to your consciences. How can we do that, when so much of our quarrel with the Council of Vicars lies in its attempt to do just that to all of God's children? Whatever your final decision, however, know this. On my own authority, in the full expectation that King Cayleb will agree, but even if he does not, I grant both of you sanctuary. Whether or not you find it in your hearts and souls to join with us in our effort to transform Mother Church back into what God would truly have her be, you may remain here, in Charis, under the protection of the Church of Charis, for however long you choose."

.IV.
Royal Palace and Monastery of Saint Zherneau, City of Tellesberg, Kingdom of Charis

A moment, if you please, *Seijin* Merlin."
Merlin paused and looked up in some surprise as Archbishop Maikel laid a large, powerful hand lightly on his shoulder.

"Yes, Your Eminence? How may I help you?"

They stood just inside the door of the chamber the rest of the Royal Council had just left, and Cayleb looked back at them with one eyebrow raised.

"Is there something we still need to talk about, Maikel?" the king asked.

"Actually, Your Majesty," Staynair said, his tone more formal than usual, "I'd like to borrow the *seijin* for the afternoon, if I might." Cayleb's surprise showed rather more clearly than Merlin's had, and the archbishop smiled. "I promise I'll have him back in time for supper, Your Majesty. I simply have a minor matter I need to discuss with him, and since I have a pastoral errand to run in the city this afternoon, anyway, I thought I might ask him to come along with me. Just as a precaution, you understand."

Cayleb's expression tightened abruptly. The attempt to assassinate Archbishop Maikel was entirely too fresh in his memory for him to misunderstand what sort of "precaution" Staynair had in mind. Especially in view of what had happened to the Royal College three days before.

"If you need additional protection, Maikel—" the king began, but Staynair shook his head.

"I'm not really especially concerned about assassins, Your Majesty," he said with a half smile. "Not this time, at least. However, I do have a visit I want to pay this afternoon, and under the circumstances, I'd really prefer not to draw a great deal of attention to it. Unfortunately, I'd be just a *tad* noticeable if I take along a passel of armsmen. Given the unfortunate events in the Cathedral, what's happened to the College, and the way feelings in general seem to be running, I'd hate for a private trip to visit an old friend who's not feeling especially well to focus any potential hostility on a simple monastery, and it's only too possible I might make certain people think I must be up to something if they realize I'm going there at all. Fortunately, I feel quite confident"—his smile grew broader—"that Captain Athrawes would be more than up to the task of keeping us both intact if I made the trip . . . incognito, shall we say?"

"Is it really important enough to risk having you running around the streets 'incognito' at a time like this?" Cayleb asked.

"He's a very old friend, Your Majesty," Staynair replied quietly, "and his health has been failing for some time now. It isn't just a visit of friendship."

Cayleb gazed at the prelate for a moment or two, then drew a deep breath and nodded. Merlin wasn't particularly surprised by the king's capitulation, even though the notion of anything happening to Maikel Staynair at this particular moment in the history of Safehold was, frankly, just this side of terrifying. That was probably even truer for Merlin than it was for Cayleb, if Merlin was going to be honest, and after the earlier attempt no one—not even Staynair—could pretend the Temple Loyalists hadn't figured out the same thing. But both Merlin and Cayleb knew nothing they could possibly say would dissuade Staynair from the discharge of his priestly office. If they could have dissuaded him, he would have been someone else . . . and he *wouldn't* have been so vital to their hopes for the future.

"Very well," the king said. Then he moved his eyes to Merlin. "Do try to keep him in one piece, please, Merlin. Again."

Staynair had the grace to wince ever so slightly at the king's final word, but he didn't let it change his mind.

"I'll do my very best, Your Majesty," Merlin assured Cayleb, and glanced at the towering Royal Guardsman who'd been waiting outside the council room door.

Sergeant Payter Faircaster was the only member of Crown Prince Cayleb's Marine bodyguard to formally transfer to the Guard when Cayleb assumed the throne. Ahrnahld Fhalkhan and the rest of Cayleb's old bodyguards were now protecting Crown Prince Zhan, Cayleb's eleven-year-old younger brother. The change of assignment had been hard on both Cayleb and the men who had protected him for so long, but the security of the heir to the Charisian throne had been a responsibility of the Royal Charisian Marines since time out of mind. Faircaster might well have stayed with the old detachment as well, but Cayleb had insisted that at least one of "his" Marines had to come along . . . in no small part because they already knew about Merlin's "visions." Having someone else along to help cover for Merlin's occasional . . . peculiarities, at least until they'd decided which of the king's new guardsmen could be admitted to that same knowledge, had struck the young king as a very good idea.

Merlin had agreed. Besides, Faircaster's calm, competent ferocity was immensely comforting to the man—or PICA—responsible for keeping the king alive. And having someone around who'd been fishing Cayleb out of scrapes since he was nine years old wasn't exactly something to sneer at, either.

"Payter," Merlin said now.

"Yes, Sir," the enormous guardsman rumbled.

"Send a page to inform Lieutenant Ahstyn that you need another man. I think Sergeant Vynair should be available. Then keep a close eye on His Majesty until Vynair turns up. Don't let him get into any trouble."

"Yes, Sir." Faircaster touched his right fist to his cuirass breastplate in salute and gave the king a stern glance, and Cayleb shook his head.

"It's always so comforting to realize how much in command I am of all about me," he remarked to no one in particular.

"That's good to know, Your Majesty." The exquisite courtesy of Merlin's response was only slightly flawed by the amusement in his strange, sapphire eyes. Then he turned back to Staynair.

"At your convenience, Your Eminence," he murmured.

▼   ▼   ▼

"Incognito," Staynair had said, and "incognito" he'd meant, Merlin thought more than a bit grumpily an hour or so later. In fact, Merlin was more than a little surprised by just how incognito Maikel Staynair could be when he put his mind to it. The archbishop was probably even more recognizable to the people of the capital than King Cayleb himself. For years, he'd appeared every Wednesday in Tellesberg Cathedral, celebrating high mass for the people of the capital as their city's bishop, and he'd been even more visible since becoming the entire kingdom's archbishop.

Despite that, and despite his flowing beard and strong-featured face, he'd faded somehow into near-total anonymity when he exchanged the orange-trimmed white cassock of his exalted ecclesiastical rank for the stark, unadorned brown robe of a simple brother of the Order of Bédard (to which he was still entitled, despite his elevation) and turned the ruby ring of his office to hide the stone against his palm. With the cowl pulled up and his head bent with proper humility, the archbishop disappeared completely.

Unfortunately, that robe was *not* one of the cassocks Owl and Merlin had replaced. Its normal cloth would offer no special resistance to blades or bullets, which was enough to make Merlin acutely unhappy, although he could hardly explain why that might be to Staynair. Which only made him even *more* unhappy, of course.

Nor did he find much to rejoice about in the reflection that a simple brother would scarcely have been accompanied by a captain of the Royal Guard, which meant Merlin had been forced to make some adjustments to his own appearance, as well. He'd left his armor, his Guard uniform, and his wakazashi behind, and he hoped his katana didn't look peculiar enough to attract undue attention. He wasn't certain how realistic that hope might be, however, since the only two men in the entire kingdom—for that matter, on the entire face of the planet—who routinely carried katanas were His Majesty King Cayleb and the famous (or infamous) *seijin*, Merlin. He was also a little surprised by how much he missed his black-and-gold livery after wearing it virtually every day for the better part of two local years.

But the hardest thing for him to disguise was his eyes. Merlin Athrawes' eyes were the same deep sapphire blue as Nimue Alban's, and he had yet to meet a single Charisian with eyes which even approached their color.

I wish to hell these people had at least invented sunglasses *or something*, he groused to himself as they made their way through the capital city's teeming, noisy, always incredibly *busy* streets. Of course, if he wanted to be honest, he could have done something about the eyes before he ever arrived in Charis. He couldn't simply reprogram their color, but he *could* have used the fabrication unit in Nimue's Cave to make himself a nice brown pair of contacts to cover their "natural" color.

I guess I didn't want to lose that last trace of Nimue, he admitted to himself. *And to be honest, I still don't . . . even if it has turned out to be a royal pain in the ass. And* one *I can't just abandon now that everyone and his brother knows "Captain Athrawes" has those "unearthly blue,* seijin *eyes." Talk about shooting myself in the foot!*

His strong suspicion that Staynair was rather amused by his predicament didn't help his mood one bit, either.

"Just how much farther is it to this monastery, Your Eminence, if you don't mind my asking?" He kept his voice low, and Staynair snorted.

"About another fifteen or twenty minutes," he replied.

"If I'd realized we were going to be hiking halfway across the city, I'd probably have insisted on a little better security," Merlin observed. He didn't quite succeed in keeping the asperity out of his voice. In fact, he didn't even try very hard, and Staynair chuckled, then shook his head.

"It's not really all that much farther," he said soothingly. "Besides, the exercise is good for us."

"Thank you for thinking of me, Your Eminence, but I get quite a lot of exercise, anyway."

Staynair chuckled again, and Merlin smiled almost against his will.

At least the inevitable mid-afternoon thunderstorms which had swept over the capital earlier had continued on their way without lingering. The air was humid in the rain's aftermath, however, and the fact that it was technically fall didn't seem to have impressed the temperature particularly. According to Merlin's built-in temperature sensors, it hovered right at thirty-two degrees on the Celsius scale no one else in the entire galaxy used any longer.

Fortunately, neither heat nor humidity meant very much to a PICA, and Staynair had grown up right here in Tellesberg. The climate didn't bother him a bit, and if *he* was in need of any exercise, it certainly didn't show in the brisk pace he'd set since they left the palace behind.

"Ah! *Here* we are," he said a few minutes later, and turned down a side street.

Merlin looked around curiously. Despite the arson which had reduced the Royal College to a heap of cinders and charred brick, Tellesberg was a more law-abiding and prosperous city than many. Even so, it had its . . . less affluent neighborhoods, and this was scarcely the better side of town. The buildings around them had the run-down look of shops and warehouses whose customers were none too plump in the purse, the odors wafting about suggested that the local sewers could have used a little attention, they'd passed at least two fire department cisterns which were no more than half-filled, and the hard and hungry eyes of one or two of the loungers they'd passed in the last few blocks had convinced Merlin that Staynair had been wise to be sure he had an adequate bodyguard even if no one at all recognized him for who he truly was.

They continued on their way for another five minutes or so, while the shops got fewer and fewer and run-down warehouses and overcrowded tenements got more and more numerous. And then, finally, Staynair turned up one last walkway to a heavy wooden door set into a distinctly battered and modest-looking wall.

Like every major Safeholdian city, Tellesberg was liberally supplied with churches and cathedrals. Monasteries and convents were also fairly common, although most of those tended to be located outside urban areas, where they could help to support themselves by farming. But this particular monastery didn't fit that description. It looked as if it had probably been here since Tellesberg's founding, and warehouses had squeezed so tightly against it on either side that it couldn't possibly have space for anything more than a very modest kitchen garden.

Staynair knocked, and then he and Merlin waited patiently until the slide on the small window in the stout wooden door opened and a monk looked out. To Merlin's surprise, the monk's brown habit bore the white horse of the Order of Truscott, not the oil lamp of the Order of Bédard. Somehow Merlin had had the impression that the monastery for which they were bound belonged to Staynair's order.

The door warden's eyes lit with obvious recognition as he saw Staynair, and the sturdy, scarred portal quickly opened. Merlin had expected it to squeak loudly, given the monastery wall's general down-at-the-heels appearance, but instead it moved with the silence of well-oiled and well-maintained hinges.

"Welcome to the Monastery of Saint Zherneau, *Seijin* Merlin," Staynair said as they passed through the opening and the door closed behind them. There was a curious note in the archbishop's voice, as if somehow the words meant more than they'd said. Merlin's internal antennae twitched, but he said nothing, only nodded and followed Staynair and the door warden across the monastery's courtyard.

The space inside the outer wall turned out to be larger than Merlin would have estimated from the outside. It was considerably deeper, and it wasn't the cobbled square or packed dirt courtyard he would have expected from the general dilapidation of the surrounding neighborhood. Instead, he found himself surrounded by greenery, ancient lichen-covered walls, and the liquid, waterfall-music magic of ornamental fish ponds. Wyverns and terrestrial songbirds perched in the branches of dwarf fruit trees which appeared to be almost as ancient as the monastery itself, and their soft whistles and chirps made a soothing contrast to the city noises outside the wall.

Staynair and he followed their guide into the chapter house and down a series of whitewashed corridors. The brick floors had been worn smooth and gullied by centuries of passing feet, and the walls were a combination of stone and brick, with the transition between building materials indicating where later additions joined the original structure. They were also quite thick, and it was cool and quiet inside them.

Their guide paused at last outside another door. He glanced over his shoulder at Staynair, then knocked once, gently.

"Enter," a voice called from the other side, and the monk opened the door and stood aside.

"Thank you, Brother," Staynair murmured, then stepped past him with a slight "follow me" head twitch at Merlin.

They found themselves in what was obviously an office, although at first glance one might have been forgiven for thinking it was a library, instead. Or possibly an outsized storage closet. The slightly musty smell of paper and ink filled the air, bookshelves filled what would otherwise have been a high-ceilinged, airy chamber almost claustrophobically full, and the desk under its single skylight sat in a shelf-surrounded space, like a clearing hacked out of a towering rain forest canopy, that looked much too small for it and the two chairs sitting in front of it.

Judging from the heap of books and papers stacked on the floor, Merlin suspected that the chairs normally served as convenient holding spots for reference works and documents. Somehow he didn't think they "just happened" to have been cleared of their burdens before he and the archbishop arrived so unexpectedly.

"*Seijin* Merlin," Staynair said, "allow me to introduce Father Zhon Byrkyt, the Abbot of Saint Zherneau's."

"Father," Merlin responded with a slight bow. Byrkyt was an elderly man, obviously at least several years older than Staynair, who wasn't precisely an infant himself. In his youth, he'd probably been somewhere between Staynair's height and Merlin's, which would have made him a veritable giant for Charis, although advancing years and a curving spine had changed that, and he looked almost painfully frail. He wore the green cassock of an over-priest, rather than the brown habit the door warden had worn. And, Merlin noted with slightly narrowed eyes, his cassock carried the quill pen of Chihiro rather than the horse of Truscott or the lamp of Bédard.

"*Seijin,*" the abbot replied. His voice sounded as if it had once been far more robust—even as he had—but his eyes were clear and sharp. They were also at least as intense as Merlin's own, and there was a curiously eager light in their brown depths. He gestured at the chairs in front of his desk. "Please, be seated, both of you," he invited.

Merlin waited until Staynair had taken one of the chairs before he sat himself. Then he settled down, standing his scabbarded katana upright against the edge of Byrkyt's desk and hoping he looked rather more relaxed than he actually felt. He didn't need a PICA's sensors to feel the strange, almost anticipatory tension which hovered about him.

That tension stretched out in silence for several seconds before Staynair broke it.

"First," the archbishop said, "allow me to apologize, Merlin. I'm reasonably certain you've already deduced that I was guilty of a certain amount of . . . misdirection, let's say, when I 'invited you' to accompany me this afternoon."

"Some slight suspicion along that line *had* occurred to me, Your Eminence," Merlin conceded, and Staynair chuckled.

"I'm not surprised," he said. "On the other hand, there are certain things which will be easier to explain here at Saint Zherneau's than they would have been in the Palace. Things which, I feel certain"—his eyes bored suddenly into Merlin's—"will come as something of a surprise to you."

"Somehow, I don't doubt that in the least," Merlin said dryly.

"What I said to Cayleb was the truth," Staynair told him. "Zhon"—he nodded at Byrkyt—"is indeed a very old friend of mine. And, alas, his health isn't good. I'm fairly confident he won't find himself in need of extreme unction this afternoon, however."

"I'm relieved to hear that, Your Eminence."

"So am I," Byrkyt agreed with a smile of his own.

"Well, yes." Staynair might actually have looked just a little embarrassed, Merlin thought, however unlikely it seemed. If he did, it didn't slow him down for long.

"At any rate," the archbishop continued, "my real objective, obviously, was to get you here."

"And the reason you wanted me here was precisely what, Your Eminence?" Merlin inquired politely.

"That's probably going to take a little explaining." Staynair leaned back in his chair, crossing his legs, and regarded Merlin steadily.

"The Monastery of Saint Zherneau is quite ancient, actually," he said. "In fact, tradition has it—and I believe the tradition is accurate, in this case, for several reasons—that the monastery stands upon the site of the oldest church in Tellesberg. It dates back literally to within a very few years of the Creation. Indeed, there are some indications that the original church was built on the Day of Creation itself."

Merlin nodded, and reminded himself that unlike any of the terrestrial religions with which he was familiar, the Church of God Awaiting truly was able to assign an exact day, hour, and minute to the moment of Creation. A date and time amply substantiated by not simply the *Holy Writ* itself, but also by *The Testimonies*, the firsthand recollections of the eight million literate Adams and Eves who had experienced it. Of course, none of the people who'd left those written journals, letters, and accounts had remembered that they'd volunteered as colonists only to have their memories completely scrubbed and reprogrammed to believe the colony command crew's personnel were archangels.

"Saint Zherneau's isn't well known outside Charis," Staynair continued. "It isn't a large monastery, and the Brethren of Zherneau have never been particularly numerous compared to any of the mainstream orders. Of course, there are quite a few small monasteries and convents, and they tend to come and go. Most of them grow out of the life and example of a particularly pious and devout spiritual leader who attracts a following of like-minded individuals during his or her own lifetime. Mother Church has always permitted such small religious communities, and the majority of them, frankly, don't often last more than a single generation or so after their founders' deaths. Generally, they're sponsored and supported by one of the major orders, and when they fade away, their holdings and manors—if any—escheat to the sponsoring order.

"Saint Zherneau's, however, is . . . unique in several respects. First, its charter was established right here in Tellesberg, not in Zion, under the authority of the first Bishop of Tellesberg, even before any archbishop had been appointed to us. Secondly, it's never been sponsored by—or restricted to the membership of—a single order. The Brethren are drawn from virtually every order of Mother Church. The monastery is a place of spiritual retreat and renewal open to all, and its brethren bring a wide diversity of perspectives with them."

The archbishop paused, and Merlin pursed his lips thoughtfully. What Staynair was describing was quite different from the vast majority of monastic communities Merlin had studied since awakening in Nimue's Cave. Most Safeholdian monasteries and convents were very definitely the property of one or another of the great orders, and those orders were zealous about defending their ownership. Once one got beyond the borders of the Temple Lands, the competition between orders was seldom as fierce as it was inside the precincts of the Temple and the city of Zion. But it always existed, and their monasteries, convents, manors, and estates represented more than simple tokens in the competition. Those institutions were the sinews and wealth which made that competition possible.

Of course, Saint Zherneau's didn't exactly strike Merlin as one of the great monastic communities. Despite its obvious age and lovingly landscaped grounds, it was, as Staynair had said, a relatively small monastery. It wasn't likely that it produced a great deal of wealth, which might well explain how it had avoided the great orders' attention, as well as the greater inclusiveness and diversity of its membership.

Somehow, though, Merlin rather doubted the explanation was quite that simple.

"I, myself, came here to Saint Zherneau's as a very young man," Staynair said. "At the time, I was unsure whether or not I truly had a vocation, and the Brethren helped me address my doubts. They were a great comfort to me when my spirit needed that comfort badly, and like many others, I became one of them. Indeed, although the population of the monastery itself at any moment is usually quite small, a great many of the Brethren, like myself, maintain our membership even after we've moved on formally to one or another of the great orders. We remain family, one might say, which means we have far more members than one might think from the size of the monastery itself, and most of us return at intervals to the monastery for spiritual retreats and to draw strength from the support of our fellow brothers.

"Interestingly enough"—the archbishop's eyes drilled into Merlin's once more—"the confessors of six of the last eight kings of Charis have all been Brothers of Saint Zherneau, as well."

Had Merlin still been a creature of flesh and blood, he would have inhaled a deep breath of surprise and speculation. But he wasn't, of course, and so he simply tilted his head to one side.

"That sounds like a remarkable . . . coincidence, Your Eminence," he observed.

"Yes, it does, doesn't it?" Staynair smiled at him, then glanced at the abbot. "I told you he was quick, didn't I, Zhon?"

"So you did," Byrkyt agreed, and smiled somewhat more broadly than his ecclesiastic superior. "As a matter of fact, he rather reminds me of another young man I once knew, although he seems rather less . . . rebellious."

"Really? And who might that have been?"

"Fishing for compliments is a most unbecoming trait in an archbishop," Byrkyt replied serenely, but his sharp brown eyes had never wavered from Merlin's face. Now he turned to face him fully.

"What Maikel is getting at, in his somewhat indirect fashion, *Seijin* Merlin, is that the Brethren of Saint Zherneau haven't, as I'm sure you've already guessed, produced that many confessors for that many monarchs by accident."

"I'm sure they haven't. The question in my mind, Father, is exactly why they've done it, and how, and why you and the Archbishop should choose to make me aware of it."

"*The* question?" Byrkyt said. "By my count, that's at least three questions, *Seijin*." He chuckled. "Well, no matter. I'll answer the last one first, if you don't mind."

"I don't mind at all," Merlin said, although, to be honest, he wasn't absolutely certain that was the truth.

"The reason Maikel decided to bring you here to meet me today, *Seijin*, has to do with a letter he received from King Haarahld. It was written shortly before the King's death, and it dealt primarily with his underlying strategy for keeping Duke Black Water's fleet in play until Cayleb—and you, of course— could return from Armageddon Reef to deal with it. In fact," if Staynair's eyes had bored into Merlin like drills, Byrkyt's were diamond-cutting lasers, "it had to do with how he knew how long he had to keep Black Water occupied."

Merlin found himself sitting very, very still. He'd never explained to either Cayleb or Haarahld exactly how he'd physically traveled four thousand miles in less than two hours to carry the warning about Black Water's new strategy to Haarahld. He'd been astounded and immensely relieved, to say the very least, by how calmly Haarahld had taken his "miraculous" appearance on the stern gallery of the king's flagship in the middle of the night, but in all honesty, he'd been so focused on the immediate threat that he hadn't really tried to nail down *why* the king had reacted with so little outward consternation.

And he'd never suspected for a moment that Haarahld might have told anyone else, even his confessor, about it.

Silence lingered in the quiet office-library. In an odd sort of way, it was almost as if Staynair and Byrkyt were the PICAs, sitting silently, waiting with absolute patience while Merlin tried to absorb the implications of what Byrkyt had just said . . . and think of some way to respond.

"Father," he said finally, "Your Eminence, I don't know exactly what King Haarahld may have written to you. I can only assume, however, that whatever it was, it was not to denounce me as some sort of demon."

"Hardly that, Merlin." Staynair's voice was gentle, almost comforting, and as Merlin watched, he smiled as if in fond memory. "He was *excited*, actually. There was always that piece of a little boy down inside him, that sense of wonder. Oh," the archbishop waved one hand, "he wasn't *totally* immune to the possibility that he was making a mistake in trusting you. That you might actually turn out to be a 'demon.' After all, we're speaking here of matters of faith, where reason is but one support, and that sometimes a frail one. Still, Merlin, there comes a time when any child of God must gather up in his hands all that he is, all that he can ever hope to be, and *commit* it. After all the thought, all the prayer, all the meditation, that moment of decision comes to all of us. Some never find the courage to meet it. They look away, try to ignore it or simply pretend it never came to them. Others turn away, take refuge in what others have taught them, what others have commanded them to think and believe, rather than making the choice, accepting the test, for themselves.

"But Haarahld was never a coward. When the moment came, he recognized it, and he met it, and he chose to place his trust in you. He wrote me about that decision, and he said"—Staynair's eyes went slightly out of focus as he recited from memory—" 'He may *be* a demon, after all, Maikel. I don't think so, but as we all know, I've been wrong a few times in my life. *Quite* a few, actually. But either way, the time has finally come. I won't fail the trust God has placed in all of us by refusing the choice. And so, I've placed my own life, my son's life, the lives of my other children, my people, and *yours*—and all the souls that go with them—in his hands. If I'm wrong to do so, then surely I will pay a terrible price after this life. But I'm not. And if it should happen that God chooses for me never to return home, know this. I accept His decision, and I pass to you and to my son the completion of the task I agreed to undertake so long ago.' "

The archbishop fell silent once more. Merlin felt the dead king's words echoing within him. It was as if he and Haarahld stood together on that stern-walk once again, and his PICA eyes burned as they faithfully mimicked the autonomous responses of their original human models.

"What task, Your Eminence?" he asked softly.

"The task of teaching his people, and all of Safehold, the truth," Staynair said. "The truth about God, about the Church, about our world and all the work of God's hands. The truth that the Church has spent so many centuries systematically suppressing and choking out of existence."

"The truth?" Merlin stared at the archbishop. Even now, even after hearing Haarahld's words literally from beyond the grave, he had never expected to hear anything like *that*, and his thoughts spun like a man dancing on ice while he fought for balance. "What truth?"

"This one," Byrkyt said quietly. "It begins, 'We hold these truths to be self-evident, that all men are created equal, that they are endowed by their Creator with certain unalienable rights, that among these are . . .' "

.V.
Marine Training Ground,
Helen Island,
Kingdom of Charis

Golden-tongued bugles sounded, and the five hundred men in the dark blue tunics and light blue breeches of the Royal Charisian Marines responded almost instantly. The compact battalion column split smoothly into its five component companies, each of which marched rapidly outward from the original column, then wheeled and formed neatly into a three-deep line.

Orders rang out from bull-throated sergeants, rifle slings came off shoulders, cartridge boxes opened, and ramrods flashed in the sunlight. Barely five minutes after the first bugle call, the early afternoon came apart in flame and smoke as the battalion fired its first volley at the targets set up a hundred and fifty yards from its position. A second volley roared fifteen seconds later, and a third fifteen seconds after that. No non-Charisian musketeers in the world could have come remotely close to matching that rate of fire. A matchlock musket did extraordinarily well to fire one shot in a minute, far less the *four* rounds a minute the Marines were managing.

And they weren't firing as rapidly as they could have. This was controlled, *aimed* volley fire, not maximum rate.

A total of six volleys cracked like thunder in just over seventy-five seconds, and the row of targets literally blew apart under the impact of three thousand half-inch rifle bullets. Very few of those bullets missed, and that, too, was something no other musketeers in the world could have matched.

While the battalion was forming up and delivering its volleys, the four pieces of artillery which had been rolling along behind it on the newly designed two-wheel carriages and limbers had come up behind the firing line, Earl Lock Island noticed from where he stood on his hilltop observation post with Brigadier Clareyk. The six-legged hill dragons harnessed to the limbers clearly didn't care much for the sounds of massed rifle fire, but equally clearly, they'd grown more or less accustomed to it. However much they might dislike it, the big beasts—they were smaller than their jungle dragon counterparts, or even the carnivorous great dragons, but they were still the size of an Old Earth elephant—were remarkably steady as their drovers turned them to face back the way they'd come while the gun crews unlimbered.

The guns were the new twelve-pounder field guns, not the much heavier siege artillery the earl had seen demonstrated several five-days ago. He hadn't yet seen the twelve-pounders in action, and as he reached down to rub the soft ears of the massive black-and-tan Rottweiler sitting alertly upright beside him, he watched with intense interest while the company forming the center of the Marine firing line marched briskly aside. The line opened smoothly, and the guns were wheeled up into position.

The gunners weren't loading with round shot; they were loading with canister, and Lock Island winced at what he knew was coming. He hadn't actually seen "canister" used yet, but he'd had it described to him. Instead of the nine to twelve small projectiles customary for a stand of grapeshot in naval service, the canister rounds were thin-walled cylinders, each packed with *twenty-seven* inch-and-a-half shot. The tubes were designed to burst apart on firing, releasing their burdens of shot and turning the cannon into the world's largest shotguns. Not only that, but these were what Sir Ahlfryd Hyndryk, Baron Seamount, called "fixed rounds." The powder charge was already attached to the tube of canister, and the entire round could be rammed home with a single thrust.

With the new ammunition Baron Seamount had designed (*with, of course, a little help from* Seijin *Merlin,* Lock Island reminded himself), the artillerists could load and fire with preposterous speed. Indeed, using the fixed rounds, they could load as quickly as the Marine riflemen who'd already shredded the waiting targets. Lock Island knew no one down there was moving as quickly as they possibly could. This was a training exercise—and demonstration—not actual combat. Which meant the officers and noncoms in charge of it weren't about to push their men hard enough to produce unnecessary casualties and injuries.

And which also meant that the rate of fire being demonstrated was "only" four or five times the rate of fire anyone else could have managed.

The guns were loaded now, he saw. Gun captains crouched behind them, peering over the simple but effective sights Seamount had devised and waving hand signals to their gun crews while the tubes were carefully aligned. Then they were waving the other gunners back, safely away from the weapons, while they took tension on the firing lanyards. One last look around to be sure everyone was clear, left hands raised in indication of readiness, and then the battery commander barked his order and the artillery bellowed with a flat, hard, concussive voice that dwarfed the sounds of rifle fire.

Each of the guns spewed its lethal canister downrange in a spreading cloud. Lock Island could see splashes of dirt kicking up where the dispersing patterns "wasted" some of their shot short of the targets. It didn't matter, though. Where the rifle bullets had ripped the wood and canvas targets into tatters, the canister simply flattened them. Well, that wasn't quite fair, Lock Island decided, raising his spyglass and peering through it. The targets hadn't been flattened; they'd simply disintegrated.

More bugles sounded, and the gunners stepped back from their weapons. The riflemen grounded the butts of their rifles, and whistles blew to signal the end of the fire exercise.

"That," Lock Island said, turning to the Marine officer standing beside him, "was . . . impressive. *Very* impressive, Brigadier."

"Thank you, My Lord," Brigadier Kynt Clareyk replied. "The men have worked hard. And not just because we've made them, either. They're impatient to show someone *else* what they can do, as well."

Lock Island nodded. He had no doubt at all who "else" Clareyk's men wanted to demonstrate their prowess to. Or, rather, *upon*.

"Soon, Brigadier. Soon," the high admiral promised. "You know better than most what the schedule looks like."

"Yes, My Lord." Clareyk might have looked just a teeny bit embarrassed, but Lock Island wasn't prepared to bet any money on it. And if truth be told, no one had a better right to be impatient than Brigadier Clareyk. After all, he was the one who'd written the training manual for the Royal Charisian Marines' new infantry tactics. And he'd also been Seamount's primary assistant in devising the world's first true *field artillery* tactics and integrating them with the infantry. He'd been a mere major then, not a brigadier; there hadn't *been* any Charisian brigadiers at the time. In fact, there hadn't been any brigadiers anywhere. The rank was less than six months old, suggested by *Seijin* Merlin as the Marines' buildup began to hit its stride.

Lieutenant Layn, Clareyk's second-in-command while he worked out the basic tactics for the new, longer-ranged, and far more accurate rifles, was now a major himself and in charge of the ongoing training program here on Helen Island.

And, Lock Island thought, looking back at the men of Clareyk's second battalion as they formed smoothly back into column formation, Layn was doing just as good a job as Clareyk had.

"Actually, High Admiral," another voice said, "I think we're probably going to need to consider moving our training operations. Or, perhaps, simply *expanding* them into other locations."

Lock Island turned to the short, almost pudgy-looking officer standing on his other side. Baron Seamount had lost the first two fingers of his left hand to an accidental explosion years before, but the mishap hadn't dimmed his passion for loud explosions one bit. Nor had it affected his sharp, incisive intelligence. Some people had been fooled by Seamount's relatively unprepossessing appearance, but Lock Island knew exactly how capable the brain behind that . . . unimpressive façade really was. And how valuable.

Although Seamount had been promoted from captain to commodore, Lock Island still felt vaguely guilty. By rights, Seamount should have had his own admiral's command streamer by now, given all he'd done for Charis. And he would have had that streamer, too . . . except for one minor problem. Despite his undeniable brilliance, despite the fact that it was his brain which had devised the basis for the new naval tactics and, with Brigadier Clareyk's able assistance, the new infantry and artillery tactics, as well, Seamount hadn't been to sea in a command capacity in almost twenty years. He'd have been hopelessly out of place actually commanding a fleet, or even a squadron. Besides, he was far too valuable where he was for Lock Island to even consider exposing him to enemy fire.

Fortunately, Seamount—who claimed he could get seasick taking a bath—appeared quite content. He got to play with fascinating new toys, especially over the past couple of years, and he was too busy stretching his brain to worry about whether his sleeve bore the single embroidered kraken of a commodore or the two gold krakens of an admiral.

"I take it that you're thinking in terms of expansion because we're running out of room here on Helen," the high admiral said now, and Seamount nodded.

"Yes, Sir. The real problem is that we don't have a great deal of *flat* room here on Helen. In some ways, that's good. As the Brigadier here pointed out to me months ago, we can't count on having nice, flat, spacious terrain when we actually have to fight, so it's not going to hurt us a bit to figure out how to fight in *cramped* terrain. And the security aspect here is very good. Nobody's going to see anything we don't want them to see. But the truth is, with the larger formations, it's hard to find the space to let them practice tactical evolutions. Too much of this island is vertical, Sir."

"That, believe me, is a point of which I'm well—one might almost say *painfully* well—aware," Lock Island said dryly. "Keelhaul, here," he gave the huge dog's massive head an affectionately gentle cuff, "actually likes coming up here. I suppose he doesn't have sufficient opportunity for exercise at sea."

Baron Seamount managed not to roll his eyes, although Lock Island suspected that the commodore was sorely tempted to do just that. The high admiral's dog's tendency to race madly up and down the decks of his flagship was legendary. Fortunately, Keelhaul—despite the dubious humor of his name—was as affectionate as he was . . . energetic. Not a minor consideration in a dog which weighed the better part of a hundred and forty pounds. Lock Island put Keelhaul's boisterousness down to his Labrador retriever grandmother; certain less charitably inclined souls put it down to the high admiral's influence. Wherever it came from, though, Keelhaul actually looked forward to their trips up the mountain. And he was calmer and less worried by the sounds of gunfire than most humans. Certainly it bothered him far less than it did the artillery's draft dragons. Which shouldn't really have been so surprising, Lock Island thought, given the amount of gunnery practice he got to listen to whenever they were at sea.

However Keelhaul felt about it, however, the high admiral's feelings were far more mixed. Fascinating as he always found Seamount's demonstrations, he and horses had not been intimate companions since he first went to sea far too many years ago. Unfortunately, his posterior had made the reacquaintance of both saddles and saddle *sores* as he trundled up and down the steep, winding road from King's Harbor to the Marines' training ground.

"The Commodore has a point, My Lord," Clareyk put in respectfully. "About the biggest formation we can really work with here is a battalion. We can squeeze two of them into the available space if we push a little, but we're really cramped when we do that. There's no way we could put both my regiments into the field as a single force given the space constraints here."

Lock Island nodded. Each of the new regiments consisted of two battalions, and each brigade was made up of two regiments, so Clareyk's total command had a total strength of just over twenty-two hundred men, counting officers, corpsmen, buglers, and runners. His actual strength on active operations would have been even higher than that, once other attached specialists were added in, and Clareyk and Seamount were right about the space limitations. That had never been a problem before, since about the largest Marine formation in pre-Merlin days had been a *single* battalion. Now, though, they weren't simply training Marine detachments for the Navy's ships; they were building an honest-to-God *army*. The first true army in Charis' history.

For the moment, that army still belonged to Lock Island, but he had no doubt a time was coming, probably in the not-too-distant future, when a Royal Army would have to be split off from the traditional Marines. There were simply aspects of what armies had to do that sea officers like himself had never been trained to do.

Maybe so, he thought with just an edge of grimness. *But the job's still mine for now, so I suppose I'd better get off my saddle-sore, horse-bitten arse—figuratively speaking, of course—and figure out how to do this right.*

"I believe you, Brigadier. I believe you both. And General Chermyn and I have already been giving some thought to the problem. For right now, though, I'm still more concerned about the security aspects. As you say, we can keep things under wraps out here on Helen a lot better than we could anywhere else. Once we've actually committed the troops to action, when 'the cat's out of the bag,' as Merlin put it the other day—and, no, I *don't* know where he got the expression from—that's not going to be such a concern."

"We understand, Sir," Seamount said. Then the roundish little commodore grinned suddenly. "Of course, we're still going to have a few things we want to maintain security about, even then."

"Ahlfryd," Lock Island said severely, turning a speculative gaze upon his subordinate, "are you up to something . . . *again?*"

"Well . . ."

"You *are* up to something." Lock Island cocked his head and folded his arms. "I suppose you'd better go ahead and tell me about it now. *And* how much I'm going to have to tell Baron Ironhill this idea's going to cost."

"Actually, I don't know that it's going to be all *that* expensive, Sir." Seamount's tone was almost wheedling, but his eyes gleamed.

"Of course you don't. *You* don't have to talk to Ironhill about these little matters," Lock Island said severely. "So try to look a little less like a boy caught with his hand in his mother's cookie jar and just go ahead and tell me."

"Yes, Sir."

Seamount rubbed his chin with his mangled left hand. Lock Island was thoroughly familiar with that "sorting out my thoughts" gesture, and he waited patiently. Then the commodore cleared his throat.

"The thing is, Sir," he began, "that I had this . . . conversation with *Seijin* Merlin the last time he and the King were out here watching an exercise."

"What sort of conversation?" Lock Island asked just a tad warily. "Conversations" with Merlin Athrawes had a distinct tendency, he'd discovered, to go off in some very peculiar directions.

"Well, we were watching some of the twelve-pounder crews training, and it occurred to me that with the new rifles, even the twelve-pounders don't really have a significant range advantage over infantry."

"They don't?" Lock Island blinked in surprise. "I thought you told me they had a maximum range of almost sixteen hundred yards!"

"Yes, Sir, they do—with round shot, which is the least effective round against an infantry target. Canister range is substantially shorter than that, though. And, Sir, with all due respect, finding clear ranges sixteen hundred yards long is going to be more problematic in a land battle than it is at sea. At sea, we don't really have to worry about things like ridgelines, trees, and ravines."

"I see." Lock Island nodded again, this time more slowly as he remembered his own thought of only minutes before. *Another one of those things sea officers don't know about from personal experience, I see.*

"It's not quite as bad as the Commodore might seem to be suggesting, My Lord," Clareyk said. Lock Island looked at him, and the brigadier shrugged. "Oh, I'm not saying it won't be a problem, My Lord. I'm just saying that finding firing lanes two miles long isn't going to be all *that* difficult as long as we make good use of things like hilltops. Or, much as the farmers are going to hate it, cropland and pastures."

"The Brigadier's right about that, of course," Seamount agreed, "but even without the question of terrain features, there's still the fact that the effective range of rifles can match or exceed the effective range of grape or canister. If a battery's exposed to the fire of a couple of hundred rifles, it's going to lose its gunners in short order."

"That's true enough, My Lord," Clareyk said a touch more grimly.

"I take it this is going somewhere?" Lock Island said mildly.

"Actually, it is, Sir." Seamount shrugged. "As I say, Merlin and the King were watching the artillery demonstration, and I raised the same point with him. You see, I'd been thinking about the new muskets. It occurred to me that if we could increase their range and accuracy by rifling *them*, why shouldn't it be possible to rifle *artillery*, as well?"

Lock Island's eyebrows rose. That idea had never occurred to him at all. Probably, he thought, because he was still too busy being so impressed by the revolutionary changes which had already overtaken the naval ordnance with which he'd grown up. Trunnions, bagged powder charges, carronades—the increase in shipboard artillery's lethality was enormous. Yet even with the new guns, sea battles tended to be fought at relatively low ranges. Longer than before the new guns, perhaps, but still far shorter than the theoretical range of their artillery might have suggested. One of the new long thirty-pounders had a maximum range of well over two miles, for example, but no gunner was going to hit a ship-sized target at that distance from a moving deck, no matter how accurate his artillery piece might theoretically be.

But the ground *didn't* move. So what sort of accuracy and execution might be possible for a *land*-based rifled artillery piece?

"And what did *Seijin* Merlin have to say in response to this fascinating speculation of yours, Ahlfryd?"

"He said he didn't see any reason why it shouldn't be possible."

Seamount met Lock Island's eyes for a moment, and both of them smiled slightly. "He did . . . suggest, however, that bronze probably wouldn't be the best material for rifled artillery pieces. As he pointed out, bronze is a soft metal, Sir. Even if we can figure out a way to make a shot take the rifling in the first place, a bronze gun's rifling grooves wouldn't last very long."

"No, I can see that."

Lock Island discovered that he was rubbing his own chin in a gesture very like Seamount's.

"Master Howsmyn told me he was making good progress with iron guns," he said after a moment.

"He is, Sir." Seamount nodded. "They're heavier, and there are still some of what Merlin calls 'quality control issues' that haven't been completely solved. Despite that, I think we'll be able to begin arming ships with iron guns instead of bronze within the next few months, or possibly even sooner.

"But that brings up another problem. The pressure inside a rifle's barrel is higher than the pressure inside a smoothbore musket's barrel, because the bullet seals the barrel and traps more of the force of the exploding powder behind it. That's one reason rifles have more range."

"And if the pressure inside a rifled artillery piece increases, and the piece is made out of iron, not bronze, we're likely to see more burst guns, since iron is more brittle than bronze," Lock Island said.

"That's what I'm afraid of, Sir," Seamount agreed. "I can't be certain how *much* it will go up, because I don't know if the bore will be sealed as efficiently in a rifled cannon as in a rifled musket. Too much depends on how we finally figure out a way to do it for me to even hazard a guess at this point. At the moment, I'm playing around with several different ideas, though. And I'm sure we can come up with a solution for the problem—assuming it actually arises—eventually."

Which means Merlin hasn't told you it's flatly impossible, Lock Island thought. *I wonder why he's so prone to throw out cryptic hints instead of just going ahead and telling us how to do it? I'm sure he's got a reason. I'm just not sure it's a reason I want to know.*

"Oh, the Commodore is *definitely* playing around with 'a few ideas,' My Lord," Brigadier Clareyk said. Seamount darted him a ferocious look which was two-thirds humorous and one-third serious, and the Marine went on. "After Merlin and the King had headed back to Tellesberg, the Commodore and I were discussing weapons in general, and he suddenly got this peculiar expression. You know the one I mean, My Lord."

"Like someone about to pass gas?" Lock Island suggested helpfully. From Clareyk's expression, the suggestion didn't seem to help as much, perhaps, as one might have hoped it would.

"No, My Lord," the brigadier said in the careful, half-breathless voice of a man trying very hard not to laugh, "not that expression. The *other* expression."

"Oh! You mean the one that always reminds me of a wyvern contemplating a chicken coop."

"That would be the one, My Lord," Clareyk agreed.

"And what, pray tell, inspired that particular expression this time around?"

"Actually, My Lord"—the brigadier's own expression was suddenly serious—"it was a very intriguing thought indeed, when I asked him about it."

"But it's one I'm still working on," Seamount interjected in a cautioning tone.

"*What's* one you're still working on?" Lock Island demanded with more than a hint of exasperation.

"Well, Sir," Seamount said, "the truth is that simply increasing the range and accuracy of a cannon by rifling it won't make the shot it fires any more effective against infantry than traditional round shot. It would just let us fire the same sort of round farther and more accurately, if you see what I mean. So I was still turning that problem over in my mind even after discussing it with Merlin. Then, last five-day, the Brigadier and I were watching a new batch of Marines training with hand grenades, and it occurred to me that, right off the top of my head, I couldn't think of any reason for it to be impossible to fire grenades—only they'd be a lot *bigger*, a lot more powerful, you understand, out of a cannon."

Lock Island blinked. If the notion of rifling artillery had opened new vistas, that was nothing compared to the possibility Seamount had just raised. And not just when it came to killing infantry at extreme ranges, either. The thought of what a "grenade" five or six inches in diameter might do to a wooden hulled warship was . . . frightening. No, it wasn't "frightening." For any experienced naval officer it would be *terrifying*. Heated shot was bad enough. It was undeniably tricky to fire, and dangerous to load, since there was always the possibility that it would burn through the soaked wad behind it and detonate the gun's charge prematurely, with nasty consequences for whoever happened to be ramming it home at the moment. Despite that, however, it could be hideously effective, because a red-hot mass of iron weighing twenty-five or thirty pounds, buried deep in the bone-dry timbers of a warship, could turn that ship into a torch. But if Seamount could fire explosive charges—explosive charges that could be reliably *detonated*, at least—it would be infinitely worse. Not just an incendiary effect, but one which would literally blow its target open and provide plenty of kindling, as well.

"Ah, have you discussed *this* particular notion with *Seijin* Merlin?" he asked after a moment.

"No, not yet, Sir. I really haven't had the opportunity."

"Well *make* the opportunity, Ahlfryd." Lock Island shook his head. "I find the entire idea more than a little frightening, you understand. But if it's possible, I want to know about it. As soon as possible."

.VI.
Captain Merlin Athrawes' Quarters,
Archbishop's Palace,
and Royal Palace,
City of Tellesberg,
Kingdom of Charis

June 12, Year of God 143
Tellesberg Enclave
Safehold

"To whoever reads this journal, greetings in the name of the true God.

"My name is Jeremiah Knowles, and I am an 'Adam.' I first opened my eyes on Safehold on the morning of Creation, and my mind and my soul were new-made, as clear and clean as the world about me. I looked upon the work of the Archangels and of God, and my heart was filled with joy and reverence.

"Like my fellow Adams and Eves, I met the Archangels. I saw the Blessed Langhorne, and the Holy Bédard. And I knew Shan-wei, the Bright One Who Fell.

"There are many others who have seen the Archangels I have seen, heard and read the Holy Writ I have heard and read. Many of us have lived out even the span of an Adam or an Eve and passed from this world, yet even now, there are hundreds of thousands—possibly millions—of us still living in this one hundred and forty-third year since the Creation. But of every one of those souls here in Tellesberg, I alone, and my three companions—Evelyn Knowles, my wife; Kayleb Sarmac, Evelyn's brother; and Jennifer Sarmac, Kayleb's wife—have known what none of those others have known.

"We know that the 'Holy Writ' is a lie . . . and that there are no 'Archangels.'"

The being known as Merlin Athrawes sat in the unlit blackness of his quarters in Tellesberg Palace, his eyes closed, looking at the pages stored in his molycirc brain, and tried to take it all in.

It was hard. Indeed, in many ways it was harder for him to absorb this than it had been for Nimue Alban to learn she'd been dead for over eight centuries. Of all the things he might have discovered, this was the one which would never have occurred to him.

He opened his eyes, using his light-gathering optics to gaze through the daylight-bright darkness and out his sleeping chamber's window at the slumbering city of Tellesberg. There'd been no time for him to read the incredible documentary treasure Maikel Staynair and Zhon Byrkyt had shown him at Saint Zherneau's. But there'd been time for him to examine every page of the manuscript journal, and he was a PICA. He had what truly was a "photographic memory," and he had pored over the stored imagery for over six hours now while all around him the rest of Tellesberg Palace and the capital of the Ahrmahks lay wrapped in the sleep he no longer needed.

"Owl," he said quietly, activating his built-in com.

"Yes, Lieutenant Commander," a silent voice said somewhere deep inside him as Owl, the Ordonez-Westinghouse-Lytton tactical computer in the hidden chamber where Nimue had awakened, replied, bouncing his signal off the carefully stealthed SNARC high above the body of water known as The Cauldron.

"Have you completed that data search?"

"Yes, Lieutenant Commander."

"Did you find the specified names?"

"I did, Lieutenant Commander. There are, however, data anomalies."

"Data anomalies?" Merlin sat straighter, eyes narrowing. "Specify data anomalies."

"Yes, Lieutenant Commander. The names you directed me to search for appear in both the Colony Administration's official roster of colonists, a copy of which was filed in my memory by Commodore Pei, and in the roster of colonists filed in my memory by Dr. Pei Shan-wei. They are not, however, assigned to the same population enclaves in both rosters."

"They aren't?" Merlin frowned.

"That is correct, Lieutenant Commander," Owl replied. A more capable AI would have explained the "data anomalies" in greater detail. Owl, on the other hand, clearly felt no need to do so.

"Where *were* they assigned?" Merlin asked, reminding himself rather firmly—again—that Owl's version of self-awareness was still . . . limited. The manual promised him that eventually the AI's heuristic programming would bring Owl to a fuller state of awareness. That he would begin recognizing rhetorical questions, responding without being specifically cued, and even start providing necessary explanations or potentially significant unexpected correlations of data search results without being specifically instructed to do so.

In Merlin's considered opinion, "eventually" couldn't possibly come too soon.

"According to Administrator Langhorne's official roster, Jeremiah Knowles, known as 'Jere Knowles,' his wife, his brother-in-law, and his sister-in-law were assigned to the Tellesberg enclave. According to Dr. Pei's roster, all four of them were assigned to the Alexandria enclave."

Merlin blinked. He'd never thought to check Shan-wei's notes on the original placement of colonists against the official record, never suspected there might be discrepancies between them. Now, however, he wondered why the possibility *hadn't* occurred to him.

Because the Commodore didn't say anything about it to you in his downloads, that's why, he thought.

"Are there additional 'data anomalies' between the two rosters?" he asked Owl. "Additional cases in which colonists appear assigned to more than one enclave?"

"Unknown, Lieutenant Commander," Owl said calmly, with the total lack of curiosity Merlin found maddening.

"Well," he said with what a human being would have recognized as dangerous patience, "find out if any such additional anomalies exist. *Now*, Owl."

"Yes, Lieutenant Commander."

The AI's tone was completely devoid of any suggestion that it had recognized Merlin's impatience. Which, of course, only made it even more maddening, Merlin reflected.

But whatever his shortcomings in terms of personality might be, Owl was a very fast worker. His analysis of the two rosters took less than two minutes, despite the millions of names in each of them.

"There are additional anomalies, Lieutenant Commander," he informed Merlin.

"Well," Merlin said twenty seconds later, "what *sort* of additional anomalies did you discover? And how many of them are there?"

"All of the anomalies discovered fall into the same category as those already known, Lieutenant Commander. They consist of colonists who appear to have been assigned to multiple enclaves. In all cases, the enclave listed in Dr. Pei's roster is Alexandria. In Administrator Langhorne's roster, they are assigned to several different enclaves. I have detected a total of two hundred and twelve such anomalies."

"I see," Merlin said slowly, his frustration with the AI's lack of spontaneity and initiative fading as he contemplated the numbers.

I know what she was up to, he thought, and his mental tone was almost awed. *My God, she was creating a second string for her bow, and she didn't even tell the Commodore. That's the only possible reason he wouldn't have told* me *about it in his message.* He frowned. *Was this something she'd intended to do all along, or did it only occur to her after they'd officially separated because of their supposed disagreement? And how did she manage to doctor the records without Langhorne and Bédard realizing what she'd done?*

There was no way for anyone to know the answers to any of those questions at this distant remove. But if Merlin didn't know how Pei Shan-wei had done it, he did know *what* she'd attempted.

He flipped ahead through the recorded pages of Jeremiah Knowles' journal to the passage he wanted.

"... *no more idea of the truth, then, than any of our fellow Adams and Eves. None of us were aware of the mental programming Bédard had carried out at Langhorne's orders. But when Dr. Pei realized what Langhorne had done, she took measures of her own. There was no way for her or any member of her staff in the Alexandria enclave to restore the memories of our past lives which had been taken from us. But, unknown to Langhorne and Bédard, she had secretly retained three NEATs. With them, she was able to reeducate a handful of the original colonists. We were among them.*"

Merlin nodded to himself. Of course that was what she'd done. It had been risky just to retain the Neural Education and Training machines, no doubt, given Langhorne's plans and willingness to crush any opposition, and actually using them on the colonists would have been even more dangerous. But it couldn't have been any riskier than her open refusal to destroy the records of the truth stored in Alexandria. Unfortunately, neither had been enough.

I can't believe this has all been just sitting here for over seven hundred local years, he thought. *I wonder if any of her other "sleepers" survived Alexandria's destruction? And if they did, did they leave a record like "Saint Zherneau's," or did they simply dive as deep into their cover identities as they could? And how in* Hell *did this journal of his manage to survive when the Brethren finally found it?*

He had no idea how to answer any of those questions, either . . . but he rather suspected that he knew someone who did.

▼   ▼   ▼

"His Eminence will see you now, Captain Athrawes."

"Thank you, Father," Merlin said as the under-priest opened the door to Archbishop Maikel's office and bowed the visitor through it.

Sunlight poured through the window that looked out across Tellesberg to the broad, blue waters of the harbor. A dense forest of masts and yards grew out of the waterfront, birds and wyverns rode the updrafts, hovering gracefully as the thoughts of God, and weather-stained sails dotted the harbor beyond them. Staynair's office was located on the lofty (for Safehold) Archbishop's Palace's third floor, and Merlin could see down into the busy streets, where people, dragon-drawn freight wagons, and horse-drawn streetcars seethed and bustled.

"*Seijin* Merlin," Staynair greeted him, holding out his ring hand with a smile. "How nice to see you again."

"And so very unexpected, I'm sure, Your Eminence," Merlin murmured as he brushed his lips across the proffered ring.

"No, not unexpected," Staynair acknowledged. He sat back down behind his desk and a wave of his hand invited Merlin to sit in the comfortable chair on the far side of it. He continued to smile as his guest settled into the chair, but the smile had turned a bit more tense, Merlin observed.

"May I assume, Your Eminence, that any conversation you and I might have here today won't be overheard by other ears?"

"Of course you may." Staynair frowned slightly. "My staff understands that unless I specifically tell them otherwise, any conversation I have in this office is as privileged as any other confession."

"I was reasonably confident that was the case, Your Eminence. Under the circumstances, however, I felt I had no option but to be certain of it."

"I suppose that's understandable enough," Staynair conceded. "And I'm quite aware that Zhon and I handed you a rather . . . significant surprise, shall we say, yesterday."

"Oh, you could certainly describe it *that* way, Your Eminence." Merlin smiled dryly.

"And I'm sure you have questions," Staynair continued. "Under the circumstances, I think it might be simpler for you to just go ahead and ask them rather than having me attempt to explain everything."

"I imagine that explaining 'everything' is going to take considerably more than a single afternoon," Merlin said, and Staynair actually chuckled.

"Very well, then, Your Eminence," Merlin continued, "I suppose my first question has to be why 'Saint Zherneau's' journal and the other documents with it weren't simply destroyed, or handed over to the Inquisition, when they were finally rediscovered?"

"Partly because they weren't 'rediscovered' at all, *Seijin* Merlin." Staynair leaned back in his chair, crossing his legs. "The Brethren of Saint Zherneau always knew exactly where all of them were; we simply didn't know *what* they were. Saint Zherneau and Saint Evahlyn left them sealed, with solemn directions for the Brethren to leave them that way for three hundred and fifty years after their deaths. Their instructions were followed to the letter."

"And the reason they weren't simply destroyed or regarded as the most heinous possible heresy when they were unsealed?"

"There, I think, you see the planning—or the impact, at least—of Saint Zherneau," Staynair said seriously. "Most of the religious philosophy and thought of Saint Zherneau and Saint Evahlyn was as orthodox as Mother Church could possibly have asked. For reasons which make perfectly good sense, I'm sure, now that you've had an opportunity to read his journal. You *did* read it overnight, didn't you, *Seijin*?"

"Yes, I did." Merlin regarded the archbishop with a speculative gaze.

"I assumed that was why you examined each page individually at Saint Zherneau's," Staynair murmured. Merlin cocked an eyebrow, and the archbishop smiled slightly. "The ability of the *seijin* to memorize things at a glance is a part of their legendary prowess. In fact, I rather suspect that was one of the reasons you decided to become one."

"I see." Merlin leaned back in his own chair and rested his elbows on its upholstered arms, steepling his fingertips across his chest. "Please, Your Eminence. Continue with your explanation."

"Of course, *Seijin*," Staynair agreed with a slightly ironic nod. "Let me see, where *was* I? Ah, yes. The single aspect in which Saint Zherneau's teachings departed from the mainstream of Church thought was the fashion in which he and Saint Evahlyn both emphasized tolerance and toleration so strongly and made it so central to their thought. The responsibility of all godly people to see all other human beings as their true brothers and sisters in God. To reason and remonstrate with those who might be in error, rather than condemning without seeking to understand. And to be open to the possibility that those who disagree with them may, in fact, prove in the end to be correct—or, at least, *closer* to correct—than they themselves had been at the beginning of the disagreement."

The archbishop paused, shaking his head. Then he looked away, gazing out his office window at the roofs and spires of Tellesberg.

"There is a reason Charis has worried the Inquisition for so long," he said quietly, "and not all of it was simple paranoia on the part of Inquisitors like Clyntahn. Despite the small size of the Monastery of Saint Zherneau, the Brethren of Saint Zherneau have wielded a disproportionate influence here in Charis for generations.

"Many of our local clergy have passed through Saint Zherneau's at one time or another. Indeed, I've often wondered what would have happened had the Inquisition been able to cross-post our clergy the way it has the mainland clergy. One thing, I suspect, is that it might have learned of Saint Zherneau's . . . influence if more of our homegrown priests had been assigned to mainland parishes. Not to mention what might have happened had the Church's senior positions here in Charis been more completely filled by foreigners. Fortunately, the Inquisition's distrust of Charisian orthodoxy has left the Church disinclined to expose other congregations to our contaminating notions, so very few of our local clergy have been posted to churches outside Charis itself. And the difficulty in getting senior churchmen to agree to serve out here at the edge of the world has worked in our favor in many ways, as well. Not least is that none of the relatively small number of truly senior clergy sent into Charis have even begun to suspect what the Brethren of Saint Zherneau have truly become here in the Kingdom and the Archbishopric."

"And what have they become, Your Eminence?" Merlin asked quietly.

"Agents of subversion," Staynair said simply. "Only a very small handful of the most senior Brethren are aware of the existence of Saint Zherneau's journal or any of the other documents. Outside that handful, none of them have ever heard of a book called *The History of the Terran Federation*, or of a document called *The Declaration of Independence*. What *every* Brother of Saint Zherneau has been taught, however, is that every individual is responsible for his or her personal relationship with God. The Inquisition would most certainly find that teaching pernicious, even though it's precisely what the *Holy Writ* says. Because, *Seijin* Merlin," the archbishop looked back from the window, his eyes dark and intense, "a personal relationship implies both toleration and questions. It implies a personal *search* for God, a need to understand one's relationship with Him for *oneself*, not simply the regurgitation of official doctrine and catechisms."

Merlin nodded slowly as he felt previously unsuspected puzzle pieces slotting into position. So that was the explanation—or *part* of the explanation, at least—for the openness, the sense of inclusiveness, which had attracted Nimue Alban to Charis and its society when she first set about seeking a proper base of operations.

"Almost every Brother of Saint Zherneau is aware that our emphasis on personal relationships with God would not find favor with the Inquisition," Staynair continued. "But not one of them, to the best of our knowledge, has ever brought the philosophy of Saint Zherneau to the Inquisition's attention. And that, Merlin, is because there is something in most men which cries out to *know* God. To find that personal, direct relationship with Him. The Brethren of Saint Zherneau—*all* of the Brethren of Saint Zherneau— recognize that wellspring of personal faith and belief within themselves. And although we never specifically address the point, all of them know it must be both protected and passed on."

"And it's also the first line of defense, isn't it, Your Eminence?" Merlin said shrewdly.

"Of course it is." Staynair's smile was crooked. "As I say, very few of the Brethren have ever learned the full truth of Saint Zherneau's writings. But by protecting and preserving the portions of Saint Zherneau's teachings of which they are aware, they also protect and preserve the portion of which they are *not* aware. For reasons I'm sure you can understand, it's been necessary to limit complete knowledge to a relatively small number of people. That's been a problem for many of us over the centuries, because it goes against the grain to deceive, even if only by omission, those who are truly our brothers. Yet we've had no choice, and so the majority of the Brethren have always viewed our purpose as gradual reform—as teaching the clergy to truly serve the souls of God's children rather than the wealth and power of Mother Church.

"Even that has scarcely been a safe mission over the years, of course. But many of our number, the majority of whom do not know of the existence of Zherneau's journal, have risen to relatively high positions in our local churches, and from those positions, they've sheltered and aided other Brethren of Saint Zherneau. Which is, of course, one reason why such a high percentage of our local priests were prepared to support our break with the Council of Vicars."

"I can see that, too," Merlin agreed.

"Don't misunderstand me, Merlin," Staynair said soberly. "When Zherneau's journal was first unsealed four hundred years ago, it was deeply shocking to the then Abbot. Only his own deep-seated faith in the teachings of Saint Zherneau kept him from doing one of the things you'd wondered about. He very seriously considered simply destroying all of it, but he couldn't bring himself to do it. Even the 'mainstream Church' has a deep and abiding reverence for written testimony. That goes back to the original Adams and Eves who wrote *The Testimonies*, I suppose. And, of course, four hundred years ago, there were far fewer literate Safeholdians than there are today."

Merlin nodded again. The Church of God Awaiting's historical and doctrinal experience included none of the textual disputes of terrestrial tradition. The documents which composed the Church's official canon had been defined by the archangels themselves, not by any potentially fallible councils of humans, which automatically placed them beyond any possibility of dispute. And there was no tradition of "false gospels" or other fraudulent documents deliberately constructed to discredit the Church's faith in its formative period. There'd *been* no "formative period," and any attempt to produce such "false gospels" would have been buried without a trace under the writings of eight million literate colonists. As a consequence, Safehold approached the historicity of the Church with a completely different mindset from that of terrestrial theologians. Every scrap of history only proved the accuracy of the Church's traditions, and so became one more pillar of support, not a seedbed of skepticism.

Of course, that could change, couldn't it? As the decades in centuries passed in a society deliberately locked into muscle and wind power, with all of the hard labor required to support such a society, that universal literacy had disappeared. By and large—there *had* been exceptions, especially in the Church—only the upper classes had retained the leisure time to become literate. And as the ability to read and write had become less and less common, the reverence of the common (and illiterate) man and woman for the written records whose mysteries they could not penetrate had become paradoxically greater and greater.

And that must have suited the Council of Vicars just fine, he thought grimly. *In fact, "Mother Church" may well have encouraged the trend, since the illiterate members of the Church became completely dependent upon their hierarchy to instruct them about the contents of those mysterious books they could no longer read for themselves. And that, in turn, became one more tool for strangling independence of thought in its cradle. On the other hand, the fact that literacy's been on the upswing again for a century or so is one of the reasons the wheels are threatening to come off their neat little mind-control machine, isn't it?*

"Despite the temptation to simply destroy the journal and other documents, he chose not to," Staynair said. "It must have been an incredibly difficult decision for him. But in addition to the journal itself, he had the letter Saint Zherneau had left for whoever finally unsealed the vault. And, of course, he had ample historical evidence to support the fact that Saint Zherneau had, indeed, been an Adam himself. That Saint Evahlyn had been an Eve. That, coupled with all of the public writings the two of them had left—including sections in *The Testimonies*—was enough to stop him from simply labeling the journal the ravings of a mad heretic. And the fact that he knew the books included with the journal had been sealed in the same vault for the better part of four hundred years proved they, too, must date from the Creation itself or immediately after it.

"Or, of course"—the archbishop's eyes bored into Merlin's—"from *before* it."

Merlin nodded once again. Personally, despite all of the Church's traditional reverence for history and historical documents, he suspected Staynair was probably understating even now the incredible depth of the spiritual struggle that long-ago Abbot of Saint Zherneau's must have faced. The degree of intellectual integrity it must have taken to make—and accept—the connections Staynair had just summarized so concisely in the face of every single word of the Church's official doctrine was difficult even to imagine.

"Forgive me, Your Eminence," he said slowly, "and please, don't take this as any sort of attack. But with this journal, and the other documents in your possession, you've known all along that the Church's entire doctrine, all of its theology and teachings, are built upon a monstrous lie. Yet not only did you never denounce the lie, but you've actually supported it."

"You would have made a splendid Inquisitor yourself, Merlin," Staynair said, his smile more crooked than ever. "I mean an Inquisitor of Father Paityr's sort, not that pig Clyntahn's, of course."

"In what way, Your Eminence?"

"You understand how to direct questions that force a man to look straightly at what he *truly* believes, not simply what he's *convinced* himself he believes.

"In answer to your perfectly valid question, however, we must plead guilty, but with extenuating circumstances. As, I feel quite confident, you already understood before you asked.

"Had we openly opposed Church doctrine, proclaimed that every word of the *Holy Writ* was a lie, we would merely have provoked the destruction of Charis centuries earlier. Perhaps the Inquisition might have settled for simply exterminating those who brought the disturbing message, but I think not. I think too much of Langhorne's and Schueler's intolerance and . . . thoroughness clings to the Inquisition even today." The archbishop shook his head. "I've read Saint Zherneau's account of what truly happened in the destruction of the Alexandria enclave, what truly happened on the dreadful night when it was transformed into Armageddon Reef. I do not have the background to understand how simply dropping rocks could have had the effect Saint Zherneau describes, but I fully accept the accuracy of his testimony. And if the Inquisition of today lacks the *Rakurai*, the Group of Four has just demonstrated that it continues to command swords in plenty.

"So, since we dared not openly oppose the Church's lies lest we achieve nothing but the destruction of the only evidence that they *were* lies, the Brethren of Saint Zherneau—those of the Brethren who knew the truth, at least—dedicated themselves to gradually building a different sort of Church here in Charis. Even that much constituted a deadly risk. We recognized that, eventually, the Inquisition would undoubtedly react as, in fact, Clyntahn has reacted. We'd hoped it wouldn't be this soon, and it probably wouldn't have been if Clyntahn hadn't become Grand Inquisitor. Yet he did, and we'd already pushed too far, made too many changes of which Mother Church disapproved. The truth of the matter is, Merlin, that Clyntahn has been right all along about the danger Charis poses to his precious orthodoxy. I rather doubt he's felt that way on the basis of any reasoned consideration of the evidence, but his instincts have not played him false where we are concerned."

"How much of this did Haarahld know?" Merlin asked quietly.

"All of it," Staynair replied simply. "He read the entire journal, read the history of the Federation. As for all of us, there was much in that history which he didn't understand, for which he had no context. But, also as for all of us, he understood enough. When you asked him why his grandfather had abolished serfdom here in Charis, he answered you honestly, Merlin. But he could have added that one of the reasons his grandfather believed all men were created equal was that he, too, had read every magnificent word of the *Declaration*."

"And Cayleb?" Merlin asked the question even more quietly, and Staynair frowned gravely.

"And Cayleb," he replied, "is one of the reasons you and I are having this conversation at this particular time."

"At this time?"

"Yes. One reason is that we are rapidly approaching God's Day, and it seemed . . . appropriate for you to be told the truth before that."

Merlin nodded once more. God's Day, which was inserted into the middle of the month of July each year, was the Church of God Awaiting's equivalent of Christmas and Easter, rolled into one. It was the highest and most holy religious festival of the year, and given what the Brethren of Saint Zherneau knew about the religion they'd dared not openly denounce for so long, he could see why Staynair would have wanted to have this conversation before he had to celebrate God's Day in Tellesberg Cathedral as Archbishop of Charis for the first time. Still—

"I can understand that, I suppose, Your Eminence. But what, exactly, does Cayleb have to do with your timing for this little revelation?"

"Ever since the vault was unsealed, there have been strenuous rules governing when and how its contents were to be made known to others. One of those rules has been that before anyone could be admitted to the truth, he must have attained the age of wisdom. Which, simply because some firm definition of when that could be presumed to have occurred was necessary, was set at the age of thirty. Another rule is that all those already privy to the truth must agree before anyone else is admitted to it, and not everyone nominated for the truth is actually told in the end. Two of the last eight monarchs of Charis were never informed, for example, because the Brethren of their time believed telling them would have constituted too great a risk. And"—Staynair's eyes turned even graver—"in both cases, their own fathers agreed with the majority of the Brethren."

"But surely that's not the case with Cayleb," Merlin objected.

"Of course not. We've always—Haarahld always—intended to inform him of the truth as soon as he reached the age of thirty. Unfortunately, the Group of Four refused to wait long enough for that. Now we have a King whose determination, courage, and wit we all trust implicitly, but who's too young, under the Brethren's rules, to be informed. And, to be perfectly honest, there are some among us who fear his youth and . . . directness. His impetuosity, perhaps. One thing young Cayleb has never been is hesitant about speaking his mind or confronting an enemy. The fear isn't that he would reject the journal's contents, but rather that if he learns the full truth, if he's shown the proof that for almost a thousand years the Church has controlled all of Safehold through the greatest lie in human history, he'll be unable to resist throwing that charge against the Group of Four, as well. And that, Merlin, is something we cannot do. Not yet.

"Schism within the Church we can contemplate, especially so long as that schism is couched in terms of reforming corruption, decadence, and abuses. But outright heresy—*true* heresy, easily provable by reference to the *Holy Writ* and *The Testimonies*—would put far too potent a weapon into Clyntahn's hands. The day is coming—*will* come—when that 'heresy' will be openly proclaimed. The Brethren of Saint Zherneau have labored to bring that day for four centuries. But for now, we must keep this a war over the Church's abuses. Over spiritual issues, yes, but spiritual issues secular rulers can grasp in *secular* terms, not over deeply divisive points of doctrine and theology."

Merlin unsteepled his fingers and leaned forward in his chair, his expression intent.

"Your Eminence, since you and Abbot Byrkyt have shown me these documents, informed me of their existence, I must assume the other Brethren who know the full truth approved your decision to do so."

His tone and raised eyebrow made the statement a question, and Staynair nodded.

"They have. In no small part, because we want your judgment as to whether or not *Cayleb* should be told. I believe he should, as do most, though not all, of the others, and all of us realize that at this moment, you're undoubtedly closer to him than any other living man. But I must confess that there's also another reason. Something which was contained in Saint Zherneau's letter, not his journal."

"Oh?"

"Yes." Staynair reached into an inner pocket of his cassock and removed a folded sheet of paper. "This is a copy of that section," he said softly, and handed it across the desk.

Merlin took it just a bit gingerly, unfolded it, and found a passage copied in Staynair's own hand.

"We, and the other Adams and Eves Dr. Pei reeducated to know the truth, were to be what she called her 'insurance policy,' " he read. "We were to be the seed, if you will, of a movement among the colonists and children of the colonists if, as she feared, Langhorne, Bédard, and Schueler moved openly against Alexandria. But she had less time than she had hoped, and there were not enough of us when they destroyed Alexandria and murdered her and all of our friends. Yet it is evident that Langhorne and most of his inner circle must also have been killed. Our best guess, especially given the changes in the *Holy Writ*, is that Commodore Pei must have managed to conceal a vest-pocket nuke and used it. I have often thought, over the years, that the confusion that must have engendered in the 'archangels'' leadership—and, quite possibly, the destruction of much of the colony administration's records—explains how we have been able to pass unnoticed out here in this distant corner of Safehold.

"But we do not know where else Dr. Pei may have placed others like us. We were never told, for obvious reasons. We do know she intended to place others here with us in Tellesberg, but there was never time, and now she never will.

"Yet know this, whoever you may be who finally reads these words. We were but one string to Dr. Pei's bow of truth. There is another. I know but little about that second string, and even that I know mostly by accident. It was never Dr. Pei's intention for us to learn about it at all—again, for obvious reasons. But I know this much. She and Commodore Pei have made other preparations, other plans, as well as this one. I will not write even the small amount I do know, lest this letter fall into the Inquisition's hands. Yet you must always remember that second string. The day will come when it sends forth its arrow, and you must recognize it when it flies. *Trust* it. It springs from fidelity you cannot even imagine, from a sacrifice deeper than space itself. I believe you will know it if—when—you see it, and this is the test: Nimue."

A PICA had no circulatory system, but deep pain stabbed through Merlin's nonexistent heart as he read that final sentence. He looked down at it for endless seconds. It was almost as if he could hear Pei Shan-wei's voice one final time through the words written by a man seven hundred and fifty years dust.

Finally, he looked up again, and Staynair looked deep into his sapphire PICA's eyes.

"Tell me, Merlin," he said, very, very softly, "*are* you Shan-wei's second arrow?"

▼   ▼   ▼

"What's this all about?" King Cayleb asked, ignoring the throne on its raised dais as he stood with his back to the small presence chamber's window. He looked back and forth between Archbishop Maikel and Merlin, his eyebrows raised, and Merlin smiled crookedly.

"You may recall, Your Majesty," he said, "that I once told you that when I could explain a certain subject more fully, I would."

Cayleb's eyes widened suddenly. Then they darted to Staynair's face. He half raised one hand, but Merlin shook his head.

"It's all right, Cayleb," he said. "It turns out Archbishop Maikel—and, for that matter, your father—had a somewhat better idea of who I am than I'd realized."

"They did?" Cayleb's expression was suddenly very intent, and the gaze he turned upon Staynair was intensely speculative.

"Oh, I think you might say that." Merlin's smile turned more crooked than ever. "You see, Cayleb, it's like this . . ."

.VII.
King Cayleb's Private Dining Salon,
Royal Palace,
City of Tellesberg,
Kingdom of Charis

M ay I refill your glass, Maikel?" King Cayleb asked late that evening, still holding the bottle of wine from which he had just refilled his own glass.

"Yes, Your Majesty. Please." The archbishop extended his glass and smiled almost mischievously. "At least one good thing's come out of Corisande," he remarked, looking at the label on the bottle.

"*Something* good has to come out of almost anywhere," Cayleb replied as he filled the glass. He seemed totally focused on the minor task, as if he found its mundaneness reassuring. Or perhaps distracting.

He finished, set the bottle back on the table, and sat back in his chair.

Officially, this was simply a private supper with his archbishop, at Maikel's request. With Gray Harbor out of the kingdom, and Staynair acting as first councilor in his place, there had been several such suppers. At which, of course, Captain Athrawes had always been the king's chosen bodyguard. That precedent had come in handy tonight.

"All right," he said quietly. "I've had at least a few hours to think over what the two of you have told me. I have to admit that it . . . hurts a little bit to discover there was a secret this profound that Father never shared with me, but I understand why he wasn't free to make that decision by himself."

"Cayleb"—Staynair's voice was equally quiet—"it was never a matter of trust or distrust. It was only a matter of the procedures which had been set up four hundred years ago. Procedures which have served the Brethren of Saint Zherneau—and, I think, the entire Kingdom—well."

"I said I understand, Maikel." Cayleb met the archbishop's eyes with a steady, level gaze. "And I think the real reason it hurts is that Father never had a chance to tell me the secret on my thirtieth birthday, after all."

"I wish he *had* had that opportunity," Merlin said softly, contemplating his own wineglass, watching the ruby light pool at its heart. "Your father was one of the finest men I've ever known, Cayleb. In fact, he was an even better man than I ever would have realized without the Archbishop's little revelation."

"Ah, yes. His *'revelation.'* An excellent word for it, Merlin. Almost"— Cayleb switched that level gaze to Merlin—"as astonishing a revelation as your own."

"Well," Merlin's smile was lopsided, "I did tell you I'd explain everything if the day ever came when I could."

"Which, in this case," Cayleb said rather pointedly, "was more a case of the day when you *had* to, wouldn't you say?"

"Fair enough." Merlin nodded. "On the other hand, there's also this. With Archbishop Maikel and the journal of Saint Zherneau to vouch for me, I figured you were a lot less likely to decide I was a lunatic. Or that you'd been wrong to trust me, after all."

"There *is* that," Cayleb agreed, and folded his arms across his chest. The intensity of his gaze faded into something else, a look of wonder, almost reverence, with what might have been still just a lingering trace of fear. Or, at least, apprehension.

"I can hardly believe it even now," he said slowly, contemplating Merlin from head to toe." To be honest, I don't know which . . . confuses me more— the fact that you're dead, or the fact that you're a woman."

"In point of fact," Staynair said mildly, "I'm not at all certain Merlin—or Nimue—*is* dead."

"Oh, trust me, Your Eminence," Merlin said in a tone that blended wryness with a lingering, aching grief, "Nimue Alban is dead. Has been, for over nine hundred of your years. As dead as all of her friends . . . and as dead as the Terran Federation."

"I've tried to visualize what you must have seen, experienced." Staynair shook his head. "I can't, of course. I don't suppose anyone could."

"In some ways, it's not that different from what you and Cayleb—and King Haarahld, of course—have faced right here in Charis," Merlin pointed out. "If we lose, everything that matters to you will be destroyed. Although, mind you, I'm hoping for a rather happier outcome this time around."

"As are we all," Staynair said dryly.

"Well, of course we are," Cayleb said, still gazing at Merlin with those perplexed and wondering eyes. "I have to say, though, Merlin, that however hard I try, I just can't visualize you as a woman."

"Which speaks well of my chosen disguise," Merlin said, then surprised himself with a chuckle. "On the other hand, that first rugby game you and Ahrnahld got me involved in was almost my undoing."

"What?" Cayleb's eyebrows knitted. "What are you talking about?"

"Cayleb," Merlin said patiently, "think about it. A PICA is fully functional, and I do mean *fully* functional. It can do anything, mimic any response, an organic human body can do . . . and I spent twenty-seven years—almost thirty of *your* years—being a woman. Trust me. There are some things that just don't change all that easily. Finding myself in the water, naked as the day I was born, and surrounded by all of those nice, equally naked, muscular, *slithery* male bodies . . . I discovered that there's this physical response men have. I'd always realized, in an intellectual sort of way, that it happened, of course, but I'd never expected to *experience* it, you might say."

Cayleb stared at him for a moment, and then he began to laugh. It started out quietly, but it didn't stay that way, and there was something deeply cleansing about the hilarity. Something that chased that lingering trace of fear—if that was what it had been—out of his eyes forever.

"Oh, my God!" he managed to gasp between roars of laughter. "*That* was why you stayed in the water! Why you were so damned careful about that towel!"

"Yes, it was," Merlin agreed rather repressively. "There've been other adjustments, but I have to admit that *that* one's probably been the most . . . interesting."

Staynair had begun chuckling himself as he realized what Merlin and Cayleb were talking about. Now he shook his head.

"Merlin," he said, still smiling, "somehow I don't think a dead woman—or a ghost—would have a sense of humor."

"I'm not so sure about that, Your Eminence."

"Then let me pose it this way. What constitutes being 'alive' for a human being?"

"I suspect most people would think *breathing* was a reasonably important criterion."

"Perhaps 'most people' would, but I'm not asking them. I'm asking you."

"I truly don't know," Merlin admitted. He looked back down into his wineglass. "Maybe it's because I've worried about it so much, chewed the problem up one side and down the other so often that I can't stand back and think about it with any sort of detachment. I've just decided that even if I'm not—alive, I mean—I might as well act as if I were. Too many people made too many sacrifices to put me here on this world, at this particular time, for me to do anything else."

"And that's why I'm certain you *are* alive, Merlin. Nimue Alban," Staynair said softly. "You were one of the ones who made those sacrifices. And you haven't done what you've already done here on Safehold out of some lingering sense of responsibility to people who have been dead for almost a thousand years. Oh, those people *are* important to you, and I understand that for you it hasn't been a thousand years since they died, either. But as Haarahld once told you, a man must be judged by his actions. And for all the lies heaped together in the *Writ*, there are truths, as well. Including the truth that a man's innermost nature will inevitably be known and revealed by his deeds.

"You've shouldered your burden out of personal outrage, Merlin Athrawes. I haven't watched you, talked to you, learned from you for two years now without taking the measure of the man—or the woman—you truly are. You feel the pain which is so much a part of life, just as you feel the joys. I've always thought you were a profoundly lonely man, and now I know why. But I have never, for one moment, doubted that you were a *good* man, and despite what those fools in Zion believe, God is a god of love, Merlin, not a god of savage discipline and mindless rejection. His way may be hard sometimes, and He may demand much from some of His servants, but whatever else He may be, He isn't stupid. He *knows* what He's asked of people like you, over the ages. And whether you realize it or not, God knows you as one of His own, as well. I have no doubt that when Nimue Alban's physical body died, God had another task, another duty, waiting for her. There are too few great souls for Him to waste one which burned that brightly. And so, He let that soul sleep until the day a machine, a . . . PICA awoke in a cave here on Safehold. You have Nimue Alban's soul, Merlin Athrawes. Never doubt it. Never question it . . . or yourself."

Merlin looked at the archbishop for endless seconds. And then, finally, he nodded once. He didn't say a single word. He didn't have to.

The others let his silence linger for a time. Then Cayleb cleared his throat.

"For what it's worth, Merlin, I agree with Maikel. Maybe it's just as well—no, it *is* just as well—you didn't try to explain all of that to me aboard *Dreadnought* before Darcos Sound. But it's like I told you that day in King's

Harbor, when you killed the krakens. You may be able to conceal *what* you are, but you can't hide *who* you are, what you feel. I'm sorry, but you're just not very *good* at it."

"Gosh, thanks," Merlin said wryly.

"Don't mention it." Cayleb grinned at him. "On the other hand, it's going to be quite some time, I imagine, before I really manage to come to grips with all of this. It's going to change a lot of my assumptions."

"I'm sure it is," Merlin acknowledged. "Still, it's not really going to change most of the constraints we face. There's still that kinetic bombardment system, floating up there in orbit. And there are still those power sources under the Temple I haven't been able to identify. Between the two of them, I think they constitute a *damned* good argument in favor of maintaining the secret just the way the Brethren have been maintaining it for the last four centuries. I, for one, have absolutely no desire to turn Charis into a second Armageddon Reef."

"Granted." Cayleb nodded. "But from what you've said, there's an enormous number of things you can teach us, show us."

"Yes and no." Merlin took another sip of wine, then set his glass aside and leaned forward in his chair, resting his folded forearms on the table.

"I can teach you, but I can't just hand you the knowledge. For a lot of reasons, including concealment from the Church and whatever remote sensors might be reporting to those power sources under the Temple. But even if I wasn't worried about that particular aspect of it, I couldn't just replace the Church as the source of all authority. People all over Safehold have to learn to do what you already do here in Charis, Cayleb. They have to learn to *think*. To reject the automatic acceptance of dogma and restrictions simply because someone else—whether it's the Church of God Awaiting or some all-knowing oracle from the lost past—tells them they *must* accept them. We have to transform Safehold into a world of people who *want* to understand the physical universe around them. People who are *comfortable* innovating, thinking of new ways to do new things *on their own*. That's one reason—the main reason, in a lot of ways—I've made suggestions, pointed out possibilities, and then stood back and let people like Baron Seamount, Ehdwyrd Howsmyn, and Rhaiyan Mychail figure out how to apply them.

"And"—he looked Cayleb straight in the eye—"it's equally important for *everyone* on Safehold, even Charis' enemies, to do the same thing."

Cayleb frowned, and Merlin shook his head.

"Think about it, Cayleb. Who's your real enemy? Hektor of Corisande? Or the Inquisition?"

"At the moment," Cayleb said after a thoughtful pause, "I'm rather more focused on Hektor. I hope you won't find that too difficult to understand." He smiled thinly. "On the other hand, I understand the point you're making.

If it weren't Hektor, Clyntahn and the Group of Four would have found someone else to use as their tool."

"Exactly. And how will you defeat the Church? Can you do it with navies and armies?"

"No," Cayleb said slowly.

"Of course not," Merlin said simply. "Your true enemy is a belief system, a doctrine, a way of thinking. You can't kill ideas with a sword, and you can't sink belief structures with a broadside. You defeat them by making them *change*, and the Church has only two options for confronting the challenge you and Charis present. Either they refuse to change, in which case they can't possibly defeat you militarily. Or they decide they have no choice but *to* change, to adopt the new weapons, the new technologies. And once they do that, they'll discover they have to change their belief structure, as well. And when that happens, Cayleb, you'll have won, because your true enemy will have committed suicide."

"You make it sound so easy," Cayleb observed with a twisted smile.

"No," the archbishop said, and the king looked at him. "Not 'easy,' Cayleb. Only *simple*."

"Exactly." Merlin nodded. "There was a military philosopher back on Old Earth before anyone had ever dreamed about spaceflight, or suspected that something like the Gbaba might be out there waiting for us. He said that in war, everything was very simple . . . but even the simplest things were hard to do."

"Really?" Cayleb's smile eased a bit. "That's interesting. Father said almost exactly the same thing to me more than once. Did he get it from one of those books of Saint Zherneau's?"

"I doubt it very much. Your father was one of the smartest men I ever met, Cayleb. I don't think he needed Clausewitz to explain that to him."

"All right," Cayleb said after a moment. "I guess I can see what you're saying. Speaking purely as the King of Charis, I'm not especially enthusiastic about it, you understand, but I see what you're saying and why. On the other hand, if the 'inner circle' of the Brethren already knows the truth about how we got here, and why, can't we at least begin spreading some of your additional knowledge around among them?"

"For those who already know about Saint Zherneau's journal, yes." Merlin shrugged. "The fact that the Inquisition didn't burn Charis to the ground years ago is pretty convincing proof that they, at least, know how to keep a secret. In fact, I'm tempted to use them to set up some additional caches of books and documents, just in case the Church gets lucky. I'm not sure that's a good idea, mind you, but I think it at least bears thinking on.

"The problem is that once we get beyond the group we already know has managed to maintain good security, every person we add to that 'inner circle' of yours constitutes a fresh risk. Whatever we may think, we can't *know* how someone is going to react to the truth, and it would take only one person who went running to the Inquisition to do enormous damage—quite possibly *fatal* damage—to everything we're all trying to accomplish."

"All right, that's obviously a valid point." Cayleb cocked his head to one side, scratching the tip of his nose gently while he thought hard. "At the same time, eventually you're going to *have* to start making the truth known to a larger number of people. I can certainly recognize the reasons for being cautious about that, but there are some people here in Charis who I think could probably weather the shock better than you might expect. And some of them could be far more useful and productive if they had more of your knowledge to work from. I'm thinking about people like Seamount, and possibly Howsmyn. Or, for that matter, Dr. Mahklyn."

Merlin nodded slowly, remembering his conversation with Cayleb the night the Royal College was burned.

"You're right about that. And you *are* the King of Charis. It's your Kingdom, they're your people, and you're the one responsible for their safety and survival. I have my mission, over and beyond the survival of Charis, but you have yours, as well."

"I may be King, but I'm not arrogant enough to believe my judgment is infallible. If it were, I wouldn't have gotten quite as many beatings as a boy." Cayleb chuckled again, then sobered. "Fortunately, there are other people here in Charis who've already demonstrated good judgment—not just about how to *keep* secrets, but about when to reveal them, too."

"You're thinking about the Brethren," Staynair said.

"That's exactly who I'm thinking about, Maikel. I have a proposal for you and the Brethren—and Merlin. I believe it's time you set up a formal process designed to actively identify and vet possible candidates for admission into the 'inner circle.' Perhaps what we really need to do is to borrow from Saint Zherneau's model and set up both inner and outer circles. I don't know about that. But I do know some sort of process needs to be in place, one that lets me make use of the Brethren's collective judgment about this sort of decision the same way I make use of the Council's, and of Parliament's, for other decisions. Except that in this case, I'll pledge to be bound by the majority recommendation of whatever 'Council of Saint Zherneau' we set up."

"There may be instances in which there's no time to ask anyone else," Merlin pointed out. "For example, I had no choice but to show you at least a part of the truth the night I took your message to your father."

"No system is perfect, Merlin. All we can do is the best we can do. Beyond that, we'll simply have to trust God."

Merlin gazed at the youthful king thoughtfully.

"What?" Cayleb said after a moment.

"I'm just . . . pleased," Merlin said.

"Pleased about what?"

"Well, one of the things I've wondered about—and worried about, to be honest—is how this planet is going to react when everyone finds out that the Church of God Awaiting has been a total fraud based on a stupendous lie."

"You're concerned that having discovered the Church is a lie, they may decide God Himself is a lie," Staynair said softly.

"Exactly, Your Eminence." Merlin turned his eyes to the archbishop. "While it may not seem likely to someone raised in a theology like the one Langhorne set up, there were plenty of people back on Old Earth—many of them good, moral, compassionate people—who rejected the existence of God for a whole range of reasons they found convincing. From the Church's perspective, that's the one downside of encouraging the sort of freedom of conscience and thought you've been proclaiming here in Charis. And in a lot of ways, rejecting God's very existence would be an intensely logical reaction once the truth finally comes out. After all, these people—your people—will have had the most convincing evidence anyone could possibly imagine that religion can be used as the most devastating tyranny in the universe."

"That's a point we've considered at Saint Zherneau's over the centuries." Staynair's slight shrug was eloquent. "Some of the Brethren have been deeply concerned over it, to be honest. But, for myself, I have no real fear on that head, Merlin."

"In that case, I envy the depth of your faith, Your Eminence."

"It isn't a matter of faith. It's a matter of logic." Merlin's eyebrows rose, and Staynair laughed softly. "Of course it is! Either God exists, or He doesn't, Merlin. Those are really the only two possibilities. If He does exist, as I believe all three of us believe He does, then, ultimately, anything which promotes truth will only tend to demonstrate His existence. And even if that weren't true, if He exists, then whatever happens will be what He chooses to allow to happen—even if, for some reason beyond my comprehension, what He chooses is to have mankind turn against Him, at least for a time."

"And if He doesn't exist?" Merlin asked quietly.

"If He doesn't, He doesn't. But if He doesn't, then none of it will matter, anyway, will it?"

Merlin blinked, and Staynair laughed again.

"I'm quite confident about which of those two possibilities apply, Merlin. But as I believe I've already told you, men must have the right to refuse to believe before they truly *can* believe. And if it turns out I've been wrong all my life, what have I really lost? I will have done my best to live as a good man, loving other men and women, serving them as I might, and if there is no God, then at the end of my life I'll simply close my eyes and sleep. Is there truly anything dreadful, anything to terrify any man, in that possibility? It isn't that I fear oblivion, Merlin—it's simply that I hope for and believe in so much more."

"Your Eminence, I don't know about the rest of Safehold, but I'm coming to the conclusion that *you* are almost disturbingly sane. And you remind me of an old folk saying from Earth. I believe you have a variant of it here on Safehold, as well. 'In the land of the blind, the one-eyed man will be king.'"

"We do, indeed, have that particular cliché," Staynair agreed. "And, of course, we have the corollary. 'The one-eyed man will be king . . . unless all of the blind men decide to kill him, instead.'" The archbishop smiled whimsically. "It puts rather an interesting perspective on things, doesn't it?"

AUGUST, YEAR OF GOD 892

Schooner *Blade* and Galleon *Guardian*, off Lizard Island, Hankey Sound

A ll right, Mr. Nethaul! Stand by the forward gun!"

"Aye, aye, Sir!"

Hairym Nethaul waved acknowledgment from his post on the schooner *Blade*'s foredeck as the fleet, flush-decked privateer swept down upon its intended prey. Captain Ekohls Raynair, *Blade*'s master and half owner, stood by the wheel, brown eyes narrowly intent as he simultaneously watched the wind, the set of his sails, and the Dohlaran galleon upon which he had set his sights.

"Let her fall off a quarter-point," he growled, and the helmsman nodded.

"Aye, Cap'n," he replied, shifting his well-masticated wad of chewleaf to the other side of his mouth, and Raynair chuckled. It would have been hard to imagine anything less navy-style than the discipline aboard *Blade*, but it got the job done. He and his schooner were seven thousand miles from Charis as the wyvern flew, and better than three times that far as they'd actually sailed. That was a long, long way, but Raynair didn't care. It had taken almost three months to make the trip, even for a fast ship like *Blade* and her three consorts, and he didn't care about that, either.

No, what Ekohls Raynair cared about was that he and his consortium partners had been right all along. It seemed abundantly clear that no one in Dohlar had entertained the least suspicion that Charisian privateers would operate so far afield. The four schooners—*Blade*, *Ax*, *Cutlass*, and *Dirk*—had cut a swath through the totally unwary Dohlaran merchant marine for almost a month now, and the expedition's books were looking very, very good.

How nice of King Rahnyld to invest all that time and effort in making us rich, Raynair thought as his ship went slicing through the water like the very blade for which she was named. *Of course, this wasn't exactly what he had in mind. But if you're stupid enough to go swimming with krakens, then you're lucky if all that happens is you get back a bloody stump.*

Rahnyld IV's ambitions to build a merchant marine from scratch were no doubt laudable, from a Dohlaran viewpoint. Raynair didn't see it that way. His father and one of his uncles had been the master and first mate (and joint owners) of a Charisian merchant ship which had come calling in the Gulf of Dohlar twelve years before and run afoul of a Dohlaran war galley in the approaches to Silkiah Bay. They hadn't even been headed for a Dohlaran port—their cargo had been bound for a spice merchant in the Grand Duchy of Silkiah—but that hadn't mattered.

King Rahnyld had decided that the Gulf of Dohlar, Hankey Sound, and Silkiah Bay ought to be closed waters. He'd started out by levying tolls on anyone passing east of the Dohlar Bank and its cluster of islands. Then he'd started pushing his area of operations farther west. Eventually, he'd extended his "protected area" as far as Whale Island, over a thousand miles from his own coastline. Claiming to exert some sort of police power over a stretch of salt water that vast was not only unheard of, it was ridiculous. Charis, for example, like virtually every other maritime power on the planet, hewed to the older rule which held that a nation could claim sovereignty only over waters in which it could—and did—exercise an *effective* control. That didn't mean just extorting money out of passing merchant ships, either. It meant dealing with pirates, preventing acts of war by other naval powers, buoying and marking navigational hazards, updating charts, and generally making the children behave. Which, in turn, meant, for all practical purposes, that territorial waters were those which lay within long cannon shot of its coastline, which was generally agreed to be about three miles. Actually, even the three-mile limit was being overly generous, as everyone understood perfectly well. And it was worth noting that somehow ships of the Harchong Empire had ended up exempt from King Rahnyld's "passage fees."

Ahbnair and Wyllym Raynair hadn't seen any reason why they should pour their hard-earned golden marks into Rahnyld's pockets, either. Especially since it was obvious the entire "passage fee" demand was intended solely to bar non-Dohlaran merchant ships from the waters Rahnyld IV regarded as "his."

No one in Charis knew exactly what had happened that afternoon in the waters between Hankey Sound and Silkiah Bay. The one thing they *did* know was that the galleon *Raynair's Pride* had been fired into, boarded, and then sunk by the Dohlaran Navy. Neither Ekohls' father, nor his uncle, had survived the experience, and only two of their crewmen had ever made it home again.

There was a reason Ekohls Raynair had been less surprised than most when Rahnyld allied himself so eagerly with Hektor of Corisande, despite the fact that Dohlar and Corisande were damned nearly on opposite sides of the world from one another. And, the truth be told, it wasn't just the profit which had attracted *Blade* and her consorts to Dohlaran waters, either.

He looked back across at the lumbering Dohlaran galleon. He could see why it was operating in the Gulf. One look at real blue water would probably have frightened the clumsy, high-sided, lubberly joke's crew to death. Fortunately, whatever the Church—or, for that matter, Rahnyld of Dohlar—might think about Charis, the imperial governor of Shwei Province appeared to understand that Charisian marks spent just as well as anyone else's. At the moment, he was doing quite well for himself, in a quiet sort of way, by allowing Raynair and his partners to dispose of prize ships and seized cargoes to Harchongese merchants at Yu-Shai, on Shwei Bay. How long that would last was anyone's guess, but for the moment at least, Raynair didn't have to worry about getting his captures all the way home to Charis.

This particular galleon seemed more stubborn than most, Raynair reflected. Her master was continuing mulishly on his course rather than accepting the inevitable. He'd clapped on all the sail he had—which wasn't all that impressive to someone who'd seen the sail plans of *Charisian* galleons—and he was plodding along as if he actually thought he could evade the sleek, low-slung schooner.

Well, he's about to find out better, Raynair thought.

▼   ▼   ▼

"Keep that damned fool's head below the bulwarks!" Captain Graygair Maigee snarled.

The offending soldier ducked hastily back into concealment, and Maigee grunted in irate satisfaction. Then he turned his attention back to the Charisian vessel bearing down upon *Guardian*.

Funny, he thought. *This all seemed like a much better idea when they were explaining it to me back in Gorath Bay. Now I'm wondering what idiot thought it up. Of course, if anybody in the damned Navy actually knew his arse from his elbow, we wouldn't have landed in this mess in the first place!*

"Do you think he'll fire into us, or put a shot across our bows, Sir?" Airah Synklyr, his first officer, asked quietly.

"How the hell do I know?" Maigee responded grumpily. It was a good question, though, he had to admit. "We'll find out when we find out, I suppose," he added.

Which, unless I miss my guess, is going to happen very soon now.

▼   ▼   ▼

"All right, Mr. Nethaul—put a shot across his bow!"

The forward gun thudded almost before Raynair had finished speaking, and he watched the plume of white water rise far beyond the galleon.

Blade and her sisters had come from the Shumair Yard in Charis. They were basically duplicates of Sir Dustyn Olyvyr's design for the Royal Navy, but with a few minor changes to suit them for their private enterprise role. Their naval counterparts carried fourteen thirty-pounder carronades apiece, but *Blade* carried only ten carronades plus the long fourteen-pounder forward on one of the new "pivot mounts." Raynair didn't know who'd thought up the "pivot mount," and he didn't really much care.

It consisted of an almost standard gun carriage that was mounted on a platform made of two heavy timbers, or skids, which were joined by four massive, evenly spaced blocks. The carriage had no wheels, however; instead, it slid along grooves cut into the skids when it recoiled. The skids themselves were secured to the deck by a pivot pin through the rearmost connecting block. The pin passed through the deck, and its lower end was secured to a two-foot-square timber. The point at which it passed through the deck was strengthened by a massive cast-iron socket that extended halfway through the belowdecks timber, and its upper end was heavily bushed where it joined to the skids, since it took the majority of the recoil forces when the gun fired. Castor wheels under the skids' front end rode a circular iron rail set into the deck, and by moving the front end along the rail and pivoting on the rear end, the entire mount could be trained around through a theoretical arc of three hundred and sixty degrees, although the ship's bowsprit and rigging blocked certain angles of fire. Rumor gave Baron Seamount credit for it, but all that Raynair really cared about was that the centerline mount permitted *Blade*'s single long gun to be brought to bear anywhere in either broadside.

There were limits to the size of gun the mount could take, and the long fourteen fired a much lighter shot than the carronades, but its range was longer, and it didn't really take the heaviest gun afloat to convince any reasonably sane merchant skipper that it was time to surrender his ship.

▼　▼　▼

"How the hell did they do *that?*" Synklyr demanded.

"D'you think *I* know?" Maigee snarled back.

In fairness, he knew it had been a rhetorical question. In fact, he wasn't certain Synklyr even realized he'd spoken aloud. None of which made him feel any happier at the fresh evidence of yet another of the apparently unending, devilish Charisian innovations.

In fact, this was the closest Maigee had yet come to the new Charisian artillery, which he more than half suspected was the real reason for most of his irritable tension. Virtually everyone in the Dohlaran Navy, from the Duke of Thorast down, was busy trying to downplay the effectiveness of the Charisian guns. Maigee supposed that was inevitable—*Obviously,* he thought sardonically, *pretending the Charisian guns don't work is much simpler than figuring out what to do about them if it turns out they* do *work, after all*—but it did damn-all for the poor bastard who found himself face-to-face with them.

He longed to pull out his spyglass and take a good, long look at the schooner's armament, but spyglasses were rare aboard merchant ships at the best of times, and especially for one as deliberately down-at-the-heels as *Guardian*.

"Stand ready, Mr. Synklyr," he said instead, then looked at his second officer. "It's time, Mr. Jynks," he said.

▼   ▼   ▼

"That's odd," Ekohls Raynair murmured to himself as the galleon finally accepted the inevitable and hove-to. He frowned, trying to decide what it was that was jabbing at the corner of his mind as *Blade* followed suit and Nethaul and a dozen heavily armed seamen took the first cutter across to take possession of their prize. There was something—

Then he found out what the "something" was.

▼   ▼   ▼

"*Now!*" Captain Maigee barked, and several things happened at once.

The waiting soldiers rose to their feet, matchlocks ready, showing themselves over the high bulwark even as other, specially arranged sections of that bulwark dropped suddenly, exposing the cannon mounted behind them. The guns were only falcons, throwing shot that weighed just under eight pounds. *Guardian* was only a converted merchant galleon, after all. She hadn't been built with artillery in mind, and each of those guns still weighed just over a ton apiece. It simply hadn't been practical to put any larger, heavier weapons aboard her, and if even a tenth of the tales about the new Charisian guns was true, her broadside was going to be far slower-firing. But the privateer had only five guns in each broadside, and *Guardian* had eighteen.

▼   ▼   ▼

Raynair's heart seemed to stop beating as the Dohlaran "merchant ship" suddenly bared its fangs. His mouth opened, but before he could get out the first order, the afternoon seemed to explode around him.

There were at least a hundred musketeers aboard that ship. Now they rose from their places of concealment and opened fire on *Blade*'s cutter. At that range, not even matchlocks were likely to miss, and the concentrated fire turned the cutter into a shattered, slowly sinking wreck filled with dead men and blood.

The fact of Nethaul's death, along with the massacre of all of the rest of his boarding party, barely had time to begin to register before the Dohlaran's broadside thundered. They were only Dohlaran guns, but there were a lot of them, and obviously *these* gunners had a damned good idea about which end of the gun the round shot came out of. Several of them managed to miss, anyway, despite the ridiculously low range. Most of them did better than that, however, and screams erupted across *Blade*'s deck as the Dohlaran fire ripped through Raynair's crew.

That was terrible enough, but that same broadside brought down *Blade*'s foremast in an avalanche of shattered spars and canvas. The foremast was actually the primary mast for a twin-masted schooner, and the tangled wreckage crippled *Blade*.

"*Fire!*" Raynair heard someone else shouting with his voice, and four of the five carronades in the schooner's port broadside belched flame.

▼   ▼   ▼

"*Yes!*" Maigee cried as the Charisian ship's mast came thundering down. That was far better than he'd hoped for, and he could see at least a dozen men already down on the schooner's shot-ripped deck.

But then the privateer disappeared behind a cloud of smoke of its own, and Maigee staggered as the fat, far heavier shot from the schooner's carronades slammed back into his own command.

Guardian had been designed and built as a merchant vessel. Her timbers were lighter, her planking was thinner, than any naval architect would have demanded. In at least one way, that worked in her favor. Because her planking was so much thinner, the shattering impact of *Blade*'s fire produced fewer and smaller splinters than would have been the case with a "proper warship's" heavier construction. On the other hand, her hull was packed with soldiers and seamen, and her lighter construction meant she was much more fragile than a warship would have been.

Maigee's ears rang with the shrieks and screams of his own wounded. One of his guns took a direct hit, and the bulky timber of its clumsy, wheelless carriage disintegrated even as still more of the Charisian's heavy shot clawed great bleeding furrows through the ship's company. *Guardian*'s guns outnumbered *Blade*'s by better than three to one, and the Dohlaran had the advantage of surprise. But *Blade*'s guns threw far heavier shot, and they fired much more rapidly.

"Reload! *Reload*, damn your eyes!" He heard Synklyr shouting out of the smoke from somewhere forward. The first lieutenant's voice sounded harsh and distorted against the backdrop of screams. The musketeers were blazing away at the Charisian ship as quickly as they could reload, but the range to the schooner was much too great for any sort of accuracy.

▼   ▼   ▼

"Hit them—*hit* the bastards!" Raynair shouted even as the bosun led a rush of seamen with axes and hatchets forward to cut away the wreckage.

Like most privateers, *Blade* carried a far larger crew than was actually required to work or fight the ship. The prize crews to take custody of their captures had to come from somewhere, after all. But the Dohlaran's deadly surprise must have killed or wounded at least thirty of Raynair's men. Counting

Nethaul and his cutter's crew, the number was closer to sixty than to fifty, a voice somewhere deep inside informed him savagely. That was at least a third of his total ship's company.

Yet there'd been a reason he'd demanded such relentless, unceasing gun drill and training during the long voyage from Charis. His port gun crews had taken heavy casualties, but replacements from the starboard guns came charging across to replace the dead and wounded. If *Blade* had been free to maneuver, things would have been very different. Unfortunately, the wreckage forward meant even the clumsy galleon could match her maneuverability.

No, there was only one thing Ekohls Raynair could do now, and he bared his teeth as *Blade*'s second broadside thundered.

.II.
Tellesberg Palace,
City of Tellesberg,
Kingdom of Charis

I s this going to meet your needs, Doctor?"
Rahzhyr Mahklyn turned from the window to face Father Clyfyrd Laimhyn, King Cayleb's personal secretary and confessor. Over the years, Mahklyn had found himself facing many a priest who seemed less than . . . fully enthusiastic over the Royal College's work. Father Clyfyrd, however, seemed gratifyingly free of any reservations. Not surprisingly, probably, in someone who had been personally recommended to the king for sensitive posts by Archbishop Maikel. Now, Laimhyn stood waiting attentively for Mahklyn to consider his question.

Not that there really ought to have been that much "considering" to do, Mahklyn reflected, glancing back out the tower window. King Cayleb's Tower—built by the present monarch's great-grandfather—stood on the side of the palace farthest from the harbor. The window offered a view across the southern third or so of Tellesberg and the vista of woodland, farms, and distant mountains beyond. It was certainly far better than the view from his old office, down by the waterfront, and the tower itself offered at least half again as much floor space. True, he was going to have to climb even more stairs to reach his present vantage point, but if he cared to ascend one more flight, he would reach the tower's flat roof, open to sunlight and wind. There was already a comfortable group of wicker chairs with padded seat cushions waiting up there under a sun canopy, and Mahklyn's imagination was fully up to the task of envisioning the sinful pleasure of sitting back in one of those chairs, notepad in lap, feet propped on a convenient stool, with a cold drink at his elbow—chilled by ice harvested from those same distant mountains and stored in the icehouse buried deep under the palace—and servants available to refresh it at need.

I think that's part of the problem, he thought sardonically. *Somehow, "pure scholarship" isn't supposed to be quite that much fun!*

Actually, as he knew perfectly well, his lingering reservations owed themselves to nothing of the sort. They represented his stubborn allegiance to the principle that the College was supposed to be officially (and as visibly as possible) independent of the Crown. Which was silly of him, since the present King Cayleb had made it abundantly clear he was going to change that relationship. For that matter, in the five-days since the fiery destruction of the College's original building, Mahklyn had come to realize that the king's decision was the right one. Unfortunately, he continued to have something he could only describe as conscience pangs whenever he thought about it.

Stop being such a twit and answer the man, Rahzhyr, he told himself firmly.

"I think the tower will do just fine, Father," he said, returning his attention to Cayleb's secretary. "I could wish we had a little more record storage space, but that, unfortunately, isn't something we're going to have to worry about for a while, at least."

He smiled, but it was an exceedingly sour smile as he once again reflected upon all of the priceless records and documents which had been destroyed. And he'd come to the conclusion that Captain Athrawes had been right from the outset about how and why that fire had been started . . . and by whom.

"If you're certain, Doctor," Laimhyn said, "I'm supposed to tell you that His Majesty would like to move you, your daughter and son-in-law, and your grandchildren into the old family section of the Palace."

Mahklyn opened his mouth in automatic refusal of the offer, but Laimhyn continued speaking before he could object to the size, luxury, and comfort of the proposed housing.

"That section of the Palace has stood virtually unused for the better part of twenty years, Doctor. In fact, we're going to have to do a little roof repair before it will be anything His Majesty would consider truly habitable. And, while I realize you and your family may feel you're rattling around like seeds in a gourd, I assure you that you won't for long. His Majesty intends to have one of the royal bedchambers converted into a working office for you, and it's highly probable that at least two or three of your senior colleagues will also be moving in. If King Cayleb's Tower will be a suitable home for the official College, the fact that it's directly across Prince Edvarhd's Court from the old family section would undoubtedly be convenient for all of you."

Mahklyn closed his mouth again. Laimhyn had placed a slight but unmistakable emphasis on his final three words, which strongly suggested to Mahklyn that they'd come from either the king himself, or from Captain

Athrawes. It had the hallmarks of their despicable cunning, at any rate. He didn't know who those "senior colleagues" might be, but he had his suspicions, and at least two of them were as creaky in the joints as he'd become. Which made the convenience argument considerably harder for him to reject than it would have been if it had been only his *own* knees he had to worry about.

Besides, Tairys will kill me if I turn down an offer like this!

"Very well, Father Clyfyrd," he said finally. "Please inform His Majesty that he's being far too generous, but that I gratefully and gladly accept his generosity."

"I'm certain His Majesty will be delighted to hear it," Laimhyn murmured, with scarcely a flicker of triumph.

"Now," he continued more briskly, "about that clerical assistance. His Majesty was thinking—"

▼   ▼   ▼

"Oh, stop grousing, Father!" Tairys Kahnklyn said with an affectionate smile as she set the salad bowl down in the center of the dinner table. "You'd think the King had offered you a cell down in the dungeons!"

"It's just the principle of the thing," Mahklyn objected gamely. "We're supposed to be independent and critical-minded, not bribed and subverted by promises of sinful luxury!"

"Personally, I'm completely in favor of sinful luxury, myself," Aizak Kahnklyn put in as he picked up the wooden tongs and began serving the salad.

Mahklyn's son-in-law was a sturdy, stocky man of average height. He had a heavy, fast-growing beard, bushy eyebrows, and powerful shoulders and upper arms, and his dark eyes looked out of cavernous sockets. People often thought that he looked as if he would have been right at home as a longshoreman down on the docks, or behind a plow on a farm somewhere. In fact, there was a sparkle of lively curiosity in those deep-set eyes, and he was one of the more intelligent and well-read men of Mahklyn's acquaintance. He and Tairys were also the College's official librarians, and if anyone had been more devastated than Mahklyn himself by the destruction of the College's records, it had to have been his daughter and his son-in-law.

"Me, too. Me, too! I *love* sinful luxury!" Eydyth Kahnklyn, Tairys and Aizak's younger daughter, announced, almost bouncing in her chair. Her twin brother, Zhoel, rolled his eyes. He did a lot of that when Eydyth's thirteen-year-old enthusiasm got the better of her. Still, Mahklyn didn't hear him raising any protest, either, and he looked at Aidryn, his oldest grandchild.

"Should I assume you support your parents and your somewhat vociferous sibling in this case?" he asked her.

"Grandpapa," the twenty-year-old replied with a smile, "if you really want to live and work in a drafty, creaky old tenement, with four flights of stairs to climb just to reach your office, and windows any nasty-minded person can chuck lit lanterns through, then you go right ahead. The rest of us will just have to make do here in the Palace."

"Hedonists, the lot of you," Mahklyn growled.

"If you really think that, then call us that without smiling, Father," Tairys said. Mahklyn ignored her challenge with the dignity appropriate to a patriarch of his advanced years. Especially since he knew perfectly well he couldn't meet it, anyway.

"Has anyone discussed it with Uncle Tohmys?" Erayk asked. At seventeen, he was the second eldest of Mahklyn's grandchildren. He favored his mother more than his father, with a tall, slender build, and he was definitely the family's worrier.

"My little brother can take care of himself, thank you very much, Erayk," his mother said now, with a smile. "He's been doing it for years, after all. And I'm quite sure that when he gets home, he'll be in favor of 'dropping the hook' here instead of our old spare bedroom."

Most of the people around the table chuckled. Tohmys Mahklyn had never married—yet, at least; he was only thirty-six, Mahklyn reminded himself—mostly because he claimed a wife and a captain's berth didn't go together. As the master of one of Ehdwyrd Howsmyn's galleons, Tohmys was away from Tellesberg much more often than he was at home, however, and Mahklyn suspected that he had quite a few lady-loves scattered about the oceans of Safehold. Unlike his sister, Tohmys had never been attracted to the scholar's life. He was much too busy pursuing more . . . lively goals, and he had no objection at all to enjoying the finer things in life.

"I'm afraid your mother's right about that much, at least," Mahklyn told his grandson.

"Of course she is," Aizak said cheerfully. "Aside from that peculiar taste of his for salt water, he's one of the sanest men I know. Do you really think your uncle would turn up his nose at quarters here in the Palace, Erayk?"

"Not Uncle Tohmys, that's for sure!" Eydyth put in with a huge grin.

"Exactly," Aizak said as he passed Mahklyn's filled salad plate to him. "And that doesn't even consider all the other advantages," he added, just a bit more quietly as he met his father-in-law's eyes across the table.

No, it doesn't, Aizak, Mahklyn agreed silently. *They'll find it harder than hell to throw any lit lanterns around* here, *won't they?*

"All right," he said. "All right! I'll stop complaining, buckle down, and suffer the imposition of all this sinful luxury in noble silence."

▼   ▼   ▼

"Your Majesty!"

Mahklyn started to spring to his feet—or as close to it as someone his age, with his knees, could manage, at least—but King Cayleb waved him back into his chair.

"Oh, stay put, Rahzhyr!" the youthful monarch scolded. "We've known each other for years, you're old enough to be my father, and this is *your* domain, not mine."

It had, Mahklyn reflected, been tactful, if not precisely accurate, of the king to say "father," and not "*grand*father."

"Your Majesty is most kind," he said, settling back into the luxuriously padded chair Cayleb had provided for him.

"My Majesty is nothing of the sort," Cayleb said tartly as Merlin Athrawes followed him through the door into Mahklyn's office carrying a leather, accordion-pleated document folder. "My Majesty is a calculating, cynically self-serving sort of Majesty. Seeing to it that you and your colleagues have everything you need to function smoothly and efficiently—and without worrying about smoke inhalation—is entirely in my own best interests."

"Of course it is, Your Majesty."

Mahklyn smiled, and the king smiled back. But then his expression turned rather more serious, and Mahklyn's eyebrows rose as Captain Athrawes closed the office door behind him.

"As a matter of fact, there's quite a lot of truth in what I just said, Dr. Mahklyn," Cayleb said. "More, in fact, than I think you know."

"I beg your pardon, Your Majesty?"

"Let me begin this way," Cayleb said, settling into one of the other chairs in the large, sunny office. "I imagine it's safe for me to assume that you've observed a few . . . minor peculiarities about *Seijin* Merlin here?"

He paused, head cocked, and Mahklyn's eyes narrowed.

"As a matter of fact, Your Majesty," he said slowly, "I have."

"Well, as it happens, that's because he's a rather peculiar sort of fellow," Cayleb said with a tight smile. "And the reason for my unannounced little visit this afternoon is to tell you about some of those peculiarities of his and why they—and you—are so important to what's happening not just here in Charis, but for all of Safehold.

"I wasn't *fully* aware of the *Seijin's* oddities myself until fairly recently," he continued. "Not until the day he and Archbishop Maikel walked in to tell me about a little history most people aren't aware of. You see, Doctor, it would appear that several centuries ago—"

▼   ▼   ▼

Just over three hours later, Cayleb leaned back in his chair and raised both hands, palms uppermost.

"So that's the truth, Doctor," he said quietly. "I know it's a lot to take in, and I know it flies in the face of everything the Church has ever taught us, but it's true. I've asked Archbishop Maikel, and he tells me he's more than willing to confirm everything I've told you. For that matter, the Brethren would be most happy to make the original documents available to you, for your own examination, at Saint Zherneau's."

"That . . . won't be necessary, Your Majesty," Mahklyn said slowly. His eyes were huge, glowing with an intense, blazing curiosity as he gazed not at the king, but at Merlin. "Oh, I'll certainly take His Eminence up on that offer—what historian could possibly *not* take it?! But I don't need to see it to believe every word you've just told me, and not simply because I've never known you to tell a lie, either. I won't pretend that I ever even suspected what you've just told me, but it explains a great many other things I *have* wondered about, over the course of my life."

"If you'll pardon my saying so, Dr. Mahklyn, you're the sort of person who *always* wonders about something," Merlin observed with a twinkle.

"One tries, *Seijin* Merlin." Mahklyn shook his head. "On the other hand, looking at you and the knowledge and capabilities your very existence represents, it's obvious I'm not going to *finish* wondering about all the things I ought to be wondering about before I run out of time."

"Are you going to be comfortable about this, now that you know, Doctor?" Cayleb asked quietly.

"A scholar isn't supposed to be *too* comfortable, Your Majesty."

"That wasn't precisely what I meant," Cayleb said dryly.

"I know that, Your Majesty." Mahklyn looked back at the king with a contrite expression. "At the same time, though, my answer wasn't completely flippant. *Seijin* Merlin and all the history you've just summarized for me is the sort of thing scholars live for. Or that we're *supposed* to live for, at any rate. I'm sure I'm going to discover aspects of that history which will be disturbing, and attempting to assimilate all of this in the face of what the Church has always taught is bound to cause the odd moment of anxiety. Compared to the fascination quotient, though—"

He shrugged, and Cayleb's shoulders seemed to relax ever so slightly, as if some previously imperceptible tension had just flowed out of him.

"I'm also beginning to understand just where *Seijin* Merlin's odd little caches of knowledge come from," Mahklyn continued.

"I don't believe I've ever actually *lied* about that, Doctor."

"No, I don't believe you have, either." Mahklyn chuckled. "As a matter of fact, I've just been running my memory back over your prefatory remarks each time you unveiled some new, useful technique or invention. You've always been very careful about the way you presented them, haven't you?"

"I've certainly tried to be," Merlin said soberly, "and largely because I've always known moments like this one have to come. There may be things I've been unable to tell you, or others, but I decided at the very beginning that it was important that I not hold back that information in a way which would undercut my credibility when I finally was able to share it."

"And if you think he's done some skillful dancing where *you're* concerned, Doctor, you should have seen him talking to Father Paityr," Cayleb put in feelingly.

"I rather think I would have liked to have seen that." Mahklyn shook his head with another chuckle. "It must have been . . . diverting."

"Oh, you have no idea, Doctor," Merlin assured him.

"Probably not," Mahklyn agreed. Then he sat upright in his own chair, leaning forward and folding his hands on the desk in front of him. "On the other hand, Your Majesty, I'm beginning to understand what you said when you first walked in. Should I assume *Seijin* Merlin has some additional kernels of knowledge to share with—and through—the College?"

"Actually, yes," Cayleb agreed. "And we'd also like you to consider additional nominees for the 'inner circle.' Obviously, you know your fellow members of the College better than either of us do. Which ones do you think would be . . . flexible enough to accept the truth?"

"I'll have to give that some thought, Your Majesty," Mahklyn said cautiously, and Cayleb snorted.

"If you *didn't* have to 'give it some thought,' I'd have you committed, Doctor! And remember, the final decision isn't solely up to you or to me. Nonetheless, it definitely would be extremely useful to have additional members of the College who could work with us on this."

"I understand, Your Majesty," Mahklyn assured him.

"Good. And now, Merlin, I believe you had something for the good doctor?"

"I do indeed, Your Majesty," Merlin said with a half bow. Then he reached into the folder he'd carried into the office and extracted a sheaf of paper. "I had this converted into manuscript form, Doctor," he said. "I thought it would probably raise fewer questions than a properly printed, hardbound copy with a publication date from *before* the Day of Creation, should someone else happen to see it. Here."

He handed it across, and Mahklyn accepted it just a bit gingerly. He opened it, then twitched in surprise.

"This is *my* handwriting!" he blurted, looking back up at Merlin.

"Actually, it's Owl's," Merlin said with a smile. "He's quite a capable forger, and I slipped him a sample of your handwriting before he produced this. I felt it would be best all around."

"But what *is* it?" Mahklyn asked.

"This, Dr. Mahklyn, is something that was written long ago, on Old Earth, by a man called Sir Isaac Newton. I've had it updated slightly—the original English was close to two thousand years old—but I think you'll find it interesting."

.III.
Royal Patent Office,
City of Tellesberg,
Kingdom of Charis

". . . and this is *your* office, Father."

Father Paityr Wylsynn followed Father Bryahn Ushyr into the large, square room and looked around. It was smaller than his old office in the Archbishop's Palace, but Wylsynn had always thought that chamber was larger and rather more magnificent than he required, anyway. This one was more than big enough, with windows in two walls and a skylight to admit plenty of light. The chair behind the desk looked comfortable, too.

"I trust this is satisfactory, Father?" Father Bryahn asked after a moment.

"Um?" Wylsynn shook himself. "I mean, certainly, Father Bryahn," he told Archbishop Maikel's aide. "It's more than adequate."

"I'm glad. We have a half-dozen trained clerks for you to choose from for your personal assistants, as well. I had them sent over this morning, and they're waiting for you to interview them. Feel free to choose any—or, for that matter, *all*—of them."

"The Archbishop is most generous," Wylsynn said, and Ushyr shrugged.

"His Eminence simply wants you to have the tools you require, Father."

"Well, he's certainly seen to it that I will." Wylsynn walked across the office to examine the neatly shelved volumes in the floor-to-ceiling bookcase behind the waiting desk. He ran his eye across the printed spines, nodding unconsciously in approval. He had all the reference works he could possibly need.

"In that case, Father, I'll take myself out of your way and let you begin settling in," Ushyr told him. "If you discover that there's anything we've overlooked, please notify us at once."

"I will," Wylsynn assured him, and walked him to the door of his new office.

Ushyr departed, and Wylsynn walked slowly back around to seat himself behind the desk. He looked around the office once more, but he didn't actually

see it at all. He was too busy asking himself if he truly knew what he was doing to worry about furnishings or office space.

That sort of second-guessing was rare for Paityr Wylsynn. From the day
he'd told his father he was prepared to accept his posting to Charis, he'd always felt he was in the "right" place. Not necessarily a *comfortable* place, but
the place he needed to be to accomplish whatever it was God desired from
him. Until, of course, Charis had decided to bid defiance to not simply the
Group of Four, but the entire hierarchy of Mother Church.

The young priest closed his eyes, reaching out to that still, quiet place at
the core of his being where he kept his faith. He touched it once more, and a
welcome sense of peace spread out from it. His worries and concerns didn't
magically disappear, but the assurance that he would be able to deal with each
of them as they arose filled him.

Of course, he thought, as he opened his eyes once again, *"deal with" isn't exactly the same thing as being positive you're doing the right thing, is it, Paityr?*

The truth, he reflected, was that he was far less concerned by his decision
to accept Maikel Staynair's authority—spiritual and secular—as the Archbishop of Charis than he was by this entire notion of a "patent office."

When the idea had first been explained to him, he'd been a little perplexed. Register new ideas and techniques? Give the people who came up
with them effective *ownership* of them and require others to *pay* them for using them? Absurd! Worse, the very concept had reeked of deliberately stoked
innovation, and that was something no member of the Order of Schueler was
likely to feel truly comfortable with. Still, he had to admit that he'd been unable to find anything in the *Writ* or *The Commentaries* which would have forbidden such an office. That might well be because it had simply never
occurred to anyone that someone might even consider creating it, but the fact
remained that there was no scriptural prohibition.

*And if these people are going to survive, they need innovative solutions to the prob-
lem of how someone outnumbered eight- or nine-to-one defends himself.*

That grim thought sent a familiar chill through him. Part of him wanted
to insist it was only a rationalization, a way to justify an unhealthy and spiri-
tually dangerous fascination with new knowledge. Yet whenever that temptation arose, he found himself recalling the horrendous, unprovoked attack
which Charis had somehow managed to fend off.

Surely God didn't want or expect His children to stand helpless while
their families were murdered and their homes were burned over their heads!
Innocent men had every right to seek the means to protect themselves against
someone else's attack, and no matter what the Church might officially say,
Wylsynn knew the attack on Charis had been totally unjustified. Not that he
was particularly surprised by the claims to the contrary coming out of Zion

and the Temple. Saddened and disgusted, yes, but not surprised. Despite his own deep and abiding faith, Paityr Wylsynn had never had any illusions about the corruption of the Group of Four and of the Council of Vicars in general.

No, that isn't quite right, he told himself harshly. *You* did *cherish at least some illusions, didn't you? Like the illusion that not even the Grand Inquisitor would set out to destroy an entire kingdom just because it irritated him.*

He'd thought, prayed, and meditated in the wake of that decision of Clyntahn's, and he'd finally come to the conclusion that what was happening here in Charis was God's will. However uncomfortable, however . . . worrisome, he might find Archbishop Maikel's beliefs, there was no question in his mind that the Archbishop of Charis stood far closer to the mind of God than the Grand Inquisitor. Maikel Staynair might be mistaken; he was *not* evil . . . and that was no longer something Wylsynn could say of Zhaspahr Clyntahn and the rest of the Group of Four. And, truth to tell, Wylsynn had become steadily more confident that Staynair wasn't mistaken, either. The implications of that, and the monumental changes in Wylsynn's own understanding of scripture and doctrine inherent in them, were frightening, but God had never promised doing His will would be easy.

And so, Father Paityr Wylsynn, Intendant of Charis, ordained priest of the Order of Schueler, found himself here, sitting in an office in a building specifically dedicated to encouraging people to think of new ways to do things.

He shook his head, lips twitching in a half smile, at the thought. Then he stood and crossed to one of his new windows, gazing out it into the afternoon.

The Patent Office had been housed in a building which belonged to Baron Ironhill's ministry. The Keeper of the Purse had rather more to do in Charis than in many of Safehold's other kingdoms, and Ironhill had moved his main staff to a considerably larger building the previous year. This one might have been too small for *Ironhill's* needs, yet it had a plethora of offices—many of them no larger than a moderately small closet—in which the new Patent Office (which also belonged to Ironhill's ministry, at least for the moment) could tuck away the innumerable clerks it was likely to require. It was also surrounded by mature nearoak and pine trees, which provided a welcome shade.

And the low wall around it was patrolled, night and day, by rifle-armed Marines.

Wylsynn's mouth tightened as he watched the afternoon sun glitter on the bayonets of the Marines stationed by the Patent Office gates. Their presence—along with what had happened to the Royal College's original home—was a grim reminder that not everyone agreed with his own assessment of events here in Charis. The thought that he had to be protected from people who thought of themselves as loyal sons of Mother Church was . . . disturbing. But so was the fate the Inquisition had dealt out to Erayk Dynnys.

No easy answers, he thought. *The* Writ *says God tests those He loves, and I've always believed that's true. But usually, what He wants of me is simple enough to recognize quickly. Not easy to do, maybe, but simple enough to* recognize.

He drew a deep breath. It was time to put the second-guessing aside. He was here not to encourage innovation—God knew there were already plenty of Charisians energetically doing that!—but to ensure that none of the newly patented processes or concepts violated the Proscriptions of Jwo-jeng. That much, he could do with no qualms at all.

And what do you do when you've seen so many new processes and concepts flow across your desk that the Proscriptions began to erode even for you, Paityr? he asked himself. *How do you say "Stop" after you've become part of telling people that change is good? His Eminence is right,* On Faith and Obedience *does say there are times when change* is *good, even necessary. But if this is one of those times, where will it end . . . and who will* you *be when you get there?*

Those were questions he had no answers to . . . yet. But there were times when any man, especially a priest, simply had to trust God to bring him to the proper final destination.

Paityr Wylsynn straightened his shoulders, crossed to the door of his new office, and looked out it at the porter for this floor.

"Father Bryahn told me he's assembled several candidates for me to interview as potential clerks," he said calmly. "Would you be kind enough to ask the first of them to step into my office?"

.IV.
House of Parliament,
Kingdom of Charis

It was the first time Merlin had seen the interior of the Charisian House of Parliament with his own eyes. Well, his own visual receptors, he supposed, if he wanted to be strictly accurate.

The chamber's plastered walls were paneled to above head height in the exotic tropical woods with which Charis' more northern forests abounded. Ceiling fans mounted on the exposed beams turned slowly and steadily overhead, pulling the heat upward, and the louvered panes of vast skylights were opened to the morning sunlight, assisting in the cooling movement of air. More sunlight streamed in through the windows set into the typically thick, heat-resistant walls of Charisian architecture. Despite the building warmth of the young day and the number of bodies gathered into one place, it was still surprisingly cool here in the chamber, which said a great deal for the skill of the men who had designed and built it.

There was no separation in Charis between the official homes of the House of Lords and the House of Commons. Each of them had its own council chambers, where much—indeed, most—of its business was accomplished in small committee meetings, but those were Parliament's working space, not its *home*. Merlin wondered how long that would last, or if it would be carried over to the newer, larger Parliament waiting over the horizon. It seemed unlikely, if only because that newer and larger Parliament would have too many members to accomplish anything efficiently without dividing itself internally into its official branches. For now, though, he found the arrangement oddly reassuring. And, if neither House had its own individual chamber, there *was* a distinct difference between the seating on the left and right sides of their shared house as one stood at the Speaker's lectern.

The seats stretched away in a multi-tiered horseshoe with the lectern between the open ends of the shoe, and the Commons sat to the Speaker's left, on comfortable benches behind individual desks well appointed with inkwells, blotters, and carafes of water. But their desks were unornamented—finely crafted and polished, to be sure, but without carving or other embellishments. They were the desks and seats provided for men who held their parliamentary office on the basis of election, not inheritance.

The Lords sat to the Speaker's right. Their benches were no more thickly padded than those of their common-born colleagues, but each of the desks on that side of the House bore on its front panel the coat of arms of the man—or, in a very few cases, the woman—seated behind it. Some of those coats of arms were simple wood carvings; others were heavily gilded and painted; and a few of them were cast in gold or silver and embellished with cut gems that caught the light from the skylights and windows with dancing flickers of red, green, and blue fire.

Despite all of that, the House wasn't really as impressive as Merlin's emotions insisted it ought to be, given his awareness of what this embryo would someday become. Of course, the British House of Parliament had always struck Nimue Alban as conspicuously modest for what had quite rightly been known as "the Mother of Parliaments." This structure, on this world, was going to claim that same title for itself, in centuries to come, assuming Charis managed to survive, so he supposed it was only appropriate that it, too, should eschew the sort of self-conscious grandeur the "Archangels'" architects had designed into the Temple.

Not that Parliament actually needed a huge home in Charis, anyway. Not yet. Despite the last few monarchs' awareness of the true history of the Terran Federation and their deliberate policy of moving in that direction, Charis was still a society which had only recently moved beyond outright feudalism. The franchise remained extraordinarily restricted, by the standards of Nimue Alban's birth country, with both property and literacy requirements. It was far larger, in proportion to its population, than that of any other Charisian realm, including the "Republic" of Siddarmark, but it was still a small body. In fact, the House of Commons, despite its nominally far larger base of representation, was only a little bigger than the House of Lords.

Of course, Merlin thought sourly, gazing out across the assembled Parliament over Cayleb's shoulder as the king, in full court regalia for the first time since his coronation, moved regally towards the Speaker's lectern, *there's a reason the Lords have so many members.*

A full third of the upper house's seats—for the most part, those with the most spectacular coats of arms of all—were held not by secular nobles, but by the bishops and senior abbots of the Church of God Awaiting. Despite whatever Haarahld or his immediate predecessors might have desired, there'd been no possible way in which they could have created a parliament without providing for the Church's massive representation within it.

Some of the men sitting in those particular seats were not the men who had sat in them prior to the Battle of Darcos Sound, however. Most of those who'd been replaced by Archbishop Maikel's new nominations and ordinations had resigned in furious protest when their fellows opted to support Cayleb and Staynair in their bid for independence from the Council of Vicars. Two of them, however, had been removed on Royal Warrant and were currently in reasonably comfortable cells awaiting trial. That was what tended to happen when the Crown had irrefutable proof that the men in question had been actively plotting the assassination of the king.

Irrefutable proof I *steered Wave Thunder to*, Merlin reflected with grim satisfaction. *I wish it hadn't existed—that there hadn't been any plots to kill Cayleb—but I might as well wish the sun wouldn't shine. And at least the rest of the Church took the arrest of two of its senior members by secular authorities on secular charges which carry the high probability of the death sentence, if sustained, far better than I was afraid it might.*

Cayleb reached the lectern, carrying the State Scepter (which, in Charis' case, was an ornately gilded and jeweled but still uncompromisingly effective mace), and Merlin suppressed an internal chuckle. That "Scepter" would undoubtedly have served quite handily to open any door which anyone might have had the temerity to close against its bearer. Which only underscored the fact that there was no nonsense here in Charis about who was whose equal. No requirement for the monarch to formally "request" admittance to the House of Commons. Haarahld VII and his immediate ancestors might have recognized their responsibility to prepare for a different day in Charis, but they'd been very careful to conserve the true power in the hands of the monarchy for now. Which was why every man, and the handful of women, in that chamber stood and bowed as Cayleb set the Scepter in the waiting brackets on the front of the lectern.

"Be seated, My Lords and Ladies," the king invited after a moment, and feet and clothing scraped and rustled as Parliament obeyed. He waited until everyone had settled once more, then turned his head, surveying all of those waiting faces with a calm Merlin suspected he didn't quite feel.

"We have summoned you in order to share with you the content and consequences of a letter we have but recently received from our trusted servant the Earl of Gray Harbor," he said then. "It concerns a decision upon the part of Her Majesty Queen Sharleyan to a proposal we committed to her by Earl Gray Harbor's personal hand."

He paused, and every person in that entire chamber sat very, very still. That stillness was the confirmation security had held, Merlin thought. Everyone knew Gray Harbor had gone to Chisholm as Cayleb's special envoy, and it had been obvious to even the least perceptive political dullard that the first councilor himself would not have been sent unless Cayleb had something significant to say to Sharleyan. But no one outside Cayleb's immediate circle of advisers knew what that something significant had been, and Parliament's eagerness to find out was palpable.

"We now announce to you," Cayleb said clearly, "Queen Sharleyan's acceptance of our offer for her hand in marriage."

For a heartbeat or two, it didn't seem to register. Then it did, and the wave of astonishment rippled through Parliament like a high wind through prairie grass. Merlin could actually *see* it sweeping across the seated representatives and peers, and despite the king's presence, despite the solemnity of the Parliament itself, a chorus of amazed voices went with it.

It was impossible even for Merlin's enhanced hearing to sort any individual remarks out of that spontaneous bedlam, and Cayleb didn't even try. He simply waited for several seconds, letting his audience's questions and exclamations run their course before, finally, he cleared his throat and raised his own voice.

"My Lords and Ladies!" he said sharply. "Is this interruption seemly?"

The king's voice cut through the hubbub, which ceased with remarkable rapidity. More than a few faces looked embarrassed by their owners' outbursts, but even in those cases, surprise and intense speculation were the overriding emotions.

"Thank you, My Lords and Ladies," Cayleb said as quiet fell once more. Then he allowed himself a small smile. "We can hardly blame you for your surprise, we suppose. Her Majesty's agreement to our offer of marriage was not an easy decision. It required a high courage, and great wisdom, to look past the inevitable rage her decision will evoke in those corrupt individuals who currently control the Temple. There can be no doubt that in her acceptance, she has irrevocably wedded"—he smiled again at his own choice of verb—"the fate of her realm to our own. She has agreed, of her own free will, to stand with us and our people in the death struggle for the soul of Mother

Church and our own survival. Make no mistake, this is a battle she has *chosen* to join, and there will be no going back from this moment for her, or for Chisholm, any more than there can be for Charis. All of this she has knowingly and willingly accepted along with our hand in marriage."

The stillness and silence was profound.

"Under the terms of our proposal to her, which we intend to disclose to you today, and which will be made available to each of you in written form, following this address, the crowns of Charis and Chisholm shall be coequal to one another for the remainder of Her Majesty's life and our own. Upon our deaths, those crowns will be united, in the persons of our children, into that of a single Charisian Empire.

"In the meantime, we and Her Majesty will be submitting to both kingdoms' parliaments the terms upon which we propose to create a new, common, and shared Imperial Parliament to advise and assist us in the equitable governance of both kingdoms in their new imperial relationship to one another. The navies and armies of our respective realms will be merged into a new Imperial Navy and Imperial Army, and commissions within the common armed forces of this, our new and greater realm, will be open to Charisians and Chisholmians alike. There shall be an Imperial Treasury, to which both kingdoms shall contribute, and our law masters, in concert with those of Chisholm, shall so reconcile the law of these two realms that the subjects of one shall enjoy all the rights, privileges, responsibilities, and duties of subjects of the other.

"And because there will always be the threat of the relationship of our realms becoming an unequal partnership, in which one kingdom becomes— or *believes* it has become—the servant of the other, rather than its equal, Tellesberg and Cherayth shall be coequal as capitals. For four months of each year—that is, for half the year, allowing for voyage time between Charis and Chisholm—Her Majesty and I will reside in Tellesberg, and govern both kingdoms from that city, and for four months of each year, she and I will reside in Cherayth, and govern both kingdoms from *that* city. No doubt it will be a difficult adjustment for both cities, but it *will* happen, My Lords and Ladies."

Cayleb paused, looking out into the stunned silence, and his face looked far less young in that moment. His eyes were as hard as his face, and when he spoke once more, his voice came crisply, clearly, ribbed with granite determination and iron purpose.

"Understand us well, My Lords and Ladies," he told his Parliament. "This will be no union of unequals. We did not offer marriage to Queen Sharleyan as anything less than a full and complete merger of our realms. As our Queen, she will share our authority in Charis, as we shall share hers in Chisholm. She will be our regent, if we be called away by war. She will have our full authority to act here in Charis as she, in her own good judgment, advised by our Council Royal and this Parliament and its imperial successor, shall see fit, and her decisions and actions shall stand approved in advance by us.

"This is no figurehead we bring you, My Lords and Ladies. This is a Queen, in all the power and accomplishment of her own reign, in her own Kingdom. One who, like us, and like our father before us, has matched herself against powerful foes, and who has met the stern test and demands of the throne to which she was called, at an even earlier age than we were, with wisdom, courage, and determination. She will be greeted, deferred to, and *obeyed* as if she had been Charisian born."

The sound of a tumbling pin would have been deafening, Merlin thought, watching the youthful king's words sink home.

"We feel sure that even a little reflection will make clear to all of you the military advantage this brings to us. The impact Queen Sharleyan's willingness to stand with us in our denunciation of the corruption of the Council of Vicars must have upon the thinking of other realms and other rulers will also require no explanation, no embellishment, from us. The advantages this will bestow for operations against our common enemies in Corisande must be equally obvious, as must the fashion in which the strength and power of our merchant marine will be reinforced and broadened.

"All of those things are true. Yet we would have you know that in our view, the greatest advantage of all which this marriage will bring to us, to our realm, and to all of Safehold, in days to come, will be the courage, the wisdom, and the intelligence of our Queen . . . and yours. Never doubt it, My Lords and Ladies. And rest assured that if any of you *should* doubt, those doubts will vanish quickly in the face of experience."

He paused once more, gazing out at the silent ranks of representatives, nobles, and priests.

"Great and terrible days are upon us all, My Lords and Ladies," he said then, quietly. "Times to test and try the mettle of any man's or woman's soul. Times in which each of us—king, bishop, noble, or commoner—must stand for those things which we hold sacred, those causes for which we will lay down our lives, if God so requires of us. In our hands lies the future of Mother Church, of Safehold, of the lives and souls and freedom of every man, woman, and child in God's vast creation. If we falter, if we fail, then the corruption which has already enveloped the Council of Vicars, already tainted Mother Church with the hunger and secular ambition of the Dark, will conquer all.

"We, Cayleb Ahrmahk, King of Charis, will die before we see that happen. We would not have brought you any Queen whose determination and courage we feared might prove unworthy of this moment, this time, in this place, and we have no fear that Queen Sharleyan's will. As Charis stands against the Darkness, so will Chisholm. So will Queen Sharleyan. And, as God is our witness, we will not cease, nor pause, nor rest, until those who would unleash warfare, rapine, and destruction upon peaceful realms out of vast and corrupt personal ambition, cloaked in the authority of Mother Church, have been purged forever from this world. To that end, we pledge our life, our fortune, and our sacred honor."

.V.
Earl of Thirsk's Townhouse,
City of Gorath,
Kingdom of Dohlar

So how well did it work?" Lywys Gardynyr, the Earl of Thirsk, asked his guest.

"That depends," that guest replied now.

Admiral Pawal Hahlynd had the unenviable task of commanding the ships assigned to protect the Kingdom of Dohlar's commerce in Hankey Sound and the approaches to Gorath Bay. Once upon a time, that had been a simple, even boring task. These days, it had become anything but.

"Depends on what, Pawal?" Thirsk asked as patiently as he could.

"Depends on how many of your 'trap ships' we have to trade for Charisian pirates," Hahlynd said sourly.

"That bad, was it?"

"Bad enough," Hahlynd agreed. Then he shook himself and inhaled deeply. "Actually, I think Maigee would have taken him in the end, if another of those damned schooners hadn't turned up. Against two of them, though—"

The admiral shrugged, his expression grim, and Thirsk nodded. He wasn't actually very surprised by the outcome, especially given the fact that the Charisians were smart enough to stay concentrated where they could support one another.

Not exactly what you expected out of "pirates," was it, Pawal? he thought sourly, then scolded himself almost instantly. Hahlynd might not have fully grasped what Thirsk had told him about the new Charisian guns or the deadly discipline of their captains and crews, but at least he'd bothered to *listen.* And not simply to listen, either. He'd actually put some of Thirsk's suggestions and recommendations into effect.

And he damned well deserved to have it work out better, the earl told himself.

"From the sound of things," Hahlynd continued, "Maigee probably managed to kill or wound at least two-thirds of the first ship's crew. And he obviously pounded the shit out of its hull." The admiral showed his teeth in a grin that was more than half snarl. "That's the only reason I can think of for a pirate to burn his own ship, at any rate."

Thirsk nodded again, this time with a bit more enthusiasm. If the Charisians had actually burned one of their ships, this far from home, then Hahlynd's estimate of the damage Thirsk's "trap ship" had managed to inflict had to be reasonably accurate. And while there were seldom enough officers of the caliber of this Maigee of Hahlynd's around—especially after the battles of Rock Point and Crag Reach, he thought bitterly—a one-for-one trade was probably the very best Dohlar could reasonably hope for.

He considered pointing out to Hahlynd that Charisian privateers were a far cry from the occasional Harchongese or Trellheim-based piratical scum the other admiral normally had to deal with. For all intents and purposes, the privateers who had decimated Dohlar's and Tarot's commerce off the east coast of Howard, and who were now ranging all the way to the *western* coast of the mainland, were auxiliary cruisers of the Royal Charisian Navy.

Thirsk was quite certain King Cayleb and Admiral Lock Island were inventively cursing the diversion of trained manpower from their navy to the privateers, but they couldn't have been surprised by it. Privateering paid better, after all . . . as long as there were enemy merchant ships upon which to prey, at least. Despite the loss of trained men to their crews, though, Thirsk somehow doubted private shipowners would have been able to get their hands on any of the new Charisian artillery pieces without at least the Royal Navy's tacit agreement. Which, given the privateers' record of success to date, had to be one of Cayleb's better investments. And, in the end, a lot of those diverted seamen would probably end back up in naval service. Privateering might pay well while it lasted, but Thirsk wasn't particularly optimistic about how much longer the Charisians would be able to find merchant ships to pounce upon.

That's one way to send the privateers home, I suppose, he thought bitterly, gazing out of the townhouse window at the beautiful blue sweep of Gorath Bay. *Once they've completely wiped out our merchant fleet, there won't be any reason for them to stay around, will there?*

"I hate to say it," he said out loud, never turning away from the view as he put his thoughts into words, "but trading one of our galleons for one of *their* privateers is probably as good as it's going to get."

"Well it's not good *enough*," Hahlynd growled. "And not just because Thorast is blaming *me* for it, either!"

"I know, Pawal," Thirsk replied. "I know."

And he *did* know. In fact, Hahlynd was one of the relatively few senior officers of the Royal Dohlaran Navy who were more concerned about finding the best way to deal with the radically new threats the Navy faced than with covering their own precious arses.

Well, one of the relatively few senior officers still serving, at least, the earl corrected himself.

"They've got to give you a command again, Lywys," Hahlynd said, almost as if he'd been reading Thirsk's mind. Not, the earl conceded, that it would have taken a genius to figure out what he was thinking. "Surely they have to realize they can't *afford* to leave you sitting ashore like a spare anchor!"

"Don't bet on it," he said sourly, and turned to face his guest fully. "Given the way Thorast and the King blame me for what happened off Armageddon Reef, I suppose I'm lucky they settled for just beaching me."

Hahlynd looked as if he would have preferred to argue. Unfortunately, King Rahnyld had been more interested in finding and punishing a scapegoat than he had in profiting from his best sea commander's experience against the Charisian Navy. And it was Thirsk's additional ill fortune that the Duke of Thorast, the closest thing Dohlar had to a navy minister—and that navy's senior officer, to boot—was married to the sister of Duke Malikai, the incomparably incompetent (and thankfully deceased) "grandadmiral" who'd gotten most of the Dohlaran Navy chopped up for kraken bait despite Thirsk's best efforts to save him from his own disastrous bungling. Thorast was scarcely likely to admit *Malikai's* culpability, especially with someone else available to take the blame. Under the circumstances, Thirsk had actually seriously considered the invitation from Baron White Ford to stay on in Tarot as the second-in-command of the Tarotisian Navy.

If it hadn't been for his family, he probably would have, he admitted to himself now. His wife had been dead for years, but all three of his daughters had husbands and children of their own. Not only would he have missed them almost more than life itself, but he'd been far from certain the king wouldn't have punished them for their father and grandfather's "failure" if Thirsk himself had been beyond his reach.

"They can't leave you cooling your heels here for long," Hahlynd argued. "You're the best and most experienced fleet commander we've got!"

"And I'm also the bone they're prepared to throw to Vicar Allayn and the 'Knights of the Temple Lands' if it comes down to it," Thirsk pointed out rather more calmly than he actually felt.

"Surely it won't come to that."

Thirsk would have felt better if Hahlynd had been able to put a little more confidence into his tone.

"I hope not." The earl turned back to the window, clasping his hands behind him as he wished his life could be as calm as those distant waters looked from here. "I'm not thoroughly convinced of that, though."

"You know," Hahlynd said a bit diffidently, "it would probably help if you'd, well . . ."

"Keep my mouth shut? Stop stepping on their toes?" Thirsk's mouth curled sardonically. "Unfortunately, Pawal, I have my own responsibilities. And not just to the King."

"I know that. It's one reason I've been over here taking your advice, trying to pick your brain for ideas. But the truth is that every time you open your mouth, you only piss off the King. And as for *Thorast*—!"

Hahlynd rolled his eyes and shook his head, and Thirsk laughed sourly.

"I can't think of anything—short of a death rattle, at least—that Thorast wants to hear out of me," he said.

In fact, he added silently to himself, *if it weren't for Fern, I think Thorast would have preferred court-martialing me and hanging me in front of Parliament as a warning to all those other "cowardly slackers"—like the ones who obviously helped me betray his brother-in-law through our own incompetence and cowardice—he's so sure are out there somewhere.*

At least Samyl Cahkrayn, the Duke of Fern and the first councilor of Dohlar, seemed to understand that Thirsk and the handful of other surviving (and disgraced) senior officers of Duke Malikai's shattered fleet were a valuable resource. He appeared to be trying to protect them, at any rate. And without a protector that highly placed, Thirsk probably would have already suffered the full consequences of the king's "extreme displeasure." Of course, it was always possible the real reason Fern was preserving Thirsk was as a potential sacrifice against a greater need. If the Group of Four ended up claiming a sacrificial victim for the failure of Vicar Allayn's oh-so-brilliant naval campaign plan, it would be hard to come up with a better one than the senior surviving admiral from the resultant fiasco.

"I'm afraid you're right where Thorast is concerned," Hahlynd admitted unhappily.

"Of course I am." Thirsk snorted. "If it's not all my fault, then it has to be his brother-in-law's, after all."

"That's certainly part of it," Hahlynd agreed. "But the way you keep pushing where the new building program's concerned isn't helping any."

"No?" Thirsk looked at him for a moment, then shrugged. "You're probably right, but that doesn't change the fact that the 'new building program' isn't going to help much against Charis, either. We don't need another galley fleet, Pawal. In fact, that's the *last* thing we need!"

Hahlynd started to say something, then changed his mind, and Thirsk snorted again.

Apparently, no one was particularly interested in his own reports on what had happened off Armageddon Reef. In his fairer moments, he tried to remind himself that the people reading those reports had to wonder whether he was telling the truth, or simply trying to cover his own arse. After all, it would make his own failure look far more excusable if he'd found himself confronting some sort of deadly new warship design and not simply an enemy commander who'd turned out to be more competent than he was. But the truth had a nasty habit of biting people who refused to confront it, and Thirsk was glumly certain his navy was going to get bitten all over again.

"This is just plain stupid, Pawal. *Galleys?*" He shook his head. "You've just been telling me what one of their *schooners* did to a *galleon* armed with the most effective broadside we could give it. Can't anyone understand that galleys have just become totally outclassed?"

"At least the new designs are going to be more seaworthy." Hahlynd sounded remarkably like someone searching for a silver lining, Thirsk thought.

"I'll grant that," he said after a moment, "and, to be fair, that's nothing to sneeze at."

His eyes turned bleak and hard as he remembered his own fleet's endless voyage to its final catastrophic meeting with the Royal Charisian Navy. The Dohlaran Navy's galleys had been designed for in-shore waters, not for the sort of blue-water crossing which had been demanded of them. They'd been shorter than most of the heavier Charisian galleys, and their drafts had been much shallower, even for their size. As a result, they'd displaced little more than a half or a third as much as a Charisian galley. That had made them much faster and more maneuverable under oars, of course . . . as long as their bottoms were reasonably clean. But it also left them far less stable under sail (which meant they could carry less of it), and far more vulnerable to even average conditions on the open sea. Which meant that *except* under oars (which meant anywhere outside coastal waters) they were actually slower and *less* maneuverable. The Charisians' galleys weren't really designed to move under oars at all, except in calms or to maneuver once combat was actually joined. They were designed primarily as sailing vessels with oars to provide auxiliary power—to give them additional speed under sail, to help them accelerate, to get them around onto a new tack more rapidly. In calm conditions, they were at a serious maneuvering disadvantage; in typical blue-water conditions, the advantage flipped entirely to their side.

Duke Malikai's flagship, *King Rahnyld*, had been the biggest ship in the entire Dohlaran Navy. She'd been almost as long as Baron White Ford's Tarotisian flagship, and stood far higher out of the water . . . yet her displacement, huge for the Dohlaran Navy, had been little more than half that of White Ford's flagship. Even White Ford's ship had been lighter and shallower draft than the majority of the Royal Charisian Navy's galleys, and the Charisian galleons were deeper draft, still. Which not only made them even more seaworthy but created ideal platforms for the new Charisian-style artillery. Speed and maneuverability under oars, like high fighting castles, had proved useless in combat against the galleons' far heavier broadsides and greater seaworthiness. For that matter, Thirsk was positive that at least a dozen, and probably more, of the ships Malikai had lost had foundered primarily because they simply had no business making an ocean crossing. So if the new designs were at least a little more seaworthy, so much the better.

Unfortunately, that only means they'll stay afloat long enough for the Charisians to turn them all into driftwood.

"It's nothing to sneeze at," he repeated, "but it's not enough, either. Remember, we aren't the only fleet Cayleb smashed."

"No, we're not. But as far as I know, we still don't have any reliable reports about what happened to Black Water and Earl Mahndyr."

Thirsk grunted. That was true enough, unfortunately.

"You're right," he said. "And I suppose it says something for the Group of Four's decisiveness, at any rate, that they've already arranged their new building program . . . even if it is the *wrong* program. It's too bad they didn't wait to read the reports first, though."

The existence of the Church's semaphore system had allowed the Group of Four to issue the various kingdoms' and empires' orders with a speed no purely secular realm could have matched. It was an advantage which had served the Church (and the Group of Four) well over the years, as Thirsk was well aware. In this case, though, that speed was actually working against them. They'd launched what had to be the biggest single shipbuilding program in the history of the world . . . and they were building the wrong ships. God only knew how much money and, even more importantly, time and skilled labor they'd already squandered buying ships which were going to be worse than useless under the new conditions of sea warfare. The fact was that the Church could probably afford the financial consequences, but if the "Knights of the Temple Lands" persisted in ignoring Thirsk's own reports, they were going to get an unholy number of other people's seamen and Marines slaughtered by the Royal Charisian Navy.

And I can't convince a single one of them to even read *my damned reports,* the earl thought despairingly. *Being "proved right" in the end is going to be damned cold comfort.*

"Well, Pawal," he said finally, "all we can do is try our best. I know it seems unlikely, but if I keep shouting loud enough, long enough, maybe someone will actually end up listening to me. I'm sure *something* more unlikely must have happened somewhere in the world since the Creation."

Hahlynd chuckled dutifully at Thirsk's feeble joke, but the earl himself didn't feel at all like laughing.

There are times, he thought, *when it's really, really hard to go on believing God is on our side.*

Of course, that was a thought he dared not express even to Hahlynd. In fact, it was one he would have preferred not expressing even to himself.

.VI.
Tellesberg Harbor,
and Tellesberg Palace,
City of Tellesberg,
Kingdom of Charis

No guns boomed in salute as the small, unarmed galleon made its way through the opening in the Tellesberg breakwater . . . but at least none of the batteries opened fire on it, either.

Which, Trahvys Ohlsyn reflected, was far better than things might have been.

The Earl of Pine Hollow stood by the ship's rail, gazing out at the city of Tellesberg while gulls and wyverns cried and whistled overhead. Like most harbors, the water close to the docks was less than pristine, although the stern injunctions of the Archangel Pasquale where things like sewers and garbage were concerned kept things from getting *too* bad. Actually, the harbor smelled better than Eraystor Bay did, Pine Hollow reflected, despite the fact that Tellesberg was considerably larger than the city of Eraystor.

In fact, it was the largest city—aside from Zion itself—Pine Hollow had ever seen, and its roofs stretched away from the incredibly busy waterfront, whose activity contrasted sharply with Eraystor's blockaded stillness, towards the mountains looming bluely to the south and southeast under their caps of eternal snow. The warehouse district was vast, with straight streets which had obviously been planned for the passage of heavy freight wagons and draft dragons. The housing clustered around the docks was modest-looking, for the most part. He could see no single family–sized houses, but the multi-story blocks of apartment houses and tenements looked well kept. Most of them appeared to be built of brick, and from where he stood at the moment, at least, there were no signs of slums. That was impressive, too, although he felt quite certain even Tellesberg under the notoriously enlightened rule of the Ahrmahks must have at least some of them.

Beyond the docks—which extended as far up the Telles River as he could see—the city rose on modest hills where the more well-to-do lived. There *were* single-family homes as one got farther away from the harbor district. Some of them were extremely imposing—obviously the town-houses of nobles or of wealthy merchants and manufactory owners (or, here in Charis, both at once, more probably)—but others were consider-ably more modest. To be honest, Pine Hollow found the existence of those modest homes much more impressive than the townhouses. In almost any other Safeholdian realm, it would have been unheard of for anyone *but* the rich and powerful to own his own home in a city as large and wealthy as Tellesberg.

The Royal Palace was plainly visible as his galleon moved towards the wharf where it had been instructed to moor. The palace was set well back, with the river washing the foot of its western curtain wall, although not so far that someone looking out of one of its tower windows didn't have an ex-cellent view of Tellesberg Bay, and Pine Hollow gazed at the large banner flying from the top of the tallest of those towers. He couldn't make out the device it bore from here, but he didn't have to see the golden kraken on the black field or the crown royal which surmounted it. The fact that it flew from the top of that particular tower informed all the world that King Cayleb was in residence, and Pine Hollow felt his stomach muscles tighten at the thought.

Don't be any stupider than you have to be, Trahvys, he told himself sternly. *Meeting Cayleb face-to-face is the entire reason you're* here*, you idiot. Wishing he were somewhere else—anywhere else—is pretty damned ridiculous when you look at it in that light.*

Somehow, that thought didn't seem to make his stomach feel any better.

A deepmouth wyvern sailed past him, barely twenty feet from the ship, and its lowered jaw hit the water in a flurry of white. The wyvern slowed un-der the braking effect of its dragging jaw, then rose once more, all four wings beating hard, as it lifted back into the air with its flexible jaw sack bulging with fishy prey. A pessimistic man, Pine Hollow decided, might be excused for seeing that as an uneasy omen of Emerald's probable fate, and he looked back at the trio of Royal Charisian Navy galleys hovering watchfully as his unarmed galleon eased her way towards the docks. He couldn't really blame them for watching him attentively, although exactly what a single galleon without so much as a matchlock musket aboard was going to do against the garrison and population of a city the size of Tellesberg eluded him. He'd de-cided to treat their presence as a mark of respect, and if he pretended very hard that he really believed that, he might be able to convince a particularly credulous three-year-old that he truly did.

His mouth twitched in a reflexive smile, and he snorted a chuckle at the thought. Which, he discovered, had actually had at least some easing effect on his stomach muscles. It was undoubtedly temporary, but he decided to make the most of it while it lasted.

▼   ▼   ▼

King Cayleb II sat on his throne as his "guest" was escorted into the throne room by a pair of extraordinarily alert Royal Guardsmen. The guardsmen's boot heels sounded loudly, firmly on the blue-swirled, lapis-like Charisian marble of the vast room's polished floor, but the Earl of Pine Hollow's lighter court shoes made almost no sound at all.

It was the first time Cayleb had ever actually laid eyes on Pine Hollow. What he saw was a typical Emeraldian, physically indistinguishable from any number of Charisians, but wearing a padded-shoulder tunic of a distinctly non-Charisian cut. The padding made his shoulders appear broader, but the truth was that the earl was broad-shouldered enough by nature to require no artificial assistance. Pine Hollow wore a heavy gold chain around his neck, token of his status as Emerald's first councilor. His eyes were as brown as Cayleb's own, and despite his exalted rank, his hair was still dark. In fact, he looked considerably younger than Cayleb had expected. Pine Hollow was more than fifteen years older than Cayleb himself, but he looked no older than Father Paityr Wylsynn. Well, perhaps a *little* older, but nowhere near grizzled enough to be the first councilor of a reigning prince.

Who may or may not be a "reigning prince" much longer, Cayleb reminded himself grimly.

Pine Hollow approached the throne and stopped, without prompting, at exactly the right distance. He managed to look remarkably calm as he delivered a deep, respectful bow. Whatever he looked like, though, Cayleb knew he couldn't possibly be as unworried as he managed to project, and the king put a checkmark on the positive side of the mental list he was making about his visitor.

Cayleb was in no tearing rush to get down to business, for more than one reason. One was that making Pine Hollow wait was more likely to shape any ensuing conversation in the direction Cayleb wanted it to take. A second and less noble one was that Cayleb took an undeniable pleasure in underscoring the relative balance of power between Charis and the prince who had attempted to have Cayleb himself assassinated. And a third had to do with another visitor whose arrival Cayleb anticipated in the next several days.

The throne room itself was a high-ceilinged, airy chamber. Ceiling fans, powered by a small waterwheel in the palace basement, rotated smoothly, keeping the tropical air moving, and the thick, heat-shedding walls were pierced by deep-set windows which looked out across a courtyard Cayleb's deceased mother had spent several years landscaping. The entire palace represented an intermediate stage in royal architecture. Its grounds were encircled by thick, well-designed curtain walls of stone, augmented at regular intervals by bastioned towers, but those walls predated the days of artillery, and the grounds inside them had been designed and landscaped as a place to live, not the interior of a grim, gray fortress. One day, Merlin had told him—one day soon, as a matter of fact—those heavy walls would be a thing of the past. Against the artillery which would be coming soon, old-fashioned walls like the one around Tellesberg Palace would become little more than annoyances to any serious attacker.

Cayleb twitched his mind back from the side path it had gone traipsing down and rested his elbows on the arms of his throne, steepling his fingers across his chest as he'd seen his father do so many times in the same throne room. The father whose death was at least partly the responsibility of the man in front of him and the prince that man served.

"Well," the king said at last into the throne room's waiting quiet, "I hardly expected to see *you* here, My Lord. Or not, at least, as an envoy."

That statement bore only a passing relationship to the truth, given that Merlin's "visions" had warned Cayleb well over three five-days ago that Pine Hollow would be arriving. In fact, Cayleb knew Nahrmahn's instructions to Pine Hollow as well as the Emeraldian earl knew them himself. Not that he had any intention of allowing Pine Hollow to guess that.

After all, it would hardly do to start giving the Inquisition genuine grounds to believe I'm dabbling in black sorcery and other forbidden arts, he thought dryly. *Why, if I did that, Mother Church might decide she didn't like me anymore.*

Pine Hollow, he noticed, had winced very slightly at his last seven words. That was good.

"Now that you're here," Cayleb continued after a brief, pregnant pause designed to underline those very words, "I suppose we should hear what you have to say."

"Your Majesty," Pine Hollow's voice was commendably steady, under the circumstances, "I feel confident you must at least suspect the reason for this rather dramatic, unannounced visit."

"Given the fact that you arrived in an official vessel, I don't imagine you're here to transfer your personal allegiance from Prince Nahrmahn to Charis," Cayleb said dryly.

"No, I'm not, Your Majesty." Pine Hollow met Cayleb's eyes very levelly, and the youthful monarch felt a stir of respect as he saw the steadiness in those eyes. They were, in their own way, a rebuke of his own levity.

"No, I don't believe you are," Cayleb acknowledged in a rather more serious tone. "In fact, given the present military balance between this Kingdom and your master's princedom—and its allies, of course—I can really think of only one thing which might have brought you here. And that, My Lord, is to discuss what sort of terms Prince Nahrmahn thinks he might be able to obtain."

"In a general sense, that's certainly accurate, Your Majesty." Pine Hollow inclined his head in a brief bow of acknowledgment.

"In that case, I might point out that he doesn't have a great deal with which to bargain," Cayleb said. "I truly mean no disrespect—the ships of your navy fought with courage and determination at Darcos Sound—but Emerald is defenseless before us. We've taken your offshore fortifications where and as we chose. Your major ports are under strict blockade, and as I believe we've demonstrated, we're capable of landing raiding parties to burn out any of the smaller ports where Commodore Zhaztro might be attempting to fit out his privateers. And we can land an army anytime we choose, at any place we choose."

Pine Hollow's eyes had flickered with surprise as Cayleb mentioned Zhaztro by name. Obviously the depth of Cayleb's knowledge about events inside Emerald had come as a less than pleasant revelation to him.

Oh, if you only knew, My Lord, Cayleb thought sardonically.

"All of that may be true, Your Majesty," the Emeraldian earl said after a moment. Then he shook his head. "No," he said, "let's be honest. It *is* true. Yet it's also true that however inevitable your victory over my Prince may be in the end, obtaining it may prove expensive. Not simply in terms of lost life and treasure, but also in terms of lost time. Despite your current advantages, which my Prince has instructed me to tell you he fully recognizes, you have a great many enemies, and no friends. No *open* friends, at least. Prince Nahrmahn has no doubt you've been continuing and even accelerating your military buildup. At the same time, however, he's well aware—as you must be—that your various enemies are engaged in exactly the same process. If you find yourself forced to spend valuable time conquering Emerald by force of arms, you may find the time you've lost doing so has allowed your more inherently formidable foes time to prepare for the next, inevitable stage in your conflict."

"Allowing, for the moment, the aptness of your analysis, My Lord," Cayleb said with an unpleasant smile, "the consequences will still be . . . less pleasant for the House of Baytz than for Charis."

"A point, I assure you, of which my Prince is well aware, Your Majesty."

"I rather thought he might be." Cayleb leaned back, crossing his legs, and cocked his head as he contemplated Pine Hollow.

"On the other hand, I must admit I'm intrigued," he said. "Whatever else Prince Nahrmahn may be, I don't believe he's deaf, blind, or stupid. Nor do I believe there's much possibility that he's unaware of who was behind his marching orders, whatever the 'Knights of the Temple Lands' might choose to pretend. Consequently, I must assume he's as well aware as we are here in Charis of who our true enemy is. Which leads me to wonder just why he might be willing to bring the wrath of the Grand Inquisitor and the Group of Four down upon his own head by daring to so much as send us an official envoy."

He eyed Pine Hollow speculatively, and the Emeraldian shrugged.

"Your Majesty, I might say that when a man has to choose between dealing with the kraken in his bathtub and the doomwhale out beyond the harbor breakwater, he tends to focus on the kraken, first. That, in point of fact, is a thought which has borne upon my Prince's thinking at this particular time. But it isn't the only consideration which brought him to send me to you. I carry with me correspondence directly from him, setting out for your consideration his own analysis of the situation. I believe you'd find it interesting reading."

"I'm sure I would." Cayleb smiled thinly. "May I also assume that this correspondence of his touches upon the terms he might hope to obtain?"

"It does, Your Majesty." Pine Hollow bowed again, then straightened. "Moreover, it will inform you that I've been appointed his official plenipotentiary. Within the limits established by my binding instructions from him, I am authorized to negotiate with you in his name, and to accept any agreement which we might reach within those limitations."

" 'Agreement which we might reach,'" Cayleb repeated softly. Then he straightened in his throne, bringing his hands down as he planted his forearms firmly on its armrests and leaned forward.

"Understand me in this much, My Lord Pine Hollow," he said quietly. "I realize your Prince was constrained against his own desires to participate in the recent attack upon my Kingdom. But I also realize that his reasons for deeming that attack . . . unwise had nothing at all to do with any deepseated love for the Kingdom of Charis. I don't believe—and never have believed—that he would have taken any joy or pleasure in the wholesale massacres, destruction, and arson the Group of Four proposed to visit upon my people, but neither do I believe he would have been dismayed by the destruction and partitioning of this Kingdom. In short, My Lord, whatever the reasons for his enmity, Prince Nahrmahn has amply declared himself the foe of Charis in times past. Now that he finds his foot firmly in the snare, he may also find himself wishing for some sort of . . . accommodation with my Kingdom and my House. Well, I won't say at the outset that any such accommodation is impossible. But I will say this. Any accommodation we may reach will be reached upon *my* terms, not his. And you may rest assured that any terms I will be willing to contemplate will preclude his ever again posing a threat to my people, to my Kingdom, and to my family. Do you understand that?"

"Of course I do, Your Majesty," Pine Hollow replied, his voice equally quiet. "Were I sitting in that throne while you stood here, in front of me, my position would be exactly the same as yours. My Prince understands that as well as I do, I assure you."

"In that case, there may be some point to your mission, after all, My Lord," Cayleb said, sitting back once more. "At any rate, I'm prepared to listen to whatever Prince Nahrmahn may have to say. If I find his proposals less than fully acceptable, there will always be time to return to the decision of the field of battle. And, to be quite honest, your point—and his—about the value of time in Charis' current situation has a certain validity."

Pine Hollow inclined his head without speaking, and Cayleb smiled.

"But that consideration lies in the future, My Lord. I have other pressing matters I must deal with today, and I intend to read your Prince's correspondence very carefully, digest it thoroughly, before you and I speak about its contents. In the meantime, I've had a comfortable suite prepared for you in Queen Marytha's Tower. I trust you'll find it adequate to your needs, and you are, of course, welcome to install any of your own servants you may deem necessary to see to your requirements."

"I thank you, Your Majesty."

"Despite all that's already happened, My Lord, there's no reason we can't be civilized about these things." Cayleb's smile turned a bit warmer and more genuine. "And whatever else may be true, you came here trusting in the hospitality and protection of my House. Under the circumstances, it behooves me to demonstrate that trust wasn't misplaced, doesn't it?"

"Since you've chosen to speak so frankly, Your Majesty," Pine Hollow replied with what might have been a shadow of an answering smile, "I'll admit that that thought—and that hope—have passed through my mind more than once since my galleon entered Charisian waters."

"Well, rest assured that you'll receive all of the courtesy due to any envoy, despite any . . . unusual aspects of the reason for your journey here to Tellesberg."

"Thank you, Your Majesty."

"In this much, at least, you're quite welcome," Cayleb said, then waved one hand at the man standing to the right of his throne in the black and gold of the Charisian Royal Guard. "Captain Athrawes will escort you to your chamber, My Lord, and see to it that the tower's guard force is informed of your status and prepared to meet any of your reasonable needs."

V ery well, Allayn," Zahmsyn Trynair's voice showed rather more irritation than he normally permitted it to as Rhobair Duchairn seated himself at the council table, "we're all here now. *Now* can you tell us what this is
all about?"

Allayn Maigwair might not have been Trynair's intellectual equal, but he
had no difficulty recognizing the asperity in the Chancellor's tone, and his
lips tightened briefly. Then he turned his head to look directly at Trynair.

"I've just received additional dispatches about the situation in the Gulf of
Dohlar, Zahmsyn." He permitted a trace of deliberate patience to color his
own tone. "I thought you might be interested in what the Duke of Fern has
to say about them. I assure you, they made . . . interesting reading. But, of
course, if you're too pressed for time . . ."

One would have had to look carefully to notice the slightly heightened
color in Trynair's cheeks, Duchairn noted. Even that, however, was a revelation of far more anger than he would ever have permitted himself to feel for
such a childish provocation under normal circumstances. Then again, these
circumstances were anything but normal, weren't they?

"Of course we have time to listen to any information that seems pertinent
and important, Allayn," the Church's Treasurer heard his own voice saying.
Both of the other vicars looked at *him*, and he smiled ever so faintly. "I'm sure
you wouldn't have requested a meeting of all four of us unless you thought
the dispatches you've received are both of those things," he continued. "On
the other hand, *all* of us have sufficiently pressing commitments on our time
to make us all a bit more . . . irritable than God would probably prefer."

Maigwair gazed at him for another second or two, then nodded, and Trynair's momentary anger seemed to fade.

"Thank you, Rhobair," the Chancellor said. "As always, you make a very
valid point. Allayn," Trynair moved his gaze back to Maigwair, "if I sounded
overly brisk, I apologize. Rhobair is right. We do all have far too many things
which require our immediate attention, but that doesn't excuse any lack of
courtesy on my part."

"Don't worry about it." Maigwair half chuckled wryly. "To be honest,
I've bitten off a few heads of my own in the last couple of months. It's hard to
be patient when so many things are going wrong at once."

"Then it's our job as God's stewards to make sure they go the right way again," Zhaspahr Clyntahn said. As usual, the Grand Inquisitor didn't seem particularly concerned with pouring any oil on troubled waters. "Which, I assume, your request for a meeting has *something* to do with?"

"You might say that." Maigwair sat back in his comfortable chair. "Or, you might say it has to do with identifying something else that's gone wrong."

"Then tell us about it," Duchairn said before Clyntahn could open his mouth again.

"I've had copies prepared for all of you, of course," Maigwair said, indicating the sheafs of notes lying on his companions' blotters. "These arrived by messenger wyvern, not via the semaphore, so there's considerably more detail. And it's the details that concern me the most. Especially in conjunction with what we're hearing from other sources.

"Basically, the situation is even worse than we'd originally thought. The Charisians are operating 'privateers' on both coasts of Howard now, as well as the east coast of Haven as far north as the Passage of Storms. There must be hundreds of them, and it seems as if every one of them has the new-design artillery. So even though they may technically be calling themselves privateers, what they really are is cruisers of the Charisian Navy. And, not to put too fine a point on it, they're wreaking havoc."

Duchairn frowned slightly. He'd found immense comfort in his renewed personal faith over the past months, which had given him a certain serenity in the face of all the calamities God seemed to be permitting to afflict His Church. Some of the other vicars—those who weren't clamoring for (or the far more numerous vicars who wished they had the courage *to* clamor for) the Group of Four's dismantlement—appeared to be withdrawing into a sort of insulated cocoon, where they could pretend their world wasn't in a state of violent upheaval. Duchairn's renewed reading of the *Writ*, however, had actually restored him to a far stronger awareness of his responsibility to meet those violent upheavals head-on. And of the entire Group of Four, he, as the Church's chief financial officer, was undoubtedly the best aware of the implications of the massive onslaught Charis had launched upon the commercial traffic of its enemies.

Ultimately, he supposed, it could be argued that Charis was playing a dangerous game by setting the example of such energetic privateering. After all, the Charisian economy was completely dependent upon its own shipping. Not only was that a major potential weakness, but the sheer value of the Charisian carrying trade promised huge profits for anyone who managed to raid it successfully, as well, and it was unlikely that the kingdom's enemies would remain blind to those minor facts forever. On the other hand, very few of the mainland realms had anything like the supply of trained seamen Charis did, which meant simply crewing enough privateers would be difficult, especially with the competition of the Church's new naval buildup drawing on that same limited pool of sailors.

Besides, he thought a bit grimly, *I suspect there's a very good reason Cayleb has been so enthusiastically encouraging the construction of so many of those damned, long-range privateer schooners and even "letting" them buy the new cannons. Once the supply of victims runs out, all of those hulls will be available for his Navy to snap up as anti-privateer cruisers, won't they? Their owners will be eager to dispose of them for a song once they've "hunted out" everyone else's merchant traffic. They may be fast, but there's no way a typical privateer is going to have the cargo capacity for a suitable bulk carrier, whatever they do, so the owners will be under a lot of pressure to dispose of them. I bet they'll settle for a tenth piece on the mark of their original prices, and the Navy's the most logical customer. Which means Cayleb didn't even have to pay the cost of their artillery out of pocket, much less their entire hulls, to provide himself with dozens—maybe even hundreds—of light naval cruisers. Talk about making war pay for itself!*

The thought twitched his lips in a hint of a sour smile of bitter admiration. From Clyntahn's irate snort, however, it was evident that he remained unimpressed by the importance—or relevance—of Maigwair's report.

"Pouncing on a few merchant ships may be irritating, but it's scarcely likely to pose any sort of true danger," he said dismissively, as if determined to illustrate that very point. "And whatever your reports may seem to indicate, not even heretics could put their accursed new weapons on 'hundreds' of privateers this quickly. No doubt people are panicking and exaggerating wildly."

Maigwair started to open his mouth, but Duchairn raised one hand in a courteous gesture and turned towards the Grand Inquisitor.

"First, Zhaspahr," he said, "no one is saying *all* of the privateers have the new guns. Most Charisian merchant galleons have always carried at least a few guns, if only to discourage pirates, and it doesn't take a lot of firepower to force a merchant ship to heave-to and surrender. So the 'old style' artillery is probably all the vast majority of them need, and it's not as if old-style guns are particularly hard for them to come by these days. God knows there're plenty of them lying around in Charis after Darcos Sound!"

Clyntahn glowered at him, but Duchairn met his gaze calmly until, finally, the Grand Inquisitor gave a grumpy, irritated nod.

"Secondly," he continued then, "if it were only 'a few merchant ships,' you might be right about how important the losses are. But it isn't 'a few,' and Allayn is perfectly correct to be concerned over the potential consequences."

Clyntahn's face tightened, but Duchairn had emerged as the Group of Four's internal peacemaker, and the beefy Inquisitor made himself nod a second time, however little he wanted to.

"You were saying, Allayn?" Duchairn invited.

"I was saying that according to Fern's report, the Dohlaran merchant fleet has taken extremely heavy losses. Apparently, these damned 'privateers' are operating virtually at will, despite the fact that they're thousands of miles from any Charisian port. They seem to be *everywhere* in the Gulf, including Hankey Sound and apparently Shwei Bay, as well. Losses are so heavy insurance rates have gone sky-high. And even *with* insurance, many owners are refusing to allow their vessels to put to sea at all. From what the Duke has to say, the Kingdom's maritime commerce has effectively come to a halt."

"So?" Clyntahn's voice was at least moderately courteous this time, Duchairn noted, and the Inquisitor shrugged heavy shoulders. "With all due respect, Allayn, and fully admitting that the impact for *Dohlar* may be significant, I fail to see what's so immediately threatening about the situation. We always knew that once these damnable heretics started raiding, the consequences were going to be severe for everyone else's merchant fleets."

"The point, Zhaspahr," Duchairn said, "is that the damage is being far worse than we'd originally anticipated. Despite what I just said, Allayn is quite right that many of these 'privateers' appear to be purpose-built vessels, armed with the best Charisian artillery. Artillery, I remind you, we still haven't managed to duplicate for our own vessels. I'm Mother Church's Treasurer General. I know how expensive our rearming program is being, which means I also have at least a feel for the sort of investment the Charisians must be making to produce the quantities of artillery their own fleet requires. Yet despite his navy's own obvious requirement for more and more guns, Cayleb is permitting *privateers* access to them. That indicates just how high a priority he and his advisers must place on those privateers' operations. And, again, speaking as Mother Church's Treasurer General, I may have a better grasp of some of the . . . indirect consequences than you do."

"So enlighten us," Clyntahn invited in a half growl.

"Allayn is probably in a better position than I am to address the consequences for our building programs," Duchairn said, "but I already know Charisian attacks have been more than a minor irritation where they're concerned. Many of the items required for the construction of our new galleys are normally transported by sea, Zhaspahr. Spars, masts, timbers, artillery, anchors—anything that's heavy, or massive, or simply big and can't be supplied in the immediate vicinity of the shipyards themselves has to be freighted in, and attempting to haul loads like that overland, even when an overland route is available, is a nightmare. If they can't be shipped by sea, costs are going to rise sky-high, and construction times are going to become far longer.

"But there's another, more direct consequence. If the Charisians succeed in effectively destroying the merchant fleets of their enemies—and producing a situation in which the surviving merchantmen cower in port rather than daring to put to sea will have the same effect capturing or sinking all of them would produce—the economies of those realms are going to take severe damage. Even our coffers are ultimately limited in terms of the subsidies and loans we can make to offset that sort of damage. And as their economies suffer, the tithes due to the treasury will also decline, with ultimately serious consequences to our own fiscal position.

"At the same time, the carnage the Charisians are wreaking isn't something realms who aren't actively at war with them are likely to fail to notice. We've all had our concerns about the ultimate reliability of Siddarmark. Well, if they see the Charisians' enemies suffering this sort of devastation, it's going to make them even less inclined to add themselves to the list of those enemies . . . and to the privateers' target list. Besides, I rather doubt that someone like Greyghor Stohnar is going to be exactly heartbroken over watching the commerce of rival rulers being hammered. After all, as their merchant fleets decline, *his* can expand to fill some of the void."

Even Clyntahn was listening attentively now, and Zahmsyn Trynair sat back in his own chair. There were times when he found the apparent rebirth of Duchairn's personal piety more than a little wearing. The Treasurer's newfound willingness to "trust in God" and to punctuate discussions of policy and planning with quotations from the *Writ* and *The Commentaries* might produce serenity for *him*, but it didn't do a great deal for all of the red-hot coals Trynair was required to juggle every day. On the other hand, his ability to convince even the increasingly belligerent Grand Inquisitor to stop and actually listen was impressive. So impressive that Trynair himself had actually considered spending some time with the *Writ*.

"But even the impact on the thinking of his potential enemies is secondary to what Cayleb is really after," Duchairn continued now. "He's systematically eliminating the carrying capacity of other realms. Effectively, he's doing exactly what we accused his father of—deliberately setting out to secure complete control of the entire world's merchant shipping. And the reason he's doing that, Zhaspahr, is that if all the other merchant carriers are eliminated, the only ones left will fly the Charisian flag. Which means the mainland realms' need for shipping to transport the cargoes essential to their own economies will drive them into using Charisian bottoms. And, in effect, that means they'll be subsidizing Cayleb's military expenses. He'll be driving the kingdoms of Haven and Howard into literally paying for his war against Mother Church."

"Then stop them from doing that," Clyntahn growled.

"That's far easier to say than to do," Duchairn countered. "The trading houses *need* that shipping just to survive, and I don't see anything we *could* do to prevent the consequences to our own cash flow. It's what I've been trying to explain all along. The entire edifice is far more fragile than it might appear from the outside, and the imperatives of economic survival are going to be as apparent to kings and princes as they are to individual bankers. Those imperatives are going to drive even godly men into the Charisians' arms if that's the only way for them to survive."

"And that's not the only worry," Maigwair put in. He'd clearly been willing to allow Duchairn to carry the major burden of the explanation, but now he leaned forward, his own expression a combination of anxiety and anger. "It's not just a matter of harming their enemies and bolstering their own economy. There's also the corrupting effect."

"Corrupting effect?" Clyntahn sat abruptly straighter in his chair as Maigwair captured his full attention at last. "What sort of 'corrupting effect'?" he demanded.

"There's an enormous amount of money being made by these 'privateers,' " Maigwair said. "Whatever else they may be, they're still Charisians when it comes to finding ways to squeeze marks out of any situation. And they've been spreading some of those marks around. I have confirmed reports that they're managing to dispose of their prizes in mainland ports. That means they don't have to put prize crews aboard them and sail them all the way back to Charis. They only need to crew them long enough to reach one of the ports which are open to them, at which point their prize crews can immediately return to them. And *that* means they can take a *lot* more ships before shortage of manpower forces them to go home and recruit new crews. Even worse, in some ways, it also means they're building cozy relationships with the authorities in those ports. They couldn't be selling captured ships there, or disposing of cargoes from their prizes, without the knowledge and consent of those authorities."

Clyntahn's jowls darkened, and anger glowed behind his eyes.

"Allayn's right," Duchairn said. "These privateers are clearly part of a coordinated Charisian strategy. Cayleb's total out-of-pocket expense is the artillery he's allowing them to purchase, and even that's only costing his navy *time*, since I'm quite certain the foundries casting those guns are showing a tidy profit in the process without any actual subsidies from the Crown. And once they run out of other people's shipping to *attack*, all of them will be available to be taken into naval service as light convoy escorts and cruisers. It's not only hurting his enemies and helping his own economy, but also freeing his navy to concentrate on Emerald and Corisande while forcing our allies to focus all of their limited remaining naval power on efforts to protect the commerce they have left. And simultaneously, as Allayn's just pointed out, giving officials of places like Harchong strong personal inducements to actively collaborate with him *and* pointing out to those rulers who aren't already on his list of active enemies that he can do the same thing to them, if he has to."

"Then obviously we need a counter-strategy, don't we?" Trynair said.

"I'd say that was a reasonable observation, yes," Duchairn agreed just a bit ironically.

"That's easy," Clyntahn growled. The other three looked at him, and he snorted.

"You've just been pointing out how destroying our allies' merchant fleets is going to hurt them, Rhobair. It's not my area of expertise, but it is yours, and I'm fully prepared to accept your analysis. But if shipping is *important* to them, it's *critical* to the heretics in Charis. All their damned fleets and all their damned privateers have to be paid for somehow, and the leeches pay for them with the money they suck out of the mainland economies. Cut that income off, and you eliminate their ability to finance their opposition to God's will."

"That's true enough," Duchairn acknowledged, watching Clyntahn through narrowed eyes.

"Well, we don't need any 'privateer' fleet to do that," the Grand Inquisitor said harshly. "All we have to do is order all mainland ports closed to Charisian shipping. We don't have to sink or burn their ships to make them useless to Cayleb and his fellow apostates."

Trynair frowned, his expression thoughtful. Maigwair appeared torn between agreement with Clyntahn and skepticism about his sweeping suggestion's apparent simplicity. Duchairn, on the other hand, shook his head.

"It's not going to be that easy, Zhaspahr," he said almost gently. "There are too many people and too many livelihoods wrapped up in it. Even the best of men, faced with the need to provide for their own families, are going to find themselves sorely tempted to continue to deal covertly with Charis if it's a choice between that and financial ruin. And make no mistake about it, for a great many of the people involved in any successful exclusion of Charisian shipping from our ports, the consequence *will* be ruin."

"If it is, it is." There was no flexibility at all in Clyntahn's voice or expression. "This is a struggle for the primacy of God Himself on His own world, Rhobair. Given that, the financial tribulations of a pack of merchants and shopkeepers is an insignificant price to pay if it weakens the hand of Shanwei's foul get."

"It may be," Duchairn responded. "But whether it is or not isn't really the point, Zhaspahr. The point is whether or not we can convince or compel those 'merchants and shopkeepers' of yours to do it in the first place. And, to be completely honest, even if we should succeed in that, the consequences for our own requirements if we intend to take the war to Charis could well be significant."

"When grass is growing in the streets of Tellesberg because they have no one to buy their goods or charter their ships, we won't need to pay for any 'requirements' to topple Cayleb and his eternally damned advisers," Clyntahn shot back. "What will be an inconvenience for us—even a serious one, perhaps—will be *fatal* for Charis. How long do you think Cayleb will last once those money-worshipping Charisians of his realize their entire kingdom is going bankrupt, and them with it?" He grunted a hungry laugh. "And once they turn on one another like the rabble they are, how much military power will it take to sweep up the pieces?"

"He has a point there, Rhobair," Trynair said quietly, and Duchairn was forced to nod.

"Yes, he does. Assuming we could enforce such a policy."

"All we have to do is give the order," Clyntahn said coldly.

"Not this time, Zhaspahr," Duchairn disagreed, facing the Grand Inquisitor's ire from the serenity of his own newly refound faith. "The Knights of the Temple Lands don't have the authority to simply issue orders like that and see them obeyed without question. Not when the temptation—the necessity, even—to *disobey* them is going to be so powerful."

"Shan-wei with the 'Knights of the Temple Lands!' " Clyntahn snarled. "It's time we stopped dancing around in the shadows, anyway."

Duchairn's expression stiffened. The Grand Inquisitor's anger had continued fermenting into fury, and the totally unexpected defiance Dynnys had shown, even in the face of his agonizing death, had goaded Clyntahn's always irascible temper into a white-hot blaze. Worse than that, in some ways, Dynnys' final statement, interrupted though it had been, had called the Group of Four's motivations into question. No one—no one outside the Council of Vicars, at least—was prepared to say so openly, but the fact that Charis' own archbishop had been prepared to indict not Charis, but the Church, from the very lip of unspeakable torment and death, had struck a totally unexpected blow against the Group of Four's authority. Indeed, much as Duchairn hated to admit it, it had struck a blow against the authority of Mother Church, herself.

And it's also undermined Zahmsyn's strategy for differentiating between the Church and the Knights of the Temple Lands, he thought. *Dynnys didn't charge the Knights with attacking Charis; he charged us, the four of us and even Mother Church herself. And if anyone believed him when he proclaimed Charis' innocence before we attacked her, it's also undermined the argument that this is all the result of some longstanding, heretical Charisian plot which has simply strayed into the open at last.*

"I have the authority to order it on the basis of the Inquisition's overriding authority to combat heresy and apostasy anywhere it emerges," Clyntahn continued.

And since when has any Grand Inquisitor ever had that *authority?* Duchairn wondered. *Within the Church, yes. And the power to summon the secular lords to support Mother Church against heresy in their own lands. But to arbitrarily order them to close their ports to another nation? To dictate the terms on which their subjects are allowed to make the livings needed to feed their own children? No Inquisitor has ever claimed that sort of power! On the other hand, when has any other Grand Inquisitor confronted the threat confronting us?*

"It would be a direct escalation," Trynair pointed out. "It would take the onus for the present situation off of Charis, to some extent at least, and place it upon Mother Church."

"And," Duchairn added, "if we do that, it will also increase the pressure on us—on Mother Church—to take powerful military action against Charis, and we're scarcely in a position to do that, I'm afraid."

"For the rest of this year, at least," Maigwair agreed. "Even after we get the ships built, it's going to take time to train crews for them. It's not as if we have the unlimited supply of seamen Charis seems to have."

"Who cares if it's 'an escalation'?" Clyntahn demanded. "This is a war between God's Church and His enemies. Between the Light of Langhorne and Shan-wei's eternal Darkness. Instead of pretending it isn't, it's time we told all of the Faithful the truth about Charis' carefully planned and long prepared rebellion against the rightful authority of God and His stewards here in the world. My agents tell me there are already whispers in the taverns and the streets about Staynair's defiance and that bastard Dynnys' so-called deathbed statement. It's time we openly admit the true nature of the struggle, time we openly call for all the Faithful to join in holy battle against that nest of Shan-wei. Better to open the wound to the cleansing air and drain the poisons of doubt before they lead still more into the paths of corruption."

Trynair's thoughtful frown deepened, and so did Duchairn's. As much as he continued to fear and distrust the consequences of Clyntahn's temper, there was much to what he'd just said. The Charisians, at least, had never tried to pretend they hadn't defied Mother Church's authority. In fact, they'd printed up thousands of copies of the text of Staynair's defiant letter to the Grand Vicar and distributed them in every port city on Safehold. The Inquisition had seized every copy it could find, but Duchairn was positive there were still plenty of them circulating. And the fact that Staynair had couched his defiance in terms of challenging the Church's corruption rather than upon any doctrinal dispute—aside, of course, from the doctrine of the Grand Vicar's paramount authority—hadn't passed unnoticed.

And coupled with Dynnys' statement, it's truly flicked Zhaspahr on the raw. But the mere fact that there's as much anger as logic driving his reasoning doesn't necessarily make it invalid. And neither does the fact that he's distorting the evidence.

Staynair is right about one thing. I may hate admitting it—I do hate admitting it—but the Council of Vicars is corrupt. We're corrupt, and it's long past time we cleaned our own house. But however right he may be about that, first we have to preserve that house. We can't let someone destroy the unity of Mother Church which has existed from the very Creation, however justified his anger and his calls for reform may be. And if that's true, then we must openly confront the actual nature of the battle we face. And, he admitted unhappily, *if that requires us to . . . misrepresent some of the particulars in order to preserve the whole, what choice do we truly have?*

"So what you're recommending is an open encyclical from the Grand

Vicar?" Trynair asked. "Not just for distribution among the bishops, but for dissemination from the pulpit, as well?"

"That's exactly what I'm recommending." Clyntahn shrugged. "I realize it will have to be carefully drafted, and that's going to take some time and thought. But I believe it's time we laid all of our cards on the table."

"If we do as you suggest, Zhaspahr," Duchairn said aloud, "it will reduce the scope and flexibility of the strategies available to us. If we draw that line, openly, before all of God's children, then those children will rightly expect us to *act*. To act as boldly and as decisively as God requires of us. Yet as Allayn's just said, we won't have that capacity to act for months to come."

"It'll take months for our message to spread and truly sink in, anyway," Zhaspahr retorted. "We can get our directives to the secular rulers involved and get our encyclical to every church on the mainland within five-days, using the semaphore. But even after we do, the common people are going to need time to absorb what we've told them. And Mother Church is going to need time to shape and direct their natural and inevitable sense of outrage."

"If we declare Holy Crusade," Duchairn said in a carefully neutral tone, "there can be no going back. Any possibility that we might be able to convince the clergy of Charis, or its people, to return willingly and repentantly to the arms of Mother Church will be gone forever. The only appeal left will be to the sword, not to reason or remonstrance."

"That decision's already been made," Clyntahn said grimly. "It was made when Cayleb and Staynair chose to dispatch their hellish letter and openly give their allegiance to Shan-wei."

Duchairn winced inside, remembering another conversation, when Zhaspahr Clyntahn, over a bottle of wine, had almost casually brought them to the point of condemning an entire kingdom to fire and destruction without warning. There was no question in Duchairn's mind of their overriding responsibility to preserve the Church and her authority as the final mortal guarantor of the souls of all men, everywhere. Yet Clyntahn's statement bothered him deeply on several levels. First, because of what it implied about who had actually made the initial decision to resort to violence. Second, because it starkly underscored the chasm of death and devastation into which Clyntahn was prepared to cast anyone who stood in his path. And, third, because Clyntahn actually *believed* what he'd just said.

That's the truly scary thing, isn't it, Rhobair? he thought. *This man is Mother Church's Grand Inquisitor, the keeper of the sanctity of her doctrines and the moral rectitude of her priests. Bad enough to think he's still prepared to make decisions at a time like this at least partially on the basis of cynical pragmatism. But if the keeper of God's doctrine is able to genuinely convince himself to believe whatever he needs to believe to suit his own purposes, preserve his own base of power within the Church, then where is the true guarantor of that doctrine?*

He had no answer to that question. Perhaps God would show him one in the end, but He clearly wasn't going to do it before the Group of Four made its decision in the name of the entire Church. And for all his doubts about the wisdom of Clyntahn's suggestion, or what had induced him to make it, Duchairn had no better answer to offer.

"Zhaspahr's right," Maigwair said. "There hasn't been any going back since Staynair's letter arrived here at the Temple, Rhobair. You know that as well as the rest of us do."

"Yes, I suppose I do," Duchairn sighed. "It's just the thought of how many people are going to die that makes me wish I *didn't* know it."

"Death is better than any heretic deserves." Clyntahn's voice was cold, his fleshy face carved out of granite. "The sooner the lot of them join their dark mistress in Hell, the better for the entire body of God's Faithful."

And what about all the people who aren't *heretics, Zhaspahr?* Duchairn asked silently. *What about the children who are going to be slaughtered along with their parents when you burn Charis' cities? Have those innocents had the opportunity to choose between heresy and the truth? And what about those Charisians who remain loyal to God and the Church and still get in the way of the holy armies you propose dispatching to slaughter their neighbors? And what about the reaction—and the reaction* is *coming, one of these days—when the rest of Charis realizes Staynair's accusations of corruption were completely justified? Are* you *going to reform the corruption? Renounce your own position of power and wealth? Begin approaching doctrine and matters of faith with a genuinely open and accepting mind?*

But despite his questions, it still came back to that single, unanswerable fact. To have any chance of restoring Mother Church to what she ought to be, what she *must* once more become, first Mother Church, whatever her present blemishes, had to be preserved.

"I don't especially like it," Trynair said with what Duchairn recognized as massive understatement, "but I'm afraid you may be right, Zhaspahr. At any rate, we must take some sort of action against the effects of the Charisian privateers Rhobair and Allayn have analyzed for us. And, *you* are certainly right about Charis' dependency on its own merchant fleet. To be honest, I want to make no suggestion that Holy War is inevitable—not yet—but you're right that we have to do *something*."

He looked around the conference table, his expression somber.

"Under the circumstances, I believe we truly may not have another option."

The afternoon sunlight was not quite unpleasantly warm on Hektor Daykyn's shoulders. The jingle and squeak of armor, weapons harnesses, and saddle leather surrounded him along with his guardsmen, and his mind was busy as he rode through the streets of Manchyr.

The day had started out better than he'd expected. The army's field maneuvers this morning had gone well, and he'd been pleased by the apparent cheerfulness of the troops. Of course, none of them were going to stand around looking despondent where he could see them, but there was a difference between men who were simply obeying orders, and men whose hearts were in their work.

Hektor rather doubted that his soldiers—most of whom, after all, were fairly bluff, unimaginative sorts—suspected how much they and their maneuvers had done to enhearten their prince. Or, for that matter, quite how much he needed enhearteneng these days. It was hard to work up much in the way of exuberance when he contemplated the sledgehammer Cayleb Ahrmahk must be busily assembling to drop on his princedom. The fact that it hadn't landed yet was at least some comfort, however, and suggested he might have at least a couple of more months before it did. And, as his troops' attitude had just reminded him, every single day he could find for himself was one more day in which he could make Cayleb's task more difficult.

Which is probably only going to be enough to give me a rather dubious—and posthumous—moral satisfaction, he admitted to himself. *Still, that's better than nothing. And it's always possible—remotely, at least—that I can put myself in a position to make enough trouble for him that it would be worth his time to at least consider negotiating.*

He snorted at his own thoughts as he considered how he would have reacted—had *planned* on reacting, in fact—if the Group of Four's invasion plans had succeeded and their positions had been reversed. The old cliché about the drowning man and the straw came rather forcibly to mind, under the circumstances.

At least it gives me something to do while I'm waiting!

He glanced back over his left shoulder at the sturdy, rather stout gray-haired man riding half a horse length behind him. Sir Rysel Gahrvai, the Earl of Anvil Rock, was one of his cousins and his senior army commander, the land-going counterpart of Earl Tartarian. Traditionally, the Army had far less prestige in Corisande than the Navy. In that much, at least, Corisande and Charis were much alike—probably inevitably, given the fact that they were both essentially just very large islands. But unlike Charis, Corisande had at least possessed a standing army composed of regular, professional troops at the beginning of the current unpleasantness. Mostly, Hektor was forced to admit, that was because he was rather less beloved by certain of his subjects (and several of his nobles), especially in Zebediah, than Haarahld of Charis had been by his. The existence of a standing army whose loyalty was to the prince who paid it and not to its own individual feudal lords had constituted a pointed suggestion to those unloving souls that they would be well advised to keep their unflattering opinions of Prince Hektor to themselves.

On the other hand, no one—least of all Hektor—had ever truly antici-pated that Anvil Rock's troops might find themselves faced with repelling someone else's invasion of Corisande. The assumption had always been that if they were going to be involved in any invasions, it would have been *them* invading someone else.

But at least Anvil Rock didn't seem too downcast. In fact, his general at-titude was as robust as Tartarian's, although Hektor suspected it was for slightly different reasons. Sir Rysel had abruptly found himself one of the most important men in the entire League of Corisande after decades of play-ing second fiddle to the Navy, and despite the gravity of the threat, he found the unusual situation rather exhilarating. Hektor might not share his cousin's exhilaration, but he was perfectly content with Anvil Rock's attitude as long as the man kept pushing his own preparations as persistently and powerfully as he had up to this point.

The prince caught the earl's eye and twitched his head, summoning Anvil Rock up beside him. The earl touched his horse with his heels, trotting a bit faster until he reached Hektor's side. Then he slowed again, riding stirrup to stirrup with him.

"Yes, My Prince?"

"I thought the maneuvers went well," Hektor said. "Please pass my com-pliments on to the field commanders."

"Of course, My Prince!" Anvil Rock's broad smile of appreciation was clearly genuine, and Hektor reached out to touch him lightly on the shoulder.

"I appreciate all your efforts, Rysel," he said. "And I realize you don't have a lot of time to make preparations. Is there anything else I can do to help you along?"

Anvil Rock considered for a few seconds, puffing his bushy mustache, then shrugged.

"Since you've asked, My Prince, there might be one thing."

"Such as?"

"I was over at the Royal Arsenal yesterday," Anvil Rock said just a bit obliquely. "Sir Taryl had invited me to watch the proof firing of the second lot of the new guns."

"Really?" Hektor cocked his head to one side. "What did you think of them?"

"I think they're very impressive. And I can certainly understand what happened to Black Water if all the Charisian ships, or even just their galleons, carried guns like them. Under the circumstances, I see why Tartarian wants as many of them as he can get, too."

Anvil Rock finished speaking, and Hektor's eyebrow rose higher.

"But?"

"I beg your pardon, My Prince?"

"I heard a 'but' rattling around in there somewhere, Rysel. Would you care to tell me why I did?"

"I suppose you did," Anvil Rock admitted. "As to why. . . ."

He gazed ahead down the broad avenue leading towards Hektor's palace for several thoughtful breaths, then shrugged again.

"My Prince, I understand why the Navy needs the new guns. And I understand that we've got to rebuild the fleet as quickly as we can. But to be honest, I don't think there's any way we're going to be able to manage all of that rebuilding before Cayleb and the Royal Charisian Navy come calling. That means they're going to be able to land troops almost anywhere they want, with no real significant resistance from our own Navy. I'm not blaming Taryl—Earl Tartarian—for that. It's not his fault. In fact, it's not *anyone's* fault, but it still means it's going to be up to the Army—and *me*—to defeat any invasions, since the Navy can't stop them from happening in the first place."

He paused, looking steadily at his prince, and Hektor nodded.

"I think you're exactly correct about that," he agreed. "And?"

"And under those circumstances, I think it might be a wiser use of our resources and the time available to us to produce cannon for the Army's use, not the Navy's. Or, at least, not *exclusively* for the Navy."

"Ah?"

Hektor frowned thoughtfully, considering what Anvil Rock had just said. And, as he did, he realized the earl had a point. A very good one, in fact.

No one on Safehold had ever heard of "field artillery." Not in the sense in which the term had once been used on a planet called Earth, at any rate. Safeholdian guns had been too big, too massive, too slow-firing. On their clumsy, wheelless "carriages," they were virtually immobile. Once emplaced, moving them again wasn't something to be considered, especially in the presence of the enemy.

But given the lightness and handiness of the new Charisian guns, that might not be true any longer. The sort of naval carriage the Charisians had developed—and which Tartarian's artisans and foundry workers had duplicated from Captain Myrgyn's sketches—wouldn't be very practical for field use, but surely something else could be worked out.

"May I assume you've been giving some thought to exactly how you might mount and use artillery in the field?" he asked aloud.

"Actually, Koryn's been thinking about it," Anvil Rock replied, and Hektor nodded. Sir Koryn Gahrvai, Anvil Rock's eldest son and heir, was also one of the earl's senior troop commanders. And despite the nepotism which had inevitably favored his career, he happened to be very good at what he did.

"And what has Koryn come up with?"

"A new carriage, for one thing," Anvil Rock said. "It's more like a two-wheeled cart than anything the Navy would use, but it looks to me as if it'll work. If it's built sturdily enough, at least. And I'm guessing they could be towed by two-horse teams fairly rapidly. Might work better with four horses, rather than two, of course. Or we might try it with draft dragons. They don't much care for the sound of gunfire, though. I think horses would probably be steadier. You'd need a lot more of them per gun, and their endurance would be lower, but they'd also be faster, over shorter distances."

"I see the two of you *have* been thinking about it," Hektor observed. "And given the circumstances we're probably going to be facing shortly, I think you're probably right about who's going to need artillery worse. Especially if you and Koryn can work out tactics to use it effectively."

"We've been kicking that around, too," Anvil Rock said. "Of course, anything we come up with at this point is going to be purely theoretical, you understand. Can't be any other way until we get some actual pieces to try out our notions, and even then—"

"Look out, Your Highness!"

Hektor's head snapped up as one of his guardsmen suddenly spurred his horse. The beast leapt forward, drawing abruptly even with Hektor's mount, and the guardsman's right hand shot out. Hektor's eyes went wide as that hand literally jerked him off of his horse, yanking him up against the guardsman's breastplate even as the bodyguard simultaneously twisted himself around sideways in the saddle. The prince was reaching for his dagger in automatic self-defense when he heard—and felt—the guardsman's sudden, convulsive gasp. The iron-hard grip which had hauled him bodily out of his saddle slackened suddenly, and Hektor found himself falling untidily to the street's cobblestones. He hit hard, sending a bolt of pain through his left forearm as he landed squarely on top of a fresh, moist pile of horse manure, but he scarcely noticed either of those things. He was staring up at the guardsman who had attacked him.

The guardsman who was slumped forward in his saddle with the two arbalest quarrels which would otherwise have struck Hektor sticking out of his back. His cuirass' backplate had slowed the missiles, but they must have been fired from very short range, because they'd punched right through it.

As Hektor watched, the guardsman started to slip sideways out of his saddle. The prince hurled himself to his feet, reaching up, grunting with effort and the fresh pain in his left arm as he caught the dead weight of the man who had just saved his life.

He went back to his knees, holding the bodyguard, watching blood bubble from the other man's nostrils.

"Window," the dying young man got out. "Saw them . . . in the window . . ."

"I understand," Hektor said, bending over him. "I understand."

"Good," the guardsman got out, and then his eyes lost focus forever.

▼　　▼　　▼

"No sign of them, whoever they were," the Earl of Coris said harshly. "We're still tearing that whole part of the city apart, but they must have had their escape route planned well in advance."

"Is that all you can say?" Sir Taryl Lektor demanded. The Earl of Tartarian sat beside Anvil Rock at the conference table, as if Hektor's top military advisers were closing ranks against his spymaster. Whether or not that was actually what they were doing, the shared unhappiness of Corisande's navy and army commanders was obvious, and Coris' mouth tightened.

"What would you prefer? That I spin fancy tales to sound more efficient? We don't have a single witness who actually saw them. The only man who *did* see them is dead, which means we don't even have a description of them, and the arbalests were still in the room they fired from. They simply dropped them and walked away, and the room itself is part of a counting house office suite that's stood empty for months. No one saw them arrive; no one saw them fire the shots; and no one was watching for them when they left. There's no way for us to tie anyone to the weapons even if we'd had any suspects in custody!"

"Calmly, Phylyp," Hektor said, turning back from the window where he'd stood gazing out over the harbor. His left forearm was in a plaster cast, supported by a sling, and despite his words, there was a tightness around his mouth which owed nothing to the pain of the broken arm.

"How do you expect me to be *calm* about this?" Coris demanded. "They came within inches of killing you today, Hektor. Don't you *understand* that?"

"Believe me, I understand it only too well." Hektor's voice was suddenly harder, colder. "And I want that guardsman's—Ahndrai's—family taken care of. He not only died to save my life, but, as you just pointed out, he was also the only man in the entire detail who even *saw* them. There aren't enough men like that to go around. There never are. So you see to it that his family knows I'm grateful. Knows they'll never want for anything."

"Of course I will," Coris said more quietly.

"Good."

Hektor turned back to the window, then looked up as the chamber door opened and a tall young woman with Hektor's hair and her dead mother's hazel eyes came quickly through it.

"Father!" The newcomer wore riding clothes. Her hair was windblown, and her eyes were dark, intent, in a worried face. "I just got back to the Palace. They just told me! Are you all right?"

"Fine, Irys," he said, reaching out his undamaged right arm. "A broken arm, but aside from that, I'm fine, I promise."

Princess Irys let her father's good arm settle around her shoulders, but she also leaned back against it, gazing up into his face with searching eyes. He didn't know exactly what she was looking for, but whatever it was, she seemed to see it, and her taut shoulders relaxed at least partially.

"Yes," she said softly. "Yes, you are."

She put her own arms around him then, squeezing tightly, and pressed her face into his shoulder. He felt the tension flowing out of her, and pressed his lips to her hair.

She's grown so tall, he thought. *So much like her mother. Where did all the years go?*

"Better?" he asked gently after a moment, and she drew a deep breath and nodded.

"Better," she confirmed, and released him and turned to face the other three men in the chamber.

She knew all of them, of course. In fact, she'd spent more than a little time helping them—and her father—ponder the unpalatable situation they faced. At seventeen, Irys Daykyn was not a typical teenager, and her grasp of the problems confronting them was as good as any of Hektor's older councilors could have boasted.

"They said it was arbalests," she said, and Hektor nodded.

"It was. Ahndrai saw them at the last minute." His nostrils flared. "He saved my life, Irys . . . and it cost him his."

"Oh, no," she said softly. Tears brimmed in her eyes for a moment. "He was so *nice*, Father."

"Yes, he was," Hektor agreed.

"Do we have any idea *who* it was?" she asked after a moment, with the air of someone who was just as happy to change the subject.

"If you mean who actually fired the quarrels, then, no," her father admitted. "Phylyp's men have recovered the arbalests themselves, but we don't have any idea who the marksmen were." He shrugged. "As far as who might have been responsible for sending them, you're just about in time to help us start speculating."

"Cayleb!" Irys more than half hissed the name. The eyes which had been filled with tears moments before glittered with fury now, and Hektor shrugged.

"Possibly. In fact, I'd have to say *probably*, under the circumstances. I'm reasonably confident it wasn't some spontaneous act of rebellion on the part of my subjects, at any rate. Beyond that, I'm not really sure of anything, though. For all I know, it could have been one of our own nobles. Someone who's afraid of what's going to happen and figures putting me out of the way might make it easier to placate Cayleb."

"My Prince, you don't really—" Coris began.

"No, I don't really think that's what happened," Hektor said, shaking his head. "I'm not quite *that* frightened of shadows yet, Phylyp! All I meant was that, as you yourself just said, we really don't know who it was."

"It was Cayleb," Irys said coldly. "Who else would want you dead badly enough to try an assassination in the middle of your own capital in the middle of the day?"

"My love," Hektor said, turning back to her with a crooked smile, "the list of people who would like to see me dead is a very lengthy one, I'm afraid. You know that. At this particular moment, Cayleb would be at the head of my own list of likely suspects. I'll admit that. But it could also have been Nahrmahn. Or Sharleyan—*she's* never made any secret of how she feels about me! For that matter, it could have been Zebediah or one of the Grand Duke's 'associates.' Or simply someone who hates me for a completely separate reason and figured suspicion would automatically focus on Cayleb instead of him. I've told you before. When something like this happens, you must never close your mind to *any* possibility until you have at least some firm pieces of evidence."

"Yes, Father." Irys inhaled again, then nodded once, sharply. "I still say Cayleb's the most likely, but you're right. Until we have something more than automatic suspicion to base our thinking on, I'll try to keep an open mind about other possible suspects."

"Good." Hektor reached out to cup the back of her head in his right palm for a moment, smiling at her. Then he turned back to Coris, Anvil Rock, and Tartarian, and his expression hardened.

"I want to know who was really behind it," he told them flatly. "Use as many men and as much gold as it takes, but find out who was behind it."

"My Prince, if mortal men can discover that, my investigators will. But, in all honesty, I have to warn you that the odds of success are problematical, at best. Generally, when something like this comes out of nowhere, the investigators either get a break in the first few hours or days, or else they *never* get one."

"That's not acceptable, Phylyp," Irys said in a cold, hard voice.

"I didn't say it was acceptable, Your Highness. I'm only warning you and your father that it's probably what's going to happen, despite the best efforts of everyone in this room. We know now that *someone* who wants the Prince dead is willing to try to bring that about. That's more than we knew this morning. I'm not saying it's *enough*, only that it's more. We'll keep trying to find out who was behind it, but in the meantime, all we can do is take precautions to make it harder for whoever it was. And, with all due respect, I think it might be wise to increase your own bodyguards, and your brothers', as well. I don't want to alarm either of you, but if it *was* Cayleb, then removing all of you might very well be what he has in mind."

"Earl Coris is right, Your Highness," Anvil Rock said quietly. "We'll all do all we can, but for now, that really amounts to little more than increasing the security around your father—and you and your brothers, of course."

"And what do we tell everyone else?" Irys' voice was still brisk, but it had lost that tang of old, cold iron. Coris' eyebrows rose, and she snorted. "Rumors must be all over the city, by now," she pointed out. "By this time tomorrow, they'll be across the Barcors and as far as Shreve or Noryst!"

That was an exaggeration, Hektor thought. It would take the Church's semaphore to carry any sort of message—or rumor—six hundred miles in barely twenty-six hours. Still, she had a point.

"There's enough uncertainty and anxiety swirling around without adding this to it," she continued. "Especially if all we can say is 'We don't know who it was' when someone asks."

"She's right about that," Hektor said. The others looked at him, and he snorted. "Of course she is! Trust me, the rumors ignorance can come up with will be worse than any possible accurate answer could have been!"

"So what should we do about it, My Prince?" Tartarian asked after a moment, and Irys laughed. It was not an especially pleasant sound.

"May I, Father?"

"Go ahead," Hektor invited, settling back on his heels, and she smiled grimly at the other three men.

"What matters most is that we put some sort of name or face on whoever it was," she told them. "That we kill any impression that it might have been some general act of defiance or rebellion from inside Corisande. And who have all of us just agreed is our most probable suspect?"

"Cayleb," Tartarian replied. Like most men, he had a tendency to forget Princess Irys wasn't yet twenty at moments like this. In fact, she was so much her father's daughter that it could be frightening at times.

"Exactly," she agreed. "Maybe it was Cayleb, and maybe it wasn't, but it obviously *could* have been him. And it's not as if we have any evidence that it *wasn't* him, either. Given the fact that we're at war with Charis, he'll strike most people as a reasonable suspect, and he's an outsider. *The* outsider, at the moment. Besides, assassination is exactly what you'd expect out of heretics. So announcing that we believe it was him will actually have a rallying effect."

"She's right," Hektor said again, smiling at her. Then he looked back at the other three. "It doesn't really matter if it actually *was* Cayleb. We certainly don't have any reason to worry about his reputation, at any rate, so I'm not likely to lie awake at night worrying about whether or not we're blaming it all on an innocent man! And it will have exactly the effect Irys has just described. In fact, aside from the fact that it got a loyal man killed, this could turn out to be very useful to us."

"As long as we don't close our own minds to the possibility that it *wasn't* Cayleb, My Prince," Coris said warningly.

Hektor arched an eyebrow, and the earl shrugged.

"Overall, I agree with you and Her Highness," he said. "Where the political consequences of this are concerned, especially. But even if this does turn out to be 'useful' in some ways, let's not forget that someone really did try to kill you this afternoon, My Prince. It's always possible they'll try again, and I don't want any of us—especially me and my investigators—to close our minds to any possible suspects or avenues of investigation until we *know* for certain who it was."

"Of course, Phylyp," Hektor agreed. "Of course. But in the meantime," he smiled unpleasantly, "let's turn our minds to how we can most suitably blacken Cayleb's reputation over this, shall we?"

.IX.
Tellesberg Harbor,
Kingdom of Charis

Merlin wondered if Cayleb realized he was slowly, rhythmically shifting his weight from foot to foot as he stood at dockside, surrounded by a storm of banners. Not to mention several score Royal Guardsmen, honor guards from both the Royal Charisian Navy and the Royal Charisian Marines, most of his Royal Council, the bejeweled ranks of what looked like at least half the House of Lords, a sizable delegation from the House of Commons, and every private citizen of his capital who could beg, borrow, buy, or steal a spot close enough to see the most momentous single arrival in Tellesberg in at least the past fifty years.

As a proper bodyguard, Merlin stood impassively behind the youthful king, watching alertly for potential threats. It was, he reflected, as he listened to the harbor batteries' saluting guns pounding out their welcome in spurts of smoke, a good thing no one had yet gotten around to perfecting the sort of artillery with which Seamount was beginning to experiment. A single howitzer shell in the middle of *this* dockside gathering would have had catastrophic consequences for the future history of Safehold.

Of course, he thought with a sense of profound satisfaction as the oared tugs maneuvered the stately galleon flying the royal blue banner with the silver doomwhale of Charis alongside the wharf, *if the Group of Four only knew, what's actually about to land on this dock is going to have even more catastrophic consequences than that for someone.*

He was hard put to avoid breaking into an enormous grin as he watched Cayleb. At this particular moment, the king's mind obviously wasn't on future political and military consequences, despite his commendable job of concentrating on those aspects of the proposed marriage when he'd presented it to Parliament. It was painfully clear that, for now, at least, those consequences had taken second place in the thoughts of a very youthful bridegroom about to meet his bride for the very first time.

▼   ▼   ▼

Sharleyan of Chisholm commanded herself to stand still and stately on the high poop deck of her galleon. The *very* high poop deck, as it happened. HMS *Doomwhale* was, in fact, one of only four galleons her navy had possessed prior to the ill-fated campaign which had ended in Darcos Sound, and unlike the Royal Charisian Navy galleons which had escorted her to Tellesberg, *Doomwhale* retained both her original cumbersome sail plan and the towering height of her massive, multi-deck castles, fore and aft. Those sleek, low-slung vessels had disposed of those features in their ruthless drive to reduce topweight and improve seaworthiness and weatherliness, and that drive had obviously succeeded. Sharleyan was far from a professional seaman herself, but her captain's envy of the Charisians' handiness had been evident even to her, despite his best efforts to conceal it.

At the moment, however, she was far less concerned with the relative merits of galleon designs than with the young man awaiting her arrival.

I am not going to run to the rail like some sort of overeager schoolgirl. I'm a reigning queen, for God's sake! I have a queen's dignity to maintain . . . and absolutely no business having all these butterflies dancing around in my middle.

She told herself that quite firmly.

It didn't seem to help a great deal.

Now stop that! You know why you made this decision, despite the opposition of people like Uncle Byrtrym. Compared to all those reasons, what does it matter what he looks like, for goodness sake?!

She snorted mentally at the direction of her own thoughts and glanced at the young woman standing on the poop deck with her.

Lady Mairah Lywkys was the only lady-in-waiting she'd brought along. Partly, that was because one of Sharleyan's first acts had been to reduce the number of ladies-in-waiting which would normally have been retained by a queen *consort* as a deliberate tactic to reduce her nobles' tendency to think of their teenaged queen as a fluttering girl in need of coddling . . . and subject to a "suitable marriage," manipulation, or removal. The same logic had applied when choosing the guest list for this voyage, and there'd never been any question as to which of her relatively short list of ladies she would choose. Mairah Lywkys wasn't simply her closest friend among the Chisholmian nobility; she was also Baron Green Mountain's niece.

But Mairah wasn't really who was on her mind at the moment, and her mouth tightened ever so slightly as she thought about the man who should have been standing at her side.

Mahrak Sahndyrs was the closest thing she'd had to a father since King Sailys' death. If anyone was going to be present for her wedding day, it should have been Mairah's uncle, she thought. But he couldn't be here. Nor was he the only person whose presence she was going to miss. She'd had no choice but to leave him behind, just as she'd been forced to leave Queen Mother Alahnah to function as her regent, while she sailed off to meet her bridegroom for the first time. They'd been the only two candidates whose ability *and* loyalty she'd been able to fully trust.

And the fact that that was true also explained the reason she'd been forced to bring the Duke of Halbrook Hollow with her.

She didn't really believe her uncle would have fomented rebellion against her in her absence, especially with his own sister sitting as her regent, but she couldn't quite convince herself she was positive of that. Much as she knew he loved her, she also knew that in this decision, she had pushed him too far. His faith—not simply in God, but in God's Church—would never let him approve of this marriage. Of the policy her acceptance of Cayleb's offer had made crystal clear for all the world to see. There had to be a dividing line somewhere between what the uncle's love for her could endure without active opposition and what Mother Church would demand of her faithful son despite that love, and Sharleyan had no intention of leaving him in a position which would compel him to face that decision now.

She wished he'd been able to bring himself to join her on deck. But he'd pleaded "seasickness," despite the calm waters of Tellesberg Bay, and retired to his cabin, instead. Which was why the man who actually *was* standing beside her was the Earl of Gray Harbor, instead of any Chisholmian.

She considered his profile from the corner of her eye. His pleasure at returning home was obvious, and she saw his eyes eagerly searching the color-ful mob crowding the wharf. The wharf's timbers had been covered in rich, thick carpets—carpets, she realized, of Chisholmian blue, and wondered where Cayleb had found enough of them. Banners of both kingdoms popped and snapped in the breeze, and the honor guards were drawn up in perfect order. Yet Gray Harbor's expression made it obvious that he cared nothing for all of that pomp and circumstance. His eyes were looking for someone—one specific someone—and she saw them narrow as he found what he sought.

"There, Your Majesty," he said quietly, although, given the tumultuous cheers echoing from the shore, it was unlikely anyone more than three feet away could have heard him even if he'd shouted. His right hand moved very slightly, the gesture almost more imagined than seen. "To the left of the royal standard," he added, and Sharleyan felt herself color ever so slightly as she followed his directions.

"Was it truly that obvious, My Lord?"

"Probably not, Your Majesty." The earl turned his head and smiled at her. "On the other hand, I have a daughter of my own."

"I will *not* be a nervous maiden," she told him, putting her earlier thoughts into words, and saw Mairah's lips twitching in an almost-smile as Gray Harbor chuckled.

"If Your Majesty will permit me to point this out, that's a little silly of you. You're still very young, you know. Older than Cayleb, true, but still young. All the world has had ample opportunity to learn that, young or not, both of you are formidable rulers. But just this once, Your Majesty, remem-ber your throne has already robbed you of countless pleasures less nobly born young women and men are allowed to enjoy. Enjoy *this* one. All matters of state aside, however true all of the arguments I've used pursuing my respon-sibility to persuade you of the statecraft and wisdom of making this decision, I assure you that the young man waiting for you over there is a very *good* young man. He'll make you happy, if any man can, and I'll promise that you'll never have to doubt his honor or feel ashamed of any decision he may make."

"God grant you're right, My Lord," she said quietly, sincerely.

"I believe He will," he replied. "Of course, I'm prejudiced. I'd be a poor first councilor if I weren't, I suppose. But I've watched Cayleb grow up, Your Majesty. I had the privilege of knowing both his father and his mother, of see-ing the sort of marriage they had . . . and taught him to desire."

Sharleyan nodded, but her eyes were on the figure Gray Harbor had dis-creetly pointed out to her.

They were still too far away for her to make out any details, but she could see he was taller than almost any of the men standing around him. Indeed, she observed with a certain satisfaction, only the black-and-gold-clad guardsman standing alertly at his back seemed to be taller.

She saw the chain Charisian custom used in place of her own presence crown glittering about his neck in gold and green fire and felt a distinct sense of relief that Cayleb had foregone court regalia. She'd expected that, but as they'd approached the harbor and she'd found herself looking for things to worry about, it had occurred to her that she might have been wrong. After all, whatever could go wrong usually did, and the last thing she needed would have been to appear underdressed beside her prospective groom. And the next worst thing would have been to appear *over*dressed.

Will you stop this nattering! she scolded herself. *Even if Gray Harbor's right, you're still a queen. You still have responsibilities, appearances to maintain.*

Besides, he can't possibly *be as good-looking as that painting.*

Despite herself, a gurgle of laughter escaped her as she finally permitted herself to think the ridiculous thought. Of all the stupid, silly things she could be worrying about at a moment like this, that had to be the most empty-headed, fluttery, *useless* one of all.

Which didn't make it go away.

Gray Harbor glanced sideways at her when she laughed, and she shook her head with a smile. It would never do for her to explain her amusement to him. Even if he did have a daughter of his own.

Oddly enough, the laughter seemed to have helped. Or perhaps it was simply that she'd finally allowed herself to admit that even a reigning queen could nurse at least a few romantic fantasies.

But I bet he really isn't as cute as his painting.

▼   ▼   ▼

The galleon nuzzled to a halt alongside the wharf under the ministrations of the oared tugboats. Hawsers came ashore, tightened about the waiting bollards as the crew took tension on them, and an ornate gangplank, its spotless white hand ropes gleaming in the sunlight, was maneuvered smoothly into position. The final saluting gun thudded, the gunsmoke drifted away through the sunlight, and there was a brief moment of near total silence, broken only by the sounds of seabirds, wyverns, and the voice of a young child loudly asking his mother what was happening. And then, as a slender, regal figure appeared at the top of the gangway at the entry port in the galleon's tall side, the trumpets massed behind Cayleb sounded their rich, golden fanfare of welcome.

Sharleyan paused as the trumpets sounded, and Merlin wondered if she realized the fanfare they were playing was reserved for the royal house of Charis alone. He didn't know about that, but his enhanced vision brought her expression to within arm's reach. He saw her eyes widen slightly, saw her head rise with even more pride, saw the color in her cheeks. And then she was coming down the gangway.

No one escorted her. Her own guardsmen hovered behind her, their faces expressionless despite an anxiety which could almost be physically touched. Thanks to the SNARC which had been keeping a protective watch over Sharleyan from the moment Gray Harbor arrived in Chisholm, Merlin knew she had specifically ordered her guard to remain aboard *Doomwhale* while she advanced by herself to meet her new husband and greet her new people.

None of them had liked it, and, indeed, Captain Wyllys Gairaht, their commander, had argued against her decision until she'd told him—in a most uncharacteristic display of temper—to shut up. And she'd told Sergeant Edwyrd Seahamper, her personal armsman since childhood, the same thing, albeit a bit less forcefully. If, she had pointed out acidly to both of her guardians, any of her proposed husband's subjects were sufficiently crazed with hate against a queen they had never even met to attempt a suicidal assassination in the face of all of the guardsmen *Cayleb* was going to have present, then no one would be able to protect her in the long run, whatever they did.

Captain Gairaht and Sergeant Seahamper clearly hadn't been concerned with "the long run." They'd been concerned with keeping her alive right now, and Merlin found himself in ungrudging sympathy with them. Despite that, Merlin knew, as the Charisians' cheers redoubled in strength and volume, that Sharleyan's instincts had not played her false. As that solitary, slender figure made its way down the gangway to greet her prospective husband's people for the first time, the symbolism of her gesture was not lost upon those people.

She's got them in the palm of her hand, Merlin thought admiringly. *And maybe the best thing about it is that she made the decision first, and got around to figuring out why only second.*

Nor was the gesture lost on Cayleb.

"Stay here—everyone!" he half-shouted through the bedlam of cheers, whistles, and shouts.

More than a few of the people among the designated official greeting party turned their heads as the king's command was relayed to them. One or two of those people's faces showed resentment, but most of them only blinked in astonishment as he summarily jettisoned the entire carefully choreographed ceremony which had been planned to welcome Queen Sharleyan.

Get used to it, people, Merlin thought with sardonic delight as Cayleb stepped forward all by himself. *These two are both bad enough by themselves where protocol is concerned. Wait until you see the two of them in action at the same time!*

▼   ▼   ▼

My God, he's better looking than the painting!

The thought flared through the back of Sharleyan's brain as Cayleb advanced to the foot of the ceremonial gangway, smiling up at her, extending a powerful, muscular hand that glittered with gem-set rings. He stood tall and straight, broad-shouldered in his thigh-length linen tunic and loose cotton silk breeches. The tunic flashed back the morning sunlight from gold and silver bullion embroidery. Tiny gems flickered amidst the traditional, swirling, wave-like patterns, and his belt of intricately decorated, seashell-shaped plaques of hammered silver gleamed with near-mirror brightness.

But it was his eyes she truly saw. Those smiling, brown eyes that met hers not with the duty of a monarch marrying to serve his people's need, but with the genuine welcome of a young man greeting his awaited bride.

▼   ▼   ▼

Merlin was out of his mind. She is so beautiful!

Cayleb knew he was staring like some oafish, backwater idiot, but he couldn't help it. Despite everything Merlin had said to him, he'd dreaded this moment, in many ways. Part of it, he'd come to suspect, was that a corner of his mind couldn't dismiss the stubborn pessimism that anything this important, this crucial to his people's survival, had to be solely a thing of cold political calculation. And sacrifice.

But the young woman reaching out her slender, fine-boned hand to him was not the stuff of calculation and sacrifice. Her black hair gleamed in the sunlight under her golden presence crown, and her huge eyes sparkled with intelligence. Her deceptively simple gown was woven of steel thistle silk, even lighter and smoother than cotton silk, and cut to an unfamiliar pattern. Charisian styles, for both men and women, favored loose-fitting, swirling garments well suited to the equatorial climate. Sharleyan's gown was far more closely tailored, revealing a richly curved figure, despite her slenderness, and she tilted back her head as he took her fingers carefully, almost delicately, between his own and raised her hand to his lips.

"Welcome to Charis, Your Majesty," he said as the cheers from the shore behind him redoubled yet again.

▼   ▼   ▼

"Welcome to Charis, Your Majesty."

Sharleyan could scarcely hear him through the tumult of voices surging all about them like some hurricane of human energy. Her own hand tightened on his, feeling the sword calluses on his fingers, the strength of his grip, and an odd sense of pleasure filled her as she realized her head didn't quite come as high as his shoulder. Earl Gray Harbor's wardrobe had prepared her for the exoticness of Charisian styles, and as she gazed at Cayleb, she realized that those loose, colorful garments were perfectly suited to his muscular figure.

Which was undoubtedly a silly thing for her to be thinking about at this particular moment.

"Thank you, Your Majesty," she said, raising her voice against the crowd sound. "Your people's welcome is . . . overwhelming."

"They've awaited you eagerly ever since your letter arrived," Cayleb explained. Then his eyes softened. "As have I."

It could have been a courtier's polite, flattering nothing. It wasn't, and Sharleyan smiled as she heard the genuine welcome, the pleasure, in his tone.

"Your portrait didn't do you justice, Your Majesty," she replied with a devilish sparkle, and saw him color slightly. Then he laughed and shook his head.

"If you can say that after actually seeing me, perhaps we'd better have the royal optician check your eyes!"

His own eyes brimmed with humor, and she laughed back. Then it was her turn to shake her head.

"Your Majesty—Cayleb—I'm sure we'll find time to know one another. For now, though, I believe your people are waiting for us."

"No, Sharleyan," he said, stepping beside her and tucking her hand into his elbow as he turned to escort her the rest of the way down the gangway. "No, *our* people are waiting for us."

.X.
Archbishop's Palace,
City of Tellesberg,
Kingdom of Charis

Forgive me, Your Eminence."

Maikel Staynair looked up from the latest stack of paperwork as Father Bryahn Ushyr opened his office door. Given the tumult and excitement of Queen Sharleyan's arrival this morning, the archbishop had managed to get very little done this day, and some of the documents on his desk simply had to be dealt with as expeditiously as possible. It hadn't been easy to carve the necessary couple of hours out of his schedule to deal with them, and Father Bryahn knew that as well as Staynair did. On the other hand, the under-priest hadn't been chosen lightly as the archbishop's personal secretary and aide. Staynair trusted his judgment implicitly, and, in normal circumstances, Ushyr was as unflappable as any archbishop might have asked. Yet there was something peculiar about his voice this afternoon. Something *very* peculiar.

"Yes, Bryahn?"

"I'm sorry to disturb you, Your Eminence. I know how busy you are. But . . . there's someone here I believe you should see."

" 'Someone'?" Staynair's eyebrows rose quizzically. "Would it happen that this *someone* has a name, Bryahn?"

"Well, yes, Your Eminence. It's just that—" Ushyr paused most uncharacteristically, then shook his head. "I believe it might be better if I simply showed her in, if that's acceptable, Your Eminence."

Staynair's curiosity was well and truly piqued. He couldn't imagine what could have flustered Ushyr this way. From what his secretary had just said, the visitor in question was obviously female, and Staynair couldn't think of a single woman in Charis—with the possible exception of Queen Sharleyan— who could have engendered that reaction in him. But he'd known the young priest long enough to accept his request, even if it wasn't exactly the normal protocol for visiting the primate of all Charis.

"Very well, Bryahn. Give me a moment or two to tidy this up," he waved one hand at the report he'd been perusing, "and then show her in."

"Yes, Your Eminence," Ushyr murmured, and the door closed quietly as he withdrew.

Staynair gazed thoughtfully at that door for several heartbeats, then shrugged, inserted a slip of paper to mark his place, and began jogging the sheets of the report into order.

Whatever might have caused his secretary's almost flustered reaction, it hadn't affected Ushyr's sense of timing, or his ability to estimate how long his archbishop needed. Staynair had exactly enough time to set the report aside, brush his desk into a semblance of neatness, and straighten himself alertly in his comfortable chair. Then the door opened, and Ushyr stepped back through it with a plainly dressed woman whose dark hair was lightly touched with silver, accompanied by two boys. The boys' features made it abundantly clear they were her sons, yet there was something else about them, as well. Something . . . familiar, although Staynair couldn't put his finger on exactly what it was. The older of them looked to be somewhere in his teens; the younger perhaps ten or eleven. That was the first thing that went through Staynair's mind, but another thought followed it almost instantly.

They were terrified. Especially the boys, he thought. Their mother hid it better, but despite the strength of character in her face, there was fear in her eyes, as well. And something else. Something dark and passionate and ribbed with iron pride.

"Your Eminence," Ushyr said quietly, "may I present Madame Adorai Dynnys."

Staynair's eyes went wide, and he surged to his feet without even realizing he had. He was around the desk and across the office to her in three quick strides, and he held out his hand.

"Madame Dynnys!" He heard the astonishment in his own voice, and it was as if he were listening to someone else. "This is most unexpected!"

Her hand trembled slightly in his fingers, and he looked into those eyes, saw the exhaustion—and the desperation—behind the fear and the pride. How she could possibly have managed to travel all the way from the Temple Lands to Charis without being identified and taken by the Inquisition was more than he could begin to imagine.

"Truly," he told her, squeezing her trembling hand gently as his own astonishment began to ebb at least a little, "God works His mysteries in ways beyond human understanding or prediction. You and your family have been in my prayers ever since Bishop Executor Zherald and Father Paityr received your husband's final letter, yet I never imagined that He would be gracious enough to allow you to reach Charis!"

"Letter, Your Eminence?" she repeated. He heard the fatigue and tension in the depths of her voice, but her eyebrows rose and her eyes sharpened. "Erayk got letters out?"

"Indeed, indeed he did," Staynair said. He extended his other hand, gripping both of hers, and shook his head. "At least one of them. I have no idea how he managed it, and I will not pretend Archbishop Erayk and I often failed to see eye-to-eye. Obviously, what's transpired here in Charis since his last visit is proof enough of that. But from the final letter he somehow arranged to have delivered to the Bishop Executor and Father Paityr, I can tell you that at the end of his life, your husband remembered the true touch of God." He shook his head again. "We've had no confirmation of his death here in Charis, but from the letter he sent—and from your own arrival here—I must assume the end he foresaw has indeed overtaken him."

"Oh, yes," she half-whispered, chin trembling at last, tears sparkling in her eyes. "Oh, yes, Your Eminence. It has. And you're right. I believe he did feel God's finger, despite all that it cost him."

"What do you mean?" Staynair asked gently, for there was something in her voice, in her manner, that said more than her words. She looked at him for a moment, then glanced at the two boys, who were watching her and the archbishop with wounded, anxious eyes.

"Your Eminence," she said obliquely, "these are my sons, Tymythy Erayk and Styvyn." Tymythy, the older of the two, bobbed his head, his expression wary, as his mother introduced him, but Styvyn only stared at the archbishop. The younger boy's grief and tension cut Staynair like a knife, and he released one of Madame Dynnys' hands to reach out to the youngsters.

"Tymythy," he said, and gripped the lad's hand in the clasp of an equal before he released it to lay that same hand lightly on the younger boy's head. "Styvyn. I know what's happened in your lives over the last few months has been frightening. I can't begin to imagine how your mother managed to get you to Charis. But know this, both of you. You're *safe* here, and so is she. No one will harm you, or threaten you, and I know I speak for King Cayleb when I tell you all three of you will be taken under his personal protection. And mine."

Styvyn's lower lip quivered. Tymythy's expression was more guarded, more wary, but after a moment, he nodded again.

"May you and I speak privately for a moment, Your Eminence?" Adorai requested. Her eyes darted once more briefly towards the boys, both of whom were still looking at Staynair, not her, and the archbishop nodded.

"Of course." He stepped to the office door and opened it, looking out into Ushyr's office space. "Bryahn, would you please take Tymythy and Styvyn here down to the kitchen and see if Cook can't find them something to eat?" He looked back over his shoulder with a smile. "It's been quite a while since I was your age, boys, but I seem to recall that it was impossible to ever really keep me fed."

The briefest of answering smiles flashed across Tymythy's face, then vanished. He looked anxiously at his mother for a moment, and she nodded.

"Go with the Father," she said gently. "Don't worry about me. As the Archbishop says, we're safe now. I promise."

"But—"

"It's all right, Tym," she said more firmly. "I won't be long."

"Yes, Ma'am," he said after one more moment of hesitation, and put his hand on his brother's shoulder. "Come on, Styv. I'll bet they've got hot chocolate, too."

He walked Styvyn out the door. The younger boy's head turned, keeping his eyes fixed on his mother until the door closed between them, and Staynair turned back to face her himself.

"Please, Madame Dynnys," he invited. "Be seated."

He ushered her to a seat at one end of the small sofa in a corner of his office, then sat at the other end, half turned to face her, rather than resuming his place behind his desk. She looked around the chamber, biting her lower lip, obviously seeking her composure, then returned her eyes to him.

"My boys know their father is dead," she said, "but I haven't told them yet how he died. It hasn't been easy, but I couldn't risk their betraying themselves until I had them someplace safe."

"They're safe now," he reaffirmed gently. "You have my promise, both personally and that of my office."

"Thank you." She looked at him steadily, then her nostrils flared. "I'm truly grateful for your promise, and I know nothing you've done was done out of personal enmity to Erayk. And yet, I hope you'll forgive me, but I can't quite separate your actions from what happened to him."

"Nor should you be able to," he replied. "Not yet, at any rate. And no one could blame you if that separation never comes to you. I won't pretend your husband was universally loved here in Charis, because he wasn't. Yet he was never hated, either—or not to the best of my knowledge, at any rate. For myself, I never considered him an *evil* man, as I do the Grand Inquisitor. I only felt he was weak and, forgive me, corrupt. Corrupt with that taint of corruption which clings to the entire Council of Vicars and all of the senior members of the episcopate."

"He *was* weak," she agreed, her eyes once more brimming with tears. "But he was stronger than I ever guessed, too. Certainly stronger than *he* ever suspected he might be. That strength came to him at the end."

"Tell me," he invited softly, and she drew a deep, ragged breath. A tear broke free and ran down her cheek, and she squared her shoulders like a soldier facing battle.

"I was there." Her voice was low, hoarse. "I had to be there. I saw every single thing they did to him before they finally let him die. It took *hours*, Your Eminence. He wasn't even a human being anymore at the end, only a broken, flayed, bleeding *thing*, and 'Mother Church' called that *justice*."

Her voice hissed as she delivered the final word like a curse. More tears broke free, but there was a fierce, blazing anger in those wet eyes as she looked at the man who had replaced her husband as the Archbishop of Charis.

"You're wrong about one thing, Your Eminence," she told him flatly. "Not every member of the Council of Vicars is corrupt. Not even every priest of the Inquisition, despite Clyntahn's poison at the very heart of the Office. That's how I know he was offered an easy death if only he would confirm the Group of Four's version of what happened here in Charis.

"He refused to do that." She met his eyes, and her chin rose with pride even as the tears spilled down her face. "My husband and I never had much of a marriage, Your Eminence. You're right, he was a corrupt man, and weak. But I tell you this, I will *never* be ashamed of Erayk Dynnys. There is nothing those lying monsters at the heart of the Church can ever say, ever do, to make me forget the choice he made, the death he died. At the end of his life, he was anything *but* weak."

"That accords well with his final letter," Staynair said softly, pulling a spotless handkerchief from the sleeve of his cassock and passing it across to her. "I didn't know any of the details of his death, obviously. But I did know he'd found the strength you speak of. And that whatever his faults may have been, at the end of his life, he saw clearly, and spoke the truth—not simply to others, but to himself. Every Wednesday, since his letter arrived, I have conducted a memorial mass for God's servant Erayk."

She nodded convulsively, clutching the handkerchief. It was several seconds before she could speak again.

"I need to tell the boys," she said then. "They have to know, and it won't be long before someone tells them anyway. Our ship left Port Harbor the evening of his execution, and the crew had none of the details. They knew he'd been executed, and the boys did, too, of course. And even though the crew didn't know the details, some of them . . . speculated about what it must have been like. They had no idea who we were, never guessed they were speaking of my sons' father. I told them I thought it was inappropriate for such young boys to hear, and I have to admit they tried to avoid speaking about it in front of them after that. But it wasn't a very large ship, Your Eminence, and I know both of them heard . . . some of it. I couldn't prevent that, although I believe—pray—that I managed to protect them from the worst. But I can't do that forever."

"Of course you can't." He leaned forward and touched her on the knee gently. "I realize it may be difficult for them to separate me, in their minds, from what happened to their father, given the fact that I'm the one who's assumed his office here in Charis. But one of the responsibilities of that office is to minister to all of God's children, so if I can be of any assistance when you tell them, please allow me to be."

"I think that perhaps if you can explain to them, or at least try to explain, *why* this is happening, it might help," she replied. Then she shook her head. "I don't know if anyone can explain that to them, Your Eminence. Not at their ages."

"Not so very long ago," Staynair said, "King Haarahld had to explain to his own cousins—two boys, both younger than your Tymythy—why their father was dead. Had to explain that their father had attempted to assassinate the Crown Prince, murder the King, and been killed by their own grandfather in the process." He smiled sadly. "Children have burdens enough without believing their fathers could be traitors, could be corrupt. Without having to accept their deaths in dishonor. From what you've said, at least *your* sons' father died speaking the truth, facing his executioners with the courage of true conviction and speaking for that conviction, despite the injustice of his execution. At their age, that will be cold comfort for his loss, especially when they learn the nature of the death he died. But they have nothing to be ashamed of. You're right about that, My Lady, and in time, they'll come to understand that. It won't erase the pain, but perhaps it will at least help them to feel the pride in their father which he so justly earned at the very end of his life. And although God knows they—and you—will need time to heal, I promise you we'll give you all of the time, all of the support, we possibly can."

"I'm glad," she said softly, and he quirked one eyebrow. She saw it, and shook her head.

"I'm glad," she repeated. "I hoped, prayed, that Erayk hadn't died for nothing. That the Group of Four truly was lying, and that the man who'd replaced my husband here in Charis truly was a man of God, not simply someone seeking political advantage, however justified he might have been to do exactly that in light of the Church's own abuses. I'm glad to see that the man who replaced him *is* a man of God."

"I try to be." He smiled at her with a mix of sadness and humor. "There are times when I'm not as confident of my success as I'd like to be. But I do try."

"I can tell." She looked at him for a moment longer, then drew a deep, steadying breath. "Father," she said, "I have sinned, and it has been three months since I last attended mass. Will you hear my confession?"

.XI.
Royal Palace,
City of Tellesberg,
Kingdom of Charis

Your Majesty?"

Sharleyan's head turned automatically towards the tall guardsman with the rakishly scarred cheek—Captain Athrawes—as he stepped deferentially into the private dining room. Then she realized Cayleb's head had done exactly the same thing, and she giggled.

She hated it when she giggled. Chuckles were acceptable. So was laughter. But *giggles* were invincibly girlish. They made her feel as if she were twelve years old again. Worse, they made her feel as if everyone else must think the same thing, yet she'd never quite been able to eradicate them, and she felt her cheeks heating with embarrassment.

But then she glanced at Cayleb. She saw the same devilish amusement dancing in his eyes, and that was too much. Giggles disappeared into laughter, and she shook her head at him.

"I think getting used to the fact that I'm a visitor in someone else's court is going to be harder than I thought it would," she said.

"Nonsense," he replied. "You may be a *newcomer* to this court, My Lady, but you certainly aren't a 'visitor.' Not here. What we're going to need is some new protocol so that we know which 'Your Majesty' is being majestied at any given moment."

"Perhaps so. But at this particular moment, I'm fairly certain Captain Athrawes means *you*."

"Indeed I do, Your Majesty," Athrawes said gravely.

The guardsman bowed respectfully, but there was a twinkle in his almost unearthly sapphire-blue eyes, and Sharleyan noted it with carefully concealed curiosity.

She'd been here in Tellesberg Palace for barely twelve hours, and she'd spent three of them locked into the inescapable, iron etiquette of the formal midday banquet which three-quarters of Charis seemed to have attended. Despite that, however, she'd already realized that Athrawes' relationship with Cayleb went far beyond the normal one of monarch and servant. In many ways, it reminded her of her own relationship with Edwyrd Seahamper, but Edwyrd had been her personal armsman since she was barely ten years old, whereas the entire world knew *Seijin* Merlin Athrawes had become Cayleb's armsman less than three years ago. Besides, there was something more even than her deep personal bond with Edwyrd in this one. Sharleyan had learned to analyze relationships with the keen eye of someone for whom the ability to know where people really stood might well mean the difference between retaining a throne and becoming one more deposed—and, quite possibly, disposed of—inconvenient child heir. That was one reason it bothered her that she couldn't put her mental finger on exactly what the bond between Cayleb and the *seijin* was, and prudence suggested that was an inability she should rectify as soon as possible.

"What is it, Merlin?" Cayleb asked now.

"Archbishop Maikel has just arrived at the Palace, Your Majesty," the *seijin* replied. "He's accompanied by an unexpected guest, and he craves a few moments of your time."

Sharleyan's mental ears pricked. There was something peculiar about the stress the *seijin* had laid upon the word "unexpected." And, she realized, there was also something peculiar about Cayleb's reaction to that emphasis. It was as if he'd been particularly surprised to hear it.

"If you need to speak with the Archbishop, I'll certainly understand, Cayleb," she said, beginning to push her chair back from the private supper table. "I'm sure the time we've already spent together today has taken you away from a great many things you needed to do. So, it's probably time—"

"No," he interrupted her, shaking his head quickly. "I meant what I said earlier. If the *Archbishop* believes he requires privacy to discuss some specific matter of the Church, that's one thing, but I didn't propose marriage simply to add one more person to the list of people I can't trust. If we're going to create the marriage—and the unified realm—I think we both want, then the time to begin is now."

"Of course," she murmured. She settled back into her chair, hoping he recognized how pleased she was by his response. It was easy to say someone was trusted; she'd discovered the hard way, very early in life, that it was harder by far to actually trust . . . and to demonstrate that one did.

And I know how . . . imperious I can be, she thought with a mental smile.

Learning to genuinely share not just trust, but authority, is going to be hard, no matter how badly we both want this to succeed. Succeed on many levels.

"Please ask the Archbishop to join us," Cayleb continued, turning back to the *seijin.*

"Of course, Your Majesty."

Captain Athrawes bowed once more, then withdrew. A moment later, the door opened again, and the *seijin* returned with Archbishop Maikel and a plainly dressed woman who was probably twenty or more years older than Sharleyan.

"Archbishop Maikel, Your Majesties," *Seijin* Merlin said.

"Your Majesty." Staynair bowed to Cayleb, then again to Sharleyan. "Your Majesty," he repeated, and Sharleyan's lips twitched at the echo of her recent conversation with Cayleb. But then the archbishop straightened, and the somberness in his eyes banished any temptation to levity on her part.

"What is it, Maikel?" Cayleb's voice was sharper, more concerned, as he, too, recognized the archbishop's mood.

"Your Majesty, Her Majesty's ship wasn't the only one to arrive in Tellesberg today, and I'm afraid our worst fears about the fate of Archbishop Erayk have been confirmed."

Cayleb's face went expressionless at Staynair's sober words, and Sharleyan felt her own do the same. As Cayleb, she was only too well aware of the fate *The Book of Schueler* prescribed for anyone judged guilty of the crimes upon which the Inquisition had arraigned Erayk Dynnys.

"Confirmed how?" Cayleb asked after only the briefest of pauses.

"Confirmed by this lady," Staynair replied, gesturing courteously to the woman beside him. "She witnessed his execution, and I believe you should hear what she has to say about it."

The pleasant supper Sharleyan had consumed seemed to congeal abruptly in her stomach. The last thing she wanted to hear over a supper table—especially *this* supper table, on this of all nights—were the savage details of Dynnys' grisly death. From Cayleb's expression, he felt much the same way. But, like Sharleyan herself, there were responsibilities he could not evade, and she felt a perverse satisfaction when he didn't even ask if she wanted to excuse herself from hearing those details with him.

"If Archbishop Maikel feels we should hear you, My Lady," the king said courteously to the other woman, "then I'm more than prepared to trust his judgment."

"Thank you, Your Majesty," Staynair said, then cleared his throat. "Your Majesties, permit me to introduce Madame Adorai Dynnys."

Cayleb straightened abruptly in his chair, and Sharleyan stiffened.

"Madame Dynnys!" Cayleb stood, stepping quickly around the supper table and extending his hand. "How in God's name did you manage to get here safely?"

"I suspect He did have more than a little to do with it, Your Majesty." Madame Dynnys' voice was deeper than Sharleyan's own soprano, and echoes of loss and grief grated in its depths like broken bits of ancient boulders, but she managed to smile.

"Please," Cayleb said, taking her hand in his and urging her towards the table, "sit down."

"That isn't necessary, Your—"

"I think it *is* necessary," he interrupted her. "And I feel certain Queen Sharleyan would agree."

"Most definitely," Sharleyan said, standing herself and pulling back a chair with her own hands.

"Thank you," Madame Dynnys said softly, with a small, sad smile of gratitude for both of them, as she sat in the proffered chair.

"I can scarcely even begin to imagine what this must have been like for you, Madame," Cayleb said, pouring a glass of wine and handing it to her. "Indeed, given the charges the Inquisition leveled against your husband, we'd all feared you and your children must have been taken into custody, as well." His mouth tightened. "Given Clyntahn's . . . personality, I felt sure he'd assume you must have been 'contaminated' by mere proximity. And as for your sons. . . ."

He let his voice trail off, and she gave a small, almost convulsive nod.

"I don't know what would have happened to me, Your Majesty, but I think you're right about the boys. I know he called them 'that eternally damned and damnable heretic's poisonous get,' at any rate." Her mouth was a hard, bitter line. "It's possible his 'colleagues' might have attempted to intervene, I suppose, however unlikely it seems. But we definitely would have been arrested, if certain . . . friends of mine in Zion hadn't gotten warning to me in time." She sipped from the wineglass. "They not only warned me, Your Majesty, but they gave all three of us refuge until they could smuggle us out of Port Harbor."

"To here."

"Where else might we have gone, Your Majesty?" There was an undeniable edge of angry despair in Madame Dynnys' voice, Sharleyan realized. And who should blame her?

"A valid question, My Lady," Cayleb acknowledged, but he met her eyes levelly. "It was never our intent for innocents to suffer, but we can't—won't—pretend we didn't know it would happen. On the other hand, my father and I—and Archbishop Maikel—had no real choice, I fear, given the fate the Group of Four had planned for all of our subjects."

"I know that, Your Majesty. And I understand both what drove your hand and what it is you hope to accomplish. Or, at least, I believe I do, especially after meeting and speaking with Archbishop Maikel." She used Staynair's title without hesitation or reservation, Sharleyan noticed. "Indeed, that understanding is one reason I came here, instead of attempting to go into permanent hiding in the Temple Lands. But, to be completely honest, another reason was that I believe your Kingdom owes my sons refuge from the many in Zion and the Temple who would kill them simply because of who their father was."

"My Lady, we owe that refuge not simply to your sons, and not even simply to yourself, but to *anyone* who finds himself or herself in danger from the corrupt men who control the Council of Vicars. In time, I hope and believe, Charis will become an openly sought refuge for all of God's children who recognize the corruption of men like the Group of Four."

"Thank you," she repeated.

"You're most welcome, in every sense of the word," Cayleb told her simply. Then he seemed to steel himself. "But now, My Lady," he continued gently, "may we hear what you've come so far to tell us?"

▼   ▼   ▼

Several hours later, Cayleb and Sharleyan stood on a balcony high on the side of King Maikel's Tower, looking out across the sparse lights of Tellesberg proper and the brighter smear of light which was the perpetually busy waterfront.

"That poor woman," Sharleyan murmured.

"Amen," Cayleb said softly, and reached out and took her hand. She turned her head, glancing at him, as she realized the action had been completely unconscious on his part. *His* eyes were still on the dark sweep of his sleeping capital as he laid her hand on his forearm and covered it with his own.

"I doubt I'll sleep very well tonight," he continued. "I've discovered that knowing what his sentence was and actually hearing how it was carried out—especially hearing it from his own *wife*—are two different things." He shook his head, his jaw tight. "The Inquisition has much to answer for. Indeed," he turned to look at her squarely, "if the truth be known, this goes beyond the Group of Four, whatever we may say."

"I realized that even before Earl Gray Harbor brought me your messages," she said steadily, and squeezed his arm gently but firmly. "That pig Clyntahn is the one immediately responsible for all of this. I've never doubted that for a moment, and every word Madame Dynnys said only confirmed it. But if the entire Church hadn't become corrupt, a man like Clyntahn could never have gained the power he has. It's tempting to blame the man and not the institution, but that's the easy answer, the one that saves us from looking truth squarely in the eye. And"—she met his gaze without flinching—"almost the very first lesson Mahrak—Baron Green Mountain—taught me after Hektor paid for my father's murder was that a monarch's first and overriding duty is to face the truth, however ugly it may be. However much she—or he—may long to avoid it."

Cayleb gazed at her in silence for several seconds, then twitched his head in an odd little half nod. She had the strange sensation that it was directed to someone else, someone not present, but he never looked away from her.

"I proposed the union of Charis and Chisholm because it seemed a military necessity," he told her. "I had reports about you and your court, of course, much as I'm sure you had about Charis and about me. From those reports, I hoped I'd find not just an alliance with your Kingdom, but an ally in *you*." His nostrils flared. "I have to tell you, Sharleyan, that even on this brief an acquaintance, it's obvious to me that the reports of your wisdom and courage failed to do you justice."

"Indeed?" She tried to keep her tone light as she studied his face as closely as she could in the available light. Then she laughed softly. "I was thinking much the same about *you*, as it happens. I do hope this isn't a case of two hesitant suitors deciding to make the best of their situation!"

"If either of us should be in that position, My Lady," he said, bowing with a gallant flourish, "it must be you. Now that I've seen you and met you, I assure you that I've decided this was one of the best notions I've ever had. On a great many levels."

He straightened, and Sharleyan felt a pleasant tingle inside at the frank desire he had allowed into his expression.

She squeezed his arm again, then turned to look back out over Tellesberg while she sorted through her own feelings. As the daughter of a king, and then as a queen in her own right, Sharleyan Tayt had accepted long ago that her marriage would be one of state. She'd also realized that as a queen in a kingdom which had shown so little tolerance for a woman's rule in the past, marriage would pose particular dangers for her, and yet there'd been her clear responsibility to provide a legitimate, acknowledged heir to her throne in order to secure the succession. With so many needs, opportunities, and threats to balance, there'd been no room in her life to worry about whether or not she might love—or even like—the man to whom she eventually found herself wed.

And then this. Barely five months ago, she'd been certain Charis—and Cayleb—were doomed, and that she would be forced to participate in their murder. She'd never imagined, in her wildest flight of fantasy, that she might actually find herself entertaining the possibility of *marrying* him. Of binding her own kingdom irrevocably to Charis and to Charis' rebellion against the oppressive authority of Mother Church. And to whatever fate that rebellion ultimately produced. Even now, there were moments when she wondered what insanity had possessed her to even contemplate such a union.

But *only* moments, and they were becoming steadily fewer.

It's Cayleb himself, she thought. *I've seen so much cynicism, so much careful maneuvering for position, and spent so much of my life watching for the hidden dagger in the hands of supposed friends. But there's no cynicism in Cayleb. That's the most remarkable thing of all, I think. He believes in responsibilities and duties, in* ideals, *not just in pragmatism and expediency, and he's got all the empty-headed, invincibly optimistic enthusiasm of one of those incredibly stupid heroes out of a romantic ballad somewhere. How in God's name could he have grown up as a crown prince without discovering the truth?*

It was all madness, of course. In the darker moments of the night, when doubt came to call, she realized that with agonizing certainty. Despite Charis' present naval advantage, the kingdom was simply too small, even with Chisholm's support, to resist indefinitely the massive power the Church could bring to bear upon them. In those dark watches of the night, it was all dreadfully clear, inevitable.

But not anymore. She shook her head, marveling at the simple awareness which flowed through her. Before she'd arrived in Charis, her belief that Charis—and Chisholm—might survive had been a thing of intellect, the triumph of analytical intelligence over the insistence of "common sense." And, she admitted to herself at last, a thing of desperation. Something she'd been forced to believe—to *make* herself believe—if there were to be any hope of her own realm's survival in the face of the Church's obvious willingness to destroy anyone even suspected of disobedience to the Group of Four.

That had changed now. Changed when she realized Cayleb in person, despite his youth, despite his undeniable charm, was even more impressive in fact than in rumor. There was something incredibly engaging about his flashes of boyish enthusiasm, but behind those flashes she saw the implacable warrior who had won the most smashing naval victories in the history of Safehold. Who was prepared to go on however long he must, to win as many more victories as his cause required, because he truly *believed* men and women were supposed to be more than the obedient slaves of corrupt men who claimed to speak with the authority of God Himself.

And even more impressive, perhaps, was the fact that his kingdom and his people believed with him. Believed *in* him. They were prepared to go as far as he led them, to face any foe—even Mother Church herself—at his side. Not at his heels, but at his *side.*

And she, she realized wonderingly, wanted to do the same thing. To face whatever storm might come, whatever odds might be, because it was the right thing to do. Because he and his father, Archbishop Maikel, his nobles and his parliament, had decided it was their responsibility. Because they'd been right when they made that decision, that choice . . . and because she wanted to share in that same ability to do what was right *because* it was right.

And the fact that he's not just cute, but probably one of the sexiest men you've ever encountered, has nothing at all to do with it, does it, Sharleyan? a corner of her brain insisted upon asking her.

Of course it doesn't, she told that pesky corner sternly. *And even if it did, this is hardly the time to be thinking about that, you silly twit! Go away! Still . . . I've got to admit that it doesn't hurt, either.*

"Can we really make this work, Cayleb?" she asked him softly, turning back to face him. "Not just us, just you and me—Cayleb and Sharleyan. All of it. After what Madame Dynnys told us this evening, with all the wealth and the manpower the Group of Four command, can we make it *work*?"

"Yes," he said simply.

"You make it sound so easy." Her voice was wondering, not dismissive, and he smiled wryly.

"Not easy, no." He shook his head. "Of all the words you might use to describe it, 'easy' is the last one I'd choose. But I believe it's something more important than easy. It's *inevitable*, Sharleyan. There are too many lies in Zion, too much deceit and corruption, more even than anyone suspects. I'm not so foolish as to think truth and justice must inevitably triumph simply because they *deserve* to, but liars ultimately destroy the things they lie to protect, and corruption, ambition, and betrayal inevitably betray *themselves*, as well. That's what's happening here.

"The Group of Four made a serious error in judgment when they thought they could just brush Charis aside, crush one more inconvenient gadfly. They were wrong about that, and the proof of that error, as much as the proof of their corruption, is what ultimately dooms them. They've made the mistake of trying to enforce their will through force and terror and the shed blood of the innocent, and they thought it would be simple, that the rest of the world would continue to accept it. But Maikel is right when he says the purpose of the Church must be to nurture and teach, not to enslave. That was the source of Mother Church's true authority, despite the existence of the Inquisition. And now that authority, that reverence, is gone, because everyone's seen the truth. Seen what the Inquisition did to Erayk Dynnys, what it's prepared to do to entire kingdoms . . . and why."

"And you really think that makes enough of a difference?"

"Yes, I do. All we really have to do is to survive long enough for that truth to percolate through the minds of other rulers, other parliaments. In the end, the Group of Four was right about at least one thing. It's our *example*, far more than our actual military strength or wealth, which poses the true threat to them."

"That's what Mahrak said," she told him. "And what I said to myself, when I could convince my emotions to listen to my intellect. But it's different, somehow, hearing *you* say it."

"Because of my noble demeanor and inspiring stature?" he asked lightly, and she shook her head with a laugh.

"Not quite," she said dryly.

"Then how?" he asked more seriously.

"Partly, I think, because you're a king yourself. A fairly impressive one, too, I'm forced to admit, and not just because of Rock Point, Crag Reach, or Darcos Sound. When you say it, it carries that ring of authority, of coming from someone in a position to truly judge possibilities.

"But even more, it comes from who you are, *what* you are. I wasn't prepared for Archbishop Maikel, or for the way the rest of your people are prepared to follow wherever you and he lead. You're scarcely the Archangels come back to earth, but I think that's actually part of your secret. You're mere mortals, and mortals are something the rest of us can understand."

"I think perhaps you give us too much credit," he said soberly. "Or perhaps I should say you give other people too *little* credit. No one can drive an entire kingdom into standing up in defiance of something like the Group of Four. That comes from within; it can't be imposed from with*out*. You know that as well as I do—it's the reason you've been able to rule Chisholm so effectively, despite the fact that your nobility obviously remembered the example of Queen Ysbell. It's the reason you were able to come here in acceptance of my proposal without seeing Chisholm go up in a flame of rebellion behind you. Your people understand as well as mine do, and that's the true reason why, in the end, we *will* win, Sharleyan."

"I think you're right," she told him, reaching out to touch the side of his face for the first time. Her fingers rested lightly against his cheekbone, against the strong line of his jaw, and she looked into his eyes.

"I think you're right," she repeated, "and that alone would make this marriage the right thing for me to do. It doesn't matter how I feel, what I want. What matters is my responsibility to Chisholm, and that responsibility is to see my people free of the Group of Four's yoke."

"And is that the only thing that matters?" he asked softly.

"Oh, no," she said. "Not the *only* thing."

He gazed down into her face for several endless seconds, and then, slowly, he smiled.

"I have to admit I hoped you'd say that," he murmured.

"Isn't this the place, in all of those sappy romances, where the hero is supposed to press a burning kiss upon the chaste maiden and sweep her off her feet in steel-strong arms?" she asked him with a lurking smile of her own.

"I see we both wasted our time when we were younger reading the same frivolous entertainment," he observed. "Fortunately, I'm sure we're both also wiser now, with better judgment and a greater grasp of reality than we had then."

"Oh, I'm sure we are," she said with a soft little chuckle.

"That's what I thought, too," he assured her, and then his lips met hers at last.

.XII.
A Palace Ballroom,
Tellesberg Palace,
City of Tellesberg,
Kingdom of Charis

Ehdwyrd Howsmyn and Ahlvyno Pawalsyn stood beside the punch bowl and watched the colorful crowd.

The two men were old friends, and one of their favorite entertainments at formal balls and parties was to count noses and see who managed to turn up fashionably later than anyone else. Howsmyn's wealth and Pawalsyn's title as Baron Ironhill—and his position as Keeper of the Purse—virtually guaranteed that both of them would be invited to any social gathering. Neither of them were particularly fond of such affairs, especially Howsmyn, but neither of them was foolish enough to think he could have gotten away with avoiding them, either. So they tended to gravitate toward a quiet corner somewhere, sometimes accompanied by a handful of their closer personal friends, and observe the plumage displays of the wealthy, the powerful, and—above all—the foolish.

"Now *there's* a gown," Howsmyn murmured, twitching his head unobtrusively in the direction of a matron of middle years who had just sailed majestically into the palace ballroom with what looked like half a dozen marriageable-age daughters bobbing along in her wake. The confection she was wearing must have cost at least enough to feed a family of five for half a year. As such, it was ample evidence of her wealth; unfortunately, it was also ample evidence of her taste.

"Well," Ironhill observed philosophically, "it may hurt your eyes, but at least Rhaiyan must have collected a pretty pile of marks from her to pay for it. And," he grinned, "speaking as the Crown's tax collector, I'm delighted to see him doing so well!"

"You really shouldn't remind me on social occasions that you're the enemy," Howsmyn replied.

"Me?" Ironhill said with artful innocence.

"Unless it was someone else who just set the new wharf taxes. Oh, and the warehouse inventory duties, too, while I'm thinking about it."

"But, Ehdwyrd, you're the one who told *me* that the Kingdom's merchants and manufacturers ought to be willing to pay a little more in order to finance the Navy."

"Obviously, that represented a moment of temporary insanity on my part," Howsmyn shot back with a chuckle. "Now that I've regained my senses, I've become aware of that hand slipping into my purse again. You know—the one with your rings on it."

"Ah, but I do it so smoothly you'll hardly even notice the pain. I promise."

Howsmyn chuckled again, then turned to survey the ballroom once more.

If pressed, he would have been forced to admit that he found this evening's gala less of a burden than most. His wife had been delighted when the invitations had been delivered, and this time he hadn't even tried to convince her she should go and have a good time while he stayed home with a book. Or perhaps arranged an emergency visit to the dentist, or something else equally enjoyable. Zhain Howsmyn was the daughter of an earl, whereas Howsmyn had been born a commoner and still hadn't gotten around to acquiring the patent of nobility which his wealth undoubtedly deserved. For the most part, Zhain had absolutely no objection to being plain "Madame Howsmyn," rather than "Lady Whatever," but she did have a much more highly developed sense of the social dynamics of Tellesberg and the kingdom as a whole.

Howsmyn was very well aware of just how great an asset his wife was. Not only did they love one another deeply, but she refused to allow him to retreat into the social hermitage which, in many ways, would have suited him far better. Whether he wanted to go to affairs like tonight's or not, he truly couldn't justify avoiding them entirely. A man of his wealth had no choice about that, but Zhain generally saw to it that he attended the ones he had to and gracefully avoided every single one that he could.

No one on the invitation list could have avoided tonight's formal ball, however. Not when it was being hosted by Queen Sharleyan of Chisholm in a ballroom she'd borrowed from her affianced husband.

Howsmyn gazed across the room to the thick cluster of exquisitely attired, lavishly bejeweled courtiers gathered around King Cayleb and his bride-to-be and felt a stab of sympathy as he watched Cayleb smiling, acknowledging greetings, and chatting away as if he were genuinely enjoying himself.

And he may well be, actually, Howsmyn thought, noting how close to Sharleyan's side Cayleb seemed to be glued. Obviously, no man with any sense was going to just wander off and leave his fiancée standing alone and forlorn at her own party. Cayleb, on the other hand, hadn't even allowed anyone else a dance with her yet. For that matter, Howsmyn rather doubted that anyone could have fitted a hand between the two of them. And, judging from Sharleyan's expression and body language, she was perfectly happy with that state of affairs.

"I think this is going to work out even better than I'd hoped," Ironhill said very quietly, and Howsmyn glanced back at his taller friend.

"I assume you're referring to the unfortunate twosome at the bottom of that feeding swarm of krakens?" he said dryly.

"They do seem to be feeding a bit more aggressively than usual tonight," Ironhill acknowledged. "Hard to blame them, really, I suppose."

"Oh, on the contrary, I find it very *easy* to blame them." Howsmyn grimaced. "Have you ever noticed how it's the most useless people who fight hardest to corner the guest of honor at something like this?"

"I don't know if that's quite fair," Ironhill said, his eyebrows rising at the unusual asperity of Howsmyn's tone. The ironmaster had never had a very high opinion of "court drones," as he was wont to call them, but he normally regarded them with a sort of amused toleration. Tonight, he sounded genuinely disgusted. "Very few of those people have the sort of access to the King that you and I enjoy, Ehdwyrd," he pointed out. "Social occasions like this one are the only real opportunity they have to get the Crown's attention."

"Oh, I know that." Howsmyn's left hand chopped at the air in a gesture which mingled acceptance of Ironhill's point with impatience. "And I also know that everyone wants to get as close to the Queen as he can, and why. I'm even aware that it's not all simply because people are looking for advantages and opportunities. But still. . . ."

He shrugged irritably, his mood obviously darkening, and Ironhill frowned.

"I've known you a long time, Ehdwyrd," he said. "Would you like to tell me exactly why you've got a spider rat up your leg tonight?"

Howsmyn looked at him again, and then, as if against his will, laughed.

"You have known me a long time, haven't you?"

"I believe I just made that same observation myself," Ironhill said with a patient air. "And you still haven't answered my question."

"It's just—"

Howsmyn broke off for a moment, then sighed heavily.

"It's just that I'm beginning to find myself in agreement with Bynzhamyn where the Temple Loyalists are concerned."

"What?" Ironhill didn't quite blink, despite the apparent non sequitur. "And what, pray tell, brought *that* on just now?"

"They've burned down the Royal College, they've attempted to murder the Archbishop in his own cathedral, and they're tacking printed broadsides denouncing the 'schismatics' and calling on 'all loyal sons of the true Church' to resist by any means necessary on walls all over the city," Howsmyn replied, his voice harsh. "I'd say that was more than sufficient reason, personally. I understand that the King and the Archbishop are leaning over backwards to avoid outright repression, but I think they may be taking it too far."

"I don't know that I disagree with you," Ironhill said. "I see the King's point, on the other hand, and I think he's entirely right when he says we can't afford to tar every single person who opposes the schism with the same brush. If we do that, we'll only succeed in driving the law-abiding members of the Temple Loyalists into the arms of the sort of people who like to play with knives, or throw lit lamps through windows. None of which gives me a clue as to why you're bringing that up at this particular moment. Did you eat something for supper that disagreed with you, Ehdwyrd?"

"What?" Howsmyn looked at him sharply, then snorted in amusement. "No, of course not."

"That's good. I was afraid it might be bellyache talking, and I was considering calling a healer to induce vomiting."

"You can be a rather crude fellow at such a highbrow gathering, can't you?" Howsmyn chuckled.

"One of the advantages of being born into the nobility, even if I am only a baron. Now, are you going to explain just what all of these cryptic utterances of yours are *really* about?"

"I guess it's just the guest list." Howsmyn shrugged. "I know there are rules about who has to be invited to something like this, but, damn it, Ahlvyno, it's time we drew a line and told the Temple Loyalists and their sympathizers that they aren't welcome guests here in the Palace anymore."

Ironhill felt his eyebrows arching again and turned to consider the crowd around the king and queen more closely. He could see several members of the nobility who'd expressed at least some reservations about the Church of Charis, but none of them had been particularly vociferous about it. For that matter, almost none of the Charisian nobility had opposed King Cayleb's and Archbishop Maikel's decisions. Not openly, at least.

"Who are you talking about, Ehdwyrd?" he asked quietly after a moment.

"What?" From Howsmyn's expression, Ironhill's question had taken him completely by surprise.

"Obviously someone over there near the King has you seriously worried, or at least pissed off. Who is it?"

"You're joking . . . aren't you?"

"No, I'm not. Who are you so worried about?"

"Well, I don't know that I'd say I was *worried* about him," Howsmyn said a bit more slowly. "Pissed off, now—that would sum it up quite nicely."

Ironhill gave him an exasperated look, and he shrugged just a bit sheepishly.

"Sorry. And in answer to your question, the person I'm pissed off at is Traivyr Kairee."

Understanding dawned in Ironhill's eyes, and he shook his head.

"Ehdwyrd, I know you and Rhaiyan both hate Kairee. For that matter, I'm not too fond of him myself. But he *is* one of the dozen or so wealthiest men in the Kingdom. Not up to your weight, perhaps, or to Rhaiyan's, but, then, you two tend to be in a class by yourselves. He's certainly wealthy enough to put him on that 'have-to-invite' list of yours, though. And he's connected by marriage to something like a quarter of the peerage, as well."

"He's a moneygrubbing bastard," Howsmyn said flatly. "He doesn't give a solitary damn about the men and women working for him, and his idea of trade is to produce his product as cheaply and as poorly as he can get away with and sell it for the most he can squeeze out of his customers. I wouldn't trust him to look after my dog for me while I was out of town for an afternoon."

Ironhill's eyebrows went up yet again at the cold, bitter loathing in Howsmyn's voice. He'd known about the bad blood between Traivyr Kairee and Ehdwyrd Howsmyn for years, of course. Everyone in Tellesberg knew about that. But this was a new level of hostility, and it worried him.

"What's brought this on just now?" he asked, turning to look back at the crowd around the king and queen.

Kairee seemed to be keeping his distance from the royal pair, the baron noticed. He was part of the crowd clustered around them, but he'd settled for the outer fringes of that crowd, where he stood in conversation with a handful of others. Several other wealthy Tellesberg businessmen were clustered around him, and they'd done their best to shanghai several of the more senior Chisholmians who'd accompanied Sharleyan to Charis. From the look of them they were busy trying to impress the visitors with what desirable avenues of investment *their* businesses represented. One or two of the Chisholmians, including the queen's uncle, looked as if they would vastly have preferred being somewhere else, but good manners precluded them from simply brushing the Charisians off.

"I suppose most of it's coming from the 'accident' in his manufactory this morning," Howsmyn conceded.

"What sort of accident?" Ironhill turned back to his friend, and Howsmyn's lips twisted in disgust.

"The sort of accident someone like him attracts like a lodestone draws iron filings. He doesn't train his people properly, he doesn't worry about the dangers of the machinery around them, and he *prefers* 'hiring' children because he can get them so much more cheaply. And he managed to get three of them killed today. A pair of brothers—ten and eleven, if you please—and their fourteen-year-old cousin who tried to get them out of the shafting."

"I hadn't heard about that," Ironhill said quietly.

"And the odds are that you wouldn't have, if you and I weren't having this conversation," Howsmyn replied bitterly. "After all, he's scarcely the only one who uses children, now is he? That's exactly why Rhaiyan and I fought so hard to get the laws against hiring children through the Council. And why we were both so unhappy about delaying their effective date to provide an '*adjustment* period.'"

Howsmyn looked as if he were tempted to spit on the polished marble floor, and Ironhill sighed.

"I understand, and I was on your side, if you'll recall. But there truly was some point to the argument that yanking everyone under the age of fifteen out of the manufactories is going to cause a lot of dislocation. And whether you like it or not, Ehdwyrd, it's also true that a lot of households who depend in full or in part on the wages their children bring home are going to get hurt along the way."

"I didn't say it would be easy, and neither Rhaiyan nor I ever argued that it would be painless. But it *needs* to be done, and Kairee is a prime example of why. Look at him—just look! Do you see a single shadow of concern on his face? And do you think for a moment that he's prepared to pay any sort of pension to those three youngsters' families for their deaths? Why should he? Until the child labor laws go into effect, there'll always be more where *they* came from."

The cold, bitter hatred in Howsmyn's voice was stronger than poison, and Ironhill shifted a bit uncomfortably. He couldn't dispute anything Howsmyn had just said. For that matter, he agreed with Howsmyn's position in general, although he sometimes thought his friend might take it to something of an extreme, trying to move too far too quickly. And there were those in the Charisian business community who took a considerably more jaundiced view of Howsmyn's and Rhaiyan Mychail's crusade to improve working conditions in their manufactories than Ironhill did. "Bleeding heart" was one of the terms bandied about from time to time, and many a businessman had been heard to mutter about the disastrous effect the policies they advocated would inevitably have on the kingdom's economy.

Which, given the fact that Ehdwyrd and Rhaiyan routinely show the greatest returns on their enterprises of anyone in Charis, is particularly stupid of them, the baron conceded to himself. *Still. . . .*

"I didn't know about the accident," he said again, quietly. "I can see exactly why that would make you angry. For that matter, it makes *me* pretty damned angry, now that I know. But how does that tie in with the Temple Loyalists?"

"You really ought to sit down and discuss that with Bynzhamyn Raice," Howsmyn told him. "I'm sure that by now Bynzhamyn must have quite a dossier on our good friend Traivyr."

"Why?" Ironhill's eyes narrowed.

"Because the same bastard who couldn't care less about workers getting themselves killed in his manufactories is outraged by the very notion of our 'godless apostasy' in daring to tell the Group of Four that we're disinclined to let them burn our homes over our heads. It turns out that we've damned every soul in Charis to an eternity with Shan-wei in Hell, to hear him tell it. Amazing how much more concerned he is over his workers' souls than over their physical well-being. Do you suppose that has anything to do with the fact that he's not going to have to pick up the ticket for their admission to Heaven?"

The bite in Howsmyn's voice could have peeled paint off a wall, and Ironhill frowned. Traivyr Kairee had always been very much a part of the religious establishment. Given his normal business practices and the way he treated his employees, however, Ironhill had always assumed his attachment to the Church stemmed from the amount of business and patronage it controlled rather than from any genuine sense of piety.

"Just how openly has he been expressing his views?" the Keeper of the Purse asked.

"Not quite as openly as he was," Howsmyn acknowledged. "Right after Cayleb arrested Ahdymsyn and named Maikel Archbishop, he was a lot more vociferous. Since then, he's pulled back a notch or two, especially since the assassination attempt. I don't think he's talking about it very much in *public* at all, anymore. Unfortunately, I can't quite avoid moving in the same circles he does—not entirely—and people who know both of us tend to talk. Believe me, he hasn't changed his position, Ahlvyno. He's just been cautious enough to go at least a little underground with it. I doubt he's fooling Bynzhamyn's investigators into thinking he's changed his mind, but just look at him smiling and nodding over there. I don't like the thought of letting someone with his sympathies into stabbing range of the King."

"I doubt he's prepared to take it quite *that* far," Ironhill said slowly. "If nothing else, it would take more guts than *I've* ever seen him display."

"Maybe not. But what he *would* damned well do is to run and tell his fellow Temple Loyalists anything he manages to pick up at Court—or anywhere else, for that matter."

"Now that, I *could* see him doing," Ironhill admitted. He frowned across the ballroom at Kairee for several more seconds, then grimaced.

"Before it slips my mind, Ehdwyrd, let me thank you for how thoroughly you've destroyed my limited enjoyment of the evening."

"Think nothing of it," Howsmyn said solemnly. "After all, that's what friends are for."

"And don't think I won't find a way to return the favor," Ironhill warned him. "On the other hand," he continued more gravely, "you've given me quite a bit to think about. Kairee is bidding on several of the Crown's current contracts. In fact, unless I'm mistaken, he's probably the low bidder on at least two of them . . . including one for five thousand of the new rifles. Under the circumstances, I think it might behoove me to consider whether or not I want someone with his attitude that deep inside what we're doing."

"I think it might, indeed," Howsmyn agreed.

"I don't know how the King is going to react to the notion," Ironhill warned him. "He's serious about this not penalizing anyone over matters of conscience as long as they haven't violated any laws."

"Ahlvyno, I respect Cayleb deeply. More than that, I'm ready to follow him anywhere he leads. But he's still a very young man, in very many ways. I understand his logic in refusing to adopt repressive measures, and I understand Maikel's position on the consciences of individuals. That doesn't mean I think they're right. Or it might be better to say I don't think they're *entirely* right. At some point, they're going to have to start making some precautionary decisions based on what amounts to suspicion. I'm not talking about arrests, or arbitrary imprisonments, and God knows I'm not talking about executions. But they've *got* to start protecting themselves against others like Kairee.

"I'll be the first to admit that the intensity of my . . . dislike for him is driving my suspicions where he's concerned, to some extent, at least. And, like you, I don't think he's got the courage to risk dying for his beliefs. But there could be others who do have the courage . . . and who do a better job of hiding just how much they disagree with what we're doing here in Charis. Those are the ones that worry me, Ahlvyno."

Ehdwyrd Howsmyn looked into his friend's eyes and shook his head, his eyes dark.

"Those are the ones that worry me," he repeated.

.XIII.
City of Ferayd,
Ferayd Sound,
Kingdom of Delferahk

How may I help you, My Lord Bishop?" Sir Vyk Lakyr asked courteously as Bishop Ernyst Jynkyns was shown into his office near the Ferayd waterfront. Father Styvyn Graivyr, Bishop Ernyst's intendant, followed
on the bishop's heels, somber in the green cassock of an upper-priest bearing
the sword and flame badge of the Order of Schueler.

Lakyr felt more than a little uneasy over what might have brought Jynkyns
to see *him*. He was neither the mayor of Ferayd, nor the governor of the district in which the port city lay, with either of whom the Bishop of Ferayd normally might be expected to have business. What he *was*, was the senior officer
of Ferayd's military garrison, which, given events elsewhere in the world of
late, helped to explain his uneasiness.

"I've already visited the Mayor, Sir Vyk," Jynkyns said. Lakyr's anxiety
clicked up another few notches, although he kept his expression merely politely attentive. "I'm sure you'll be hearing from him—and quite probably
from the Governor, as well—shortly. Since, however, this matter directly
concerns Mother Church, I thought it would be best if I came and discussed
it with you in person, as well."

"I see," Lakyr said. Then he paused and shook his head. "Actually, My
Lord, I *don't* see. Not yet, at least."

"That's honest, at any rate, Sir Vyk." Jynkyns smiled. It was a brief smile,
and his face quickly sobered once again.

"In point of fact, Sir Vyk," he said, "I'm here on the direct instructions of
Chancellor Trynair and Grand Inquisitor Clyntahn."

Lakyr felt his facial muscles congeal, but he simply nodded.

"The Office of Inquisition, and the Council of Vicars, have determined
that the pernicious doctrines, misrepresentations, blasphemies, and lies being
spread by the apostate heretics of Charis are even more poisonous and corrupting to all of God's people than was at first believed," Jynkyns said. Something in
the bishop's tone sounded to Lakyr like a man who wasn't in complete agreement with what he was required to say, but the prelate went on unflinchingly.

"Because of the corrosiveness of the blasphemous teachings of the so-
called 'Church of Charis,' the Grand Inquisitor has determined that it is in-
cumbent upon him to limit their spread by any means possible. And, since it
has been well established that the merchant ships of the Kingdom of Charis

carry its heretical teachings with them wherever they may go, as witness the copies of the apostate Staynair's falsehood-riddled 'letter' to His Holiness which have been so broadly distributed, Grand Inquisitor Clyntahn has resolved to close all ports of all God-fearing realms against their entry and the seduction of their lies. Accordingly, you are to take steps to close Ferayd to them in future . . . and to seize and intern any Charisian-flag vessels currently in the port. According to my own dispatches, the King is in agreement with the Chancellor and the Grand Inquisitor in this matter. Mother Church has made the semaphore available to him, and I believe you will be receiving confirmation of these instructions from him shortly."

Lakyr felt as if someone had just punched him unexpectedly. For a moment, he could only stare at Jynkyns, unable to immediately comprehend what the bishop had said. Then his brain started working again, and he wondered why he'd felt surprised.

Because this is going to effectively destroy Ferayd's economy, that's why, a stubborn voice said in the back of his brain. The city had grown wealthy and powerful because it was the major port of the Kingdom of Delferahk . . . and because its relative proximity to Charis made it a natural transshipment point for cargoes from and to ports all over the west coast of Howard, as well. *It's like spanking a baby with an ax!*

"If those are my orders from King Zhames and from Mother Church, My Lord Bishop," he said, "I will, of course, carry them out to the best of my ability. However, I feel I should point out that there are at least twenty-five Charisian-flag vessels in the harbor at this very moment. For that matter, there are probably more than that; I haven't checked with the harbormaster lately, but there have been more of them even than usual since . . . ah, since that business in Darcos Sound." He cleared his throat a bit nervously, then continued. "Not only that, but at least half of them are lying to anchor, waiting for dockside berths, not tied up alongside one of the wharves. That's going to make them rather difficult to seize if they realize what's happening and try to make sail."

"You'll have the assistance of several galleys," Father Styvyn said rather abruptly. A flicker of annoyance flashed across Jynkyns' face and his lips pressed firmly together for perhaps a single heartbeat, but he didn't rebuke Graivyr for inserting himself into the conversation.

Of course he didn't, Lakyr thought. *Graivyr's not exactly noted for his humility and easygoing temperament at the best of times. God only knows what he's likely to report to the Temple if he decides someone—even the Bishop—is obstructing the Grand Inquisitor's decrees. Which is a point I'd better bear in mind, as well.*

"That will undoubtedly help a great deal, Father," he said aloud. "It's still going to be tricky, though. We'll do the best we can, I assure you, but it's entirely possible that at least a few of them will evade us."

"Then sink them if they try," Graivyr said coldly.

"Sink them if there's no other way to stop them," Jynkyns corrected quietly. The look Graivyr gave him was not the sort Lakyr was accustomed to seeing a mere upper-priest give a bishop, but Jynkyns met it levelly.

"Of course that's what I meant, My Lord," the intendant said after a brief hesitation.

"Ah, that might be more easily said than done, I'm afraid, Father," Lakyr said delicately. Both clerics turned back to him, and he shrugged. "At the moment, none of the island batteries are manned. I have skeleton gun crews for the waterfront batteries, but not for the outer batteries. If they get out of the harbor proper, they'll have a free run through any of the main channels."

"Then *get* them manned." Graivyr sounded as if he thought he were speaking to an idiot, and Lakyr felt his jaw muscles tighten.

"It's not that simple, Father," he said, trying very hard to keep any emotion out of his voice. "I don't *have* the gunners for those batteries. We don't normally keep them manned during times of peace, you know."

Which, he carefully did *not* say aloud, *is because they're over a hundred frigging miles from the city, you . . . uninformed soul.*

The large islands between Ferayd Sound and the Southern Ocean, and the extensive shoals around them, helped shelter the huge bay from the often fractious weather off the southern tip of Howard. The islands also offered handy places to put batteries to cover the shipping channels, but manning fortifications like those was expensive . . . and Zhames II of Delferahk had a well-deserved reputation for pinching marks until they squealed. Aside from what were little more than bare minimum caretaker detachments, the island batteries were never manned in peacetime.

"It would take several days at a minimum—more probably the better part of two or three five-days, to be honest, even if you permitted me the use of Mother Church's semaphore—for me to request the necessary gun crews, get them here, and then get them transported all the way out to the islands," he continued in that same painfully neutral tone. "My impression was that you intend for me to close the port to Charis promptly. If that is, indeed, the case, there won't be sufficient time to get the gunners we need to man the channel forts."

"I see." Graivyr looked as if he wanted to find fault with Lakyr's explanation and felt nothing but irritation when he couldn't.

"You're correct about how quickly we need this done, Sir Vyk," Jynkyns said. "And"—he glanced at Graivyr—"all God can ask of any man is that he do the best he can within the capabilities he has. I feel confident that you, as always, will do just that."

"Thank you, Bishop." Lakyr gave him a slight but heartfelt bow.

"In that case, we'll leave you to begin making your preparations," the bishop said. "Come, Styvyn."

Graivyr looked briefly rebellious. Because, Lakyr realized, the intendant wanted to take personal command of the entire operation. Since he couldn't do that, the next best thing would have been to spend several hours telling Lakyr how *he* should go about doing it.

And wouldn't that result in a fine mess, Lakyr thought sardonically from behind the careful shield of his eyes. *Not that it isn't likely to wind up as exactly that, anyway. And just how do Clyntahn and the Chancellor expect Charis and King Cayleb to react to all this?*

He had no answer for his own question . . . yet.

▼   ▼   ▼

Edmynd Walkyr, master after God of the galleon *Wave* (when his wife wasn't on deck, at least), stood by the galleon's after rail and worried.

That was where he always did his worrying, by and large. And he preferred to do it after sunset, as well, when none of his crew could see his expression and be infected by his worries. And, of course, when Lyzbet couldn't see him and offer to clout him on the ear as her own, thankfully unique antidote for anxiety.

Not that she really would . . . in front of the crew, at least.

I think.

His lips twitched at the thought, but his amusement was brief, and he quickly returned to his worrying as he gazed across the dark harbor's waters at the dim lights of the Ferayd waterfront.

I don't care what she says, he told himself firmly. *Next voyage, Lyzbet's staying home. And so is Greyghor.*

He didn't expect that to be an easy decision to enforce. Like at least a third, and more probably half, of the total Charisian merchant fleet, *Wave* and her sister ship *Wind* were family-owned. Edmynd and his brother Zhorj were the master and first officer, respectively, of *Wave*, and Edmynd's brother-in-law, Lywys, and Edmynd's youngest brother, Mychail, held the same positions aboard *Wind*. Family members usually formed the nucleus of the crews aboard such vessels, and Edmynd's wife, Lyzbet, acted as *Wave*'s purser. There were sound reasons for that arrangement, and under normal circumstances, when all a man had to worry about was wind, weather, shipwreck, and drowning, it didn't especially disturb Edmynd's sleep.

But circumstances weren't normal. Not remotely normal.

He leaned both hands on the rail, fingers drumming while he frowned. Ever since the Group of Four's unprovoked onslaught upon Charis, tensions had run incredibly high. Well, of course they had! When the Grand Inquisitor himself connived at the destruction of an entire kingdom, merchant ships *from* that kingdom could expect to find themselves in what might charitably be called "an uncomfortable position."

Still, things hadn't seemed all that unsettled on the first voyage Edmynd had made after the Battle of Darcos Sound. He'd left Lyzbet home for that one—not without a battle of wills which had left him longing for something as peaceful as a hurricane—but he'd experienced no problems, really. The Tellesberg-Ferayd circuit was *Wave*'s usual run, and the factors and merchants with whom he normally dealt here in the Kingdom of Delferahk had seemed relieved to see him again. Given the quantity of goods which had built up in Ferayd's warehouses, awaiting transshipment, not to mention all the merchants who'd been waiting for consignments from Charis which had been delayed by the war, that probably shouldn't have been as surprising—or as big a relief—as it had been.

Unfortunately, it had also suggested (as Lyzbet had predictably pointed out) that there was no reason she shouldn't come along on the next voyage. Which she and their oldest son, Greyghor, had. And he wished to Heaven that he'd left both of them home again.

It's that letter of the Archbishop's, he thought unhappily. *I can't disagree with anything he said, but that's what it is.*

The last time he'd been here, that letter had been in transit. Now it had arrived, and the Church's reaction had been . . . unfavorable. The fact that, as far as Edmynd could tell, every mainland port had been flooded with thousands of printed copies of the same letter hadn't helped matters, either. Before, everyone had wanted to pretend it was still business as usual, that the attack on Charis really had been made by her purely secular enemies—and, of course, by the equally secular "Knights of the Temple Lands." Now that Archbishop Maikel's challenge had been so publically thrown down, that was impossible. Worse, what had really happened had been wildly distorted in the Church's accounts . . . with the predictable result that many people were prepared to assume it was *Charis* who had lied.

Most of Ferayd's merchants were still eager to see Charisian galleons and Charisian goods, but they weren't that eager to see *Charisians*. Or, rather, they weren't eager to be *seen* seeing Charisians. No doubt much of that was because associating with someone who'd been designated as an enemy of the Church carried with it the active threat of official displeasure. But there was also an undertone, a virulent hostility which had nothing to do with officialdom, bubbling away beneath the surface.

There was always an element, in any harbor city, which resented the wealth and strength of the seemingly omnipresent Charisian merchant marine. Local shipowners who resented the Charisians for taking "their" legitimate cargoes. Local seamen who blamed Charis for their frequent bouts of unemployment. Local artisans who resented the flood of Charisian goods that undercut the prices they could charge. Even local shipbuilders who resented the fact that everyone "knew" Charisian-built ships were the best in the world . . . and went ship-shopping accordingly. There was always *someone*, and now those someones had the added "justification" (not that they'd really needed any additional reasons, as far as Walkyr had ever been able to see) that obviously *all* Charisians were heretics out to destroy Mother Church.

There'd been some ugly incidents in the waterfront taverns, and one party of Charisian seamen had been set upon in an alley and severely beaten. The city guard hadn't exactly worn itself to the bone trying to figure out who'd been responsible for the attacks, either. By now, by unspoken agreement, the masters of the Charisian ships crowding Ferayd's harbor and waiting their turns at wharfside were keeping their men aboard ship at night, rather than allowing them their customary runs ashore. Many of them—like Walkyr himself—had made quiet preparations against possible riots down here on the waterfront, as well, although he hoped it would never come to that. On the other hand, he wasn't at all certain it wouldn't . . . and it said a great deal about just how tense things were that the crews weren't even complaining about their captains' restrictions.

No, he told himself firmly. *When I get Lyzbet and Greyghor home again, they're damned well staying there. Lyzbet can throw all the tantrums—and pots—she wants, but I'm not going to see her hurt—or worse—if this situation gets any further out of hand.*

His mind flinched away from the thought of anything happening to her, and he drew a deep breath, then looked up at the moonless sky with a sense of decisiveness.

Of course, he told himself, *there's no great need for me to rush into telling her about my decision before we get back to Tellesberg, now is there?*

▼   ▼   ▼

"All right," Sergeant Allayn Dekyn growled, "does anybody have any last-minute questions?"

No one did, predictably. Which, Dekyn thought, equally predictably guaranteed that some damnfool idiot *didn't* understand something he damned well ought to have asked about. It was always that way; every sergeant knew that.

Even without all of the extra things waiting to go wrong tonight.

Dekyn grimaced and turned to look down the length of the poorly lit pier from his position in the ink-black lee of a stack of crates. Personally, he thought this entire operation was about as stupid as they came. Which was *not* a thought he intended to express aloud to anyone. Especially not anywhere some overzealous pain-in-the-arse could go running to the Inquisition.

Allayn Dekyn was as loyal a son of Mother Church as anyone. That didn't mean he was deaf, dumb, or stupid, though. He was more than willing to agree the Charisians had gone much too far in openly defying the Council of Vicars' authority, and even the authority of the Grand Vicar himself. Of course they had! But still. . . .

The sergeant's grimace deepened. Whether they'd gone too far or not, he couldn't pretend he didn't understand a lot of what had driven them. For that matter, he sympathized with their complaints, and even with their explicit charges of corruption against the Church's hierarchy. But however much *he* might have sympathized with Charis, the Inquisition obviously did *not*, and he felt glumly certain that the reason for tonight's activities owed far more to the Inquisition's desire to teach the heretics a lesson than it did to anything else remotely rational. And its timing probably owed more to the Inquisition's impatience than it did to any sort of actual planning. The middle of a pitch-black night wasn't the best time Dekyn could have thought of to be putting armed men, many of whom had no experience at all down here on the water-front, aboard totally unfamiliar ships on less than one day's notice.

Well, that's probably not entirely fair, he told himself. *If we're supposed to take over the ships out in the anchorage, too, we need the cover of darkness, I guess. And at least they assigned us arbalests instead of matchlocks, so we won't stand out in the dark like a flock of damned blink-lizards! But Langhorne knows there's a Shan-wei of a lot of things that can go wrong trying to do this all in the middle of the night! And I might not be a sailor, but it occurs even to me that doing this when the tide is going* out *isn't exactly brilliant, either.*

He shook his head, then gave his platoon one more glower—more out of habit than for any other reason—and waited as patiently as possible for Captain Kairmyn's signal.

▼   ▼   ▼

Had Sergeant Dekyn only known it, he was scarcely the only Delferahkan who cherished reservations about the upcoming operation's timing and his own part in it. Captain Hauwyrd Mahkneel, of the galley *Arrowhead,* agreed with him completely about that much, at least.

Mahkneel's ship had been detailed to cover the main shipping channel out of Ferayd Sound. It would have been nice if they'd been able to find another ship to support *Arrowhead,* especially if they wanted to do this on a moonless night while the tide was going out. The channel between Flying Fish Shoals and Spider Crab Shoal began almost a hundred miles from the waterfront itself, and it was over twelve miles wide. Expecting a single galley to guard that much water against the flight of any of the Charisian merchant ships in the harbor went beyond ridiculous to outright stupid, in his considered opinion.

Not that anyone had been particularly interested in asking his opinion, of course.

He stood atop the galley's aftercastle, looking up at the heavens. At least the timing meant that any fleeing galleons wouldn't reach his own position until after dawn, so he ought to have light to spot them. Assuming the weather cooperated. The stars were clear enough . . . for now, but he didn't much like the way that growing bank of clouds was blotting out the starscape to the north as the wind carried the overcast steadily southward.

And that was another thing, he groused to himself. Not only had the people who'd planned this overlooked the interesting little fact that any fugitives were going to catch the ebb tide at *both* ends, but the wind wasn't likely to cooperate, either. The sound was just past high water, which, given the thirteen-and-a-half-hour tidal cycle and the probable speed of any fleeing galleons under the current wind conditions, meant the tide would be ebbing *again*, setting strongly through the channels to the open sea, by the time any fugitives got this far south. That, along with the fact that the wind was almost straight out of the north-northwest, would favor any galleon making for the main channel or for the East Pass, between East Island and Breakheart Head, as well. And with wind and tide both in its favor, even something as fundamentally clumsy as a galleon—and Charisian galleons, at least a third of which seemed to have the new sail plans, were far less clumsy than most—might well elude even a well-handled galley.

At which point none of Mahkneel's superiors would particularly care how well-handled *Arrowhead* might have been. Or about the fact that Mahkneel had been required to give up over half his hundred and fifty Marines and a quarter of his three hundred oarsmen for the boarding parties Sir Vyk Lakyr had required. It was tempting to blame Lakyr for that, but Mahkneel knew the garrison commander hadn't had any more choice about his orders than Mahkneel himself did if he was going to scare up the necessary personnel and boats.

And when you come right down to it, it's past time someone *did something about these damned heretics and their lies*, Mahkneel thought grimly. *This may not be the smartest possible way to go about it, but at least someone's finally* doing *something!*

"All hands will be ready to man their stations an hour before first light, Sir," a voice said, and Mahkneel turned away from the rail as Rahnyld Gahrmyn, *Arrowhead*'s first officer, appeared beside him.

"I notice you didn't say all stations will be fully manned and ready, like a good first lieutenant should, Master Gahrmyn," Mahkneel observed with a tart smile.

"Well, no, Sir," Gahrmyn admitted. "First lieutenants are supposed to be truthful, after all. And given how thin we're stretched, I thought that probably would have been something of an exaggeration."

"Oh, you did, did you?" Mahkneel chuckled sourly. "An 'exaggeration,' hey?"

Gahrmyn had been with him for almost two years now. The captain had cherished a few doubts about the lieutenant initially. After all, Mahkneel was a sailor of the old school, and he'd been more than a little leery of an officer who spent his off-duty time reading and even *writing* poetry. But over the months they'd served together, Gahrmyn had amply demonstrated that however peculiar his taste in off-duty recreation might be, he was as sound and reliable an officer as Mahkneel had ever known.

"Well, 'exaggeration' sounds better than calling it an outright lie, doesn't it, Sir?"

"Maybe." Mahkneel's smile faded. "Whatever you call it, though, it's a damned pain in the arse."

"I don't believe anyone's likely to disagree with you about that, Sir. *I'm* not, anyway."

"I wish they'd been able to find at least one other galley to help us cover the channel," Mahkneel complained for what was—by his own count—at least the twentieth time.

"If they'd given us another few days, they probably could have," Gahrmyn pointed out.

"I know. I know!" Mahkneel glowered back in the general direction of the city . . . and of the oncoming clouds. "I don't like the smell of the wind, either," he complained. "There's rain behind those clouds, Rahnyld. You mark my words."

Gahrmyn only nodded. Mahkneel's feel for weather changes was remarkable.

"While I'd never want to appear to be criticizing our esteemed superiors, Sir," he said instead, after a moment, "I must say I'm not certain this is the wisest way to go about this."

"Wallowing around all by ourselves in the dark like a drunk, blind whore at a formal ball?" Mahkneel cracked a hard laugh. "What could be unwise about *that*?"

"I wasn't just referring to the timing, Sir," Gahrmyn said.

"No?" Mahkneel turned back around to look at him in the faint backwash from the port running light. "What do you mean, then?"

"It's just. . . ." Gahrmyn looked away from his captain, gazing out into the darkness. "It's just that I have to wonder if closing our ports is the best way to deal with the situation, Sir."

"It's not going to be pleasant for Ferayd, I'll grant you that," Mahkneel replied. "It's going to be even less pleasant for those damned heretics, though!"

The captain couldn't see Gahrmyn's expression as the lieutenant looked away from him, and perhaps that was as well. Gahrmyn paused for a few seconds, considering his next words carefully, then turned back towards Mahkneel.

"I'm sure it is going to be painful for Charis, Sir. As you've said, though, it's also going to be painful for Ferayd. And this isn't the only port where that's going to be true. I'm afraid that *ordering* the ports closed is going to be a lot easier than *keeping* them closed once the trade really starts drying up."

"You may have a point," Mahkneel acknowledged. "But if that happens, it's going to be up to us and the rest of the Navy to see to it that anyone who might be tempted to cooperate with these godless apostates gets shown the error of *his* ways, too."

"I just hope we'll have enough ships to do the job, Sir."

"Mother Church is building enough that we ought to," Mahkneel half grunted. Something about Gahrmyn's last comment bothered him. The lieutenant had an unfortunately valid point about the difficulties the Navy was likely to face keeping the bottle corked. There'd always be at least some men shortsighted enough to be more concerned with money in their pockets than where and how their souls would spend eternity, after all. And it was going to take a *lot* of galleys to enforce Vicar Zhaspahr's orders; anyone but an idiot had to see that coming! But Mahkneel had the oddest feeling that Gahrmyn's observation hadn't been what the lieutenant had started out to say.

"I hope you're right, Sir," Gahrmyn continued, a bit more briskly. "And, with your permission, I'll just go and take one last turn around the ship before I turn in. Given how shorthanded we are, I don't see how it could hurt."

"Neither do I, Rahnyld," Mahkneel agreed with a smile, and the lieutenant touched his left shoulder with his right fist in salute and disappeared back into the darkness.

▼   ▼   ▼

"Does it seem to you that there was a lot of boat traffic this morning, Kevyn?"

Kevyn Edwyrds, first lieutenant of the Charisian galleon *Kraken*, turned in some surprise at the question from behind him. Captain Harys Fyshyr had turned in over two hours ago, and, like most professional seamen, he understood the value of getting as much sleep as a man could *whenever* he could. Which was why Edwyrds hadn't expected him to reappear on deck in the middle of the night when *Kraken* lay snuggly at anchor in sheltered waters.

"Excuse me?" the lieutenant said. Fyshyr cocked his head at him, and Edwyrds shrugged. "I didn't quite catch the question, Sir," he explained.

"I asked whether or not it seemed to you that there'd been a lot of boat traffic this morning."

"As a matter of fact," Edwyrds frowned, "now that you mention it, there actually seemed to be *less* boat traffic than usual, all day today. We only had three or four bumboats trying to come alongside this afternoon, instead of the usual couple of dozen."

"I wasn't talking about *regular* boat traffic," Fyshyr said. "Although, now that you mention it, that's another interesting point. It's just that after I'd turned in, I got to thinking. Did you notice that every galley left the harbor almost before dawn this morning?"

"Well, no, Sir," Edwyrds admitted slowly. "I can't say I did—not really. Of course, I didn't have the morning watch, either."

"I didn't think too much about it, myself," Fyshyr said. "Not then. But like I said, I got to thinking after I turned in tonight, and I've got this memory kicking around the back of my brain. I could swear I saw at least two or three navy launches rowing *into* the harbor shortly after the galleys they belonged to *left* the harbor."

Edwyrds frowned again, more deeply. He hadn't really noticed that himself, but Captain Fyshyr wasn't the sort to imagine things. And the Delferahkan Navy, like several navies, allowed its captains to paint their ships' boats to suit their fancies. Most of them—especially the ones who wanted to advertise their wealth—adopted highly individualistic paint schemes which made them readily identifiable. And which also meant that if Fyshyr thought he'd seen launches which belonged to specific galleys, he'd probably been right.

"That doesn't make much sense, Sir," he said after a long, thoughtful moment.

"No, it doesn't, does it?" Fyshyr managed to keep any exaggerated patience out of his voice. Actually, it wasn't very hard to do, despite Edwyrds' tendency to restate the obvious, given how highly he valued his first officer. Edwyrds might not exactly be the sharpest arrow in the quiver, but he had copious common sense to make up for any lack of brilliance, and he was fearless, unflappable, and totally reliable in moments of crisis. Not to mention the minor fact that he'd held a commission in the Royal Charisian Navy for almost a decade, which made him particularly valuable for *Kraken*, given that the galleon was no longer the innocent cargo carrier she appeared to be.

"I think," the captain went on after a moment, "that it might not be a bad idea to very quietly rouse the watch below."

"Yes, Sir," Edwyrds agreed. Then he paused and cleared his throat. "Ah, Sir. Would you like me to go ahead and clear away the guns? *Without* opening the ports?"

Fyshyr gazed at his first lieutenant speculatively.

Either Kevyn's got more imagination than I gave him credit for, or else I really am on to something, he thought. *God, how I'd like to find out Kevyn's just being more alarmist than usual!*

"I think that might be a very good idea, actually," he said. "But quietly, Kevyn—*quietly*."

▼   ▼   ▼

"I trust you've impressed your men with the necessity of showing these heretics sufficient firmness, Captain Kairmyn?"

"Of course I have, Father," Tomhys Kairmyn replied, and turned to look Father Styvyn in the eye. He would have preferred avoiding that particular necessity, but the intendant was one of those Inquisitors with near total confidence in his ability to read the truth in other men's eyes. Which made it most unwise to appear as if one were attempting to refuse him that opportunity.

Father Styvyn Graivyr gazed into Kairmyn's eyes intensely, as if he'd just read the captain's mind.

Which I certainly hope he hasn't, Kairmyn thought, *given that Sir Vyk's instructions were almost exactly the reverse of his!*

"Good, Captain," Graivyr said after a moment. "Good."

The intendant turned away once more, gazing out from the dense black shadows of the warehouse. There was very little to see—yet—and the upperpriest inhaled audibly.

"I realize," he said, almost as if he were speaking to himself, "that not everyone truly realizes the danger of the precipice upon which we all stand. Even some members of the episcopate don't seem to fully recognize what's happening."

That, Kairmyn thought, *is almost certainly a reference to Bishop Ernyst.*

The reflection didn't make him particularly happy.

"I suppose it's hard to blame them," Graivyr continued. "All men want to believe in the goodness of other men, and no one wants to believe mere mortals could overset God's own plan for man's eternal well-being. But even the Archangels"—he touched his heart, then his lips—"discovered to their sorrow that sin can destroy any goodness, can corrupt even an archangel herself. These Charisians"—he shook his head slowly—"have set their hand to Shan-wei's own work. And, like their eternally cursed mistress, they've begun by mouthing pious concerns that cloak their true purpose."

Kairmyn watched the intendant's back, listening to the deep-seated anger—the frustration—in the other man's voice.

"Any man, even the Grand Vicar himself, is only mortal," Graivyr said. "That's what makes their accusations so damnably convincing to those of weaker faith. Yet whatever His Holiness' mortal frailties in his own person, when he speaks as Langhorne's Steward, he speaks with the infallibility of God Himself. There may be . . . imperfections among the vicarate. There may be isolated instances of genuine corruption among the priesthood. That's one of the things the Office of Inquisition was commissioned by the Archangel Schueler to root out and punish, after all, and the Inquisition's tasks will never be completely accomplished, however zealously we strive. But when sinful men challenge the primacy of God's own Church, however carefully they may couch their challenge in seeming reason, it's Shan-wei's work, not

Langhorne's, to which they've set their hands. And"—he wheeled once more, half glaring through the darkness at Kairmyn—"they must be *stopped*. Shan-wei's poison must be cut out of the body of the Faithful as a surgeon cuts away a diseased limb, purged with fire and the sword."

Kairmyn wished he had the courage to ask the intendant whether or not the bishop had authorized his presence here this night. Or, for that matter, if Bishop Ernyst even knew where Graivyr was. But he dared not—any more than he'd dared to question Graivyr when the intendant turned up with a dozen of his fellow Schuelerites to be assigned to the various troop detachments detailed to tonight's operation.

And for all I know, he's completely right about what's happening in Charis, what it means for the rest of us. I'm only a soldier—what do I know about God's will? About the Grand Vicar's infallibility? What the Charisians say sounds reasonable, given what they say the "Knights of the Temple Lands" really meant to happen to them, and why. But how do I know they're the ones telling the truth when Mother Church herself insists their charges are all lies? Father Styvyn's right about at least one thing, after all—they don't call Shan-wei "Mother of Lies" for nothing!

"Father," he said finally, "I'm a soldier, not a priest. I'll do my best to follow my orders, but if it's all the same to you, I'll leave decisions about doctrine and theology to those better suited and trained to make them."

"That's exactly what you ought to do, Captain." Graivyr's voice was warmer, more approving, than anything Kairmyn had heard from him so far. Then the intendant turned back to look out into the night, nodding his head.

"Exactly what you ought to do," he repeated softly.

▼　　　▼　　　▼

"Will you *please* come to bed?" Lyzbet Walkyr demanded.

"What?" Edmynd Walkyr turned back from the rail as his wife appeared behind him. She looked at him for a moment, then folded her arms and shook her head.

"I said that it's time you came to bed," she told him severely.

"Yes, I know. I'm just . . . getting a little fresh air."

"Standing up here trying to gather the courage to tell me you plan on leaving me home next time, you mean."

Edmynd winced slightly at the directness of her acerbic challenge, but then he shrugged.

"That's part of it, I guess," he admitted. "I'm sorry. I know it's going to make you unhappy—which probably means I'll be lucky to get back to sea myself without getting my head split open with a cookpot! But, there it is. I'm not going to have something happen to you, Lyz. I'm sorry, but I just can't do that."

He couldn't see her face very well on the darkened poop deck, but he recognized the softening in her body language. He didn't speak all that often of the depth of his love for her, although he knew she knew how deep it truly was. She stood there for another moment, then crossed to his side and put her arms about him.

"Don't you dare cheat that way," she said softly, laying her cheek against his chest. "And don't think you can turn me up all soft and obedient with a little sweet talk!"

"Oh, believe me, I'd never think *that*," Edmynd told her, hugging her back.

"Good." She stood back, holding him by his upper arms as she gazed up into his face in the dim backwash of the anchor lights. "I wouldn't want you thinking I'm going soft in my old age. But"—she leaned closer and kissed him—"if that's the way you're going to be about it, I suppose I'm going to have to put up with it. *This* time, anyway."

Edmynd was wise enough not to breathe any prayers of gratitude where she might hear them.

"In that case," he said, instead, "let me make one more swing around the deck, and then I'll be happy to come below and turn in."

"Good," she repeated, in an entirely different tone, and he grinned as he heard the challenge—and promise—in her voice.

He gave her another quick kiss, patted her on her still remarkably firm and shapely posterior, and started forward.

▼   ▼   ▼

"All right, let's go!" Sergeant Dekyn whispered harshly, and his platoon started moving silently—or as close to silently as twenty-five cow-footed infantry troopers were ever likely to move—down the length of the dimly illuminated pier.

He glanced over his shoulder at the under-priest who'd attached himself to the platoon. Dekyn didn't much care for the priest's fervent manner. And he cared even less for the feeling that the platoon had two sergeants now. Or for the fact that the second one was senior to Dekyn himself.

Enough room for things to go straight to Hell already without having the troops looking to someone else for orders at the same time, he thought grumpily. *Why, oh why, can't officers and priests just stay the Shan-wei out of the way and let the sergeants get on with handling the details?*

He returned his attention to the task at hand as he and his men neared the first vessel on their list. They were just coming even with the lantern at the foot of the ship's gangway when there was a sudden shout from farther up the pier.

"You, there! Stand aside! We're coming aboard!"

"*Shan-wei!*" Dekyn swore as he recognized the voice.

He'd never thought a great deal of Sergeant Zohzef Stywyrt, who ran the company's second platoon. In his considered opinion, Stywyrt was stupid enough to make a perfectly serviceable officer, but they'd both been present when Captain Kairmyn gave them their orders. Which meant even *Stywyrt* should have gotten his men aboard the very first ship on his list before he started shouting challenges from pierside!

"Okay, let's pick it up!" he barked at his own men as shouts from the Charisian galleon's harbor watch responded to Stywyrt. The Charisians didn't sound very happy—or cooperative—and Stywyrt shouted something louder and considerably more obscene.

"*Idiot!*" Dekyn muttered under his breath. "What the *fuck* does he—?"

The sergeant's question chopped off as the shouts were abruptly punctuated by the unmistakable "chunnnng" sound of an arbalest's steel bow and a throat-tearing scream.

"God*damn* it!" Dekyn snarled.

Less than a minute into what's supposed to be a quick, quiet job, and that stupid son-of-a-bitch's already letting his men shoot civilians!

▼   ▼   ▼

Greyghor Walkyr was fourteen Safeholdian years old. He'd spent almost a third of his life at sea on one of the family's two galleons, but this was the first voyage when he'd been allowed to actually begin discharging some of the duties of a real officer, rather than being stuck as a glorified cabin boy. It had been a heady experience, but even that hadn't been enough to blind him to the tension gripping his parents, especially since their arrival here in Ferayd. He didn't fully understand all the issues involved—in fact, he didn't *fully* understand *any* of the issues involved—in Charis' confrontation with the Church. He'd been too focused on his own suddenly expanding professional horizons to worry a great deal about that.

Still, he'd felt the anxiety, and—like his mother (and, for that matter, every other member of the crew, as well)—he knew exactly where his father went to worry about things aboard *Wave*. He wasn't about to intrude upon his parents. His ears would have rung for five-days from the clout his mother would have fetched him if he'd dared to do anything of the kind! On the other hand, a junior officer, even one in the early stages of his training and career, had certain responsibilities. Which was why Greyghor had taken to making his own quiet rounds of the ship before turning in at night.

He'd been careful not to get too close to his father and mother as he waited for them to go below so he could be about his self-assigned additional duties without the undoubtedly sarcastic comments they would have made if

they'd realized what he was up to. But he was close enough to see his
mother's head snap up as voices shouted somewhere farther along the pier.
Greyghor was still trying to figure out exactly which direction the shouting
had come from when it was interrupted by the most horrible scream he'd
ever heard in his life.

He jerked to his feet from where he'd been seated on a coil of rope and
started across the deck towards his mother just as she crossed to the pierside
bulwark with three or four quick strides. She grasped the rail, looking down
towards the pier.

"Who are you?!" she shouted suddenly. "What d'you think you're doing?!"

The shout from dockside was too indistinct for Greyghor to understand.
Something about "Mother Church's name," he thought, even as he heard his
father shouting something urgent at his mother from farther forward.

"Stand off!" his mother barked. She charged down the steep poop deck
ladder to the main deck and towards the head of the gangplank. *"Stand off, I tell
you!"*

"We're coming aboard!"

This time, Greyghor understood the shout from the pier, despite the
Delferahkan accent of the shouter.

"The Shan-wei you are!" his mother shouted back, and snatched a belaying pin from the pinrail beside the entry port. "This is my husband's ship,
and you bastards aren't—"

The meaty, ripping "thud" the arbalest quarrel made as it tore through
his mother's body in a spray of blood was the most horrible sound Greyghor
Walkyr had ever heard.

The impact threw her aside, without even crying out.

"Mother!" Greyghor shrieked. He thundered across the deck towards her
even while he heard fresh shouts—angry, conflicting shouts—coming from
the pier.

▼   ▼   ▼

"Whystlyr, you goddamned *idiot!*" Allayn Dekyn bellowed. "I told you *no
shooting*, damn it!"

"But the heretic bitch was going to—" the trooper began to protest.

"I don't give a fuck what *she* was going to do! We're not out here to kill
goddamned *women* who're only—"

▼   ▼   ▼

Greyghor reached his mother. Life aboard a square-rigged sailing ship was
seldom easy, and never truly safe. Greyghor had seen men killed in accidents
and in falls from aloft, seen at least one man lost overboard and drowned.

And as he looked at his mother, lying in the spreading pool of blood with the terrible wound in her chest, he knew death when he saw it once more.

He didn't call her again. Didn't shout for his father. He didn't even think. He only leapt to the rail where his father had ordered the swivel-mounted wolf loaded after the galleon *Diamond*'s crewmen had been beaten in one of Ferayd's alleys.

The light guns Charisians called "wolves" came in several bores and weights of shot. The one mounted on the swivel on *Wave*'s bulwark had an inch-and-a-half bore and threw a round shot that weighed just under half a pound. At the moment, however, it had been loaded with an entire bag of musket balls, instead, and Greyghor Walkyr's eyes blazed as he yanked it around, trained it on the men starting up the gangway, and snatched up the slow match whose glow had been hidden from dockside by the bulwark.

He touched that glowing match to the wolf's priming, and a lightning-bolt muzzle flash shredded the night.

▼   ▼   ▼

Allayn Dekyn never really registered the muzzle flash. There was no time before the charge of musket balls, like buckshot from an enormous shotgun, streaked straight down the gangway and ripped him, the trooper who'd fired the fatal shot, and three more of his platoon into bloody rags.

The Inquisitor who'd attached himself to the sergeant's platoon bellowed in shock as Dekyn's blood splashed over him in a hot, salty wave. For an instant, he couldn't move, could hardly even breathe. But then the poisonous power of his own panic touched his hatred for the "heretics" of Charis, and he whipped his head around to glare at the platoon's surviving twenty men.

"What are you *waiting* for!?" he shrieked in a voice sharp-edged with terror-born fury. "Kill the heretics! *Holy Langhorne and no quarter!*"

▼   ▼   ▼

"*Damn* it!" Tohmys Kairmyn swore savagely as the flash of *Wave*'s wolf lit the entire waterfront like the *Rakurai* of Langhorne. "What the *hell*—?"

He chopped himself off abruptly, remembering the upper-priest standing at his side, but the question continued furiously through his brain. So much for Sir Vyk's orders to do this *quietly!*

"It had to be the heretics," Father Styvyn grated. Kairmyn looked at him, and the intendant shrugged angrily. "That was no arbalest, Captain! I may not be a soldier, but even I know that much. And that means it came from the accursed heretics. Of course their very first response is to resort to the cowardly murder of men serving God's will! What else should you expect from Shanwei's murderous get?"

Kairmyn couldn't fault the Schuelerite's analysis of who'd fired that shot, although he might have quibbled with the last couple of sentences. Which, unfortunately, did nothing to stop what was about to happen out there in the darkness.

▼   ▼   ▼

All along the harbor's piers, Delferahkan soldiers and sailors who'd been quietly approaching their assigned objectives heard and saw the wolf's discharge. So did the harbor watches aboard the Charisian ships they'd come to seize, and the Delferahkans heard shouts from aboard those vessels, heard ships' bells clanging the alarm, heard bare feet beginning to run across deck planking as the rest of the galleons' crewmen responded to the duty watch's shouts.

For a moment, the boarding parties hesitated. But only for a moment. Then the orders of their own sergeants, the passionate shouts of the Inquisitors who'd attached themselves to the boarders, sent them charging forward, rushing the gangways in an effort to get aboard before more resistance could be organized.

Startled merchant seamen, still running towards the rails of their own ships while they tried to figure out what was happening, found themselves face-to-face with armed soldiers, charging up the gangways to their ships. Quite a few of those seamen turned and ran, but Charisian sailors weren't noted for their timidity. Storm, shipwreck, and pirates tended to weed out the weaklings ruthlessly, and like Lyzbet Walkyr, defiance and a fierce defense were their natural response to any threat to their ships.

Men snatched up belaying pins and marlinespikes. Others, whose captains, like Edmynd Walkyr, had felt the tension building, grabbed the cutlasses which had been quietly broken out, instead, and here and there along the waterfront, other loaded wolves flashed and thundered.

▼   ▼   ▼

"*Langhorne!*" Kevyn Edwyrds exclaimed.

He and Harys Fyshyr found themselves side by side at *Kraken*'s after rail, staring towards the dockside. *Kraken* hadn't been able to find room alongside one of the piers when she arrived, and she was anchored a good fifteen hundred yards out into the harbor. Which was close enough to see and hear even light artillery being fired in the middle of the night.

"Those *bastards!*" Fyshyr snapped an instant later. "They're trying to seize our ships!"

"You're right about that, Sir. And look there!"

Fyshyr followed Edwyrds' pointing finger, and his lips drew back in a snarl as he saw the pair of launches pulling towards *Kraken*. The rowers had clearly been surprised by the sudden tumult from the port. Even as he watched, their stroke redoubled, but they obviously hadn't expected the alarm to be raised this soon, and they were still at least ten minutes away from *Kraken*.

And ten minutes will be more *than long enough*, he thought viciously.

"All hands!" he bellowed. *"All hands, repel boarders!"*

.XIV.
Ferayd Harbor and
Main Shipping Channel,
Ferayd Sound,
Kingdom of Delferahk

Sir Vyk Lakyr swore violently as another broadside lit the night. At least his harbor batteries were finally beginning to shoot back, but that was re-markably little comfort under the circumstances.

He stood in an open freight door on the second floor of one of the dock-side warehouses, under the gaunt, looming arm of the gantry used to raise crates and casks to it. He'd chosen his lofty perch as an improvised command post when the bedlam, shouts, shots, and screams had made it painfully obvi-ous his effort to accomplish his orders with a minimum of violence and bloodshed had come to nothing. He had no idea what had initially precipi-tated the violence, but even the fragmentary reports he'd already received made it abundantly clear that what had been supposed to be a quiet, orderly property seizure had turned instead into something with all the earmarks of a massacre.

Not that it had all been one-sided, he thought grimly. None of the Charisian merchant ships' companies were large enough to hold off his troops and borrowed naval seamen more than briefly, but some of them, at least, had clearly cherished at least some suspicion about what was coming. Many of them had had weapons ready to hand, and they'd managed to fight back hard—hard enough to inflict more than enough casualties to infuriate his men. And the even more infuriated, *consecrated* voices of the Inquisitors who'd attached themselves to his boarding parties without Father Styvyn's having happened to mention their intention to Sir Vyk had helped turn that completely natural anger and fear into outright bloodlust.

Even as he watched, another of the Charisian galleons caught fire, joining the two already blazing at dockside. At least it didn't appear that the flames were going to communicate themselves to any of the warehouses, but they provided a suitably hellish illumination, and he could see at least one galleon which was still holding off every attempt to get aboard. It looked as if the crews of two or three other Charisians must have managed to get aboard her—probably by swimming when their own ships were taken—and even as he watched, another wolf fired from the ship's high bulwarks. There were even matchlocks firing down from her, and someone was throwing lit hand grenades down onto the wharf, as well.

That, he was grimly certain, was only going to make the attackers even more savage when they finally overpowered the defenders, although it was unlikely anything could have made them *less* savage after what had already happened.

And the fact that I'm technically the one in command of this rat-fuck means I'm *the one who's going to be blamed for it by the Charisians,* he thought even more grimly.

He didn't much care for that, for a lot of reasons, including the fact that no man wanted to be remembered as a bloody murderer, especially when he'd done his very best to *avoid* getting anyone killed. At the moment, however, he had other things to occupy his worry, and his teeth clenched as yet another broadside thundered out of the dark, sweeping the embrasures of one of his waterfront batteries with a storm of grapeshot.

Obviously, at least one of the galleons anchored out there had been a disguised privateer. The good news was that the number of guns which could be concealed behind disguised gunports was limited. The bad news was that the guns in question—much heavier, from the sound of things, than he would have thought could have been successfully concealed—were clearly some of those new, quick-firing Charisian pieces he'd heard about . . . and the gun crews behind them manifestly knew what they were doing with them.

The galleon swept steadily, majestically, across the waterfront under topsails and jibs alone, firing savagely at the harbor batteries. Here and there, one of the slower-firing defending guns got off a shot in reply, but even though Lakyr couldn't make out many details through the smoke, darkness, and glare, it didn't look to him as if his gunners were scoring very many hits. And they obviously weren't coming even close to matching the Charisians' rate of fire.

▼   ▼   ▼

Screams from forward told Captain Fyshyr *Kraken* had just taken another hit. That was the fourth, and whatever her other qualities might have been, Fyshyr's ship had never been designed and built as a true warship. In some ways, her thinner scantlings actually worked in her favor, since they tended to produce fewer and smaller splinters than the heavier sides of a warship. On the other hand, they also offered negligible resistance to the round shot slamming into her, and he'd already had at least seven men killed and twice that many wounded.

Which is less than we've cost *the bastards!* he thought with savage satisfaction.

Kraken's broadside and bulwark-mounted wolves had caught the pair of

Delferahkan launches headed for her completely by surprise. The wolves alone probably would have been enough to slaughter the launch crews, but the twelve thirty-pounder carronades in her port broadside, sweeping the water with double charges of grapeshot, had reduced the launches themselves to splintered driftwood. There'd been no survivors from either of them.

Nor had *Kraken* been idle since. She was the only Charisian ship in the entire harbor which could truly be considered armed, and she could only be in one place at a time, but she'd intercepted—and slaughtered—boarding parties headed for two other anchored galleons, and her own boarding parties had retaken three more. Fyshyr had too few men to divert to still more boarding parties without depleting his gun crews or dangerously weakening *Kraken*'s own ability to stand off boarding attempts. But in addition to the five ships her direct intervention had saved, three more had managed to join up with her. All of them had at least a few wolves—enough to discourage any more boat crews from trying to get alongside them, now that their crews knew what was happening, at any rate—and Fyshyr had taken his own ship in as close to the waterfront batteries as he dared, scourging their embrasures with grapeshot in an effort to suppress their fire while other Charisian ships tried to fight their way out of the chaos closer in.

It didn't look as if very many of them were going to make it.

A third galleon caught fire, and Fyshyr's teeth ached from the pressure of his jaw muscles. He had no idea who'd set the flames aboard any of those ships, but unlike the seamen of most other nations, who had a tendency to sink like stones in deep water, Charisian seamen, by and large, swam like fish. *Kraken* had already recovered at least a dozen swimmers from the harbor water, and their gasped-out, fragmentary accounts—plus the number of bodies Fyshyr himself had seen floating in the flame-mirrored harbor—made it horrifyingly clear what was going on aboard the beleaguered merchantmen. Even if they hadn't, he'd been close enough to see one of the galleons himself, silhouetted against the flames beyond her, as Delferahkan boarders dragged struggling Charisians to the side of their ship. Blades had flashed in the fuming glare, and then the suddenly limp, no longer struggling bodies had splashed into the water like so much refuse.

"That's it, Sir!" Kevyn Edwyrds shouted almost in his ear. Fyshyr looked at him, and *Kraken*'s first officer grimaced. "No one else is getting out of *that*, Sir!" Edwyrds said, waving one arm at the chaos, violence, and flames roaring along the wharves. "It's time to go!"

Fyshyr wanted to argue, to reject Edwyrds' evaluation, but he couldn't. There were too many Delferahkan troops swarming over the galleons tied up at dockside. For that matter, most of the anchored Charisian merchantmen had already been taken by boated boarders, as well. *Kraken* and the eight ships following in her wake were the only escapees he could see, and the others weren't going to make it to sea without *Kraken*'s continued protection.

"You're right," he admitted. "Shape a course for Spider Crab Shoal; we'll take the main channel."

▼   ▼   ▼

Captain Mahkneel paced slowly, steadily back and forth along the aftercastle rail, hands clasped behind him as he wondered how things were working out in Ferayd. If everything had gone according to schedule—and as planned— then every Charisian ship in the harbor had been taken hours ago. Of course, things very seldom did go according to schedule—and as planned—did they?

He grimaced at the thought, then glanced up at the steadily lightening sky to the east. It was only an indistinct, featureless gray, for the clouds he'd observed the night before had thickened and spread, until only a thin band of clear, starry sky remained visible along the southern horizon. The wind had picked up, as well, raising whitecaps as it came rolling across Ferayd Sound, and swung a little farther around to the north. *Arrowhead*'s motion was markedly rougher than it had been, with a hard, bouncing pitch as she plowed into the wind, and the first drops of rain had pattered down across the galley's upper decks almost two hours ago. At least it wasn't still raining at this particular moment, but visibility wasn't going to be very good, even after the sun came up, and he grunted unhappily as he admitted that to himself.

If any of the bastards did get away, we'll probably be seeing them sometime in the next few hours, he thought. *Although exactly what we're supposed to do if there's more than one or two of them at a time eludes me.*

He snorted in unwilling, ironic amusement, then gave himself a shake. At least there ought to be time to get the men fed before anything exciting happened.

▼   ▼   ▼

"Any sign of anyone else, Kevyn?" Hairys Fyshyr asked as he made his way back on deck, brushing biscuit crumbs from his tunic.

"Only the one ship, Sir," Edwyrds replied. The first officer's face looked drawn and weary, as well it might after a night like the one just past, Fyshyr thought. There'd been little sleep for anyone, and despite the steadily freshening wind, the top speed of *Kraken*'s little convoy was little more than eight or nine knots. Even to get that much speed had required them to carry more sail than most merchant skippers were willing to risk at night, when their lookouts were unlikely to see squall lines sweeping towards them in time to reduce sail for safety. Given the possibility that the galleys he'd seen leaving harbor the morning before might be lurking about to pounce on any fugitives, however, none of the other skippers had raised any protest when Fyshyr insisted on making all possible speed.

"Only the one ship," Fyshyr repeated, and heard the harshness in his own voice. There'd been twenty-seven Charisian merchant ships, in addition to *Kraken*, in Ferayd. Of that total of twenty-eight, only ten, barely more than a third, had managed to win free . . . so far, at least.

And I don't think any of the others would have made it without us, he thought bitterly. *So what's happened* other *places?*

It was not a question whose answer he expected to like when he finally found out. Unless King Zhames of Delferahk had run mad all on his own, this had to be the work of Clyntahn and the Group of Four. The accounts he'd already heard from the survivors *Kraken* had plucked from the harbor waters all emphasized their attackers' shouts about killing "heretics." And they'd also made it abundantly clear that the Delferahkans hadn't differentiated between men, women, and children. He could scarcely imagine how the Kingdom of Charis was going to react when it learned of this, but he already knew that anything he *could* imagine was going to come far short of the reality.

More to the point at this particular moment, the only reason anyone had managed to escape from Ferayd was the fact that no one in Delferahk had realized *Kraken* had been fitted out as a privateer. Which meant the chances of anyone escaping from any of the other ports where similar scenes were undoubtedly being enacted had to be poor.

And if I'd *been the one planning this. . . .*

"They'll have a picket off the channel mouth," he said out loud.

"Yes, Sir," Edwyrds agreed. "Either there, or further south, inside the channel itself."

"Maybe both." Fyshyr leaned both hands on the bulwark, fingers drumming while he gazed back at the other galleons, visible in the steadily strengthening predawn grayness, following along astern.

"It's what I'd do," Edwyrds said with a nod. "On the other hand, Sir, they didn't have very many galleys in port when this whole thing started. How many pickets can they have?"

It was Fyshyr's turn to nod. Edwyrds' question was well taken; there *hadn't* been many galleys available at Ferayd. For that matter, the entire Delferahkan Navy probably had less than thirty galleys all told. And unless the local authorities had been given more warning of what was expected of them than Fyshyr suspected was the case, there wouldn't have been time for the three or four galleys already at Ferayd to have been reinforced.

For that matter, if they'd had more galleys available, they'd probably have used them for the boarding actions. They'd have been a lot more efficient than boat attacks, at any rate.

"Well," he said, turning back to Edwyrds, "if they've been sitting out

here, guarding the channel all this time, then they don't know what happened
back at Ferayd. How it worked out, I mean. And they don't know about *us* any
more than those other bastards did."

"No, Sir, they don't," Edwyrds agreed slowly, his eyes narrowing.

"Let's get the ports closed again," Fyshyr said briskly. "I think we can
leave half the wolves mounted—they'll expect any galleon to have at least a
few of those aboard, and they'd be surprised if they didn't see any sign of
them. But for the rest of it. . . ."

He let his voice trail off, and the smiles he and his first officer exchanged
would have done credit to their ship's namesake.

▼   ▼   ▼

"Sail ho!"

Hauwyrd Mahkneel looked up sharply at the lookout's announcement.

"Five sail—no, at least *seven* sail—bearing nor'-nor'west!"

"Seven?" The captain shook his head. *"Seven?"*

"Something must have gone wrong, Sir." Mahkneel hadn't realized he'd
spoken aloud until Lieutenant Gahrmyn responded to him. He turned and
looked at the other man, and Gahrmyn shrugged. "I don't know what it
might have been, Sir, but obviously something did. If I had to guess, I'd wager something tipped Sir Vyk's hand early and these are the ones who managed to make sail and avoid the boat parties."

Mahkneel grunted. Gahrmyn's explanation was almost certainly the right
one, but that didn't help him very much. Seven ships would be almost a quarter of the total number of Charisian galleons in Ferayd when *Arrowhead* departed for her part in this operation, and he had exactly one galley with which
to stop them.

And if any *of them get away, someone's going to want* my *arse fried on a spit, and
never mind the fact that I can only intercept one of them at a time!*

"Clear for action, Master Gahrmyn," he said crisply.

"Aye, aye, Sir."

Gahrmyn touched his shoulder in salute, turned away, and began shouting orders of his own. Bosuns' whistles blew, the deep-voiced drums began to
roll, and feet pattered wildly as *Arrowhead*'s crew responded to the summons
to battle.

"Deck, there! I can see at least *nine* of 'em now!" the lookout shouted, and
Mahkneel grimaced.

The numbers weren't getting any better, but at least these were merchant
ships, not war galleons. *Arrowhead*'s broadside armament might be little more
than a joke compared to what King Cayleb's galleons were reported to mount,
but eight falcons, each throwing an eight-pound shot, ought to be sufficient to
deal with any mere merchantman. And if it wasn't, the forecastle's chase

armament—one fifty-pound doomwhale and a flanking pair of thirty-pounder krakens, mounted to fire straight ahead—certainly would. The problem wasn't whether or not he could stop any galleon with which he managed to come to grips, but the fact that he didn't see any way a single galley could "come to grips" with *nine* of them before most of them, at least, sailed right past him.

Well, the Writ *says Langhorne knows when a man's done the best he can. I'm just going to have to hope Mother Church and the King are equally understanding.*

"Do you want to use the chase guns or the falcons, Sir?" Lieutenant Gahrmyn asked.

"A single shot from the doomwhale would turn one of these people inside out," Mahkneel said.

"Yes, Sir. I know."

"On the other hand. . . ."

Mahkneel rubbed his chin thoughtfully. What he'd just said to Gahrmyn was undoubtedly true. The chasers were far more gun than would be needed to stop any merchantman ever built . . . but they would certainly be more impressive than his falcons. And he could use the chase armament to plug away at them from astern if they decided to keep running, as well. Under these sea conditions, his gunners' accuracy wouldn't be anything to brag about. In fact, they'd be lucky to hit their target at all at any range much above sixty or seventy yards. But they might *get* lucky, and even if they didn't, merchant seamen faced with the prospect of fifty-pound shot pitching into their hulls might just decide against tempting fate.

"Have the Gunner go ahead and load the chasers," he said after a moment. "And tell him I'll want the warning shot fired from the doomwhale." Gahrmyn's eyebrows rose, and Mahkneel chuckled sourly. "I don't much like heretics, Rahnyld, but I'd just as soon not kill anyone I don't have to. And if *you* were a merchant seaman, how would you feel about having a doomwhale fired across your bow?"

"Actually, Sir," the first lieutenant said with the first genuine smile Mahkneel had seen out of him since they'd received their orders, "I think that after I got done pissing myself, I'd probably strike my colors as quickly as humanly possible!"

▼   ▼   ▼

"What do you think he's going to do, Sir?" Kevyn Edwyrds asked quietly as the Delferahkan galley came plowing through the strengthening whitecaps towards them.

The low-slung galley was making heavier going of it than the galleons, but there was an undeniable rakish gracefulness to her, compared to the high-sided, round-bowed galleons. She was a coastal design, far smaller and with a much shallower draft than any Charisian galley. She couldn't have displaced much more than a third of *Kraken*'s thousand tons, and she had much lower and sleeker castles fore and aft than a Charisian galley would have shown. That smaller size made her faster under oars in calm conditions, but it also left her at a greater disadvantage in a seaway. Bursts of spray exploded over her sharply raked bow, and green water swept back on either side to cream whitely over the angularity of her rowing frame. It must, Fyshyr thought, be . . . lively aboard her. Which wasn't going to do a thing for her gunnery.

"From the looks of things, he's planning to put a shot across our bows from one of the chasers," the captain said out loud. "If he fires at anything over a hundred yards, we'd be safer if he were shooting *at* us, I think."

"He might just get lucky, Sir."

"He might. Still, I'm thinking he'll probably want to get closer than that before he fires the first shot. It's going to take him a good ten minutes to re-load an old-style gun under these conditions, maybe longer. So, if he fires one shot—probably from the main chase, although he *might* use one of the flankers—and we don't stop, he'll want to be close enough to make sure he's got at least a decent chance of hitting us with the other two."

"So how do you want to handle it, Sir?"

Fyshyr kept his eyes on the oncoming galley while he considered Edwyrds' question. *Kraken*'s carronades were loaded and ready, although her camouflaged gun ports were still closed. The question in his mind was whether or not that camouflage would hold up.

Part of him was tempted to fire as soon as the galley entered his effective range. Which, he admitted to himself, wasn't going to be much above a hundred yards, maximum, under these conditions even for his gunners. But in order to fire, they'd have to open the ports and run out the guns, and that was going to take at least a few seconds. Long enough for an alert galley's gun crews to get off their own shots first. Of course, there was always the question of just how accurate and *effective* those shots might be, especially if they were rushed, wasn't there? Still. . . .

"We'll hold our course for now," he said. "If we can, I want to encourage him to waste at least one of the shots from those chasers of his."

▼   ▼   ▼

Mahkneel glowered at the untidy gaggle of galleons.

They showed no sign of stopping, despite the fact that only a drooling id-iot could have misunderstood his own intentions, but at least they hadn't done the one thing he'd been most afraid of. If they'd scattered, tried to evade *Arrowhead* independently, the galley could never have caught more than one or two of them at most, under these conditions. But they hadn't done that. Instead, they'd stayed huddled together like frightened sheep, which suited him just fine.

"That one, I think," he said to Gahrmyn, pointing at the leading galleon. It was bigger than most of the others, and it had drawn a good quarter mile in front of its fellows. And while the others were crowding up to windward, staying as far from *Arrowhead* as they could, the leader had actually fallen off the wind a bit, which was going to bring him closer to Mahkneel's guns.

"Aye, aye, Sir."

The lieutenant saluted, then made his way forward to personally pass the word to the gunner, and Mahkneel nodded in satisfaction. That sort of thoroughness was typical of Gahrmyn.

▼ ▼ ▼

"That's right," Fyshyr half crooned to himself, watching the Delferahkan closing on *Kraken*. "Just a *little* closer. . . ."

▼ ▼ ▼

"Very well, Master Gahrmyn!" Mahkneel shouted through his leather speaking trumpet.

The first lieutenant straightened from where he'd been personally peering along the barrel of the massive, four-and-a-half-ton doomwhale in the open-backed forecastle. He didn't reply to Mahkneel's order, except to wave one hand in acknowledgment, then nod to the gun captain.

The gun captain bent over the breach of his weapon for a moment, checking its sighting for himself, then stepped aside and pressed the red-hot iron in his right hand to the primed venthole. Smoke flashed upward from the priming, and then the massive gun spewed fire and smoke as it went leaping back along the deck on its wheelless timber mounting. The shock of recoil slammed the soles of Mahkneel's feet, transmitted through *Arrowhead*'s deck planking as the breeching tackle snubbed the gun's movement, and the white fountain as the round shot plowed into the water well over a hundred yards beyond the galleon was visible despite the whitecaps.

And now what are you going to do, my fine heretical friend? the captain thought sardonically.

▼ ▼ ▼

"Well, that was certainly unfriendly," Hairys Fyshyr murmured. Then he raised his voice.

"*Now*, Master Edwyrds," he shouted.

▼ ▼ ▼

Mahkneel was looking straight at the Charisian galleon. Even so, it took him two or three precious heartbeats to realize what he was seeing as the gun port lids, carefully painted to match the rest of the galleon's hull, opened abruptly. They rose as if they'd been snatched up by a single hand, and the short-snouted carronades thrust out of the sudden openings.

He opened his mouth, but Gahrmyn had seen it as well. The first lieutenant needed no orders, and *Arrowhead*'s flank chasers bellowed almost as one. In fact, they fired too soon, while the bow was rising, and both of them went high. One of them missed entirely, and even though the other smashed into the Charisian's hull, it hit too far up her side to be effective. It tore a round, splinter-fringed hole through the bulwark, but then it continued onward on an upward trajectory to plunge into the sea far beyond the galleon without inflicting any further damage.

Arrowhead was less fortunate.

▼　　▼　　▼

Kraken's deck bucked as twelve tons of carronades recoiled in a single, brutal bellow. Smoke billowed, momentarily blinding, despite the brisk wind. Then it was snatched away, rolling downwind like a shredding bank of fog, and Fyshyr bared his teeth as he saw the galley once again.

▼　　▼　　▼

"Hard a port! *Hard a port!*" Mahkneel shouted, fighting to get *Arrowhead* round so her own broadside armament would bear while the forward gunners reloaded. Unfortunately, the galley had scarcely begun to answer the helm before the Charisian fired.

Despite their relatively narrow target, despite the fact that both their target and the deck beneath them were moving, and despite the shot which had already hammered into their own ship, the Charisian gunners made no mistake. At least eight round shot, each of them as heavy as either of *Arrowhead*'s flank chasers could have fired, crashed into the galley's bow.

Men shrieked as the heavy shot plowed aft, killing and maiming anyone in their paths. One struck the starboard rowing frame, ripping lengthwise along it and cutting off sweeps like a scythe reaping wheat. Two more screamed down the oardeck itself, accompanied by lethal showers of splinters, and *Arrowhead* staggered as the intricately coordinated choreography of her rowers was brutally interrupted.

More iron swept aft at the upper deck level, punching completely through the forecastle, exploding out its open back like demons, and carving their own paths of carnage through the deckhands and the Marines waiting for orders to board the fat, helpless galleon after its surrender. One shot crashed directly into the timber bed carriage of the starboard chase flanker, dismounting the weapon and killing almost its entire crew, and yet another slammed into the capstan and sprayed a fan of splinters and bits of iron across the deck.

"*Get her around!*" Mahkneel bellowed at his helmsman, and the helm went hard over. Despite the wild, flailing confusion of her starboard oars, *Arrowhead* retained enough momentum to respond, and the galley swept around, fighting to bring her port falcons to bear.

That was when Hauwyrd Mahkneel discovered that the preposterous reports about how quickly Charisian artillery could fire weren't preposterous, after all.

▼   ▼   ▼

"*Yes!*" Hairys Fyshyr shouted as his second broadside crashed into the Delferahkan. His gun crews knew how urgent speed was, but they were taking time to aim, as well, firing on the downroll so that every shot hammered into their target's hull, and another storm of iron smashed into the galley.

Arrowhead was more heavily built than *Kraken*, but not nearly so heavily as a Charisian galley, and her turn had exposed her side instead of her narrow beam, giving *Kraken's* gunners a longer, bigger target. The heavy round shot smashed into her timbers, shattering and splintering, killing and maiming, and he could hear the screams of wounded and dying men as the galley's momentum carried her still closer.

The Delferahkan managed to get the rest of the way around, and her broadside of light falcons barked. At least three of the eight-pound shot slammed into *Kraken*, and someone cried out in pain. But the galleon's smoke-streaming carronades had already recoiled, their crews were already reloading, and the galley had scarcely fired before *Kraken's* broadside bellowed for a third time.

▼   ▼   ▼

Mahkneel staggered, clinging to the rail for balance, as the Charisian's fire crashed into his ship again and again while she wallowed. *Arrowhead's* rowers were in hopeless disarray, she'd lost all forward way, dead and wounded lay heaped about the decks as she fell helplessly off to leeward, Lieutenant Gahrmyn was down—dead or wounded, Mahkneel didn't know which—and as he watched, the "merchantman" which had already so mangled his command altered course. She turned downwind, angling to cross his broken, bleeding ship's stern at a range of mere yards, and he knew there was nothing at all he could do to stop her.

He watched the Charisian's guns running back out yet again, saw them flash fresh fire, felt the impact of their iron on his ship as if in his own flesh, and knew it was over.

"Strike the colors!" he heard someone else shouting with his own voice. *"Strike the colors!"*

▼   ▼   ▼

Fyshyr watched the green and orange Delferahkan colors come down like a wounded wyvern, and his lips drew back in a snarl. Behind his eyes, he saw again those bodies being thrown over the side of their own ship like so much harbor garbage. Heard again the survivors' reports of murder and massacre, of dead women and slaughtered children, and the screaming encouragement to slaughter the "heretics" in God's name.

His guns thundered yet again, and fierce exultation blazed in his heart as their iron shot smashed into the galley's splintering hull. They'd chosen to start the slaughter, he thought savagely. Now they could deal with the consequences.

"They've struck, Sir!" Edwyrds cried in his ear, and Fyshyr nodded.

"I know," he said flatly, as yet another broadside thundered into the mangled, bleeding carcass of his enemy.

"Damn it, Sir—*they've struck!*" Edwyrds shouted.

"So what?" Fyshyr wheeled on his first officer, then shot out one arm, pointing back the way they'd come. "Did they give *us* any warning, like an 'officer and a gentleman' is supposed to do? Did the people we're not even at war with stop when they were murdering *our* people? *Our* women and children? Burning *our* ships? Killing *our* friends?"

Edwyrds looked at him for a moment, then shook his head and leaned closer.

"No, Sir, they didn't. But these people were clear out here when it happened. And even if they hadn't been, *we're not them.* Do you really want us to turn into exactly what Clyntahn's already *accused* us of being?"

Fyshyr's eyes went wide in astonishment as bluff, unimaginative Kevyn Edwyrds threw that question into his teeth. For a long, breathless moment, while the guns roared yet again, they stood there, eyes locked . . . and it was the captain's gaze which fell.

"No, Kevyn," he said, and his voice would have been all but inaudible even without the thunder of battle raging around them. "No. I won't be that."

He drew a deep breath, looked once more at the broken, bleeding galley, and then raised his voice.

"Cease fire!" Hairys Fyshyr shouted. "Cease fire!"

S ir Rayjhis Dragoner tried hard to feel grateful for his posting as he gazed
pensively out the window.

Usually, he didn't find that a particularly difficult task. Of all the em-
bassies to which an ambitious diplomat might find himself assigned, the one
in the city of Siddar was probably the plum. Any Charisian was still going to
have to put up with the fundamental, almost unconscious arrogance mainlanders displayed to almost anyone from what even the best of them had
a tendency to refer to as "the out islands," of course. The Siddarmarkians
weren't quite as bad about that as most of their fellows, but they were still
quite bad enough to go on with.

Yet all minor complaints aside, the Republic was the most comfortable fit
any Charisian was going to find among the mainland realms. Siddarmark was
firmly addicted to its ancient, republican form of government, and its society
and social customs were far less rigidly stratified than most of Safehold's
more powerful states could boast. That didn't prevent the Republic from sus-
taining its own great dynasties—in effect, if not in name, an hereditary nobility as powerful as anyone else's—and although there was considerably less
prejudice here against those whose wealth came from "trade" than there was
in the other mainland realms, there was still more than there was in Charis.
Yet despite all that, Siddarmarkians were more comfortable than most with
Charis' sometimes outrageous social notions, and their shared identity *as* Siddarmarkians included a powerful, self-aware strand of stubborn independence of mind which they embraced consciously and deliberately as a
defining aspect of their national personality.

No doubt, Dragoner thought, that independence explained much of the
traditional tension between the Republic and the Temple Lands. Despite the
nightmares which obviously plagued the Knights of the Temple Lands from
time to time, no Siddarmarkian lord protector had ever been likely to seriously
contemplate launching a war of conquest against them, however tempting a
target their wealth might make them. That hadn't kept generations of Church
chancellors from worrying about the possibility that one day some lunatic lord
protector *would*, however. And even worse, in some ways (mostly because it
was a considerably more realistic possibility), was the Church's fear that the
stubbornly intransigent Siddarmarkians might someday refuse to submit to

some Church decree. If that ever happened, the well-trained, professional, well-equipped pikemen of the Republican Army would make a fearsome foe. And unlike Charis, it would be a foe which literally lived right next door to the Temple Lands themselves.

That independence of mind was also one of the reasons Siddarmark, traditionally, had maintained close commercial ties with Charis. The Siddarmarkian merchant class was heavily represented in the Republic's elected Assembly of the People. In fact, coupled with the wealthy farming class, they dominated the Assembly, thanks in no small part to the rigorous property requirements of the franchise. The merchants' interest in supporting friendly relations with Charis was obvious, and despite a certain traditional prejudice against bankers and merchants in general, the farmers' interest was even stronger. No one in Siddarmark was able to supply manufactured goods at anything remotely like the price Charisians could offer, and Charis was Siddarmark's largest single market, by far, for raw cotton, silk, tea, tobacco, and wheat. It was a lucrative trading relationship which both nations had every reason to preserve.

All of which explained why the Charisian Ambassador to the Republic had an easier job than most diplomats could ever hope for. Under normal circumstances, at least.

Circumstances, however, were no longer "normal," and Sir Rayjhis rather doubted they ever would be again.

He grimaced while he continued gazing out his office window across the sunlit roofs of Siddar to the dark blue, sparkling waters of North Bédard Bay. North Bédard Bay—normally called simply "North Bay," to distinguish it from the even broader waters of Bédard Bay proper, to the south—was over two hundred miles wide, and the passage between the two bodies of water was little more than thirty miles across. The shipping channels were even narrower than that, and the Republic, at enormous expense, had built Castle Rock Island (and the powerfully gunned fortifications on it) in the shoal water between the two main channels where they approached one another most closely. In many ways, Castle Rock was the Republic's Lock Island, although neither lobe of Bédard Bay had ever been as critical to the Republic's development as Howell Bay had been to that of Charis.

It still made Siddar a remarkably secure harbor, however. Piracy had never been much of a problem here, and the waterfront and warehouse district were usually bustling hives of almost Charisian-like activity. And as one of the premier ports of West Haven, Siddar was also home to one of the largest communities of Charisians outside the kingdom itself.

All of which had made the city a prey to conflicting, dangerous tides of public opinion ever since the conflict between Charis and her enemies had exploded into open warfare. Tension had run high enough when everyone had been busy trying to pretend the Knights of the Temple Lands and the

Council of Vicars—or, at least, the Group of Four—were two separate entities. Since Archbishop Maikel's denunciatory letter had arrived in Zion (and,
so far as Sir Rayjhis could tell, every port city on Safehold simultaneously),
that pretense had been stripped away like the frail mask it was. And the level
of tension in the Republic had soared accordingly.

Even people who don't like the Group of Four are worried as hell, Dragoner
thought. *And it's a lot worse than that where the hardline Temple Loyalists are concerned. The only good thing is that the more extreme Loyalists had already made themselves thoroughly unpopular with the Siddarmarkians before this whole mess ever blew
up. Unfortunately, there's no way this is going to get any way but worse. What in God's
name did Cayleb and Staynair think they were* doing?!

His grimace deepened as he faced an unpalatable truth. Despite his own
reservations about the Group of Four, his own certainty that whatever else
they might represent, it wasn't God's will, Sir Rayjhis Dragoner was one of
the Charisians who was horrified by the sudden open schism between Tellesberg and the Temple. Conflicting loyalties pulled him in two different directions, and he found himself hoping—and praying regularly—that somehow
the inevitable confrontation between the kingdom he loved and the Church
he revered might somehow be averted.

But it's not going to be, he thought sadly. *Not with the lunatics on both sides
pushing so hard. Still,* he admitted almost grudgingly, *I suppose it's hard to blame
Cayleb, given what the Group of Four tried to do. And whatever else I may think of
Staynair's letter, he's right about the abuses and corruption in the Church. But surely
there has to be a better way to reform those abuses! Mother Church has ministered to
men's souls ever since the Creation itself. Can't* anyone *see where splitting the Church
is bound to lead?*

It was a question which had a certain burning significance for him in
more than one way. Like himself, the entire Charisian community here in
Siddar found itself split between enthusiastic supporters of what were already
being called the Church of Charis and the Temple Loyalists. He suspected
that Siddar's distance from Tellesberg had a great deal to do with the nature of
the division here. Unless he was sadly mistaken, the Loyalists constituted
only a relatively tiny minority of the kingdom's home population, whereas
they constituted at least half of the Charisians living here in Siddar.

*Unfortunately, most Siddarmarkians don't seem able to distinguish between one
group of Charisians and another one,* he reflected glumly. *What's worse, I'm not
sure the* Church *can, either. It's bad enough that Charisians, even individual families,
are split and divided. That the division is turning into anger, even hatred, between people
who used to be friends, between brothers, between parents and children. But if those who
want to remain loyal to the Church find themselves lumped in with the Church's enemies by the Group of Four, any possibility of reconciliation is going right down the toilet.
And* then *what do I do?*

He had no answer for that question. No answer besides the oaths of loyalty he'd sworn, the duties he'd agreed to accept when he became King Haarahld's ambassador to Lord Protector Greyghor.

He was still gazing out the window when someone knocked quietly on his office door. His eyebrows rose, and he turned with a frown. It was late afternoon, and his calendar had been thankfully clear for a change. But the pattern of knocks—two, one, three, two—was his secretary's warning code that he had an important visitor.

He turned away from the window, crossed quickly to his desk, and settled into the chair behind it.

"Come!" he called in a pleasant tone, preparing to rise in artful surprise as his unexpected guest was ushered in.

As it happened, he didn't have to pretend to be surprised, after all.

"Ambassador, Master Khailee would like a few moments of your time," Zheryld Mahrys, his secretary, said.

"Of course," Dragoner said automatically. "Thank you, Zheryld."

"You're welcome, Ambassador."

Mahrys withdrew with his normal quiet efficiency, and Dragoner settled his professional diplomat's expression into place as he found himself alone with his visitor.

Rolf Khailee was a tallish man, with the light complexion and fair hair which was common in the Republic but which still seemed odd to Dragoner's Charisian eyes. He was of middle years, with a strong nose which suggested—correctly, in his case, as it happened—that he was related to the powerful Stohnar Clan. In fact, he was Lord Protector Greyghor's fourth cousin . . . and his name was not "Rolf Khailee." It was Avrahm Hywstyn— *Lord* Avrahm Hywstyn—and he was a mid-level official in the Republic's Foreign Ministry. Precisely what he did there was something of a mystery to most people, although his relationship with the lord protector undoubtedly suggested several interesting possibilities.

Sir Rayjhis Dragoner didn't need any "suggestions," however. He was one of the relatively small number of people who knew that Lord Avrahm was his powerful cousin's finger on the pulse of the Republic's relations with the realms which were most important to it. And he was also the conduit through which the Republic's ruler sometimes passed particularly sensitive messages or bits of information to someone else's ambassador. Of course, no one, not even—or especially—Lord Protector Greyghor, was going to admit anything of the sort, and so Hwystyn's alternative persona as Master Rolf Khailee. Dragoner knew perfectly well that the masquerade never fooled anyone, but that wasn't really the point. It provided a degree of *official* separation. It was certainly no more far-fetched than the pretense that the Knights of the Temple Lands weren't also the Council of Vicars, at any rate, and no one was likely to press the Lord Protector of Siddarmark too hard on any diplomatic fictions he chose to maintain.

Besides, the real reason Avrahm uses Khailee is to underscore the fact that whatever he's about to tell me is important . . . and that he was never here.

"This is an unexpected pleasure, 'Master Khailee,' " he said calmly. "May I offer you some refreshment?"

"That's very kind of you, Ambassador," his guest said. "Unfortunately, I'm rather pressed for time this afternoon. Perhaps some other day."

"Of course," Dragoner murmured, and gestured courteously at the comfortable chair facing his desk. He waited until "Khailee" had seated himself, then settled back into his own chair. "May I ask what brings you here this afternoon?" he asked politely.

"As a matter of fact," the Siddarmarkian said, "a rather remarkable message crossed my desk this morning. A message from Chancellor Trynair to Lord Wallyce."

Dragoner managed to keep his face only politely attentive, despite the quiver of shock which went through him. Lord Frahnklyn Wallyce was the Republic's Chancellor, Earl Gray Harbor's equivalent here in Siddarmark. The fact that "Khailee" was here instead of an official messenger from the Chancellor's office sounded all sorts of warning bells. And the fact that "Khailee" was here about a message between Wallyce and the Chancellor of the Council of Vicars was the next best thing to terrifying.

The hell with the "next best thing," Rayjhis, he told himself. *It damned well is terrifying, and you know it!*

"Indeed?" he said, as calmly as he could.

"Indeed." His guest sat very straight, his eyes intent. "It was transmitted by semaphore for the Lord Protector's urgent attention. Unfortunately, the Lord Protector is out of the city this afternoon. He won't be returning until quite late this evening."

"I hadn't heard that," Dragoner said, listening very carefully to what "Khailee" *wasn't* saying, as well as what he was.

"Chancellor Trynair requested that his message be presented to the Lord Protector as quickly as possible, and with the utmost confidentiality. Unfortunately, that leaves us with something of a problem. Since we're not entirely certain where the Lord Protector is at this particular moment—we know his schedule, but we can't be certain he's managed to keep it—we can hardly send a copy of it racing about, trying to find him. So, in order to comply with the Chancellor's request for confidentiality and security, we've transmitted the message to Protector's Palace to await his return and sent messengers looking for him to tell him that it's arrived."

"That sounds commendably thorough," Dragoner said.

"Thank you. However, that's also what brings me here today—as one of those messengers, as it were. It just happens that the Lord Protector had mentioned he might be dropping by your embassy on his way home. Obviously, his schedule isn't exactly written in stone, so I can't be certain he actually will be visiting you. If you should happen to see him, however, would you pass on a message for me?"

"I'd be delighted to be of service in any way I could," Dragoner assured him.

"I appreciate that, Ambassador." The Siddarmarkian's mouth smiled, but his eyes never did. "Would you please tell him we've received a directive from the Chancellor, transmitted on behalf of the Grand Inquisitor. Obviously, I can't go into the details of such a confidential communiqué, but, if you could, also inform him that we require his authorization for the harbormaster, director of customs, and the port admiral to enforce the Grand Inquisitor's directive. And"—he looked directly into Dragoner's eyes—"we also need his instructions as to where and how he would like us to house the crews and officers of the merchant ships involved in the enforcement of that directive until the Church is able to make her own arrangements for them."

Dragoner's stomach muscles clenched into a constricted knot. He knew his expression was giving away entirely too much, but his professional diplomat's reflexes had deserted him for the moment.

"Of course," he heard himself say.

"Thank you." "Master Khailee" pushed back his chair and stood. "Well, Ambassador, as always, it's been a pleasure. However, I'm afraid I must go. There are several other places I need to leave messages for the Lord Protector, just in case he should happen by. And I'm afraid it's rather urgent. We really need his decision on these matters no later than dawn tomorrow."

"I understand." Dragoner rose and escorted his guest to the door. "I hope you find him in time, and if I should happen to see him, I'll certainly pass on your message."

"In that case, Ambassador, I'll bid you good day," the Siddarmarkian said. He bobbed his head in a courteous little bow, then he stepped through the door and it closed behind him.

Dragoner gazed at the closed door for several taut seconds, then shook himself. He knew—or, at least, he was reasonably certain he knew—why Lord Protector Greyghor had seen to it that he received "Khailee's" warning, despite the very real risk he and his cousin had both run. And, as the Charisian Ambassador, there was no doubt in Dragoner's mind about precisely what he ought to *do* with that warning. But even as he thought that, the son of the Church within him recoiled from the thought of deliberately sabotaging a direct order from the Grand Inquisitor speaking for the Council of Vicars.

But he isn't *speaking for the entire Council,* Dragoner told himself almost despairingly. *He's speaking for the Group of Four, and God only knows what* their *final objective is now! Yet, even if that's true, it doesn't magically absolve me of my responsibility to honor the expressed will and decrees of Mother Church. But, if I do, if I don't act on this information, then. . . .*

He leaned forward, pressing his forehead against the door's cool wood while conscience fought with duty and conviction warred with unwilling recognition. And then, finally, he drew a deep breath, straightened his spine, and opened the door. Young Mahrys was waiting, and Dragoner smiled at him.

"Find me some messengers, Zheryld," he said. "People you can trust to keep their mouths shut afterwards."

"Yes, Sir. Ah, what message will they have to carry?" Mahrys asked, and Dragoner's smile turned into something entirely too much like a rictus.

"Let's just say that any Charisian vessel here in Siddar is about to discover she has urgent business somewhere else. *Anywhere* else, if you take my meaning."

Despite himself, Mahrys' eyes widened. Then the color seemed to drain out of his face, and he swallowed hard.

"Yes, Sir," he said, after a long, tense moment. "As a matter of fact, I think I know just the men we need."

▼　　▼　　▼

"This is getting depressingly familiar," Cayleb Ahrmahk said as he turned up the wick of the bedside lamp.

"I'm sorry about that." Merlin quirked a brief, lopsided smile. "I'm afraid it's getting a bit harder to find opportune moments to pass unobtrusive messages now that you're a king, instead of a mere crown prince."

"Or, at least, to pass them without anyone else noticing that you're doing it," Cayleb agreed with a yawn. He swung his legs over the side of his bed and stood, then grimaced. "And I imagine it's going to get even worse after the wedding," he said sourly.

"Cayleb—"

"I understand!" Cayleb interrupted Merlin's response, and his grimace turned into a lopsided smile of his own. "Little did I think when I agreed to abide by the Brethren's decision about who we could tell that it was going to turn around and bite me on the arse this quickly."

"No one wants to make this any more difficult than it already is," Merlin began. "And you know—"

"Yes, I do know you and Maikel both think we should go ahead and tell her. Well, so do I. And, frankly, I'm going to find it very difficult to justify *not* telling her once we're married. I can't quite shake the feeling that this is going to come under the heading of one of those interesting little secrets of state joint rulers are expected to *share* with one another, Merlin."

Merlin nodded. In fact, he knew Cayleb really did understand that Merlin strongly agreed with him. This was something Sharleyan *had* to be told about, even if it was only the "By the way, did we mention that the *seijin* has visions?" version. Unfortunately, the more cautious among the Brothers of Saint Zherneau also had a point. However intelligent, however committed Sharleyan might be—however flexible she might appear, or actually be—they simply hadn't had long enough to get a feel for how she might react to the shattering implications of Saint Zherneau's journal.

Personally, Merlin felt confident she would handle it far better than others might fear. But that was at least in part because he'd spent the last two years watching her through his SNARCs. He'd seen her, listened to her, and observed her ability to keep necessary secrets of state, and he'd developed a lively respect for both her intelligence and her intellectual resilience. For her moral courage and ability to face even unexpected realities. And, as the man who had once been Nimue Alban, he had an even more lively respect for her ability to do all of that in a kingdom where reigning queens had never before prospered. The Brethren lacked that particular avenue of insight, however, and they were only too well aware of their responsibilities as the keepers of Saint Zherneau's secret.

Cayleb had known Sharleyan literally only for a few days. It was obvious to everyone, though, that the two of them were delighted by the mutual discoveries they were making, and Merlin had no doubt many of the Brethren suspected that Cayleb's judgment was . . . less than fully impartial, as a consequence. As for Cayleb, he'd managed to remind himself it was entirely possible the Brethren's concerns were well founded. Getting himself to *believe* they were was something else, of course.

On the other hand, he's like his father in a lot of ways, Merlin reflected. *Including the fact that when he gives his word, it means something.*

"Oh, don't worry, Merlin," Cayleb said a bit gruffly, as if he'd been reading Merlin's mind. He waved one hand in an impatient gesture, then crossed from the pool of lamplight around his bed to the bedchamber's window. He gazed out through the gauzy, gently stirring drapes for several seconds at a night drenched in moonlight, then turned back.

"And now that I'm over my waked-up-in-the-middle-of-the-night snit, what did you come to tell me about this time?"

"It's not good," Merlin said. Cayleb's face tightened at his tone, but he didn't look very surprised, Merlin observed. "Somehow, I suspect you'd already figured that out, though," he added.

"Let's just say I don't expect you to be dragging me out of bed at this hour to tell me something that's not important. And that I can think of relatively few things we might reasonably describe as both 'important' and 'pleasant news' these days."

"Unfortunately," Merlin agreed. Then he inhaled deeply. "I've just been reviewing Owl's take from the SNARCs," he continued, reflecting upon what a great relief it was to no longer worry about circumlocutions when he told Cayleb about something like this. The youthful King of Charis was still working his way through to a genuine understanding of what advanced technology implied, but he'd amply demonstrated his resiliency, and what he already understood only whetted his appetite to understand still more. That was the good news; the bad news was that even with Owl to help monitor, there was simply too much going on in the world for any single being—even a PICA—to keep track of, and it was getting worse as events snowballed. The fact that Merlin still didn't know what those unidentified power sources under the Temple were, and that because he didn't, he didn't dare insert a SNARC into the Group of Four's council chambers, didn't help any, either. Thanks to him, Cayleb's intelligence resources were incomparably better than those of anyone else on the planet, but they still weren't perfect, and he was picking up too late on too many things. Or even missing them altogether, he thought with a harsh self-anger he knew was unreasonable, as the images of massacre and burning ships replayed themselves behind his artificial eyes.

Too many things like this, *for example.*

"There are several things you need to know about," he continued aloud, "but the most important are from Siddarmark and Delferahk."

"Siddarmark and *Delferahk?*" Cayleb repeated, then snorted when Merlin nodded. "Those two are just a *little* far apart to be ganging up on us, aren't they?"

"Yes and no, unfortunately," Merlin said grimly. "And it wasn't exactly their idea, either. You see—"

SEPTEMBER,

YEAR OF GOD 892

It was odd, the Earl of Pine Hollow thought as he was escorted into the Tellesberg Palace throne room once more. He hadn't believed he could feel more nervous than he had on the occasion of his first visit here.

Unfortunately, I was wrong.

He followed the pair of guardsmen, one in the black and gold of Charis and the other in the silver and blue of Chisholm, across the polished stone floor, under the silently turning fans. It was much the same room as before, he noticed . . . aside from the minor fact that the raised dais was a bit larger and that it no longer supported only a single throne.

No wonder he wanted time to "think about his response." Despite his own internal tension, Pine Hollow found it hard not to smile as he looked at the attractive young woman sitting in the throne to Cayleb's right. *I can hardly believe the two of them managed to put this entire marriage together without anyone in Emerald catching so much as a sniff of it! Nahrmahn was right about Sharleyan all along, though. And he was right about something else, too. Cayleb is dangerous enough by himself; the two of them together are going to turn Hektor into kraken bait, and when that happens, I'd rather be in the boat with them than in the water with Hektor.*

The Earl of Gray Harbor stood between the two thrones, effectively at the shoulders of each of the two monarchs seated in them, and Archbishop Maikel stood to the king's left. Aside from the first councilor, the archbishop, and their personal bodyguards, Cayleb and Sharleyan were alone. That was interesting. The lack of additional councilors—and witnesses—argued, among other things, that the two of them intended to speak . . . frankly. Whether that was a good thing or a bad thing for Emerald remained to be seen, of course.

He stopped at the correct distance from the pair of thrones, bowed to both of the seated monarchs, then straightened and stood waiting respectfully.

"Well, My Lord," Cayleb said after several thoughtful moments, "I did say we'd talk again, I believe."

"Indeed, you did, Your Majesty." Pine Hollow allowed himself a small smile. "At the time, however, you allowed me to assume that there would be only one monarch present when we did."

"As you see, our spymasters are better than yours." Cayleb smiled back, and his tone was light, almost whimsical. His eyes, however, Pine Hollow noted, *didn't* smile.

"In point of fact, Your Majesty, we'd already deduced that in light of certain other small surprises we've suffered of late. I believe it had something to do with what happened to our fleet—among other people's"—he allowed his eyes to flit briefly sideways to Sharleyan—"in the recent . . . unpleasantness."

"An interesting choice of words," Cayleb observed. He, too, glanced at the queen seated beside him. Then he looked back at Pine Hollow. "It was indeed 'unpleasant,' My Lord. And, in the event, rather more unpleasant for some than for others. If we were inclined to spend our time rehashing all of our mutual reasons for enmity, we'd still be sitting here this time next year, however. So, bearing in mind the reason your Prince sent you here, Queen Sharleyan and I propose to move forward, rather than look back. Neither of us, however, is blind to the past, My Lord. In fact, we remember everything that's passed, and it would be wise of you and your Prince to bear that in mind. And to remember what I said a moment ago. Our spymasters are very, very good."

Pine Hollow inclined his head in silent acknowledgment of Cayleb's point. It wasn't one he or Nahrmahn was ever likely to forget.

"You may have noted, My Lord, that I said *Queen Sharleyan and I* propose to move forward. Allow me to be specific, just in case the contacts I'm certain you've been cultivating here in Tellesberg have failed to provide you with the full specifics. When Her Majesty and I wed one another in a few days' time, we will lay the foundation for a new realm, the Empire of Charis. Queen Sharleyan will continue to rule Chisholm in her own right, and I will continue to rule Charis in my own right, but both of those kingdoms will become subordinate to and included in the Empire of Charis. The crown of that empire will be held initially by me, but Queen Sharleyan will be my coruler, not simply my consort. She will become not simply my wife, not simply my senior councilor, but my regent and my deputy. Any decision she reaches in my absence will be as valid as any decision I myself might have reached. And should I predecease her, the Empire's crown—and the crown of 'the Old Kingdom of Charis'—will pass first to her, and only after *her* death to our eldest child.

"What this means for you and for Emerald, My Lord, is twofold. First, the terms which will be offered to your Prince are those upon which Her Majesty and I have *mutually* agreed. They aren't the terms of Charis, and they aren't the terms of Chisholm; they are *our* terms, and they aren't subject to negotiation. Your choice, My Lord, is to accept them or to reject them. Is that point clear?"

"It is, Your Majesty." Pine Hollow kept his voice even, although it was difficult. It was obvious Cayleb was doing his very best to avoid grinding Emerald's pride into the dirt any more thoroughly than he must, but the fact remained that he—*and Sharleyan*, Pine Hollow reminded himself—were dictating terms. The fact that they had the power to do that made the experience no more enjoyable from the other side.

"Very well," Cayleb said. "In that case, understand the second consequence for Emerald. Your Prince's independence must come to an end and Emerald must become a part of the new Empire of Charis.

"There are two ways in which this might be accomplished, and to be perfectly honest, the one which most appeals to me on a personal basis, for many reasons, would be to depose Prince Nahrmahn and formally annex Emerald as a part of the Kingdom of Charis. As you and I are both aware, I have many personal reasons to feel less than fond, shall we say, of your Prince, and I suppose it's only human of me to wish to make that point abundantly clear to him.

"However, after further consideration and after discussing the matter fully with Queen Sharleyan, we've decided to adopt a second approach. Instead of adding your princedom to the territory of the Kingdom of Charis, which we would be fully entitled to do, having secured our claim by force of arms, we propose to add the Princedom of Emerald to the *Empire* of Charis as an intact unit."

Pine Hollow's mental ears pricked. He felt his shoulders stiffen, but he managed to keep any hint of emotion out of his expression.

"Assuming Prince Nahrmahn is prepared to accept the sovereignty of the Empire of Charis and its ruler, and to give expression to any requirements for domestic change that ruler may make upon him, accepting that the imperial crown has the right to issue whatever instructions it, in its own good judgment, finds most appropriate, he will be permitted to retain the crown of the Princedom of Emerald and will become the second-ranking noble of the Empire. Only the heir apparent to the imperial crown will take precedence over him."

This time, Pine Hollow couldn't keep the astonishment—and vast relief—from showing. Cayleb noted it, and smiled thinly.

"It would be well, My Lord, for you and Prince Nahrmahn to disabuse yourselves of any notion that this means it will be 'business as usual' for him in Emerald. The Emperor—or Empress—of Charis *will* be the master—or mistress—of the Empire. Your Prince will retain his throne only at the pleasure of the Emperor. He would be well advised to remember that firmly, because I assure you, Queen Sharleyan and I most definitely will."

Pine Hollow nodded silently, and Cayleb's smile grew slightly warmer.

"Neither the Queen nor I are blind to the realities of human nature, or to the fact that from your Prince's viewpoint, his reasons for enmity with Charis have been just as valid and just as real as Charis' reasons for enmity with him. Bearing that in mind, and rather than rely solely upon the power of the sword to enforce his obedience to our decree, we would prefer to find another means to encourage and sustain his obedience and cooperation. To be blunt, My Lord, we believe there are many ways in which Prince Nahrmahn could be of enormous value to the Empire of Charis, just as we recognize that there are many ways in which he might be tempted to create problems, instead. And so, as a means of demonstrating our sincerity when we state that Prince Nahrmahn will be the Empire's second-ranking noble, one of the conditions of any treaty between us will be the betrothal of his eldest daughter to Crown Prince Zhan of Charis."

Pine Hollow's eyes flew wide. *That* was a possibility which had never occurred to him or to Nahrmahn. He knew his expression was giving away entirely too much, but Cayleb—and Sharleyan, he noticed—only smiled.

"The Queen has no brothers or sisters," Cayleb continued after a moment. "Nor, obviously, does she have a child of her body. As such, Zhan will be our joint heir until such time as we produce children of our own. And, equally obviously, Zhan and Zhanayt will stand very close to the succession even after we do produce children of our own. As a pledge on our part that we will support and defend Prince Nahrmahn as we would any other vassal of the Crown, so long as he remains mindful of his own obligations *to* the Crown, we propose to unite his family with our family. We realize there are some years difference in age between Zhan and Princess Mahrya, but the difference is less than in many marriages made for far less weighty purposes. And, to be perfectly honest, we believe Princess Mahrya would be well suited to become Empress Consort of Charis should it chance that the Queen and I die without heirs of our bodies."

"Your Majesty—Your Majesties—this is far more generous than my Prince or I dared to contemplate," Pine Hollow said, and for perhaps the first time in his life as an envoy or a councilor to the Crown, there was not even a trace of diplomatic hyperbole in his response. "To be honest, my Prince feared—and was prepared to face—your demand for his imprisonment, or even his execution. Certainly he never contemplated the possibility that you might offer to unite his house with yours—with *both* of your houses—instead."

"I will be frank, My Lord," Sharleyan said, speaking for the first time. "The terms King Cayleb has just described to you originated almost entirely from his suggestions, not mine. As you, I was astounded by the generosity of his proposals. Had I been in his place, I think I would have found it far more difficult to have responded in such a way after such a long and intense period of hostility. Nonetheless, on mature reflection, I believe he's shown as much wisdom as generosity in this instance. While I would never go so far as to say I believe Prince Nahrmahn's conscience is as pure as the driven snow, I will say, as someone who was compelled, against her will, to support her King-dom's most bitter enemy in a totally unjustified war against an innocent friend, that I realize full well that not all which has passed between Emerald and Charis was of Prince Nahrmahn's doing. In that sense, at least, we've all been victims of the Group of Four and of the corruption which has so con-taminated and tainted the Church. As Cayleb said to me when we discussed this matter, it's long past time for us to turn our attention to the challenges—and the great enemy—we hold in common. The *Writ* teaches that reconcilia-tion is one of the godly virtues. Very well. Let us be reconciled with Prince Nahrmahn, and with Emerald, and then let us go forward together to face the great struggle of our lives."

"Your Majesty," Pine Hollow said with a profound bow, "I see the reports of your wisdom which our admittedly inferior Emeraldian spymasters"—he allowed himself a wry smile—"have managed to bring us in Eraystor have failed to do you justice. As my Prince's plenipotentiary, I accept your most generous terms in his name. Nor do I fear that he will feel any temptation to override my acceptance."

"So long as both of you understand this, My Lord," Cayleb reentered the conversation. Pine Hollow looked at him, and the king's eyes were hard. "First, there will be no second chance. So long as Prince Nahrmahn keeps faith with us, we will keep faith with him. But should he prove faithless, there will be no generosity, no mercy, the next time."

"I understand, Your Majesty," Pine Hollow said quietly.

"Then understand this second point equally clearly, My Lord. By these terms, by this marriage, we will bring an end to the enmity between the House of Ahrmahk and the House of Baytz. But in so doing, your Prince—as Queen Sharleyan and myself—will have declared his personal war—the war of our *houses*, not simply the war of our realms—against the Group of Four, the Council of Vicars, and the Grand Vicar himself. There will be no going back, Earl Pine Hollow. This decision, this declaration, is forever. The only possible outcomes are victory or total destruction, and I advise you and your Prince to think long and hard upon the nature of the death the Grand In-quisitor visited upon Erayk Dynnys. That is the fate which awaits any of the Temple's enemies who fall into its power."

"I understand that, as well, Your Majesty," Pine Hollow said even more quietly, meeting Cayleb's eyes levelly. "Indeed, Prince Nahrmahn himself said very much the same thing to me. I won't pretend I was happy to hear it, or that the thought of raising my own hand, far less my sword, against Mother Church didn't fill me with dismay. I'm a son of Mother Church, and all I ever wanted was to be loyal to her. But how can any man of conscience be loyal to someone who, as my Prince put it, 'whistled up our Princedom like a hired footpad and ordered us to cut an innocent man's throat'?"

"A valid question, My Lord," Sharleyan said softly. "Alas, there are those who will insist obedience to God's Church requires them to acquiesce even in acts such as that, when commanded to do so by men who wear the orange."

"I was such a man, Your Majesty," Pine Hollow acknowledged. "And in some small corner of my soul, I wish I still were. My heart misses that certainty. But, as Archbishop Maikel's letter made painfully clear, there is indeed a distinction between God Himself and the Archangels, on the one hand, and mortal, corrupt men who claim to speak in God's name, upon the other. What we owe to God, we do not owe to those who pervert all He is to serve their own ends."

"If that's truly Prince Nahrmahn's opinion as well as your own, My Lord," Cayleb said, "then Queen Sharleyan and I will welcome him warmly. Just as"—he smiled suddenly—"I'm certain the Group of Four will welcome *all* of us 'warmly,' if, perhaps, in a somewhat different fashion, should they ever have the opportunity!"

.II.
Tellesberg Cathedral,
City of Tellesberg,
Kingdom of Charis

Tropical sunlight poured through Tellesberg Cathedral's stained-glass clerestory, spilling down over the richly adorned statuary and the towering mosaic of the Archangels Langhorne and Bédard which reared high above the worshippers. Organ music had filled the huge cathedral virtually without interruption since an hour after dawn, and superbly trained choirs, drawn from the entire Kingdom of Charis, had taken their turns, lifting their voices in hymns of praise, of supplication, and of blessing. The walls were trimmed with the white blossoms of the mountain spike-thorn which was the traditional bridal flower of Charis, and more of the gorgeous blossoms were heaped and piled in and around the sanctuary.

Most mountain spike-thorn came in various shades of deep, rich red, but the white spike-thorn's trumpet-shaped blossoms boasted throats of deep, almost cobalt blue, fading to purest white, edged in deep golden yellow, at the trumpet's "bell." It was part of the Charisian marriage tradition for family and well-wishers to bring their own sprays of spike-thorn, and the packed cathedral was filled with drifts of flowers whose sweetly scented perfume overpowered even the incense.

King Cayleb and Queen Sharleyan had attended a private predawn mass, before the cathedral was opened to the public. Now, six hours later, the enormous structure was packed to overflowing, and a tense aura of anticipation hovered in its air like smoke. The waiting worshippers were a sea of brilliant fabrics, gems, and jewelry, but there were plainer strands woven through that richly textured matrix. By long tradition, a third of the cathedral's seating was reserved for commoners on a first-arrival basis whenever a member of the royal family was married, baptized, or buried. Most of the "commoners" who took advantage of that tradition were themselves at least moderately wealthy, but there were always some who were not, and today, those of humbler status seemed to be in the ascendant.

Well, of course they are, Merlin Athrawes thought as he waited patiently for King Cayleb and his bride and watched the imagery superimposed on his field of view. The sensors he and Owl had sown so thickly throughout the cathedral in the wake of the failed assassination attempt drove that display, giving him a panoramic view of the entire cathedral which he could manipulate and study as he chose.

The people of this Kingdom genuinely love Cayleb and his family, his thought continued, *and Sharleyan's taken them by storm. She's young, she's exotically foreign, she's beautiful (or the next best thing, at least!), and she's come thousands of miles to marry their King, even if that means standing up against the Church and the Grand Vicar himself beside him . . . and them. The balladeers and the newspapers and public broadsides have turned her into the next best thing to an icon, and in her case, it didn't even take a lot of exaggeration. This time, even the poorest people in Tellesberg want to be there, want to see her marry Cayleb.*

He made one last careful examination of the cathedral's interior, then nodded mentally in approval. The other members of the Royal Guard were exactly where they were supposed to be, the Marine sharpshooters Cayleb had permanently detailed to the cathedral were in position, and all of the security plans and measures he and Colonel Ropewalk had devised seemed to be in place. It grieved him that they had to take such additional pains to guarantee Cayleb's security, but Staynair's attempted assassination and the fire which had gutted the Royal College's original home left them no choice. And Merlin's position as the commander of Cayleb's personal guard detail made him, in effect, the second-in-command of the entire Royal Guard, despite his relatively junior official rank.

However much most people may love Cayleb, the ones who don't really don't these days, Merlin reflected gloomily. *And I'd be a lot happier if I thought the "Temple Loyalists" weren't getting themselves organized. Or if I at least knew enough about who they are and where they're doing the organizing to keep an eye on them. That attempt on Staynair was bad enough, and it came within a whisker of succeeding . . . largely because I didn't (and don't) know enough about them and the people like them to spot it coming ahead of time.*

Actually, he would have preferred not having to spy on any of Cayleb's subjects, for a lot of reasons, including the fact that it felt like a violation, especially when there was absolutely nothing anyone could have done about it, even if they'd realized it was happening. Keeping an eye on political figures like Nahrmahn or Hektor was one thing; playing the role of Peeping Tom on private citizens was something else again, and the fact that he saw no alternative didn't make him one bit happier. In fact, it made him *less* happy. "Necessity" was a poisonously seductive argument, however genuinely unanswerable it might be upon occasion, and Merlin didn't want to get into the habit of justifying the abuse of his capabilities.

That bit about "power corrupting" worries me, he admitted to himself. *The Group of Four's proof enough that it really does, and, in some ways, my "power" is even greater than theirs. Or it could be, at any rate. It's bad enough knowing that I'm for all intents and purposes potentially immortal without giving myself any easy rationalizations for treating people who* aren't *immortal as if I'm somehow "naturally superior" to them. I don't want to be giving away pieces of my soul that way . . . assuming Maikel's right about my still having one, of course.*

I wonder if—

His introspection was abruptly interrupted as the door opened and Cayleb and Sharleyan came through it.

Cayleb was magnificent in white breeches and a traditional Charisian tunic of tawny-amber cotton silk, trimmed in rich green, and embroidered with the black and gold kraken of his house. The rubies and sapphires of the formal Crown of State glittered on his dark hair like flashes of red and blue fire; the crimson cloak of his full court regalia, trimmed in the snowy white fur of a mountain slash lizard's winter pelt, was thrown over his shoulders; and the katana Merlin had given him rode at his side in a newly made black scabbard set with faceted gems and clasped in silver.

Sharleyan had attended the dawn mass in one of the sumptuous, tailored gowns she'd brought from Chisholm, but for this ceremony, she wore a Charisian wedding gown. The decision had been hers—Cayleb had actually been in favor of her wearing a Chisholm-style gown as a symbol of the unification of their two kingdoms—but as soon as she'd made her desire known, the seamstresses of Tellesberg had erupted in a virtual death match to see who would be allowed to design and craft the queen's gown. The competition had been not simply intense, but characterized by scrupulously polite, utterly venomous exchanges. Merlin had been a little surprised when it was all settled without actual bloodshed, and he suspected there were going to be several multi-generational feuds between competing dressmakers and their progeny unto the fifth or sixth generation.

Despite that, he—and Cayleb—had been forced to admit that the queen's choice had been an inspired one. Word that she'd insisted on donning Charisian fashion for her wedding had gotten out, and it had quickly become yet another factor in the way her Charisian soon-to-be subjects had taken her to their collective heart.

Not only that, Merlin thought, absorbing her appearance through the eyes of both the man he had become and the woman Nimue Alban had been, Charisian fashion suited her perfectly. Her hair was arranged in an artfully flowing style which looked simple and unpremeditated, despite the fact that it had taken Sairah Hahlmyn, Mairah Lywkys, and two assistants literally hours to coax into position. Her gown mirrored the coloration of the white mountain spike-thorn, with a long, paneled skirt of cobalt blue that swirled and danced around her slender legs when she moved, and a bodice of almost eye-watering white, adorned with fine sprays of Charisian pearls and a delicate froth of diamonds. The bodice, like the panels of the skirt, was edged in golden thread, and the cloak over her shoulders was trimmed in the same white fur as Cayleb's, but matched the deep, rich blue of her gown's skirt. The fact that the national colors of Chisholm—and of the House of Tayt— were royal blue and silver was a happy coincidence which she had turned into a deliberate symbolism that was lost on no one. Her embroidered court shoes mirrored the blue and white of her wedding gown and flashed back sunlight from gems and silver bullion thread whenever her skirt's motion allowed them to peep into visibility, while their heels were high enough that the crown of her head just topped Cayleb's shoulder.

I can't imagine anyone looking more like a queen, Merlin thought while fabric rustled throughout the hallway as the waiting courtiers swept deep bows and curtsies. *And she certainly has the figure to carry that tailored bodice and skirt perfectly!*

Unlike the courtiers, Merlin and Sergeant Seahamper, as the two men directly responsible for keeping the bride and groom alive, neither bowed nor curtsied, and Merlin found his lips trying to twitch into a smile.

Every single one of the Chisholmian Royal Guardsmen who'd accompanied Sharleyan to Tellesberg was a thoroughgoing professional, completely devoted to their queen. They'd made a deliberate and conscientious effort to fit into the existing Charisian Royal Guard's structure and procedures, and Captain Gairaht, their CO, was young, smart, and hardworking. He'd established an excellent working arrangement with Colonel Ropewalk, the Charisian Guard's commander, and with Merlin, but just as Merlin was Cayleb's personal armsman, as well as the commander of the king's personal guard detail, Seahamper was *Sharleyan's* personal armsman, and Gairaht left the day-to-day details of running her guard detail in Seahamper's callused, competent hands.

Merlin was glad he had. He'd come to like and respect Edwyrd Seahamper, and the Chisholmian guardsman's devotion to Sharleyan was absolute. Not only that, but the fact that he'd been her armsman literally since childhood also meant he was the one member of her detail who could sit her down and lecture her in approved, exquisitely polite finger-waving fashion when it was necessary. Unfortunately, Seahamper wasn't quite as unflappable and impassive as he liked to pretend. In fact, his attitude towards Sharleyan often reminded Merlin of a doting but exasperated parent, especially when she insisted on doing something foolish like walking down a ship's gangplank to a totally foreign kingdom without so much as a single bodyguard.

At least a few members of the Charisian Royal Guard thought Seahamper was on the fussy, paranoid side. After all, it would hardly have made sense for Cayleb to invite Sharleyan to Charis in order to marry her if he—or his guardsmen—intended to let anything happen to her, and some of them were actually inclined to take offense at his apparent lack of confidence in their competence. Merlin, on the other hand, found it difficult to blame him, especially when he reflected on the fact that Seahamper lacked his own access to things like SNARCs.

Now he and Seahamper made brief eye contact, nodded to one another, and began diplomatically chivying their youthful charges out of the palace to the waiting carriage.

And, of course, Merlin thought sardonically, *to the* rest *of the guard detail.*

▼   ▼   ▼

They completed the short journey from the palace to the cathedral without incident, which might have owed at least a little something to the hundred and fifty picked Royal Guardsmen of the "honor guard" around the carriage. Those guardsmen offered no protection from the deafening waves of cheers which seemed to come from every direction, however. Banners in the colors of both Charis and Chisholm waved madly, spectators leaned out of open windows, cheering and waving, and the street before the carriage's perfectly matched four-horse team was a drift of flower petals, while still more petals sifted down like rainbow-hued snow. Given the wild fervor of the crowds lining the entire route from the palace to the cathedral, Merlin and Seahamper's security arrangements seemed comfortably redundant. While Merlin had no doubt that somewhere in that swirling chaos of cheering, whistling, shouting humanity there had to be quite a few people who were outraged and infuriated by the notion of this marriage and what it represented, none of them were foolish enough—or suicidal enough—to make their presence known on Cayleb's wedding day.

Not that he or Seahamper intended to lower their guard.

At the cathedral, the king and queen were quickly and efficiently ushered to their places in the royal box. Crown Prince Zhan and Princess Zhanayt were already there, waiting for them, and the Duke of Darcos, in the sky-blue dress tunic and dark blue trousers of a Royal Navy midshipman, had managed to get back to Tellesberg in time for the wedding after all.

There were three other people in the royal box this day, however, and Adorai Dynnys and her sons stood as Cayleb and Sharleyan entered it. Archbishop Erayk's widow was more richly, though still somberly, dressed than on the night of her arrival in Tellesberg, and her sons seemed less frightened. There were shadows in the boys' eyes, however—shadows put there by their mother's confirmation of how their father had died. Nor were they the only ones who had heard that heart-wrenching tale. At Adorai's own request, Maikel Staynair had made the cathedral itself available to her, and it had been crowded to capacity while she described her husband's agonizing execution not simply to her sons, but to the entire Kingdom of Charis.

Erayk Dynnys had not been held in universal affection by Charisians, yet as they learned how he had died—and what his final words had been—many of his harshest critics had found themselves echoing their new archbishop's prayers for Dynnys' soul. And several members of the Charisian clergy whose support for their new archbishop and the newborn "Church of Charis" had been at best tepid had found themselves reconsidering their positions in the wake of the atrocity visited upon their *old* archbishop.

But the atmosphere in Tellesberg Cathedral was very different this day. As Cayleb and Sharleyan appeared at the front of the royal box, a torrent of cheers overpowered the rich-voiced organ and the choir. The mighty structure seemed to quiver on its foundation, and the tumult redoubled when the king and queen raised their hands in acknowledgment of the thunderous greeting.

It took quite a while for the cheering to subside. Then, finally, when the packed pews were calm once again, the organ launched into a soaring prelude which had been composed specifically for this wedding. The cathedral doors swung wide, and Archbishop Maikel Staynair and the assembled bishops of the Church of Charis entered through a storm of music.

If Staynair was troubled in the least by memories of what had almost happened to him in this cathedral, neither his expression nor his body language so much as hinted at it. His golden crown flashed in the stained-glass-filtered sunlight, the rubies glowing like small red suns in their own right. The richly embroidered and adorned robes of his high office (suitably modified by Owl, whether anyone knew it or not) gleamed with their own thread of gold and silver, their own pearls and gems. The other bishops' vestments were almost as richly embroidered and adorned as his, but as bishops visiting in another's cathedral, they wore their traditional priest caps rather than their own coronets. There was, however, an enormous difference between their normal priest caps and the jeweled and magnificently embroidered ones they wore today.

The choir's superb voices rose as the clerics processed down the cathedral's central aisle behind the scepter-bearers, the candle-bearers, and the thurifers. Despite Merlin's soul-deep hatred for the "religion" Langhorne and Bédard had foisted upon the inhabitants of Safehold, even he was forced to acknowledge the sheer beauty and majesty of its pageantry and liturgy as he watched Staynair, still reaching out to touch children's heads in brief blessing as he passed.

And the fact that all of these people truly believe *in what they've been taught is part of it,* he thought. *There's power in faith, even when that faith is being used and abused, and I can't believe God doesn't listen to these people, however they may have been lied to. All of this faith, all of this belief . . . surely He has to recognize its strength, its passion. How could He condemn anyone for worshipping Him in the only way they've ever been taught?*

The procession of bishops unraveled as the prelates took their positions, and Staynair turned to face the entire crowded cathedral from the foot of the steps leading to his archbishop's throne. He stood there, until the music finally swept away into silence. Still he said nothing, only smiling, while that silence stretched itself into a perfect and purified stillness. It was so quiet that it seemed as if no one in that entire vast cathedral dared to so much as breathe, and only then did he speak into the waiting hush.

"My children," he said then, "this is a great and joyous day. It is always a source of joy for the people of a well-ruled kingdom when their monarch weds. Not only does that marriage become a promise and a guarantor of the future succession of the Kingdom, but any ruler—be it king or queen—who finds the spouse of his or her heart, so that they may stand side by side, united against all the world may send against them, is a stronger and a better monarch.

"King Haarahld, may God and the Archangels smile upon him, found exactly that bride in Queen Zhanayt, and now I may tell you that, of my own knowledge, King Cayleb has found that bride in Queen Sharleyan, as well. Marriages of state are all too seldom marriages of the heart, my children. Never doubt that *this* marriage is both."

He smiled up at the royal box, where Cayleb and Sharleyan sat side by side, and Cayleb reached out—unconsciously, Merlin was almost certain—to take Sharleyan's hand in his own.

"This marriage, however, is more than simply the union of a young man and a young woman," Staynair continued. "It is more even than the normal dynastic marriage which secures the inheritance of a title or a crown. In this marriage, we see the union not only of man and wife, but of Charis and Chisholm, of two realms which will become one. Of the commitment and fierce resolve of two peoples to stand for truth and to defend that which all men not blinded by avarice, greed, personal ambition, intolerance, or bigotry know to be worth dying to preserve. And so, we have much to be grateful for this day, much for which to return thanks to God. There will be days of darkness before us, my children, for the struggle to which we have set our hearts, our minds, and our hands will not be an easy one, nor will the battle be quickly won. But when those days of darkness come, when gloom lies all about you and you are most tempted to despair, remember this day. Remember this King and this Queen, who come before you now to consecrate their vows to one another in your sight, and in the sight of God. Remember that they have chosen to promise their lives to one another . . . and to *you*."

The silence was even more absolute, if that were possible, and then the archbishop smiled once more—a huge and beaming smile, flooding the sober silence his words had created with a vast tide of joy and anticipation as he raised both hands and Cayleb and Sharleyan rose. They descended the carpeted steps from the royal box, between sweet-scented drifts of spike-thorn, to stand hand in hand before him. For all the importance of this wedding, all the hopes and fears and promises riding upon it, the ceremony they had chosen was very ancient, and very simple. Any young bride and groom, however humble their circumstances, might have chosen it, and there was a message in that, as well. They faced the primate of all Charis, and he looked beyond them to the waiting tide of faces.

"And now, dearly beloved," he told the people behind those faces, "we have gathered together here in the sight of God and the Archangels, and in the face of this company, to join together this man and this woman in holy matrimony; which is an honorable estate, instituted of God and the Archangels, signifying unto us the mystical union that is between God and His Church; which is a holy estate which the Archangel Langhorne adorned and beautified with his presence in his time here upon Safehold, and is commended of the Archangel Bédard to be honorable among all men: and therefore is not by any to be entered into unadvisedly or lightly; but reverently, discreetly, advisedly, soberly, and in the fear of God. Into this holy estate these two persons present come now to be joined. If any man can show just cause why they may not lawfully be joined together, let him now speak, or else hereafter forever hold his peace."

.III.
Tellesberg Palace,
City of Tellesberg,
Kingdom of Charis

Your Majesties, Prince Nahrmahn and Princess Ohlyvya."

Nahrmahn Baytz stepped past the bowing chamberlain with a lifetime's aplomb. From his expression, no one could have guessed that the rotund little prince wasn't walking into his *own* throne room. His wife was as tall as he was and far more slender, and she, too, had a lifetime's experience as a noblewoman and a princess consort, yet she couldn't match his apparent calm.

No one could have called her overtly *nervous*; at the same time, no one could have doubted she would much have preferred to be somewhere else.

They crossed the same polished stone floor Baron Pine Hollow had crossed before them, and Nahrmahn considered how the throne room—or its inhabitants, at least—had changed as they halted before the same pair of thrones. Cayleb wore the Charisian Crown of State, which had recently become the imperial Crown of State, as well, while Sharleyan wore an only marginally smaller crown without the Crown of State's rubies. Despite the crowns, neither of them were in full court regalia, at least, for which Nahrmahn was profoundly—if privately—grateful. Ohlyvya looked stately and beautiful in full regalia; Nahrmahn looked like a round, fuzzy ball which had somehow acquired a head and feet.

Stubby little feet.

I suppose it's a good thing I decided to do this before I actually laid eyes on Cayleb in the flesh, as it were, for the first time, the Emeraldian prince thought with a touch of whimsy. *If I'd had time to see how tall, broad-shouldered, and disgustingly handsome he is with my own eyes and work up a proper state of livid jealousy, I might not have been able to do it after all. Having your head chopped off is much less irritating than admitting that the man you're about to surrender to looks so much more like a king than you do.*

That thought carried him to the foot of the waiting thrones, and he bowed deeply while Ohlyvya curtsied.

"Your Majesties," he murmured.

"Actually, Prince Nahrmahn," Cayleb said dryly, "we've decided upon a slightly revised protocol. Since my wife and I"—Nahrmahn wondered if Cayleb himself heard the profound, proud satisfaction in the emphasis he placed upon the word "wife"—"are both reigning heads of state in our own rights, and since there's always the possibility of confusion, it's been decided that while it's correct and proper to address either of us individually as 'Majesty' in the absence of the other, the proper protocol now is that in Charis, when both of us are present, I am properly addressed as 'Your Majesty' while *she* is properly addressed as 'Your Grace.' In Chisholm, where we'll also be spending approximately half the year, *she* will be properly addressed as 'Your Majesty,' while I'll be properly addressed as 'Your Grace.' "

"Ah, I see, Your Majesty." Nahrmahn felt his lip trying to twitch in something he suspected would have been a smile if he'd allowed it to show itself. "I can readily understand where that might have created confusion. Of course, I'm quite sure that when word of your marriage—not to mention your coronation as Emperor—reaches Zion, the reaction will be substantially worse than 'confusion.' "

"One can only hope," Cayleb replied, then leaned back in his throne and cocked his head. "And while we're on the topic of news reaching Zion, I'm sure they'll be equally perturbed by the news of your arrival here, and the reason for your visit. May I suppose that your arrangements with Commodore Zhaztro and Duke Solomon have adequately . . . secured your rear, shall we say, against Bishop Executor Wyllys and *his* reaction to your decision?"

Nahrmahn managed not to blink any eyes or let his jaw drop in slack astonishment. And, he reminded himself a moment later, Cayleb's remark didn't necessarily imply any special knowledge about his own recent activities. He'd already had ample evidence that the Ahrmahks were a dismayingly intelligent and competent dynasty. It wouldn't have taken someone as bright as Cayleb very long to reason out what Nahrmahn must have done to protect himself against the Church's reaction. And having figured out *what* he'd done, it would have been only a single short, simple step to deducing who he'd selected to do the doing.

Still, it's an impressive conversational gambit, he admitted to himself.

"I believe the good Bishop Executor is currently a guest in Eraystor Palace, Your Majesty," he said calmly. "I'm sure my staff is providing for all of his needs, and he's entirely welcome to remain our guest until such time as we manage to resolve any . . . misunderstandings."

"Perhaps we could send Bishop Zherald to help him reason his way to the truth," Sharleyan suggested. Nahrmahn looked at her politely, and she shrugged. "Bishop Zherald has placed his services at Archbishop Maikel's disposal, following Archbishop Erayk's murder at the Inquisition's hands. It might be that his own experience in Bishop Executor Wyllys' role might enable him to lead the Bishop Executor to a more accurate understanding of what the schism between the Church of Charis and the Church of Zion truly means."

"He might, indeed, be able to exert a beneficial influence, Your Grace." Nahrmahn bowed to her once again. "At any rate, I don't see any way it could hurt."

"Then, if the Archbishop is willing to dispatch him to Eraystor, we'll certainly do so," Cayleb said. "In the meantime, however, there are certain formalities to be attended to."

"Indeed there are, Your Majesty," Nahrmahn acknowledged.

"In that case, I believe there's only one preliminary question which must be asked and answered under the eyes of our court and our advisers as well as the eye of God. And that question is whether or not you understand, fully accept, and enter without reservation upon the terms provisionally accepted upon your part by Baron Pine Hollow?"

"Your Majesty, I do." Nahrmahn bowed again, more deeply. "And since, as you say, we stand currently under the eyes of your court and your advisers, I would also beg leave to say this. The terms which you and Her Grace have seen fit to offer to my subjects, to my House, and to me as an individual are far more generous than I ever anticipated or might reasonably have asked for. Because of that truth, and because of my awareness of it, I wish to express my deep and profound gratitude."

"The terms are what they are, My Lord," Cayleb replied after a moment. "I won't deny I was strongly tempted to be . . . less generous. But vengeance for past enmities is a petty thing, and a poisonous one. There are far more things happening in the world these days than the traditional squabbling and sparring between Emerald and Charis. Those things leave no time for our small, local disputes, and I don't propose to leave any festering cankers to poison all of us when we confront the greatest challenge of our lives. Her Majesty and I didn't offer these terms because of how much we love you; we offered them out of a realistic understanding of the need to make reliable allies out of past enemies in the face of the threat represented by the Group of Four."

"The fact that generous terms may also be wise makes them no less generous, Your Majesty," Nahrmahn said.

"Perhaps not. But now it's time to deal with those formalities."

"Of course, Your Majesty."

Nahrmahn gave his wife's hand a last, unobtrusive squeeze, then released it and stepped forward to the waiting cushion. That cushion's placement was an indication of just how much things had changed. It wasn't directly in front of Cayleb's throne. Instead, it was placed between the two thrones, and as he went to his knees on it, Archbishop Maikel held out a gold and gem-clasped copy of *The Holy Writ*. The prince kissed the book's cover, then laid his right hand upon it while he looked up into Cayleb's and Sharleyan's eyes.

"I, Nahrmahn Hanbyl Graim Baytz, do swear allegiance and fealty to Emperor Cayleb and Empress Sharleyan of Charis," he said speaking clearly and distinctly, "to be their true man, of heart, will, body, and sword. To do my utmost to discharge my obligations and duty to them, to their Crowns, and to their House, in all ways, as God shall give me the ability and the wit so to do. I swear this oath without mental or moral reservation, and I submit myself to the judgment of the Emperor and Empress and of God Himself for the fidelity with which I honor and discharge the obligations I now assume before God and this company."

There was a moment of silence. Then Cayleb laid his hand atop Nahrmahn's on the *Writ*, and Sharleyan laid *her* hand atop Cayleb's.

"And we, Cayleb Zhan Haarahld Bryahn Ahrmahk and Sharleyan Ahdel Alahnah Ahrmahk, do accept your oath," Cayleb replied steadily. "We will extend protection against all enemies, loyalty for fealty, justice for justice, fidelity for fidelity, and punishment for oath-breaking. May God judge us and ours as He judges you and yours."

For an endless moment, all three of them looked into one another's eyes at the heart of a profound stillness. And then, finally, Cayleb smiled crookedly.

"And now, My Lord, you should probably stand up. I believe you and I—and Her Grace—have quite a bit that needs discussing."

▼   ▼   ▼

It had not, Prince Nahrmahn reflected as he gazed out of the window of his family's sumptuous suite at the clouds welling up above the Styvyn Mountains to the west, lit with the crimson and gold fire of sunset, been the sort of day he'd once looked forward to spending in Tellesberg. In one way, it was a great relief. He'd come out of the conflict with a crown still on his head, even if its authority had been rather severely diminished, and with a close familial relationship with what bade fair to become one of the most—if not *the* most—powerful dynasties in the history of Safehold. On the other hand, it was probably at least as likely that the dynasty in question, to which his and his family's fortune was now inescapably tied, would find itself exterminated by a vengeful Church. And, he acknowledged to himself, there was also that other minor bit about who he'd expected to be swearing fealty to whom.

"I think I rather like them, actually," a voice said from behind him, and he turned from the window to face Ohlyvya.

"I presume you're referring to our new sovereign lord and lady?" he said, with a slightly crooked smile, and she snorted.

"Actually, I was referring to the second and third under cooks!" she said, and he laughed.

"I never really *disliked* Cayleb or his father, my dear. They were adversaries, and I'll admit—if only to you—that I found their persistence in surviving everything Hektor or I attempted rather trying, upon occasion. But it was never *personal* for me the way it was for Hektor. Although, to be totally fair," his smile faded slightly, "given my involvement in efforts to eliminate both of them, I'm astonished that Cayleb *appears* to cherish so little animosity."

"I don't think either of them do 'cherish' much animosity," she said seriously.

One of Nahrmahn's eyebrows rose, but he only waited for her to complete her thought. Ohlyvya Baytz was a very intelligent woman. More than that, she was the one person in the entire world Nahrmahn trusted without any reservation. Like Cayleb's and Sharleyan's, theirs had been an arranged marriage of state, but it had become far more than that over the years, and Nahrmahn had often wished it had been possible to name Ohlyvya to his official Royal Council. That, unfortunately, had been out of the question, but that hadn't prevented him from listening very carefully to her on the infrequent occasions when she'd offered an opinion.

And, he thought, *now that we have an Empress who's also a queen in her own right, naming a woman to a mere prince's council probably just got a lot more possible, didn't it?*

"I'm not saying either of them exactly loves you yet, dear," she continued now, with a ghost of a smile, and reached up to lay one hand against his cheek. "I'm sure that once they get to know all the sterling qualities hiding under that shy and modest exterior of yours they'll *come* to love you, but in the meantime, there are those minor matters of assassination attempts and wars."

"Assassination attempts?" Nahrmahn did his very best to look totally innocent . . . with a notable lack of success.

"Oh, don't be silly, Nahrmahn!" Ohlyvya scolded. "Despite your best efforts to 'protect me' from the sordid realities, I have heard all the rumors about that assassination attempt on Cayleb, you know. And even though I love you as both my husband and the father of my children, I've never cherished any illusions about the seriousness with which you played 'the great game,' I think you've called it."

This time Nahrmahn's eyes widened in genuine surprise. Ohlyvya had seldom expressed herself quite so bluntly. And she was right about at least one thing. He truly had attempted to shield her from the frequently distasteful and unpleasant decisions he'd found himself compelled to make as a player of the game.

Let's be honest with ourselves here, Nahrmahn, he told himself. *Yes, you were "compelled" to make some of those decisions, but the real reason you played the game was because you enjoyed it so much. Unfortunately, you didn't end up winning it . . . although I suppose I could also argue that I haven't exactly lost it yet, either.*

Something of his thoughts must have shown in his expression, because his wife shook her head.

"I'm not complaining, Nahrmahn. There have been times I've been *tempted* to complain, that's true. In fact, there have been more than a few times when I wanted to kick you smartly in the posterior. On the whole, though, I've been able to tell myself—honestly, I think—that most of the things you've done, including the ones that have caused me the greatest concern for the state of your soul, came about as a result of the situations you faced. Conflict between Emerald and Charis, for example, was probably inevitable, whatever you wanted, just because of geography.

"But," she continued very seriously, looking into his eyes so that he could see the truth in hers, "I'd be lying if I said I wasn't rather relieved at the way it finally worked out. I know our parents never expected it, Nahrmahn, but I truly do love you, you know. And I love our children. Knowing Cayleb isn't going to be looking for your head, or seeing the boys as a threat that needs to be . . . dealt with, takes an enormous weight off of my mind and heart."

Nahrmahn raised his left hand, cupping its palm over the hand still on his cheek. His right hand reached out to settle on the back of her neck and draw her forward as he leaned to meet her until their foreheads touched. It wasn't often she expressed her feelings for him that clearly, and he closed his eyes for a moment while he savored it.

"It doesn't end here, you know," he told her then, his voice low. "Cayleb was right when he told Trahvys this is only the beginning. By siding with Cayleb, I've sided against the Temple, and Clyntahn's a far more vindictive enemy than Cayleb could ever be. Not to mention the fact that the Church controls many times the resources, wealth, and manpower Cayleb does, even with Chisholm added to this new 'empire' of his."

"Clyntahn is a bigoted, fornicating, self-serving, gluttonous, wine-swilling, sanctimonious pig with delusions of godhood and a self-righteous sense of zealotry," Ohlyvya said flatly, with a venom Nahrmahn had never heard from her before.

He blinked in surprise at hearing it now and drew back far enough to look into her eyes once more. She looked back without flinching, and he saw a fire burning behind them. One he'd never suspected might be there . . . which was an oversight for which he would find it hard to forgive himself.

"I'm not exactly *blind*, you know, dear," she told him tartly. "But my point at the moment is that someone like Clyntahn would have a hard enough time standing up to Cayleb and Sharleyan by themselves. With you added to the mix, that pig in Zion is as overmatched as I'd be trying to arm wrestle that Captain Athrawes of Cayleb's!"

Despite himself, Nahrmahn smiled. She glared at him for a moment, and then she chuckled and leaned forward, resting her cheek against his chest.

"I know you've never thought of yourself as the very image of the dashing warrior prince, love," she said. "Well, neither have I. But I've always thought of you as something rather more important than that—someone who looks at the future and his own responsibilities without flinching and without deluding himself. And while I'd never want you to get a swelled head over it, you're also one of the *smartest* men I know."

"If I'm so smart, then why did I just end up swearing fealty to Cayleb, instead of the other way around?" he asked in a half-jesting tone.

"I didn't say you were infallible, dear; just smart. Besides, to use that charming idiom your son has picked up from those dreadful novels of his, you can only play the cards you're dealt. I believe someone's just offered you an entirely new deck, though. And from what I've seen of you this time around, I don't think you're even tempted to try dealing off the bottom."

"Not anymore," he acknowledged, then shook his head, half in wry amusement and half in bemused disbelief. "Even if I were tempted—which, to my own considerable surprise, I'm not—it would be incredibly stupid of me. There aren't any bridges back to Zion now, love, and there's no way I could possibly take over and maintain the core of opposition to the Temple which Cayleb's been able to put together. Trying to betray him at this point would be like deciding to cut the throat of your best helmsman in the middle of a hurricane. And I'm very much afraid"—his smile was tart enough to sour milk—"that this voyage is going to be long enough that I'll be completely out of practice before things ever get stabilized enough for me to contemplate any sort of treachery."

"Good." She nestled more firmly against him. "Good," she repeated.

"Do you know," he said softly, bending to kiss the part of her hair, "I believe I agree with you."

▼   ▼   ▼

The clouds of the evening before had turned into a solid, dark gray overcast. Rain slashed down from the wet charcoal heavens, beating on the roof of Tellesberg Palace, rushing down gutters and downspouts, gurgling down the drainage channels beside the capital's roads. Commerce in Tellesberg never stopped, of course. Even during the recent war against the Group of Four's cat's-paws, the purely local shipping of Howell Bay had kept a fair amount of freight moving and the ships to carry it busy. Now that the oceans of the entire world were once again open to Charisian galleons, the waterfront's activity had resumed its normal frenetic level. Even while rain pounded down, lightning flashed, and thunder rumbled, the heavy freight wagons—most drawn by dragons, although here and there a smaller wagon drawn by horses or mules moved down the smaller, narrower streets—continued to flow.

Prince Nahrmahn was impressed. As he stood at the open window of the small, private council chamber looking out into the rain, he saw the visual evidence of the prosperity and industry which made the Kingdom of Charis so much more dangerous a foe than the simple size of its population might have suggested.

The door opened behind him, and he turned from the window as Bynzhamyn Raice, Baron Wave Thunder, entered the chamber.

"Your Highness," King—*no*, Nahrmahn corrected himself, *Emperor*—Cayleb's senior spy said with a bow.

"My Lord," Nahrmahn replied with something much closer to a nod than a bow.

"First, I'd like to thank you for making the time available to meet with me," Wave Thunder continued as the two of them walked to the smallish but beautifully polished conference table at the center of the chamber.

"I suspect His Majesty would probably have insisted if I'd proven difficult, My Lord." Nahrmahn chuckled. "I'm quite familiar with the process of . . .'debriefing,' I believe Baron Shandyr calls it. And in all fairness, His Majesty was quite polite about 'suggesting' I sit down for a short chat with you. Obviously, if there's anything I can tell you, I'm at His Majesty's service and yours."

"Actually, Your Highness," Wave Thunder said, waiting until Nahrmahn had seated himself and then settling into a chair of his own on the opposite side of the table, "you may be surprised about the actual purpose of our 'short chat.' To be honest, His Majesty—and I—are less interested in the information you may possess than in the additional insight you may be able to offer into our analysis of the information we already have."

"Indeed?" Nahrmahn raised both eyebrows, and it was Wave Thunder's turn to chuckle.

"Indeed," he confirmed, while a fresh, closer peal of thunder crashed overhead. "In fact, to be perfectly blunt, Your Highness, one of the secondary purposes of this meeting is to acquaint you with the intelligence capabilities we already possess."

"Ah, I see." Nahrmahn smiled thinly. "As a pointed reminder of Cayleb's ability to . . . monitor my own activities, I presume."

"To some extent," Wave Thunder agreed imperturbably, and his own smile was a bit broader than Nahrmahn's had been. "I hope you won't mind my saying that, despite a few initial reservations of my own, it's something of a relief to be able to discuss this with someone who understands how these things are done, Your Highness."

"I'll take that as a compliment, My Lord—provisionally, at least."

"Believe it or not, that was how it was intended."

The baron opened the briefcase he'd brought with him and extracted a fairly thick stack of folders. He laid them on the table in front of him, then cocked his head at Nahrmahn.

"I realize Baron Shandyr hasn't had much luck reestablishing your own spy networks here in Charis, Your Highness," he said. "I also know you've been quite patient with him, despite your own obvious frustration, and that his operations have continued with their normal high rate of success *outside* Charis."

Nahrmahn's eyebrows rose again at the frankness in Wave Thunder's calm voice. The baron saw his expression and shook his bald head.

"There's a reason he's been so unsuccessful here in Charis, and it has nothing to do with his competence or how hard he's tried. As you yourself are aware, Your Highness, the only way a secret can truly be kept is if it isn't told to anyone. I believe that's a practice with which you're quite familiar, just as you're also aware it can occasionally be frustrating to your subordinates. For example, Earl Pine Hollow was quite surprised some months ago to discover you'd already been in contact with King Gorjah's first councilor."

This time Nahrmahn's eyebrows lowered suddenly, and he frowned.

"There are two reasons I used that particular example," Wave Thunder continued calmly. "First, because it demonstrates the extent to which we've penetrated Emerald, and how long ago we managed to do it. Second, because it demonstrates that you're familiar with the idea of what we call here in Charis 'the need to know.' It's one of our fundamental policies that information is kept in individual compartments, and that only those who 'need to know' something in order to do their jobs are made privy to that information. It indicates not *distrust* on our part, although, as you yourself are aware, a certain degree of distrust is a necessary precaution, but rather the protection of critical information by limiting its spread."

"You're right, My Lord," Nahrmahn said slowly, still frowning, although it was a frown of thoughtfulness now, not one of astonishment. "I am familiar with the need to keep things close, although I've never used that description of the logic. 'Need to know.' " He seemed to roll the words on his tongue, tasting them as he repeated them, and then nodded slowly. "I have to say it's an appropriate turn of phrase, though."

"I'm glad you understand, Your Highness." Wave Thunder sat back in his chair. "One of those 'need to know' things is precisely how our spies go about gathering much of the information and knowledge which comes to us here. Frankly, we have great respect for your ability as an analyst, and we intend to make the best use of it we can. However, as often as not—and, to be honest, probably *more* often than not—you may never know how the information we're asking you to analyze came into our possession in the first place."

"I trust you'll forgive me for pointing this out, Baron, but quite frequently the source of a piece of information has enormous bearing on its reliability, and that, in turn, has obvious implications for its analysis."

"Your Highness," Wave Thunder smiled even more broadly, "it truly *is* a pleasure to discuss these matters with someone who understands the niceties of the spymaster's art. However, one of the reasons I brought these"—he tapped the stack of folders—"is to give you a demonstration of how reliable our spies are."

"In what way, if I may ask?" Nahrmahn inquired when the Charisian paused.

"Pick a day—any day you wish—from the third five-day of May," Wave Thunder invited.

Nahrmahn blinked at him, then shrugged.

"Very well," he said. "I pick Thursday."

"Very good, Your Highness." Wave Thunder sorted through the folders until he found the one he wanted. He separated it from the others, then laid it carefully on the table in front of him and opened it.

"On Thursday, May the fourteenth," he said, looking down at the notes before him, "you summoned Commodore Zhaztro and Earl Pine Hollow to Eraystor Palace. You met in the Blue Salon, where you discussed the recent capture of the Church dispatch boat carrying dispatches from Bishop Executor Thomys to Bishop Executor Wyllys. Commodore Zhaztro informed you that there was no way to guarantee the safe passage of even Church dispatch boats into Eraystor Bay in the face of our blockade. He suggested, however, that not even our navy could blockade every minor port, and that it would be possible for Church couriers to use those secondary ports. You pointed out that the Bishop Executor felt using such minor ports would be undignified, but you also instructed the Commodore to draw up a list of them for future use, after which you dismissed him and had a most interesting conversation with the Earl. In the course of that conversation you shared with him your own analysis of the confrontation between Charis and the Group of Four and your belief that things would get far worse before they get better."

Wave Thunder glanced up from his notes. Despite decades of experience at self-discipline and self-control, Nahrmahn's jaw had dropped as the Charisian spymaster continued his deliberate, devastatingly accurate summarization of the meeting at which only three men had been present.

"I would make two points at this moment, Your Highness," the baron said calmly. "First, it was in fact your words to Earl Pine Hollow, and several other, similar conversations with him, which played a not insignificant part in the terms which Emperor Cayleb was prepared to offer Emerald. And, secondly, if you're thinking either Commodore Zhaztro or Earl Pine Hollow must have betrayed your confidence for us to have this information, let me turn to a later point in that same day."

He turned pages unhurriedly until he found the one he wanted, then cleared his throat.

"Later that same evening," he resumed, "you had a private meeting with Baron Shandyr. At that meeting, you touched once again, if less strongly, upon the same analysis of the Church's position you had shared with Earl Pine Hollow earlier. You also pointed out to the Baron—as, indeed, you had pointed out to the Earl earlier—that the Group of Four's entire plan had been as stupid as it was arrogant. And you pointed out that Prince Hektor was unlikely to risk his own security to come to Emerald's aid. In fact, your exact words were 'Why should that bastard risk one pimple on his precious arse for us?' After which"—the baron looked up at Nahrmahn once again—"you instructed the Baron to review his arrangements for passing the execution order, if you'll pardon the choice of words, to the assassins you have in place in Manchyr."

Nahrmahn's astonishment had gone far beyond mere shock as Wave Thunder calmly closed the folder once again.

"As you can see, Your Highness," he said, "for us to have obtained this information through any avenue with which you may be familiar, both Earl Pine Hollow and Baron Shandyr would have to have been agents of Charis. Which, I assure you—and I'm quite sure you already know it to be the truth—neither of them would have dreamed of becoming."

"I . . ."

Nahrmahn's voice trailed off, and he shook himself. Then he cleared his throat and sat back in his chair, gazing intently into Wave Thunder's eyes.

"I certainly wouldn't have believed either of them would have betrayed me," he said at last. "On the other hand, I can't see any other way for you to have learned the details of two separate private conversations."

"Your Highness, I allowed *you* to pick the day," Wave Thunder pointed out. "If you would care to pick another day—as, for instance, the following Friday, when you had a private conversation with Commodore Zhaztro, or perhaps Monday, when Bishop Executor Wyllys met with you to 'discuss' your suggestion that 'Mother Church's messengers creep about, like poachers or smugglers, from one wretched little rathole to another'—I'm quite prepared to share the summaries of those other days with you, as well."

"But how—?"

Nahrmahn chopped the question off. He stared at Wave Thunder for several more seconds, then inhaled deeply.

"I begin to understand what you meant about 'needing to know,' My Lord. Understanding it will make my curiosity burn no less brightly, but I'm not about to ask you to compromise your access to information that detailed. And please believe me when I tell you that the realization that you and the Emperor have access to it should quite neatly depress any temptation on my part to even contemplate betraying my oath of fealty to him. After all," the Emeraldian prince showed his teeth briefly, "it's extraordinarily difficult to concoct an effective plot without even talking to your fellow conspirators!"

"I must confess I'm relieved to hear that, Your Highness. And if I'm going to be totally honest, that was, in fact, one of the conclusions both His Majesty and I hoped you would reach. Nonetheless, I was also completely honest when I said we would all appreciate any insight into this information which you might be able to help us to gain."

"I'll be delighted to help in any way I can," Nahrmahn assured him.

"I'm glad. Ah, there *is* one other minor point I need to touch upon, however, Your Highness."

"Which would be what, Baron?"

"His Majesty is aware that you and Baron Shandyr did, in fact, order Hektor's assassination," Wave Thunder said rather delicately. "Now, in the normal course of things, the Emperor would shed no tears if Hektor were to . . . suffer a fatal accident, shall we say? And, to be honest, it would seem a most appropriate fate for someone like Hektor. Unfortunately, we believe any attempt upon Hektor's life would have no more than an even chance of success, at best. And, more to the point, perhaps, there's no doubt in our minds as to who the Corisandians will blame for any such attempt at this time. While we cherish no illusions about the opinions already held in

Corisande where Charis is concerned, we're deeply concerned about the propaganda value the Group of Four might be able to extract from such an attempt. In fact, in many ways, Hektor's assassination—especially if it could be reasonably charged that Charis was responsible—would be more valuable to the Group of Four than Hektor himself, alive, is. With his navy neutralized, and his realm open to invasion whenever we choose to strike, he's scarcely a military asset any longer, nor is there any way the 'Knights of the Temple Lands' could come to his assistance, even if they wished to. So, since he no longer has value as a living ally, someone like Chancellor Trynair, at the very least, would be quick to recognize his greater value as a dead martyr, treacherously slain by murderous Charisian assassins."

Nahrmahn considered that, then nodded.

"I can see your point, My Lord," he acknowledged, not even attempting to pretend he hadn't given exactly the instructions Wave Thunder had said he had. "At the time, for obvious reasons, I was less concerned about how Hektor's demise might affect Charis than I was about how a sudden power vacuum in Corisande might have attracted Charisian attention there and away from *me*. Obviously, that portion of my calculations requires some rethinking under the new arrangement."

"Oh, indeed it does, Your Highness," Wave Thunder agreed with a smile. "And your comment about 'rethinking' brings me to my final point for this meeting. You see, Prince Nahrmahn, Emperor Cayleb doesn't believe you'll find it possible to stop scheming and plotting. Oh," the Charisian raised one hand and waved it back and forth, like a man brushing away an irritating fly, "that doesn't mean he suspects you of some fell intent to betray the oath you just swore. It simply means you are who you are, Your Highness, and this is the way your mind works. More than that, you're very good at it—much better than Hektor even begins to suspect—and it would be foolish of His Majesty to allow such a sharp and serviceable sword to rust into uselessness through disuse. Which is why he has a proposal he would like you to consider."

"What sort of proposal, My Lord?" Nahrmahn asked, his eyes narrowed in speculation.

"His Majesty, with Her Majesty's concurrence, wishes for me to remain here, in my existing post as the Kingdom of Charis' senior spy. It makes particularly good sense in light of the fact that I'm also the man in charge of our domestic security and investigations. Given the potential for internal unrest which the schism with the Church creates, this is scarcely the time for me to be taking my finger off of that particular pulse.

"By the same token, they wish for Baron Shandyr to retain *his* post in Emerald, and Sir Ahlber Zhustyn to do the same thing in Chisholm. That, however, leaves a glaring vacancy which they're considering calling upon you to fill."

"You can't be serious, My Lord," Nahrmahn said. Wave Thunder cocked his head, raising one eyebrow, and Nahrmahn shook his head. "It's been less than three days since I swore fealty to Cayleb, and less than three *years* since I attempted to have him assassinated. Whatever else he may be, Cayleb is neither an idiot nor a fool!"

"You're absolutely right, he isn't," Wave Thunder agreed. "Nonetheless, he and Empress Sharleyan propose precisely what you were thinking about. The Empire will require an *imperial* spymaster, and you, Your Highness, have both the aptitude and the rank and authority to fill that post admirably."

"But only if Cayleb can *trust* me!" Nahrmahn protested.

"First, His Majesty wouldn't have offered you the terms he offered you if he'd felt you'd be likely to betray him. You've just seen the sort of information upon which he based that assessment, and I assure you it wasn't a judgment which was arrived at lightly. Second, do you truly believe, given what you've just learned, that he would be unaware of any actions on your part if you should succumb to the temptation to plot against him? And, third, Your Highness, Emperor Cayleb and Empress Sharleyan—and I, for what it matters—believe you truly mean the things you've said about the Group of Four, Mother Church's corruption, and the inevitable consequences of the events Clyntahn and Trynair have set in motion. In short, we believe you have no reasonable motive to betray any trust the Crown might place in you, and every reason to support the Crown against Clyntahn and his cronies. You may rest assured that neither the Emperor nor the Empress is so foolish as to forget to . . . keep an eye on you until they're certain their judgment is accurate, of course. But as the Emperor pointed out, after so many years of 'playing the great game,' as I believe you've put it upon occasion, it's foolish to think you'll somehow be able to magically stop, however genuine your resolve to do so might be. That being the case, he prefers to channel your natural bent into a useful occupation, rather than letting it tempt you into some sort of . . . mischief, instead."

" 'Mischief,' is it?" Nahrmahn repeated with a snort, and Wave Thunder shrugged.

"Actually, Your Highness, I believe his exact words to the Empress were, 'We're never going to be able to shut that man's brain off, whatever we do. So, the way I see it, either we find a way to make it work *for* us, or else we disconnect it—and the head it lives in—from the rest of his body. And that's so *messy*.' "

Despite himself, Nahrmahn sputtered with laughter. He could just see Cayleb saying exactly that, even picture the glint in the emperor's brown eyes.

And the fact is, he's got a point. I really do intend to behave myself, but even I'm not positive I'll be able to manage that. Yet even so—

"My Lord," he said frankly, "I'm not at all certain His Majesty isn't making a very serious mistake here. And whatever *I* may think about it, I strongly suspect that certain of his own nobles aren't going to be any too enthralled by the notion of suddenly finding *me* in such a critical post. Despite all that, though, I have to confess I'm . . . intrigued by the possibility."

"I realize it's come at you as something of a surprise," Wave Thunder said with generous understatement. "Obviously it's something you're going to have to think about, and His Majesty realizes that. In fact, he recommends you discuss it with your wife. He and the Empress have a lively respect for her intelligence, and she undoubtedly knows you better than anyone else in the world. Including, if you'll forgive me for pointing this out, yourself. See what she thinks about it before you give the Emperor your answer."

"Now that, My Lord," Nahrmahn Baytz said with total sincerity, "sounds like a very good idea, indeed."

.IV.
The Temple,
City of Zion,
The Temple Lands

R hobair Duchairn wondered if he would ever again cross the Plaza of Martyrs without recalling the bloody horror of Erayk Dynnys' execution. The chill bite of fall lay heavy on the city of Zion, despite the sunniness of the day, but his shiver had nothing to do with the temperature as he gazed up at the soaring colonnade of the Temple of God and the mirror-polished dome beyond it, with the heroic sculpture of the Archangel Langhorne raising the scepter of his holy authority high, and remembered that dreadful day. Then he paused in place, eyes closing in silent prayer, although he could not have said exactly what it was for which he prayed.

Troubling times, he thought to himself as he opened his eyes once more and continued across the plaza towards the Temple. *Troubling times . . . and frightening ones.*

The triteness of his own thoughts was irritating, yet that made them no less accurate. The strength of his newly refound faith helped, and he'd found many passages of the *Writ* of tremendous comfort, but not a single scriptural passage told him what he ought to be doing.

Well, Rhobair, that's not quite accurate, is it? he thought sardonically. *You know exactly what you ought to be doing. The only question is how you go about doing it.*

He paused again, the spray of the countless fountains chilly as the brisk breeze blew it across him, and gazed at the very spot where Dynnys had died. The fallen archbishop's execution had been the most horrible thing Duchairn had ever seen, ever imagined. He was no Schuelerite. He'd read the penalties the Archangel Schueler had ruled must be meted out to the apostate and the heretic, yet he'd never allowed his mind to dwell upon them. They'd been one of those unpleasant aspects of life, something the *Writ* called for, but which Rhobair Duchairn had never expected to actually see, far less help to inflict. And he *had* helped. There were times, especially when the dreams came in the middle of the night, when he longed to pretend he hadn't. But the decision to execute Dynnys had been made by the Group of Four, and so Rhobair Duchairn bore his share of the blood guilt. Worse, he was fully aware that the initial decision to execute the former Archbishop of Charis had been made as a matter of pragmatism, an act of expediency. And Dynnys' final words, his defiance of the Grand Inquisitor from the very lip of the grave, those worried Duchairn.

The man had been promised an easy death—or, at least, an easier one—if only he'd played his part. Duchairn hadn't been supposed to know about that arrangement, but he had, and that made Dynnys' defiance even more perplexing. Unless, of course, the most obvious explanation was also the correct one and the man had actually believed what he'd said.

Which he undoubtedly did, Duchairn told himself, gazing at the spot where the tortured wreck of a human being had finally been permitted to die. *That's what truly torments you about it, isn't it, Rhobair? Whatever's happening now, you— you and the other three—set it into motion. Whatever Charis has done since you and your friends orchestrated the attack upon it, you were the ones who began it. You pushed Charis into its damnable actions. Any animal will fight for its life, for the lives of its young, if you push it into a corner, and that's exactly what you did to Charis, and Dynnys knew it. Not only knew it, but had the courage to proclaim it even after the Inquisition had decreed his death.*

It was a thought which had come to him frequently of late, and with the strength of his reborn faith, he made himself face it head-on once again. He'd prayed to God and to Langhorne, begging them to forgive him for the disastrous decisions which had provoked the unthinkable, but the fact that he deeply and sincerely repented his responsibility *for* them did nothing to relieve him of his responsibility to do something *about* them. It would have been his duty to confront the disaster and to somehow bring the Church of God Awaiting victoriously through the ordeal which faced her no matter how it had come about; the part he'd played in provoking that ordeal only made his responsibility deeper.

And however difficult the journey may be, he told himself once again, *ultimately there can be only one destination. This is God's Church, instituted by the Archangels themselves for the salvation of all men's souls. Whatever those misguided souls in Charis may believe, Mother Church must be preserved intact. And because she must, she will.*

There can be no other outcome . . . as long as we who defend her remain true to her, to the Writ, *to the Archangels, and to God.*

He believed that. He *knew* that. What he *didn't* know was whether or not God would ever forgive him for the acts to which he had already set his hand.

He looked one more time at the spot where Erayk Dynnys had died his gruesome death, wondering how many others the Inquisition would send to the same dreadful fate before the challenge to Mother Church's rightful supremacy had been dealt with. Then he shook his head, tucked his hands into the warm comfort of his cassock's full sleeves, and continued on his way.

▼   ▼   ▼

"Well, I see we're all here . . . at last," Zhaspahr Clyntahn said waspishly as Duchairn walked into the conference chamber.

Warm air flowed easily, effortlessly, throughout the chamber, maintaining the temperature at its customary level of perfect comfort. The imperishable conference table—the work, like the entire Temple, of the Archangels' own hands—was as perfect and unmarred by use as it had been on the very Day of Creation, and the illumination radiating from the ceiling itself flowed down with a shadowless brightness no candle or lamp flame could ever hope to challenge. As always, that irrefutable evidence that he was, indeed, in the presence of the Divine reassured Duchairn that whatever errors mere humans might make, God was capable of setting them all right in the end, as long as His servants were only true to their faith.

"I'm sorry I'm late," he said now, crossing to his place at that mystic table. "I had several pastoral matters to deal with, and I'm afraid the time got away from me."

" 'Pastoral matters,' was it?" Clyntahn snorted. "I'd think preserving Mother Church would take precedence over almost any other 'pastoral matter' *I* could think of."

Zahmsyn Trynair stirred slightly in his chair at the head of the table. Clyntahn had become even more caustic and abrasive since Dynnys' execution. It was as if the ex-archbishop's final defiance had goaded the Grand Inquisitor into even greater belligerence and vengefulness. And in some peculiar fashion, Duchairn's obviously resurgent faith actually made Clyntahn even more impatient with the Treasurer General. It was almost as if he feared Duchairn's faith would further soften the resolution of the vicar he'd always regarded as the least resolute of the Group of Four to begin with.

Or perhaps it was simpler than that. Perhaps what had happened with Dynnys had made him wary of what Duchairn might yet do in the name of *his* refound faith.

"Whatever you need to talk about, Zhaspahr," Duchairn said serenely, "my arriving here five minutes early or five minutes late isn't going to have any world-shattering consequences. And since that's the case, I saw no need to cut short the counsel and advice one of my bishops required."

"And how do you—" Clyntahn began irately, but Trynair raised his hand.

"He's right, Zhaspahr," the Chancellor said. The Grand Inquisitor turned his glare upon him in turn, but Trynair only looked back at him calmly. "I agree that a certain degree of urgency in responding to this sort of thing is undoubtedly in order, but we can't afford to simply drop everything and come running whenever some . . . unfortunate bit of news arrives. First, because even with the semaphore, whatever it is that brings us together must already have happened quite some time ago, and our response to it is going to take just as long to reach out from Zion. So frantic haste on our part isn't going to affect things very much, one way or the other. Second, however, is the fact that as vicars of Mother Church, we have many responsibilities, like the ones Rhobair was dealing with this afternoon. We can't allow the schism Charis has created to distract us from all of those other responsibilities. And, third, because it's essential we not allow anyone to *believe* we've been distracted from those responsibilities by it. Never forget that there are those who are merely waiting for the best opportunity to assail us. If we allow them to believe we've been so badly panicked that the schism crisis is the only thing we can think about, those weaker brethren among the vicarate may be tempted to openly defy our guidance."

Clyntahn's jowls had darkened, and he'd opened his mouth to retort angrily, but Trynair's slow, calm, reasonable tone had stopped him. Now he glowered at the Chancellor for another few heartbeats, then shrugged.

"Oh, very well," he growled.

Duchairn simply folded his hands in front of him on the table and waited patiently. He remained wary of the Grand Inquisitor's power and increasingly irascible temper, but he no longer *feared* Clyntahn. Which was probably at least a little unreasonable of him, given what Clyntahn had already done to Erayk Dynnys. And, he realized as he sat waiting, the fact that he was no longer afraid of the Grand Inquisitor quite probably explained Clyntahn's increasing impatience with him. Zhaspahr Clyntahn didn't like the thought of not being feared.

There's something I need to consider more deeply in that, the Church's Treasurer thought. *It says something about him, but it says something about* me, *too.*

"At any rate, we are all here now," Trynair continued. "And since you were the one who requested this meeting, Zhaspahr, why don't you go ahead and tell us why?"

"Two things, really," Clyntahn replied. The Grand Inquisitor's irritation remained evident, but he straightened in his chair and some of the petulance faded from his expression. "One is a message from Bishop Executor Wyllys, and the other is a message from Father Styvyn in Delferahk."

"Father Styvyn?" Allayn Maigwair repeated the name, then grimaced. "Which 'Father Styvyn,' Zhaspahr?"

"He's Bishop Ernyst's intendant in Ferayd," Clyntahn said, and Duchairn's weren't the only eyebrows which rose in surprise.

"And what exactly makes this message from . . . Father Styvyn, was it?" Trynair looked at Clyntahn, who bobbed his head in a curt nod. "Well, what makes this message from him so important?"

"I'll get to that in a moment." Clyntahn waved his right hand as if he were pushing something aside on the table in front of him. "It's important, but I think we need to look at the Bishop Executor's message first."

Trynair nodded, and Duchairn braced himself. He had no illusions about any message Wyllys Graisyn might have sent. Given the tenor of the Emeraldian bishop executor's recent correspondence, it was obvious Emerald's military position was about as close to hopeless as mere mortals could expect to come. And Graisyn's more recent analyses of Prince Nahrmahn's options—and inclinations—hadn't exactly provided cheerful bedtime reading.

"Well, it isn't official yet—or, at least, it wasn't when Graisyn composed his message—but there's not much question that Nahrmahn's turning his coat," Clyntahn growled. All of his listeners sat up in their chairs, eyes narrowing, and he shrugged heavy shoulders. "I know Graisyn's been telling us for months that Emerald wouldn't be able to hold out long once Cayleb put his troops ashore, but I don't think even he saw this coming."

"How good is his information?" Maigwair asked.

"That's always the question, isn't it?" Clyntahn showed his teeth in a tight grin. "Apparently, neither he nor his intendant could confirm or deny the rumors swirling around Eraystor, but they *were* able to confirm that Pine Hollow's been sent off somewhere. And most of the rumors agree that there's only one logical place for Nahrmahn to be sending him. And now, apparently, Nahrmahn himself has sailed off somewhere, as well. Would any of you care to place a small wager on what *his* destination might have been?"

Duchairn's face tightened in dismay. As Clyntahn said, there'd been little doubt the Charisians could conquer Emerald anytime they got around to it. But having Emerald *conquered*, bad as it might have been, was a very different prospect from having Emerald voluntarily align itself with the House of Ahrmahk's defiance of Mother Church's authority.

"I can't believe Nahrmahn would do such a thing," Maigwair said, but his tone was that of a man trying to convince himself, and Clyntahn snorted again.

"I can." The Grand Inquisitor's eyes glowed with anger. "Why shouldn't

Nahrmahn follow Charis' example? They're right next to each other; they're both halfway around the world from Zion, which leaves them ripe for any heresy that comes along; and Nahrmahn's always had the moral character of a dockside whore."

It was typical of Clyntahn, Duchairn reflected sourly, that he could condemn someone else's moral character with absolutely no sense of hypocrisy.

"I'm afraid Zhaspahr has a point," Trynair said. "And, in some ways, it's probably difficult to blame Nahrmahn if he has sought an accommodation with Cayleb."

"*I* can damned well blame him," Clyntahn retorted.

"I didn't say he shouldn't be condemned for it, Zhaspahr," Trynair pointed out. "What I said was that it's difficult to blame him, and on a purely secular level, that's nothing but the simple truth. In fact, that's what's truly dangerous about this."

"The fact that it neatly removes one distraction we were counting on to keep Charis occupied is scarcely a minor consideration, I'd think," Maigwair put in.

"Actually, it is," Trynair disagreed coolly. Maigwair bristled, but the Chancellor shook his head. "Think it through, Allayn," he said. "Emerald was never going to be a *serious* 'distraction' for Charis without a navy to prevent its invasion. Not really, or not for very long, at least. But now Nahrmahn—assuming Graisyn's suspicions prove accurate—has made a political accommodation with Cayleb. I'm not sure how well it's going to work out for him, but I'm assuming that since he sent Pine Hollow ahead, and then followed himself, the terms have to be at least livable. As a matter of fact, if Cayleb is as clever as his father was, he'll probably have offered Nahrmahn remarkably generous terms. He's got a big enough stick in this new navy of his that he can afford to offer some very juicy carrots with his other hand. And if he does, then he's going to make it increasingly tempting for other potential Nahrmahns to reach understandings with him instead of trying to fight him."

"Zahmsyn has a point," Duchairn said unhappily. The other three turned to look at him, and he shrugged. "If Nahrmahn's really done this, then it strikes directly at the reliability of all of the secular lords. He's made a *political* calculation and acted upon it in what can only be construed as deliberate, open defiance of Mother Church. He's put politics and his own personal survival in front of his overriding duty to protect Mother Church's sanctity and authority. Don't think for a moment that there aren't other secular rulers who'd feel exactly the same way in his place. And now they're going to have an example of someone who actually did jettison his loyalty and responsibilities to the Church out of pure political expediency. Do you truly think, assuming he gets away with it, that his example's going to be lost on the next 'Nahrmahn' on Charis' list?"

"Exactly." Trynair nodded vigorously. "This is something which was probably going to rear its head inevitably, whatever happened. Given all the reasons for bad blood between Charis and Emerald, I didn't expect to see it quite this soon, but that only makes the example even worse. If *Nahrmahn* does this successfully, especially when all the world knows Haarahld and Cayleb both held him responsible for attempting Cayleb's assassination, it's going to tell everyone that Cayleb is willing to be 'reasonable.' And if we can't punish Nahrmahn effectively for it, that example is going to generate a lot of temptation to do exactly the same thing when the Royal Charisian Navy comes calling on other princes and kings."

"Then stop it in its tracks," Clyntahn growled.

"And precisely how do you propose to do that, Zhaspahr?" Trynair asked, and his tone was rather more tart than he normally used when addressing the Grand Inquisitor. "If Graisyn's correct, and Nahrmahn's already sailed, he's already accepted Cayleb's terms. He'd hardly sail off to Tellesberg while he's still at war with Charis if he *hadn't* already accepted them, now would he? And do you truly believe he wouldn't have taken precautions against anything Graisyn might do in his absence? In fact, I'm astonished Graisyn got a message off to us at all."

"Don't be *too* astonished," Clyntahn told him. "The dispatch boat from Emerald to Hammer Island left from Shalmar Keep, not Eraystor."

The Grand Inquisitor grimaced, and Duchairn knew why. Shalmar Keep, the capital of the Duchy of Shalmar, was at the extreme northern end of Emerald Island, more than nine hundred miles from Nahrmahn's capital.

"And Graisyn's message wasn't even complete," Clyntahn continued in a harsh voice. "The transmission was interrupted somewhere between Eraystor and Shalmar . . . assuming it wasn't cut off in Eraystor itself."

"Wonderful." Maigwair's expression could have been used to ferment beer, Duchairn thought. "So now you're telling us Nahrmahn's seized the semaphore in Emerald."

"At the very least," Clyntahn agreed. "And I think we can safely assume he wouldn't have seized just the semaphore towers, now can't we?"

"I'm sure you're right about that, too, Zhaspahr," Trynair said. "Which makes my own point even more urgent."

"Agreed." Duchairn nodded. "On the other hand, Zhaspahr, you said you had two messages—one from Emerald and one from Delferahk. Why don't we set Nahrmahn aside for the moment? We're going to have to make some hard decisions in his case, but it might be as well to let that pot simmer away in the backs of our brains for a few minutes. Besides, if these messages are going to have an impact on one another, we probably need to hear both of them before we get too deeply involved with figuring out what to do about *one* of them."

"That makes sense," Trynair agreed, and turned back to Clyntahn. "What about this message from Ferayd, Zhaspahr?"

"I'm not sure it has any bearing at all on Nahrmahn and Emerald." Clyntahn sounded irritated all over again, as if he resented having his ire redirected.

"Perhaps not," Trynair said patiently. "On the other hand, we have to hear it sooner or later, so we might as well go ahead and hear it now."

"Oh, very well." Clyntahn leaned back in his chair. "According to Father Styvyn, the seizure of the Charisian merchant ships in Ferayd didn't go what one might call smoothly."

"What does that mean, exactly?" Duchairn asked, feeling a familiar unpleasant tightening sensation in his stomach muscles.

"It means the frigging heretics were too fucking stupid to do the smart thing," Clyntahn grunted. "When the Delferahkan troops tried to board their ships, they resisted. Which was stupid of them. *Terminally* stupid, as a matter of fact."

"Some of them were killed, you mean?" Duchairn pressed.

"No, I don't mean 'some of them' were killed," Clyntahn half sneered. "I mean *all* of them were."

"What?" The one-word question came from Trynair, not Duchairn, and Clyntahn looked at the Chancellor.

"I mean that once they started killing Delferahkans, the gloves came off," he said, and shrugged. "That's the sort of thing that happens when you're stupid enough to piss off armed troops in someone else's port."

"Are you saying there were no Charisian survivors at all?" Duchairn demanded.

"There may have been a handful." Clyntahn shrugged again. "According to Father Styvyn, there couldn't have been any more than that. Not aboard the ships the Delferahkans managed to keep from leaving port, at any rate."

"You mean some of them got away?" Trynair sounded even unhappier than he had a moment before.

"A half dozen or so," Clyntahn confirmed. "Apparently, they were the ships anchored too far out to be boarded directly from dockside. And at least one of them was apparently one of the Charisians' damned privateers, presumably in disguise. At any rate, it was heavily armed with the new artillery, and it covered the others while they ran for it."

Trynair looked at Duchairn, and the Treasurer General understood the Chancellor's dismay perfectly. Any escapees from Ferayd must be well on their way back to Charis by now, complete with their version of what had happened. And despite Clyntahn's cavalier attitude, Duchairn was sickly certain the Charisians would be able to describe what had happened as a "massacre" with complete accuracy. Worse, many of the ships involved would have been family-owned enterprises, and given traditional Charisian practice where crewing such ships was concerned, a lot of those dead Charisians would have been women and children.

Has it come to this so quickly? Duchairn demanded. *And why is the message about this from this Father Styvyn, and not his bishop?*

He could think of at least one reason for the intendant to have sent his own messages independent of the bishop, and he didn't like that reason one bit. But if Clyntahn suspected that the Inquisition's agent in Ferayd was getting his report in early in an effort to put his own spin on a disaster at least partially of his own creation, no sign of it crossed the vicar's face. For that matter, Clyntahn seemed totally oblivious to the potentially disastrous consequences of the incident.

And for all we know, this isn't the only "incident" like it, either, Duchairn thought. *It could be simply the first one we've* heard *about. So far.*

"This is very serious news," Trynair said, with what Duchairn privately considered to be dizzying understatement. "Once word gets back to Charis, they're going to denounce this entire unfortunate affair as a deliberate massacre carried out at the Inquisition's direct orders."

"It was nothing of the sort," Clyntahn said. "On the other hand, I'm not going to pretend I'm shedding any tears for a batch of heretics who got exactly what their own heresy and stupidity deserved. For that matter, they got off *lightly*."

"I'm not asking you to pretend anything." Trynair kept his voice level, his tone even. "I'm simply pointing out that Charis is going to proclaim to the entire world that we ordered the deliberate slaughter of merchant seamen—and their *families*, Zhaspahr—as part of our campaign against the schismatics. They'll use it to justify their rebellion . . . and whatever counter-atrocities they decide to stage."

Clyntahn looked at the Chancellor as if he were speaking a completely unknown language, Duchairn thought. And from the Grand Inquisitor's perspective, perhaps Trynair was. After all, they'd been prepared to unleash fire, slaughter, and devastation on the entire Kingdom of Charis from the outset, so why should anyone get particularly upset over the deaths of a few dozen—or a few hundred—Charisian sailors and their wives and children?

"All right," Clyntahn said after a moment. "If you're so worried about how the Charisians can use this, then let's use it ourselves. Father Styvyn's dispatch makes it abundantly clear it was the Charisians who began the fighting. And, I might add, the Delferahkans' casualties weren't exactly light. Since they started it, I think we should tell the world exactly that. The Delferahkan authorities attempted to peacefully sequester their vessels, and instead of submitting to the instructions of the legal authorities, they resisted with deadly force. I'm sure the Charisians are going to hugely exaggerate their own casualties, so I don't see any reason why we should downplay the Delferahkans' losses. In fact, I think we should probably declare that anyone who was killed attempting to carry out Mother Church's orders to sequester those ships should be declared a martyr of God."

It wasn't "Mother Church's" decision to close the mainland ports against Charis, Duchairn thought grimly. *It was yours, Zhaspahr. And it was done on your authority. Amazing how your new formulation of what happened gets you off of that particular hook, isn't it?*

But that wasn't the worst of it—not by a long chalk. If they declared the dead Delferahkans martyrs, then they moved an enormous stride closer to declaring all-out Holy War against Charis. No doubt that was inevitable, in the fullness of time, but Rhobair Duchairn was in no hurry to embrace that cataclysm.

And is that simply moral cowardice on your part, Rhobair? If that's our inevitable destination, why hesitate? It's God's will that His Church's authority be maintained in accordance with His plan, so how can you justify trying to avoid doing whatever is re- quired to accomplish His ends?

"I don't know. . . ." Trynair said slowly.

"I think Zhaspahr's right," Maigwair said. The others looked at him, and it was his turn to shrug. "The smartest thing we can do is to use the sema- phore to see to it that our version—the true version"—he actually managed to say that with a straight face, Duchairn noted—"reaches all the mainland realms before any lies Charis may choose to tell. And if these men were killed carrying out Mother Church's orders, then what *are* they, if they aren't mar- tyrs?"

"Exactly!" Clyntahn agreed vigorously.

Trynair looked at Duchairn again, and the Treasurer General knew ex- actly what the Chancellor's eyes were asking him. He started to open his mouth to disagree with Clyntahn and Maigwair, then hesitated.

"Besides," Maigwair continued while Duchairn wavered, "when you look at this news alongside Nahrmahn's decision to betray us—Mother Church, I mean—there's a pattern."

"A pattern?" Trynair didn't quite manage to keep his incredulity out of his tone, and Maigwair's lips tightened.

"What I mean," he said, "is that as you pointed out just a few minutes ago, other secular rulers are going to be tempted to seek some sort of accom- modation or understanding with Charis if they find themselves between the rock and the hard place. I think we need to give them a reason to think long and hard about that. And we need to make it clear to everyone in Charis ex- actly what stakes they're allowing their king to play for."

"How?" Duchairn asked with a distinctly sinking sensation.

"I say we formally excommunicate Cayleb, Staynair, and every single person who signed Staynair's appointment as archbishop, or Cayleb's writ of succession, or Staynair's letter to the Grand Vicar. We excommunicate Nahrmahn, Pine Hollow, and anyone else who reaches an 'understanding' or 'accommodation' with Charis. And we place all of Charis and all of Emerald under the interdict."

Duchairn's sinking sensation accelerated abruptly, but Clyntahn's eyes flashed.

"That's exactly what we ought to do," he agreed harshly. "We've been tiptoeing around from the outset, trying to avoid 'inflaming the situation,' when we've all known all along exactly where it has to end! What we should have been doing instead was putting the damned schismatics on notice, telling them exactly where they're going to end up if they persist in this defiance. And we need to tell every single one of Cayleb's subjects what sort of disaster their precious King is leading them directly to!"

"This isn't a step to take lightly," Duchairn cautioned. "And if we do take it, it isn't one we'll be able to take back later."

Excommunicating Cayleb and the others would be bad enough. Under Church law, it would absolve every child of God from obedience to them. Indeed, it would make *continuing* to obey them an act of defiance against the Church and against God. Assuming most Charisians were prepared to follow Church doctrine, it would in effect dissolve all legal authority in the kingdom. Yet, in many ways, the interdict would be even worse. As long as the interdict was in effect, *all* Church sacraments, offices, and functions within Charis would be suspended. There would be no baptisms, no weddings, no masses, no burials. And that would continue until the interdict was lifted.

Inflicting such severe and weighty punishment was, as Duchairn had said, never something to be undertaken lightly. Its consequences for the souls of those caught up in it might well be dreadful.

That was bad enough, yet it was scarcely all that might follow from Maigwair's proposed actions. The declaration of excommunication and the interdict was only one tiny step short of the declaration of Holy War, and once Holy War was openly declared, there could be no stepping back from a life or death grapple between the Church and those opposed to her.

And the one thing this isn't going to do is convince Charis to return willingly to the fold, he thought. *Cayleb and Staynair would never have gone as far as they have already if they weren't prepared to go all the way, and even Zhaspahr's reports make it clear the overwhelming majority of Charisians agree with their King and their new "Archbishop." So even if we declare Cayleb excommunicate and all of Charis under the interdict, they won't care. Or, at least, they won't pay any attention. They'll continue in their allegiance to him, which will mean we've created a situation in which they'll be in direct, open defiance of Mother Church. And that will leave us with no choice but to declare Holy War in the end, whatever we might wish.*

I wonder if that's exactly why Zhaspahr and Allayn are so in favor of this? Because it will commit us once and for all, before the entire world, to the complete destruction of Charis?

"It may not be a step to be taken lightly," Clyntahn said, "but it's a step we'll have to take sooner or later, Rhobair, and you know it. Given what Zahmsyn's already said, I think we have no choice but to go ahead and do it now. Take the offensive and preempt whatever distorted version of events Charis might choose to publish to the world. Unless, of course, you have a better idea?"

▼   ▼   ▼

Icy rain pelted down from a midnight-dark sky, although it was technically still an hour or so before official sunset. Wind lifted sheets of water, blowing it into the faces of anyone foolish enough to be out and about in it and weaving delicate veils of dancing mist where it whipped the water cascading from eaves.

None of the visitors converging on the Church of the Holy Archangel Bédard had either the time or the inclination to stop and observe the weather. The landscaped shrubbery and ornamental trees around the church flogged limbs to which the last colorful sprays of leaves still clung or waved branches already bared by approaching winter as the wind lashed at the church's solid stonework, and that was a far better metaphor for the visitors than any fanciful visions of dancing water.

The Church of the Holy Archangel Bédard was quite old. Tradition had it that Archangel Bédard's had been built within only a year or two of the Temple itself; although unlike the Temple, it was manifestly the work of mortal hands. And despite its antiquity, it was little used these days. It lay within less than two miles of the Temple, and any who could preferred to walk the additional few thousand yards to worship at the Temple. Despite that, its age, and the fact that the Bédardists considered it the mother church of their order, meant it was carefully maintained, and like every church, its doors were perpetually unlocked, open to any worshipper at any hour, as the law required.

Yet the Temple's proximity meant the church was undeniably all but forgotten by the vast majority of the Faithful, and so it was left to itself most of the time, drowsing away in the shadows of its larger, newer, and more prestigious brothers and sisters. Indeed, most of the time people seemed to forget it was even there, which was what made it appropriate to the ends of the men gathering within it despite the pounding rain.

The last visitor arrived, slipping through the heavy wooden doors into the church's anteroom. He surrendered his cloak to a waiting under-priest, revealing the orange cassock of a vicar of the Church of God Awaiting, and then walked briskly into the church proper. The residual scent of centuries of incense, candlewax, and the printer's ink of prayer books and hymnals, greeted him like a comforting hand, despite the wet, autumnal chill which could be clearly felt even here, and he drew the perfume of Mother Church deep into his lungs.

Twenty-odd other men waited for him. Most of them wore the same orange cassock he wore, but there were others in the more modest attire of archbishops and bishops. There were even a couple of mere upper-priests, and all of them turned to look at him as he arrived among them.

"I beg your pardons, Brothers." Vicar Samyl Wylsynn's deep, beautifully trained voice, well suited to his priestly calling, carried easily through the sound of rain pounding on the church's slate roof and pattering against the stained-glass windows. "I had an unexpected visitor—on purely routine Church business—just as I was preparing to leave."

Several of the other men had tensed visibly at the words "unexpected visitor," only to relax with almost audible sighs of relief as Wylsynn finished his sentence. He smiled wryly at their reactions, then waved one hand at the pews at the front of the church.

"I believe we should probably be about *our* business, now that the late arrival is among you," he said. "It would never do to have to explain what the lot of us are doing out here on a night like this if someone should happen by."

As he'd intended, his choice of words engendered a fresh air of urgency, and the others settled quickly into the pews he'd indicated. He himself walked to the rail around the sanctuary, genuflected to the traditional mosaics of the Archangels Langhorne and Bédard, then rose and turned to face them once again.

"First," he said gravely, "allow me to apologize for summoning all of you on such short notice. And for asking you to gather for an unscheduled meeting. All of us are only too well aware of the risks involved in improvising meetings such as this, but I believe it's essential we and all other members of the Circle be made aware of the Group of Four's most recent decisions."

No one else spoke, and he could literally feel the intensity of their eyes as they gazed at him.

"They're reacting to two new messages," he continued. "One is from Emerald, and strongly suggests that Prince Nahrmahn has elected to align himself with King Cayleb and the 'Church of Charis.' Whether he's done so out of conviction or out of the pragmatic need to survive is more than anyone here in Zion can possibly guess at this moment. Somewhat to my own surprise, I find myself inclining to the theory that it may, indeed, be a matter of conviction, or at least a combination of the two. I base this in no small part upon past conversations with Earl Pine Hollow's younger brother, but I emphasize that it can be only an opinion at this time. Nonetheless, judging from what my sources in Clyntahn's office have been able to tell me, I believe our

Grand Inquisitor's interpretation of Nahrmahn's actions is essentially accurate, whatever the Prince's motives may have been.

"The second message is from Ferayd, in the Kingdom of Delferahk. My sources were able to get me an actual copy of the original semaphore message, which doesn't quite match exactly what Clyntahn reported to the other three. According to the original message, the attempt to seize the Charisian galleons in the port turned into a bloodbath after someone in one of the boarding parties shot and killed a woman armed only with a belaying pin. There's no question, according to the dispatch, but that the Delferahkans shot first and that their very first victim appears to have been a woman whose sole 'crime' was to attempt to prevent them from boarding her husband's ship."

Wylsynn's face was grim, his eyes bleak, and he felt the same anger radiating from his audience.

"Once the Charisians realized they were under attack and began attempting to defend themselves, it turned even uglier," he told them. "In fact, according to this Father Styvyn's letter, only fourteen Charisians survived to be taken into custody by the Inquisition."

"Only *fourteen*, Your Grace?" a voice asked. The shock in Archbishop Zhasyn Cahnyr's voice was mirrored in his expression, and Wylsynn nodded.

"I'm afraid so, Zhasyn," he said heavily. "Even in a personal message to Clyntahn, this Father Styvyn didn't want to be too explicit, but there's no real question. The Delferahkan troops massacred virtually every Charisian they got their hands on, and from the very careful way 'Father Styvyn' chooses his words, I'm quite certain that one reason the troops 'got out of hand' was because they were being egged on by him and his fellow Schuelerites."

Wylsynn himself wore the sword-and-flame of the Order of Schueler, and shame made his voice even flatter and harder than it might have been otherwise.

"May God have mercy on their souls," Vicar Gairyt Tanyr murmured.

"Amen," Wylsynn agreed quietly, bowing his head. There was a moment of silence, made somehow stiller and more intense by the sound of the autumn storm lashing the church's exterior. Then Wylsynn raised his head once more.

"No one in the Office of Inquisition is going to admit what actually happened. In fact, Clyntahn hasn't even admitted the full truth to the other three. I'm not sure why. It may be that he's afraid of Duchairn's possible reaction. At any rate, the official position of Mother Church is going to be that the Charisians provoked the Delferahkans who were only attempting to peacefully board and 'sequester' their vessels. It was the *Charisians'* fault there was any fighting at all, and their resistance was obviously a result of their heretical rejection of Mother Church's legitimate authority to order their vessels detained. Clyntahn is also planning on grossly exaggerating the number of Delferahkan casualties while understating the number of Charisian dead."

Someone muttered something indistinct which Wylsynn felt quite certain went poorly with the speaker's high clerical rank.

"In addition to all of that," he continued, "there's the reason they're in such a hurry to get their version of events out. It seems at least some of the Charisians got away—in fact, one of the galleons must have been a heavily armed privateer, judging by the amount of carnage it appears to have wreaked on its way out of Ferayd Sound. That means it isn't going to be very long before Charis starts telling *its* version of what happened, and the Group of Four wants to be sure it already has its story straight and issued for public consumption before any inconvenient little truths turn up to challenge it."

"Much as I despise Clyntahn, I can understand his reasoning, Samyl," Vicar Hauwerd Wylsynn said. Hauwerd looked a great deal like his older brother, with the same auburn hair and gray eyes, although he was a member of the Order of Langhorne, not a Schuelerite. At the moment, his expression was just as grim as Samyl's, as well.

"Oh, we all *understand* it, Hauwerd," Samyl replied. "And they're undoubtedly correct that almost any of the mainlanders who hear the 'official' version are more likely to believe it than the Charisians' version, especially if they hear the Church's version first and get it set into their minds. Unfortunately, no one on the other side is going to believe it for a moment, and the fact that the Church is obviously lying is only going to be one more nail in the coffin of any hope of reconciliation."

"How realistic is that hope, anyway?" Vicar Chiyan Hysin asked.

Hysin had been born into one of the powerful Harchongese dynasties. In the Empire, more than in most Safeholdian realms, the nobility and the traditional church dynasties tended to be identical, and Hysin's older brother was a duke. Despite that, and despite the Harchongese tradition of arrogance and extreme conservatism, Hysin had been a member of the Circle since he'd been an under-priest. There were points in the doctrine of reform on which he and Wylsynn disagreed, but his dual status as secular aristocrat and Knight of the Temple Lands gave him an often invaluable perspective. And unlike most members of the Circle—including, Wylsynn admitted, himself—Hysin had always been skeptical of any possibility of peacefully resolving the Charisian schism.

"I don't know that there ever was any realistic hope," Wylsynn admitted now. "What I *do* know, though, is that if there ever was any such hope, the Group of Four is doing its very best to demolish it as quickly as possible. Not only are they planning to declare that every Delferahkan killed at Ferayd is a martyr of Mother Church, but they intend to excommunicate Cayleb, the entire clergy of the 'Church of Charis,' every Charisian noble who accepted Cayleb's succession and Staynair's appointment as Archbishop, and also Nahrmahn, his entire family, and anyone else who may have supported, joined in, or even simply passively accepted his decision to seek terms from Cayleb. And just for good measure, they intend to place all of Emerald and all of Charis under the interdict."

"They've gone mad, Your Grace!" Cahnyr blurted.

"It sounds that way, doesn't it?" Wylsynn agreed. "As a matter of fact, the only thing that really surprised me when I heard about all of this is that they've stopped short of simply going ahead and declaring Holy War right now. Clyntahn, for one, not only sees that as inevitable but is actually eager to be about it, I think."

"They didn't go ahead and declare it yet because Trynair, at least, is smart enough to realize they have to prepare the ground for it first," Hysin said. The others looked at him, and the slightly built, dark-haired vicar shrugged. "There's never been a true Holy War in all of history," he pointed out. "Not, at least, since Shan-wei's defeat. Even the most faithful are going to have qualms about embracing *The Book of Schueler*'s ordinances where Holy War is concerned. Despite the general belief in Dynnys' guilt, there was a great deal of shock and revulsion right here in Zion when they tortured him to death on the Temple's front steps, and that was actually *mild* beside what Schueler laid down for cases of large-scale heresy." The Harchongese vicar's oval eyes were hard with remembered anger and disgust. "If they expect to treat entire kingdoms to the same sort of punishment, they're going to have to whip up enough hatred, enough anger, to carry the rest of the Church hierarchy—and the common folk—along with them. Which is precisely what they're doing here."

"And what can we do to stop them?" Tanyr asked.

"I don't know," Wylsynn admitted. "We and our predecessors have been waiting for over twenty years now for the opening we need, and it's persistently eluded us. We have all the evidence we've collected over those years to prove the corruption and doctrinal perversion of people like the Group of Four. But we still don't have the opening wedge we need to make use of it."

Several heads nodded in bitter agreement, and Wylsynn managed not to grimace in even more bitter memory. He'd come so *close* to beating Clyntahn out as Grand Inquisitor, and if he had, he would have been in a position to use all of the evidence, all of the proof, people like him, Ahnzhelyk Phonda, Adorai Dynnys, and so many others had carefully gathered and substantiated. Of course, it was just as probable he would have gone the same way as his ancestor, Saint Evyrahard. But at least he'd been willing to try, and unlike the murdered Evyrahard, he'd carefully built at least a small core of fiercely loyal supporters who would have tried hard to watch his back as he recalled his own order and the Office of Inquisition to their high purpose of policing

Mother Church, and not simply terrorizing God's children in the *name* of Mother Church.

"We certainly don't have any opening now," Hysin agreed. "At the moment, opinion's setting strongly in the Group of Four's support on the Council."

"Can't *any* of those idiots see where this is headed?" Hauwerd Wylsynn demanded. Everyone recognized it as a rhetorical question, born of bitterness and frustration, but Hysin shrugged once more.

"Frightened men see only what offers them a chance of survival, Hauwerd. Charis' military victories would be frightening enough without adding Cayleb and Staynair's open defiance into the mix. Deep down inside somewhere, all of them must recognize how corrupt we've become here in Zion and, especially, in the Temple. They're terrified of what may happen if the windows are pried open and all of their dirty little secrets are revealed openly to the flock they've been supposed to be shepherding, and the Charisians are threatening to do exactly that. Anything that lets them cling to the possibility of continuing 'business as usual' is bound to attract powerful support."

"Until they discover that it isn't going to let them do that at all," Vicar Erayk Foryst put in.

"*If* they discover it," Hysin replied. "Don't forget how long we've already been waiting for our opportunity. If the confrontation with Charis turns into a full-blown Holy War, then the Council as a whole is going to voluntarily surrender what's left of its decision-making power to the Group of Four on the basis that fighting and winning such a conflict requires unity and centralized direction. And that, Erayk, is precisely what Clyntahn is counting on."

"I don't think it's *all* cynical calculation on his part," Vicar Lywys Holdyn said. The others looked at him, and he snorted. "Don't misunderstand me. Cynical calculation would be more than enough for Clyntahn, but we'd be foolish to risk forgetting that streak of zealotry of his." Holdyn's mouth twisted as if he'd just tasted something sour. "I think he's one of those people who believes the ferocity with which he forces *other* people to behave buys *him* a degree of license. The 'good' he does so hugely outweighs his own sins that God will overlook them."

"If that *is* what he believes, he's going to pay a terrible price," Samyl Wylsynn observed quietly.

"Oh, I don't doubt that for a moment," Holdyn agreed. "If God knows His own, so does Shan-wei, and no mere mortal—not even the Grand Inquisitor of the Church of God Awaiting—can fool either of them when he meets them face-to-face. But in the meantime, he's in a position to wreak immense harm, and I don't see a way we can stop him."

"Unless he and the Group of Four continue to suffer reverses like Crag Reach and Darcos Sound," Tanyr pointed out. "If it's mainly fear which inspires the rest of the Council to follow them—and I think you're essentially correct about that, Chiyan—then still more, equally spectacular disasters are bound to shake the other vicars' confidence in Trynair and Clyntahn. A horrible number of people are going to be killed and maimed in the process, but if Cayleb and any allies he manages to gain can throw the Church obviously back on the defensive, I think the Group of Four's support will vanish."

"Which is a bit like saying that if the house burns down, at least you won't have to fix the leaks in the roof," Hauwerd Wylsynn observed.

"I didn't say it was an ideal solution, Hauwerd. I simply pointed out that the Group of Four's arrogance may yet be its own downfall."

"And if the Group of Four falls," Samyl Wylsynn pointed out to his brother, "then the door will be open for the Circle. Perhaps once the rest of the Council has had a chance to recognize that brute force isn't going to succeed, it will be willing to admit at least the possibility that the true answer lies in reforming the abuses the Charisians have so rightly identified and protested."

"Even if that happens, do you honestly believe this 'Church of Charis' will ever voluntarily return to Mother Church?" Foryst asked, shaking his head, and Wylsynn shrugged.

"To be honest? No." He shook his own head. "I'm beginning to come to Chiyan's view of the future, I'm afraid. By the time we're able to convince the Council that the Group of Four is leading all of us to disaster—*if* we ever manage to convince the others of that—too much blood will have been shed, and too much hatred will have been engendered. I'm very much afraid that whatever else happens, the schism between Charis and the Temple is unhealable."

The silence in the rain-lashed church was profound as the Circle's leader finally admitted that.

"In that case, is Clyntahn's determination to forcibly suppress the schismatics really wrong?" Holdyn asked. All of them looked at him, and he waved one hand in the air before his face. "I'm not saying the man isn't a monster, or trying to suggest that his initial solution to the 'Charisian problem' wasn't loathsome in the eyes of God. But if we've reached a point where the Charisians will never return voluntarily to Mother Church, what other option than *forcing* them to return will lie open to us as the vicars of God's Church?"

"I'm not certain forcing them to return, by any means, is the right course," Wylsynn replied, facing the issue squarely. "With all due respect for the traditions of Mother Church, perhaps the time's come for us to simply accept that the people of Charis are not going to submit to what amounts to foreign rule of their own church any longer."

He looked around the other, worried faces and wondered how many of them were thinking what he was. The Church's "traditions" didn't always perfectly reflect historical truth. That was one of the things which made Maikel Staynair's appointment as Archbishop of Charis—and his letters to the Temple—so dangerous. It was enormously ironic that the rebellious arch-bishop had chosen to base so much of his argument on Grand Vicar Tomhys' writ, *On Obedience and Faith*. That writ of instruction's true purpose had been to establish the doctrine of the Grand Vicar's infallibility when he spoke in the name of God. Which, as Wylsynn, for one, knew perfectly well had been a new and radically different formulation of doctrine, justified on the basis of "necessary change." And the same writ had moved the Church's confirma-tion of bishops and archbishops from the archdiocesan level to that of the vic-arate itself.

That had been in the year 407, and in the five centuries since, it had be-come the Church's tradition that it had *always* been so. Indeed, most people—including many of the clergy, who should have known better—truly believed that to have been the case. Which was what made the fact that Staynair had used the same writ's authorization of canonical change when events within the world made it necessary so damnably ironic . . . and dangerous. For the Church to deny the authority of Tomhys' writ in Charis' case was to deny its authority in *all* cases. Including that which, ultimately, had made the vicarate the undisputed master of the Church in the first place.

From Wylsynn's perspective, that would almost certainly be a very good thing. From the perspective of the Group of Four and those like them, it was anathema, complete and total.

"All of you know my son was Dynnys' intendant," he continued. "In fact, he understood from the beginning the reasons why I actually helped Clyn-tahn engineer his 'exile' to Tellesberg rather than trying to fight it. I've shared most of his private letters with other members of the Circle. He's convinced—and I have great faith in his judgment—that whatever else the Charisians may be, they aren't servants of Shan-wei, and that their general hostility towards Mother Church is directed at her *hierarchy*—at the Group of Four . . . and at the rest of the vicarate because of our failure to restrain people like Clyntahn. So I believe we have to ask ourselves a fundamental question, Brothers. Which is more important? The outward unity of Mother Church, enforced by swords and pikes against the will of God's children? Or the con-tinued, joyous communion of those children with God and the Archangels, even if it be through a hierarchy other than our own? If the only point of true doctrinal disagreement lies in the infallibility of the Grand Vicar and the overriding authority of the vicarate, isn't it perhaps time we considered saying to our brothers and sisters in Charis that they are still our brothers and sisters, even if they refuse to submit to the authority of the Temple? If we let them go their own way to God, with our blessing and continued prayers for their salvation, rather than attempting to force them to act in violation of their own consciences, perhaps we can at least blunt the hatred between Tellesberg and the Temple."

"Accept the schism as permanent, you mean?" Hysin asked. The Harchongese vicar seemed surprised to hear such sentiments from any Schuelerite, even a Wylsynn.

"So long as it's only schism, and not true heresy, yes," Wylsynn agreed.

"That's getting much too far ahead of ourselves," Tanyr said after a moment. "First, we have to survive, and somehow Clyntahn and the others have to be taken out of the decision-making positions of Mother Church." He smiled without any humor at all. "That's quite enough of a challenge for *me*, I think."

"To be sure." Wylsynn nodded.

"Actually, in some ways, I find Duchairn more worrisome than Clyntahn at the moment," Hysin said. Several others looked at him questioningly, and he frowned. "Unlike the rest of the Group of Four, I think Duchairn's actually rediscovered the *Writ*. Everything I've seen suggests a genuine resurgence of faith on his part, but he's still wedded to the rest of the Group of Four. In an odd sort of a way that actually serves to legitimize the Group of Four's policies in a way Clyntahn doesn't . . . and can't."

"Because it's obvious that unlike Clyntahn, he's not making cynical calculations—anymore, at least—you mean?"

"That's exactly what I mean, Hauwerd." Hysin nodded. "Even worse, I think he may well prove a rallying point for vicars who might otherwise support the Circle. Vicars who're genuinely tired and heartsick over the Church's abuses may see in him and in his regenerated faith the model for their own regeneration. And I'm very much afraid that whatever *we* may think about the acceptability of a permanent schism, Duchairn isn't prepared to entertain that concept at all."

"Perhaps it's time we started thinking about recruiting him for the Circle," Foryst suggested.

"You may be right," Samyl Wylsynn said after several seconds of careful thought. "But even if it might prove possible to recruit him, we need to be very, very cautious about how we approach him. First, because we might be wrong—he might regard us as traitors, as an internal threat to Mother Church's unity at the greatest moment of crisis in her history. But, second, because he's so close to Clyntahn. And Trynair, of course; let's not forget that our good Chancellor is scarcely an idiot, however much he may act like one upon occasion. But I would be absolutely astonished to discover that Clyntahn isn't using the Inquisition to keep tabs on his three 'allies.' If he is, and if we approached Duchairn even a little clumsily, it could be disastrous for everyone."

"Agreed," Foryst said. "And I'm not suggesting we rush right out and invite him to our next meeting. But I do think it's time we began considering this possibility seriously, and thinking about ways we might approach him if the time should come when it seems appropriate. Arguments to convince him we're right, and ways of presenting those arguments that aren't likely to trigger any alarms in Clyntahn."

"I see you haven't lost your taste for formidable challenges, Erayk," Hysin said dryly, and a chuckle ran around the seated vicars and bishops.

"Very well," Samyl Wylsynn said after the chuckle had died. "We've all been brought up to date, and we've all had a chance to discuss our current thinking where the schism—and the Group of Four—are concerned. I don't believe we're in a position to decide on any new policies or strategies at this point. Not, at least, until we've had an opportunity to see how the Group of Four's version of events in Ferayd, Charis, and Emerald plays out once it's finally presented to the rest of the Council. Between now and then, I think all of us need to pray and meditate in hopes that God will show us our true path."

Heads nodded gravely, and he smiled more naturally and openly than anyone had since their arrival.

"In that case, Brothers," he said, "won't you join me in a moment of prayer before we venture back out into all that wind and rain?"

.V.
Army Training Ground and Manchyr Cathedral,
Duchy of Manchyr,
Kingdom of Corisande

The SNARC's deployed sensor was parked on Hektor of Corisande's right shoulder, where it provided Merlin with, among other things, an exquisitely detailed view of the prince's ear hair. There were times—many of them—when Merlin had felt severely tempted to use the sensors' self-destruct capability to remove Hektor from the equation once and for all. The remotes had been designed to be capable of working together with their clones to destroy specifically targeted circuits in enemy installations with their incendiary/shaped-charge "suicide pills," and it wouldn't have been particularly difficult for him to maneuver several of them deep into the Corisandian's ear canal and use their combined charges to eliminate him while he slept.

Unfortunately, he wouldn't be able to disguise what had happened, and even if Safeholdian healers had been trained by rote according to *The Book of*

Pasquale rather than on any scientific basis, an explosive burst of flame sufficient to burn holes through tempered steel plates inside an ear canal would be
hard for any postmortem exam to miss. The questions *that* would raise—
including the inevitable allegations that the Charisians must have done it using black arts provided to them by their true mistress, Shan-wei (which, after
all, would be uncomfortably close to the truth)—scarcely bore thinking
upon.

It's bad enough that everyone in Corisande already thinks we tried to kill him once,
Merlin reflected, swiveling the sensor's field of view away from the prince's
hairy earlobe and back out across the grassy hillside on which Hektor, his
daughter, and the Earl of Coris sat their horses with Earl Anvil Rock. *Adding
charges of witchcraft to the mix couldn't make anything better!*

The thought brought a slight smile to his lips, but his amusement vanished as he reflected upon what Hektor had come here to see.

Manchyr was six hours ahead of Tellesberg. Although it would be some
hours yet before the sun rose over Cayleb's capital, the morning was already
well advanced in Corisande, and the troops who'd been detailed to demonstrate their new weapons for Hektor had been waiting for him and the
princess for almost an hour.

"All right, Rysel," Hektor said. "Your reports have been interesting enough.
I'm looking forward to seeing the actual guns."

"I don't think you'll be disappointed, My Prince," Anvil Rock told him.

"I'm not expecting to be," Hektor assured the earl.

Anvil Rock grinned at him, then nodded to the youthful officer standing
beside him. The young man picked up a flag from the grass at his feet and
waved it vigorously overhead. Someone down at the deployed battery of guns
saw it and waved another flag in response, and the waiting gun crews swung
into action.

The guns themselves looked odd, especially in comparison to the pieces
Seamount was in the course of providing for Charis. The barrels were short
and stubby, which only made sense, Merlin supposed, since they'd been
copied directly from the sketches Captain Myrgyn had sent home. Myrgyn
had sketched only the carronades the Charisian galleys had mounted in their
broadsides, not the long guns they'd mounted as chase weapons, and most of
the new Corisandian artillery was being made to that pattern.

Earl Tartarian had recognized the implications of the carronades' shorter
inherent range once the Navy had begun test firings, and the third pour of
naval artillery had increased barrel length to extend the weapons' range.
Anvil Rock and his son were familiar with the modified, longer naval pieces,
but they'd chosen to stick to the carronade pattern for their new field artillery.
That let them put considerably heavier guns into the field for the same weight
of metal, and even the "field carronades," as Merlin had decided they needed

to be called to separate them from proper field *guns*, had several times the effective range of smoothbore matchlock muskets. Against that sort of infantry weapon, the artillery Anvil Rock had designed made excellent sense. Unfortunately—or, perhaps, *fortunately*, from Merlin's perspective—Anvil Rock wasn't aware of the fact that the Charisian Marines were now armed with *rifles*, not smoothbores.

Not that his carronades aren't going to be a big enough pain in the ass to go on with, Merlin thought grimly. *And he and his son were certainly right about the throw-weight side of things. They're going to be deploying twenty-four-pounders on carriages the size of the ones we're using for* twelve-pounders, *and there are going to be plenty of instances in which we can't make use of our rifles' maximum ranges against them. Which is going to* hurt. *A lot.*

And if they haven't figured out about rifles, Anvil Rock's over-clever, pain-in-the-ass son has obviously figured out the implications of the flintlocks our artillery uses instead of slow match.

The new musket-sized flintlocks already being issued to the Corisandian Army might still be smoothbores, but they were going to fire a lot faster and be a lot handier than the old-style matchlocks. Fortunately, the Corisandians had run into a bottleneck producing the smaller, lighter wooden stocks for the converted weapons, but they were still going to have a lot more of them available than Merlin and Cayleb had hoped.

The gun crews had been busy while he pondered the gloomy implications of the field carronades' existence and the new muskets. They'd made full use of the concept of bagged charges, as well, he observed. They were still using meal powder, at least—Myrgyn's notes clearly hadn't told them how corned powder was made—which meant it was weaker, weight for weight, and that even the individually bagged charges had a tendency to separate into their constituent ingredients if they were carried very far. But while that was all well and good, they'd still improved their artillery's rate of fire considerably.

And that's another place where their shorter gun tubes are going to help them, Merlin reflected. *Their gunners are going to be able to fire more rapidly than ours can, which means that* shoe, *at least, is going to be on the other foot . . . and pinching hell out of our toes, at that.*

The distant flag down by the artillery waved once again, and then the guns boomed. The flat, hard, dull concussion pounded at the witnesses' ears, their horses twitched under them at the unfamiliar noise, and the weapons' shorter barrels made their muzzle flashes even more impressive. Perfectly round, dirty-white smoke rings drifted off on the gentle breeze, and the guns' round shot smashed into the waiting targets with terrific force.

Baron Seamount favored straw-stuffed mannequins as demonstration targets, and Merlin had always found the clouds of flying, golden hay highly—even gruesomely—effective for making his point. Earl Anvil Rock, on the other hand, favored casks of water, and the huge, sun-shot spray patterns as the round shot tore through the barrel staves were spectacular. So was the rate of fire the gunners demonstrated as they moved through the routine of serving their pieces as smoothly and efficiently as any Charisian gun crew.

I do wish the other side could be composed solely of idiots, Merlin thought glumly, watching the nascent Corisandian field artillery demonstrate its paces for Prince Hektor. *Those things are going to be copper-plated bitches to deal with, especially in any sort of close terrain. And given how much less metal there is in each carronade, their foundries can turn out more of them—and faster—in the time they've got.*

In the long run, he felt confident, Seamount's longer field guns ought to be able to master their shorter-ranged Corisandian counterparts. But "the long run" wasn't something he especially wanted to rely upon, not when "the short term" was going to be punctuated with Charisian bodies. At least the lack of any Corisandian experimentation with rifles meant Charisian infantry was going to retain a major advantage in any sort of ranged combat. That alone ought to pretty much guarantee tactical superiority on the battlefield.

On the other hand, the French rifles were superior to the Prussians' in the Franco-Prussian War, and that didn't keep the Prussian artillery from kicking the French Army's ass. Now there's a cheerful thought, Merlin!

He grimaced, continuing to watch the demonstration play out across the backs of his eyelids as he sat in his darkened room. Cayleb wasn't going to be happy to hear about this, he decided, but that could have its good points, as well. Now that Nahrmahn was no longer the enemy, the question as to what constituted the next natural strategic objective for Charis had been drastically simplified. Now, watching the new weapons Hektor was putting into the field, it was obvious to Merlin that it was time to accelerate their timetable for the invasion of Corisande.

I just hope we can accelerate it enough, he thought.

▼   ▼   ▼

"That was truly impressive, Rysel," Prince Hektor told Anvil Rock with simple sincerity as the gun crews swabbed out the bores of their weapons.

"You can thank Koryn for most of it." Anvil Rock smiled, his pride in his eldest son evident. "Well, him and Charlz Doyal. We'll have three complete batteries in service by the end of next five-day, and they're concentrating on grapeshot and canister for field use. I don't suppose we'll be battering any walls down anytime soon."

"I don't imagine so." Hektor smiled thinly. "In point of fact, I'm fairly confident *Cayleb* expects to be the one doing any wall-battering. I'm going to rely on you and Koryn to see to it that he's disappointed in that respect."

"We'll do our best, My Prince." Anvil Rock touched his breastplate in formal salute, half bowing in the saddle, and Hektor nodded.

"I know you will, Rysel. I know you will."

Anvil Rock straightened, then glanced down the hill to where the artillerists were almost done with their post-demonstration cleanup.

"My Prince, it would do morale a world of good if you could have a few words with the men."

"I'd be delighted to," Hektor said with a smile. "And do you think having Irys say a little something might help, too?"

"My Prince," Anvil Rock smiled at the princess, "most of these men are young, impressionable, and away from home for the first time in their lives. Having a beautiful young princess tell them how wonderful they are is bound to help morale! But it would probably be a good idea for me to go and warn them they're about to be visited by royalty before you suddenly turn up."

"'*Beautiful!*'" Irys sniffed, then smiled at her cousin. "Go and warn them to be suitably stricken by my incomparable loveliness, you mean, don't you, Uncle Rysel?"

"Actually," Anvil Rock said with an expression of unusual sobriety, "you need to spend a little more time looking into your mirror, Irys. Since all those knobby tomboy knees and scraped elbows became things of the past, you've started to look a lot like your mother. And, to be perfectly honest, your mother was the one thing I ever truly envied your father over." His eyes softened for a moment, then brightened with a gleam of humor. "Of course, it *was* an arranged marriage. Otherwise, I'm certain, she would have opted for my own incomparable masculine grace and charm. I certainly tried hard enough to convince her to elope with me, but she was always a slave to family duty."

"No doubt," Hektor said dryly, then smiled himself. "I think it's time you trotted on over and warned your artillerists about our impending arrival. I'd hate to be forced to deprive myself of my best field commander by beheading you for lèse-majesté on the very eve of invasion."

"Of course, My Prince!" Anvil Rock slapped his breastplate again, wheeled his horse, and went cantering down the gentle slope in a spatter of damp clods of earth.

"Did Uncle Rysel really want to marry Mother?" Irys asked her father softly as the earl rode away.

"No." Hektor shook his head, smiling faintly after Anvil Rock. "Oh, he adored her, no question of that. But he was already very happily married, and he loves his wife, too. Actually," he turned to look at his daughter, "everyone adored your mother, I sometimes think. And Rysel's right. You do look more and more like her every day, despite your hair. Hers was closer to chestnut. Your brother got that. It's a pity he didn't get anything else."

"Father—" Irys began, and Hektor grimaced.

"I'm not going to start in on him again, I promise. And you're right. He *is* young, and there's still time for him to grow into the crown. Or, there ought to be, anyway. But as much as you love him, I can't help wishing he could develop at least a *little* of the urgency you seem to feel over our imminent invasion by Charis. I'd feel a lot happier over the succession if he would."

Irys' expression was obviously unhappy, but she only nodded.

"And speaking of the succession," Hektor continued, lightening his tone deliberately as he turned to the Earl of Coris, who'd sat his horse to one side while he and Irys talked, "are there any further clues as to who was behind that assassination attempt?"

"No, My Prince," Coris admitted. "My agents have interviewed every shop owner, street vendor, and beggar in Manchyr looking for witnesses who might be able to identify the assassins or tell us where they went after the attack. We've even tried—without success—to find the maker of the arbalests on the off-chance that he might remember who bought them from him. The only thing I can tell you for certain is that their proof marks aren't Corisandian."

"They aren't?" Hektor rubbed his chin contemplatively. "That's interesting. Do we have any idea whose proof marks they are, since they aren't ours?"

"I suspect they're Harchongese, My Prince. Unfortunately, Harchong is rather outside our normal area of interest. I'm trying to get confirmation of that, but so far without much luck."

"But they're not Corisandian, and they're from far enough away— wherever they were actually made—that you're finding it difficult even to identify the maker," Irys said, her hazel eyes as thoughtful as her father's. "That's significant itself, don't you think?"

"Possibly." Coris nodded. "The same thought had occurred to me, Your Highness. Foreign weapons, difficult to trace, might well suggest this was carefully planned by foreigners. I don't think we ought to jump to any conclusions in that regard, however. That's not to say I'm not strongly inclined towards the same one you're suggesting, only that I'm trying to keep my mind open to other possibilities."

"I understand, My Lord." Irys smiled at him. "And I'm grateful to you for reminding me of the need to consider possible culprits besides Cayleb."

"If anyone in the entire Princedom, besides the two of you, is blaming anyone but Cayleb for it, *I* haven't heard anything about it," Hektor said wryly.

"Good!" Irys turned back from Coris and showed him her teeth. "If it wasn't Cayleb, *I'm* not going to shed any tears over seeing him blamed for it anyway. And judging from the reactions I've been seeing, the idea that he tried to kill you has truly infuriated quite a few of your subjects, Father!"

"Amazing how a foreign assassination attempt can make people forget all the reasons they have for being . . . irritated with their own prince, isn't it?" Hektor observed with a chuckle.

His daughter's eyebrows furrowed, and he chuckled again, harder.

"Irys, no matter how good a prince may be—and I've never made any pretensions to sainthood, sweetheart—at least some of his subjects are going to be unhappy with him about something. It happens. I couldn't make everyone happy even if I tried, and it's not really the fault of those I make *unhappy* that they don't like me very much. That's one reason I try not to step too heavily on any one group—here at home, at least—and one reason to balance the nobility and its demands and desires against the commons and *their* demands and desires. I don't lose any sleep over the fact that I can never satisfy everyone, but the ruler who forgets that at least some of his subjects have *legitimate* reasons to be unhappy with him isn't likely to continue to rule very long."

She nodded very seriously, and he smiled at her.

Rysel is even righter than he knows, he thought. *You're so much like your mother. And Hektor isn't enough like me . . . or your mother. But at least he'll have you, won't he, Irys? And maybe he'll actually be smart enough to listen to you. I'm sure a more unlikely miracle has happened somewhere in history . . . even if I can't think of one right offhand.*

"Earl Anvil Rock is waving his flag again down there, My Prince," Coris observed.

"Then let's ride down and enhance a little morale, shall we, Irys?" Hektor said lightly, and turned his horse towards the waiting artillerists.

▼   ▼   ▼

"I hate relying on anyone from Siddarmark," Bishop Executor Thomys Shylair said unhappily.

"As do I, My Lord," Father Aidryn Waimyn, Bishop Executor Thomys' intendant, agreed. "At the moment, however, we don't have very much choice, do we?"

Shylair shook his head, but his expression didn't get any happier, and Waimyn was scarcely surprised. Unfortunately, they truly didn't have much choice at the moment. It was painfully evident that the Royal Charisian Navy—and for all Waimyn knew, veritable swarms of Charisian privateers—were going to gleefully take, sink, or destroy every Church dispatch boat they encountered. On the other hand, the accursed heretics had every motive to avoid irritating the Republic of Siddarmark. Which meant, galling as it was to admit it, that Shylair's dispatches to the Council of Vicars and the Office of Inquisition in Zion stood a much better chance of reaching their destinations aboard a Siddarmarkian merchant ship than they would have aboard one of Mother Church's own vessels.

"I'm afraid Archbishop Borys and the Chancellor aren't going to be very happy to read our messages even when—*if*—they receive them," the bishop executor continued. "And I doubt very much that Vicar Zhaspahr's going to be delighted to hear Hektor is dabbling with the same 'improvements' as the Charisians!"

"I doubt he will be," Waimyn agreed.

On the other hand, the intendant thought, *it's not as if* Hektor *has a lot of choice, either. And whatever the Grand Inquisitor may choose to decree from Zion, the truth is that I can't see anything in the new artillery that comes close to violating the Proscriptions, either.*

That was not a point he intended to make in any of his own correspondence. He understood that anything of Charisian origin was going to be suspect in Zhaspahr Clyntahn's eyes. In fact, to some extent, he was in wholehearted agreement with the head of his own order in that regard. And whether or not there was anything impermissible about the new artillery, the fact remained that its introduction was symptomatic of Charis' infernal fascination with new and dangerous things. Waimyn often thought Charisians were in love with change for the sake of change itself, however vociferously they might protest that they were seeking only increased efficiency within the allowed bounds of the Proscriptions. And the fact that they were so far away from Zion and the Temple generated its own tendencies towards dangerous independence of thought, as Waimyn knew from his own experience here in Corisande. Corisandians were nowhere near so demonically fixed on overturning the established order wherever they found it, yet even they were far more . . . freethinking than any servant of the Inquisition could ever find truly comfortable.

Despite all of that, however, Waimyn firmly believed that, in the end, Mother Church—*and, yes, even Vicar Zhaspahr, for that matter!*—was going to have to adopt at least some of the Charisian innovations. The new artillery, for example, and the acceptance of the primacy of the cannon-armed galleon over the traditional galley. The advantages those things bestowed upon Charis were simply too great to be overcome without duplicating them.

And won't that *make the Grand Inquisitor happy?* Waimyn thought acidly.

"I wish we could at least tell them something about who tried to kill Hektor," Bishop Executor Thomys said.

"I thought the entire world knew it was Cayleb, My Lord," Waimyn said with a chuckle, and Shylair snorted.

"If you truly believe that, Aidryn, I have some nice property on the bottom of Temple Bay I'd like to sell you!"

"Oh, *I* don't believe it, My Lord, but that probably makes us the only two men in the entire League of Corisande—outside of Prince Hektor and Earl Coris, of course—who don't. And you have to admit it's had a salutary effect on support for the Prince here in Corisande."

"Yes, it has," Shylair acknowledged. "In fact, I shouldn't admit it, but there are times I almost wish whoever it was had succeeded."

Waimyn's eyes narrowed, and the bishop executor shook his head quickly.

"I said *almost*, Aidryn. Still, the truth is that unless Cayleb's a lot more incompetent than his performance to date has given us any reason to think, he's going to beat Hektor. Despite any of these new Charisian 'innovations' Hektor may choose to adopt, he's going to lose in the end. When he does, it's going to be one more blow at Mother Church's position, and knowing Hektor, there's always the chance he'll at least try to reach some sort of last-minute accommodation with Cayleb, if the only alternative is outright defeat. And *that*, Aidryn, will be even more destructive to Mother Church. Hektor dead at Charisian hands, and a martyr to God's cause, could at least be a rallying point. Hektor alive, and a prisoner of Charis, languishing in some noisome dungeon somewhere, might even be useful to us. But Hektor alive and *negotiating* with Charis is going to be anything but an asset."

"That's true enough, My Lord," Waimyn agreed, but he also shook his head. "Somehow, though, I doubt it's ever likely to happen. If there's one person on the face of Safehold Cayleb of Charis hates with every fragment of his being, it's Hektor of Corisande, especially since his father's death. Unless I'm seriously mistaken, about the only negotiating token Cayleb would be willing to receive from Hektor would be his own beating heart."

"I know. I know!" Shylair waved one hand. "I didn't say it was likely, Aidryn. That doesn't stop it from keeping me awake at night from time to time, though."

Waimyn nodded in understanding. He rather liked the bishop executor, although he'd always thought of Shylair as something of an intellectual lightweight. He'd hardly have ended up assigned to someplace like Corisande and an archbishop like Borys Bahrmyn otherwise. But God knew the man was under enough stress for any three bishops executor. Small wonder if his imagination was turning to even the most unlikely of scenarios.

Still, the intendant thought, *if there's one thing in the entire world I'm confident of it's that not even Langhorne himself could work out any sort of 'negotiated settlement' between Hektor of Corisande and Cayleb of Charis!*

.VI.
Tellesberg Palace
and
The Sailor's Lady Tavern,
City of Tellesberg,
Kingdom of Charis

The mood in the throne room was ugly.

Although the official report hadn't been delivered yet, the rumors about its content had spread like wildfire since *Kraken* and the merchantmen under her protection had arrived in Tellesberg, two hours earlier. Captain Fyshyr had sent an immediate letter to the palace, announcing his return and alerting his king (only Cayleb was technically an "emperor" now) and queen (who was also an empress, and who he'd had no notion he was about to acquire when he'd sailed) that he had vital news. Now, Fyshyr walked across the polished stone floor towards the paired thrones, and his grim expression warned everyone that the rumors had been only too accurate.

It was the first time the captain had ever visited the palace or personally encountered his king, and it was obvious he was nervous. On the other hand, the importance of his mission seemed to be providing an antidote for any jitters he might be inclined to feel. The chamberlain escorting him touched his elbow and whispered something into his ear, stopping him the proper distance from the thrones, and Fyshyr bestowed a somewhat awkward but profoundly respectful bow upon his sovereign.

"Your Majesty," he said, then added a hasty, "and Your Grace," in Sharleyan's direction as he obviously remembered his last-minute coaching.

"Captain Fyshyr," Cayleb responded. The captain straightened, and the emperor looked him straight in the eye. "I've read your letter with great concern, Captain. I realize you were able to give me only the barest details in it, but before you say anything else, I wish to acknowledge before these witnesses"—he waved one hand at the court officials and sundry aristocrats around them—"how grateful the Crown and I personally are to you. You did well, Captain. Very well. As well"—this time Cayleb looked away, letting his eyes survey the people his hand had already indicated—"as I could have expected even from a Charisian seaman."

Fyshyr flushed with pleasure, but the grimness of his expression didn't falter, and Cayleb sat back in his throne.

"And now, Captain," he said, "I'm afraid it's time for you to tell us what you've come here to say. I want everyone to hear it directly from you."

"Yes, Your Majesty." Fyshyr drew a deep breath, visibly bracing himself, then began. "We were anchored in Ferayd Sound, Your Majesty. There'd been some tension, but until that night, we didn't have any real reason to expect that—"

▼   ▼   ▼

"—so after we'd picked up *Arrowhead*'s survivors, I came straight home to Tellesberg," Captain Fyshyr finished just over an hour later. "I had my clerk interview all the Charisians we'd picked out of the harbor on our way out, and I brought them with me to the Palace for you to speak with personally, if you wish. Your chamberlain has them."

The mood in the throne room had been ugly when Fyshyr arrived; now it had been whetted to an edge of incandescent fury. There'd actually been a handful of interruptions—mostly as profane as they'd been angry—as the captain reported what had happened. Especially what the single survivor they'd picked up from the galleon *Wave* had had to say about how the massacre had started.

Empress Sharleyan had hardly been surprised. Although she'd only recently become a Charisian by marriage, the people of Charis weren't *that* different from Chisholmians, and volcanic outrage had surged up in her with actual physical force as she listened. One look at Cayleb's profile had shown both his matching anger and the harsh discipline which held it in check, yet there was something else about his expression. Something which puzzled her. Not his fury, or his discipline, but his . . . preparedness. He'd had time to read Fyshyr's preliminary letter, of course. Sharleyan had read it with him, in fact. So obviously this hadn't all come at him completely cold. But that was true for her, as well, and yet she had the distinct impression that he'd already guessed far more of the details they were about to hear than she had.

Don't be silly, she scolded herself. *You're still getting to know him, you twit! You already knew he was one of the most disciplined men you've ever met, so why should you feel surprised when he shows it?*

Which was obviously true, but still didn't dismiss that slight sense of puzzlement.

"I'd already said you did well, Captain." Cayleb's voice drew her out of her thoughts once more. "I now wish to repeat that. In fact, you performed outstandingly." He looked across at Earl Gray Harbor. "My Lord, I want this man's name added to the Order of Queen Zhessyka. See to it."

"Of course, Your Majesty." Gray Harbor bowed slightly, and Fyshyr flushed with embarrassment once more. The knightly Order of Queen Zhessyka had been instituted by the House of Ahrmahk almost two centuries earlier. It could be awarded only to those who had distinguished themselves in battle in the service of Charis, and it was not lightly given.

No, it isn't, Merlin thought from his position behind Cayleb's throne. *But if it's ever been well deserved, this is the time.*

"I assure you that you'll soon be receiving additional proof of the Crown's gratitude, Captain," Cayleb continued, turning back to Fyshyr. "When you return to your ship, please tell the rest of your ship's company they won't be forgotten, either."

"Thank you, Your Majesty," Fyshyr got out, speaking rather more awkwardly than he had when he'd been confining his remarks to mere matters of life, death, and massacre.

"And also inform them," Cayleb said grimly, "that King Zhames and the Church in Delferahk will soon receive a message of rather a different sort from me and from all of Charis."

"Thank you, Your Majesty," Fyshyr repeated, and this time there was no awkwardness at all in his hard-eyed response.

"And now, if you will, Captain," Cayleb continued, standing and nodding to the chamberlain who'd waited patiently through the captain's entire lengthy account, "please go with the chamberlain. Quarters here in the Palace have been prepared for you. Go and refresh yourself, but please hold yourself in readiness if I should send for you."

"Of course, Your Majesty. Your Grace." This time Fyshyr remembered Sharleyan, and she felt her lips trying to twitch in an inappropriate smile despite the gravity of the occasion.

Fyshyr bowed to them again, and this time Cayleb returned it with a formal nod of his own head. He stood there, waiting while Fyshyr followed the chamberlain out of the throne room, then turned back to Gray Harbor.

"My Lord, I believe it's time the Council discussed this . . . incident."

▼   ▼   ▼

"—and burn the bastards' city to the ground!"

"Aye, with them *in* it!"

The first speaker turned his head, peering through the thick fume of tobacco smoke which hazed the main taproom of The Sailor's Lady. The tavern was one of the two or three biggest on the entire Tellesberg waterfront. The Red Dragon and The Golden Keg each had their champions as being larger than The Lady, but there wasn't any true question as to which was queen of the sailors' drinking establishments. The fact that The Lady's owner was always careful to set an excellent table, as well, and that one could always count on finding fresh vegetables waiting for one after even the longest voyage, had more than a little to do with that.

But the air of contented homecoming which so often filled The Lady's taproom and dining rooms was notably absent today.

"Let's see how *their* women and children like it!" someone else snarled.

"Here, now!" a burly, broad-shouldered seaman with grizzled hair braided in a long pigtail said sharply. "There weren't no *women* trying to come aboard our ships! No, nor any children, either!"

"No, but they started—"

"Shut your damned trap!" the seaman barked, coming off of his stool at the bar like a galley breaking an enemy's column. He forged through the crowd like an angry doomwhale, and it parted before him like nearcod while the man who'd been shouting—and who looked much more like some counting house clerk than a seaman—stepped back quickly. He was still stepping back when a solid wall stopped him, and he froze as the sailor glared at him.

"Aye, I want our own back," he told the unfortunate clerk, nailing him to the floor with fiery eyes. "But whatever it may be *they're* inclined to do, and whatever those mother-loving Inquisition bastards might think, I'll not have the blood of women and children on my hands! No, and not on my *Kingdom's* hands, neither!"

"Hey, now," the barkeep said soothingly. "Tempers are hot, and they're going to get hotter. Let's not be going for each other."

"Yes!" someone else said. "Sit back down. Let me buy you another round."

The sailor settled back down, and the clerkish man disappeared. The exchange had interrupted, however briefly, the steadily mounting firestorm of outrage which had enveloped The Sailor's Lady ever since the seagoing community of Tellesberg had discovered the truth was even worse than the rumors had been.

The man who'd just departed had been very much out of place in that taproom at that time. The men—and women—in it were overwhelmingly professional seamen and their wives. Every one of them had known someone who'd been in Ferayd, and every one of them knew it could just as easily have happened to them, or to their husbands, brothers, sisters.

Or children.

The fury seething barely below the surface was a bitter, ugly thing. The majority of those present might have agreed with the grizzled seaman, but at least some of them had obviously agreed with the clerk, instead. And even those who hadn't agreed with him wanted vengeance, as well as justice. The long-standing anger against Corisande and the Group of Four hadn't gone away, hadn't abated. But this was different. It was new, it was ugly, it was *personal* . . . and it was the direct doing of the Church.

There was no question of that in the minds of the men and women gathered in The Sailor's Lady. Every single one of the handful of survivors from the ships which had been tied up at dockside in Ferayd had reported exactly the same thing. Reported the presence of Schuelerite priests in the boarding parties. Reported the shouted exhortations to "Kill the heretics!"

Even some of those who'd entered the tavern as Temple Loyalists now shared the bone-deep hatred that had aroused, and the infuriated reaction was already spreading beyond the waterfront district and into the city of Tellesberg as a whole.

"I still say burn the bastards' city down!"

"Why, as to that," the grizzled seaman growled, looking up from his beer mug, "I'm with you there! Aye, and ready to ship out tonight to do it, too!"

A general rumble of agreement snarled through the taproom, and the owner poked his head through the archway from the dining room.

"Don't be getting greedy, lads—or you, either, lassies—but the next round is on the house!" he announced.

"Aye, and here's the toast!" someone shouted. *"Death to the Inquisition!"*

▼　　▼　　▼

The mood in the council chamber was quieter than the one in The Sailor's Lady's taproom, but it was no less bare-clawed.

Prince Nahrmahn was present in his new position as Councilor for Imperial Intelligence. The newfangled title still sounded more than a little peculiar, but it was no less odd than seeing the man who'd been one of Charis' mortal enemies until so very recently sitting at the same table with the Royal Council of Charis.

Actually, with the *rest* of the Royal Council of Charis.

At least the news from Delferahk's managed to distract the "Old Guard" from their suspicions about Nahrmahn, Merlin thought from his place just inside the council chamber door. *For now, at least.*

"—subjects are going to expect prompt, severe action, Your Majesty," Ahlvyno Pawalsyn was saying. "And it's hard to blame them, either. For that matter, if this is allowed to pass unanswered, it's much more likely the Group of Four will actually succeed in closing the mainland ports against us and keeping them that way."

"But if we take strong action against Delferahk, then we up the stakes all around, don't we, My Lord?" Paityr Sellyrs, Baron White Church and Keeper of the Seal, seemed almost as worried as he was angry. Not surprisingly, perhaps, Merlin thought dryly, given what a huge percentage of his personal wealth was tied up in the merchant ships he owned. Most of the other councilors looked at him, and he shrugged.

"I'm not saying action isn't called for, Ahlvyno!" he said, carefully confining his remarks to Baron Ironhill, rather than looking in his monarch's direction. "Obviously, it is. I'm only saying that when we're already at war with Corisande and Tarot, and the Church seems to be on the point of declaring Holy War, we don't need to be adding *another* war to all of that."

"With all due respect, My Lord," Sharleyan said, "it isn't 'another war';

it's the same one we're already fighting with those ... people in Zion. They've simply chosen to open another front."

"Her Grace is right," Gray Harbor said firmly. "This has Clyntahn's touch written all over it."

"You think the massacre was intentional, Rayjhis?" Admiral Lock Island asked.

"I'm not really prepared to decide about that either way," Gray Harbor replied without so much as twitching an eyelid in Captain Athrawes' direction. "On the one hand, it would have been an especially stupid thing for them to do on purpose. On the other hand, it might not strike *them* that way. Especially not Clyntahn and Maigwair. The two of them would probably favor anything that drives a deeper wedge between us and any appearance of reasonableness."

"You're saying they might have deliberately engineered a massacre in order to goad us into a disproportionate response of our own?" Sharleyan said thoughtfully. "One they could use to good advantage when they paint us as the bloody-handed villains trying to destroy God's Church?"

"I'm saying they *might* have thought that way, Your Grace." Gray Harbor shrugged slightly. "At the same time, remember that you should never ascribe to malice what can be put down to incompetence. So far, this is the only port where we've had anything like this happen. Of course, it's also the first port where we know our shipping has been seized, at all. I doubt very much that King Zhames would have run amok this way on his own, however, and the presence of Schuelerites in the boarding parties would obviously argue against that, as well. But if we assume this has been part of a general offensive against our merchant ships and crews, then the same thing may have happened in dozens of seaports. Or, conversely, ships may have been seized elsewhere with a minimum of violence. If it turns out this is the only place a massacre resulted, then I'd think it indicates there was no direct order from the Temple for bloodshed."

"God knows it wouldn't be the first time troops got out of hand, misunderstood their orders, or just plain fu—er, *fouled* up their execution, Your Grace." General Hauwyl Chermyn was not officially a member of the Council, but his role as the senior officer of the Royal Charisian Marines (and the fact that he'd happened to be in Tellesberg for an entirely separate series of meetings with Lock Island and Cayleb) had brought him to the council chamber. Clearly, he wasn't accustomed to his present situation, as witness his fiery blush as he shifted in mid-verb out of deference to Sharleyan, but there wasn't an ounce of quitter in him, and he continued gamely. "If there wasn't 'supposed to be' any fighting, then if any of our people *did* fight back, the troops may well have exceeded their orders. I'm not saying that would justify anything they did. I'm only saying it happens, and that it wouldn't have taken an order from the Grand Inquisitor to *make* it happen this time."

"I find myself in agreement with the General's comments, Your Majesty. Indeed, his observations accord well with my own estimate of what's happened," Nahrmahn said. If the rotund little Emeraldian felt out of place sitting at the council table, there was no sign of it in his expression or his manner. One or two people frowned, but it was little more than an automatic reflex. Even those who remained least reconciled to the bizarre and unnatural notion of the Prince of Emerald as the father-in-law (by betrothal) of the Charisian crown prince had quickly realized that the "fat little bugger," as King Haarahld had been wont to call him, had a far nimbler brain than most of them had ever suspected.

"And that estimate is, Your Highness?" Cayleb asked.

"My personal belief, which I hasten to add is based solely on my own analysis of the Group of Four's probable motives, not on any concrete evidence, is that what occurred at Ferayd was not intended when the orders to sequester our shipping"—Merlin wondered if calling Charisian merchant ships "our shipping" felt as peculiar to Nahrmahn as *hearing* him call them that felt to everyone else—"were initially given. Or, at least, not specifically ordered. While it's probably true Clyntahn would feel a certain satisfaction, and Maigwair definitely wouldn't *mind* that it had happened, neither Trynair nor Duchairn would have wanted it."

"That does make sense," Ironhill acknowledged after a moment. "Duchairn certainly wouldn't want anyone we're not already at war with to do anything which would cause us to retaliate against their own shipping on a grand scale. And it's pretty obvious Trynair's doing all he can to delay the next major clash until the Temple finishes building up its naval forces."

"Which so far appear to consist entirely of galleys," Lock Island noted with profound satisfaction.

"Well, I don't really care *why* it happened," Sir Rahnyld Seacatcher, Baron of Mandolin, growled. "The point is that it *has* happened, Your Majesty. And it happened because those bastards in Zion—beg pardon, Your Grace—*ordered* it, whether they specifically wanted a massacre or not. So, as far as I'm concerned, it's time to teach a lesson to anyone who seizes our shipping and murders our seamen!"

There was a general almost-snarl of agreement. Cayleb, Sharleyan noticed, failed to join it. And so did Earl Gray Harbor, Archbishop Maikel, and Baron Wave Thunder. She'd quickly discovered that those three were the most accurate barometer for what Cayleb himself might be thinking, and she frowned mentally as she considered Mandolin's argument.

A part of her agreed fiercely. In fact, she was just a little surprised to discover how "Charisian" she'd come to feel over the last few five-days. She told herself she would have felt the same way if it had been Chisholmian merchant ships and seamen and their families, and that was true. But she was still a little bemused to find herself identifying so powerfully with her new husband's subjects as her own.

Another part of her agreed solely on the basis of cold political and military calculation. Whether the massacre had been intentional or not, it had, as Mandolin had pointed out, happened. Allowing it to pass unavenged for any reason would be seen as an indication of weakness by Charis' enemies and potential friends alike.

Yet despite that, *another* part of her dreaded the expansion of warfare which seemed implicit in Mandolin's position. Not simply because it would mean more people would be killed, but because of the way it would dilute the combat power of the new Charisian Empire.

We don't need a distraction from Hektor right now, she thought, and realized with something very like surprise that Cayleb must already have recognized that point. In fact, it seemed as if his closest allies in the council must have seen it also, and she wondered when and how they might have found time to discuss it.

You're making mysteries out of nothing again, she told herself. *They've known Cayleb since he was a boy. Of course they'll have realized how his mind is working without his having to tell them. God knows Mahrak does that for you often enough!*

All of which was perfectly logical . . . and did nothing to change her stubbornly persistent feeling that something more was involved.

"You've made an excellent point, Sir Rahnyld," Cayleb said. "I'd like to remind everyone, however, that we have a rather pressing problem to the east, as well. Does anyone at this table really want to think about what Hektor may be able to do if we give him any more months to work with than we have to?"

The thoughtful silence which answered him was profound, Merlin observed dryly.

"Obviously, we can't know everything Hektor might be doing," Gray Harbor said . . . not entirely accurately, Merlin thought. "On the other hand, we all know he isn't exactly a drooling idiot, unfortunately. We have to assume he's making preparations for the invasion he knows as well as we do is coming."

"Actually, Prince Nahrmahn and I may have a report on his preparations sometime in the next few days, Rayjhis," Wave Thunder said. "I'm expecting to hear from certain agents of mine sometime quite soon now."

Nahrmahn simply nodded, his expression serene, as if he had some idea of what Wave Thunder was talking about, and Merlin felt a smile tickling the corners of his mouth.

"That will be very welcome, Bynzhamyn," Gray Harbor said with a nod of his own. "However, the point we all need to bear in mind right this minute is the one His Majesty's already raised. If we allow this massacre to divert us from our focus on Hektor, it may cost us dearly."

"I agree." Sharleyan was a bit surprised by how firmly her own two-word sentence came out, but she didn't let that faze her. "Obviously, I have my own reasons for wanting to see Hektor dealt with. Nonetheless, I think it should be clear to all of us that he represents a far greater potential danger to us than Delferahk ever could. Not only do we already know he's our enemy, even without the Church's prompting, but he's closer to us. And, as Earl Lock Island's just pointed out, all indications are that the Group of Four is laying down only new *galleys*, whereas I think we'll all agree Hektor is far too smart—and far too well aware of what just happened to his navy—to make that particular mistake."

"Precisely." Cayleb nodded and smiled at her.

"I have to agree, as well," Lock Island said, far more reluctantly. "At the same time, though, Your Grace, Baron Mandolin's point is very well taken. We have to respond to this."

"Oh, I agree, Bryahn," Cayleb said. "I simply want everyone to bear in mind that the nature of our rather pressing commitments means that some of the things we might *like* to do are mutually exclusive."

"Very well, Your Majesty, we'll all bear that in mind," Lock Island said, eyeing his youthful monarch speculatively. "Now suppose you tell us what you've already decided *we're* going to decide to do about this?"

Sharleyan still felt more than a little surprised when one of Cayleb's councilors showed the temerity to speak to him that way. Very few monarchs would have tolerated it, yet Cayleb actually seemed to *encourage* it, out of his closest advisers, at least.

And the fact that they feel comfortable enough with—and confident enough in—him to actually do *it probably explains why he gets so much out of them.*

"Actually, I have had a thought or two on the subject," Cayleb admitted mildly, and despite the gravity of the events which had brought them together, more than one of his councilors raised a hand to hide a smile.

"In simplest terms, we do need to respond, but we also need to retain the majority of our fighting power for use against Hektor and Corisande. Also, I believe it's important that whatever response we make be clearly appropriate to the provocation. We're going to have a fight on our hands getting anyone to accept—or to openly admit that they do, at least—that our version of events is the truth, instead of the lies we all know the Group of Four are going to manufacture to justify their actions and blacken ours. We don't need to make their mouthpieces' task any easier."

Even Mandolin nodded, and the emperor continued.

"So far as we now know, the only place where this has happened is Ferayd.

It's possible we'll find out differently, in which case we may have to reconsider things. If, however, it turns out that this did happen only at Ferayd, then our legitimate quarrel will be with King Zhames and his Kingdom. We may protest the seizure of our ships by other realms, but under the accepted law of nations, protesting is the appropriate response at this point *unless* there's been deliberately inflicted, avoidable loss of life. Which is precisely what seems to have happened at Ferayd.

"In addition, there's the . . . complication that all of the witnesses agree the Inquisition was directly involved. In fact, that Inquisitors deliberately *incited* the massacre." The youthful emperor's expression turned bleak, his eyes into brown flint. "Whatever Clyntahn and the Group of Four may claim, those Inquisitors *knew* they were goading King Zhames' troops into murdering women and children aboard those ships. Somehow I find it difficult to believe a *child* could be guilty of heresy, whatever its parents might have done, and I think it's time we reminded of the Inquisition of what the *Writ* says about the murder of innocents." Those flinty eyes went to Maikel Staynair's face. "I believe the relevant text is in *The Book of Langhorne,* isn't it, Maikel? Chapter twenty-three, if I recall correctly?"

The archbishop looked back at him for a moment, then nodded slowly.

"I believe you're thinking about verse fifty-six, Your Majesty," he said." 'Woe be unto the murderers of innocence, for the blood of the innocent cries out to the ear and heart of God, and He will not hold His hand against its shedders. Better for them never to have been born, for His curse is upon them, His wrath will find them out, and He will use the hand of the righteous to destroy them utterly.' "

"Yes, that's the passage I had in mind," Cayleb agreed grimly.

"Excuse me, Your Majesty," Baron White Church said in a very careful tone of voice, "but—"

"I'm not planning on holding the entire city of Ferayd responsible for those deaths and stringing up every head of household in the city limits, My Lord," Cayleb interrupted the Keeper of the Seal. "But I do intend to call the guilty to account. Whoever they may be."

There was dead silence in the council chamber for several seconds. Sharleyan glanced at the faces of the men seated around the council table and felt that silence singing in her bones. White Church looked profoundly unhappy, and one or two others certainly looked . . . less than eager, yet she was almost surprised by how little true resistance she sensed.

And why should I be surprised? She shook her head mentally. *As White Church himself pointed out, we're already at war with the Church, and with enough just cause for* twenty *kingdoms!*

"And how will you establish that guilt, Your Majesty?" Staynair asked quietly at length.

"I don't propose to select two or three dozen Temple Loyalist priests at random and hang them as examples or reprisals, Maikel." Cayleb's expression lightened slightly, and he snorted. "Mind you, there are times I find the temptation to do precisely that greater than at others. However, if we're not going to act without evidence right here in Charis, we can't do the same thing somewhere else, either. Not unless we want to open ourselves to the deserved accusation that our actions are just as capricious and reprehensible as those of Clyntahn himself, and no matter how angry I may be, I refuse to put myself into the same category as Zhaspahr Clyntahn! On the other hand, I don't suppose that anyone in Ferayd—and especially not anyone from the Office of the Inquisition—is particularly concerned about any possible consequences stemming from their actions in this case. Which probably means there hasn't been any cover-up yet. Or, at least, not any *effective* cover up. And if there hasn't, then I think it's time they, and the Grand Inquisitor, discover they're wrong about those consequences. No one is going to act without evidence. If, however, that evidence exists, and if it can be found, then the men who incited the murder of Charisian children in front of their mothers' and fathers' eyes, *will* face the justice meted out to any murderer of children. I don't care who they are, I don't care what their names are, and I don't care about whatever vestments they may wear. Is that clear to everyone around this table?"

He swept his eyes around the table. White Church still looked deeply unhappy, but even he met that flint-brown gaze without flinching, and Cayleb nodded.

"Good," he said softly. Then he inhaled deeply.

"However," he continued in a deliberately lighter voice, "lest all of you decide I'm turning all wishy-washy by insisting on evidence, I do believe a significant slap on the wrist is due to King Zhames, Ferayd, and Delferahk generally. Just as a gentle reminder that we're none too happy with *them,* either. And since we'd like for others to profit from their example, I want that slap delivered firmly. *Very* firmly."

"Administered exactly how, Your Majesty?" Lock Island asked just a little cautiously.

"We're not going to need the entire Navy for the invasion of Corisande," Cayleb replied. "Enough to provide security for the invasion transports, of course. And enough light units to provide the flank security we'll need and to blockade Hektor's ports. But no matter how hard he's been working on replacing *his* navy, he can't have any more than a handful of ships . . . yet. It's partly because of the need to keep that from changing that I refuse to be diverted from Corisande at this point.

"We, on the other hand, have over fifty galleons in commission by now. I imagine we could let you have twenty or thirty of them for something besides invading Corisande, Bryahn. I'm thinking we should hand them over to

Admiral Rock Point and tell him to go . . . remonstrate with Ferayd. He can have a few Marines, too. Enough to pretty much burn the entire waterfront district of Ferayd to the ground, let's say."

Cayleb's voice had gone iron-hard once more with the last sentence. Even so, it was warmer than the brown eyes looking levelly into Lock Island's.

"I want no counter-massacre here, Bryahn. Be sure all your captains understand that. Justice against those we know are guilty, yes, but I don't want our people provoked into anything that could even be *called* a counter-massacre. I don't doubt that even if we managed to refrain from injuring a single soul, the Group of Four would announce we'd raped and murdered half the city. In the end, though, the truth is going to get out. When it does, I want it to bite Clyntahn on the arse, not us. But having said that, I also don't want a single unburned ship floating in that harbor, or a building standing within two miles of that waterfront. Is that understood?"

"Yes, Your Majesty," Lock Island said formally, without a trace of levity.

"Good. I also want all of our captains, and all of our privateers, to understand that it's hunting season for anything flying the Delferahkan flag. Again, make it clear I will tolerate no unnecessary brutality or vengeance killing. But I don't want a single Delferahk-flagged merchant ship anywhere on the seas of Safehold two months from today."

"Yes, Your Majesty," Lock Island repeated.

"If it should turn out that any of the other realms have treated our people the way Delferahk has, they'll receive the same treatment, one port city at a time. In the meantime, though, we need to be concentrating our primary effort on Corisande and Hektor. So, since we have you and General Chermyn both present, what can you tell us?"

"Mainly that so far we're on schedule, Your Majesty. The transports are collecting now, although if we've lost as many merchantmen as we may have to this new move by the Group of Four, it could put a crimp into our plans. Aside from that possibility, I don't see any significant problems. The troop strengths should reach the required level on schedule, at any rate."

"Ah, if I might, Your Majesty?" Prince Nahrmahn said, raising one plump hand in a polite attention-seeking gesture.

"Yes, Your Highness?" Cayleb replied.

"I simply wished to say, first, that I agree wholeheartedly with the priorities you've just established. And, second, that I've had a certain amount of correspondence with Grand Duke Tohmas."

"What sort of 'correspondence'?" Cayleb asked, his eyes narrowing intently.

"It was purely of an exploratory nature, you understand, between myself as Prince of Emerald and him as the Grand Duke of Zebediah," Nahrmahn said in a self-deprecating tone. "As such it was, of course, well before Emerald became a territory of the Empire. In fact, it began well before the recent . . . unpleasantness the 'Knights of the Temple Lands' demanded of Her Grace and me. It's continued since, however. Until, ah, quite *recently*, in fact."

"I see." Cayleb kept his eyes on Nahrmahn, Sharleyan noticed. Earl Gray Harbor, on the other hand, glanced at Cayleb, rather than the Emeraldian prince. Or perhaps not. For just a moment, the first councilor's eyes actually seemed to slip past the emperor, instead.

"And the nature of this correspondence was . . . ?" Cayleb continued before she had any time to consider that possibility, and the question promptly refocused her own attention fully upon Nahrmahn.

"As I say, it was of an exploratory nature," Nahrmahn repeated. "Nonetheless, I suspect from some of the points we discussed that it's entirely possible he might be prepared to be . . . rather more reasonable than you and your advisers may have been assuming. In fact, I believe it's entirely possible he might be open to the possibility of providing Admiral Lock Island and General Chermyn with a forward base much closer to Corisande than, say, Chisholm."

"I see," Cayleb said slowly. He cocked his head to one side, considering his younger brother's father-in-law-to-be thoughtfully. Then he nodded. "I'll want to be more fully informed on that previous correspondence of yours, Your Highness. I believe, however, that if the possibility you've suggested actually exists, it could prove quite valuable."

Nahrmahn said nothing. Instead, he inclined his head in a half bow of assent.

"Very well," Cayleb said then, with an air of finality as he laid his palms flat on the council table and pushed his chair back from it. "I believe that completes our business for the day, Gentlemen?"

There was a general rumble of agreement. Of course, there always was, Merlin thought, and wondered what would happen if one day one of Cayleb's councilors disagreed with him, instead.

"In that case," the emperor continued, "I'll ask you all to excuse Her Grace and me. We have an appointment with the survivors from Ferayd." His mouth tightened briefly, then his nostrils flared as he stood, extending his hand to Sharleyan to assist her to her feet. "I hope they'll take a certain comfort from learning that Delferahk and Ferayd will soon learn the error of their ways. At any rate, *I'll* take a great deal of comfort from telling them so."

OCTOBER, YEAR OF GOD 892

The breeze piled whitecaps across King's Harbor as Empress Sharleyan stepped out onto the battlements of the Citadel. It was a most impressive sight, she thought, gazing down at the tiny model ships lying at anchor across the sun-sparkled, white-veined blue marble. The wind was a cool, vigorous relief from the day's heat, and the flags and banners along the battlements danced and clapped wildly, as if applauding the scene stretched out before her. Edwyrd Seahamper, on the other hand, seemed less impressed by the spectacular vista than he was relieved by the fact that up here on the battlements, she was safe from any lurking assassins.

"I really don't believe you're going to be required to sell your life dearly in my service, Edwyrd," she said to the man who had spent his life keeping her safe since she was a little girl.

"With all due respect, Your Majesty, I don't really think so, either. Not today, at any rate."

She turned her head, gazing at him with a fond smile. Then the smile faded just a bit, and she reached out and laid one hand on his upper arm.

"Do you still think this was all a dreadful mistake, Edwyrd?" she asked, her quiet voice almost lost in the rippling thunder of the flags snapping and popping on the breeze.

"Your Majesty, it would never have been my place to say anyth—"

"Don't be silly, Edwyrd." She squeezed his chain mail–covered arm. "I don't believe you've actually had to *say* anything since I was eleven!"

Despite himself, the guardsman's mouth twitched on the shivering edge of a smile, and she laughed.

"Edwyrd, Edwyrd!" She shook his arm gently. "It's such a pity you've spent so much time working on that poker face of yours, when the only person you really want to fool can read you like a book!"

"Well, it's hardly my fault you've always been too smart by half, Your Majesty," he replied.

"No, it's not. And you still haven't answered my question. Do you still think this was all a dreadful idea?"

Seahamper looked at her for a moment, then turned to gaze out over the harbor. It wasn't often he and the queen—*Empress, you dolt!* he corrected himself—found themselves alone like this. Indeed, she had even less privacy now than she'd had when she was "only" the Queen of Chisholm.

"Your Majesty," he said finally, his eyes still on the galleons anchored so far below them, "I don't know. I have to admit, the Emperor's a better man—a better *husband* for you—than I'd ever truly hoped you'd find. It's good you've found someone I think you can actually love, and who can love you back." He looked at her last. "It's not many a king or a queen who can say that, when all's said and done. But whether or not this 'Empire of Charis' is a good idea or a bad idea. . . . That's more than I can say."

"It was only a matter of time, you know, Edwyrd," she said softly. It was her turn to turn back to the anchorage, her eyes unfocused as they stared into the blue distance of Howell Bay, stretching limitlessly to the diamond-hard horizon beyond the harbor breakwater. "Whatever I wanted, whatever I might have preferred, the day was coming when I would have had no choice but to defy the Council of Vicars on my own. I'd always been afraid of that. When Clyntahn and the rest of the Group of Four decided to destroy Charis, and to use *us* to do it, I knew my fears had been justified."

Seahamper folded his hands behind him in a "parade rest" stance, looking at her sword-straight spine.

"And then, somehow, Charis survived. Not just survived, but devastated the fleets sent against her . . . including my own. And while I was still wondering what I was supposed to do, how Chisholm and everything I cared for might somehow find a way to survive, Cayleb proposed."

She shook her head, breathing deep of the tropical air. To her northern sensibilities, Charis was often swelteringly hot, and the sunlight had to be experienced to be believed. She was glad the healers had advised her to be careful about exposing herself to it; one or two members of her party, including Mairah Lywkys, who'd been less cautious had experienced agonizing sunburns, as a result.

But those things were as much a part of the exotic beauty with which Cayleb's kingdom had entranced her as the year-round fresh fruit, the coconuts, the rich and varied cuisine, and the spectacular forests crawling up the flanks of the Charisian Mountains like tropical green fur. It was all so *different* from anything she'd grown up with, like some sort of magical fairyland, and yet there were so many similarities between Charisians and her own Chisholmians. Differences, too, of course. Perhaps even more of them than there were similarities. But if the differences were more numerous, the similarities were vastly more important, because under the skin, where their hearts and souls lived, they were so *much* alike.

"Your Majesty, the Duke doesn't approve," Seahamper said very quietly as Sharleyan's silence stretched out, and she drew a deep, sad breath.

"No, he doesn't," she admitted.

Halbrook Hollow had made his ongoing opposition to—and resentment of—her marriage to Cayleb abundantly clear. Not publicly, perhaps. Even the queen's—or empress'—uncle had to be careful about challenging her policies in public, and however much he disapproved, he would never have permitted himself to show open disagreement, for a whole host of reasons. But Sharleyan knew. So did most of her advisers, and while he might not have voiced open disagreement, his attitude made it abundantly clear that his fundamental sympathies lay with the Temple Loyalists, not the Church of Charis. That much was becoming unhappily apparent to almost everyone.

Including Cayleb, she thought sadly. Her husband had never explicitly mentioned her uncle's feelings, but the very way he *hadn't* mentioned them told someone as perceptive as Sharleyan a great deal.

"He's not the only one, either," Seahamper said, finally permitting himself to actually voice at least a part of what concerned him. "I'm no lord, Your Majesty, nor likely to be one. God knows, I've never even wanted to be an officer! But I've guarded your back since you were a girl, and maybe I've learned a thing or two along the way, whether I wanted to or not. And there are people in Chisholm who don't like this marriage, this new 'Empire,' one bit. And they *won't* like it, wherever it goes."

"I know there are." She folded her arms under her breasts and turned back to him. "More of them in the nobility than among the commoners, I think, though."

"With all due respect, Your Majesty, it's the nobility that worries me most," Seahamper said frankly.

"And rightly so, I suppose. Goodness knows we're a lot more likely to see scheming nobles than any sort of spontaneous popular rebellion. Against the *Crown*, at least. But even if Chisholmians aren't as 'uppity' as Charisians— yet!—they're still a lot less hesitant about making their feelings felt than the subjects of a lot of other kingdoms. That's something Uncle Byrtrym himself helped the nobility learn it has to keep in mind."

Seahamper nodded slowly, although his expression was still worried. She had a point. The common folk of Chisholm had taken their "girl queen" to their hearts when her father died. The fact that Queen Mother Alahnah had been enormously popular hadn't hurt, of course, but it had been the dauntless courage they'd sensed in the "mere slip of a girl" upon whom the crown had so unexpectedly and suddenly descended which had truly won them. And the magic had never faded. Even now, when he knew so many of them cherished reservations about her open defiance of the Church, that deep reservoir of love had carried them with her.

But even the ocean has a bottom, he told himself, trying to keep the worry he felt out of his expression.

"I'm just . . . not happy about being away from home so long, Your Majesty," he said.

"What? No fear of fanatical Charisian assassins, loyal to the Church?" she teased.

"As to that, I've fewer worries in that regard than I had before we arrived, and that's no lie." He shook his head, smiling ruefully. "I'll confess it, Your Majesty. I don't know how you do it, but you've got the Charisians eating out of your hand, too!"

"Nonsense." It was her turn to shake her head, and she did, rather more forcefully than he had. "Oh, I won't deny they've taken me to their hearts, but that has less to do with me than it does with Cayleb, I think. They truly love him, you know. I think they'd have been prepared to welcome *anyone* if they thought she'd make him happy."

"Aye?" Seahamper quirked one sardonic eyebrow. "And the fact that the beautiful young sovereign queen of another kingdom, thousands of miles away, chose to make their quarrel with the Church hers had nothing to do with it?"

"I didn't say that."

"No, you didn't," Seahamper snorted. "Still and all, I'm less anxious than I was, and that's a fact. Of course, it doesn't hurt any that the Royal—I mean *Imperial*—Guard knows exactly how unholy a disaster it would be for Charis if they let anything happen to you! I don't think your folk back home would take that kindly, at all."

"No, I don't imagine they would," she agreed with a quirky little smile.

"And with good reason," Seahamper growled, his expression turning sober once again. Then he cocked his head. "Still," he conceded, "I'll not deny I was relieved once I got their measure."

"You're *admitting* you're impressed by someone else's armsmen?" She stepped back, leaning dramatically against the battlements for support as she pressed one hand to her heart, her eyes wide, and despite himself, he chuckled. But he also shook his head reprovingly at her.

"It's no laughing matter, Your Majesty, and well you know it. And if you didn't, Baron Green Mountain does! Would you like to hear what the Baron had to say to me before we left for Tellesberg?"

"Actually, no." She grimaced. "I expect he said a lot of the same things to *me*, if not quite so forcefully. Although, you know, the real reason he was so . . . cranky was my decision to leave him home in Cherayth."

" 'Cranky,' was he, Your Majesty?" Seahamper snorted again.

"Among other things. But he also admitted I was right, finally. I had to leave him to keep an eye on things."

"What you mean, Your Majesty," Seahamper said a bit grimly, "is that he's the only man you can trust out of your sight for four or five months at a time."

"Well, yes," Sharleyan acknowledged.

"I think that's what worries me most, Your Majesty," Seahamper said frankly. "I'm not truly concerned for your safety here in Charis. If I'd been inclined to stay that way, Captain Athrawes would've cured me by now. That man's even more impressive than the tales about him, in some ways. But I am worried about what's happening in Chisholm while we're here."

"To be honest, that's my worst concern, as well." She glanced back out across the harbor. "But it's a chance we have to take, and at least I have mother and Mahrak to manage things for me while I'm in Charis. And, to be honest, I think Cayleb is right. One of us has to be the first to spend time in the other's kingdom, and given the decisions that have to be made—and the fact that even the most dull-witted nobleman in Cherayth must know that at this moment Charis is the military linchpin—it has to be me in Charis, and not him in Chisholm."

"I know that, Your Majesty." He surprised her just a bit by sweeping her a bow. "I only hope you're right about the Baron's ability to juggle all the dragon's eggs we left behind."

"So do I, Edwyrd," she said softly, her eyes once again on the anchored galleons so far below. "So do I."

▼   ▼   ▼

"May I have a moment, Merlin?"

Merlin turned at the question and found himself facing Commodore Seamount. The rather portly officer—in some ways, Merlin had decided, Seamount reminded him of Prince Nahrmahn—had a fat folder under his left arm and the right sleeve of his uniform tunic was thickly smudged with chalk dust, a sure sign he'd been in his office above the Citadel's main powder magazine scrawling diagrams, questions, and notes on its slate-covered walls.

"Of course, My Lord." Merlin bowed slightly, and Seamount snorted.

"There's no one else watching us," he pointed out. Merlin straightened and arched one eyebrow, and Seamount shrugged. "I appreciate the courtesy, *Seijin* Merlin, but don't you and I have better things to do with our time than waste it bowing and scraping?"

"Courtesy, My Lord, is never wasted," Merlin replied a bit obliquely.

"Smoothly put, *Seijin*," Seamount chuckled. Merlin gazed at him for a moment longer, then gave up.

"Very well, My Lord. What is it I can do for you today?"

"That's better!" Seamount grinned, then pulled the folder out from under his arm and waved it in the general direction of Merlin's nose.

"I take it there's something *inside* the folder?" Merlin asked politely.

"Yes, there is. These are my latest notes on the artillery project."

"I see." Merlin's lips twitched, and he tugged at his waxed mustachio. "Ah, just *which* artillery project would that be, My Lord?"

"All of them!" Seamount said impatiently, and Merlin shook his head.

The official reason for Cayleb and Sharleyan's visit to Helen Island was to sit down with Bryahn Lock Island, General Chermyn, their senior officers, and their staffs to finalize their plans for the invasion of Corisande and officially set that project in motion. Or, rather, to discuss the changes those plans would require in the wake of the Ferayd Massacre, as it was already coming to be known. They wouldn't be boarding any troops for quite some time, after the way Admiral Rock Point's punitive expedition had been given priority over everything else, and in some ways that was a good thing. It gave them more time to deal with the inevitable last-minute snafus, at any rate.

The *real* reason for the trip to Helen, though, in a lot of ways, was that Sharleyan had wanted to see the place where so many of the innovations which had spelled Charis' survival had been hatched. And then, of course, there'd been the fact that Cayleb was never shy about seizing upon any opportunity to get out of the palace.

The actual meetings with Lock Island, Chermyn, and their officers had gone more smoothly than Merlin had allowed himself to hope they might. No one in Charis (or anywhere else on Safehold) had ever attempted to project a fifty thousand–man invasion army across thousands upon thousands of miles of seawater. On the other hand, the Royal Charisian Navy had amassed a vast amount of experience when it came to handling purely *naval* logistics. The unavoidable delay imposed by Ferayd had helped, as well. It had not only given them more time to finish building the invasion force's weapons—from flintlock rifles, to breastplates, to saddles and bridles, to Seamount's field artillery—but had given the invasion planners additional time to go over their numbers again and again (using the new Arabic numerals and abacuses Merlin had introduced by way of the Royal College). The result was that no military operation in which Nimue Alban had ever been involved—including Operation Ark—had been more thoroughly planned out.

That doesn't guarantee the plans will work, *of course,* he reflected. *But at least if they don't, it won't be because there wasn't time to dot all the i's and cross all the t's!*

Because of that, this particular set of meetings had been almost a formality, in many ways. But they'd been a useful formality, especially when it came to bringing Sharleyan fully up to speed. That, alone, would have made the trip thoroughly worthwhile in Merlin's opinion.

And I wish the Brethren would get off their collective . . . dime and decide we can bring her fully inside! Damn it, the woman's even smarter than I thought she was! We need her brains, and we need her insight, and we need them now, *not four or five damn years from now!*

No sign of his frustration was allowed to touch his expression, and he reminded himself—again—that Sharleyan had been Empress of Charis for less than a full month. It was hard to remember sometimes, given how completely she'd entered into the planning and projects Cayleb had already set into motion. Several of her suggestions, especially on the diplomatic front, had constituted major improvements, and Cayleb had discovered that she was probably the best sounding board he'd ever had. Which, of course, only increased his own frustration with the Brethren of Saint Zherneau's caution.

I'd say with their glacial *caution, except that no one in Charis has ever actually seen a glacier,* Merlin thought tartly, then gave himself a mental shake and returned his focus to Seamount.

" 'All of them' takes in a fair amount of ground, My Lord," he pointed out. "Could we possibly be a bit more specific?"

"Well, all right," Seamount said. "Do you want to discuss them here in the hallway, or would you care to step into my office?"

▼   ▼   ▼

The walls of Seamount's office were, indeed, covered with fresh diagrams, Merlin observed. Several of them were quite interesting. It was obvious Seamount had been concentrating on ways to devise explosive shells for smoothbores, which made sense, given the number of smoothbore artillery pieces already in service. Not to mention the minor fact that there were *no* rifled artillery pieces in service anywhere in the world.

"The biggest problem with the explosive shot—I'm thinking about calling them 'shells,' since they're basically hollow shells filled with gunpowder—is getting them to explode when and where they're supposed to," the baron said.

"Yes?" Merlin encouraged in a neutral tone carefully selected to tease Seamount. The Charisian knew it, too, and his eyes gleamed.

"Well, there's this *minor* difficulty," he said. "Put most simply, it needs a fuse. One possibility, I suppose, would be to use a short-barreled weapon—something even shorter than a carronade, which could probably lob the shells the same way a catapult lobs stones. Anyway, something with a barrel short enough that one of the gunners could reach down it and light the fuse on the shell after it's loaded into the gun. Of course, I imagine most people would be a little unhappy standing around with a lit fuse on a shell inside a gun which might choose that particular moment to misfire." The baron shook his head. "Waiting for the explosion could be just a little hard on the nerves, I suspect."

"I can see that," Merlin agreed, manfully resisting the powerful temptation to smile.

"I'd gotten that far," Seamount continued more seriously, "when it occurred to me that there was no need to light the fuse by hand if I could use the gun's muzzle flash to do the same job, so I started trying to come up with a fuse which could be 'self-igniting' and give a reasonably reliable and consistent burn time. I've tried slow match and quick match, and I've tried other approaches, as well. The one that seems to work best, at least in tests, is a hollow wooden plug filled with fine-grained powder. We've finally managed to come up with a composition which actually burns at a predictable, reliable speed, and by using a fairly thin-walled plug, we can actually select for different burn times. We've discovered that if we mark the outside of the plug in increments and punch a hole through it so that the fuse's powder train ignites at a different point in the fuse channel, we can adjust the interval between firing and the shell's explosion with a surprising degree of accuracy."

In this case, Merlin knew, "we've" actually meant "I've," and he folded his arms as he allowed his own expression to match the Charisian's increased seriousness.

"I can see where that would have been difficult," he said. "From what you've already said, though, I suspect that isn't the real problem."

"No, it isn't," Seamount said with what Merlin recognized as massive restraint. "The problem, *Seijin* Merlin, is that it doesn't matter how reliably the fuse can be timed if the propelling charge keeps blowing the damned fuse *into* the shell and setting it off *inside* the gun!"

"Oh!" Merlin nodded, tugging on his mustache again. He frowned in obvious thought, although he wasn't thinking about exactly what Seamount might have thought he was. The difficulty lay less in solving Seamount's problem than in managing to avoid solving it too quickly.

"Let me see if I have this straight," he said, after several seconds. "You don't want the gunner to have to physically light the fuse on these 'shells' of yours for every shot, so you've developed one that the propelling charge's flash ignites. And from what you're saying, the fuse you've come up with lets you time things with a reasonably accurate reliability . . . when it works at all. But when the gunpowder behind the shell goes off, the fuse is a weak point in the shell wall and it goes off prematurely?"

"Basically, yes." Seamount shrugged. "For quite some time I wasn't certain whether the shell wall was fracturing around the fuse, or if the fuse itself was simply being blown bodily into the shell's interior. I suspected that it was the latter, but since no one's had any experience with this kind of projectile before, I couldn't rule out the possibility that the shells I'd designed simply had walls that were too thin to stand the shock of firing. There was no real way to tell from what was left after the shell exploded, so I tried firing a couple of hundred shells with solid plugs instead of fuses. The rate of premature detonations went down enormously, but they were still occurring, so I sat down and thought about it for while.

"Eventually, I realized that at least part of what was happening was that the gunpowder filling was moving inside the shell cavity when the round was fired, and the friction heat that generated was causing the premature detonations. So I tried stabilizing the charges by pouring in hot tar to hold everything in place. I had to be careful to preserve an open channel for the fuse's flash to reach the main charge, but that wasn't too difficult.

"After I started using the tar, we got no more premature detonations . . . as long as we stuck with the solid plugs, instead of using live fuses. That seemed like pretty conclusive evidence that the shell wall was strong enough, but I wanted to be sure. So, I filled several dozen shells with flour, instead of gunpowder, put live fuses into them, and fired them into shallow water where divers could recover them. When I examined them, it was obvious that the fuse itself—or enough of it to do the job, at any rate—was being blown into the shell, but that the walls weren't cracking under the stress of firing, which confirmed my suspicions about the cause."

He paused for a moment, his expression that of a man torn between satisfaction that at least a part of his design had proved workable and that he'd devised a technique for proving that it had, on the one hand, and frustration over his inability to fix the part of the design that *hadn't* proved workable, on the other hand.

"It doesn't happen every time, of course," he said then. "But it does happen a lot of the time, and getting gunners to adopt something this newfangled is going to be hard enough even if they're not afraid each shell is going to explode either inside the gun or the instant it clears the muzzle. It's just a little difficult for them to feel all warm and happy about something that's likely to *kill* them, you know."

"Well, yes, I can see that, I suppose." Merlin smiled slightly. Then he tugged on his mustache again, his smile turning into a frown as he pondered.

"Tell me," he said finally, "from what you've just said, it sounds as if you were loading the guns with the fuse hard up against the propelling charge."

Seamount nodded, and Merlin raised one eyebrow.

"Have you considered loading your 'shell' with the fuse facing *away* from the propelling charge, instead?"

"What?" Seamount frowned.

"I asked, if you'd—"

"Just a minute!" Seamount's raised hand stopped him, and the stubby commodore's eyes narrowed as he thought hard and furiously, indeed. Then he started nodding. Slowly at first, then faster and faster.

"Of course! I should have thought of that myself! The flash from the propelling charge sweeps all the way *around* the shell, doesn't it?"

"I'd certainly think so, at any rate," Merlin agreed.

"Of course it does! And if it sweeps around and lights the fuse in the front instead of hammering it into the shell cavity from the back. . . ."

Seamount stepped over to one of the slate-covered walls, snatched up a piece of chalk, and began jotting notes to himself. He read over them, shook his head impatiently, erased one line and chalked a correction, then nodded and looked back over his shoulder at Merlin.

"You're a very useful fellow to have over on a visit, *Seijin* Merlin," he said dryly. "Somehow, you always manage to point me in the right direction, don't you?"

"One tries," Merlin murmured.

"Oh, one certainly does," Seamount agreed.

"Was there anything else I might help you with, My Lord?" Merlin asked, sounding as little as if he were changing the subject as he could manage.

"Actually, there are two other problems I wanted your opinion on."

"Of course, My Lord."

"Both of them have to do with the new rifled guns," Seamount began. "I've tried several approaches to getting their rounds to take the rifling. One that seemed promising was to encase the projectile in a soft metal, like lead, that could be forced into the rifling much as we've done with the new rifle bullets. Unfortunately, the lead keeps stripping off and the rounds don't take the rifling consistently.

"One of my bright young assistants suggested that what we might do was to cut the cannon's bore like a helix, so that it was twisted itself. Not a round bore, you understand, but something a bit more trapezoidal that twisted around its own central axis to force the shot to spin without requiring rifling at all. Frankly, I think that would probably work, but I'm concerned about bore erosion. Which is why I'm still convinced that some form of grooved rifling is the answer; it's just a question of figuring out how to make the shot physically engage with the grooves.

"So far, the most promising thing I've tried is to cast the shot with metal studs." Chalk cracked like a staccato explosion as he tapped one of the diagrams on his wall. "As you can see, the idea is that when the gunners insert the shot into the muzzle, they engage the rifling with the studs. Then the shot rides down, rotating as it goes, until it comes to rest against the propelling charge. When it's fired, the studs ride back up the grooves, which imparts a rapid spin to the shot, and off it sails to its target."

He turned back from the wall to smile fiercely at Merlin, and Merlin smiled back.

"The problem is this," Seamount continued, his smile fading slightly. "First, as we'd expected from the beginning, bronze is too soft, especially using the stud-and-groove system. The insides of the barrels simply shred after only a very few rounds. Secondly, I've already discovered that even with the stud-and-groove approach, bore pressures are rising dangerously."

"What do you mean, 'even with the stud-and-groove approach'?"

"I expected bore pressure to go up drastically when I tried the lead coating system. After all, the shot was sealing the bore a lot more thoroughly, so it was inevitable the pressures would go up, the same way they went up in the rifles when we started using hollow-based bullets in them. But I'd rather hoped that enough of the propelling gases would be able to escape around the shot, which is smaller in diameter than the bore, using the stud system. Which, by the way," he added parenthetically, "is one reason I'm irritated with myself for not realizing those same gases could ignite the fuse on their way past the shell. Anyway, I'd hoped the windage between the shell body and the bore wall would let the gases escape and relieve the pressure."

"I can see that," Merlin acknowledged.

"Well, I suppose at least some of the gases are doing just that," Seamount told him. "Unfortunately, I don't think enough of them are. And there's another factor, too—one I hadn't really thought about initially. The shells we're developing for the existing smoothbores are the same size as the round shot they already fire, and because they're filled with gunpowder rather than solid iron, the shells are actually lighter than the shot the guns were originally proved for. But in a *rifled* gun, the shot doesn't have to be round. In fact, you don't *want* a spherical round. Since a more cylindrical shape lends itself more efficiently to rifling, anyway, you end up with an elongated projectile. For an explosive shell, that will give me a larger internal cavity, which means I'll be able to pack in more explosive, and the fact that it's hollow will tend to hold the weight down, at least to some extent. For a solid shot, though, the overall weight of the shot goes up very sharply, and even with a gunpowder filling, a properly designed shell strong enough to stand the shock of firing without disintegrating is going to have thick enough cavity walls for it to weigh more than a round shot for the same gun. And that greater weight means the gun has to work harder to throw shells at the same velocities at which it throws round shot, and that drives up bore pressure, too."

"All right," Merlin said, nodding to show he was following so far.

"We can cast iron guns and then cut the rifling grooves into them," Seamount said. "On the other hand, we've already got hundreds—thousands, actually—of the new bronze guns. I'm sure we could find something else to do with all of that bronze, but it seems an awful pity after we've gone to all the trouble of casting them in the first place to simply throw them away—as artillery pieces, I mean. That's one problem. The other problem, frankly, is that cast iron is a lot more brittle than bronze. I'm not sure it's going to be up to the stresses that are going to be exerted once we start casting large-caliber rifled guns. Not without going to truly enormous pieces—probably at least as big as or bigger than the old Great Doomwhale."

Which, Merlin reflected, had weighed almost six tons.

"But what would you use instead?" he asked aloud.

"At the moment, I'm thinking in terms of wrought iron," Seamount replied, not to Merlin's great surprise. "It'll be expensive—even more expensive than bronze—but Master Howsmyn says his ironmasters are equal to the task. I think he's probably right about that, but producing reliable wrought-iron gun tubes is going to be expensive in terms of manufacturing *time*, as well."

Merlin nodded again. He wasn't surprised by the difficulties Seamount had encountered. Indeed, if he was surprised at all, it was by how quickly the Charisian had experienced them. Which was foolish of him, he supposed. If Sir Ahlfryd Hyndryk had demonstrated anything, it was that his mind was every bit as quick and focused as Prince Nahrmahn's, if in very different directions.

The problem, as Seamount had just pointed out, was that cast iron was brittle. Safeholdian foundry techniques were remarkably advanced for a culture where steam power had been prohibited, yet they still weren't up to mass production of steel by a considerable distance. The technology itself lay within their grasp, but there were still obstacles to be overcome.

The fact that Safeholdian foundries had been using waterwheels for centuries helped, but it was only in the last few decades that men like Edwyrd Howsmyn and his "mechanics" had begun applying power to the process more generally. Initially, the waterwheels' only true function had been to power blowers to raise the temperature in Safeholdian blast furnaces and fineries. The processes for turning blast furnace iron into wrought iron and steel had been no further advanced than perhaps 1700 Europe.

Howsmyn had been one of the pioneers—all of whom had been located right here in Charis—who had championed replacing charcoal with coke made from the kingdom's generous quantities of coal. He'd also taken the lead in developing what had been called the "puddling process" back on Old Earth, with the result that *his* foundries' output of wrought iron—very high quality wrought iron, in fact—was several times that of any other foundries on Safehold. But even though that was true, wrought iron was still more expensive, primarily because of the greater amount of labor, processes, and time involved in its manufacture, than cast iron.

There was plenty of room for refinement in his current relatively crude techniques, but what he'd done so far hadn't truly required Church approval, since it was based entirely on novel applications of techniques which had already been approved. On the other hand, all of them were basically empirical. They'd been worked out by men with lifetimes of practical experience forging iron and steel, but with no theoretical understanding of *why* the improvements they'd come up with worked. Any systematic effort to tweak Howsmyn's current capacity was going to require the development of that theoretical understanding, and that *was* going to be a problem in the face of the Proscriptions of Jwo-jeng.

The crux of Seamount's current problem, however, was that the only alternatives for artillery pieces were bronze, cast iron, and wrought iron. Bronze was an excellent material for smoothbore muzzleloaders, but, as Seamount had just complained, it was both expensive and too soft to stand up to the strains of rifling for very long. Cast iron was relatively cheap, and the foundry techniques for working with it were well established, but even using sandcasting to reduce porosity, cast-iron guns were much more brittle than bronze and likely to crack or burst under the stresses of the bore pressures Seamount was anticipating. Which really left only *wrought* iron. If Ehdwyrd Howsmyn said his foundries could produce the needed guns out of wrought iron, Merlin had no doubt they could, but Seamount was right that they weren't going to be cheap.

"All right," he said finally, "I've got a couple of thoughts.

"First, as far as the existing guns and the bore pressures are concerned. If I'm understanding you correctly, you're saying that if we're willing to accept a lower shell *velocity*, we could probably keep pressures within the acceptable limits for the existing gun tubes, even with the heavier shell *weights*. Is that pretty much correct?"

Seamount nodded, and Merlin shrugged.

"In that case, why don't you ask Master Howsmyn if it would be possible to produce a relatively thin-walled, rifled tube, like an inner sleeve of wrought iron, that we could slide down inside the bore of an existing smoothbore? What I'm thinking is that if we did that, and fixed it firmly at the muzzle, probably by cutting threads into the outside of the muzzle and literally screwing its forward end into place, then fired a fairly powerful charge out of the gun, wouldn't it expand the inner sleeve and more or less weld it into place as a permanent liner that would protect the bronze against bore erosion?"

"I . . . don't know," Seamount said slowly. "It sounds like it ought to make sense. At any rate, it's certainly something to ask Howsmyn about."

Chalk rattled as he jotted additional notes. He stood back to read over them and frowned thoughtfully.

"The strength of the existing gun tubes would still limit shot weight and velocity," he said. "You're right about that. But we've got enough margin to handle heavier projectiles than the guns are firing now, I think. And the increase in accuracy, not to mention the use of an explosive filler, would make the idea more than worthwhile if we can figure out how to do it."

"That's what I thought, too," Merlin agreed. "On the other hand, I had another thought when you were talking about why wrought iron was better than cast iron."

"Ah?" Seamount turned back from the slate wall, eyebrows rising.

"Yes. You said cast iron is too *brittle* to stand up to the bore pressures you're expecting."

Seamount nodded, just a touch impatiently, and Merlin shrugged.

"Well, what occurred to me was that while you're right, that wrought iron is less brittle, that might not be the only way to get the strength you're looking for."

Seamount looked perplexed, and Merlin waved one hand, like a man trying to pluck the exact word he wanted out of the air.

"What I'm saying is that you're thinking in terms of a solid mass of metal strong enough to stand up to the discharge of these new rifled artillery pieces of yours."

"Of course I am. You're not suggesting we make them out of *wood*, are you?"

"Not quite." Merlin grinned at the asperity which had seeped into Seamount's tone. "The point that had occurred to me was that perhaps Master Howsmyn should be looking into another approach. What if instead of trying to cast the cannon as a single, massive piece of metal, then reaming out and rifling the bore, he used a relatively thin wrought-iron tube, like the 'sleeve' we were talking about a few moments ago. But instead of sticking it down inside an existing bronze gun tube and expanding it, what would happen if he wrapped it very tightly in wire, instead?"

Seamount opened his mouth, as if to automatically dismiss the idea, then froze. His eyes widened in sudden speculation.

"What you're saying is that we could *wrap* the reinforcement around a fairly light tube," he said slowly. "I don't see any reason that couldn't work, as long as we wrapped it tightly and thickly enough."

"I'd think a wire-wrapped approach would be a lot less brittle than cast iron or even wrought iron," Merlin agreed. "Surely the individual wires would have a tendency to flex and stretch without cracking or bursting the way solid metal might under the same pressures."

"Not only that," Seamount said with gathering enthusiasm, "but you wouldn't have to wonder if there were flaws, the way you do with iron. You'd be able to examine every inch of wire individually before it went into the gun!"

"Yes, you would." Merlin's approving surprise wasn't at all feigned. Once again, Seamount's agile brain was leaping ahead as soon as the possibilities were pointed out to him.

"I don't know if it's practical, at least with Master Howsmyn's existing equipment," the Charisian said, almost bouncing up and down on his toes as his mind careened through the vista of possibilities and the accompanying manufacturing problems which would have to be overcome. "For one thing, we'd be talking about a lot of wire, and I have no idea what his wire-drawing capacity might be. And I'm fairly certain that it would have to be wrapped really tightly, tighter than we can manage with muscle power, which is going to require his mechanics to figure out how to do it using *water* power. If they can't do it with what they have *now*, though, I'm sure they can figure out how to build whatever they need to build in order to build whatever they need in order to do it!"

He wheeled back to the wall of slate, chalk clattering as he wrote furiously. Then he spun back around to Merlin just as quickly, pointing at him with the piece of chalk.

"I don't believe for a minute that you 'just happened' to think of this, *Seijin* Merlin." It could have been accusing, but it wasn't. "On the other hand, I'm not going to ask any more questions today. I've got the oddest feeling that if I were to do that, we'd find ourselves getting into explanations you'd really rather not make."

Merlin managed to keep his expression under control. It wasn't the first time one of Seamount's comments had headed in the same direction, but this one was more explicit than most, and he decided not to mention a third problem the little commodore was about to encounter with rifled guns. The fuse system he'd worked out for his smoothbore shells would work just fine, relying on flash for the original ignition. But sticking that sort of fuse design onto the nose of a rifled round was likely to prove more problematical. Since a rifled shell was always going to land nose-first, a nose-mounted fuse would tend to be crushed on impact, or else driven back into the shell. In the first case, the shell probably wouldn't detonate at all; in the second case, it would detonate effectively instantaneously, before it had time to penetrate sufficiently into the target.

I'll just let you come across that little difficulty for yourself, My Lord, he thought dryly. *I'm sure it will occur to you soon enough. It probably won't do all that much good, but I can at least* pretend *I don't have all of the answers. Besides, I want to see how* you *approach the problem. One thing I'm sure of—it'll be interesting.*

"Don't worry, Merlin," Seamount continued, his eyes gleaming almost as if he'd just read Merlin's mind. "I promise to be good. But I'll be interested to see Howsmyn's reaction to 'my' suggestions about how to approach this. You realize you're about to set off another round of 'infernal innovation,' don't you?"

"The thought hadn't even crossed my mind," Merlin said with immense—and completely false—sincerity.

"Oh, of course it hadn't!" Seamount chuckled, shook his head, and turned back to his chalked notes. "I'm glad Father Paityr is back on board with Archbishop Maikel, because this is going to be at least as upsetting to certain people I could think of as the first batch of artillery improvements were."

Oh, I hope *so, Sir Ahlfryd,* Merlin thought, watching the commodore ponder his notes. *I do hope so!*

L arys Shaikyr, master after God of the galleon *Raptor*, looked away from his conversation with Hahl Urbahn, his first officer, as fresh cannon fire rumbled and crashed like Langhorne's own thunder. The schooner *Slash Lizard* was dashing down from windward once again, hammering away at the flagship of the convoy's escort, and Shaikyr shook his head in exasperation. The crippled galley had fallen well astern of the rest of the convoy, crawling on a handful of crippled oars while white water jetted from her pumps in clear proof of damage below the waterline.

"Signal *Slash Lizard* to break off action!" Shaikyr told his signal party sharply.

"Aye, Sir," the senior signalman acknowledged, and Shaikyr looked back at Urbahn.

"We can always finish him off later, assuming he doesn't just go ahead and sink on his own," he growled.

"Yes, Sir." Urbahn nodded, then grinned crookedly. "I think some of our skippers are beginning to forget how to think like *privateers!*"

"Then they'd best remember." Shaikyr shook his head. "I'm just as determined to carry out the King's—I mean, the Emperor's—instructions as the next man. But there's reason in all things, Hahl. And even if I wasn't worried about the money at all, wasting time attacking galleys that're already crippled is the best way I can think of to let the real prizes slip away!"

Urbahn nodded, and the two of them returned their contemplation to the galleons fleeing before them . . . and the three Delferahkan war galleys which were still more or less intact and trying desperately to cover the merchant ships' escape.

They're gutsy, those captains, Shaikyr acknowledged to himself as he glowered at the remaining galleys. *They've already seen what happened to the rest of the escort, and they're* still *trying to hold us off.*

Under the current relatively light wind conditions, those galleys could have shown most of the attacking Charisian privateers a clean pair of heels if they'd chosen to run for it. Some of the faster schooners, like *Slash Lizard* or *Fist of Charis*, probably would have been able to catch them anyway, but the bigger, slower galleons like *Raptor* could never have hoped to overtake them.

Fortunately, the Delferahkan *galleons*, which were what the privateers truly wanted, were substantially slower and less weatherly than *Raptor* or

Shaikyr's other three galleons. With their old-fashioned sail plans and tower-ing freeboards, they might as well have been sea anchors as far as the galleys were concerned. All the gallantry in the world couldn't have changed what was going to happen to that convoy, and the galleys' commanders had to know that, yet still they stayed stubbornly between the privateers and their prey.

War Hammer, the leading galleon of Shaikyr's "squadron," was close enough already to begin engaging the rearmost galley with her forward chasers. Another twenty or thirty minutes, and she'd be able to bring the galleons under fire, as well. And the schooners *Windcrest* and *Sea Kiss* had already over-taken the merchant ships, keeping well up to windward of the galley escorts and out of the reach of their broadside guns. *Windcrest*, in fact, was already slanting downward on a course to intercept the leading Delferahkan galleon, and there was nothing at all the galleys could do about it.

The panorama, Shaikyr reflected, would make a magnificent painting. Although he'd never had any formal training, he had a self-taught, private passion for canvas and oils, and a back corner of his mind was busy recording all the details for the future. The green of the ocean water, shading to a steadily deeper and darker cobalt as it stretched away towards the horizon. The high, white clouds drifting like infinitely tall, infinitely vast galleons across an even deeper sea of blue. Sunlight striking downward, flashing off the green and blue mirror of water, touching the dirty-white spurts of pow-der smoke, glinting on helmets, pikeheads, swords, and boarding axes. The complex patterns of weathered canvas, shrouds, and wind shadows, and the long spider-legs of the galleys stirring the sea to froth as the oarsmen pulled furiously. The sheer visual impact of moments like this touched something deep inside Larys Shaikyr.

But however spectacular the panorama might be, there were practical things to consider, as well, and he smiled with cold satisfaction as *War Ham-mer*'s round shot began slamming into the lightly built galley. Even without his spyglass, he could see the galley's starboard oars flailing in sudden confu-sion as the Charisian fire began to rip across the ship's oardeck. The closer sound of the galleon's artillery swallowed up the distant thunder of *Windcrest*'s guns, but the sudden billow of gunsmoke surging above the schooner told him she'd brought her target into at least extreme range, as well.

Or maybe not, he told himself. *We don't want to break any more eggs than we have to, so she may just want to pointedly suggest that it's time to heave to before she does bring the bastards into range.*

Frankly, that was just fine with Larys Shaikyr. He was as infuriated as anyone else over the Ferayd Massacre, but he was also a pragmatic business-man . . . and a fifteen-percent shareholder in *Raptor*. Vengeance for cold-blooded murder was a fine thing, and he wouldn't pretend, even to himself, that it wasn't exactly what he wanted. But vengeance was already on its way to Ferayd, in the form of Admiral Rock Island and his fleet. It would arrive soon enough, and in the meantime, there were bills to pay, as well.

War Hammer's target was beginning to fall astern of her consorts as her oars floundered in greater and greater confusion. That was one of the problems with galleys, he reflected with grim satisfaction. Losing a sail or, even worse, a mast could have serious consequences for any galleon, but a galley under oars depended upon the synchronized, carefully controlled effort of literally hundreds of oarsmen. Aboard a ship like *War Hammer*'s current prey, there might be four or five men on each oar, whereas one of the Charisian Navy's larger galleys would have had as many as ten men to each sweep, half of them facing aft and pushing while the other half faced forward and pulled. Keeping that many men working smoothly, as an integrated team, even under perfect conditions, could be a daunting task.

With five-inch round shot pitching in among the rowers, mangling them, sending knife-edged clouds of splinters swirling through them, splashing even unwounded men with the blood of someone who'd been pulling the same oar beside them only a heartbeat before, keeping the sweeps moving in any sort of organized fashion was simply out of the question.

More cannon thundered as *Sea Kiss* came down on the merchant ships in *Windcrest*'s wake, and he bared his teeth as one of the galleons—which hadn't even been brought under *threat* of fire yet, as far as he could see—suddenly let her sheets fly, spilling the wind from her sails in token of surrender.

"I believe we're almost in range to give *War Hammer* a hand, Hahl," he observed.

"I believe you're right, Sir." Urbahn returned his thin smile and touched his left shoulder in salute. "I'll just go have a talk with the Gunner and bring that to his attention, shall I, Sir?"

"I think that would be an excellent idea," Shaikyr agreed, and watched the first officer heading forward to where *Raptor*'s gunner was fussing over the chase weapons on the galleon's foredeck.

Then he returned his attention to the convoy which was his prize. There were only six galleons in it, which meant he had enough privateers to chase each of them down and still have two left over to finish off the galleys. Normally, Shaikyr, like any prudent privateer, would have preferred to leave the galleys astern once they were too crippled to interfere with his operations. After all, galleys weren't worth very much these days. They didn't carry valuable cargoes, and no sane Charisian admiral would even contemplate adding a captured *galley* to his fleet. That meant the possibility of prize money would have been virtually nonexistent, and even Delferahkan artillery was likely to inflict at least some damage and—especially—casualties.

In this instance, however, he had every intention of finishing those galleys off—yes, and taking intense satisfaction in the doing. He would have been inclined to under any circumstances, after what had happened in Fer- ayd. The fact that Emperor Cayleb had pledged the resources of the Crown to support operations against Delferahk, and the fact that the Crown would be paying privateers "head money" for the crews of captured or destroyed war- ships, exactly the way it did to regular Navy crews, meant that inclination would actually show a profit. Of course, the privateers in question also had to accept the Crown's rules for awarding prize money. Under those rules, the ships which brought prizes in were entitled to only a fourth part of their ac- tual value, with the remainder going to the Crown, but that wasn't entirely bad. More than one privateer had returned from a cruise with no prizes at all. Sometimes fortune simply deserted a hunter, after all, and game was begin- ning to become increasingly scarce for everyone. But as long as they were cruising in Delferahkan waters, the Crown would cover their operating ex- penses and at least a minimal lump sum payment to their ships' companies. Under those circumstances, the amount they did receive from the prize court's awards would be pure profit.

Which meant Shaikyr could do his patriotic duty punishing Delferahk rather than chasing after the normally richer prizes of Dohlaran or Tarotisian merchant shipping and still show *Raptor*'s financial backers a profit. Not as great a one as they might have realized from the same number of Dohlaran prizes, but at least a reliable one.

Raptor's chasers began to bellow. The powder smoke rolled steadily downwind on the light breeze, and round shot began to seed the water around her target with white feathers.

Not much longer, friend, Shaikyr thought nastily. *And you'd better be grateful we* are *sailing under Crown orders. I am, anyway. Because if I weren't, if it were up to me, there wouldn't* be *any prisoners. But the Emperor's a better man than I am, thank God. Which means I won't be facing God's justice someday with the blood of a massacre on* my *hands.*

He took one more painter's look at sky, sun, water, and ships, then put that thought away and turned to his second officer.

"Stand to at the port battery," he said coldly. "We'll have some work for them in a few minutes, I believe."

▼   ▼   ▼

"Captain?"

Shaikyr looked up as Dunkyn Hyndyrs, *Raptor*'s purser, appeared in the chart room doorway. The captain had been studying the local charts, consid- ering where to take his hunting pack next, and he blinked against the bright sunlight framing the purser as he stood in the open door.

"Yes?"

"Captain, I think maybe you'd better come on deck."

"What?" Shaikyr straightened. "What's wrong?"

"Nothing's *wrong*, Sir," Hyndyrs said in a very careful tone. "I'm just afraid things are about to get a little noisy, and I thought you'd prefer to be there when they do."

"Noisy?" Shaikyr's eyes were beginning to adjust to the brightness halo-ing Hyndyrs', and he frowned as the purser's expression registered. He looked, the captain thought just a bit uncharitably, like someone who'd swallowed a spider and wasn't entirely certain it was going to stay swallowed.

"What's going on, Dunkyn?"

"A boat from *Windcrest* just came alongside," Hyndyrs replied. "It brought a note from Captain Zherahk. Along with the bill of lading for one of the prizes."

"And?" Shaikyr growled a bit impatiently.

"And there's a *reason* those galleys were so stubborn, Sir," Hyndyrs told him. "The entire convoy was under charter to the Delferahkan crown. Four of the galleons were loaded mainly with naval stores for the Temple's ship-building project. Another one is carrying several hundred tons of copper and tin ingots, apparently for casting into artillery, also for their new fleet. I'm sure the Emperor and the Navy will be suitably glad to see all of those cargoes. But the sixth wasn't under charter to Delferahk, at all. Not really. It was under charter to the 'Knights of the Temple Lands.' "

Shaikyr's impatience disappeared abruptly, and he settled back on his heels.

"Number six wasn't carrying naval stores or copper and tin, Sir." Hyndyrs shook his head. "She's loaded with gold and silver bullion. I don't begin to know how much of it yet, but whatever I might estimate right now would almost certainly be low, I think. She was carrying over six months' worth of the Temple's payments to the shipyards building new galleys for the Church at Ferayd. And, on top of that, the Council of Vicars has apparently authorized the payment of subsidies to the ports which are losing the most money because they've been closed to our shipping. And, according to the galleon's skipper—who is *not* a happy man right this minute, Captain—there's also a goodly chunk of money which was destined to pay pensions to the survivors of the brave Delferahkans who were murdered by those nasty Charisians."

"Langhorne!" Shaikyr murmured. A prize like the one Hyndyrs was describing came along possibly once in a privateer's lifetime, and he felt the sudden tingle of wealth running along his nerves. But then his expression altered abruptly.

"*Langhorne!*" he repeated in a very different tone, and Hyndyrs chuckled harshly.

"Yes, Sir. That's one of the reasons I expect it to get noisy when I tell the men."

" 'Noisy' may not begin to describe it," Shaikyr said sourly as his own earlier thoughts came back to him. *Raptor* and the other ships operating with her were under Crown warrant. Which meant the Crown was going to pocket three-fourths of the treasure ship's value while the privateers who'd actually captured her got only a quarter to split among them.

You know, Larys, he told himself, *it's amazing how much better that arrangement sounded to you an hour or so ago, isn't it?*

"Well," he said finally, laying his dividers on the opened chart, "I suppose I'd better come." He detected a certain lack of enthusiasm in his own voice, and smiled crookedly at Hyndyrs. "The men aren't exactly likely to be singing loud hosannas when we remind them about the prize court, are they?"

"I'd say that was probably a fairly safe prediction, yes, Sir," Hyndyrs agreed.

"I don't really blame them," Shaikyr admitted. "On the other hand, from the way you've described things, even a quarter share of the total, distributed over every man and ship's boy, is still going to be at least four or five years' earnings for most of them."

"I realize that, Sir," Hyndyrs said, and smiled encouragingly. "You just go right on telling them that. I'm sure that by the time those ship's boys are, oh, fifty or sixty years old, they'll come to accept things without complaining."

.III.
Tellesberg Palace,
City of Tellesberg,
Kingdom of Charis

In many ways, Safeholdian music wasn't all that different from the music Nimue Alban had known during her biological life. In other ways, it was . . . weird.

Yes, definitely *weird,* Merlin thought, standing his post yet again to watch over the king—*no, dummy,* he reminded himself yet again, *the Emperor*—and his wife.

The familiar part included a whole host of stringed instruments from humanity's past: guitars, violins, cellos, violas, even balalaikas and (here in Charis, at least) banjos. Personally, Merlin could have done without the banjos just fine. Most of the traditional brasses and wind instruments were still around, as well, although a few new ones had been added. Or, Merlin suspected, perhaps it would be more accurate to say that some extremely old ones had been resurrected. After all, it was unlikely that the citizens of Safehold, in a mere eight and a half centuries, could have reproduced all of the musical variants humanity had managed on Terra in well over fifty thousand years. One of the instruments Merlin wasn't familiar with was a brass, its tube so long the marching variants required a second musician to help carry it, but which was played using the same tongue and breath control as the Old Earth bugle. There was another one which looked something like a French horn crossed with a tuba. Then there were woodwinds—the piccolos, flutes, and fifes—not to mention the piano, the pipe organs of the various churches and cathedrals, and even harpsichords. Percussion instruments were well represented, as well, with drums, cymbals, xylophones (especially in Chisholm), and everything in between.

And then there were the bagpipes. Several versions of them, actually, from the multi-pipe version with which Nimue had been familiar, all the way up to a decidedly peculiar confection which combined the bag of the traditional bagpipes with something very like a trombone.

But it wasn't so much the instruments themselves which struck Merlin as peculiar as it was the *combinations* of instruments Safeholdians favored. For example, Nimue Alban had never imagined a concerto written for guitar, banjo, fife, drums, and bagpipes. Merlin, unfortunately, no longer had to imagine it.

There were a few other mixes and matches which occasionally made him wonder if some sort of bizarre genetic drift had affected Safeholdians' hearing. It was the only answer he could come up with for the theoretically tuneful goulashes they'd come up with.

Fortunately, the music favored for formal dances like the present one tended to be somewhat more restrained, and usually based around combinations of instruments which didn't leave Merlin feeling as if his artificial hearing had been assaulted with a blunt musical instrument. In fact, the current music arising from the orchestra parked along one wall of Tellesberg Palace's grand ballroom was almost soothing. It reminded Merlin somewhat of waltz music, although it also incorporated what Nimue would have called a "swing beat."

Merlin was just as glad he wasn't out there dancing with the others. Nimue had been an excellent dancer, and she'd always enjoyed the opportunity when it came her way. Merlin, on the other hand, had never been tutored in Safeholdian dance techniques . . . which appeared to incorporate both waltz-like measures and something like a square dance on steroids, interspersed with the tango and something which reminded him of what had once been called "the Charleston." How flesh-and-blood dancers survived it in a climate like Tellesberg's was one of those mysteries which defied rational explanation.

Some of his fellow guardsmen sometimes resented—or perhaps regret-ted would be a better way to put it—the duty which kept them standing guard during festivities like tonight's. Merlin didn't. If pressed, he would have admitted that he hadn't realized, despite his experience as one of Crown Prince Cayleb's personal bodyguards, that the King of Charis' personal arms-man would spend such a huge chunk of his life simply standing around look-ing sufficiently menacing to deter any thought of assault upon the king's person. Cayleb's transition from king to emperor hadn't done a thing to ease those particular requirements, either.

But whereas his fellow guardsmen's feet might ache, Merlin Athrawes' artificial sinews never felt fatigue unless he chose to feel it. And whereas those same fellow guardsmen might occasionally think of something else they could be doing with that same time, Merlin was actually grateful for the sometimes endless periods he spent standing outside a chamber door, or against the wall behind Cayleb's chair or throne. There was never enough time for him to adequately review the take from the literally hundreds of re-mote sensors his SNARCs had deployed, after all. To be gifted with large chunks of time when he could simply stand in one place and review the intel-ligence tidbits Owl had flagged for human (or, at least, Merlin's) evaluation was welcome. The fact that Nimue had always been capable of multi-tasking and that Merlin could do the same meant he could engage in that review while simultaneously keeping an eye on Cayleb. It wasn't something he'd even be tempted to do under other circumstances, but as only one member of a four- or five-man security detail inside Tellesberg Palace, he was willing to take the chance of operating at a few percentage points less than his full capa-bility while he studied the transmissions from Owl. Especially when that "full capability" included many times human strength, enhanced hearing, and the sort of reaction speed possible for someone whose nervous impulses moved a hundred times faster than those of any organic human.

At the moment, given the dense, glittering crowd which filled the grand ballroom to capacity, reviewing sensor reports was the last thing on his mind. He didn't really anticipate any desperate attack upon Cayleb or Sharleyan, but the sheer number of people packed together could provide highly effec-tive cover for an assassin with a knife, as the attempt on Archbishop Maikel had made only too clear. It wouldn't necessarily have to be some suicidal fa-natic from the Temple Loyalists in this case, either. The size of the crowd it-self could provide plenty of cover for any assassin cool enough to blend back into it once he'd struck the fatal blow.

You know, Merlin told himself rather severely, *you do have a tendency to look on the dark side of these festive occasions, don't you?*

There was an undeniable edge of truth to the self-question. During

Nimue's lifetime, evenings like this had possessed an almost frenetic aura. Everyone attending them had known the Gbaba were out there, and that humanity was losing. That every formal ball they attended was one of a dwindling number of balls any human being would ever attend again. It had, to say the least, put a damper on the festivities.

It had for Nimue, at least. Or perhaps it was only that she'd been sufficiently sensitive to the moods of others that the crowds around her had caused her to feel that sense of depressing mortality. Merlin sometimes thought that must have been the case, given Nimue's preference for solo forms of entertainment. Sailing, for example. Rock climbing, hang gliding, hikes. Reading, or splashing paint on a canvas. It was as if she'd been spending the limited number of years available to her soaking up the natural universe through her very pores.

There was actually a faint ghost of some of those currents of Gbaba-spawned tension in Charis these days. Even the most ardent of Cayleb's supporters had to feel the occasional moment of dread when he or she contemplated the odds against Charis' survival. Adding Chisholm and Emerald to the newborn Charisian Empire had obviously helped, but given the fact that at least eighty percent of the human race lived on one of the mainland continents under the direct control of the Church of God Awaiting, doubling the Charisian population hadn't really shifted the overall odds very far.

Tonight, however, no one seemed to be thinking gloomy thoughts. The ballroom's polished floor of black marble, inlaid with the kraken motif of the Kingdom of Charis' coat of arms in a warm, honey-gold marble from the Lizard Range in the Duchy of Ahrmahk, gleamed in the light of the chandeliers' countless flames. The marble was like a pool of deep, dark water, its surface mirroring the dancers upon it, and those dancers glittered and gleamed with their own finery in the same light, touched with the red, blue, and golden fire of rubies, sapphires, and topaz. Gold and silver chains, bullion embroidery, rustling cotton silk and the even more expensive steel thistle silk. . . .

A commercially oriented ear—and what Charisian ear wasn't commercially oriented?—could have literally heard the sweet, musical clinking of all the coins which had changed hands to create that rich, swirling interplay of fabric, precious metals, and gems.

For example, the steel thistle silk, which had been all but unobtainable outside the borders of the Empire of Harchong until very recently, was remarkably present tonight. The cotton gin technology which Merlin had suggested to Ehdwyrd Howsmyn and Rhaiyan Mychail had, indeed, proved capable of extracting the tiny, spiny, toxic seeds from raw steel thistle fiber. Unlike cotton silk, steel thistle had to be run through the ginning process multiple times, using a progressively finer comb to extract all the seeds, so it seemed likely to remain the more expensive of the two, despite the fact that steel thistle grew faster than cotton silk and in a much greater range of climates. But its price was already beginning to fall, despite Mychail's best efforts to increase the supply only gradually. In fact, Mychail had even suggested that the cost of the material might fall far enough for it to be considered for sailcloth.

The very notion had struck both Cayleb and Earl Lock Island as preposterous, yet they'd come to the conclusion that it actually had much to recommend it. For one thing, steel thistle was almost indestructible, with a remarkable resistance to rot and virtual immunity to mildew, so even if initial purchase costs might be high, *replacement* costs would be much lower. It was also enormously strong, stronger than anything Terra-based humanity had been able to produce before the days of artificial fibers. Coupled with its extraordinarily fine weave, which would give it a considerable efficiency advantage in driving power over any organic-based sail which had ever been produced on Earth, there was much to be said for the "preposterous" notion.

For tonight, though, any suggestion that the noblest, most expensive fabric ever known on Safehold might be put to such a plebeian use would have been greeted with mingled incredulity and horror by the guests displaying their wealth and sartorial splendor by wearing it to the most important social event of the year, after Cayleb's coronation and his and Sharleyan's wedding.

The guests of honor weren't dancing at the moment, however, and Merlin's lips twitched with wry sympathy as he glanced in their direction. Crown Prince Zhan and his wife-to-be, Princess Mahrya, sat side by side, watching the dancers. The fact that Zhan was still less than eleven Safeholdian years old—barely ten standard years—while Mahrya was almost nineteen Safeholdian years of age made them an ill-matched couple on the dance floor. Mahrya wasn't especially tall for her age (not surprisingly, Merlin thought, given her parentage), but she was still the better part of a foot taller than Zhan, even though he was already showing promise of matching Cayleb's inches.

Still, they'd danced with surprising gracefulness in the evening's first dance. In fact, Merlin had been astonished by how calm they'd both managed to look under the massed eyes of the entire royal and imperial court. No doubt the fact that they'd been reared and trained literally from the cradle for moments precisely like tonight had helped, but he'd still been surprised by their apparent aplomb and self-possession as they swirled through the measures of the opening dance of the ball in honor of their official betrothal.

He'd realized only later that Mahrya was deliberately (and surprisingly skillfully) diverting her younger fiancé's thoughts from the evening's central tension. Despite the difference in their ages, she seemed genuinely pleased with the betrothal, and not just because she would be marrying the current heir to the Charisian throne. Merlin sincerely doubted that she cherished any smolderingly romantic thoughts about an eleven-year-old, but she obviously liked Zhan. And, as Cayleb had pointed out, the difference in their ages— barely six and a half years, standard—was actually far from uncommon when it came to arranged marriages of state.

Zhan, for his part, had been seriously inclined to pout when he'd been informed that his older brother intended to marry him off to the eldest daughter of Nahrmahn of Emerald. Zhan hadn't been disposed to look favorably on *anything* coming out of Emerald or Corisande, even before his father's death. Since the Battle of Darcos Sound, that hatred had hardened rather alarmingly. But the fact that Mahrya was so much older than he was, with a figure ripening into intensely intriguing contours, had served to discount at least some of the Emeraldian taint clinging to her. The discovery that she shared his own love for books, and that despite the age differential and her undoubted (and obvious) intelligence she showed absolutely no tendency to talk down to him, had eliminated still more of that taint in Zhan's eyes. Princess Ohlyvya, Mahrya's mother, had been another factor in the betrothal's favor. She was darker than Zhan's dead mother, but there was much about her that reminded the orphaned crown prince of Queen Zhanayt.

The reaction Mahrya had drawn from the older male adolescents of the court had sealed Zhan's approval of the arrangement, Merlin thought, lips twitching in another smile. It was fortunate the princess had inherited both her figure and her coloration from her mother, not her father. She was going to be as slender as Princess Ohlyvya, but she was already well past that coltish, awkward stage of adolescence, and unless Merlin was mistaken, she was likely to prove even more curvaceous than her mother. At least a few nobly born Charisian teenagers seemed to experience some difficulty restraining themselves from drooling whenever she strode gracefully past them. In fact, she appeared to effortlessly evoke a response from the male of the species which Nimue Alban at seventeen would have envied with every hormonally activated bone in her body. Zhan had been quick to note how his proposed betrothal to her had raised his stock among his older contemporaries in a way which even his newfound status as Crown Prince of Charis had been unable to do.

This is one notion of Cayleb's that's going to work out very well, I think, Merlin told himself, his sapphire eyes watching Emperor Cayleb and Empress Sharleyan swirling gracefully about the dance floor. *I doubt very much that Zhan is truly aware of all the political implications of this betrothal. Even if he were, I don't think they'd matter a great deal to him—certainly not as much as those stirring hormones of his do! But everyone else recognizes those implications only too well. Given the formal provisions of the treaties establishing the Empire, it's unlikely Nahrmahn's grandson or granddaughter will ever inherit the imperial crown, even if something happens to Cayleb in the upcoming campaign. But whether that happens or not, this marriage will guarantee his close association with the House of Ahrmahk, and a lot of the people who were most worried about Emerald as a threat to Charis are just delighted to have Nahrmahn working for Charis, instead.*

As was Merlin, himself. He was perhaps a little less surprised than others by the strengths Nahrmahn brought to Cayleb and Sharleyan's council, but that only made him even happier to have Nahrmahn working for Cayleb, rather than trying to have him assassinated. Diverting *anyone* from assassinating the emperor would have been worthwhile in its own right; gaining the full-fledged support of someone as irritatingly capable as Nahrmahn had proven himself was even more worthwhile. Merlin never doubted that there were moments when Nahrmahn deeply regretted the way in which his decades of plotting and scheming against Charis had come to such an abrupt and final—and *unsuccessful*—end. Still, he'd made out almost as well as he might have if he'd won, especially after the Group of Four had chosen to make him Hektor's lackey, and he seemed rather surprised by the fact that he actually *liked* Cayleb and Sharleyan. At the moment, he was more comfortable admitting that liking for Sharleyan than he was for Cayleb, but once the remaining ruffled feathers of his masculine ego had recovered, he would probably grudgingly admit (to Princess Ohlyvya, at least) that Cayleb was at least moderately likable in his own right.

And I'll bet Ohlyvya will hardly even say "I told you so" more than two or three times. Merlin chuckled mentally at the thought, then checked his built-in chronometer.

Another couple of hours, and then the ball would begin to wind down. Mostly, although no one was about to admit it, because they were already well past the prospective groom's bedtime.

▼   ▼   ▼

"Well, *this* seems to be working out reasonably well, at any rate." Emperor Cayleb sipped at a cup of punch as he and his empress sat regaining their breath. A discreetly interposed wall of Imperial Guardsmen actually afforded them a few moments of genuine privacy, and he chuckled as he gazed at his younger brother. "Zhan was certain this was going to be a disaster," he added.

"No wonder, given the way most of your people seem to have spent their time talking about Emerald and Prince Nahrmahn the entire time he's been alive." Sharleyan sniffed. "I'm not trying to say they weren't justified, but expecting a boy Zhan's age to leap with joy when he found out he was about to be married off to the ogre's daughter would have been silly."

"I know." Cayleb chuckled again. "On the other hand, it's remarkable how quickly he started getting over that once he laid eyes on her."

"Didn't you tell me you were pleasantly surprised at the way *your* arranged marriage worked out?"

"Stop fishing for compliments, dear." Cayleb lifted her hand to his lips and pressed a kiss upon the back of her wrist, his eyes smiling up at her. Then he straightened. "I didn't say I was pleasantly *surprised*," he continued. "I said I was pleasantly *relieved*."

"I knew it was something tactful like that," Sharleyan said dryly.

"Well," he smiled wickedly, "I hope the noble and selfless dedication I've brought to the task of begetting an heir for our new dynasty has convinced you I don't feel *too* much like a martyr to international politics."

Sharleyan blushed. One would have had to look very closely to see the rising color in her cheeks, given the lighting and her complexion of antique ivory, but *Cayleb* saw it, and his smile turned into a broader grin. Sharleyan reached across and whacked him on the knuckles with her fan—a practical necessity, and not simply a fashion accessory here in Charis—then found herself fighting hard against an attack of giggles as he winked suggestively at her. The fact was that Cayleb's ardor was . . . remarkable, she told herself with a slight but pardonable complacency. He was not only extraordinarily good-looking, but young, fit, and a trained warrior, with all the hardihood and . . . endurance that implied. She might have been forced to avoid entanglements, or any hint of a potential scandal, before her marriage, but the two of them were making up for lost time quite handily. Even better, almost everyone in Charis seemed pleased for both of them, and that could be entirely too rare when a member of a royal family brought home "that foreign woman" as his bride.

"As a matter of fact, the possibility that you'd managed to resign yourself to your fate had crossed my mind," she told him after a moment. "And," she added in a softer voice, "so have I."

"I'm glad," he said simply.

"Yes, well," she gave her head a slight shake, "to return to your younger brother's future nuptials. I think he's *already* 'resigned to his fate.' And," she added frankly, "given Mahrya's figure, I'd be astonished if he weren't. He may be young, but he's definitely male! It seems to run in the family."

"That's what Father always said, at any rate," Cayleb agreed.

"And did your father, pray tell, suggest to you that it might be a good idea to keep an eye on your younger *sister*, as well, Your Majesty?"

"Zhanayt?" Cayleb blinked. "What about Zhanayt?"

"Men!" Sharleyan shook her head. "Even the best of you seem to think that all you have to do is beat your hairy chests to encourage the female of your choice to swoon and fall into your manly arms! Doesn't it occur to *any* of you that we women have minds of our own, as well?"

"Believe me, My Lady," Cayleb said sincerely, "if my mother had allowed any silly notion that you don't to take root in my brain in the first place, the first few days of marriage to you would have disabused me of it. But what, exactly, does that have to do with Zhanayt?"

"Haven't you seen the way she's been looking at Nahrmahn the Younger?" Sharleyan said, and Cayleb's eyes widened.

"You're not serious!"

"Never more so, my dear." Sharleyan shook her head. "She's three years older than Zhan, you know. Trust me, she's even more aware of how . . . interesting the opposite sex is than *he* is right now. Not only that, but she sees everyone else getting married right and left. I'm not saying she cherishes any overwhelming need to leap into young Nahrmahn's arms. For that matter, I wouldn't be a bit surprised if someone else displaced him in her thoughts in the next several months. But given her rank and his, he's about the only youngster here in Tellesberg she could realistically consider. And the fact is that he really isn't all that bad looking. For that matter, I can actually see what Princess Ohlyvya sees in his *father*, although it wouldn't hurt Nahrmahn the Elder a bit to lose a little weight. Like half his body weight, perhaps."

"My God, you *are* serious!" It was Cayleb's turn to shake his head. Then he frowned. "I suppose, in some ways, it could be a beneficial match," he said slowly.

"I hate to think in cold-blooded dynastic terms, Cayleb," Sharleyan replied in a rather more serious tone, "but however beneficial it might be, I have to suspect that an even more advantageous match is likely to offer itself—possibly quite soon—in Zhanayt's case."

"Yes?" He raised an eyebrow at her, and she waved her fan gently.

"The match between Zhan and Mahrya is already going to bind the House of Ahrmahk and the House of Baytz together," she pointed out. "I happen to think Nahrmahn the Younger is actually quite a pleasant young man, but I don't think we need to put Zhanayt on the Emeraldian throne as princess consort just to ensure his future loyalty to the imperial crown. He's bright enough to see the advantages, and by the time he takes the throne, Emerald will have been part of the Empire for decades, and he and his family will be deeply involved in and committed to governing it. I don't think he'll have the least motive or inclination to be anything except a loyal supporter of the Crown. But Corisande is going to be rather a different case. To be perfectly blunt, there's no way I'd trust any member of *Hektor's* house as far as I could throw one of those new guns of Baron Seamount's. There's been far too much blood spilt between Corisande and the House of Ahrmahk and the House of Tayt, and Corisande *isn't* going to be peacefully and willingly integrated into the Empire. I don't know about you, but given all that, I could never trust one of Hektor's children, far less Hektor himself."

"I'm afraid I agree with you," Cayleb said, and his nostrils flared. "In fact, it's given me the occasional nightmare. I don't have the stomach for slaughtering all the possible pretenders to the Corisandian throne, but I'm not at all sure that simply removing Hektor from it and leaving his children alive to plot against us—or to be used as cat's-paws by someone else . . . like Zhamsyn Trynair or Zhaspahr Clyntahn, for example—is going to be enough."

"I'm quite certain it isn't," Sharleyan said bluntly. "I'm no more in favor of killing children just to keep them from being potential future threats than you are, but the fact remains that we have a responsibility here. One that doesn't end when we take Hektor's head. That's what I'm thinking about where Zhanayt is concerned."

"In exactly what way?" Cayleb asked, but his tone suggested he was following Sharleyan's thoughts quite well now.

"What we're going to have to do is to find some Corisandian noble who's sufficiently popular in Corisande to have at least some chance of gradually winning public acceptance as our vassal *and* Prince of Corisande, but smart enough—or pragmatic enough, at any rate—to realize we can't allow him to survive if he isn't a *loyal* vassal. And then we're going to have to bind him to us as closely as possible. Which may well mean. . . ."

She allowed her voice to trail off, and Cayleb nodded. It wasn't an entirely happy nod.

"I see your logic," he conceded. "I hate to think of putting Zhanayt on the marital auction block so cold-bloodedly, though."

"Did that stop you from proposing to someone you'd never even met?" she asked gently. "Did it stop you from doing exactly that with Zhan?"

"No, but that's—"

"That's *different*," she finished for him. "Cayleb, I think I really do love you, but to be perfectly honest, that wasn't something I counted on, and it wasn't something that was necessary, either. Can you honestly tell me it was different for you?"

"No," he admitted softly.

"But Zhanayt is your baby sister." Sharleyan smiled just a bit wistfully. "I wish sometimes that I'd had at least one sibling, just so I could really experience what you're feeling about Zhanayt right now. Of course, if I had—and especially if it had been a younger *brother*—Mahrak would have had an even harder time keeping me alive and on the throne, I suppose. But the fact is, you were ruthless enough to make a necessary marriage of state for yourself, and you were ruthless enough to do the same thing with Zhan, for the same reasons. If the time comes, my love, you *will* make the same decision for Zhanayt. I only hope it works out as well for her as it has for us and as it seems likely to for Zhan and Mahrya."

"And what do you think the odds of that are?" he asked even more softly.

"Honestly?" She met his eyes unflinchingly. "Not that high," she said then. "The fact that you and I are able to do more than merely tolerate one another because we have to already puts us ahead of the game, Cayleb. The fact that Mahrya looks like being an ideal mate for your younger brother puts us even farther ahead. But it has to even out somewhere, you know."

"Yes, I do," he half murmured, and she reached out to squeeze his hand.

"However it works out in the end, there's no need for us to rush to meet it," she told him. "One of the very first lessons Mahrak taught me when I inherited the crown was that more troubles than not work *themselves* out with the passage of time. I'm not trying to suggest to you that you have to start scheming about who you're going to marry Zhanayt off to right this minute. I'm only suggesting that it might be wise for you to not encourage any possible yearnings on her part at this time."

Cayleb looked at her for a moment and started to open his mouth. Then he changed his mind and lifted her hand with his to kiss it once more. She looked a question at him, obviously wondering what he'd begun to say, but he only shook his head with another smile.

I really wish I could tell you how thoroughly events have proven that Merlin was right when he told me to make you my partner, *and not just my wife*, he thought.

▼   ▼   ▼

"I thought that went fairly well," Cayleb said again, later that night, to a considerably different audience.

Sharleyan had gone on to bed, and he'd discovered that, since his marriage, he felt much less temptation to stay up late drinking too much wine or telling too many bad jokes with Merlin or some other crony. At the moment, however, he didn't have much choice, and he, Archbishop Maikel, Rahzhyr Mahklyn, and Merlin sat on a palace balcony sipping Desnairian whiskey while they gazed up at the stars. The distant chips of light—lights, he knew now, which were every one of them a sun as fiercely bright as Safehold's own—glittered like jewels in the heavens' velvet vault, with that cool hush that comes only in the hours before dawn. It was scarcely a setting most people would have associated with a meeting between an emperor and three of his most trusted advisers, but that suited Cayleb just fine. If he simply had to deal with matters of state instead of the bedroom, he could at least do it as comfortably as possible.

"As a matter of fact, I thought it went quite well myself," Staynair agreed.

"And a good thing, too, if you'll pardon my saying so, Your Majesty," Mahklyn put it. "I'm delighted to have that particular arrangement made and solidly accepted well before you go sailing off to invade Corisande."

Merlin nodded, although the doctor's observation showed a far greater degree of pragmatism and political awareness than he'd ever expected to hear out of him. He'd known all along that the perpetually bemused look Mahklyn presented to the rest of the world was deceiving, but he'd never appreciated how acute the older man's political insights were likely to prove when he chose to exercise them.

And he's been exercising them a lot more ever since Cayleb moved the Royal College into the Palace, hasn't he? Merlin thought. *Well, that and since the Brethren cleared him for the complete story of Saint Zherneau.*

Judging from Cayleb's next words, the same thought might well have been passing through the emperor's brain.

"I agree with you, Rahzhyr," he said. "But that brings me back to my on-going concern. I *am* going to be leaving the Kingdom within the next few five-days now. And Sharleyan is going to be ruling as my regent, with Rayjhis as her first councilor. Don't you think it's about time for the Brethren to make up their minds to let me tell at least one of them the full story?"

Mahklyn had the good sense to keep his mouth firmly shut. Cayleb's tone was determinedly pleasant, but that only emphasized the very real anger at the backs of his brown eyes.

"Cayleb," Staynair said after glancing at Merlin, "I understand your impatience. Truly, I do. But it's simply not reasonable to expect the Brethren to reach that decision this quickly."

"With all due respect, Maikel, I disagree," the emperor said flatly. Staynair started to open his mouth again, but Cayleb raised his hand in a gesture which, while far from discourteous, was undeniably imperious, and continued speaking.

"The fact is that Merlin was absolutely right when he told me how smart this woman was," he said. "In fact, if anything, I think Merlin *under*estimated her. She's not just 'smart'; she's a hell of a lot more than that, and keeping her in the dark about something this fundamental is depriving us of one of our most valuable resources. Not only that, but as I believe I've mentioned before, she's my *wife*, as well as the Empress of Charis. As Empress, she very definitely has Merlin's 'need to know.' And as my wife, she has every *right* to expect me to be open and honest with her, especially when it comes to something as fundamental as this!"

None of the other three spoke for several seconds. Then Merlin cleared his throat, which, despite the tension, won an involuntary grin from Cayleb. The emperor still might not fully grasp everything involved in the concept of a PICA, but he was aware that Merlin would never have any *physical* need to clear his throat.

"First, Cayleb, let me say I agree with you completely. But, however deeply I may agree with you, there are certain practical realities we simply can't ignore. And one of them is that the Brethren are still concerned by that possible 'youthful impetuosity' of yours. Let's face it, you just married a beautiful, smart, and—if you'll pardon me for saying it—sexy young woman. Nothing could be more natural than for you to be besotted with her. Or, at least, for all of those factors to push you into making something less than a careful, fully reasoned decision where she's concerned."

"Kraken shit," Cayleb said bluntly. "Oh, I suppose a sufficiently older, close-minded, cranky monk under an oath of celibacy in a bare monastery cell somewhere might think that way. I'll even go so far as to drop the oath of celibacy. But I'm a king, Merlin. In fact, I'm a bloody *emperor* now! This isn't just a decision to be made by a new husband. It's a decision to be made by a ruling head of state on what's effectively the eve of his departure for the invasion of a hostile princedom. I know the odds are against my getting myself killed. But don't any of you forget that the odds were against my father getting *himself* killed, too. It *can* happen. And if it does, and if Sharleyan has to be told the truth after my death, how do you think that's likely to affect her willingness to accept the trustworthiness of the Brethren—or of you and Maikel, for that matter?"

"That's a very telling argument," Staynair said after a moment. "And, by the way, one I agree with wholeheartedly. But there's an aspect of this that Merlin left out of his analysis a moment ago."

"Such as?" Cayleb challenged.

"The truth is that in the past few months the Brethren have admitted more people into what we might call the 'inner circle' than in the preceding ten *years*, Cayleb. Don't forget that some of these people, like Zhon Byrkyt, have spent literally a lifetime—and a *long* lifetime at that—protecting that secret, worrying about what would happen if their security arrangements had even the tiniest flaw. At the moment, they're feeling exposed and off-balance. To be blunt about it, they don't want to tell *anyone* else unless they absolutely have to."

"That's not the best basis upon which to be making decisions, Maikel," Cayleb pointed out, and the archbishop nodded.

"I couldn't agree with you more about that. Unfortunately, it's what's happening. And as important—even vital—as it may be to bring the Empress fully into the 'inner circle' as soon as possible, it's equally important that we maintain the confidence of those already inside that circle."

"Much as I hate to admit it, Cayleb, I think he has a point," Merlin said quietly. Cayleb half glared at him, and Merlin shrugged. "I don't say not telling her is a good decision. I'm just afraid that at this particular moment, given the pragmatic constraints of the situation, there really isn't any 'good' solution available to us. So we're just going to have to do the best we can choosing between less than optimal ones."

Cayleb made an irate grunting sound, but his grimace also indicated at least unwilling acceptance, if not outright agreement. He wasn't quite done, though, and he leaned back in his chair once again.

"All right," he said. "I'll concede where Sharleyan is concerned . . . for now, at least. But what about Rayjhis? He's going to be her primary political adviser here while I'm gone, and God knows he spent the last two or three decades showing that he knows how to keep secrets of state secret! Don't you think it's about time we told *him* the truth?"

"Actually," Staynair said, "I'm afraid that I rather think the time to tell Rayjhis the *entire* truth will never come at all, Cayleb."

The emperor looked at him in obvious surprise, and Staynair sighed.

"I've known Rayjhis Yowance since he was little more than a boy, Your Majesty," he said rather more formally than had become his wont with Cayleb. "He was still a midshipman, and I was only a novice, when we first met. I hold him in the deepest affection, and I would cheerfully trust him with my life or the life of my Kingdom. But I have to tell you that as disillusioned as he may be about the Group of Four, as committed as he may be to the separation between the Church of Charis and the Church of the Temple, I don't believe he is—or ever will be—prepared to accept the full truth about Langhorne, Bédard, and Pei Shan-wei. I'm actually more than a little frightened about how he might react even to the discovery that Merlin, here, isn't actually 'alive' after all. He believes in the Archangels, Cayleb. Deep inside, where the very things that make him so strong, so determined and trustworthy, come together, he *believes*. I don't think he'll be able to step beyond that. And, to be completely honest with you, I don't know that we have any right to ask him to do that."

Cayleb's eyes narrowed as he gazed at the archbishop. It was obvious he was thinking hard, and the better part of a full minute dragged past before he exhaled noisily.

"I'm afraid you may be right," he said then, slowly. "I guess it's just that I've never thought of Rayjhis as being . . . parochial, or narrow-minded."

"This is neither parochialism nor closed-mindedness," Staynair said. "It's faith—the faith he's been taught literally since the cradle. And it's what's going to make this struggle so extraordinarily ugly once its full dimensions become known to all. Which, as I suggested to Merlin once, is the reason we can't afford to make those full dimensions known yet."

"I agree, Cayleb," Merlin said. "And, on a pragmatic level, I have to say I don't really think it matters a great deal where Rayjhis is concerned."

"No?" Cayleb cocked his head, and Merlin shrugged.

"Whatever he might or might not be able to accept about Shan-wei, he's obviously accepted my '*seijin*' abilities. I think he's pretty sure they go beyond mere *seijin*-hood, in fact. But the fact that both your father and Maikel here have accepted those abilities as serving the Light and not the Dark is enough for him. And I know he's learned to allow for them and to make the most effective possible use of them. There's an old saying, one I haven't come across here on Safehold, but one I think we'd all do well to bear in mind upon occasion. 'If it isn't broken, don't fix it.' "

"I agree," Staynair said, nodding vigorously. "Rayjhis is a very good, very loyal, and very capable man, Cayleb. You know that as well as I do. And you also know he's been using that goodness, loyalty, and capability in effective partnership with Merlin for almost three years now. Admittedly," the archbishop smiled without any humor at all, "their relationship got off to a rocky start, but since he accepted that Merlin was on Charis' side, he's worked wholeheartedly with him. I don't think we need to tell him anything more than we've told him so far—all of which, mind you, has been the truth, if not the *entire* truth. And if, as you've suggested is possible, anything should 'happen to you' in Corisande, there are already several people here in Tellesberg, including myself, who do know the full secret and who Rayjhis already trusts."

"All right." Cayleb nodded again, then laughed a bit sourly. "I seem to be being defeated on all fronts tonight. I hope it isn't an omen for how well things are working out for Domynyk at Ferayd!"

"If it's an omen of any sort, let's hope it's an omen from the theater," Merlin suggested, and all three of the others chuckled. Safehold's theater tradition continued to enshrine the ancient belief that a bad rehearsal was the best guarantee of a good performance.

"Still, that does bring up something else I've been thinking about, Merlin," Cayleb said, turning to the man who had once been Nimue Alban.

"That sounds ominous," Merlin remarked, and Cayleb snorted.

"Not quite that bad, I think. The thing that's occurred to me is that all of us, except you, of course, have only the most imperfect understanding of what humanity was like before Langhorne and the Church of God Awaiting."

"I'm afraid that's unfortunately true," Merlin acknowledged.

"Well, what I've been wondering about is this thing Zherneau called a 'NEAT' in his journal. He said Shan-wei used it to reeducate him after Langhorne and Bédard had erased all of his earlier memories."

He paused, and Merlin nodded.

"And did 'Nimue' have one of the things—whatever it is—in her 'cave'?" the emperor asked.

"As a matter of fact, she did—I mean, I do," Merlin said.

"Well, I got the impression from his journal that they were capable of teaching someone an enormous amount in a very short time. So I've been wondering if it wouldn't make sense for us to use one of those machines to 'educate' some of the rest of us, just in case anything untoward were to happen to you."

"Actually, I think that would be a splendid idea, especially where you, Maikel, and Rahzhyr are concerned. Unfortunately, we can't."

"Why not?"

"Because 'NEAT' is an acronym, which stands for 'Neural Education and Training,'" Merlin said. All of his Safeholdian listeners looked blank, and he raised his right hand, holding it cupped before him as if to contain something.

"What that means is that it directly interfaces—connects with—the human neural system. Your nerves and brain. It's rather like the technology Nimue used to record her personality and her memories when she uploaded them to me."

It felt more than a little peculiar to be having this conversation, Merlin reflected. On the other hand, it probably would have felt equally peculiar to have held it with anyone from Terra. Not least because of the fact that he was so far past the mandated ten-day legal maximum which had been permitted under Federation law for a PICA to operate in autonomous mode.

"The problem is that for a NEAT to interface with a human being, the human being has to have the necessary implants." They looked even blanker, and he sighed. "Think of it as . . . the fitting a water hose screws into aboard one of the water hoys the harbormaster uses to refill a ship's water tanks. It's a very, very tiny . . . mechanism, for want of a better word, that has to be surgically implanted into someone before they can connect to a NEAT. Shan-wei was able to reeducate Zherneau and the others because all of the 'Adams' and 'Eves' had already received their implants. Everyone on Old Earth received them shortly after birth. No one here on Safehold has them, though. So without something to attach the 'hose' to, I can't just pour knowledge into your heads."

"I'm extremely sorry to hear that," Mahklyn said. Merlin glanced at him, and the doctor chuckled a bit harshly. "Reading over the texts you've had copied for me is exciting enough, Merlin. Having the same knowledge 'magically' made available to me would be even more marvelous. And it would save so much time, too."

Merlin chuckled. Mahklyn was in the process of completely revolutionizing Safeholdian mathematics. It would be some time yet before he was prepared to publish, because at the moment he was busy reading the works not only of Newton, but of several of Newton's contemporaries—and successors—for himself. Brilliant as he undoubtedly was, that was a huge amount of theory and information to soak up, and the task of translating it into his own words, so that it was obviously a native Safeholdian development, and not something which came from the "dark knowledge of Shan-wei" was likely to take the entire remainder of his life . . . and then some. His discomfort at passing off the gigantic work of others as his own was manifest, but at least he seemed to have accepted that he had no choice.

"I don't doubt that it would," Merlin said now. "Unfortunately, we can't do it."

"Well, there it is," Cayleb said philosophically. All of the others looked at him, and he smiled crookedly. "Three strikes, and out," he said.

"I don't think that's a completely fair way to look at things, Cayleb," Staynair said mildly. "None of them were really *strikes*, you know."

"You can call them whatever you like, Maikel. For me, they were strikes. On the other hand," Cayleb shoved himself up out of his chair, "that's not necessarily a terrible thing. After all, if I've just struck out here, then it's only reasonable for me to head off to the showers. And," he smiled wickedly, "to bed. If I can't tell Sharleyan everything I'd like to tell her, I can at least make it obvious to her just how much I'm going to miss her while I'm away."

.IV.
Ferayd Sound,
Kingdom of Delferahk

They're *what?*"

Sir Vyk Lakyr jerked upright in his chair, staring at the very young officer on the far side of his desk. Lieutenant Cheryng had become a rather frequent visitor in Lakyr's office since the bloody August fiasco here in Ferayd, because he was in charge of Lakyr's clerks and message traffic. There'd been a lot more of that traffic over the last two and a half months, and very little of it had been pleasant. In fact, Lakyr was more than a little surprised that he was not only still in command of the Ferayd garrison, but that he'd actually been promoted when that garrison was reinforced by providing the gunners for its batteries. He wasn't certain if that meant King Zhames recognized that it hadn't been his fault, but he *was* certain that he might yet be dismissed if the Church demanded it. Which, given the fact that it was the Church's own bloodthirsty Inquisitors who had truly provoked the massacre, was still entirely possible.

It had become less probable, however, when the Church proclaimed its version of what had happened here. Lakyr didn't know whether he was more outraged or infuriated by the blatant lies, but one reason for his anger was that he couldn't quite shake a sense of gratitude, as well. By placing all of the blame on the Charisian victims, rather than on anyone—especially the Inquisition—here in Ferayd, it had diverted at least some of the heat from him, as well. What had astonished him, at least initially, was how many people living right here in Ferayd actually believed the Church's version. When he'd first realized that was the case, Lakyr had been forced to remind himself that it had all taken place in the middle of the night, and that the first thing anyone in Ferayd—outside his own units and the Inquisition—had known about it was the sudden eruption of cannon fire in the harbor.

But if he'd understood Lieutenant Cheryng correctly, everyone involved was about to get a painful demonstration of the ancient principle that, for good or ill, all actions had consequences.

"Major Fhairly says that at least fifteen Charisian galleons are standing in through the East Pass, Sir," the lieutenant repeated now, in response to his question. "He believes there are more of them than he's seen so far. Or, rather, than he'd seen when he dispatched his message."

Lakyr's jaw clenched. Major Ahdym Fhairly commanded the defensive batteries on East Island, which covered the narrowest portion of East Pass, the easternmost of the three navigable passages into Ferayd Sound proper. But East Island was a hundred and thirty miles from Ferayd itself.

"How long did his message take to reach us?"

"Only about four hours, Sir. He sent his dispatch boat across to the mainland, and the semaphore chain transmitted it from there."

Only *about four hours*, Lakyr thought. *I wonder if Fhairly is still alive?*

"All right," he said aloud, "it'll take them at least fifteen or sixteen hours to get here, even after they clear the pass. That wouldn't put them off the harbor until after dark, and I doubt they're going to want to launch any significant attacks without enough light to see what they're doing."

He glanced up and paused as he saw Cheryng's expression.

"Yes, Lieutenant?"

"Sir, it's just— Well, what if they don't get past East Keep at all?"

The youngster sounded as if his feelings had been hurt by his commander's automatic assumption that Fhairly wouldn't manage to stop them, Lakyr thought. He started to reply sharply to the question, then reminded himself that he, too, had once been a young and inexperienced lieutenant.

"I'd have to say it's . . . unlikely Major Fhairly and his men will be able to stop them, Taiwyl," he said almost gently. "The Major's already reported fifteen galleons. That's at least seven hundred guns, if our reports on their ships' average armaments are accurate. Major Fhairly has only twenty-five. Admittedly, his are protected by stone parapets, but they also can't move. Not to mention the fact that at high tide—and from the timing of his message, the Charisians arranged their arrival to coincide with high tide—even at East Island, the navigable channel is almost six miles wide. His guns have a maximum range of only *three* miles under absolutely optimum conditions, and their chance of hitting anything at that distance is . . . remote. Unless they choose to engage him, he's not going to be able to do more than annoy them."

Cheryng looked surprised, although what Lakyr had just said ought to have been obvious to him. Then again, just looking at a map, it was easy to overlook the sheer width of the channel. Lakyr had often suspected that that was precisely what the people who'd authorized the construction of East Keep in the first place had done.

"And that," Lakyr continued grimly, "is why I feel confident we're going to be seeing the Charisian Navy right off the port sometime around dawn tomorrow. We've got until then to get ready to greet them."

▼   ▼   ▼

A fresh rumble of thunder washed over East Keep as the galleons sailing regally past pounded the batteries, and Major Fhairly spat out a muddy mouthful of rock dust.

"This is fucking *useless*, Sir!" his second-in-command shouted almost in his ear. "We're not even marking the bastards!"

That, Fhairly thought, wasn't entirely true. He was confident they'd managed to land at least a few hits of their own. But there couldn't have been very many of them, and there hadn't been *any* in the last hour or so.

It was the sheer number of guns they'd managed to cram aboard those ships. That, and their obscene rate of fire. Every single one of those galleons mounted more guns than his entire battery in each broadside, and every single one of those guns fired four or five times as rapidly as his did . . . and clearly threw a heavier shot when they did fire. They'd started out using round shot, but as their fire had plowed into and around his guns' embrasures and his own artillerists' fire had begun to slacken, they'd come in closer until they were sweeping his positions with grapeshot from barely three hundred yards out as they sailed past. In fact, three of the bastards had actually shown their contempt for anything he might yet manage to do by coming in to less than *two* hundred yards and *anchoring* there. They'd anchored by the stern, with springs on their cables, turning themselves into stable, unmoving gun platforms, and they were pouring a devastatingly accurate storm of grapeshot across his position.

His subordinate was right, and he knew it. They'd already taken over thirty fatal casualties, and he had at least that many more who'd been wounded. That was twenty percent of his total effective force, and the men still in action weren't accomplishing a thing. The galleons anchored off the battery had Fhairly's guns totally suppressed, and the other war galleons—and the dozen or so transports with them—were making their way past the defensive works completely unhampered.

He poked his head up, looking over the parapet as the Charisian fleet sailed by. He didn't recognize the standard they flew, but from the colors, it had to be the flag of the new "Charisian Empire" he'd been hearing rumors about. If it was, the new "Imperial Navy" didn't seem to have gotten any less capable than the "Royal Navy" had been.

Had he not been covered with the rock dust blasted from the walls of his own fortress and half-deafened by the merciless bellowing of artillery, he might have had more appreciation of the martial spectacle in which he had become an unwilling participant. The morning sky was a perfect blue dome, unmarked by a single cloud, and the blue waters of East Pass—fourteen miles wide, at this point, although the navigable channel was much narrower—sparkled in the bright morning sunlight. But not everywhere.

A forest of masts and sails, of tarred ratlines, of standards and signal flags, moved majestically up the channel under topsails and headsails alone. The war galleons were very different from their transport consorts. They were unnaturally low to the water, their hulls a stark black, relieved only by the white strakes along their gun ports. There was none of the gilding, the elaborate carving, and the brave paint of proper warships, but he supposed they didn't really need any of that. Not when those gun ports were open and belching steady flame and destruction at his men.

The more brightly painted merchant ships which obviously had been pressed into service as troop transports made a striking contrast, and even through the blanket of smoke and dust enshrouding East Keep, he could see the blue tunics of Charisian Marines lining the transports' sides to watch the spectacle as the walls of gunsmoke erupted from the warships' sides with such deadly, steady rapidity.

He looked at it all for perhaps one minute, then ducked back into cover, put his back against the inner face of the parapet, and looked at his second-in-command once more.

"You're right," he grated. The words cost him physical pain much worse than the cut a flying fragment of stone had opened across the side of his head at the very start of the engagement. "Tell the men to cease fire and get under cover. Then lower the standard."

▼   ▼   ▼

"Signal from *Destiny*, Sir."

Sir Domynyk Staynair, Baron Rock Point, looked up from his conversation with his flag captain.

"Yes, Styvyn?"

"East Keep has surrendered, Sir," Lieutenant Erayksyn said. "The Marines have gone ashore and taken the garrison into custody. Captain Yairley reports that Major Zheffyr's men have secured the battery and are preparing its demolition."

"Excellent news, Styvyn!" Rock Point smiled broadly, then glanced back at Captain Darys. "Yairley seems to be developing rather a talent for this sort of thing, doesn't he, Tym?"

"Yes, My Lord, he does."

Darys smiled back. He and Rock Point had both known Dunkyn Yairley since he was a midshipman. They were perfectly well aware of the occasional spasms of self-doubt he experienced . . . and also of the way that he somehow invariably managed to get the job done, anyway.

"If he keeps this up, I'm afraid we're going to have to go ahead and promote him to commodore," Rock Point continued. "Even if that does mean he'll have to give up those enjoyable boating excursions of his."

This time Darys chuckled out loud, but Rock Point's expression sobered as he turned back to Lieutenant Erayksyn.

"A signal to *Destiny*, Styvyn."

"Yes, Sir?"

"Well done. *Chihiro* 7:23."

"Aye, aye, Sir," Erayksyn acknowledged.

"Very well, Styvyn. Run along and send it." Rock Point made shooing motions with both hands, and the lieutenant headed back towards the signal party.

"*Chihiro* seven, Sir?" Darys said, raising one eyebrow, and Rock Point smiled rather more grimly.

"It seemed appropriate, somehow," he said.

▼　▼　▼

Captain Sir Dunkyn Yairley read the brief dispatch without comment, then handed it back to the signals midshipman.

"Thank you, Master Aplyn-Ahrmahk," he said, and turned to gaze out over the rail, with his hands clasped behind him, while the words of the verse from the *Writ* ran through his memory. "And Holy Langhorne said unto him, 'Surely, God will give over His enemies to the destiny prepared for those who serve corruption, to be conquered and humbled for their sins, and to be bound hand and foot and sent into captivity by the just.'"

I suppose he means it as a compliment based on the ship's name, he thought. *But it's more than that, too. And given what happened in Ferayd, it's certainly an appropriate choice of text.*

He thought for another few moments, then turned back from the rail and beckoned the youthful Duke Darcos back to him.

"Signal to the flagship," he said. "*Langhorne* 23:7."

"Aye, aye, Sir."

The youngster grinned at him, obviously pleased with his choice of scripture. Then he hurried back over to make the indicated signal, and Yairley's smile was thin as he gazed at the battery where his landing parties were busy. The Delferahkans who had manned the guns, wounded and unwounded alike, had been removed to safety at the far side of East Island. Then the guns had been loaded with quintuple charges and four round shot each, and quick match had been laid from gun to gun. Another length of quick match had been laid into the magazine itself. Both of them branched from the same length of slow match, which had been cut to give the last boat time to get clear after it was lit. The overcharged guns would go off first, almost certainly splitting their breeches and making them useless for anything except scrap. Then the powder magazine would explode with sufficient force to reduce East Keep itself to a heap of rubble. When the smoke cleared, East Island would be home to nothing but wreckage.

Or, as his chosen verse from *The Book of Langhorne* said, "The inheritance of the wicked is the whirlwind, and I will cast down all the works and strong places of those who would oppress the people of God."

▼   ▼   ▼

Sir Vyk Lakyr climbed down off his horse and watched the groom lead it away.

I really ought to be in bed, he reflected. *The one thing I know I'm going to need is rest. Unfortunately*, his lips twitched in a humorless smile, *sleep is also the one thing I know isn't going to happen.*

Actually, he thought as he turned and headed into his office in the city's citadel, that *wasn't* the one thing he knew was going to happen. Reports had come in over the course of the day as lookouts spotted the steadily moving sails drawing inexorably closer to Ferayd. The semaphore system had kept Lakyr informed of that implacable approach, although that was a mixed blessing. It hadn't done a great deal to inspire peace of mind, and he was also aware that his lookouts hadn't seen anything the Charisians hadn't chosen to let them see. Once they had cleared East Pass, they hadn't had to pass close enough for any shore-bound lookout to see and report them. For that matter, most of the semaphore posts themselves were effectively defenseless against naval landing parties. The Charisians could have cut the signal chain at any of several points . . . if they'd chosen to.

The only question in Lakyr's mind was *why* any of them had allowed themselves to be seen. He supposed it might be simple arrogance, but somehow he doubted that.

I suppose it's possible they're deliberately letting us know they're coming so we can get the civilians out of the way, he reflected. *I'd like to think that was the case, at any rate. Even if it is better than the bastards who ordered the slaughter of their civilians deserve.*

He grimaced and shook his head.

Better not even be thinking that way, Vyk. Whatever else, the Church is still the Church. The fact that the men who serve her at any given moment may be less than worthy of her can't change that. Besides, the way things seem to be headed, there's not going to be any room for divided allegiances.

He entered his lamplit office and found Captain Kairmyn waiting for him. The captain stood quickly as Lakyr walked into the room, but the garrison commander waved him back into his chair.

"Sit," he commanded, and grinned sourly. "If you've been as busy as I have today, your feet can probably use the break."

"That they can, Sir," Kairmyn acknowledged as he settled back.

"For myself, at this particular moment, it's my arse," Lakyr confessed, circling the desk and seating himself rather more gingerly in the padded chair behind. Kairmyn cocked his head, and Lakyr shrugged. "I've just completed a circuit of the entire waterfront. We're as ready as we're going to get, and I've ordered the men to get some rest while they still can."

Kairmyn nodded in understanding, and Lakyr stretched hugely, twisting his shoulders to try to work out some of the tension kinking his spine. Then he looked back at the younger officer.

"I take it your men are ready, Captain?"

"Yes, Sir. They are. But, Sir, I still wish you'd—"

"Don't say it, Tomhys." Lakyr's raised hand interrupted him. "Someone has to be in charge of the detachment. I picked you because you're one of the best men for the job. If it happens that I have . . . additional motives for selecting you, that's my business, not yours."

"But—"

"Don't make me repeat myself, Captain," Lakyr said, his tone much sterner than it had been.

For a moment or two, Kairmyn seemed to hover on the point of continuing his protest. Then he thought better of it—or, more probably, realized it wasn't going to do him any good—and nodded.

"Yes, Sir. In that case, though," he stood, "I suppose I'd better be going. Good luck, Sir."

"And to you, Captain." Lakyr rose to return Kairmyn's salute as the captain came to attention. Then the younger man nodded once, turned, and left the office.

Lakyr sank back into his chair, gazing at the open doorway for several seconds, then shrugged and turned to the sheaf of messages Lieutenant Cheryng had stacked neatly on his blotter. Most of them were simply readiness reports, and the handful that weren't didn't really require any action or decisions from him. It was too late for anything he might have done at this point to affect what was going to happen come morning.

He finished the last message, set it aside, and tipped back in his chair, thinking about the youthful captain he'd just sent off to take charge of the military escort he'd provided to maintain order among the civilians he'd ordered to evacuate the city. Kairmyn was right about the reason Lakyr had selected him for that duty, of course. What had happened to the Charisian sailors and their families here in Ferayd hadn't been Tohmys Kairmyn's fault. In fact, it had happened because the very careful orders he'd given beforehand had been totally disregarded. Unfortunately, the Charisians couldn't know that.

Lakyr had absolutely no idea how much Cayleb of Charis knew about the details of what had happened here. It was unlikely, to say the least, that there'd been time for the Church's propaganda to reach Charis before this fleet was dispatched. It was remotely possible, however, and if Cayleb had seen the Church's version and compared it to the reports of his own people who had escaped the carnage, he'd be perfectly justified in assuming the massacre had been planned from the beginning. And if it should happen that he had assumed that, and the officer who'd been in direct command of the troops responsible for it fell into his hands, the consequences for that officer might be . . . severe.

And rightly so, if it had *been planned*, Lakyr thought. *Which suggests certain unpleasant possibilities for my own immediate future if things go as badly as I'm afraid they may.*

Well, if they did, they did. And at least he'd gotten Kairmyn safely out of the way.

▼   ▼   ▼

"Sir! *Sir!*"

Major Gahrmyn Zhonair jerked upright, snatching at the hand shaking his shoulder. He hadn't meant to doze off. In fact, he'd expected the straight-backed chair to be uncomfortable enough that he couldn't.

Unfortunately, he'd been wrong. Which didn't mean it hadn't been uncomfortable enough to leave him feeling as if his spine had been beaten with a club.

"What?" he demanded. The word came out sounding harsher than he'd intended, and he cleared his sleep-dried throat and tried again.

"What?" he repeated in a more normal voice.

"Sir, we've seen something—out in the harbor!"

"Show me!" Zhonair snapped, the last rags of sleep vanishing abruptly.

He followed the sergeant who'd awakened him out onto the nearest gun platform. It was still at least an hour or so until dawn, and the largely evacuated city of Ferayd was dark behind him. The sky was crystal clear, prickled with heaps of glittering stars, but there was no moon. Which probably had something to do with the reason the Charisians had chosen this particular night to come calling.

The starlight was too dim to be called illumination, but it was at least a tiny bit better than nothing, and he strained his eyes as he followed the sergeant's pointing finger. For several moments he saw nothing at all. Then his eyes narrowed as they caught the faint, faint gleam of starlight on canvas.

"I see it," he said quietly. "But where's the guard boat that ought—"

He flinched at the abrupt, blinding flash of lightning as a cannon fired out in the harbor with absolutely no warning.

▾　　▾　　▾

Admiral Rock Point's head came up as he heard the sudden crash of a firing thirty-pounder. The sound came from the east, somewhere astern of his flagship, and his peg leg clunked on the deck planking as he moved to *Destroyer's* stern rail. He looked out across the harbor, trying to find the gun which had fired, but the night had closed back in.

"Gunfire, one point on the starboard quarter!"

The lookout's cry floated down from overhead, not that it did a great deal of good at the moment. Still, it gave Rock Point an approximate idea of where it had come from, and he frowned as he summoned up a mental image of the harbor and matched it against his detailed sailing instructions.

Probably *Indomitable* or *Justice*, he decided. Assuming they were where they were supposed to be at any rate. And a single gunshot suggested either an accidental discharge, which was going to land someone neck-deep in trouble, or else an encounter with a guard boat.

Well, it's not as if anyone doesn't already know we're out here, he thought. *The only thing that really surprises me, if it was a guard boat, is that we haven't already run into dozens of the things. For that matter, we may have and I just don't know anything about it, assuming they settled the business with cutlasses!*

He didn't envy the crews of any launches or cutters ordered to patrol the harbor. To be sure, they had a better chance of spotting a galleon than a galleon had of spotting a single, smallish, low-lying boat. On the other hand, there wasn't very much they could do except run if they did encounter one of Rock Point's ships. As that single cannon shot emphasized, they certainly didn't have the firepower to do anything else.

Actually, Rock Point's greatest concern had been that the Delferahkan Navy might be present in the form of *galleys* being used as "guard boats." The biggest potential danger of approaching in darkness had been the possibility of its allowing galleys to get close enough to galleons to try ramming or boarding them. The chance of any galley managing that through the accurate fire of a galleon who'd seen it coming was minute; the chance of a galley managing the same feat in the dark was significantly higher.

Given the quality of his own crews, Rock Point had accepted the risk with a fair degree of equanimity. That didn't mean he'd been eager to see what would happen if the Delferahkans tried it, though, and he wondered why they hadn't.

Either they're smart enough to have figured out what would probably happen to any galley which did intercept one of us, or else they didn't happen to have any galleys in port when we arrived.

Personally, he suspected the former. To be sure, a galley might get along-side one of his galleons under these visibility conditions, if its skipper was smart and skilled. But the Delferahkan Navy's galleys were mainland designs—smaller than Charisian galleys, with smaller crews. Rock Point's gun-heavy galleons each carried between eighty and a hundred and twenty Marines, depending on their size, and had more than enough seamen to support them. It would take at least two, more probably three, galleys of the Delferahkan type to overwhelm the crew of one of his ships, and the rest of his squadron wouldn't exactly be standing around twiddling their thumbs while that happened. So unless the Delferahkans had managed to assemble at least twenty or thirty galleys (and the losses their fleet had taken against the marauding privateers who had preceded Rock Point's fleet into these waters made it unlikely that they still had that many in the first place), trying to use them in some sort of nighttime interception would have been an exercise in futility.

On the other hand, it could have been an exercise in futility that was still painful as hell for whichever ship they happened to hit. So I'm *not going to complain that they didn't do it.*

He snorted and stumped back across the quarterdeck to Captain Darys.

"Well, we've knocked on the door now, My Lord," the flag captain said wryly.

"And here I was hoping they wouldn't guess we were coming," the admiral replied dryly. Then he shook his head.

"About an hour or so, I make it," he said more seriously.

"About that," Darys agreed.

"In that case, I hope they didn't wait until they heard our 'door knocker' to start getting people out of harm's way."

The admiral's voice was much grimmer, and Darys nodded silently. The flag captain, like his admiral, had been pleased by their orders' emphasis on avoiding civilian casualties to the greatest possible extent. That, in fact, was the reason they'd deliberately alerted the Delferahkans to their approach. It was always possible the commander of the port's defenses might be sufficiently stupid to fail to consider the possibility that any attacking Charisian squadron might land troops. Assuming the commander in question had the intelligence God had given a slash lizard, however, it was going to occur to him that simply sending ships to sail up and down in the harbor wouldn't accomplish very much.

What it came down to in the end was whether or not the man in charge of defending Ferayd had a realistic appreciation for the chance that his batteries might manage to drive off the Charisian galleons. And whether or not he had the moral courage to risk being accused of defeatism if he ordered an evacuation before the first shot was even fired.

Rock Point hoped Sir Vyk Lakyr had both of those things. Unlike any of the other officers and men of his squadron, the admiral knew from *Seijin* Merlin's visions that the garrison commander had deliberately sought to minimize casualties. That didn't make the admiral feel any more kindly towards Delferahk, but it did tell him—or, at least, *remind* him—who the Empire's true enemy was. And whether Delferahk had been a willing participant in the massacre, or simply hadn't been able to stop it, it couldn't be allowed to pass unpunished. Emperor Cayleb was right about that, too. Ferayd had to be turned into an object lesson to the Empire's enemies, and for the Empire's subjects, the massacre itself had to be punished.

And that, he thought grimly, turning back to the east where a hint of grayness was creeping into the heavens, *is exactly what we're about to do.*

▼   ▼   ▼

"Oh, *shit,*" someone whispered.

It took Major Zhonair a moment to realize it had been himself and even then, the recognition was a distant and unimportant thing as he gazed out from his battery's walls.

There were *dozens* of Charisian galleons out there. They obviously had detailed charts of the harbor and its defenses, too, because they'd used the darkness to get themselves perfectly positioned. Twenty-three of them were sailing slowly, in a remarkably neat line, directly across the harbor towards him, while another ten or fifteen hovered farther out, watching over the transports. The approaching line was already little more than three or four hundred yards out, and its ships were angling steadily closer. The rising sun gleamed on their sails, gilding the tan and gray, weather-stained canvas with gold, and what had to be the new Charisian Empire's flag—the silver and blue checkerboard of the House of Tayt quartered with the black of Charis and the golden kraken of the House of Ahrmahk—flew from their mizzen peaks. Hundreds of guns poked stubby fingers out of their opened gun ports, and the utter silence of their approach sent a shiver of dread through Zhonair's bones.

"Stand to!" he shouted. *"Stand to!"*

His drummer sounded the urgent tattoo, although it was scarcely necessary, since the guns had been fully manned for the last hour and a half. As he'd expected, though, the drumroll was picked up by the battery to his right, as well, and relayed all along the waterfront and back into the city. His own men crouched over their guns, waiting for the inexorably advancing Charisian line to enter their field of fire, and Zhonair raised his spyglass to peer through it at the enemy.

▼   ▼   ▼

"Very well, Captain Darys," Rock Point said formally. "I believe it's time."

"Aye, aye, My Lord," Darys replied, then turned and raised his voice.

"Master Lahsahl! Open fire, if you please!"

"Aye, aye, Sir!" Lieutenant Shairmyn Lahsahl, *Destroyer*'s first lieutenant, acknowledged, and drew his sword.

"On the *up* roll!" he barked, raising the sword overhead.

▼   ▼   ▼

The ship leading the Charisian line, the one flying the command streamer of an admiral, disappeared behind a sudden wall of flame-cored smoke.

Zhonair ducked instinctively, and something large, iron, and fast-moving whizzed viciously over his head. More iron crashed into the face of his battery, and he heard someone scream. And then, as if the first broadside had been a signal—which it undoubtedly *had* been—every other ship in that line seemed to spurt fire and smoke virtually simultaneously.

The concussion of that many heavy cannon, firing that closely together, was indescribable; the impact of that many tons of iron was terrifying.

The battery's protective stonework was the better part of two centuries old. It had originally been intended to protect catapults and ballistae from similar engines and archery, before cannon had even been thought of. Its replacement with more modern fortifications had been discussed off and on for decades, but the expense would have been enormous, and the dozens of guns *behind* the stonework had been judged sufficient for security's sake.

But that had been before those dozens of guns found themselves opposed to *hundreds* of guns, each of which fired far more rapidly than the defensive batteries could possibly hope to match. The twenty-three ships in Admiral Rock Point's line mounted over thirteen hundred guns. Almost seven hundred of them could be brought to bear on the harbor defenses simultaneously, and Rock Point had planned his approach carefully. Although Ferayd's defensive batteries mounted a combined grand total of over a hundred and fifty guns, only thirty of them would bear on his line as he approached from one end of the waterfront's fortifications.

In the first six minutes of the engagement, each of those thirty guns fired once. In return for their thirty round shot, Rock Point's line fired almost three *thousand* back.

The aged stonework, never intended to withstand that sort of punishment, didn't simply crumble. Huge chunks of stone and mortar flew under the savage impact of better than forty tons of iron, and rock dust erupted from the fortifications' face like a second fog of gunsmoke. And even though the guns' individual embrasures were relatively small targets, obscured by the flying rock dust and the firing ships' own powder smoke, there was no way they could all be missed in that torrent of Charisian fire.

Zhonair crouched behind the battlements, his mind cringing as the incredible bellow of the Charisian artillery seemed to consume the world. Smoke and dust were everywhere, catching at his throat, choking him. The solid stone under his feet quivered, vibrating like a frightened child as the brutal storm of iron scourged it. He couldn't even hear his own guns firing—assuming they were—but he heard the shrill shrieks as a gun less than thirty yards from him took a direct hit.

The Charisian round shot came in just below the muzzle, striking the solid timber of the piece's "carriage," and the entire gun flew into the air. The tube separated entirely from the carriage, most of which disintegrated into splinters as long as a man's arm. At least a third of the crew was killed outright when the round shot continued on its way, plowing right through their midst. Most of the others were crushed to death when the ten-foot gun tube came smashing down across them once more.

The major stared at the tangled, shattered bloody wreckage which had been eighteen human beings only an instant before. More Charisian fire slammed into his position, again and again. The outer face of the battery wall literally began to disintegrate with the third salvo, and as the range dropped, at least a half dozen of the Charisians began firing grapeshot, as well, sweeping the wall. Dozens of the small, lethal shot came whipping in through the embrasures, and more of Zhonair's gunners disappeared in gory sprays of blood, torn flesh, and shattered bone.

Zhonair thrust himself back to his feet, charging into the midst of the chaos, shouting encouragement. He didn't know exactly *what* he was shouting, only that it was his duty to be there. To hold his men together in this hurricane of smoky thunder and savage destruction.

They responded to his familiar voice, laboring frantically to reload their slow-firing guns while the Charisians slammed broadside after broadside into their position. One of the crenellations shattered under the impact of enemy shot. Most of the stone tumbled outward, crashing down the face of the battery into the water at its foot, but a head-sized chunk of it flew through the air and struck a man less than six feet from Zhonair. The gunner's blood erupted across the major, and he scrubbed at his sticky eyes, trying to clear them.

He was still scrubbing at them when the incoming round shot struck him just below mid-chest.

▼   ▼   ▼

"Sir, their Marines are ashore in at least three places."

Lakyr turned towards Lieutenant Cheryng. The youngster's face was white and strained, his eyes huge.

"Only one of the batteries is still in action," the lieutenant continued, "and casualties are reported to be extremely heavy."

"I see," Lakyr said calmly. "And the enemy's losses?"

"One of their galleons has lost two masts. They've towed her out of action, and another was apparently on fire, at least briefly. Aside from that—"

Cheryng shrugged, his expression profoundly unhappy, and Lakyr nodded. The Charisians had worked their way methodically along the waterfront, concentrating their fire on one defensive battery or small group of batteries at a time. Traditional wisdom had held that no ship could engage a well-sited, properly protected battery, but that tradition had depended upon equal rates of fire. He had no doubt that the Charisians had suffered damage and casualties well beyond those Cheryng had just reported, although they obviously hadn't suffered enough to decide to break off the attack. Which was scarcely astonishing. He'd hoped to do better than that, but he'd never had any illusions about successfully standing off the attack.

And I'm not going to get any more men killed than I have to trying to do the impossible, he thought grimly, and looked at the clock on his office wall. *Three hours is long enough—especially if they've already got Marines ashore, anyway. It's not like the King gave me more* infantry *along with the gunners, after all.*

"Very well, Lieutenant," he said, speaking more formally than he normally did when addressing Cheryng. "Instruct the signal party to raise the white flag."

NOVEMBER,
YEAR OF GOD 892

I suppose it's time."

Empress Sharleyan Ahrmahk turned from the huge stern windows' panoramic vista of Tellesberg Harbor's incredibly crowded waters at the sound of her husband's voice.

It was the first day of November, a date she had been dreading for five-days, and now it was here.

Cayleb stood beside the dining cabin table which had been one of her gifts to him. She'd managed to commission it without his finding out she had, and the obvious pleasure he'd taken from the surprise had pleased her immensely. Now the hand-rubbed, exquisitely finished wood's exotic grain and patterns gleamed in the single brilliant shaft of morning sunlight falling through the opened skylight, and the thick rugs which cushioned the deck's planking glowed like pools of crimson light in the cabin's shadowed dimness. The bullion embroidery of his tunic flashed and flickered, the sunlight through the skylight struck green and golden fire from the chain of office about his neck, and something was trying to close her throat as she gazed at him.

"I know it's time," she said, then paused and cleared her throat. "I . . . just don't want it to be."

"Me either," he said with a flash of white teeth in a fleeting smile.

"I know you have to go. I've known you'd be going ever since I arrived in Tellesberg. But"—Sharleyan heard the slight quaver in her own voice—"I didn't expect it to be this hard."

"For both of us, My Lady."

Cayleb's voice was quiet, and he crossed to her in two long strides. He caught both her slender hands in his powerful, sword-callused ones, raised them to his lips, and kissed their backs.

"It wasn't supposed to be like this," she told him, freeing one hand and laying it gently against his cheek.

"I know." Again, that flashing smile she'd discovered could melt her heart. "It was supposed to be a marriage of state, with you secretly hardly able to wait to see my back despite all of the proper public platitudes." He shook his head, his eyes glinting in the dimness. "How in the world can I expect to kick Hektor's arse the way he deserves to have it kicked when I couldn't even get *that* right?"

"Oh," she said as lightly as she could, "I'm sure you'll fumble through to victory somehow, Your Majesty."

"Why, thank you, Your Majesty."

He kissed the hand he still held for a second time, then drew her close and tucked an arm about her.

She savored that arm's strength even as she marveled at the depth of the truth hidden in his lighthearted description of what their marriage could have been. What she'd more than half *expected* it to be.

It didn't seem possible. They'd been married for little more than one month. She'd known him for less than three. And yet this parting was like cutting off her own hand.

"I don't want you to go," she admitted softly.

"And I don't want to leave you behind," he replied. "Which makes us just like thousands of other husbands and wives, doesn't it?" He looked down into her eyes, and his own were grave. "If we have to ask this of them, I suppose it's only fair that we have to pay in the same coin."

"But we've had so little *time!*" she protested.

"If God's good, we'll have the years yet to make up for that." He turned to face her fully, and she laid her cheek against his chest. "And I assure you that I'm looking forward to every one of those years," he added in a wicked whisper into her ear as his right hand slid down her back to caress her posterior.

That was one good thing about Charisian fashion, she thought. Chisholmian gowns tended to be well buttressed with petticoats against her northern kingdom's cooler climate. Charis' lighter and thinner gowns were far less armored.

"It's a good thing there are no witnesses to discover what a crude and vulgar fellow you really are, Your Majesty," she told him, raising her head and turning her face up towards his.

"Maybe it is. But it's a very bad thing that I don't have enough time to *prove* what a crude and vulgar fellow I am," he told her, and bent to kiss her.

She savored the moment, pressing against him, and then—as if on cue—each of them inhaled deeply and they stepped back slightly from one another.

"I truly do hate leaving you behind, for a lot of reasons," he told her. "And I'm genuinely sorry to be dropping full responsibility on you when you've had so little time to settle in here in Tellesberg."

"I can't pretend I didn't know a moment like this would be coming, though, can I?" she countered. "And at least I'll have Earl Gray Harbor and the Archbishop to advise me."

"There's just never enough *time*." He grimaced in frustration. "You should have had more time. There are so many things I still need to tell you, explain to you." He shook his head. "I shouldn't have to be dashing off like this with so much still only half-done."

She started to reply, then settled for shaking her own head with a slight smile. In theory, he didn't actually *have* to "dash off." His naval and land commanders were perfectly capable of fighting any battles which had to be fought. But there might well be—indeed, almost certainly *would* be—political decisions which needed to be made at the battlefront, promptly and decisively, without the five-days and five-days of delay involved in sending dispatches back and forth across the thousands of miles between Corisande and Charis. Besides, the fighting men of Charis had an almost idolatrous faith in Cayleb Ahrmahk. Not surprisingly, perhaps, given the Battles of Rock Point, Crag Reach, and Darcos Sound. His presence with them, she knew, would be worth a squadron of galleons.

And, just as importantly, it gives us the opportunity to show that this newfangled "Empire" of ours truly is a marriage of equals. The King of Charis may be going off to war, but that war is the Empire's, not just Charis' alone. And the Queen of Chisholm is staying home to govern not just Chisholm, but the entire Empire in his absence . . . and in her own name, as well as his.

"You do realize, don't you," she said after a moment, "that this little military excursion of yours is probably going to put a serious crimp into our plans to move the capital back and forth between Tellesberg and Cherayth?"

"I hope it won't be too bad," he replied seriously. "If we have to, we could probably leave Rayjhis home to serve as our joint regent here in Charis while we officially move the capital—and you—back to Cherayth, I suppose."

"I think that would be the wrong decision." She pursed her lips thoughtfully. "I won't pretend I'm not anxious about how well Mahrak and Mother are managing in my absence. But they're very capable people, and the fact that you're going to stage through Chisholm for the invasion is going to give them a chance to meet *you*, the same way your Charisians have met me. And unless I'm seriously mistaken, the fact that you—and your Charisians—trust me enough to leave me here in Tellesberg in your absence to govern the entire Empire is going to more than offset any concern in Chisholm about whether or not the seat of government is going to move back and forth exactly as scheduled."

"Of course I trust you!" He sounded surprised that there could be any question of that, and she tapped his chest with a slender index finger and a smile.

"*I* know that," she told him half scoldingly. "Getting everybody else to believe it may not be quite that simple, though. And this, I think, is one of the best ways we could have come up with to accomplish that."

"Even if it is a pain in the arse for us," he agreed.

"And there's another side to it, as well," she said.

"Such as?"

"One of the advantages of having co-rulers is that we *can* leave one of us here, managing things in Tellesberg, while the other one goes off to deal with other problems. I know we both have first councilors we trust implicitly, Cayleb, but that's not really the same thing, and you know it. If this works out the way I think it's going to, we'll have a degree of flexibility I don't think anyone else has ever had before. And, to be honest, we're going to need that kind of flexibility just to keep something the size of the Empire semi-organized and moving in the same direction."

He nodded soberly, and in an odd sort of way which he doubted he'd ever be able to explain to anyone else, her serious, pragmatic analysis only increased the tenderness—and regret—he felt as the moment of departure swept down upon them. In some ways, he'd been almost guiltily grateful for the Ferayd Massacre. Putting together Rock Point's fleet, and finding the transports for *his* Marines, had disrupted Lock Island's carefully choreographed schedule for the invasion of Corisande. That had given them time to produce several thousand more desperately needed rifles . . . and delayed Cayleb's own departure for another blessed pair of five-days. Ten more days he'd had with Sharleyan.

Which only made this moment even harder.

"Be careful." His hands slid around to rest upon her shoulders as he looked deep into her eyes. "Be very careful, Sharleyan. Rayjhis and Maikel and Bynzhamyn and all the rest will guard you, but never forget the Temple Loyalists are out there somewhere, and they've already shown they're not shy about resorting to bloodshed. Most of 'my' Charisians are already prepared to love you as one of our own, but three of them tried to murderer Maikel, and someone else burned down the Royal College, and we still don't know who it was or how much organization there may have been behind it. So don't forget there are still daggers out there. And that not all of them are going to be made out of steel."

"I won't." The corners of her expressive eyes crinkled with an odd sort of amusement, and she snorted. "Don't *you* forget that you're talking to someone who grew up in Queen Ysbell's shadow! I know all about political machinations and court intrigues. Yes, and about assassins, too. And if *I* were likely to forget, Edwyrd will see to it that I don't!"

"I know. I know!" He held her close again, shaking his head. "I just can't stand the thought of something . . . happening to you."

"Nothing is going to happen to *me*," she assured him. "You just see that nothing happens to *you*, either, Your Majesty!"

"With Bryahn, General Chermyn, and Merlin all looking out for me?" It was his turn to snort, and he did it rather magnificently, she thought. "I won't say that *nothing* could happen—after all, there's always lightning, forest fires, and earthquakes—but somehow I don't see anything less than one of those getting through to me."

"See that it stays that way." She reached up and caught the lobes of both ears, holding his head motionless. "I've already told Captain Athrawes that he'd better not come home to Charis without you."

"I'll bet that put the fear of God into him," Cayleb said, smiling appreciatively.

"I don't know about God," she told him. "But I did my best to put the fear of someone a bit less powerful but more . . . immediate, shall we say, into him."

Cayleb laughed out loud. Then he sobered once again.

"It really is time, love," he said softly.

"I know. 'Time and the tide wait for no man,'" she quoted.

"Not without every general, admiral, and ship's master in the entire invasion fleet seriously considering regicide, at any rate. Charisian seamen *hate* missing the tide."

"Then I suppose we'd better get this over with."

Despite her cheerful tone, she felt her lower lip trying to quiver. She suppressed the reflex sternly and tucked her hand into the elbow of his proffered arm as he escorted her out of the cabin where they'd actually managed to find genuine privacy even onboard a crowded warship.

The deck outside that cabin made the ship's crowding abundantly clear.

Cayleb's flagship was the newest and most powerful unit of what had just become the *Imperial* Charisian Navy. She was an improvement on the *Dreadnought* which had served as Cayleb's flagship for the Armageddon Reef campaign. That ship had gone down after the Battle of Darcos Sound, and originally, this ship had been intended to carry the same name. But Cayleb had decreed a change. Charisian tradition prohibited naming warships for people who were still alive, so instead of the name he really would have preferred, his new flagship had been christened "*Empress of Charis.*"

As Sharleyan stepped onto the main deck of the ship which wasn't quite officially her namesake, she was once more struck by how enormously the standards of naval design and naval combat had changed in the course of only three years. Charisian galleys had been the biggest and most seaworthy in the world. That had meant they were also the slowest in the world under oars alone, but even the largest of them had been no more than two-thirds the size of *Empress of Charis.* Cayleb's new flagship measured over a hundred and fifty feet between perpendiculars and, with her far deeper draft, displaced almost fourteen hundred tons. She mounted thirty long krakens on her gundeck and thirty-two carronades on her spar decks. Combined with the new, long fourteen-pounders mounted as chase guns, fore and aft, that brought her total armament up to sixty-eight guns, and no other warship in the world could hope to stand up to her. Except, of course, for the sisters anchored all about her.

She seemed downright huge to Sharleyan. And she was. The largest ship in the *Chisholmian* Navy had shown little more than half her displacement and had mounted only *eighteen* guns. Yet the empress knew from conversations with her husband, Lock Island, and Sir Dustyn Olyvyr that Sir Dustyn was already applying the lessons he'd learned designing *Empress of Charis* to the next even larger and still more powerful class.

She no longer even looked like a galleon. *Dreadnought* and her sisters had already dispensed with the towering fore and aftercastles, but *Empress of Charis* showed even less freeboard than they had, proportionately, and she was effectively flushdecked, with no raised forecastle or aftercastle at all. Or, rather, the narrow spardecks which had been incorporated into *Dreadnought* had been broadened so that they formed virtually a complete, upper gundeck, and her gently curved sheer ran unbroken all the way from prow to transom. Because of her greater size, she actually carried the sills of her gundeck gun ports higher than the older ship had, and just looking up at her soaring, powerful sail plan could make Sharleyan dizzy. But her cutwater was sharply raked, and despite their vast size, she and her sister ships looked low-slung, lean, and dangerous. Her every line carried a sleek, predatory gracefulness, and the new Imperial Navy was continuing another Charisian tradition. Other navies might paint their ships in gaudy colors; Charisian warships' hulls were black. The galleons carried white stripes along their sides, marking the line of their gun ports, and the port lids were painted red. Aside from their figureheads, that was virtually the only color their hulls showed, in stark contrast to the ornamental carving, gilding, and paint of other navies.

It was, Sharleyan had discovered, a deliberate statement. Charisian warships needed no decoration, no proud carving or glittering gold leaf, to overawe an opponent. Their reputation took care of that quite handily, and the very lack of those things gave them a severe sort of beauty, the grace of function unhampered by a single unnecessary element.

"You named a beautiful ship for me, Cayleb," she said in his ear, speaking loudly as the seamen manning *Empress of Charis'* yards began cheering the instant they stepped onto the deck.

"Nonsense. I named her for the office, not for the person holding it!" he replied with a wicked grin, then twitched as she pinched his ribs fiercely. He looked down at her, and she smiled sweetly.

"There's worse than that waiting when you get home, Your Majesty," she promised him.

"Good."

His grin grew even broader, then faded as they reached the entry port and the bosun's chair waiting to lower her to the deck of the fifty-foot cutter moored alongside the flagship. The cutter flew the new imperial flag, and the golden kraken of the House of Ahrmahk swam sinuously across it, rippling in the brisk breeze. The same flag, except for one detail, flew from the mizzen peak of every warship in the anchorage, but Sharleyan's cutter showed the silver crown of the Empress above the kraken, while the flag flying above *Empress of Charis* showed the golden crown of the Emperor.

The two of them stood gazing down at the cutter for a moment, and then Cayleb inhaled deeply and turned to face Sharleyan.

"My Lady Empress," he said, so softly she could scarcely hear him through the cheers rising now from the cutter's crew and spreading outward to every ship. She could see the sailors spread out along the spars, the Marines manning the sides, of all those ships, and she realized they weren't cheering for Cayleb. Or, not for Cayleb alone. They were cheering for *her*, as well.

The line-tenders started drawing the bosun's chair down to the deck for her, and she managed not to grimace. The thought of being lifted over the side and lowered to the cutter on a line like a parcel scarcely seemed dignified, but it was undoubtedly better than trying to manage her skirts while clambering down the battens nailed to the ship's side. It would be more modest, at any rate, and she was far less likely to find herself inadvertently and unexpectedly soaked. And, anyway, it wasn't like—

Her thoughts were abruptly interrupted as Cayleb's arms went around her. Her eyes widened in astonishment, but that was all she had time for before she found herself being kissed—ruthlessly, energetically, and delightfully competently—in front of the entire watching fleet.

For one heartbeat, sheer surprise held her stiff and unresponsive in his arms. But only for a heartbeat. It was, of course, a flagrant and scandalous breach of all proper rules of decorum, she thought as she melted into his embrace, not to mention the way it violated etiquette, protocol, and common decency, and she couldn't have cared less.

For a moment, everyone else seemed equally dumbfounded by the abrupt departure from the occasion's planned, dignified choreography, but then the cheers began again—different cheers, this time. Cheers that rippled with laughter and were punctuated by clapping hands and whistles of encouragement. Sharleyan would recall that later, treasure the pleasure—pleasure for Cayleb and for her—implicit in those cheers, those whistles, that clapping. At the moment, it scarcely registered. Her mind was on other things entirely.

It was a long, ardent, and *very* thorough kiss. Cayleb was a methodical man, and he took the time to do it right. Finally, however—due to a simple lack of air, no doubt—he straightened once more, smiling down at her through the whistles and stamping feet. Beyond him, she saw Earl Lock Island, Commodore Manthyr, and Captain Athrawes trying very hard not to grin like schoolboys, and the delighted laughter around her redoubled as she shook her finger under her husband's nose.

"Now you've gone and proven what a lewd, uncultured lout you are!" she scolded, her eyes sparkling. "I can't *believe* you did something that improper in front of everyone! Don't you realize how you've violated protocol?!"

"Damn protocol," he told her unrepentantly and reached out to touch the side of her face with his right hand while his left steadied the descending bosun's chair for her. His fingers were feather-gentle on her cheek, moving caressingly, and his eyes glowed. "That was fun, and I intend to do it again . . . often. But for today, if we don't get you into this chair and off this ship, we're all going to miss the tide, and then we'll probably have an outright rebellion on our hands."

"I know."

She allowed him to help her into the chair, although she was scarcely so feeble that she required the assistance. He checked personally to make sure everything was secure, and then the bosun's pipes wailed and the Marines snapped to attention and presented arms as she was lifted from the deck. The ship's bell began to strike, its deep, musical voice ringing out even through the tumult of renewed cheering. It struck twenty-four times in the formal salute to a crowned head of state.

"Take care of him, Merlin!" she heard herself cry suddenly. "Bring him back to me!"

She hadn't meant to say anything that maudlin. Certainly not in front of all those other eyes and ears! Fortunately, the cheering all around her was so overwhelming no one possibly could have heard her.

Except for one man.

"I will, Your Majesty."

Somehow, the *seijin* had heard her, and his deep voice cut through the roaring surf of all those other raised voices, projected for her to hear. She looked back at him, standing by Cayleb's shoulder, like a shield at her husband's back, and his unearthly sapphire eyes gleamed in the sunlight as he touched his left shoulder with his right fist in formal salute.

Sharleyan Ahrmahk was no sheltered hothouse flower. She'd learned long ago that life was no heroic ballad in which good always triumphed magically over evil. She'd been no older than twelve when her father's death had taught her that and brought her girlhood to a shattering end.

Yet, in that moment, as her eyes met Merlin Athrawes' bright blue gaze, she felt a sudden irrational yet overwhelming confidence. She looked at him as the bosun's chair rose higher, then began to dip towards the waiting cutter, feeling that assurance flowing out of him and into her, and her eyes prickled with a sudden rush of tears.

Every eye in that harbor was looking at her. Every spyglass was trained upon her, and she knew it. Knew they could see her fighting back her tears like some sort of schoolgirl.

She didn't care. Let them think what they liked, believe what they chose. She would cling to that last glimpse of the husband she'd come so unexpectedly to love and to a sapphire promise to bring him home to her once more.

Characters

ABYLYN, CHARLZ—a senior leader of the Temple Loyalists in Charis.

AHBAHT, LYWYS—Edmynd Walkyr's brother-in-law; XO, merchant galleon *Wind*.

AHBAHT, ZHEFRY—Earl Gray Harbor's personal secretary. He fulfills many of the functions of an undersecretary of state for foreign affairs.

AHDYMSYN, BISHOP EXECUTOR ZHERALD—Erek Dynnys' bishop executor.

AHRDYN—Archbishop Maikel's cat-lizard.

AHRMAHK, CAYLEB ZHAN HAARAHLD BRYAHN—King of Charis.

AHRMAHK, CROWN PRINCE ZHAN—younger brother of King Cayleb.

AHRMAHK, KAHLVYN CAYLEB—younger brother of Duke Tirian, King Cayleb's first cousin once removed.

AHRMAHK, KING CAYLEB II—King of Charis (see Cayleb Zhan Haarahld Bryahn Ahrmahk).

AHRMAHK, PRINCESS ZHANAYT—King Cayleb's younger sister.

AHRMAHK, QUEEN ZHANAYT—King Haarahld's deceased wife; mother of Cayleb, Zhanayt, and Zhan.

AHRMAHK, RAYJHIS—Duke of Tirian, Constable of Hairatha, King Cayleb's first cousin once removed.

AHRMAHK, ZHENYFYR—Dowager Duchess of Tirian, mother of Rayjhis and Kahlvyn Cayleb Ahrmahk, daughter of Rayjhis Yowance, Earl Gray Harbor.

AHRTHYR, SIR ALYK, EARL OF WINDSHARE—the commander of Sir Koryn Gahrvai's cavalry.

AHSTYN, LIEUTENANT FRANZ, CHARISIAN ROYAL GUARD—the second-in-command of King Cayleb II's personal bodyguard.

AHZGOOD, PHYLYP, EARL OF CORIS—Prince Hektor's spymaster.

APLYN-AHRMAHK, MIDSHIPMAN HEKTOR, ROYAL CHARISIAN NAVY—a midshipman assigned to HMS *Destiny*, 54. An adoptive member of the House of Ahrmahk as the Duke of Darcos.

ATHRAWES, CAPTAIN MERLIN, CHARISIAN ROYAL GUARD—King Cayleb II's personal armsman; the cybernetic avatar of Commander Nimue Alban.

BAHNYR, HEKTOR, EARL OF MANCORA—one of Sir Koryn Gahrvai's senior officers; commander of the right wing at Haryl's Crossing.

BAHRMYN, ARCHBISHOP BORYS—Archbishop of Corisande.

BAHRNS, KING RAHNYLD IV—King of Dohlar.

BANAHR, PRIOR FATHER AHZWALD—head of the priory of Saint Hamlyn, city of Sarayn, Kingdom of Charis.

BAYTZ, HANBYL, DUKE OF SOLOMON—Prince Nahrmahn of Emerald's uncle and the commander of the Emeraldian Army.

BAYTZ, NAHRMAHN HANBYL GRAIM—see Prince Nahrmahn Baytz.

BAYTZ, PRINCE NAHRMAHN GAREYT—second child and elder son of Prince Nahrmahn of Emerald.

BAYTZ, PRINCE NAHRMAHN II—ruler of the Princedom of Emerald.

BAYTZ, PRINCE TRAHVYS—Prince Nahrmahn of Emerald's third child and second son.

BAYTZ, PRINCESS FELAYZ—Prince Nahrmahn of Emerald's youngest child and second daughter.

BAYTZ, PRINCESS MAHRYA—Prince Nahrmahn of Emerald's oldest child.

BAYTZ, PRINCESS OHLYVYA—wife of Prince Nahrmahn of Emerald.

BREYGART, COLONEL SIR HAUWERD, ROYAL CHARISIAN MARINES—the rightful heir to the Earldom of Hanth.

BRYNDYN, MAJOR DAHRYN—the senior artillery officer attached to Brigadier Clareyk's column at Haryl's Priory.

BYRKYT, FATHER ZHON—an over-priest of the Church of God Awaiting; abbot of the Monastery of Saint Zherneau.

CAHKRAYN, SAMYL, DUKE OF FERN—first councilor of Dohlar.

CAHNYR, ARCHBISHOP ZHASYN—Archbishop of Glacierheart; a member of the reformists.

CHALMYRZ, FATHER KARLOS—Archbishop Borys' personal aide.

CHARLZ, MASTER YEREK, ROYAL CHARISIAN NAVY—Gunner, HMS *Wave,* 14.

CHERMYN, GENERAL HAUWYL, RCM—the senior officer of the Charisian Marine Corps. He will be the SO for the Marines in the invasion of Corisande.

CHERYNG, LIEUTENANT TAIWYL—a junior officer on Sir Vyk Lakyr's staff; he is in charge of Lakyr's clerks and message traffic.

CLAREYK, BRIGADIER KYNT, RCM—CO, Third Brigade, Royal Charisian Marines. One of the senior Marine officers assigned to the invasion of Corisande. He is also the originator of the training syllabus for the RCMC.

CLYNTAHN, VICAR ZHASPAHR—Grand Inquisitor of the Church of God Awaiting; one of the so-called Group of Four.

COHLMYN, SIR LEWK, ROYAL CHARISIAN NAVY—Earl Sharpfield, Queen Sharleyan's senior naval commander. Also the equivalent of her Navy Minister.

DAHRYUS, MASTER EDVARHD—an alias of Bishop Mylz Halcom.

DAIKYN, GAHLVYN—King Cayleb's valet.

DAIVYS, MYTRAHN—a Charisian Temple Loyalist.

DARCOS, DUKE OF—see Midshipman Hektor Aplyn-Ahrmahk.

DARYS, CAPTAIN TYMYTHY, ROYAL CHARISIAN NAVY ("TYM")—CO, HMS *Destroyer*, 54. Flag captain to Admiral Staynair.

DAYKYN, CROWN PRINCE HEKTOR—Prince Hektor of Corisande's second oldest child and heir apparent.

DAYKYN, PRINCE DAIVYN—Prince Hektor of Corisande's youngest child.

DAYKYN, PRINCE HEKTOR—Prince of Corisande.

DAYKYN, PRINCESS IRYS—Prince Hektor of Corisande's oldest child.

DAYKYN, PRINCESS RAICHYNDA—Prince Hektor of Corisande's deceased wife; born in the Earldom of Domair, Kingdom of Hoth.

DEKYN, SERGEANT ALLAYN—one of Kairmyn's noncoms, Delferahkan Army.

DOYAL, SIR CHARLZ—Sir Koryn Gahrvai's senior artillery commander.

DRAGONER, SIR RAYJHIS—Charisian ambassador to the Siddarmark Republic.

DRAGONMASTER, BRIGADE SERGEANT MAJOR MAHKYNTY ("Mahk"), RCM—Brigadier Clareyk's senior noncom.

DUCHAIRN, VICAR RHOBAIR—Treasurer General of the Church of God Awaiting; one of the so-called Group of Four.

DYNNYS, ADORAI—Archbishop Erayk Dynnys' wife. Her alias after her husband's arrest is Ailysa.

DYNNYS, ARCHBISHOP ERAYK—former Archbishop of Charis.

DYNNYS, STYVYN—Archbishop Erayk Dynnys' younger son, age eleven.

DYNNYS, TYMYTHY ERAYK—Archbishop Erayk Dynnys' older son, age fourteen.

EDWYRDS, KEVYN—XO, privateer galleon *Kraken*.

ERAYKSYN, LIEUTENANT STYVYN, ROYAL CHARISIAN NAVY—Admiral Staynair's flag lieutenant.

ERAYKSYN, WYLLYM—a Charisian textiles manufacturer.

FAHRMYN, FATHER TAIRYN—the priest assigned to Saint Chihiro's Church, a village church near the Convent of Saint Agtha.

FAIRCASTER, SERGEANT PAYTER, CHARISIAN ROYAL GUARD—one of King Cayleb II's armsmen. A transfer from Crown Prince Cayleb's Marine detachment.

FHAIRLY, MAJOR AHDYM—the senior battery commander on East Island, Ferayd Sound, Kingdom of Delferahk.

FHALKHAN, LIEUTENANT AHRNAHLD, ROYAL CHARISIAN MARINES—commanding officer, Crown Prince Zhan's bodyguard.

FORYST, VICAR ERAYK—a member of the reformists.

FRAIDMYN, SERGEANT VYK, CHARISIAN ROYAL GUARD—one of King Cayleb II's armsmen.

FYSHYR, HAIRYS—CO, privateer galleon *Kraken*.

GAHRMYN, LIEUTENANT RAHNYLD—XO, galley *Arrowhead,* Delferahkan Navy.

GAHRVAI, SIR KORYN—Earl Anvil Rock's eldest son and CO of Prince Hektor's field army.

GAHRVAI, SIR RYSEL, EARL OF ANVIL ROCK—Prince Hektor's senior army commander and distant cousin.

GAIRAHT, CAPTAIN WYLLYS, CHISHOLMIAN ROYAL GUARD—CO of Queen Sharleyan's Royal Guard detachment in Charis.

GALVAHN, MAJOR SIR NAITHYN—the Earl of Windshare's senior staff officer.

GARDYNYR, ADMIRAL LYWYS, EARL OF THIRSK—King Rahnyld IV's best admiral, currently in disgrace.

GRAISYN, BISHOP EXECUTOR WYLLYS—Archbishop Lyam Tyrn's bishop executor.

GRAIVYR, FATHER STYVYN—Bishop Ernyst's intendant. A man after Clyntahn's own heart.

GRAND VICAR EREK XVII—secular and temporal head of the Church of God Awaiting.

GYRARD, CAPTAIN ANDRAI, ROYAL CHARISIAN NAVY—CO, HMS *Empress of Charis.*

HAHLMYN, FATHER MAHRAK—an upper-priest of the Church of God Awaiting; Bishop Executor Thomys' personal aide.

HAHLYND, ADMIRAL PAWAL—CO, anti-piracy patrols, Hankey Sound. (A friend of Admiral Thirsk.)

HAHSKYN, LIEUTENANT AHNDRAI, CHARISIAN IMPERIAL GUARD—a Charisian officer assigned to Empress Sharleyan's guard detachment. Captain Gairaht's second-in-command.

HAIMYN, BRIGADIER MAHRYS, RCM—CO, Fifth Brigade, Royal Charisian Marines.

HALCOM, BISHOP MYLZ—Bishop of Margaret Bay.

HARMYN, MAJOR BAHRKLY, EMERALD ARMY—an Emeraldian army officer assigned to North Bay.

HARYS, CAPTAIN ZHOEL—CO, Corisandian galley *Lance.*

HOLDYN, VICAR LYWYS—a member of the reformists.

HOWSMYN, EHDWYRD—a wealthy foundry owner and shipbuilder in Tellesberg.

HOWSMYN, ZHAIN—Ehdwyrd Howsmyn's wife.

HWYSTYN, SIR VYRNYN—a member of the Charisian Parliament elected from Tellesberg.

HYLLAIR, SIR FARAHK, BARON OF DAIRWYN—the Baron of Dairwyn.

HYNDRYK, COMMODORE SIR AHLFRYD, ROYAL CHARISIAN NAVY—Baron Seamount, Charisian Navy's senior gunnery expert.

HYNDYRS, DUNKYN—purser, privateer galleon *Raptor*.

HYRST, ADMIRAL ZHOZEF, ROYAL CHISHOLMIAN NAVY—the third ranking officer of the RCN. SO in Command, Port Royal.

HYSIN, VICAR CHIYAN—a member of the reformists (from Harchong).

HYWSTYN, LORD AVRAHM—a cousin of Greyghor Stohnar, and a mid-ranking official assigned to the Siddarmarkian foreign ministry.

HYWYT, COMMANDER PAITRYK, ROYAL CHARISIAN NAVY—CO HMS *Wave,* 14 (schooner). Later promoted to captain as CO, HMS *Dancer,* 56.

ILLIAN, CAPTAIN AHNTAHN—one of Sir Phylyp Myllyr's company commanders.

JYNKYN, COLONEL HAUWYRD, ROYAL CHARISIAN MARINES—Admiral Staynair's senior Marine commander.

JYNKYNS, BISHOP ERNYST—Bishop of Ferayd. He is not an extremist and does not favor excessive use of force.

KAHNKLYN, AIDRYN—Tairys Kahnklyn's older daughter.

KAHNKLYN, AIZAK—Rahzhyr Mahklyn's son-in-law.

KAHNKLYN, ERAYK—Tairys Kahnklyn's oldest son.

KAHNKLYN, EYDYTH—Tairys Kahnklyn's younger daughter.

KAHNKLYN, HAARAHLD—Tairys Kahnklyn's middle son.

KAHNKLYN, TAIRYS—Rahzhyr Mahklyn's married daughter.

KAHNKLYN, ZHOEL—Tairys Kahnklyn's youngest son.

KAIREE, TRAIVYR—a wealthy merchant and landowner in the Earldom of Styvyn.

KAIRMYN, CAPTAIN TOMHYS—on of Sir Vyk Lakyr's officers, Delferahkan Army.

KEELHAUL—Earl Lock Island's rottweiler.

KESTAIR, MADAME AHRDYN—Archbishop Maikel's married daughter.

KESTAIR, SIR LAIRYNC—Archbishop Maikel's son-in-law.

KHAILEE, MASTER ROLF—a pseudonym used by Lord Avrahm Hywstyn.

KNOWLES, EVELYN—an Eve who escaped the destruction of the Alexandria Enclave and fled to Tellesberg.

KNOWLES, JEREMIAH—an Adam who escaped the destruction of the Alexandria Enclave and fled to Tellesberg, where he became the patron and founder of the Brethren of Saint Zherneau.

LADY MAIRAH LYWKYS—Queen Sharleyan's chief lady-in-waiting. She is Baron Green Mountain's cousin.

LAHFTYN, MAJOR BRYAHN—Brigadier Clareyk's chief of staff.

LAHRAK, NAILYS—a senior leader of the Temple Loyalists in Charis.

LAHSAHL, LIEUTENANT SHAIRMYN, ROYAL CHARISIAN NAVY—XO, HMS *Destroyer,* 54.

LAIMHYN, FATHER CLYFYRD—King Cayleb's confessor and personal secretary, assigned to him by Archbishop Maikel.

LAKYR, SIR VYK—SO, Ferayd garrison, Kingdom of Delferahk. About the equivalent of a brigadier general.

LATHYK, LIEUTENANT RHOBAIR—XO, HMS *Destiny*, 54.

LAYN, MAJOR ZHIM, RCM—Brigadier Kynt's subordinate for original syllabus development. Now the senior training officer, Helen Island Marine Base.

LEKTOR, ADMIRAL SIR TARYL, EARL OF TARTARIAN—Prince Hektor's senior surviving naval commander.

LOCK ISLAND, HIGH ADMIRAL BRYAHN, ROYAL CHARISIAN NAVY—Earl of Lock Island, CO, Royal Charisian Navy, a cousin of King Cayleb.

MAHKELYN, LIEUTENANT RHOBAIR, ROYAL CHARISIAN NAVY—fourth lieutenant, HMS *Destiny*, 54.

MAHKLYN, DR. RAHZHYR—head of the Royal Charisian College.

MAHKLYN, TOHMYS—Rahzhyr Mahklyn's unmarried son.

MAHKLYN, YSBET—Rahzhyr Mahklyn's deceased wife.

MAHKNEEL, CAPTAIN HAUWYRD—CO, galley *Arrowhead*, Delferahkan Navy.

MAHLYK, STYWYRT—Captain Yairley's personal coxswain.

MAHNTAYL, TAHDAYO—usurper Earl of Hanth.

MAHNTYN, CORPORAL AILAS—a scout-sniper assigned to Sergeant Edvarhd Wystahn's platoon.

MAHRYS, ZHERYLD—Sir Rayjhis Dragoner's secretary.

MAIGEE, CAPTAIN GRAYGAIR—CO, Royal Dohlaran Navy galleon *Guardian*.

MAIGWAIR, VICAR ALLAYN—Captain General of the Church of God Awaiting; one of the so-called Group of Four.

MAIYR, CAPTAIN ZHAKSYN—one of Colonel Sir Wahlys Zhorj's troop commanders in Tahdayo Mahntayl's service.

MAKAIVYR, BRIGADIER ZHOSH, RCM—CO, First Brigade, Royal Charisian Marines.

MANTHYR, COMMODORE GWYLYM, ROYAL CHARISIAN NAVY—was flag captain to Crown Prince Cayleb in the Armageddon Reef campaign.

MYCHAIL, ALYX—Raiyan Mychail's oldest grandson.

MYCHAIL, MYLDRYD—one of Rhaiyan Mychail's married granddaughters-in-law.

MYCHAIL, RHAIYAN—a business partner of Ehdwyrd Howsmyn and the Kingdom of Charis' primary textile producer.

MYCHAIL, STYVYN—Myldryd Mychail's youngest son.

MYLLYR, SIR PHYLYP—one of Sir Koryn Gahrvai's regimental commanders.

NETHAUL, HAIRYM—XO, privateer schooner *Blade*.

NYLZ, ADMIRAL KOHDY, ROYAL CHARISIAN NAVY—one of King Cayleb's newly promoted fleet commanders.

OHLSYN, TRAHVYS—Earl of Pine Hollow, Prince Nahrmahn's of Emerald's first councilor and cousin.

OLYVYR, SIR DUSTYN—chief constructor of the Royal Charisian Navy.

PAHLZAR, COLONEL AHKYLLYS—Sir Charlz Doyal's replacement as Sir Koryn Gahrvai's senior artillery commander.

PAWALSYN, AHLVYNO—Baron Ironhill, Keeper of the Purse (treasurer) of the Kingdom of Charis, a member of King Cayleb's council.

PHONDA, MADAME AHNZHELYK—proprietor of one of the City of Zion's most discreet brothels.

QUEEN YSBELL—an earlier reigning Queen of Chisholm who was deposed (and murdered) in favor of a male ruler.

RAHLSTAHN, ADMIRAL GHARTH, EMERALD NAVY—Earl of Mahndyr, CO, Emerald Navy.

RAICE, BYNZHAMYN—Baron Wave Thunder, member of the Council of King Cayleb, Cayleb's spymaster.

RAIMYND, SIR LYNDAHR—Prince Hektor of Corisande's treasurer.

RAIYZ, FATHER CARLSYN—Queen Sharleyan's confessor.

RAIZYNGYR, COLONEL ARTTU—CO, 2/3rd Marines (Second Battalion, Third Brigade), Charisian Marines.

RAYNAIR, CAPTAIN EKOHLS—CO, privateer schooner *Blade.*

RAYNO, ARCHBISHOP WYLLYM—Archbishop of Chiang-wu; adjutant of the Order of Schueler.

RAYNO, KING ZHAMES II—the King of Delferahk.

RAYNO, QUEEN CONSORT HAILYN—the wife of King James II of Delferahk; a cousin of Prince Hektor of Corisande.

ROCK POINT, BARON OF—see Admiral Sir Domynyk Staynair.

ROHZHYR, COLONEL BAHRTOL, RCM—a senior commissary officer.

RYCHTAIR, NYNIAN—Ahnzhelyk Phonda's birth name.

SAHLMYN, SERGEANT MAJOR HAIN, RMMC—Colonel Zhanstyn's battalion sergeant major.

SAHNDYRS, MAHRAK—Baron Green Mountain; Queen Sharleyan's first councilor.

SAIRAH HAHLMYN—Queen Sharleyan's personal maid.

SARMAC, JENNIFER—an Eve who escaped the destruction of the Alexandria Enclave and fled to Tellesberg.

SARMAC, KAYLEB—an Adam who escaped the destruction of the Alexandria Enclave and fled to Tellesberg.

SAWAL, FATHER RAHSS—an under-priest of the Order of Chihiro, the skipper of one of the Temple's courier boats.

SEACATCHER, SIR RAHNYLD—Baron Mandolin, a member of King Cayleb's Council.

SEAFARMER, SIR RHYZHARD—Baron Wave Thunder's senior investigator.

SEAHAMPER, SERGEANT EDWYRD, CHISHOLMIAN ROYAL GUARD—a member of Queen Sharleyan's normal guard detail; her personal armsman since age ten.

SELLYRS, PAITYR—Baron White Church, Keeper of the Seal of the Kingdom of Charis; a member of King Cayleb's Council.

SHAIKYR, LARYS—CO, privateer galleon *Raptor*.

SHAIN, CAPTAIN PAYTER, ROYAL CHARISIAN NAVY—CO, HMS *Dreadful*, 48. Admiral Nylz's flag captain.

SHANDYR, HAHL—Baron of Shandyr, Prince Nahrmahn of Emerald's spymaster.

SHUMAY, FATHER AHLVYN—Bishop Mylz Halcom's personal aide.

SHYLAIR, BISHOP EXECUTOR THOMYS—Archbishop Borys' bishop executor.

STANTYN, ARCHBISHOP NYKLAS—Archbishop of Hankey in the Desnairian Empire. A member of the reformists.

STAYNAIR, ADMIRAL SIR DOMYNYK, BARON ROCK POINT, ROYAL CHARISIAN NAVY—younger brother of Bishop Maikel Staynair. CO, Eraystor blockade squadron.

STAYNAIR, ARCHBISHOP MAIKEL—senior Charisian-born prelate of the Church of God Awaiting in Charis; named prelate of all Charis by King Cayleb.

STAYNAIR, MADAME AHRDYN—Archbishop Maikel's deceased wife.

STOHNAR, LORD PROTECTOR GREYGHOR—elected ruler of the Siddarmark Republic.

STYWYRT, SERGEANT ZOHZEF—another of Kairmyn's noncoms, Delferahkan Army.

SUMYRS, SIR ZHER, BARON BARCOR—one of Sir Koryn Gahrvai's senior officers; commander of the left wing at Haryl's Crossing.

SYMMYNS, TOHMYS, GRAND DUKE OF ZEBEDIAH—the senior nobleman of Zebediah. Raised to that rank by Prince Hektor to ride herd on the island after its conquest.

SYMYN, LIEUTENANT HAHL, ROYAL CHARISIAN NAVY—XO, HMS *Torrent*, 42.

SYMYN, SERGEANT ZHORJ, CHARISIAN IMPERIAL GUARD—a Charisian noncom assigned to Empress Sharleyan's guard detachment.

SYNKLYR, LIEUTENANT AIRAH—XO, Royal Dohlaran Navy galleon *Guardian*.

TANYR, VICAR GAIRYT—a member of the reformists.

TAYSO, PRIVATE DAISHYN, CHARISIAN IMPERIAL GUARD—a Charisian assigned to Empress Sharleyan's guard detachment.

TAYT, KING SAILYS—deceased father of Queen Sharleyan of Chisholm.

TAYT, QUEEN MOTHER ALAHNAH—Queen Sharleyan of Chisholm's mother.

TAYT, QUEEN SHARLEYAN—Queen of Chisholm.

THOMPKYN, HAUWERSTAT—Earl White Crag; Sharleyan's lord justice.

TIANG, BISHOP EXECUTOR WU-SHAI—Archbishop Zherohm's bishop executor.

TRYNAIR, VICAR ZAHMSYN—Chancellor of the Council of Vicars of the Church of God Awaiting, one of the so-called Group of Four.

TRYNTYN, CAPTAIN ZHAIRYMIAH, ROYAL CHARISIAN NAVY—CO, HMS *Torrent*, 42.

TYMAHN QWENTYN—the current head of the House of Qwentyn, which is one of the largest, if not *the* largest banking and investment cartel in the Republic of Siddarmark. Lord Protector Greyghor holds a seat on the House of Qwentyn's board of directors, and the cartel operates the royal mint in the city of Siddar.

TYRN, ARCHBISHOP LYAM—Archbishop of Emerald.

TYRNYR, SERGEANT BRYNDYN, CHISHOLMIAN ROYAL GUARD—a member of Queen Sharleyan's normal guard detail.

TYRNYR, SIR SAMYL—Cayleb's special ambassador to Chisholm; was replaced / supplanted / reinforced by Gray Harbor's arrival.

URBAHN, HAHL—XO, privateer galleon *Raptor*.

URVYN, LIEUTENANT ZHAK, ROYAL CHARISIAN NAVY—XO, HMS *Wave*, 14.

USHYR, FATHER BRYAHN—an under-priest. Archbishop Maikel's personal secretary and most trusted aide.

VYNAIR, SERGEANT AHDYM, CHARISIAN ROYAL GUARD—one of King Cayleb II's armsmen.

VYNCYT, ARCHBISHOP ZHEROHM—primate of Chisholm.

WAIMYN, FATHER AIDRYN—Bishop Executor Thomys' intendant.

WAISTYN, BYRTRYM—Duke of Halbrook Hollow, Queen Sharleyan's uncle and treasurer. He does not favor an alliance with Charis but is loyal to Sharleyan.

WALKYR, EDMYND—CO, merchant galleon *Wave*.

WALKYR, GREYGHOR—Edmynd Walkyr's son.

WALKYR, LYZBET—Edmynd Walkyr's wife.

WALKYR, MYCHAIL—Edmynd Walkyr's youngest brother; XO, merchant galleon *Wind*.

WALKYR, SIR STYV—Tahdayo Mahntayl's chief adviser.

WALKYR, ZHORJ—XO, galleon *Wave*. Edmynd's younger brother.

WALLYCE, LORD FRAHNKLYN—Chancellor of the Siddarmark Republic.

WYLSYNN, FATHER PAITYR—a priest of the Order of Schueler and the Intendant of Charis. He served Erayk Dynnys in that capacity and has continued to serve Archbishop Maikel.

WYLSYNN, VICAR HAUWERD—Paityr Wylsynn's uncle; a member of the reformists and a priest of the Order of Langhorne.

WYLSYNN, VICAR SAMYL—Father Paityr Wylsynn's father; the leader of the reformists within the Council of Vicars and a priest of the Order of Schueler.

WYSTAHN, AHNAINAH—Edvarhd Wystahn's wife.

WYSTAHN, SERGEANT EDVARHD, ROYAL CHARISIAN MARINES—a scout-sniper assigned to ⅓rd Marines.

YAIRLEY, CAPTAIN ALLAYN, ROYAL CHARISIAN NAVY—older brother of Captain Sir Dunkyn Yairley.

YAIRLEY, CAPTAIN SIR DUNKYN, ROYAL CHARISIAN NAVY—CO, HMS *Destiny,* 54.

YOWANCE, RAYJHIS—Earl Gray Harbor, First Councilor of Charis.

ZAIVYAIR, AIBRAM, DUKE OF THORAST—effective Navy Minister and senior officer, Royal Dohlaran Navy, brother-in-law of Admiral-General Duke Malikai (Faidel Ahlverez).

ZHAKSYN, LIEUTENANT TOHMYS, RMMC—General Chermyn's aide.

ZHANSTYN, COLONEL ZHOEL, RMMC—CO, ⅓rd Marines (First Battalion, Third Brigade). Brigadier Clareyk's senior battalion CO.

ZHAZTRO, COMMODORE HAINZ, EMERALD NAVY—the senior Emeraldian naval officer afloat (technically) in Eraystor.

ZHEFFYR, MAJOR WYLL, ROYAL CHARISIAN MARINES—CO, Marine detachment, HMS *Destiny*, 54.

ZHONAIR, MAJOR GAHRMYN—a battery commander in Ferayd Harbor, Ferayd Sound, Kingdom of Delferahk.

ZHORJ, COLONEL SIR WAHLYS—Tahdayo Mahntayl's senior mercenary commander.

ZHUSTYN, SIR AHLBER—Queen Sharleyan's spymaster.

Glossary

Anshinritsumei—literally "enlightenment," from the Japanese. Rendered in the Safehold Bible, however, as "the little fire," the lesser touch of God's spirit. The maximum enlightenment of which mortals are capable.

Blink-lizard—a small, bioluminescent winged lizard. Although it's about three times the size of a firefly, it fills much the same niche on Safehold.

Borer—a form of Safeholdian shellfish which attaches itself to the hulls of ships or the timbers of wharves by boring into them. There are several types of borer, the most destructive of which actually eat their way steadily deeper into a wooden structure. Borers and rot are the two most serious threats (aside, of course, from fire) to wooden hulls.

Catamount—a smaller version of the Safeholdian slash lizard. The catamount is very fast and smarter than its larger cousin, which means that it tends to avoid humans. It is, however, a lethal and dangerous hunter in its own right.

Cat lizard—a furry lizard about the size of a terrestrial cat. They are kept as pets and are very affectionate.

Chewleaf—a mildly narcotic leaf from a native Safeholdian plant. It is used much as terrestrial chewing tobacco over most of the planet's surface.

Commentaries, The—the authorized interpretations and doctrinal expansions upon the Holy Writ. They represent the officially approved and sanctioned interpretation of the original scripture.

Choke tree—a low-growing species of tree native to Safehold. It comes in many varieties and is found in most of the planet's climate zones. It is dense-growing, tough, and difficult to eradicate, but it requires quite a lot of sunlight to flourish, which means it is seldom found in mature old-growth forests.

Cotton silk—a plant native to Safehold which shares many of the properties of silk and cotton. It is very lightweight and strong, but the raw fiber comes from a plant pod which is even more filled with seeds than Old Earth cotton. Because of the amount of hand labor required to harvest and process the pods and to remove the seeds from it, cotton silk is very expensive.

Council of Vicars—the Church of God Awaiting's equivalent of the College of Cardinals.

Dagger thorn—a native Charisian shrub, growing to a height of perhaps three feet at maturity, which possesses knife-edged thorns from three to seven inches long, depending upon the variety.

Deep-mouth wyvern—Safeholdian equivalent of a pelican.

Doomwhale—the most dangerous predator of Safehold, although, fortunately, it seldom bothers with anything as small as humans. Doomwhales have been known to run to as much as one hundred feet in length, and they are pure carnivores. Each doomwhale requires a huge range, and encounters with them are rare, for which human beings are just as glad, thank you. Doomwhales will eat *anything* . . . including the largest krakens. They have been known, on *extremely* rare occasions, to attack merchant ships and war galleys.

Dragon—the largest native Safeholdian land life-forms. Dragons come in two varieties, the common dragon and the great dragon. The common dragon is about twice the size of a Terran elephant and is herbivorous. The great dragon is smaller, about half to two-thirds the size of the common dragon, but carnivorous, filling the highest feeding niche of Safehold's land-based ecology. They look very much alike, aside from their size and the fact that the common dragon has herbivore teeth and jaws, whereas the great dragon has elongated jaws with sharp, serrated teeth. They have six limbs and, unlike the slash lizard, are covered in thick, well-insulated hide rather than fur.

Five-day—a Safeholdian "week," consisting of only five days, Monday through Friday.

Fleming moss—(usually lower case) An absorbent moss native to Safehold which was genetically engineered by Shan-wei's terraforming crews to possess natural antibiotic properties. It is a staple of Safeholdian medical practice.

Grasshopper—a Safeholdian insect analogue which grows to a length of as much as nine inches and is carnivorous. Fortunately, they do not occur in the same numbers as terrestrial grasshoppers.

Gray-horned wyvern—a nocturnal flying predator of Safehold. It is roughly analogous to a terrestrial owl.

Great dragon—the largest and most dangerous land carnivore of Safehold. The great dragon isn't actually related to hill dragons or jungle dragons at all, despite some superficial physical resemblances. In fact, it's more of a scaled-up slash lizard.

Group of Four—the four vicars who dominate and effectively control the Council of Vicars of the Church of God Awaiting.

Hairatha Dragons—the Hairatha professional baseball team. The traditional rivals of the Tellesberg Krakens for the Kingdom Championship.

Hill dragon—a roughly elephant-sized draft animal commonly used on Safehold. Despite their size, they are capable of rapid, sustained movement.

Ice wyvern—a flightless aquatic wyvern rather similar to a terrestrial penguin. Species of ice wyvern are native to both the northern and southern polar regions of Safehold.

Insights, The—the recorded pronouncements and observations of the Church of God Awaiting's Grand Vicars and canonized saints. They represent deeply significant spiritual and inspirational teachings, but, as the work of fallible mortals, do not have the same standing as the *Holy Writ* itself.

Intendant—the cleric assigned to a bishopric or archbishopric as the direct representative of the Office of Inquisition. The intendant is specifically charged with assuring that the Proscriptions of Jwo-jeng are not violated.

Jungle dragon—a somewhat generic term applied to lowland dragons larger than hill dragons. The gray jungle dragon is the largest herbivore on Safehold.

Kercheef—a traditional headdress worn in the Kingdom of Tarot which consists of a specially designed bandana tied across the hair.

Knights of the Temple Lands—the corporate title of the prelates who govern the Temple Lands. Technically, the Knights of the Temple Lands are *secular* rulers who simply happen to also hold high Church office. Under the letter of the Church's law, what they may do as the Knights of the Temple Lands is completely separate from any official action of the Church. This legal fiction has been of considerable value to the Church on more than one occasion.

Kraken—generic term for an entire family of maritime predators. Krakens are rather like sharks crossed with octupi. They have powerful, fish-like bodies, strong jaws with inward-inclined, fang-like teeth, and a cluster of tentacles just behind the head which can be used to hold prey while they devour it. The smallest, coastal krakens can be as short as three or four feet; deep-water krakens up to fifty feet in length have been reported, and there are legends of those still larger.

Kyousei hi—literally "great fire" or "magnificent fire." The term used to describe the brilliant nimbus of light the Operation Ark command crew generated around their air cars and skimmers to help "prove" their divinity to the original Safeholdians.

Langhorne's Watch—the thirty-one-minute period immediately before midnight in order to compensate for the extra length of Safehold's 26.5-hour day.

Master Traynyr—a character out of the Safeholdian entertainment tradition. Master Traynyr is a stock character in Safeholdian puppet theater, by turns a bumbling conspirator whose plans always miscarry and the puppeteer who controls all of the marionette "actors" in the play.

Monastery of Saint Zherneau—the mother monastery and headquarters of the Brethren of Saint Zherneau, a relatively small and poor order in the Archbishopric of Charis.

Mountain spike-thorn—a particular subspecies of spike-thorn, found primarily in tropical mountains. The most common blossom color is a deep, rich red, but the white mountain spike-thorn is especially prized for its trumpet-shaped blossom, which has a deep, almost cobalt blue throat, fading to pure white as it approaches the outer edge of the blossom, which is, in turn, fringed in a deep golden yellow.

Narwhale—a species of Safeholdian sea life named for the Old Earth species of the same name. Safeholdian narwhales are about forty feet in length and equipped with twin hornlike tusks up to eight feet long.

Nearoak—a rough-barked Safeholdian tree similar to Old Earth oak trees, found in tropic and near-tropic zones. Although it does resemble an Old Earth oak, it is an evergreen and seeds using "pine cones."

Nynian Rychtair—the Safeholdian equivalent of Helen of Troy, a woman of legendary beauty, born in Siddarmark, who eventually married the Emperor of Harchong.

Persimmon fig—a native Safeholdian fruit which is extremely tart and relatively thick skinned.

Prong lizard—a roughly elk-sized lizard with a single horn which branches into four sharp points in the last third or so of its length. They are herbivores and not particularly ferocious.

Proscriptions of Jwo-jeng—the definition of allowable technology under the doctrine of the Church of God Awaiting. Essentially, the Proscriptions limit allowable technology to that which is powered by wind, water, or muscle. The Proscriptions are subject to interpretation, generally by the Order of Schueler, which generally errs on the side of conservatism.

Rakurai—literally "lightning bolt." The *Holy Writ*'s term for the kinetic weapons used to destroy the Alexandria Enclave.

Saint Zherneau—the patron saint of the Monastery of Saint Zherneau in Tellesberg.

Sand maggot—a loathsome carnivore, looking much like a six-legged slug, which haunts beaches just above the surf line. Sand maggots do not normally take living prey, although they have no objection to devouring the occasional small creature which strays into their reach. Their natural coloration blends with their sandy habitat well, and they normally conceal themselves by digging their bodies into the sand until they are completely covered, or only a small portion of their backs show.

Sea cow—a walrus-like Safeholdian sea mammal which grows to a body length of approximately ten feet when fully mature.

Seijin—sage, holy man. Directly from the Japanese by way of Maruyama Chihiro, the Langhorne staffer who wrote the Church of God Awaiting's Bible.

Slash lizard—a six-limbed, saurian-looking, furry oviparous mammal. One of the three top predators of Safehold. Mouth contains twin rows of fangs capable of punching through chain mail; feet have four long toes each, tipped with claws up to five or six inches long.

SNARC—Self-Navigating Autonomous Reconnaissance and Communication platform.

Spike-thorn—a flowering shrub, various subspecies of which are found in most Safeholdian climate zones. Its blossoms come in many colors and hues, and the tropical versions tend to be taller-growing and to bear more delicate blossoms.

Spider-crab—a native species of sea life, considerably larger than any terrestrial crab. The spider-crab is not a crustacean, but rather more of a segmented, tough-hided, many-legged seagoing slug. Despite that, its legs are considered a great delicacy and are actually very tasty.

Spider rat—a native species of vermin which fills roughly the ecological niche of a terrestrial rat. Like all Safehold mammals, it is six-limbed, but it looks like a cross between a hairy gila monster and an insect, with long, multi-jointed legs which actually arch higher than its spine. It is nasty tempered but basically cowardly, and fully adult male specimens of the larger varieties of spider rat run to about two feet in body length, with another two feet of tail. The more common varieties average between 33 percent and 50 percent of that body/tail length.

Steel thistle—a native Safeholdian plant which looks very much like branching bamboo. The plant bears seed pods filled with small, spiny seeds embedded in fine, straight fibers. The seeds are extremely difficult to remove by hand, but the fiber can be woven into a fabric which is even stronger than cotton silk. It can also be twisted into extremely strong, stretch-resistant rope. Moreover, the plant grows almost as rapidly as actual bamboo, and the yield of raw fiber per acre is 70 percent higher than for terrestrial cotton.

Surgoi kasai—literally "dreadful (great) conflagration." The true spirit of God, the touch of His divine fire which only an angel or archangel can endure.

Tellesberg Krakens—the Tellesberg professional baseball club.

Testimonies, The—By far the most numerous of the Church of God Awaiting's writings, these consist of the firsthand observations of the first few generations of humans on Safehold. They do not have the same status as the Christian gospels, because they do not reveal the central teachings and inspiration of God. Instead, collectively, they form an important substantiation of the *Writ's* "historical accuracy" and conclusively attest to the fact that the events they collectively describe did, in fact, transpire.

Wire vine—a kudzu-like vine native to Safehold. Wire vine isn't as fast-growing as kudzu, but it's equally tenacious, and unlike kudzu, several of its varieties have long, sharp thorns. Unlike many native Safeholdians species of plants, it does quite well intermingled with terrestrial imports. It is often used as a sort of combination of hedgerow and barbed wire by Safehold farmers.

Wyvern—the Safeholdian ecological analogue of terrestrial birds. There are as many varieties of wyverns as there are of birds, including (but not limited to) the homing wyvern, hunting wyverns suitable for the equivalent of hawking for small prey, the crag wyvern (a small—wingspan ten feet—flying predator), various species of sea wyverns, and the king wyvern (a very large flying predator, with a wingspan of up to twenty-five feet). All wyverns have two pairs of wings, and one pair of powerful, clawed legs. The king wyvern has been known to take children as prey when desperate or when the opportunity presents, but they are quite intelligent. They know that man is a prey best left alone and generally avoid areas of human habitation.

Wyvernry—a nesting place and/or breeding hatchery for domesticated wyverns.

A Note on Safeholdian Timekeeping

The Safeholdian day is 26 hours and 31 minutes long. Safehold's year is 301.32 local days in length, which works out to .91 Earth standard years. It has one major moon, named Langhorne, which orbits Safehold in 27.6 local days, so the lunar month is approximately 28 days long.

The Safeholdian day is divided into twenty-six 60-minute hours, and one 31-minute period, known as "Langhorne's Watch," which is used to adjust the local day into something which can be evenly divided into standard minutes and hours.

The Safeholdian calendar year is divided into ten months: February, April, March, May, June, July, August, September, October, and November. Each month is divided into ten five-day weeks, each of which is referred to as a "five-day." The days of the week are: Monday, Tuesday, Wednesday, Thursday, and Friday. The extra day in each year is inserted into the middle of the month of July, but is not numbered. It is referred to as "God's Day" and is the high holy day of the Church of God Awaiting. What this means, among other things, is that the first day of every month will always be a Monday, and the last day of every month will always be a Friday. Every third year is a leap year, with the additional day—known as "Langhorne's Memorial"—being inserted, again, without numbering, into the middle of the month of February. It also means that each Safeholdian month is 795 standard hours long, as opposed to 720 hours for a 30-day Earth month.

The Safeholdian equinoxes occur on April 23 and September 22. The solstices fall on July 7 and February 8.